SEA *of* TRANQUILITY

Emily St. John Mandel was born in Canada and studied dance at The School of Toronto Dance Theatre. Her novels include *Last Night in Montreal*, *The Singer's Gun*, *The Lola Quartet*, *Station Eleven*, *The Glass Hotel* and *Sea of Tranquility*. She lives in New York City and Los Angeles.

SEA

of

TRANQUILITY

Emily St. John Mandel

PICADOR

First published in the USA 2022 by Alfred A. Knopf,
a division of Penguin Random House LLC, New York

First published in the UK 2022 by Picador

This paperback edition published 2023 by Picador
an imprint of Pan Macmillan
The Smithson, 6 Briset Street, London EC1M 5NR
EU representative: Macmillan Publishers Ireland Ltd, 1st Floor,
The Liffey Trust Centre, 117–126 Sheriff Street Upper,
Dublin 1, D01 YC43
Associated companies throughout the world
www.panmacmillan.com

ISBN 978-1-5290-8351-4

A few sentences in this book appeared, in different form, in a short story
published in the anthology *Imaginary Oklahoma* in 2013, an article published
in *The New Republic* in 2014 and an essay published in *Humanities* in 2016.

3 5 7 9 8 6 4

A CIP catalogue record for this book is available from the British Library.

Printed and bound by CPI Group (UK) Ltd, Croydon, CR0 4YY

Visit www.picador.com to read more about all our books
and to buy them. You will also find features, author interviews and
news of any author events, and you can sign up for e-newsletters
so that you're always first to hear about our new releases.

For Cassia

Contents

1

Remittance /

1912

2

In Halifax he finds lodging by the port, a boardinghouse where he's able to secure a corner room on the second floor, overlooking the harbour. He wakes that first morning to a wonderfully lively scene outside his window. A large merchant ship has arrived, and he's close enough to hear the jovial curses of the men unloading barrels and sacks and crates. He spends much of that first day gazing out the window, like a cat. He planned to go west immediately, but it's so easy to linger in Halifax, where he falls prey to a personal weakness he's been aware of all his life: Edwin is capable of action but prone to inertia. He likes sitting by his window. There's a constant movement of people and ships. He doesn't want to leave, so he stays.

"Oh, just trying to puzzle out my next move, I suppose," he says to the proprietor, when she makes gentle inquiries. Her name is Mrs. Donnelly. She's from Newfoundland. Her accent confounds him. She sounds like she's from Bristol and also from Ireland, simultaneously, but then sometimes he hears Scotland. The rooms are clean and she's an excellent cook.

Sailors pass by his window in jostling waves. They rarely look up. He enjoys watching them but dares not make any movement toward them. Besides, they have each other. When drunk they put their arms around one another's shoulders and he feels a piercing envy.

(Could he go to sea? Of course not. He discards the idea as soon as it arises. He once heard of a remittance man who reinvented himself as a sailor, but Edwin's a man of leisure through and through.)

He loves watching the boats come in, steamships pulling into the harbour with an aura of Europe still clinging to their decks.

He takes walks in the mornings and again in the afternoons. Down to the harbour, out to quiet residential areas, in and out of little shops under the striped awnings on Barrington Street. He likes to ride the electric streetcar to the end of the line, and then come back, watching the shift from small houses to larger houses to the commercial buildings downtown. He likes buying things that he doesn't especially need: a loaf of bread, a postcard or two, a bouquet of flowers. This could be a life, he finds himself thinking. It could be as simple as this. No family, no job, just a few simple pleasures and clean sheets to fall into at the end of the day, a regular allowance from home. A life of solitude could be a very pleasant thing.

He begins buying flowers every few days, which he places on his dresser in a cheap vase. He spends a long time gazing at them. He wishes he were an artist, to draw them and in so doing to see them more clearly.

Could he learn to draw? He has time and money. It's as good an idea as any. He makes inquiries with Mrs. Donnelly, who makes inquiries with a friend, and a short time later Edwin is in the parlour of a woman who trained as a painter. He spends quiet hours sketching flowers and vases, learning the fundamentals of shading and proportion. The woman's name is Laetitia Russell. She wears a wedding ring, but the location of her husband is unclear. She lives in a tidy wooden house with three children and a widowed sister, an unobtrusive chaperone who knits endless scarves in a corner of the room, so that for the rest of his life Edwin associates drawing with the clicking of knitting needles.

He's been living at the boardinghouse for six months when Reginald arrives. Reginald, he can tell at once, is not prone to inertia. Reginald has immediate plans to go west. He's two years older than Edwin, a fellow old Etonian, third son of a viscount, and his eyes are beautiful, a deep greyish blue. Like Edwin, his plans involve establishing himself as a gentleman farmer, but unlike Edwin, he's actually taken steps to achieve this and has been corresponding with a man who wishes to sell a farm in Saskatchewan.

"Six months," Reginald repeats at breakfast, not quite believing it. He stops spreading jam on his toast for a moment, seemingly unsure if he heard correctly. "Six *months*? Six months *here*."

"Yes," Edwin says lightly. "Six very agreeable months, I might add." He tries to catch Mrs. Donnelly's eye, but she's focusing intently on pouring tea. She thinks he's a little touched, he can tell.

"Interesting." Reginald spreads jam on his toast. "I don't suppose we're hoping to be called home, are we? Clinging to the edge of the Atlantic, staying as close as we can to king and country?"

This stings a little, so when Reginald lights out for the west the following week, Edwin accepts an invitation to join him. There's pleasure in action, he decides, as the train leaves the city. They've booked first-class passage on a delightful train that features an onboard post office and barbershop, where Edwin writes a postcard to Gilbert and enjoys a hot shave and a haircut while watching the forests and lakes and small towns slip past the windows. When the train stops at Ottawa he doesn't disembark, just stays on board, sketching the lines of the station.

The forests and lakes and small towns subside into plains. The prairies are initially interesting, then tedious, then unsettling.

There's too much of them, that's the problem. The scale is wrong. The train crawls like a millipede through endless grass. He can see from horizon to horizon. He feels terribly overexposed.

"This is the life," Reginald says, when at last they arrive, standing in the doorway of his new farmhouse. The farm is a few miles outside Prince Albert. It is a sea of mud. Reginald purchased it, sight unseen, from a disconsolate Englishman in his late twenties—another remittance man, Edwin can't help but suspect—who's thoroughly failed to make a go of it here and is headed back east to take a desk job in Ottawa. Reginald is very carefully not thinking about this man, Edwin can see that.

Can a house be haunted by failure? When Edwin steps through the door of the farmhouse, he feels immediately ill at ease, so he lingers out on the front porch. It's a well-built house—the previous owner was well-funded once—but the place is unhappy in a way that Edwin can't entirely explain.

"There's . . . a lot of sky here, isn't there?" Edwin ventures. And a lot of mud. Really an astonishing amount of mud. It glitters under the sun as far as he can see.

"Just wide-open spaces and fresh air," Reginald says, gazing out at the horrifically featureless horizon. Edwin can see another farmhouse, far away, hazy with distance. The sky is aggressively blue. That night they dine on buttered eggs—the only thing

Reginald knows how to cook—and salt pork. Reginald seems subdued.

"I suppose it's quite hard work, farming?" he says, after a while. "Physically taxing."

"I suppose so." When Edwin imagined himself in the new world, he always saw himself in his own farm—a verdant landscape of, well, of some unspecified crop, tidy but also vast—but in truth he never thought much about what the work of farming might actually entail. Taking care of horses, he supposes. Doing a bit of gardening. Digging up fields. But then what? What do you actually do with the fields, once you've dug them up? What are you digging for?

He feels himself teetering on the edge of an abyss. "Reginald, my old friend," he says, "what does a fellow have to do to get a drink around here?"

"You *reap*," Edwin says to himself, on his third glass. "That's the word for it. You dig up the fields, you sow things in the fields, then you reap." He sips his drink.

"You reap what?" Reginald has a pleasant way about him when he's drunk, as if nothing could possibly offend him. He's been leaning back in his chair, smiling into the empty air.

"Well, that's just it, isn't it," Edwin says, and pours himself another glass.

3

After a month of drinking, Edwin leaves Reginald on his new farm and continues west to meet up with his brother Niall's school friend Thomas, who entered the continent via New York City and sped west immediately. The train through the Rocky Mountains takes Edwin's breath away. He presses his forehead to the window, like a child, and openly gapes. The beauty is overwhelming. He maybe took the drinking a little far, back in Saskatchewan. He'll be a better man in British Columbia, he decides. The sunlight hurts his eyes.

After all that wild splendour, it's an odd jolt to find himself in Victoria, in those tamed and pretty streets. There are Englishmen everywhere; he steps out of the train and the accents of his homeland surround him. He could stay here for a while, he thinks.

. . .

Edwin finds Thomas in a tidy little hotel in the city centre, where Thomas has taken the best room, and they order tea with scones in the restaurant downstairs. They haven't seen one another in three or four years, but Thomas has changed very little. He has the same reddish complexion he's had since childhood, that perpetual impression of just having stepped in off the rugby pitch. He's trying to become a member of the Victoria business community, but he's vague on what kind of business he wants to be in.

"And how's your brother?" Thomas asks, changing the subject. He means Niall.

"Making a go of it in Australia," Edwin says. "He seems happy enough, judging by his letters."

"Well, that's more than most of us can say," Thomas says. "No small thing, happiness. What's he doing down there?"

"Drinking away his remittance money, I'd imagine," Edwin says, which is ungentlemanly but also the probable truth. They have a table by the window, and his gaze keeps drifting to the street, the shop fronts, and—visible in the distance—the unfathomable wilderness, dark towering trees crowding in around the periphery. There's something ludicrous about the idea that the wilderness belongs to Britain, but he quickly suppresses this thought, because it reminds him of his last dinner party in England.

4

The last dinner party began smoothly enough, but trouble started when the conversation turned, as ever and always, to the unimaginable splendour of the Raj. Edwin's parents were born in India, Raj babies, English children raised by Indian nannies—"If I hear one more word about her goddamned ayah," Edwin's brother Gilbert muttered once, never finishing the thought—and raised on tales of an unseen Britain that, Edwin couldn't help but suspect, had been slightly disappointing when they first laid eyes on it in their early twenties. ("More rain than I'd expected," was all Edwin's father would say on the matter.)

There was another family at that last dinner party, the Barretts, of similar profile: John Barrett had been a commander in the Royal Navy, and Clara, his wife, had also spent her first few years in India. Their eldest son, Andrew, was with them. The

Barretts knew that British India was an inevitable detour in any evening spent with Edwin's mother, and as old friends, they understood that once Abigail got the Raj out of her system, conversation could move on.

"You know, I so often find myself thinking of the beauty of British India," his mother said. "The colours were remarkable."

"The heat *was* rather oppressive, though," Edwin's father said. "That's one thing I didn't miss, once we came here."

"Oh, I never found it *terribly* oppressive." Edwin's mother had a far-off look that Edwin and his brothers called her British India expression. There was a haziness about her that meant she was no longer with them; she was riding an elephant or strolling through a garden of verdant tropical flowers or being served cucumber sandwiches by her goddamned ayah or something, who knows.

"Nor did the natives," Gilbert said mildly, "but I suppose that climate's not for everyone."

What inspired Edwin to speak just then? He found himself dwelling on the matter years later, at war, in the terminal horror and boredom of the trenches. Sometimes you don't know you're going to throw a grenade until you've already pulled the pin.

"Evidence suggests they feel rather more oppressed by the British than by the heat," Edwin said. He glanced at his father, but his father seemed to have frozen, his glass halfway between the table and his lips.

"Darling," said his mother, "whatever can you mean?"

"They don't want us there," Edwin said. He glanced around

the table, at all the silent staring faces. "Not a great deal of ambiguity on that point, I'm afraid." He listened to his own voice as if from some distance away, with wonderment. Gilbert's mouth had fallen open.

"Young man," his father said, "we have brought nothing but civilization to these people—"

"And yet one can't help but notice," Edwin said, "that on balance, they rather seem to prefer their own. Their own civilization, that is. They managed quite well without us for some time, didn't they? Several thousand years, wasn't it?" It was like being strapped to the roof of a runaway train! He actually knew very little about India, but he remembered having been shocked as a boy by accounts of the 1857 rebellion. "Does anyone want us *anywhere*?" he heard himself ask. "Why do we assume these far-flung places are ours?"

"Because we *won* them, Eddie," Gilbert said, after a brief silence. "One assumes that the natives of England were perhaps not unanimously delighted by the arrival of our twenty-second great-grandfather, but, well, history belongs to the victors."

"William the Conqueror was a thousand years ago, Bert. Surely we might strive to be somewhat more civilized than the maniacal grandson of a Viking raider."

Edwin stopped talking then. Everyone at the table was staring at him.

"'The maniacal grandson of a Viking raider,'" Gilbert repeated softly.

"Although one should be grateful, I suppose, that we're a

Christian nation," Edwin said. "*Imagine* what a bloodbath the colonies would be if we weren't."

"Are you an atheist, Edwin?" Andrew Barrett inquired, with genuine interest.

"I don't quite know what I am," Edwin said.

The silence that followed was possibly the most excruciating of Edwin's life, but then his father began speaking, very quietly. When Edwin's father was furious, he had a trick of beginning speeches with a half-sentence, to catch everyone's attention. "Every advantage you've ever had in this life," his father said. Everyone looked at him. He began again, in trademark fashion, only slightly louder, and with deadly calm: "Every advantage you've ever had in this life, Edwin, has derived in some manner or another from the fact of your being descended from, as you so eloquently put it, the *maniacal grandson of a Viking raider.*"

"Of course," Edwin said. "It could be so much worse." He raised his glass. "To William the Bastard."

Gilbert laughed, in a nervous way. No one else made a sound.

"I do beg your pardon," Edwin's father said to their guests. "One might reasonably mistake my youngest son for a grown man, but it seems he's still a child. To your room, Edwin. We've heard quite enough for one evening."

Edwin rose from the table with great formality, said, "Good night, everyone," went to the kitchen to request that a sandwich be delivered to his room—the main course hadn't yet been served—and then retired to await his sentence. It came before midnight, with a knock on the door.

"Come in," he said. He'd been standing by the window, staring fretfully out at the movements of a tree in the wind.

Gilbert came in, closed the door behind him, and sprawled into the ancient stained armchair that was among Edwin's most treasured possessions.

"Quite the performance, Eddie."

"I don't know what I was thinking," said Edwin. "Actually, no, that's not true. I do know. I am absolutely certain there was not a single thought in my head. It was like a kind of void."

"Are you unwell?"

"Not at all. Never better."

"It must have been rather thrilling," Gilbert said.

"It was, actually. I won't say I regret it."

Gilbert smiled. "You're to go to Canada," he said gently. "Father's making arrangements."

"I was always going to go to Canada," Edwin said. "It's planned for next year."

"Now you're to go a little sooner."

"How much sooner, Bert?"

"Next week."

Edwin nodded. He felt a touch of vertigo. There had been a subtle shift in the room's atmosphere. He was going to go forth into an incomprehensible world and the room was already receding into the past. "Well," Edwin said, after a moment, "at least I'll still be on a different continent to Niall."

"You're at it again," Gilbert said. "Do you just say whatever comes into your head now?"

"I recommend it."

"We can't all be so careless, you know. Some of us have responsibilities."

"By which you mean a title and an estate to inherit," Edwin said. "What a terrible fate. I'll weep for you later. Will I receive the same remittance as Niall?"

"A little more. Niall's is just meant to support him. Yours comes with conditions."

"Tell me."

"You're not to come back to England for a while," Gilbert said.

"Exile," Edwin said.

"Oh, don't be melodramatic. You were always going to go off to Canada, as you said."

"But how long's a while?" Edwin turned away from the window to stare at his brother. "I'd thought I could go to Canada for a time, establish myself somehow, and then come home at regular intervals for visits. What did Father say, exactly?"

"I'm afraid the phrase that sticks in memory is 'tell him he's to stay the hell out of England.'"

"Well, that's rather . . . unambiguous."

"You know how Father is. And of course Mother is going along with it." Gilbert stood, and paused for a moment by the door. "Just give them time, Eddie. I'd be astonished if your exile were permanent. I'll work on them."

5

The trouble with Victoria, in Edwin's eyes, is that it's too much like England without actually being England. It's a far-distant simulation of England, a watercolour superimposed unconvincingly on the landscape. On Edwin's second night in the city, Thomas takes him to the Union Club. It's enjoyable at first, a shot of home, pleasant hours slipping past in the company of a few other old boys from the homeland and some truly exceptional single-malt scotch. Some of the older men have been in Victoria for decades, and Thomas seeks out their company. He stays close, asks their opinions, listens seriously to them, flatters them. It's embarrassing to watch. Thomas is clearly hoping to establish himself as a steady kind of man with whom one might wish to go into business, but it's obvious to Edwin that the older men are only being polite. They're not interested in outsiders, even outsiders from the correct country, with the correct ancestors and the correct accent, who've gone to the correct school. It's a closed society that admits Thomas only on the periphery. How long will Thomas have to stay here, circling around inside this clubhouse, before they'll accept him? Five years? Ten? A millennium?

Edwin turns his back on Thomas and goes to the window. They're on the third floor, with a view of the harbour, and the last light is fading from the sky. He feels restless and ill at ease. Behind him, men are relating tales of sporting triumphs and uneventful voyages by steamship to Quebec City, Halifax, and New York. "Would you believe," an arrival at the latter port is saying, somewhere behind him, "my poor mother was under the impression that New York was still part of the Commonwealth?"

Time passes; night falls over the harbour; Edwin rejoins the other men.

"But the unfortunate truth of the matter," one says, in the depths of a conversation about the importance of being an adventuring sort, "is we've no real future back in England, have we?"

A pensive silence falls over the group. These men are second sons, one and all. They are ill-prepared for a working life and will inherit nothing. To his own great surprise, Edwin raises a glass.

"To exile," he says, and drinks. There are disapproving murmurs: "I would hardly call this *exile*," someone says.

"To building a new future, gentlemen, in a new and far-distant land," says Thomas, ever the diplomat.

. . .

Later, Thomas finds him standing by the window.

"You know," he says, "I may have heard something or other in passing about a dinner party, but I'm not sure I quite believed it till now."

"I'm afraid the Barretts are incorrigible gossips."

"I think I've had about enough of this place," Thomas says. "I thought I could make a go of it here, but if you're going to leave England, surely there's something to be said for actually leaving England." He turns to face Edwin. "I've been thinking about going north."

"How far north?" Edwin is beset by a worrisome vision of igloos on the frozen tundra.

"Not very far. Just up Vancouver Island a little."

"You have prospects there?"

"Specifically, my friend's uncle's timber company," Thomas says. "But in the abstract, wilderness. Isn't that why we're here? To leave a mark on wilderness?"

What if one wanted to disappear into wilderness instead? A strange thought on a northbound boat a week later, steaming up the broken coast of the west side of Vancouver Island. A landscape of sharp beaches and forest, mountains rising up behind. Then all at once the broken rocks subside into a white-sand beach, the longest Edwin has ever seen. He sees villages on the shore, smoke rising, those wooden columns with wings and painted faces—totem poles, he remembers now—erected here and there. He doesn't understand them and therefore finds them menacing. After a long time the white sand subsides into rocky crags and narrow inlets again. Every so often he sees a canoe in the distance. What if one were to dissolve into the wilderness like salt into water. He wants to go home. For the first time, Edwin begins to worry about his sanity.

The passengers on the boat: three Chinese men going to work in the cannery, a very tense young woman of Norwegian origin travelling to join her husband, Thomas and Edwin, the captain and two Canadian crewmen, all in the company of barrels and sacks of supplies. The Chinese men talk and laugh in their own language. The Norwegian woman stays in her cabin except for meals, and never smiles. The captain and crew are cordial but uninterested in talking to Thomas and Edwin, so Thomas and Edwin spend most of their time together up on deck.

"What those utterly inert fellows in Victoria don't quite understand," Thomas says, "is that the entirety of this land is here for the taking." Edwin glances at him, and sees into the future: since Thomas was rejected by the Victoria business community, he'll spend the rest of his life railing against them. "They're ensconced in their very English city, and, look, I do understand the appeal, but we have an opportunity here. We can create our own world in this place." He drones on about empire and opportunity while Edwin gazes out over the water. The inlets and coves and little islands are on their starboard side, and just beyond them rises the immensity of Vancouver Island, its forests ascending into mountains whose summits are lost in low cloud. On the port side, where they're standing, the ocean extends uninterrupted until, as far as Edwin can figure it, the coast of Japan. He has the same queasy sense of overexposure that he felt on the prairies. It's a relief when the boat finally makes a slow right turn and begins travelling up an inlet.

They reach the settlement of Caiette in the early evening. There isn't much to it: a pier, a small white church, seven or eight houses, a rudimentary road that leads up to the cannery and the logging camp. Edwin stands by the pier with his steamer trunk beside him, at a loss. This place is precarious, that's the only word for it. It's the lightest sketch of civilizations, caught between the forest and the sea. He doesn't belong here.

"That bigger building up there's a boardinghouse," the captain says kindly to Edwin, "if you wanted to stay here for a spell, get your bearings."

It's troubling to realize he's so obviously lost. Thomas and Edwin walk up the hill together to the boardinghouse and secure rooms on the upper floor. In the morning Thomas departs for the logging camp, while Edwin slips immediately into the same stasis that overcame him in Halifax. It isn't quite listlessness. He makes a careful inventory of his thoughts and decides that he isn't unhappy. He just desires no further movement, for the time being. If there's pleasure in action, there's peace in stillness. He spends his days walking on the beach, sketching, contemplating the sea from the porch, reading, playing chess with other boarders. After a week or two, Thomas gives up trying to persuade him to come to the logging camp.

Edwin is astonished by the beauty of this place. He likes to sit on the beach, and just gaze out at the islands, little tufts of trees rising out of the water. Canoes pass by sometimes, on unknowable errands, and the men and women in the boats sometimes ignore him and sometimes stare. Larger boats come in at regular intervals, bringing men and supplies for the cannery and the camp. Some of them know how to play chess, which is one of Edwin's great pleasures. He's never been very good at chess, but he enjoys the sense of order in the game.

"What are you doing here?" they sometimes ask.

"Oh, just contemplating my next move, I suppose," he always replies, or words to that effect. He has a sense of waiting for something. But what?

6

On a sunny morning in September, he's out for a walk when he comes upon two Indigenous women laughing on the beach. Sisters? Good friends? They speak in a rapid language unlike anything he's ever heard, a language punctuated by sounds he can't imagine being able to replicate, let alone render in the Roman alphabet. Their hair is long and dark, and when one of them turns her head, light glances off a pair of enormous shell earrings. The women are wrapped in blankets against a cold wind.

They fall silent and watch him as he approaches.

"Good morning," he says, and touches the brim of his hat.

"Good morning," one replies. Her accent has a beautiful lilt. Her earrings hold all the colours of the dawn sky. Her companion, whose face bears a scattering of smallpox scars, just looks at him and says nothing. This isn't out of keeping with Edwin's experience of Canada—if anything, he reflects, it would come as the shock of his life if after half a year in the New World he were to find himself suddenly able to charm the locals—but the flat uninterest of the women's gaze is unnerving. This is a moment, he realizes, when he could express his views on colonization to people on the other side of the equation, so to speak, but he can't think of anything to say that doesn't sound absurd under the circumstances—if he tells them he believes colonization to be abhorrent, surely the logical next question will be *Then what are you doing here?*—so he says nothing further, and then they're behind him and the moment has passed.

He keeps walking, and then at some distance, still feeling their eyes on his back and wishing to convey an impression of having some sort of important errand to attend to, he turns toward the wall of trees. He never goes into the forest, because he's afraid of bears and cougars, but now it holds a strange appeal. He'll step in a hundred paces, he decides, no more. Counting off a hundred paces might calm him—counting has always calmed him—and if he walks straight for the full hundred then surely he can't get lost. Getting lost is death, he can see that. No, this whole place is death. No, that's unfair—this place isn't death, this place is indifference. This place is utterly neutral on the question of whether he lives or dies; it doesn't care about his last name or where he went to school; it hasn't even noticed him. He feels somewhat deranged.

7

The gates of the forest. The phrase comes immediately to mind, but Edwin's not sure where he picked it up. It sounds like something from a book he might have read as a boy. The trees here are old, and enormous. It's like stepping into a cathedral, except the underbrush is so thick that he has to fight his way through. He stops a few paces in. He sees a maple tree just ahead, large enough that it's created its own clearing, and that seems like a pleasant destination—he'll walk to the maple tree, he decides, he'll step out of the underbrush and linger a moment, then he'll go back to the beach immediately and never enter the forest again. This is an adventure, he tells himself, but it doesn't feel like an adventure. Mostly it feels like being slapped in the face with salal branches.

He fights his way through to the maple. It's quiet here, and he has a sudden certainty that he's being watched. He turns, and there—as incongruous as an apparition—is a priest, standing no more than a dozen yards away. He's older than Edwin, perhaps in his early thirties, and has very short black hair.

"Good morning," Edwin says.

"Good morning," the priest says, "and forgive me, I didn't mean to startle you. I like to walk here on occasion." There's something about his accent that eludes Edwin—it's not quite British, but not quite anything else. He wonders if the man's from Newfoundland, like his landlady back in Halifax.

"It does seem a peaceful destination," Edwin says.

"Quite so. I won't intrude on your contemplation, I was just on my way back to the church. Perhaps you'll stop in later."

"The church at Caiette? But you're not the usual priest," Edwin says.

"I'm Roberts. Filling in for Father Pike."

"Edwin St. Andrew. Pleased to meet you."

"Likewise. Good day."

The priest seems no more practised at walking through underbrush than Edwin. He crashes away between the trees, and within minutes Edwin is alone again, gazing up at the branches. He steps forward—

8

—into a flash of darkness, like sudden blindness or an eclipse. He has an impression of being in some vast interior, something like a train station or a cathedral, and there are notes of violin music, there are other people around him, and then an incomprehensible sound—

9

When he returns to his senses he's on the beach, kneeling on hard stones, vomiting. He has a vague memory of having fought his way out of the forest in a blind panic, a nightmare of shadow and blurred green, branches lashing his face. He rises shakily, and walks to the water's edge. He wades in up to his knees—the shock of cold is wonderful, it's the thing that will restore his sanity—and kneels to wash vomit from his face and shirt, then a wave knocks him over, so that by the time he stands he's choking on seawater and soaked through and through.

He's alone on the beach now, but he sees movement among the buildings of Caiette, in the middle distance. The priest disappearing into the white church on the hill.

When Edwin reaches the church, the door is ajar, and the room is empty. The door behind the altar is open too, and through it he sees a few gravestones in the green quiet of the tiny cemetery. He slips into the last row of pews, closes his eyes, and rests his head in his hands. The building is so new that the church still holds the fragrance of freshly cut wood.

"Did you fall in the ocean?"

The voice is gentle, the accent still indecipherable. The new priest—Roberts, he remembers—stands at the end of his pew.

"I knelt in the water. To wash vomit from my face."

"Are you unwell?"

"No. I . . ." It seems silly now, and a little unreal. "I thought I saw something in the forest. After I saw you. I heard something. I don't know. It seemed . . . supernatural." The details are already slipping away from him. He walked into the forest, and then what? He remembers darkness; notes of music; a sound he couldn't identify; all of it over in a heartbeat. Did it really happen?

"May I sit with you?"

"Of course."

The priest sits beside him. "Would it help to unburden yourself?"

"I'm not Catholic."

"I'm here to serve everyone who walks through those doors."

But the details are already fading. In the moment, the strangeness Edwin encountered in the forest was utterly destabilizing, but now he finds himself thinking of a particularly bad morning at school. He was nine, maybe ten, and he realized that he couldn't read the words in front of him, because the letters were wriggling into incoherence and there were spots swimming in his vision. He stood from his desk to ask to go see the matron, and he fainted. Fainting was darkness, but also sound: a murmuring and chirping like a chorus of birds, a blank void followed rapidly by an impression of being comfortably at home in bed—wishful thinking on the part of his subconscious, presumably—and then he woke into utter silence. Sound returned gradually, like someone turning a dial, silence fading into clamour and racket, the exclamations of other boys and the rapid steps of the approaching teacher—"Stand up, St. Andrew, no more malingering"—and was the moment just now in the forest really so different?

There were sounds, he reasons, and darkness, just like in that first instance. Perhaps he just fainted.

"I thought I saw something," Edwin says slowly, "but as I say it, I realize that perhaps I didn't."

"If you did," Roberts says gently, "you wouldn't be the first."

"What do you mean?"

"It's just, I've heard stories," the priest says. "That is, one hears stories."

This clumsy amendment strikes Edwin as a kind of camouflage, Roberts changing his patterns of speech to sound more English. More like Edwin. There's a wrongness about the man that Edwin can't entirely pinpoint.

"If I may ask, Father, where are you from?"

"Far away," the priest says. "Very far away."

"Well, that's all of us, isn't it," Edwin says, a little irritably. "Excepting the natives, of course. When we met in the forest just now, you said you were filling in for Father Pike, didn't you?"

"His sister was taken sick. He left last night."

Edwin nods, but there's something about this that rings utterly false. "Odd that I didn't hear anything about a boat going out last night, though."

"I have a confession to make," Roberts says.

"I'm listening."

"When I saw you in the forest, and I said I was going back to the church, well, I turned back for just a moment, as I was walking away."

Edwin stares at him. "What did you see?"

"I saw you walk under a maple tree. You were looking up, into the branches of the tree, and then—well, I had the impression that you could see something I couldn't. Was there something there?"

"I saw . . . well, I *thought* I saw—"

But Roberts is watching him too intensely, and in the quiet of this one-room church, at the far edge of the Western world, Edwin is oddly spooked. He's still a little ill—he has a pounding headache—and colossally weary. He doesn't want to talk anymore. He wants only to lie down. Roberts's presence here doesn't make sense to him.

"If Pike left last night," Edwin says, "he must have swum."

"But he did leave," Roberts says, "I assure you."

"Do you know how starved this place is for news, Father, really any news whatsoever? I live in the boardinghouse. If a boat had gone out last night, I would have heard about it at breakfast." The obvious next thought occurs to him: "Speaking of things I should have heard about, how did you get here? No boat's arrived in the past day or two, so am I to assume you strolled in through the forest?"

"Well," Roberts says, "I'm not sure how my mode of transportation is strictly relevant—"

Edwin rises, which forces Roberts to rise too. The priest backs into the aisle, and Edwin brushes past him.

"Edwin," Roberts says, but Edwin's already at the door. Another priest is approaching, climbing the stairs that lead up from the road: Father Pike, just returning from a visit to the cannery or the logging camp, his shock of white hair all but shining in the sunlight.

Edwin looks over his shoulder, into an empty church with its back door hanging open. Roberts has fled.

Mirella and Vincent /

2020

1

"I'd like to show you something strange." The composer, who was famous in an extremely limited, niche kind of way, i.e., in zero danger of being recognized on the street but most people in a couple of smallish artistic subcultures knew his name, was obviously uncomfortable, sweating as he leaned in close to his mic. "My sister used to record videos. This next one is a video of hers that I found in storage, after her death, and it's got some kind of glitch in it that I can't explain." He was quiet for a moment, adjusting a knob on his keyboard. "I wrote some music to go with it, but right before the glitch, the music will go silent, so we can appreciate the beauty of technical imperfection."

The music began first, a dreamlike swelling of strings, suggestions of static just under the surface, and then the video: his sister had walked with her camera along a faint forest path, toward an old-growth maple tree. She stepped under the branches and angled her camera upward, into green leaves flashing in the sunlight, in the breeze, and the music stopped so abruptly that the silence seemed like the next beat. The beat after that was darkness: the screen went black, just for a second, and there was a brief confusion of overlapping sounds—a few notes of a violin, a dim cacophony like the interior of a metropolitan train station, a strange kind of *whoosh* that suggested hydraulic pressure—then in a heartbeat the moment was over, the tree was back, and there was some chaotic camerawork as the composer's sister seemingly looked around wildly, forgetting that she had the camera in her hand.

The composer's music resumed, that video shifting seamlessly into one of his newer works, this one involving a video that he'd shot himself, five or six minutes of an aggressively ugly street corner in Toronto, but with orchestral strings labouring to produce the idea of hidden beauty. The composer was working rapidly, playing sequences of notes on keyboards that emerged a beat later as violin music, building the music up in layers as the Toronto street corner ticked by on the screen over his head.

In the front row of the audience, Mirella Kessler was in tears. She'd been friends with the composer's sister—Vincent—and hadn't known that Vincent had died. She left the theatre soon after, and spent some time in the ladies' lounge, trying to pull herself together. Deep breaths, a fortifying layer of makeup. "Steady," she said aloud, to her face in the mirror. "Steady."

· · ·

She'd come to this concert in the hope of speaking to the composer, in order to find out Vincent's whereabouts. There were certain questions she'd wanted to ask. Because in a version of her life so distant that it seemed now like a fairy tale, Mirella had had a husband—Faisal—and she and Faisal had been friends with Vincent and with Vincent's husband, Jonathan. There were several magnificent years, years of travel and money, and then the lights went out. Jonathan's investment fund turned out to be a Ponzi scheme. Faisal, unable to live in the face of financial ruin, took his own life.

Mirella had never spoken with Vincent again after that, because how could Vincent not have known? But a decade after Faisal's death she was at a restaurant with Louisa, her girlfriend of a year, and the first shiver of doubt crept in.

They were having dinner at a noodle place in Chelsea, and Louisa had been telling her about an unexpected birthday card from her Aunt Jacquie, whom Mirella had never met because at any given moment half of Louisa's family was feuding. "Jacquie's kind of awful most of the time," Louisa said, "but she came by it honestly, in my opinion."

"Why, what happened to her?"

"I never told you this story? It's epic. Her husband had a secret second family."

"Seriously? What a soap opera."

"It gets better." Louisa leaned forward to deliver the punch line: "He parked the second family *across the street*."

"What?"

"Yeah, it was amazing. Okay," Louisa said, "picture this scene. Hedge-fund guy, Park Avenue apartment, nonworking wife, two kids in private school. Peak Upper East Side. Then one day Aunt Jacquie checks the Amex statement, and there's a tuition payment to a private school that neither of her children attend. So she hands the statement to Uncle Mike, like, 'What's this crazy charge,' and apparently he almost has a heart attack on the spot."

"Go on."

"So my cousins, at the time they're in like eighth grade and ninth grade, something like that, but turns out Uncle Mike's also the father of the kindergartner across the street. He put the five-year-old's tuition payment on the wrong Amex."

"Wait, *literally* across the street?"

"Yeah, the buildings face each other. The doormen at both addresses probably knew for years."

"How could she not know?" Mirella asked, and just like that the past had swallowed her whole and she was talking about Vincent.

"A man who works long hours can hide anything," Louisa said. She was still talking about her aunt, and hadn't noticed that Mirella was elsewhere. "Lucky for you I don't work."

"Lucky for me," Mirella echoed, and kissed Louisa's hand. "What a crazy story."

"It's the across-the-street thing that gets me," Louisa said. "That geography was *brazen*."

"I can't decide if it's very lazy or very efficient." Mirella was pretending to still be there in the restaurant with Louisa, eating noodles, but she was far away. Vincent had sworn she hadn't known about her husband's crimes, in deleted voicemails and in a deposition.

"Mirella." Louisa's hand rested gently on Mirella's wrist. "Come back."

Mirella sighed, and set down her chopsticks.

"Did I ever tell you about my friend Vincent?"

"The wife of the Ponzi scheme guy?"

"Yeah. That story about your aunt made me think of her. Did I tell you I saw her once, after Faisal died?"

Louisa's eyes widened. "No."

"It was a little over a year after his death, so March or April of 2010. I went into a bar with some friends, and Vincent was the bartender."

"Oh my god. What did you say to her?"

"Nothing," Mirella said.

She hadn't recognized her at first. In the days of money, Vincent had had long wavy hair like all the other trophy wives, but in the bar her hair was cut very short, and she wore glasses and no makeup. In the moment the disguise had struck Mirella as vindication—*of course you're trying to hide, you monster*—but now a certain ambiguity had entered the scene: a reasonable alternate explanation for the short hair/glasses/no makeup was that one or another of her husband's defrauded investors could walk in at any moment. Manhattan was lousy with defrauded investors in those days.

"I pretended not to know her," she said now, to Louisa. "As revenge, I guess. It wasn't my best moment. She always said she didn't know what Jonathan had been doing, but I just thought, *Of course you knew. How could you possibly not have known. You knew and you let Faisal lose everything and now he's dead.* That was all I could think about in those days."

Louisa nodded. "Stands to reason that she'd know," she said.

"But what if she didn't?"

"Is it plausible that she didn't know?" Louisa asked.

"I didn't think so, at the time. But you're telling me this story about your poor Aunt Jacquie, and, well, if you can hide a five-year-old, you can hide a Ponzi scheme."

Louisa held Mirella's hands across the table. "You should talk to her."

"I have no idea how to find her."

"It's 2019," Louisa said. "No one's invisible."

But Vincent was. In those days Mirella was working as a receptionist at a high-end tile showroom near Union Square. It was the kind of place that required few customers, because when people spent money here, they spent tens of thousands of dollars. The morning after her dinner with Louisa, whiling away a silent hour behind a reception desk the size of a car, Mirella searched for Vincent. She tried Vincent's husband's surname first. A search for "Vincent Alkaitis" produced old society photos, some with Mirella in them—parties, galas, etc.—and also pages of Vincent at her husband's sentencing hearing, blank-faced, in a grey suit, and absolutely nothing else. The most recent images were from

2011. "Vincent Smith" turned up dozens of different people, mostly men, none of them the Vincent she was looking for. She couldn't find Vincent on social media, or anywhere else.

She leaned back in her chair, frustrated. High over her desk, a light was buzzing. Mirella wore a great deal of makeup at work, and when she was tired in the afternoons, sometimes her face felt heavy. Out on the white-tiled prairie of the sales floor, a lone sales rep was walking a customer through every conceivable colour of the company's signature composite material, which looked like stone but wasn't.

Vincent's parents were long dead, but she'd had a brother. Dredging up the brother's name required a deep dive into memory, which was a place Mirella generally tried to avoid. She glanced at the door to make sure no customers were approaching, then closed her eyes, took two deep breaths, and typed "Paul Smith + composer" into Google.

This was how she found herself at the Brooklyn Academy of Music four months later, waiting outside the stage door for Paul James Smith. She'd been hoping he could tell her how to find Vincent. But now Vincent was dead, apparently, which meant it was going to be a very different conversation. The stage door was on a quiet residential street. Mirella paced while she waited, not far, just a few feet in either direction. It was late January but unseasonably warm, well above freezing. Only one other person waited with her: a man of about her own age, mid-thirties, in jeans and a nondescript blazer. His clothes were too big. He nodded to her, she nodded back, and they settled into an awkward wait. Some time passed. A couple of staffers left without looking at them.

Then finally Vincent's brother emerged, looking a little haggard, although in fairness no one looked especially healthy in the orange glow of the streetlights here.

"Paul—" Mirella said, at the same moment that the other man said, "Excuse me—" and then they exchanged apologetic glances and fell silent, Paul glancing back and forth between them. A third man was approaching rapidly, a pale guy in a fedora and trench coat.

"Hello," Paul said, in a general way, to all of them.

"Hello!" said the newcomer. He took off his hat and revealed himself to be mostly bald. "Daniel McConaghy. Huge fan. Great show."

Paul gained an inch of height and a few watts of radiance as he stepped forward to shake the man's hand. "Well, thank you," he said, "always great to meet a fan." He looked around expectantly at Mirella and the guy in the oversized clothes.

"Gaspery Roberts," the oversized-clothes guy said. "Wonderful show."

"Hope you're not offended," the man in the fedora said, "I don't think your hands are dirty or anything, I've just gotten really into Purell since this thing in Wuhan hit the news." He was rubbing his hands together, with an apologetic smile.

"Fomites aren't a major mode of transmission with Covid-19," Gaspery said. *Fomites? Covid-19?* Mirella had never heard either term, and the other two were frowning too. "Oh, right," Gaspery said, seemingly to himself, "it's only January." He snapped back into focus. "Paul, could I maybe buy you a drink and ask you a couple quick questions about your work?" He had a faint accent that Mirella couldn't place.

"That sounds awesome," Paul said. "I could definitely use a drink." He turned to Mirella.

"Mirella Kessler," she said. "I was friends with your sister."

"Vincent," he said quietly. She couldn't quite parse his expression. Sadness but also a flash of something furtive. For a moment no one spoke. "Hey," he said, with forced cheer, "should we *all* get a drink?"

They wound up at a little French restaurant a few blocks away, across the street from a park that looked from Mirella's vantage point like a hill barely contained by a high brick retaining wall. She didn't know Brooklyn at all so everything was mysterious here, no points of reference beyond a vague notion that if she were to step outside the restaurant door, the spires of Manhattan would be somewhere to the left. The initial shock of the news of Vincent's death had faded a little, replaced by a limitless exhaustion. She was sitting next to the guy in the fedora, whose name she had forgotten, and across from Gaspery, who sat next to Paul. The fedora was going on and on about Paul's brilliance, his obvious influences, artistic debt to Warhol, etc.; he'd loved Paul's work from the beginning, that groundbreaking experimental collaboration with the video artist—what was his name again?—at Miami Basel, what a leap it had been when

Paul suddenly started using his own videos instead of collaborating with others, and so on and so forth. Paul was glowing. He loved being praised, but who doesn't. She was facing the window, and her gaze kept drifting over Gaspery's shoulder to the park. If there were an earthquake and the retaining wall broke, would the park spill across the street and bury the restaurant? She returned her attention to the table when she heard Vincent's name.

"So your sister, Vincent, she's the one who filmed that strange video in your performance tonight?" This was Gaspery, his name memorable because she hadn't heard it before.

Paul laughed. "Name one of my videos that *isn't* strange," he said. "I did an interview last year, with this guy who kept calling me *sui generis,* and at a certain point I was like, 'Guy, you can just say *strange. Strange, weird,* or *eccentric,* take your pick.' Interview went a whole lot better after that, let me tell you." He laughed loudly at his own anecdote, and the fedora laughed too.

Gaspery smiled. "I meant that video with the forest path," he persisted. "With the darkness, the strange sounds."

"Oh. Yeah. That was Vincent's. She said I could use it."

"Was it filmed near where you grew up?" Gaspery asked.

"You've done your research," Paul said approvingly.

Gaspery inclined his head. "You're from British Columbia, aren't you?"

"Yeah. Tiny little place called Caiette, northern Vancouver Island."

"Oh, near Prince Edward Island," the fedora said confidently.

"Didn't really grow up there, though," Paul said, apparently not hearing this. "Vincent grew up there. Same dad, different moms, so I was just there summers and every second Christmas. But yeah, that's where the video was filmed."

"That . . . that moment in the video," Gaspery said, "that anomaly, for lack of a better word. Did you ever see anything like it in person?"

"Only on LSD," Paul said.

"Oh," the fedora said, brightening suddenly, "I didn't realize there was a psychedelic influence on your work." He leaned forward, in a confiding way. "I went pretty deep with psychedelics, myself. Once you get into heroic doses, you start to have certain realizations about the world. So much is an illusion, right?"

Gaspery shot him a troubled look. Mirella watched him while she waited for an opportunity to ask about Vincent. Gaspery seemed foreign in a way that she couldn't quite parse.

"And then once you grasp *that,*" the fedora was saying, "it all just falls into place, right? Buddy of mine, he was struggling to quit cigarettes. Guy must've tried six or eight times. Not happening. Couldn't do it. Then one day he takes LSD, and *bam*. He calls me up the next evening, says, 'Dan, it's a miracle, I haven't even *wanted* a cigarette today.' I tell you, it was—"

"What happened to her?" Mirella asked Paul. She knew she was being rude but she didn't care, she was sitting there growing older by the minute, sinking into grief, and she wanted to know what had happened to her friend so she could leave these people.

Paul blinked at her, as if he'd forgotten she was there.

"She fell off a ship," he said. "About a year and a half—no, two years ago. It was two years last month."

"What kind of ship? Was she on a cruise?"

The fedora was glowering at his drink, but Gaspery was listening to the conversation with great interest.

"No, she was . . . I don't know how much you know about what happened to her in New York," Paul said, "that crazy thing with her husband, where it turned out he was a crook—"

"My husband was an investor in his Ponzi scheme," Mirella said. "I know all about it."

"Jesus," Paul said. "Did he—"

"Wait," the fedora said, "are we talking about Jonathan Alkaitis?"

"Yes," Paul said. "You know the story?"

"That crime was *insane*," the fedora said. "What was the size of the fraud, twenty billion dollars? Thirty? I remember where I was when that story broke. Call comes in from my mom, turns out my dad's retirement savings were—"

"You were telling me about the boat," Mirella said.

Paul blinked. "Right. Yeah."

"You have a bit of an interrupting problem," the fedora said, to Mirella. "No offence."

"No one's talking to you," Mirella said. "I asked a question of Paul."

"Yeah, so Vincent and I, we were out of touch for a few years," Paul said, "but after Alkaitis abandoned her and fled the country,

I guess Vincent got some training and certifications and went to sea as a cook on a container ship."

"Oh," Mirella said. "Wow."

"Sounds like an interesting life, right?"

"What happened to her?"

"No one really knows," Paul said. "She just disappeared from the ship. Seems like it was an accident. No body."

Mirella didn't know she was going to cry until she felt tears spilling down her face. All of the men at the table looked acutely uncomfortable. Only Gaspery thought to pass her a napkin.

"She drowned," she said.

"Yeah. I mean, it seems like it. They were hundreds of miles from land. She disappeared in bad weather."

"Drowning was the thing she was most scared of." Mirella dabbed at her face with the napkin. In the quiet, the small noises of the restaurant swelled around them: a couple arguing softly in French at a nearby table, clattering from the kitchen, the restroom door closing.

"Well," Mirella said, "thanks for telling me. And thank you for the drink." She didn't know who was paying for the drink, but she knew it wasn't her. She rose and walked out of the restaurant without looking back.

Outside, she felt directionless. She knew she should get in an Uber and go home, just go home and sleep and not do anything stupid like go for a walk after dark in an unfamiliar borough, but Vincent was dead. She'd find somewhere to sit for a few minutes, Mirella decided, just to collect her thoughts. The neighbourhood seemed fairly tame to her and it wasn't that late, also she was afraid of nothing, so she crossed the street and entered the park.

The park was quiet, but by no means unoccupied. People moved through pools of light, couples with arms around one another's shoulders and small groups of friends, a woman singing to herself. She sensed free-floating menace in the air, but it wasn't directed toward her. How could Vincent be dead? It was impossible, everything about it. She found her way to a bench and put on her headphones so she could pretend not to hear if anyone spoke to her, and willed herself toward invisibility. She would sit here for a while, she would sit here and think about Vincent, or sit here until she could find a way to stop thinking about Vincent, then she would go home and go to bed. But her thoughts shifted toward Jonathan, Vincent's former husband, living out his life in a luxury hotel in Dubai. The thought of him being there, wherever he was, ordering room service and asking to have the sheets changed and swimming in the hotel pool—*while Vincent was dead*—was an abomination.

A man walked in front of her and sat on the bench. She turned and it was Gaspery, so she took off the headphones.

"Forgive me," he said, "I saw you go into the park, and it's not a bad neighbourhood, but—" He didn't finish the thought, because he didn't have to. For a woman alone in a park after nightfall, every neighbourhood is a bad neighbourhood.

"Who are you?" Mirella asked.

"I'm a kind of investigator," Gaspery said. "You'll think I'm crazy if I get into the details."

There was something familiar about him, it seemed to her now, something about his profile that rang a distant bell, but she couldn't quite place him.

"What are you investigating?"

"Look, I'll be frank with you, I have no interest in Mr. Smith or his art," Gaspery said.

"That makes two of us."

"But I'm interested in, well, in a certain kind of anomaly, like that moment in the video when the screen goes black. I waited outside the stage door to ask him about it."

"It is a strange moment."

"Can I ask, did your friend ever talk about that moment? Since it was her video, after all."

"No," Mirella said, "not that I remember."

"Stands to reason," Gaspery said. "She would've been quite young when she shot that video. The things we see when we're young, sometimes they don't stay with us."

The things we see when we're young.

"I think I've seen you before," Mirella said. She was looking at his face in profile in the dim light. He turned to look at her, and she was certain of it. "In Ohio."

"You look like you've seen a ghost."

She rose from the bench. "You were under the overpass," she said. "In Ohio, when I was a kid. That was you, wasn't it?"

He frowned. "I think you're mistaking me for someone."

"No, I think it was you. You were under the overpass. Right before the police came, before you were arrested. You said my name."

But he looked genuinely confused. "Mirella, I—"

"I have to go." She fled, not quite running, but walking in the flying unstoppable way that she'd perfected over years in New York City, darting out of the park, back down to the street, where in the fishbowl glow of the French restaurant the fedora and Vincent's brother were still deep in conversation. Gaspery hadn't followed her. She was grateful that he was wearing a white shirt; he would all but shine in the dark. She plunged into the shadows of a residential street. She flew past old brownstones standing beautiful in the streetlights, iron fences, old trees; faster and faster, toward the bright lights of a commercial avenue up ahead, where a yellow cab was gliding across the intersection like a chariot, like some kind of miracle—a yellow cab in Brooklyn!— and she hailed it and climbed aboard. A moment later the taxi was speeding over the Brooklyn Bridge, Mirella crying quietly in the backseat. The driver glanced at her in the rearview mirror, but—oh, the grace of strangers in this crowded city!—said nothing.

2

When Mirella was a child, she lived with her mother and her older sister, Susanna, in a duplex in exurban Ohio. The housing development was located in a territory composed of strip malls and big-box stores. Farmland extended to the back of the Walmart parking lot. Some miles away, there was a prison. Mirella's mother worked two jobs and spent very little time at home. In the early mornings—well before dawn in the wintertime—Mirella and Susanna's mother rose after a few hours of sleep, poured milk over her daughters' cereal and did their hair while blearily drinking coffee, and drove them to school. She kissed her daughters goodbye and they were at school for the next ten hours—early drop-off, then school, then after-school programming—until at the end of the afternoon they boarded a bus that dropped them a half-mile from home.

It was a bad half-mile. They had to walk under an overpass.

The overpass scared Mirella, but in all the years she lived there, from when she was five until she dropped out of school and took a bus to New York City at sixteen, there was only one truly terrible incident. Mirella was nine, which made Susanna eleven, and they did hear the gunshots as the school bus pulled away, but the sounds were clear only in retrospect. In the moment, they looked at each other in the winter twilight and Susanna shrugged. "Probably just a car backfiring or something," she said, and Mirella, who would have believed anything Susanna told her, took her sister's hand and they walked together. Snow was falling. The mouth of the overpass was a dark cave waiting to swallow them. *It's fine,* Mirella told herself, *it's fine, it's fine,* because it was always fine, but this particular time it wasn't. As they stepped into the shadows, the sound came once more, impossibly loud now. They stopped.

Two men lay on the ground a few yards ahead of them. One was perfectly still; the other was twitching. In the dim light, at this distance, she couldn't see exactly what had happened to them. A third man was sitting slumped against the wall, a handgun dangling loose in his hand. A fourth was running away—his footsteps echoed—but Mirella glimpsed him for only an instant, scrambling up the embankment at the far end of the overpass and out of sight.

For a long time all of them—Mirella, Susanna, the man with the gun, the two dead or dying men on the ground—were frozen in a winter tableau. How much time? It felt like forever. Hours, days. The man with the gun had a sleepy, sedated look about him; his head nodded forward once or twice. Then came the police lights, blue and red washing over him, and this seemed to wake him up. He stared at the gun in his hand, as if unsure how it had arrived there, then he turned his head, and looked directly at the girls.

"Mirella," he said.

Then came shouting and confusion, a swarm of dark uniforms—"*Drop your weapon! Drop your weapon!*"—and although the event objectively happened, she and Susanna really were interviewed by the police, and there really was a story in the papers the next day ("Two Shot Dead Under Overpass: Suspect in Custody"), it was easy to convince herself in the years that followed that she'd only imagined this last part, that he hadn't really said her name. How could he have known her name? Susanna didn't remember hearing anything.

But all these years later, in the back of a Manhattan-bound taxi, safe in another life, here was a certainty she couldn't shake: the man in the tunnel was Gaspery Roberts.

She closed her eyes, trying to relax, but her phone vibrated in her hand. A text from her girlfriend: *Are you coming to Jess's party?*

It took a moment to remember. She texted back—*On my way*—and waved to catch the driver's eye in the rearview mirror.

"Excuse me."

"Ma'am?" he said, a little wary because she'd just been crying.

"May I give you a new destination? I need to get to Soho."

3

She had to walk all the way through the party before she found Louisa, smoking a cigarette on a terrace that was really just a tiny patch of blacktop roof. She kissed her and then sat awkwardly beside her on a narrow stone bench.

"How are you doing?" Louisa asked. They lived separately but spent a great deal of time together.

"Not bad at all," Mirella said, because she didn't want to talk about it. It was troublingly easy to lie to Louisa. She knew it was unfair to compare people, everyone knows that, but a difficulty she was having at this moment was that Louisa seemed infinitely less interesting to her than Vincent. Louisa had a kind of unspoiled quality, an air of having been cushioned from life's sharper edges, which was less appealing now than it had been. "I'm a little tired," Mirella said. "I didn't sleep that well."

"How come?"

"I don't know, just one of those random bad nights."

Another difficulty of the evening: this was Jess's party, and Jess was Mirella's friend, not Louisa's. In Mirella's old life, her long-ago life wherein everything was different, she'd been to this terrace with Faisal. Now, as then, the space was dressed up with fairy lights and potted palms, but still felt a little like the bottom of a hole. This was the downside to having retained a few friends from her time with Faisal—there were dangerous places here and there, places where she could get sucked into memories of another life, and this terrace was among them. On another night, at another party—fourteen years ago? thirteen?—she and Vincent had stood out here, a little drunk, looking straight up at the tiny patch of dark sky because Vincent swore she could see the North Star.

"It's right there," Vincent said. "Look, follow my finger. It's not that bright."

"That's a satellite," Mirella said.

"*What's* a satellite?" Faisal asked, stepping out onto the balcony. They'd arrived separately, and this was the first time she'd seen him all day. She kissed him and didn't quite fail to see the way Vincent glanced in their direction before returning her gaze to the sky. A difference between Mirella and Vincent was that Mirella truly loved her husband.

"There," Mirella said, pointing. "It's moving, right?"

Faisal squinted. "I'll have to take your word for it," he said.

"I think I need new glasses." He glanced around the cramped space, his arm around her waist. "Wow," he said, "what a thrillingly boho firetrap."

It was true. Buildings rose up on all sides. Three walls belonged to other buildings, and the fourth held the door that led back into the party. All these years later, sitting out here with Louisa, Mirella closed her eyes momentarily in order to not see Faisal gazing up at the sky.

"What did you do all day?" Louisa asked.

There had been a time when Mirella liked Louisa's questions—what a gift, she'd once thought, to be with someone who was so *interested,* interested in everything she'd done all day, someone who cared enough to ask—but tonight it was an intrusion.

"Went for a walk. Did some laundry. Stared at Instagram, mostly." Gaspery Roberts couldn't possibly have been the man under the overpass, now that she thought about it, because that was decades ago and he hadn't aged.

"Was that satisfying?"

"Of course not," Mirella said, a little sharper than she'd intended, and Louisa gave her a surprised look.

"We should go somewhere," Louisa said. "Maybe rent a cottage, get out of the city for a few days."

"That sounds nice." But Mirella was startled by the unhappiness that flooded through her at the suggestion. She very much did not want to go to a cottage with Louisa, she realized.

"But first," Louisa said, "I need another drink." She went inside and Mirella was alone for a while, then a woman came over to ask for a light and offered to tell Mirella's fortune in return. Mirella held her hands out as instructed, palms up, embarrassed by the way they trembled. How could she have fallen out of love with Louisa so suddenly, so cleanly? How could the man in the tunnel in Ohio have surfaced all these years later in New York? How could Vincent be dead? The fortune-teller put her hands over Mirella's hands, their palms almost touching, and closed her eyes. Mirella liked being able to watch her unobserved. The fortune-teller was older than Mirella had thought at first, somewhere in her thirties, first lines visible on her face. She was wearing a complicated arrangement of scarves.

"Where are you from?" she asked.

"Ohio."

"No, I mean originally."

"Still Ohio."

"Oh. I thought maybe I heard an accent."

"The accent's from Ohio too."

The fortune-teller's eyes were still closed.

"You have a secret," she said.

"Doesn't everyone?"

Her eyes opened. "You tell me yours, I'll tell you mine, and we'll never see each other again," she said.

It was an attractive proposition. "Okay," Mirella said. "But you go first."

"My secret is, I hate people," the woman said, very sincerely, and for the first time Mirella liked her.

"All people?"

"All except maybe like three," she said. "Your turn."

"My secret is, I want to kill a man." Was this true? Mirella wasn't sure. It had a ring of truth about it.

The fortune-teller's eyes darted over Mirella's face, like she was trying to work out if this was some kind of joke. "A specific man?" she asked. She smiled tentatively—*You're kidding, right? Please tell me you're kidding?*—but Mirella didn't smile back.

"Yes," Mirella said. "A specific man." It became real as she said it.

"What's his name?"

"Jonathan Alkaitis." When had she last said the name out loud? She repeated it to herself, more quietly this time. "Actually, maybe I just want to talk to him. I don't know."

"Pretty big difference," the fortune-teller said.

"Yeah." Mirella closed her eyes against the dark of the sky, the tumult of the nearby party, the reek of cigarette smoke, the fortune-teller's face. "I guess I'll have to make up my mind."

"Okay," the fortune-teller said, "well, thanks for the light." She slid away from Mirella and vanished into the party, through an open door like a portal into a lost world. It was a cold night, and the moon was brilliant over New York City. Mirella stood looking at it for a moment, then returned to the party, which felt like a dream she'd had once, all abstract colour and commotion and lights. Louisa was dancing in the living room. Mirella stood watching her for a moment, then waded through the crowd.

"I've got a headache," Mirella said. "I think I'm going to go."

Louisa kissed her, and Mirella knew it was over. She felt nothing. "Call me," Louisa said.

"Adieu," Mirella said as she backed away through the crowd, and Louisa, who spoke no French and didn't understand the implication, blew her a kiss.

3

Last Book Tour on Earth /

2203

THE FIRST STOP ON THE BOOK TOUR WAS NEW YORK CITY, where Olive did signing events at two bookstores and then found an hour to walk in Central Park before the bookseller dinner. The Sheep Meadow at twilight: silvery light, wet leaves on the grass. The sky was crowded with low-altitude airships, and in the distance the falling-star lights of commuter aircraft streaked upward toward the colonies. Olive paused for a moment to orient herself, then walked toward the ancient double silhouette of the Dakota. Hundred-story towers rose up behind it.

The Dakota was where Olive's new publicist, Aretta, was waiting, in charge of all events in the Atlantic Republic. Aretta was a little younger than Olive, and deferential in a way that made Olive nervous. When Olive walked into the lobby, Aretta stood quickly, and the hologram with whom she'd been speaking blinked out. "Did you have a nice walk in the park?" she asked, already smiling in anticipation of a positive reply.

"It was lovely, thank you," Olive said. She didn't add *It made me wish I could live on Earth,* because the last time she'd confided in a handler, it was repeated at dinner—"Do you know what Olive told me on the ride over?" a librarian in Montreal had reported breathlessly to a restaurant table full of waiting librarians, "She told me she was a little nervous before her talk!"—

so now as a matter of policy Olive didn't reveal anything even remotely personal to anyone ever.

"Well," Aretta said, "we should probably be getting to the venue. It's about six or seven blocks, should we maybe just . . . ?"

"I'd love to walk," Olive said, "if you don't mind." They walked out together into the silver city.

Did Olive actually wish she could live on Earth? She vacillated on the question. She'd lived all her life in the hundred and fifty square kilometres of the second moon colony, the imaginatively named Colony Two. She found it beautiful—Colony Two was a city of white stone, spired towers, tree-lined streets and small parks, alternating neighbourhoods of tall buildings and little houses with miniature lawns, a river running under pedestrian archways—but there's something to be said for unplanned cities. Colony Two was soothing in its symmetry and its order. Sometimes order can be relentless.

In the signing line after the lecture in Manhattan that night, a young man knelt on his side of the table so that he was more or less at eye level with Olive, and said, "I have a book to sign"—his voice trembled a little—"but what I really wanted to tell you is that your work helped me through a bad patch last year. I'm grateful."

"Oh," Olive said. "Thank you. I'm honoured." But in these moments *honoured* always felt inadequate, which made it feel

like the wrong word, which made Olive feel somehow fraudu-
lent, like an actor playing the role of Olive Llewellyn.

"Everyone feels like a fraud sometimes," Dad said the following
day, on the drive from the Denver airship terminal to the tiny
town where he lived with Olive's mother.

"Oh, I know," Olive said. "I'm not suggesting it's an actual
problem." Olive's understanding of her own life was that she
didn't have any actual problems.

"Right." Dad smiled. "I'd imagine your life's a little disorienting these days."

"Perhaps just a little." Olive had forty-eight hours to see her
parents before the tour resumed. They were passing through
an agricultural zone, enormous robots moving slowly over the
fields. The sunlight here was sharper than at home. "I'm grateful
for all of it," she said. "Disorienting or not."

"Sure. Must be hard to be away from Sylvie and Dion, though."

Now they were in the outskirts of the little town where her
parents lived, passing through a district of robot repair foundries.

"I just try not to think about it," Olive said. The grey of the
foundries was subsiding into brightly painted little shops and
houses. The clock in the town square glinted in the sunlight.

"The distance is unbearable if you let yourself dwell on it."
Her father's gaze was fixed on the road. "Here we are," he said.
They were turning onto her parents' street, and there, so close,
her mother stood in the doorway. Olive leaped down from the

hovercraft the moment it stopped, and ran into her mother's arms. *If the distance is unbearable,* she didn't ask, then or in the two days she stayed with her parents, *then why do you live so far from me?*

Olive's parents' house couldn't be called her childhood home— her childhood home had been sold a few weeks after she left for college, when her parents decided to retire on Earth—but there was peace here. "It was so good to see you," her mother whispered when she left. She held Olive for just a moment, and stroked her hair. "Come back soon?"

A hovercraft was waiting outside the house, the driver hired by one of Olive's North American publishers. She had an event at a bookstore in Colorado Springs that night, followed by an early-morning flight to a festival in Deseret.

"I'll bring Sylvie and Dion next time," Olive said, and stepped back into the tour.

A book tour paradox: Olive missed her husband and daughter with a desperate passion, but also she liked very much being alone in the empty streets of Salt Lake City at eight-thirty in the morning on a Saturday in the bright autumn air, birds wheeling in white light. There's something to be said for looking up at a clear blue sky and knowing that it isn't a dome.

In the Republic of Texas the next afternoon, she wanted to go for a walk again, because on the map, her hotel—a La Quinta that faced another La Quinta, a parking lot between them—was just across the road from a cluster of restaurants and shops, but what the map didn't show was that the road was an eight-lane express-way with no crosswalk and constant traffic, mostly modern hov-ercraft but also the occasional defiantly retro wheeled pickup truck, so she walked along the expressway for a while with the shops and the restaurants shining like a mirage on the other side. There was no way to cross without risking her life, so she didn't. When she got back to her hotel she felt something scratching her ankles, and when she looked down her socks were spiked with little burrs, astonishingly sharp black-brown stars like miniature weapons that had to be extracted very carefully. She set them on the desk and photographed them from every angle. They were so perfectly hard and shiny that they could've passed for biotech, but when she pulled one apart, she saw that it was real. No, *real* wasn't the word for it. Everything that can be touched is real. What she saw was it was a thing that grew, a castoff from some mysterious plant they didn't have in the moon colonies, so she wrapped a few of them in a sock and carefully stowed the sock away in her suitcase to give to her daughter, Sylvie, who was five and collected that kind of thing.

"I was so confused by your book," a woman in Dallas said. "There were all these strands, narratively speaking, all these characters, and I felt like I was waiting for them to connect, but they didn't, ultimately. The book just ended. I was like"—she was some distance away, in the darkened audience, but Olive saw that she was miming flipping through a book and running out of pages—"I was just like, *Huh? Is the book missing pages? It just ended.*"

"Okay," Olive said. "So just to clarify, your question is . . ."

"I was just, like, *what,*" the woman said. "My question is just . . ." She spread her hands, like *help me out here, I've run out of words.*

The hotel room that night was all black and white. Olive had dreams about playing chess with her mother.

Did the book end too abruptly? She fixated on the question for three days, from the Republic of Texas to western Canada.

"I'm trying not to be pessimistic," Olive said, on the phone to her husband, "but I've barely slept in three days and I doubt I'll be terribly impressive in my lecture tonight." This was in Red Deer. Outside the hotel room window, the lights of residential towers glimmered in the dark.

"Don't be pessimistic," Dion said. "Think of that quote I've got pinned up in my office."

"'It's a great life if you don't weaken,'" Olive said. "How's work going, speaking of your office?"

He sighed. "I got assigned to the new project." Dion was an architect.

"The new university?"

"Yeah, kind of. A centre for the study of physics, but also . . .

I signed an ironclad confidentiality agreement, so don't tell anyone?"

"Of course. I won't tell a soul. But what's so secret about the architecture of a university?"

"It's not quite . . . I'm not sure it's exactly a university." Dion sounded troubled. "There's some serious weirdness in the blue-prints."

"What kind of weirdness?"

"Well, for starters, there's a tunnel under the street connecting the building to Security Headquarters," he said.

"Why would a university need a tunnel to the police?"

"Your guess is as good as mine. And the building backs up on the government building," Dion said, "which, I mean, at first I thought nothing of it. That's prime downtown real estate, so you know, why shouldn't the university build next to the government building, but the two buildings aren't separate. There are so many passageways between them that it's functionally the same building."

"You're right," Olive said, "that seems weird."

"Well, it's a good project for my portfolio, I guess."

Olive understood from his tone that he wanted to change the subject. "How's Sylvie?"

"Doing fine." Dion immediately pivoted the conversation to some trivial matter involving the grocery order and Sylvie's school lunches, from which she understood that Sylvie probably wasn't in fact doing particularly well in her absence, and she was grateful for his kindness in not telling her this.

. . .

In the morning she flew to a city in the far north for a day of interviews, and then she had an evening lecture, and then there was a long signing line and a late dinner, followed by three hours of sleep and a three-forty-five a.m. airport pickup.

"What do you do, Olive?" the driver asked.

"I'm a writer," Olive said. She closed her eyes and rested her head against the window, but the driver spoke again:

"What do you write?"

"Books."

"Tell me more."

"Well," Olive said, "I'm travelling because of a novel called *Marienbad*. It's about a pandemic."

"That's your most recent?"

"No, I've written two others since then. But *Marienbad*'s being made into a film, so I'm on tour for a new edition."

"That's so interesting," the driver said, and started talking about a book she wanted to write. It seemed to be some kind of sci-fi/fantasy epic, the modern world except with wizards, demons, and talking rats. The rats were good. They helped the wizards. They were rats because in all the books the driver had read that involved helpful talking animals, the animals were just too big. Horses and dragons and whatnot. But how do you discreetly move through the world with a dragon or a horse? It's untenable. Try taking a horse into a bar sometime. No, what you want, she said, is a pocket-sized animal sidekick, a rat for example.

"Yeah, I guess rats are more portable," Olive said. She was trying to keep her eyes open, but it was very difficult. The massive transport truck in front of them kept weaving over the centre line. Human-driven, or a flaw in the software? Unsettling either way. The driver was talking about the possibilities of the multiverse: rats can't talk here, she pointed out, but does it logically follow that they can't talk *anywhere*? She seemed to be waiting for a reply.

"Well, I don't know much about rat anatomy," Olive said, "like if their voice boxes and vocal cords or whatever are up to the task of human speech, but I'll have to think about it, maybe rats in different universes could have different anatomy . . ." (She may have been mumbling by that point, or possibly not speaking at all. It was so hard to stay awake.) The back of the transport truck was beautiful, a diamond-patterned textured steel that glinted and shone in the headlights.

"I mean, for all we know," the driver was saying, "there's a universe where your book is real, I mean nonfictional!"

"I hope not," Olive said. She could only keep her eyes half-open, so the lights in her field of vision were streaked into vertical spikes, the dashboard, the tail lights, the reflections off the back of the truck.

"So your book," the driver said, "it's about a pandemic?"

"Yes. A scientifically implausible flu." Olive couldn't keep her eyes open anymore, so she surrendered, she closed her eyes and let herself fall into the kind of half-sleep from which she knew she could be summoned by a voice—

"Have you been following the news about this new thing," the driver said, "this new virus in Australia?"

"Kind of," Olive said, with her eyes closed. "It seems like it's been fairly well contained."

"You know, in my book," the driver said, "there's a kind of apocalypse too." She talked for some time about a catastrophic rip in the space-time continuum, but Olive was too tired to follow.

"I've kept you up this whole time!" the driver said brightly, as the car pulled into the airport. "You didn't get to sleep at all!"

Twelve hours later, Olive was delivering her *Marienbad* lecture, which leaned heavily on her research into the history of pandemics. The lecture was so familiar at this point that it required very little in the way of conscious thought, and her mind was wandering. She kept thinking about the conversation with the driver, because she remembered saying *It seems like it's been fairly well contained,* but here's an epidemiological question: If you're talking about outbreaks of infectious disease, isn't *fairly well contained* essentially the same thing as *not contained at all*? *Focus,* she told herself, and pulled herself back to the reality of the podium, the hard bright light, the microphone.

"In the spring of 1792," she said, "Captain George Vancouver sailed northward up the coast of what would later become British Columbia, aboard the HMS *Discovery*. As he and his crew travelled northward, the men found themselves increasingly unsettled. Here was this temperate climate, this incredibly green landscape, and yet it seemed strangely empty. Vancouver wrote in his shipboard diary: 'We travelled nearly one hundred fifty miles of those shores, without seeing that number of inhabitants.'" A pause to let that sink in, while Olive took a sip of water. A virus is either contained or it isn't. It's a binary condition. She hadn't been sleeping enough. She set down her water glass.

"When they ventured ashore, they found villages that could have housed hundreds, but those villages were abandoned. When they ventured farther, they realized that the forest was a graveyard." This was the part of the lecture that had been easy before giving birth to her daughter, and was now almost impossible. Olive paused to steady herself. "Canoes with human remains were strung three or four metres up in the trees," she said. *Human remains that were not Sylvie. Not Sylvie. Not Sylvie.* "Elsewhere, they found skeletons on the beach. Because smallpox had already arrived."

In the signing line after that night's lecture, signing her name over and over again, Olive's thoughts kept drifting toward disaster. *To Xander with best wishes Olive Llewellyn. To Claudio with best wishes Olive Llewellyn. To Sohail with best wishes Olive Llewellyn. To Hyeseung with best wishes Olive Llewellyn.* Was there going to be another pandemic? A new cluster of cases had appeared in New Zealand that morning.

The hotel room that night was mostly beige, with a painting of some extravagantly petalled pink Earth flower—a peony?—over the bed.

. . .

"A year earlier," Olive told another crowd, same lecture/different city, "in 1791, a trading ship, the *Columbia Rediviva*, had sailed those same waters. They were trading sea otter skins." What did a sea otter even look like? Olive had never seen one. She resolved to look this up later. "They had a similar experience. They found a depopulated land, and the very few survivors they encountered had terrible stories and terrible scars. ''Twas evident that these Natives had been visited by that scourge of mankind the smallpox,' wrote a crew member, John Boit. Another sailor, John Hoskins, was moved to outrage: 'Infamous Europeans, a scandal to the Christian name; is it you,' he wrote, 'who bring and leave in a country with people you deem savages the most loathsome diseases?'"

A sip of water. The audience was silent. (A passing thought that felt like triumph: *I am holding the room.*) "But of course," she said, "there's always a beginning. Before smallpox could be brought from Europe to the Americas, smallpox had to arrive in Europe."

She got out of bed that night and walked into a side table, because she'd been thinking about the layout of the previous night's hotel room.

The next morning, on a long drive between cities, the driver asked if Olive had kids back home.

"I have a daughter," Olive said.

"How old?"

"Five."

"What are you doing here, then?" the driver asked.

"Well, this is how I provide for her," she said, in her mildest voice, and didn't add *Fuck you, I know you would never ask a man that question*, because after all it was just the two of them alone in the car, this man and Olive. Watching the trees slip by outside the window; they were passing through a forest preserve. Imagining Sylvie was here beside her, imagining that if she wanted to she could reach out and hold that warm little hand.

"You grew up there? In the colonies?" he asked abruptly, after some time had passed. They'd been talking about the moon colonies earlier.

"Yes. My grandmother was one of the first settlers."

She liked to picture her grandmother sometimes, twenty years old, rising out of the Vancouver Airship Terminal in the first light of dawn, her ship streaking out into the dark.

"Always meant to go up there," the driver said. "Never made it."

Remember that you're lucky to get to travel. Remember that some people never leave this planet. Olive closed her eyes, in order to better imagine that Sylvie was sitting beside her.

"You smell nice, by the way," the driver said.

The next four hotel rooms were white and grey and had identical layouts, because all four hotels were part of the same chain.

"Is this your first time staying with us?" a woman at a reception desk for the third or fourth hotel said to her, and Olive wasn't sure how to answer, because if you've stayed in one Marriott, haven't you stayed in all of them?

Another city:

"Before smallpox could be brought from Europe to the Americas, smallpox had to arrive in Europe." Olive was regretting her decision to wear a sweater. The lights in Toronto were too hot. "In the middle of the second century, Roman soldiers returning from their siege of the Mesopotamian city of Seleucia brought a new illness back to the capital.

"Victims of the Antonine Plague, as it came to be called, developed fevers, vomiting, and diarrhea. A few days later, a terrible rash would appear on their skin. The population had no immunity." Olive had delivered the lecture so many times that she felt at this point like a neutral observer. She listened to the words and cadences from some distance away.

"When the Antonine Plague raged through the Roman Empire," Olive told the audience, "the army was decimated. There were parts of the empire where one in three people died. Here's something interesting: the Romans wondered if they'd brought this calamity upon themselves, by their actions in the city of Seleucia."

She was in that night's hotel room—mostly beige and blue, with pink accents—when Dion called. This was unusual: generally speaking, she called him. Dion sounded tired. He'd been working long hours, he said, and the new university project was creepy, and Sylvie was being difficult. When he'd picked Sylvie up at school today she hadn't wanted to leave and had made a scene and everyone had felt sorry for him, he could see it in their soft expressions. "Have you been following the news about this new illness in Australia?" he asked. "I'm kind of worried about it."

"Not really," Olive said. "To be honest, I've been too tired to think."

"I wish you could come home."

"I'll be home soon."

He was silent.

"I should go," she said. "Good night."

"Good night," he said, and hung up.

"In the city of Seleucia," Olive told a crowd at the Mercantile Library in Cincinnati, a day or two later, "the Roman army had destroyed the temple of Apollo. In that temple, the historian Ammianus Marcellinus wrote, Roman soldiers had discovered a narrow crevice. When the Romans opened this hole wider, in the hope that it might contain valuables, Marcellinus wrote that there 'issued a pestilence, loaded with the force of incurable disease, which . . . polluted the whole world from the borders of Persia to the Rhine and Gaul with contagion and death.'"

A beat. A sip of water. Pacing is everything.

"This explanation might seem a little silly to us now, but they were grasping wildly for an explanation for the nightmare that had befallen them, and I think that in its outlandishness, the explanation touches upon the root of our fear: illness still carries a terrible mystery."

She looked over the crowd and saw, as always at this point in the lecture, that particular look on the faces of some of the audience, a specific grief. In any given crowd, several people will inevitably be incurably sick, and several others will have recently lost someone they love to illness.

"Are you worried about the new virus?" Olive asked the library director in Cincinnati. They were sitting together in the director's office, which Olive had immediately ranked as possibly her favourite of all the offices she'd ever seen. It was located beneath the stacks, which were hundreds of years old and made of wrought iron.

"I'm trying not to be," the director said. "I'm hoping it'll just fizzle out."

"I suppose they usually do," Olive said. Was this true? She was unsure as she spoke.

The library director nodded, her eyes wandering. She clearly didn't want to talk about pandemics. "Let me tell you something magnificent about this place," she said.

"Oh, please do," Olive said. "It's been a while since anyone's told me anything magnificent."

"So we don't own the building," the director said, "but we hold a ten-thousand-year lease on the space."

"You're right. That's magnificent."

"Nineteenth-century hubris. Imagine thinking civilization

would still exist in ten thousand years. But there's more." She leaned forward, paused for effect. "The lease is renewable."

The window in that night's hotel room opened, which after a dozen rooms with nonopening windows felt like something of a miracle. Olive spent a long time reading a novel by the window, in the beautiful fresh air.

The next morning, leaving Cincinnati, Olive saw a sunrise from the airport lounge. Heat shimmering over the tarmac, the horizon cast in pink. *Paradox: I want to go home but I could watch Earth's sunrises forever.*

"The truth is," Olive said, behind a lectern in Paris, "even now, all these centuries later, for all our technological advances, all our scientific knowledge of illness, we still don't always know why one person gets sick and another doesn't, or why one patient survives and another dies. Illness frightens us because it's chaotic. There's an awful randomness about it."

At the reception that night, someone tapped her shoulder, and when she turned around it was Aretta, her publicist from the Atlantic Republic.

"Aretta!" she said. "What are you doing in Paris?"

"I'm off work," Aretta said, "but one of my best friends works for your French publisher and she got us tickets for the reception, so I thought I'd say hi."

"It's good to see you here," Olive said, and meant it, but someone was pulling her away to speak to a group of sponsors and booksellers, so for a while afterward Olive stood in a circle of people who wanted to know when her next book was coming out and whether she was enjoying France and where her family was.

"You must have a very kind husband," a woman said, "to look after your daughter while you do this."

"What do you mean?" Olive asked, but of course she knew what the woman meant.

"Well, he's looking after your daughter, while you do this," the woman said.

"Forgive me," Olive said, "I fear there's a problem with my translator bot. I thought you said he was kind to care for his own child." As she turned away, she realized that she was grinding her teeth. She looked for Aretta but couldn't find her.

The next four hotel rooms were beige, blue, beige again, then mostly white, but all four had silk flowers in a vase on the desk.

"What's it like?" the interviewer asked. It was difficult to stop thinking about the woman in Paris, but Olive was trying. *Keep moving.* Olive and the interviewer were onstage in Tallinn. The lights were very hot.

"What do you mean?" It was a strange opening question.

"What's it like writing such a successful book? What's it like being Olive Llewellyn?"

"Oh. It's surreal, actually. I wrote three books that no one noticed, no distribution beyond the moon colonies, and then . . . it's like slipping into a parallel universe," Olive said. "When I published *Marienbad,* I somehow fell into a bizarre upside-down world where people actually read my work. It's extraordinary. I hope I never get used to it."

The driver who took Olive to her hotel that night had a beautiful voice and sang an old jazz song as he drove. Olive opened the hovercraft window and closed her eyes in order to live more completely in the music, cool air in her face, and for several minutes she was perfectly happy.

"It's amazing how time slows when I'm travelling," Olive said, on the phone to Dion. She was lying on her back on the floor of another hotel room, staring up at the ceiling. The bed would have been more comfortable, but her back hurt and the hard floor was helping. "I feel like I've been on the road for six months. I'm not sure how it's still November."

"It's been three weeks."

"Like I said."

There was silence on the line.

"Look," Olive said, "the thing is, it's possible to be grateful for extraordinary circumstances and simultaneously long to be with the people you love."

She felt a softening between them before he spoke. "I know, love," Dion said gently. "We miss you too."

"I've been thinking about your project," she said. "Why a

university would need an underground passageway to police headquarters and—"

But Dion's device was ringing. "I'm sorry," he said, "it's my boss. Talk soon?"

"Talk soon."

She'd been on an airship crossing the Atlantic when the answer to the puzzle came to her.

Research teams had been working on time travel for decades, both on Earth and in the colonies. In that context, a university for the study of physics with an underground passageway to the police headquarters and countless literal back doors into government made perfect sense. What is time travel if not a security problem?

She kept searching for the song the driver in Tallinn had been singing, but she couldn't find it. The lyrics evaded her. She kept entering search terms into her device (*love + rain + death + money + lyrics + song*) and getting nowhere.

In Lyon, at a festival dedicated to mystery fiction, Olive's French publicist brought her to a media room where the interviewer, a woman who worked for a magazine, was programming an array of hologram cameras. "Olive," the interviewer said, "I love your work."

"Thank you, that's really nice to hear."

"Will you sit in that chair, please?"

Olive sat. An assistant affixed a mic to her shirt.

"So this is a feature I'm doing with all of the authors at the festival," the interviewer said, "just a brief interview feature. It's a fun thing for our audience."

"A fun thing?" Olive was troubled. Her French publicist shot the interviewer a look of alarm.

"Shall we get started?"

"Sure." Ten holographic cameras floated through the air and surrounded Olive like a ring of stars, building their composite impression.

"So these questions," the interviewer said, "they have a mystery focus!"

"Because we're at a mystery festival," Olive said.

"Exactly. Okay. Number one: What's your favourite alibi?"

"My favourite . . . alibi?"

"Yes."

"I don't really . . . I just say I have other plans. When I don't want to do something."

"I understand you're married to a man," the interviewer said. "When you met your husband, what was your first clue that you loved him?"

"Well," Olive said, "I guess just a sense of recognition, if that makes sense. I remember the first time I saw him, I looked at him and I knew he'd be important in my life. Is that a clue, though?"

"What's your idea of the perfect murder?"

"I remember reading a story once where a guy got stabbed with an icicle," Olive said. "I guess that's sort of perfect, a crime where the murder weapon melts. Do you mind if I ask, though, do you have any questions that have to do with my work?"

"I just have one more. Okay, last question. Sex with or without handcuffs?"

Olive unclipped the mic from her shirt as she stood. She placed the mic carefully on the chair. "No comment," she said, and left the room before the interviewer could see the tears in her eyes.

In Shanghai, Olive spent a combined total of three hours talking about herself and about her book, which meant talking about the end of the world while trying not to imagine the world ending with her daughter in it, and then returned to her hotel, where she noticed in the corridor that she was having difficulty walking in a straight line. She never drank, but drunkenness and fatigue look the same sometimes. Olive weaved down the hallway and stumbled into her room. She closed the door behind her and stood just inside for a long time, her forehead resting on the cool wall above the light switch. After a while, she heard her own voice, repeating *It's too much. It's too much. It's too much.*

"Olive," the room's AI system said softly, when some time had passed, "do you desire assistance?" When Olive didn't answer, it repeated the inquiry in Mandarin and Cantonese.

"Olive, this is totally random, but I was your agent's babysitter," a woman told her, in a signing line in Singapore the next day.

. . .

"What message would you like your readers to take away from *Marienbad*?" another interviewer asked.

Olive and the interviewer were onstage together in Tokyo. The interviewer was a hologram, because for unspecified personal reasons he'd been unable to leave Nairobi. Olive suspected the personal reason was illness: the interviewer kept freezing up, but the sound had no lag, which meant the interviewer wasn't freezing due to a bad connection, he was freezing because he kept pressing the Cough button on his console.

"I was just trying to write an interesting book," Olive said. "There's no message."

"Are you sure?" the interviewer asked.

"Will you sign a used book?" a woman asked, in a signing line.

"Of course, I'd be happy to."

"Also," the woman said, "is this your handwriting?"

Someone, not Olive, had already written in this woman's copy of *Marienbad: Harold: I enjoyed last night. xoxoxoxo Olive Llewellyn.*

Olive stared at the message and felt just a touch of vertigo. "No," she said, "I don't know who wrote that."

(She was distracted for days afterward by the thought of a shadow Olive moving over the landscape, on a kind of parallel tour, writing uncharacteristic messages in Olive's books.)

· · ·

In Cape Town, Olive met an author who'd been out on the road with his husband for a year and a half, touring in the service of a book that had sold several times as many copies as *Marienbad*.

"We're trying to see how long we can travel until we have to go home," the author said. His name was Ibby, short for Ibrahim, and his husband was Jack. The three of them were sitting together in the evening on the rooftop terrace of the hotel, which was filled with authors attending a literary festival.

"Are you trying to avoid going home?" Olive asked. "Or you just like travelling?"

"Both," Jack said. "I like being on the road."

"And our apartment's mediocre," Ibby said, "but we haven't decided what to do about it. Move? Redecorate? Could go either way."

There were dozens of trees up here, in enormous planters, with little lights sparkling in the branches. Music was playing somewhere, a string quartet. Olive was wearing her designated fancy tour dress, which was silver and went to her ankles. *This is one of the glamorous moments,* Olive thought, filing it carefully away so she could draw on it for sustenance later. The breeze carried a scent of jasmine.

"*I* heard some good news today," Jack said.

"Tell me," Ibby said. "I've been in a kind of book festival tunnel all day. Inadvertent news blackout."

"Construction just began on the first of the Far Colonies," Jack said.

Olive smiled, and almost spoke, but she was momentarily wordless. Planning for the Far Colonies had begun when her grandparents were children. She would always remember this moment, she thought, this party, these people whom she very much liked and might never see again. She'd be able to tell Sylvie where she was when she heard the news. When had she last experienced true awe? It had been a while. Olive was flooded with happiness. She raised her glass.

"To Alpha Centauri," she said.

In Buenos Aires, Olive met a woman who wanted to show her a tattoo. "I hope this isn't weird," she said, and rolled up her sleeve to reveal a quote from the book: *We knew it was coming,* in a beautiful curly script on her left shoulder.

Olive's breath caught in her throat. It wasn't just a line from *Marienbad,* it was a tattoo in *Marienbad.* In the second half of the novel, her character Gaspery-Jacques had the line tattooed on his left arm. You write a book with a fictional tattoo and then the tattoo becomes real in the world and after that almost anything seems possible. She'd seen five of those tattoos, but that didn't make it less extraordinary, seeing the way fiction can bleed into the world and leave a mark on someone's skin.

"That's incredible," Olive said softly. "It's incredible to see that tattoo in the real world."

"It's my favourite line from your book," she said. "It's just true of so much, isn't it?"

• • •

But doesn't everything seem obvious in retrospect? Blue dusk over the prairies, gliding toward the Dakota Republic in a low-altitude airship. Olive stared out the window and tried to find some peace in the landscape. She had a new invitation for a festival on Titan. She hadn't been since she was a kid and retained only vague memories of crowds at the Dolphinarium and some oddly tasteless popcorn, the warm yellowish haze of the daytime sky—she'd been in a so-called Realist colony, one of the outposts whose settlers had decided on clear domes in order to experience the true colours of the Titanian atmosphere—and strange fashions, this thing all the teenagers were doing that involved painting their faces like pixels, big squares of colour that were supposed to defeat the facial-recognition software but that had the side effect of making them look like deranged clowns. Should she go to Titan? *I want to go home.* Where was Sylvie at this moment? *This is easier than having a day job, though, just remember that.*

"I remember reading somewhere," an interviewer said, "that the title of your first book actually came from your last day job?"

"Yes," Olive said, "I came across it at work one day."

"Your first novel was, of course, *Swimming Stars with Gold-flitter.* Will you tell me about that title?"

"Sure, yes. I was working in AI training. So, you know, correcting awkward renderings from the translator bots. I remember sitting there by the hour in this cramped little office—"

"This was in Colony Two?"

"Yes, Colony Two. My job was to sit there all day, rewording unfortunate sentences. But there was one that stopped me cold, because it may have been awkward and error-ridden, but I loved it." Olive had told this story so often that it was like reciting lines from a play. "It was a description of votive candles with little poems on the candleholders. The description had somehow been rendered as *seven motives for verse*, and then one of the candle descriptions was *swimming stars with goldflitter*. The beauty of those phrases, I don't know, it just stopped me cold."

Stopped me cold. Two days later she was on a panel with another writer at a festival in the city-state of Los Angeles, and the implication of that phrase had just occurred to her. What stops you, and turns you cold? Death, obviously. Olive couldn't believe she'd never thought of this. Los Angeles was under a dome, but still the light through the windows was blinding. This meant she couldn't see the audience, which was frankly ideal. All those faces staring at her. No, at them: the other writer's name was Jessica Marley and Olive was glad Jessica was here with her, even though she didn't actually like her very much. Everything offended Jessica, which is inevitable when you move through the world in search of offence.

"Well, some of us don't have doctorates in literature, Jim," Jessica said to the interviewer, in response to some imperceptible provocation. The look on his face mirrored Olive's thought at that moment: *Well, that escalated quickly.* But a man in the audience was standing up with a question about *Marienbad*. Almost all of the questions were about *Marienbad,* which was awkward because Jessica was there too, Jessica with her book about coming of age in the moon colonies. Olive was pretending that she hadn't read *Moon/Rise,* because she'd hated it. Olive had lived the real thing, and it wasn't nearly as poetic as Jessica's book suggested. Growing up in a moon colony was fine. It was neither great nor dystopian. It was a little house in a pleasant neighbourhood of tree-lined streets, a good but not extraordinary public school, life lived at a consistent 15° to 22° Celsius under carefully calibrated dome lighting, scheduled rainfalls. She didn't grow up *longing for Earth* or experience her life as *a continual displacement,* thank you.

"I wanted to ask Olive about the death of the prophet in *Marienbad,*" the man in the audience said. Jessica sighed and slumped a little in her chair. "It could have been a much bigger moment, but you decided to make it a relatively small, not-climactic event."

"Really? I thought of it as climactic," Olive said, as mildly as possible.

He smiled, humouring her. "But you chose to make it really small, almost inconsequential, when it could have been cinematic, something really big. Why is that?"

Jessica sat up straight, excited by the possibility of combat.

"Well," Olive said. "I suppose everyone has a different idea of what constitutes a big moment."

"You're a master of deflection," Jessica murmured, without looking at her. "You're like some kind of deflection ninja."

"Thank you," Olive said, although she knew it wasn't a compliment.

"Let's move on to the next question," the interviewer said.

"You know the phrase I keep thinking about?" a poet asked, on a different panel, at a festival in Copenhagen. " 'The chickens are coming home to roost.' Because it's never good chickens. It's never 'You've been a good person and now your chickens are coming home to roost.' It's never good chickens. It's always bad chickens."

Scattered laughter and applause. A man in the audience was having a coughing fit. He left quickly, bent over in an apologetic way. Olive wrote *no good chickens* in the margin of her festival program.

Was the death of the prophet in *Marienbad* too anticlimactic? It seemed possible. Olive was sitting alone at a hotel bar near the Copenhagen festival, drinking tea and eating a wilted salad with too much cheese on it. On the one hand the prophet's death *was* dramatic, after all he'd been shot in the head, but maybe there should've been some kind of battle scene, maybe the death really was too casual, in the way he went from perfect health to death over the course of a paragraph and the story kept moving without him—

"May I get you anything else?" the bartender asked.

"Just the check, please," Olive said.

—but on the other hand, isn't that reality? Won't most of

us die in fairly unclimactic ways, our passing unremarked by almost everyone, our deaths becoming plot points in the narratives of the people around us? But obviously *Marienbad* was fiction, i.e., reality wasn't relevant to the question at hand, and maybe the death of the prophet really was a flaw. Now Olive was holding the pen over the check, but there was a difficulty: she'd forgotten her room number. She had to go to the front desk to retrieve it.

"It happens more often than you'd think," the clerk at the front desk said.

At the airship terminal the next morning, she sat next to a business traveller who wanted to tell her about his job, which had something to do with detecting counterfeit steel. Olive listened for a long time, because the monologue distracted her from how much she missed Sylvie. "And what do you do?" the other traveller asked finally.

"I write books," Olive said.

"For children?" he asked.

When Olive circled back to the Atlantic Republic, seeing her AR publicist again was like seeing an old friend. Aretta and Olive sat together at a dinner for booksellers in Jersey City.

"How's it been since I saw you last?" Aretta asked.

"Fine," Olive said, "it's all going fine. I have no complaints." And then, because she was tired and she knew Aretta a little by now, she broke her own rule about never revealing anything personal, and said, "It's just a lot of people."

Aretta smiled. "Publicists aren't supposed to be shy," she said, "but I get a little overwhelmed at these dinners sometimes."

"Me too," Olive said. "My face gets tired."

That night's hotel room was white and blue. The thing with being away from her husband and daughter was that every hotel room was emptier than the one before.

The last interview of the tour was the following afternoon in Philadelphia, where Olive met a man in a dark suit who was her age or a little younger, in a beautiful meeting room at a hotel. The room was on a high floor with a wall of glass, and the city rolled away beneath them.

"Here we are," said Aretta brightly. "Olive, this is Gaspery Roberts, *Contingencies Magazine*. I have to make a couple of quick calls, so I'll leave you two." She receded. Olive and the interviewer sat in matching green velvet chairs.

"Thank you for meeting with me," the man said.

"My pleasure. Do you mind if I ask about your name? I'm not sure I've ever met a Gaspery."

"I'll tell you something even stranger," he said. "My first name is actually Gaspery-Jacques."

"Seriously? I thought I'd made up the name for that character in *Marienbad*."

He smiled. "My mother was astonished when she came across the name in your book. She thought she'd made it up too."

"Perhaps I came across your name somewhere and didn't consciously remember it."

"Anything's possible. It's hard to know what we know sometimes, isn't it?" He had a gentle way of speaking that Olive liked, and a faint accent that she couldn't quite place. "Have you been in interviews all day?"

"Half the day. You're my fifth."

"Ouch. I'll keep this brief, then. I'd like to ask you about a specific scene in *Marienbad*, if I may."

"Okay. Sure."

"The scene in the spaceport," he said. "Where your character Willis hears the violin and he's . . . transported."

"It's an odd passage," Olive said. "I get a lot of questions about it."

"I'd like to ask you something." Gaspery hesitated. "This might seem a bit—I don't mean to pry. But is there an element of—I'm wondering if that bit of the book was inspired by a personal experience."

"I've never been interested in auto-fiction," Olive said, but it was difficult to meet his eyes now. She'd always found something steadying in looking at her own clasped hands, but she didn't know if it was the hands or the shirt, the impeccable white cuffs. Clothes are armour.

"Listen," Gaspery said, "I don't mean to make you uncomfortable or put you on the spot. But I'm curious if you experienced something strange in the Oklahoma City Airship Terminal."

In the quiet, Olive could hear the soft hum of the building, the sounds of ventilation and plumbing. Perhaps she wouldn't have admitted it if he hadn't caught her toward the end of the tour, if she hadn't been so tired.

"I don't mind talking about this," she said, "but I'm afraid I'll seem too eccentric if it makes it into the final version of the interview. Could we go off the record for a moment?"

"Yes," he said.

Bad Chickens /

2401

1

No star burns forever. You can say "It's the end of the world" and mean it, but what gets lost in that kind of careless usage is that the world will eventually literally end. Not "civilization," whatever that is, but the actual planet.

Which is not to say that those smaller endings aren't annihilating. A year before I began my training at the Time Institute, I went to a dinner party at my friend Ephrem's place. He was just back from a vacation on Earth, and he had a story about going on a walk in a cemetery with his daughter, Meiying, who was four at the time. Ephrem was an arborist. He liked to go to old cemeteries to look at the trees. But then they found the grave of another four-year-old girl, Ephrem told me, and he just wanted to leave after that. He was used to graveyards, he sought them out, he'd always said he didn't find them depressing, just peaceful, but that one grave just got to him. He looked at it and was unbearably sad. Also it was the worst kind of Earth summer day, impossibly humid, and he felt like he couldn't get enough air. The drone of the cicadas was oppressive. Sweat ran down his back. He told his daughter it was time to go, but she lingered by the gravestone for a moment.

"If her parents loved her," Meiying said, "it would have felt like the end of the world."

It was such an eerily astute observation, Ephrem told me, that he stood there staring at her and found himself thinking, *Where did you come from?* They got out of the cemetery with difficulty—"She had to stop and inspect every goddamned flower and pinecone," he said—and never went back.

Those are the worlds that end in our day-to-day lives, these stopped children, these annihilating losses, but at the end of Earth there will be actual, literal annihilation, hence the colonies. The first colony on the moon was intended as a prototype, a practice run for establishing a presence in other solar systems in the coming centuries. "Because we'll have to," the president of China said, at the press conference where construction on the first colony was announced, "eventually, whether we want to or not, unless we want all of human history and achievement to get sucked into a supernova a few million years down the line."

I watched footage of that press conference in my sister Zoey's office, three hundred years after the fact. The president behind the lectern with her officials arrayed around her, a crowd of reporters below the stage. One of them raised his hand: "Are we sure it's going to be a supernova?"

"Of course not," the president said. "It could be anything. Rogue planet, asteroid storm, you name it. The point is that we're orbiting a star, and all stars eventually die."

"But if the star dies," I said to Zoey, "obviously the Earth's moon goes with it."

"Sure," she said, "but we're just the prototype, Gaspery. We're just proof of concept. The Far Colonies have been populated for a hundred and eighty years."

2

The first moon colony was built on the silent flatlands of the Sea of Tranquility, near where the Apollo 11 astronauts had landed in a long-ago century. Their flag was still there, in the distance, a fragile little statue on the windless surface.

There was substantial interest in immigration to the colony. Earth was so crowded by then, and such swaths of it had been rendered uninhabitable by flooding or heat. The colony's architects had set aside space for substantial residential development, which sold out quickly. The developers lobbied successfully for a second colony when they ran out of space in Colony One. But Colony Two was built a little too hastily, and within a century the lighting system on the main dome had failed. The lighting system was meant to mimic the appearance of the sky as viewed from Earth—it was nice to look up and see blue, as opposed to looking up into the void—and when it failed there was no more false atmosphere, no more shifting pixelations to give the impression of clouds, no more carefully calibrated preprogrammed sunrises and sunsets, no more blue. Which is not to suggest that there wasn't light, but that light was extremely un-Earthlike: on a bright day, the colonists looked up into space. The juxtaposition of utter darkness with bright light made some people dizzy, although whether this was physical or psychological was up for debate. More seriously, the failure of the dome lighting removed the illusion of the twenty-four-hour day. Now the sun rose rapidly and spent two weeks crossing the sky, after which there were two straight weeks of night.

The cost of repair was deemed prohibitive. There was a degree of adaptation—bedroom windows were outfitted with shutters, so people could sleep during the nights when the sun was out, and street lighting was improved for the days without sunlight— but property values declined, and most people who could afford it moved to Colony One or the recently completed Colony Three. "Colony Two" drifted out of common parlance; everyone called it the Night City. It was the place where the sky was always black.

I grew up in the Night City. My walk to school took me past the childhood home of Olive Llewellyn, an author who'd walked those same streets two hundred years ago, not too far out from the moon's first settlers. It was a little house on a tree-lined street, and I could tell that it had been pretty once, but the neighbourhood had gone downhill since Olive Llewellyn had been a child there. The house was a wreck now, half the windows covered up and graffiti everywhere, but the plaque by the front door remained. I paid the house no attention, until my mother told me she'd named me after a peripheral character in *Marienbad,* Llewellyn's most famous book. I didn't read the book— I didn't like books—but my sister Zoey did and reported back: the Gaspery-Jacques in the book wasn't anything like me.

I decided not to ask her what she meant. I was eleven when she read it, which would have made her thirteen or fourteen. By then she was already a serious, driven kind of person who was obviously going to excel at everything she attempted, whereas by eleven I already had the first suspicions that I might not be exactly the kind of person I wanted to be, and it would be awful if she were to tell me that the other Gaspery-Jacques were, say, a strikingly handsome and generally impressive person who was extremely focused on his schoolwork and never committed petty theft. But nonetheless I began to secretly regard Olive Llewellyn's childhood home with a degree of respect. I felt connected to it.

There was a family living there, a boy and a girl and their parents, pale, miserable-looking people who possessed this weird talent for conveying an impression that they were up to no good. They had an air of having gone to seed, the whole family. Their last name was Anderson. The parents spent a lot of time on the porch, arguing quietly or staring into space. The boy was surly and got into fights at school. The girl, who was about my age, liked to play with a hologram in the front yard, an old-fashioned mirror hologram who danced with her sometimes, and that was actually the only time I saw the Anderson girl smile anywhere near her house, when she was spinning and leaping and her holographic double was spinning and leaping too.

When I was twelve, the Anderson girl was in the same class as me, and I learned her name was Talia. Who was Talia Anderson? She loved to draw. She did backflips on the field. She looked much happier at school than she did at home.

"I know you," she said abruptly one day, when we were in the cafeteria line together. "You're always walking by my house."

"It's on my way," I said.

"On your way to what?"

"Well, on my way to everywhere. I live at the end of the cul-de-sac."

"I know," she said.

"How do you know where I live?"

"I walk by your house too," she said. "I cut through your neighbour's lawn to get to the Periphery."

At the end of our lawn there was a screen of leaves. Push through them and you'd get to the Periphery Road, which circled the interior of the Night City dome. Cross the road and there was a strange, wild area, no more than fifty feet deep, a strip of wilderness between the road and the dome. Scrub brush, dust, stray plants, garbage. It was a forgotten kind of place. Our mother didn't like us playing there, so Zoey never ventured across the Periphery Road—she always did as she was told, which I found maddening—but I liked the wildness of it, the mild sense of danger inherent in a forgotten kingdom. That day after school

I crossed the empty road for the first time in a few weeks, and stood for a while with my hands pressed to the dome, looking out. The composite glass was so thick that everything on the other side looked like a dream, distant in a muffled kind of way, but I saw craters here and there, meteors, grey. The opaque dome of Colony One glowed in the near distance. I found myself wondering what Talia Anderson's thoughts were when she gazed out at the moonscape.

Talia Anderson transferred out of my class and left the neighbourhood halfway through the year. I didn't see her again until my mid-thirties, when we were both employed by the Grand Luna Hotel in Colony One.

I started work at the hotel about a month after my mother died. She'd been sick for a long time, years, and at the end Zoey and I all but lived at the hospital. That last week we were there every day and every night, exhausted comrades keeping watch, while our mother murmured and slept. Death was imminent and remained imminent, for much longer than the doctors predicted. Our mother had worked at the post office since we were very young, but in her last hours she thought she was doing post-doctoral work in a physics lab again, murmuring in a confused way about equations and the simulation hypothesis.

"Do you understand what she's talking about?" I asked Zoey at one point.

"Most of it," Zoey said. In those hours Zoey sat by the bed

with her eyes closed, listening to our mother's words as if listening to music.

"Can you explain it to me?" It was like being on the outside of a secret club, nose pressed to the glass.

"The simulation hypothesis? Yeah." She didn't open her eyes. "Think of how holograms and virtual reality have evolved, even just in the past few years. If we can run fairly convincing simulations of reality now, think of what those simulations will be like in a century or two. The idea with the simulation hypothesis is, we can't rule out the possibility that all of reality is a simulation."

I'd been awake for two days and felt like I was dreaming. "Okay, but if we're living in a computer," I said, "whose computer is it?"

"Who knows? Humans, a few hundred years into the future? An alien intelligence? It's not a mainstream theory, but it comes up every so often at the Time Institute." She opened her eyes. "Oh god, pretend I didn't say that. I'm tired. I shouldn't have."

"Pretend you didn't say what?"

"The Time Institute part."

"Okay," I said, and her eyes closed again. I closed my eyes too. Our mother had stopped murmuring, and now there were just her ragged breaths, with too much time between each one.

When at last the end came, Zoey and I were sleeping. She woke me in the exhausted grey light of early morning, and we sat together for a long time in silence, in reverence, before the stilled figure of our mother on the bed. We dealt with the formalities, hugged goodbye, went our separate ways. I returned home to my cramped apartment, and several days passed where I spoke only with my cat. There was the funeral, then more stillness. I needed a new job—I'd been without one for some time and was burning through my savings—and so a month after the funeral I found myself in the basement office of a hotel Human Resources officer, a vaguely familiar-looking woman with blond hair, accepting a position that had been advertised as "hotel detective" but whose exact parameters were unclear.

"To be absolutely honest," I told her, "I'm not entirely clear on what a hotel detective position might entail."

"It's just hotel security," she said. I realized I'd forgotten her name. Natalie? Natasha? "The job title wasn't my idea. You won't actually be a detective. Just a security presence, as it were."

"I want to be sure I'm not misrepresenting myself," I said. "I left school a few months shy of my criminal justice degree."

"Can we be honest here, Gaspery?" There was definitely something familiar about her.

"Please."

"Your entire job is to pay attention to what goes on around you and call the police if you see anything suspicious."

"I can do that."

"You sound doubtful," she said.

"I'm not doubtful for myself. I mean, I don't doubt I could do it. It's just, I'm—couldn't anyone do this job?"

"You'd be surprised. It's the attention part that's hard to hire for," she said. "Distraction is a problem, generally speaking. You remember that test you had to take on your first interview?"

"Sure."

"That was to measure attentiveness. Your score was high. Tell me, do you agree with your test results? Can you pay attention?"

"Yes," I said. I was pleased as I said this, because I'd never really thought of myself in this way before, but it seemed to me that I'd been paying close attention my entire life. I hadn't been successful at very many things, but I'd always been good at watching. That was how I knew my ex-wife had fallen in love with someone else, just by being attentive. There were no obvious clues, just a subtle shift in— but the HR person was talking again, so I reeled myself in from the past.

"Wait," I said. "I know you."

"From before this meeting, you mean?"

"Talia," I said.

Something changed in her face. A mask dropped. Her voice was different when she spoke again, less amused by the world. "I go by Natalia now, but yes." She was quiet for a moment, looking at me. "We went to school together, didn't we?"

"End of the cul-de-sac," I said, and for the first time in the interview, she gave me a genuine smile.

"I used to stand at the Periphery for hours," she said, "looking out through the glass."

"You ever go back there? To the Night City?"

"Never," she said.

3

Never to the Night City. The phrase had a rhythm that pleased me, so it lodged itself in my head. I thought of it often in my first weeks on the job, because the job was terminally boring. The hotel had retro pretensions, so I wore a suit cut in an antique style and a peculiarly shaped hat called a fedora. I walked the halls and stood watch in the lobby. I paid attention to everyone and everything, as instructed. I've always enjoyed watching other people, but people in hotels turned out to be surprisingly boring. They checked in and checked out. They appeared in the lobby at odd hours, asking for coffee. They were drunk, or they weren't. They were businesspeople, or they were with their families on vacation. They were tired and frazzled from their journeys. People tried to sneak in dogs. In the first six months I had to summon the police only once, when I heard a woman scream in a hotel room, and even then I wasn't the one who did the calling;

I called the night manager, who called the police for me. I wasn't there when the woman was carried out by paramedics.

The job was quiet. My mind wandered. *Never to the Night City*. What had Talia's life been like there? Not great, obviously, any idiot could see that. Some families are better than others. When her family moved out of the Olive Llewellyn house, some other family moved in, but I found I couldn't remember this other family beyond a general impression of dereliction. At the hotel I saw Talia only occasionally, passing through the lobby on her way home from work.

In those days I lived in a bland little apartment in a block of other bland little apartments on the far edge of Colony One, close enough to the Periphery that the dome barely cleared the roof of the apartment complex. Sometimes on dark nights I liked to cross the street to the Periphery, to look through the composite glass at Colony Two glittering in the distance. My life in those days was as bland and limited as my apartment. I tried not to think about my mother too much. I slept through the days. My cat always woke me in the late afternoon. Around sunset I ate a meal that could reasonably be called either dinner or breakfast, put on my uniform, and went to the hotel to stare at people for seven hours.

I'd been at the hotel for about six months when my sister turned thirty-seven. Zoey was a physicist at the university, and her area of expertise had something to do with quantum blockchain technology, which I was never able to understand although she'd made several good-faith efforts to explain it to me. I called to wish her a happy birthday, and realized in the beat before she picked up that I hadn't congratulated her on receiving tenure. Which was when, a month ago? I felt a familiar variety of guilt.

"Happy Birthday," I said. "And also congratulations."

"Thank you, Gaspery." She never dwelt on my lapses, and I couldn't entirely parse why this made me feel so awful. There's a low-level, specific pain in having to accept that putting up with you requires a certain generosity of spirit in your loved ones.

"What's it like?"

"Being thirty-seven?" She sounded tired.

"No, being tenured. Does it feel different?"

"It feels like stability," she said.

"So what are your birthday plans?"

She was quiet for a moment. "Gaspery," she said, "is there any way you could come to my office this evening?"

"Of course," I said. "Of course."

When had she ever asked me to her office? Just once, years ago, when she first started there. The university wasn't that far away from my apartment, but also it was fundamentally a different universe. When had I even seen her last? It had been a few months, I realized.

I called in sick to work and then lay on the sofa for a while to bask in my sudden freedom. Marvin, my cat, climbed heavily onto my chest, where he stretched out his legs and fell asleep purring. The night extended before me, all those magnificently empty hours shining with possibility. I dislodged Marvin, showered and put on nice clothes, stopped by a bakery for four cupcakes—red velvet, which I hoped was still Zoey's favourite—and by six-thirty p.m. the sun was setting in a wash of oranges and pinks on the far side of the dome. I'd lived for a year in Colony One and the dome lighting still looked like theatre to me. Were cupcakes enough? Should I buy flowers? I bought a bouquet of something unflashy and yellow, and was at the Time Institute gate by seven thirty. I took off my dark glasses for the iris scan and was still holding the glasses awkwardly in my hand six iris scans later, when I found Zoey pacing in her office. She didn't look like a woman celebrating a birthday. She took my flowers with a distracted air, and I could tell from the way she set them on her desk that she'd forgotten about them by the time they left her hand. I wondered if someone had just broken up with her, but Zoey's romantic life had always been a forbidden topic.

"Oh, thank god," she said when I held out a cupcake. "I completely forgot dinner."

"You seem agitated."

"Can I show you something?"

"Sure."

She touched a discreet console on her office wall, and a projection filled half the room. There was a man on a stage, surrounded by bulky antique machines of some kind, inscrutable instruments. Above his head was an old-fashioned screen, a rectangle of white floating there in the dim light. It seemed to me that the scene we were looking at was quite old.

"A friend sent this to me," Zoey said. "She works in the art history department."

"Who is he? The guy in the projection."

"Paul James Smith. Twenty-first-century composer and video artist."

She pressed play, and the room filled with three-hundred-year-old music in a vague, shifting genre. Ambient, I supposed. I didn't know much about music but found this guy's composition faintly annoying.

"Okay," she said, "now pay attention to the white screen above him."

"What am I looking for? It's blank."

"Watch."

The screen came to life. The video had been shot in a forest on Earth. The quality was a little jerky; the videographer had been walking on a forest path, toward an enormous leafy tree, some Earth species that didn't grow in the colonies. The music stopped, and the man looked up at the screen above him. The screen went dark. There was a strange cacophony of noise— notes of a violin, the indistinct murmur of a crowd, the hydraulic *whoosh* of an airship taking off—and then it was over, the forest was back, and for a moment the image was dizzying, as if the videographer had forgotten that they were holding a camera. The forest faded out, but the music continued.

"Listen carefully," Zoey said. "Listen to the way the music's changed. You hear how the violin notes from the video are there in Smith's music? That same motif, that five-note pattern?"

I couldn't hear it, and then I could. "Yes. Why is that important?"

"Because it means that . . . that weirdness, that glitch, whatever it was, it was part of the performance. It's not a technical problem." She stopped the recording. She looked troubled in a way I didn't understand. "It goes on," she said, "but the rest of the performance is uninteresting."

"You brought me here to show me that," I said, just checking.

"I need to talk this through with someone I trust." She picked up her device, and I heard my own device chime with an incoming document.

She'd sent me a book: *Marienbad*, by Olive Llewellyn.

"Mom's favourite novel," I said. I was thinking of our mother, reading on the porch at twilight.

"Have you read it, Gaspery?"

"I've never been much of a reader."

"Just jump to the highlighted passage and tell me if you notice anything."

It was disorienting, leaping into the middle of a book I'd never read. I started a few paragraphs before the passage she'd highlighted:

We knew it was coming.

We knew it was coming and we prepared accordingly, or at least that's what we told our children—and ourselves—in the decades that followed.

We knew it was coming but we didn't quite believe it, so we prepared in low-key, unobtrusive ways—"Why do we have a whole shelf of canned fish?" Willis asked his husband, who said something vague about emergency preparedness—

—Because of that ancient horror, too embarrassingly irrational to be articulated aloud: if you say the name of the thing you fear, might you attract that thing's attention? This is difficult to admit, but in those early weeks we were vague about our fears because saying the word *pandemic* might bend the pandemic toward us.

We knew it was coming and we were breezy about it. We deflected the fear with careless bravado. On the day reports broke of a cluster in Vancouver, which was three days after the British prime minister announced that the initial outbreak in London was fully contained, Willis and Dov went to work as usual, their sons Isaac and Sam went to school, and then they all met up for dinner at their favourite restaurant, which was crowded that night. (Bit of a horror movie in retrospect: imagine clouds of invisible pathogens drifting through the air, floating from table to table, swirling in the wake of passing servers.) "If it's in Vancouver it's obviously here," Dov said to Willis, who said, "I'd bet money on it," and refilled Dov's water glass.

"If what's in Vancouver?" Isaac asked. He was nine.

"Nothing," they said in unison, and felt no guilt at all because it didn't feel like a lie. Pandemics don't approach like wars, with the distant thud of artillery growing louder every day and flashes of bombs on the horizon. They arrive in *retrospect*, essentially. It's disorienting. The pandemic is far away and then it's all around you, with seemingly no intermediate step.

Dov, practising his lines in front of the bedroom mirror after the community theatre closed: "Is this the promised end?"

We knew it was coming but we behaved inconsistently. We stocked up on supplies—just in case—but sent our children to school, because how do you get any work done with the kids at home?

(We were still thinking in terms of getting work done. The most shocking thing in retrospect was the degree to which all of us completely missed the point.)

"God," Willis said, a few days before the schools closed, but after the news headlines had started, "this all seems so retro."

"I know," Dov said. They were both in their forties, which is to say they were old enough to remember Ebola X, but those sixty-four weeks of lockdown had faded to the hazy province of childhood memory, a span of time that was neither awful nor pleasant, months populated by cartoons and imaginary friends. You couldn't call it a lost year, because it did have nice moments. Their parents were competent enough at parenting to shield them from the horror, which meant it was lonely but not unbearable. There was a lot of ice cream and extra screen time. They'd been glad when it was over, but after a few years had passed they didn't think of it much.

"What does *retro* mean?" Sam asked.

As Willis glanced at his younger son, he did have the thought—he clung to this later—that perhaps school wasn't such a great idea. Nonetheless, the old world hadn't slipped away just yet, so in the morning he packed Sam's and Isaac's lunches and dropped them off at the academy, stepped back out into the bright sunlight, and caught a transporter to the airship terminal. Just an ordinary morning under a harmless blue sky.

In the terminal he stopped to listen to a musician, a violinist playing for spare change in one of the cavernous entry corridors. The violinist was an old man who played with his eyes closed, coins accumulating in a hat by his feet. He played an ancient-looking violin—it looked like it was made of real wood—and Willis was by no means an expert in acoustics, but it seemed to him that there was a kind of warmth in the sound. Willis was listening to the music, to the way it rose up over the susurration of the morning commuter crowd, but then—

—a flash of darkness, weird sudden light—

—a fleeting hallucination of forest, fresh air, trees rising around him, a summer's day—

—and then he was back in the Oklahoma City Airship Terminal, in the cool white of the west entry corridor, blinking and disoriented. *Something just came over me,* he found himself thinking, but this was inadequate as an explanation, because *what* had just come over him? That flash of darkness, then the forest rising around him, what was that?

It hit him all at once: an afterlife.

The darkness was death, he told himself. The forest was the after.

Willis didn't believe in an actual afterlife, but he did believe in the subconscious, he believed in knowing without consciously knowing, and almost without thought he was walking away in the wrong direction, away from his commute. He didn't know where he was going until he found himself on the doorstep of his sons' school.

"But why are you pulling your boys out of school?" the principal asked. "I've been following the news closely, Willis, and there's just that tiny cluster of cases in Vancouver."

I closed the file and put my device in my pocket, unsettled in a way I couldn't explain.

"Do you see it?" Zoey asked. "The way the video mirrors the passage in the book?"

I did see it. A person in a forest in the twenty-first century sees a flash of darkness and hears noises from an airship terminal two centuries later. A person in an airship terminal in the twenty-third century sees a flash of darkness and is struck by the overwhelming sensation that he's standing in a forest.

"She could have seen the video," I suggested. "Olive Llewellyn, I mean. She could've seen it and worked it into her fiction." I was pleased with myself for this suggestion.

"I thought of that," Zoey said. *Of course you did*, I didn't say aloud. That was a major difference between us: Zoey always thought of everything. "There's something else, though. My team's spent the last month researching the region where the composer grew up, and this afternoon we found a letter." She was scrolling through files on her projection, but it was set to privacy mode, so it appeared from my angle that she was moving her hand through clouds. "Here," she said.

A projection snapped into place in the air between us. It was a handwritten document in a foreign alphabet.

"What is this?"

"I think it might be supporting evidence. It's a letter," she said. "From 1912."

"What alphabet's this?" I asked.

"Seriously?"

"What, should I be able to read it?" I peered closer, and recognized a word. No, two. It was almost English, but warped and slanted; there was a certain beauty to it, but the letters were misformed. Some kind of proto-English?

"Gaspery, that's cursive," she said.

"I don't know what that is."

"Right," she said, with that maddening patience I'd come to expect from her. "Let me switch to audio."

She toggled something in the clouds, and a man's voice filled the room.

Bert,

Thank you for your kind letter of 25th April, which made its way across the Atlantic and across Canada at a snail's pace and arrived in my hands only this evening.

How am I, you ask? The honest answer, brother, is that I'm unsure. This comes to you from a candlelit room in Victoria— you'll forgive, I hope, the dash of melodrama, but I feel that I've earned it—where I've taken up lodging in a pleasant boarding-house. I have given up all thought of establishing myself in business and wish only to return home, but this is a comfortable exile and my remittance provides for my day-to-day necessities.

I've had a very strange time here. No, that's not quite it. I've had a somewhat dull time here—my fault, not Canada's—except for a strange interlude in the wilderness, which I shall attempt to recount. I had travelled north from Victoria with Niall's old friend from school, Thomas Maillot, whose surname I'm possibly misspelling. For two or three days we moved north up the coast on a tidy little steamboat, weighed down with provisions, until at last we arrived at Caiette, a village consisting of a church, a pier, a one-room schoolhouse, and a handful of houses. Thomas continued on to a logging camp, a short distance up the coast. I elected to remain for the moment in the boardinghouse in Caiette, for the sake of enjoying the beauty of that place.

One morning in early September, I ventured into the forest, for reasons too tedious to relate, and a few paces in, I came upon a maple tree. I stopped there a moment, to catch my breath, and then there occurred an incident that struck me at the time as some kind of supernatural event, but seems to me in retrospect to have been perhaps some kind of fit.

I was standing there in the forest in the sunlight, and then all at once there was darkness, as abruptly as a candle snuffed out in a room, and in the darkness I heard the notes of a violin, an inscrutable noise, and with this a strange impression of being somehow fleetingly indoors, in some echoing cavernous space like a train station. Then it was over and I stood in the forest. It was as though nothing had happened. I staggered back out to the beach and was violently sick on the rocks. The following morning, concerned for my well-being and determined to quit that place and return to some semblance of civilization, I began the return journey to the little city of Victoria, where I remain.

I have a perfectly adequate room at a boardinghouse by the harbour, and amuse myself with walks, books, chess, and the occasional bit of watercolour painting. As you know, I've always adored gardens, and there's a public garden here in which I've found great solace. Not to trouble anyone, but I did consult a doctor, who is confident in his diagnosis of migraine. Seems a peculiar sort of

migraine that doesn't involve any pain in one's head, but I suppose
I'll accept it in lieu of an alternate explanation. I cannot forget it,
however, and the memory unsettles me.

   I hope you are well, Bert. Please convey my affection and respect
to Mother and Father as well.

Yours,
Edwin

The audio stopped. Zoey swiped the projection into the wall and came to sit with me. There was a heaviness about her that I'd never seen before.

"Zoey," I said, "you seem more upset than . . . I'm not sure I completely understand."

"Which operating system do you use on your device?"

"Zephyr," I said.

"Same. You remember that weird Zephyr bug a couple years ago, this only lasted a day or two, but sometimes you'd open a text file on your device and you'd hear whatever music you'd been listening to last?"

"Sure. That was annoying." I only vaguely remembered it.

"It was file corruption."

I sensed something vast and terrible, swimming just outside of my grasp.

"You're saying . . ."

Zoey's elbows were on the table, and as she spoke, she rested her forehead in her hands.

"If moments from different centuries are bleeding into one another, then, well, one way you could think of those moments, Gaspery, is to think of them as corrupted files."

"How is a moment the same as a file?"

She was very still. "Just imagine that they are."

I tried. A series of corrupted files; a series of corrupted moments; a series of discrete things bleeding into one another when they shouldn't.

"But if moments are files . . ." I couldn't finish the sentence. The room we were in seemed much less real than it had only a moment ago. *The desk is real*, I told myself. *The wilted flowers on the desk are real. The blue paint on the walls. Zoey's hair. My hands. The carpet.*

"You see why I didn't go out to celebrate my birthday," she said.

"It's just . . . Look, I agree that it's weird, but we're talking about Mom's thing, aren't we? The simulation thing?"

She sighed. "Believe me, the thought's occurred to me. It's very possible that my thinking is clouded. You know she's the reason I became a scientist."

I nodded.

"And look," she continued, "I know it's all circumstantial, I'm not crazy. It's just a series of descriptions of some kind of bizarre experience. But the *coincidence*, Gaspery, the way these moments seem to bleed into one another, I can't help but see it as some kind of evidence."

4

If we were living in a simulation, how would we know it was a simulation? I took the trolley home from the university at three in the morning. In the warm light of the moving car, I closed my eyes and marvelled at the detail. The gentle vibration of the trolley on its cushion of air. The sounds—the barely perceptible whisper of movement, the soft conversations here and there in the car, the tinny notes of a game escaping from a device somewhere. *We are living in a simulation,* I told myself, testing the idea, but it still seemed improbable to me, because I could smell the bouquet of yellow roses that the woman sitting beside me held carefully in both hands. *We are living in a simulation,* but I'm hungry and am I supposed to believe that that's a simulation too?

"I'm not saying these things add up to any kind of definite proof that we're living in a simulation," Zoey had said, an hour ago in her office. "I'm saying I think there's enough here to justify an investigation."

How do you investigate reality? My hunger is a simulation, I told myself, but I wanted a cheeseburger. Cheeseburgers are a simulation. Beef is a simulation. (Actually, that was literally true. Killing an animal for food would get you arrested both on Earth and in the colonies.) I opened my eyes and thought, *The roses are a simulation. The scent of roses is a simulation.*

"What would an investigation look like?" I'd asked her.

"I think you'd want to visit all those points in time," Zoey said. "You'd want to speak with the letter writer in 1912, the video artist in 2019 or 2020, and the novelist in 2203."

I remembered the news stories when time travel was invented and then immediately made illegal outside of government facilities. I remembered a chapter from a criminology textbook dedicated to the near-annihilating nightmare of the so-called Rose Loop, when history had changed twenty-seven times before the rogue traveller was taken out of commission and his damage undone. I knew that one hundred forty-one of the two hundred and five people serving life sentences on the moon were there because they'd attempted time travel. It didn't matter if they'd been successful or not; the attempt was enough to send you away for life.

"Gaspery," Zoey had said, "I'm not sure why you look so shocked. What does the sign on the building say?"

"Time Institute," I admitted.

She looked at me.

"I thought you were a physicist," I said.

"Well . . . yes," she said. There was a knowledge-and-achievement gap the size of the solar system in that pause between words. I heard that old kindness, that familiar sense that she was extending generosity toward me. We can't all be geniuses, I wanted to tell her, but we'd had that conversation when we were teenagers and it had gone poorly, so I didn't.

We are living in a simulation, I told myself as the trolley stopped a block from my apartment, but this fell so far short of, well, of the *reality,* for lack of a better word. I couldn't convince myself. I didn't believe it. There was a scheduled rainfall in—I glanced at my watch—two minutes. I stepped out of the trolley and walked very slowly, on purpose. I've always loved rain, and knowing that it isn't coming from clouds doesn't make me love it less.

5

In the weeks that followed, I tried to reacclimatize to the rhythms of my life. I rose at five in the afternoon in my tiny apartment, listened to music while I cooked, fed my cat, walked or took the trolley to work. I was at the hotel by seven p.m., gazing out at the lobby from behind dark glasses—most staffers didn't wear dark glasses, but as a light-sensitive native of the Night City who couldn't tolerate the diffuse glare of the dome, I had special dispensation from HR—and I stood there thinking of all of the things around me that might not be real. The stone of the lobby floor. The fabric of my clothes. My hands. My glasses. The footsteps of a woman crossing the lobby.

"Evening, Gaspery," the woman said.

"Talia. Hi."

"You were taking a very concentrated interest in the lobby floor."

"Can I ask you an extremely random question?"

"Please do," she said. "I've had a boring day."

"Do you ever catch yourself thinking about the simulation hypothesis?" It seemed worth asking. It was all I could think about.

She raised her eyebrows. "That's the idea that we're possibly living in a simulation, isn't it?"

"Yeah."

"Actually, yes. I have thought about it. I don't believe we're living in a simulation." Talia was gazing past me, past the lobby, to the street. "I don't know, maybe this is naïve of me, but I feel like a simulation should be better, you know? I mean, if you were going to the trouble to simulate that street, for example, couldn't all of the streetlights work?"

The streetlight across the street had been flickering for a number of weeks.

"I see your point."

"Well, anyway," Talia said, "good night."

"Good night." I returned to the exercise of noticing everything and telling myself that none of the things I noticed were real, but now I was distracted by her point. Something no one ever talked about in those days was the shabbiness of the moon colonies. I think we were all a little embarrassed by it.

"Yeah, I think it's fair to say the glamour's worn off," Zoey said when I saw her later that night. My shift ended at two a.m., so I'd called to ask if I could come over and see her. I'd known she'd be up—she'd never fully transitioned out of the Night City either, and, like me, she preferred to stay up all night—and she was taking a couple of days off work, so I took the trolley to her apartment. I'd been to this apartment only a handful of times, and had forgotten how dark it was. She'd painted the walls in a deep shade of grey. She had a collection of old-fashioned paper books—mostly history—and a framed painting on the wall that we'd made together when we were children. I was moved by it. We'd been about four and six, something like that, and we'd painted ourselves: a boy and a girl holding hands under a tree in exuberant colours.

"Where did the glamour go?" I asked. She'd poured me a generous glass of whisky, which I was sipping very slowly because I've never had much of an alcohol tolerance. She was already on her second drink.

"To the newer colonies, I suppose. Titan, I guess. Europa. The Far Colonies." We were at her kitchen table. She lived across the street from the Time Institute, which I'd known intellectually without fully absorbing. What did Zoey have? She'd been very close with our mother, and now that Mom was gone, what Zoey had was her work. Her work and almost nothing else, to all appearances, but who was I to judge. I leaned back in my chair, gazing over the Time Institute rooftops at the luminescent spires of beyond. Could I immigrate to the Far Colonies? Fantastical thought. But of course the thought that followed was *If we're living in a simulation, it's not like the Far Colonies are real either.*

"What happened to them?" I asked. "The letter writer back in the twentieth century, Edwin whatever his name was, and Olive Llewellyn?"

Zoey had somehow finished her second glass—I was still only halfway through my first—and poured herself a third.

"The letter writer went to war, returned home to England a broken man, and died in an insane asylum. Olive Llewellyn died on Earth. A pandemic broke out while she was on a book tour."

"Zoey," I said, "has your investigation started yet?"

"Sort of. Preliminary discussions are under way. The bureaucracy around travel is intense."

"Will you get to . . . Will you be the one to travel?"

"I almost left the Time Institute a few years ago," she said. "I agreed to stay on condition that I never have to travel again."

"You've travelled through *time*," I said, and my awe at my sister was boundless in that moment. "Where did you go?"

"I can't talk about it." Her expression was grim.

"Can you at least tell me why you don't want to do it anymore? I'd think it'd be . . ."

"You'd think it'd be interesting," she said. "It is. At first it's fascinating. It's a portal to a different world."

"Right, that's how I imagined it."

"But before you go, Gaspery, you might spend two years engaged in research. When you're going to a given point in time, you're there to investigate some specific thing, and you read up on everyone you expect to encounter. There are people at the Time Institute, hundreds of staff, whose entire job is researching long-dead people to compile dossiers for travellers, and your job is to study those dossiers until you know everything in them." She stopped to drink. "So, Gaspery, picture this scene. You step into a party, at some long-ago point in time, and you know exactly how and when each and every person in that room is going to die."

"That's pretty creepy," I admitted.

"And some of them are going to die in the most preventable ways, Gaspery. You might be talking to a woman, let's say she has young children, and you know she's going to drown at a picnic next Tuesday, and because you can't mess with the time line, the one thing you absolutely cannot say to her is 'Don't go swimming next week.' You have to let her die."

"You can't pull her from the water."

"Right."

For a while I wasn't sure what to say, so I gazed out the window at the rooftops and spires and wondered if letting someone die for the sake of the time line was something I could do. Zoey drank quietly.

"The job requires an almost inhuman level of detachment," she said finally. "Did I say *almost*? Not *almost* inhuman, *actually* inhuman."

"So someone will have to travel through time to investigate this," I said, "but it won't be you."

"It will be several people, but I don't know who. It's not exactly a popular job."

"Send me," I said. Because what I was thinking in that moment was that the theoretical woman who was going to drown next Tuesday was going to drown anyway.

She looked at me, surprised. Two spots of pink had appeared on her cheeks, but otherwise she seemed perfectly sober.

"Absolutely not."

"Why not?"

"One, it's a horrifically dangerous job. Two, you're not qualified."

"What kind of background would you have to have, to travel back in time and talk to people? That's what it is, isn't it? I mean, what are the qualifications?"

"There's a barrage of psychological testing, followed by years of training."

"I could do that," I said. "I could go back to school, I could do whatever training was required. You know I almost finished my criminology degree. I know how to conduct an interview."

She was quiet.

"You want to keep the circle small here," I said, "don't you? Imagine the panic if word got out that we're living in a simulation."

"We don't know that we're living in a simulation, and I don't know that *panic* is quite the word. More like terminal ennui."

I decided to look up *ennui* later. There are words you encounter all your life without knowing what they mean.

"Zoey," I said, "I'm not doing anything with my life."

"Don't say that," she said, too quickly.

"This is just . . . this situation," I said, "this thing, whatever it is, this possibility I guess, it's the most interested I've been about anything in maybe my entire life."

"Then get a hobby, Gaspery. Take up calligraphy or archery or something."

"Can you just think about it, Zoey? Talk to whoever you have to talk to? Can I be considered? If we're talking about travelling through time here, then there's no real rush, is there? I'd have time to prepare, I could do whatever you want, go back to school, psychological training, whatever—" I realized I was babbling, so I stopped.

"No," she said. "Absolutely not." She drained her glass. "When I say it's a dangerous job, Gaspery, I mean I wouldn't want anyone I love to do it."

6

I didn't see Zoey again for three weeks after that, and there was an away message on her device. I went to work, I came home from work, I paced my apartment and talked to the cat. Finally, on a day off from the hotel, I left her a voicemail to say I was coming to her office. She didn't respond, but I boarded a trolley to the Time Institute in the late afternoon. She'd told me her schedule. I knew she'd be there. I watched the pale streets slipping past, the old stone buildings with missing pieces of masonry and the ramshackle illegal dwellings pressed close against them—the influence of the Night City seeping in, a whiff of disorder that I found invigorating—and I had a strange, wild notion that she might be dead. She worked too much and drank too much. In that first year after our mother died, my thoughts often veered toward disaster.

I stood outside the Time Institute, white stone monolith, and called her one more time. Nothing. It was around six o'clock. A few people emerged from the building, singly or in pairs. I found myself studying their faces, wondering what it might be like to have a job with stakes attached to it, and then one of the faces was Ephrem's.

"Eph," I said.

He looked up, startled.

"Gaspery! What are you doing here?"

I'd talked to Ephrem at my mother's funeral, briefly, but that day was a blur. We hadn't spoken at any length since the last dinner party I'd attended at his house, a year ago now. Perhaps it was just the dome lighting—dimming gently but also increasingly silvery, in a rough approximation of an Earth twilight—but Ephrem looked older than I remembered, older and more careworn.

"I was about to ask you the same thing," I said. "What's an arborist doing at the Time Institute?" He hesitated, and in that beat, I saw an opening. There was something he didn't want to tell me, and there was something I wasn't supposed to know. "You work here, don't you?"

He nodded. "Yes. For some time now."

"Then do you know about the project Zoey's working on? The simulation thing?"

"For god's sake, Gaspery, don't say another word." Ephrem was smiling, but I could tell he meant it. "It's been a while. Shall we grab a cup of tea?"

"Love to."

"Come see my office," he said. "I'll get some tea sent up."

We walked together in silence through the atrium, past Security, into an elevator and through successive white corridors that all looked the same to me, a maze of blank doors and opaque glass.

"Here we are," he said.

His office was identical to Zoey's but had a bonsai tree in the window. A tea service was waiting for us on the table, with three cups. I'd known Ephrem half my life, but had I ever really asked him about his work? He'd told me he was an arborist, I'd asked him the occasional question about a tree, but apparently I knew much less about my friend than I'd thought. His office was on a high floor, overlooking the spires of Colony One. In the distance, I saw the Grand Luna Hotel.

"How long have you been here?" I asked.

"About a decade." He was pouring tea, but he paused for a moment, considering. "No, seven years. It only feels like a decade."

"I thought you were an arborist."

"I miss that job, to be honest. I'm afraid trees are just a hobby now. Will you join me?"

I moved over to his meeting table, which was exactly like Zoey's. I was overcome by the strangeness of the moment, the disorienting sense of one reality slipping away and being replaced by another. *But I've known you for years,* I wanted to say, *and you're an arborist, not a suit at the Time Institute. We graduated high school together.*

"Were trees easier?" I asked.

"Than my current job? Yes. Very much so." His device vibrated. He glanced at the screen and winced.

"Why didn't you tell me you worked here?"

"It's just . . . it's awkward," he said. "By *awkward*, I mean classified. The thing is, I can't really answer questions about my job, so I don't like to talk about it."

"Must be strange," I said, "doing something secret." By *strange*, I meant wonderful.

"I try not to lie about it. If you'd asked where I was working, I'd have said I was doing some work with the Time Institute, and let you assume it was somehow tree-related."

"Okay," I said. The silence extended around us. I didn't know how to ask for what I wanted. *Hire me, let me in, let me be a part of whatever it is you people are doing here.* "Ephrem," I began, but the door opened just then, and Zoey came in. Her expression was set in a way I hadn't seen since childhood. Zoey was furious. She sat across from me, ignored her tea, and stared into my eyes until I was forced to look away.

"I've been losing staring contests with my sister since I was five," I said to Ephrem. "Maybe four." He rewarded me with a weak smile. No one spoke. My gaze drifted back to the bonsai tree.

Finally, mercifully, Ephrem cleared his throat.

"Listen," he said. "No one's broken any rules here. When

Zoey spoke with you about the anomaly, Gaspery, it hadn't been classified yet."

Zoey looked at her tea.

"Of course," Ephrem said, "that doesn't mean you should be standing outside the Time Institute repeating the things she told you."

"I'm sorry," I said. "Ephrem, can I ask, is it real?"

"What do you mean?"

"The things Zoey told me about seemed like a pattern, but, well, it was our mom's thing," I said. "Simulation hypothesis."

"I remember her talking about it," he said gently.

"I think that when you lose someone, it's easy to see patterns that aren't there."

Ephrem nodded. "True. I don't know if there's anything there," he said. "But I wasn't close with your mother, which makes me a somewhat neutral party in this question, and I think there's enough to make it worth investigating."

"Can I help?" I asked.

"*No,*" Zoey muttered, barely audible.

"Zoey did tell me that you wanted to work here." I noticed that Ephrem was very carefully not looking at Zoey.

"Yes," I said, "I would."

"*Gaspery,*" Zoey said.

"Why do you want to work here?" Ephrem asked.

"Because it's interesting," I said. "I'm more interested in this than—well, than anything I can remember, honestly. I hope that doesn't make me seem desperate."

"Not at all," Ephrem said. "It just makes you sound interested. All of us are interested, or we wouldn't be here. Do you know what we do here?"

"Not really," I said.

"We safeguard the integrity of our time line," he said. "We investigate anomalies."

"Have there been others?"

"Usually it turns out to be nothing," Ephrem said. "My first case at the Institute involved a doppelgänger. According to our best facial-recognition software, the same woman appeared in photographs and video footage taken in 1925 and 2093. I was able to collect DNA and establish that they were two different women."

"You said *usually*," I said.

"On a few occasions," Ephrem said, "we haven't been able to make a determination one way or the other." I could tell he was unsettled by this.

"Is there something you're looking for?" I asked.

"There are several things we're looking for." He was quiet for a moment. "The aspect of our work that relates to the anomaly," he said, "is a continuing investigation into whether we're living in a simulation."

"Do you think we are?"

"There's a faction," he said carefully, "myself among them, that believes time travel works better than it should."

"What do you mean?"

"I mean that there are fewer loops than one might reasonably expect. I mean that sometimes we change the time line and then the time line seems to *repair* itself, in a way that doesn't make sense to me. The course of history should be irrevocably altered every single time we travel back in the time line, but, well, it isn't. Sometimes events seemingly change to accommodate the time traveller's interference, so that a generation later it's as if the traveller were never there."

"None of which is proof of a simulation," Zoey said quickly.

"Right. For obvious reasons," Ephrem said, "it's difficult to confirm."

"But you could move a step closer to confirmation by identifying a glitch in the simulation," I said.

"Yes, exactly."

"Gaspery," Zoey said, "I know it's interesting, but it's a troubling line of work."

"Zoey and I have some disagreements regarding the Time Institute," Ephrem said. "I think it's fair to say that our experiences here have been different."

"Yeah, that's fair," Zoey said flatly.

"But what I can tell you," Ephrem said, "is that it's an interesting place to work."

"What *I* can tell you," Zoey said, "is that Ephrem missed his recruitment goals this year, last year, and the year before."

"The training and the job both require immense discretion," Ephrem said, ignoring her, "and a great deal of focus."

"I can focus," I said. "I can be discreet."

"Well," Ephrem said, "I'll set up a screening interview for you."

"Thank you," I said. "This will sound . . . look, I don't mean to sound pathetic, but I've literally never had an interesting job before."

Ephrem smiled. "I'm not worried about the screening interview. You'll pass easily. This calls for a celebration."

But if it called for a celebration, why was my sister speaking so little, why did she look so grim? *A troubling line of work.* Look, I wanted to tell her, as Ephrem ordered three glasses of champagne, I would rather do a dangerous job than a job that makes me comatose with boredom, but I was afraid if I said this she might start to cry.

7

A week later I arrived at the hotel fifteen minutes before my shift, and went to Talia's office.

"Gaspery," she said.

I started to close the door, but she shook her head and rose from behind her desk. "Let's go for a walk."

"I only have a few—"

"You know, it's interesting." She gestured for me to walk out ahead of her. "I studied the history of work in university, and if there's one historical constant over the centuries, it's that no one especially wants to mess with HR." She opened the side door and we emerged into daylight by the loading dock. "I told your supervisor that I needed to meet with you. No one will mind."

Today's weather programming called for clouds, so the daylight was dim and greyish. I found it unsettling.

"It's hard to get used to," Talia said. She'd seen me glance uneasily at the sky. We were walking toward the path that ran alongside the Colony One river. All three colonies had rivers, for mental health reasons, running along identical white stone riverbeds, with identical white stone bridges arcing across them. They were engineering marvels. They all sounded exactly the same. "Why did you leave the Night City?" she asked.

"Bad divorce," I said. "I just wanted a fresh start." There was comfort in the sameness of the river sound; if I didn't look up, if I didn't pay attention to the strange greyish fake-cloudy-day light, I could pretend I was home. "Why did you come here?"

"I'm from here," she said. "I didn't move to the Night City till I was nine."

"Oh."

We were approaching a bridge. In the Night City, the bridge would've had a selection of derelicts napping or getting high underneath, in the peace and shadows of the embankment, but here there was just an old man on a bench, sitting alone and staring at the water.

"You came to my office to give your notice," Talia said.

"How did you know?"

"Because my boss's boss's boss told me to speak with a couple of suits from the Time Institute three days ago. I could tell from their questions that they were vetting you for a position."

Is there an unease that's specific to the sense of an invisible bureaucracy in motion around you? Talia stopped walking, so I stopped too, and I gazed down at the water. When I was a kid I used to float little boats down the Night City river, but the Night City river was a dark and sparkling thing, reflecting both sunlight and the blackness of space. The Colony One river was pale and milky, reflecting the fake clouds on the dome.

"We used to live there," Talia said, pointing, and I looked up and across the river at one of the oldest and most splendid of the grand apartment buildings, a white cylinder of a tower with a garden on every balcony. "My parents worked for the Time Institute."

I wasn't sure what to say. There was no non-catastrophic reason I could think of why a family would go from one of the most fashionable addresses in Colony One to a falling-down house in the Night City.

"They were both travellers," Talia said. "Until a mission went wrong in some kind of awful way, after which my parents were unable to work, and within a year we were in that run-down neighbourhood in the Night City."

"I'm sorry." I resented having to say this, because the thing was, I loved the Night City, and that run-down neighbourhood was my home. My family—me, Zoey, our mom—weren't there because we *had* to be there, we were there because in my mother's words, "at least this place has some character to it, not like those sterile colonies with the fake lighting," although as I remembered this, I was also remembering that we couldn't afford to fix the roof when it leaked.

Talia was looking at me. "Drunks are indiscreet," she said.

"As I'm sure you're aware, if you've ever thought about the question for more than five minutes, sending someone back in time inevitably changes history. *The traveller's presence itself is a disruption,* that's the phrase I remember my dad using. There's no way to go back, engage with the past, and leave the time line perfectly unchanged."

"Right," I said. I wasn't sure what she was getting at, but listening to her made me so uneasy that I couldn't meet her eyes.

"Sometimes the Time Institute goes back in time and undoes the damage, ensures that the traveller doesn't do the thing that changes history. You know, the little thing, like you hold open the door for the woman who goes on to create a civilization-ending algorithm or whatever. Sometimes they go back and undo the damage, but not always. Do you want to know how they make that decision?"

"That sounds extremely classified," I said.

"Oh, it *is,* Gaspery, but I like you and also I've developed a reckless streak in my old age, so I'm going to tell you anyway." (She was, what, thirty-five? In that moment, I found her thrillingly jaded.) "Here's the metric: they only go back and undo the damage *if the damage affects the Time Institute.* What am I, Gaspery? How would you describe me?"

This felt like a trap. "I . . ."

"It's okay," she said, "you can say it. I'm a bureaucrat. HR is bureaucracy."

"Okay."

"As is the Time Institute. The premier research university on the moon, possessor of the only working time machine in existence, intimately enmeshed in government and in law enforcement. Even *one* of those things would imply a formidable bureaucracy, don't you think? What you have to understand is that bureaucracy is an organism, and the prime goal of every organism is self-protection. Bureaucracy exists to protect itself." She was gazing across the river again. "We lived on the third floor," she said, pointing. "The balcony with the vines and rosebushes."

"It's nice," I said.

"Isn't it? Look, I understand why you'd want to work with the Time Institute," she said. "It must seem like an exciting opportunity. It's not like you've got much of a career path at the hotel. But just know that when the Institute is done with you, they'll throw you away." She spoke so casually that I wasn't sure if I'd heard her correctly. "I have a meeting," she said. "You should probably start your shift in the next hour or so." She turned and left me there.

I looked back at the apartment building. I'd been to one of those apartments once, years ago, for a party, and I'd been fairly drunk at the time, but I remembered vaulted ceilings and spacious rooms. What I was thinking was that if anything went wrong with the Time Institute, I would never be able to say I hadn't been warned.

But I felt such impatience with my life. I turned back to the hotel, and found that I couldn't go in. The hotel was the past. I wanted the future. I called Ephrem.

"Could I start early?" I asked. "I know the plan was to give the hotel two weeks' notice, but could I just start the training now? Tonight?"

"Sure," he said. "Could you be here in an hour?"

8

"Would you like some tea?" Ephrem asked.

"Please."

He typed something into his device, and we sat together at the meeting table. A sudden memory: drinking chai tea with Ephrem and Ephrem's mother after school one day at Ephrem's apartment, which was nicer than mine. Ephrem's mother had a job she could do from home, I remembered; she'd been staring at a screen. Ephrem and I were both studying, so it must have been just before an exam, during a period when I'd been experimenting with (a) tea and (b) being a good student. I was about to bring up this moment—*Do you remember?*—when there was a soft chime at the door, and a young man came in with a tray, which he left on the table with a nod. *Chai tea is real*, I told myself, and then I realized: Ephrem must remember that long-ago moment too, because he'd only ever served me chai when I'd come here.

"Here you are." Ephrem passed me a steaming mug.

"Why didn't Zoey want me to work here?"

He sighed. "She had a bad experience a few years back. I don't know the details."

"Yes, you do."

"Yes, I do. Look, this is just a rumour, but I heard she was in love with a traveller, then the traveller went rogue and got lost in time. That's literally all I know."

"No, it isn't."

"Literally all I know that isn't classified," Ephrem said.

"How do you get lost in time?"

"Suppose you were to intentionally fuck with the time line. The Time Institute might decide not to bring you back to the present."

"Why would anyone intentionally fuck with the time line?"

"Exactly," Ephrem said. "Don't do that, and you'll be fine." He leaned over to touch a console on the wall, and a time line with photographs of people was suspended in the air between us. "I've been working on an investigation plan for you," he said. "We don't want to place you in the centre of the anomaly, because we don't know what the anomaly is, or how dangerous it might be. We want you to interview people who we think have seen it."

He enlarged a very old photograph, black-and-white, of a worried-looking young man in military uniform. "This is Edwin

St. Andrew, who experienced something in the forest at Caiette. You'll visit him, and see if he'll talk about it."

"I didn't know he was a soldier."

"He won't be when you speak with him. You'll talk to him in 1912, and then later he'll go on to have a very bad time on the Western Front. More tea?"

"Thank you." I had no idea what the Western Front was and hoped it would be covered in my training.

He swiped the time line to the side, and I was looking at the composer from the footage Zoey had shown me. "In January 2020," Ephrem continued, "an artist named Paul James Smith gave a performance that involved a video, and it seems like that video maybe shows the anomaly that St. Andrew described a century earlier, but we don't know where exactly that video was taken. We don't have complete footage of his concert, just the clip Zoey showed you. You'll speak to him and see what you can learn."

Ephrem swiped again, and I saw another photograph, an old man playing a violin in an airship terminal, his eyes closed. "This is Alan Sami," Ephrem said. "He played the violin for several years in the Oklahoma City Airship Terminal, circa 2200, and we believe it's his music that Olive Llewellyn references in *Marienbad*. You'll interview him and find out more about the music. Really just find out anything you can." He moved on through the time line, and there was Olive Llewellyn, my mother's favourite author, long-ago resident of Talia Anderson's childhood home. "And here's Olive Llewellyn. I regret to report that absolutely no one keeps surveillance footage for two hundred years, so there's no record of whatever Olive Llewellyn may or may not have experienced there prior to writing *Marienbad*. You'll interview her on her last book tour."

"When was her last book tour?" I asked.

"November 2203. Early days of the SARS Twelve pandemic. Don't worry, you won't get sick."

"I've never heard of it."

"It was one of our childhood immunizations," Ephrem said.

"Will there be other investigators assigned to the case?"

"Several. They'll look at different angles, interview different people, or interview the same people in a different way. You may meet some of them, but if they're good at their jobs, you'll never know who they are. From your perspective, Gaspery, this is not a complicated assignment. You'll conduct a few interviews, and then hand off your findings to a more senior investigator, who will take over and make the final determination, and if all goes well, there will be other investigations for you. You could have an interesting career here." He was gazing at the time line. "Where I think you'll start," he said, "is by interviewing the violinist."

"Okay," I said. "When do I talk to him?"

"In about five years," Ephrem said. "You have some training to do first."

9

The training wasn't like immersing myself in a different world. It was like immersing myself in successive different worlds, these moments that had arisen one after another after another, worlds fading out so gradually that their loss was apparent only in retrospect. Years of private instruction in small rooms in the Institute, years of passing by people who may or may not have been my fellow students in the halls—no one wore name tags here—and years of studying quietly in the Time Institute library, or in my apartment late at night with my cat asleep on my lap. Five years after I left the hotel, I reported for the first time to the travel chamber.

It was a midsize room made entirely of some kind of composite stone. At one end was a bench, moulded into a deep indentation in the wall. The bench faced an extremely ordinary-looking desk. Zoey was waiting there, with a device that looked unnervingly like a gun.

"I'm going to shoot a tracker into your arm," she said.

"Good morning, Zoey. I'm fine, thanks for asking. Nice to see you too."

"It's a microcomputer. It interacts with your device, which interacts with the machine."

"Okay," I said, giving up on pleasantries. "So the tracker sends information to my device?"

"Remember that time I gave you a cat?" she said.

"Of course. Marvin. He's napping at home as we speak."

"We sent an agent back to another century," Zoey said, "but the agent fell in love with someone and didn't want to come home, so she removed her own tracker, fed it to a cat, and then when we tried to forcibly return her to the present, the cat appeared in the travel chamber instead of her."

"Wait," I said, "my cat's from another century?"

"Your cat's from 1985," she said.

"What," I said, at a loss for words.

She took my hand—when was the last time we'd touched one another?—and I observed her grim concentration as she shot a silver pellet into my left arm. It hurt much more than I would've imagined. She opened a projection over the desk, and turned her attention to the floating screen.

"You should have told me," I said. "You should have told me my cat was a time traveller."

"Honestly, Gaspery, what difference would it make. A cat's a cat."

"You never were an animal person, were you."

Her mouth was set in a thin line. She wouldn't look at me.

"You should be happy for me," I said, while she was adjusting something in her projection. "This is the only thing I've ever really wanted to do, and I'm doing it."

"Oh, Gaspery," she said absently. "My poor little lamb. Device?"

"Here."

She took my device, held it close to the projection, and handed it back to me.

"Okay," she said. "Your first destination has been programmed. Go sit in the machine."

Gaspery Roberts: Okay, it's on. Thank you for taking the time to speak with me.

Alan Sami: You're welcome. Thank you for lunch.

GR: Now, just for the benefit of my recording, you're a violinist.

AS: I am. I play in the airship terminal.

GR: For spare change?

AS: For pleasure. I don't need the money, to be clear.

GR: But you do collect change, in that hat at your feet . . .

AS: Well, people were throwing change at me, so I did at one point decide to just turn my hat upside down in front of me, so that all the change would at least land in one place.

GR: May I ask, why do you do it, if you don't need the money?

AS: Well, because I love it, son. I love playing the violin, and I love seeing people.

GR: I'd like to play a short clip for you, if I may.

AS: Of music?

GR: Music with some ambient noises. I'll play it, and then I'm going to ask you to tell me anything you can about it. That sound all right?

AS: Sure. Go ahead.

[. . .]

GR: That was you, right?

AS: Yes, that's me in the airship terminal. Poor-quality recording, though.

GR: How can you be sure it's you?

AS: How can I . . . really? Well, son, because I know the music and I heard an airship. That *whoosh* just at the end.

GR: Let's focus on the music for a moment. That piece you were playing, can you tell me about it?

AS: My lullaby. I composed it, but I never gave it a title. It was something I made up for my wife, my late wife.

GR: Your late . . . I'm sorry.

AS: Thank you.

GR: Is there—did you ever record yourself playing it, or write down the score?

AS: Neither. Why?

GR: Well, as I mentioned, I'm an assistant to a music historian. I've been tasked with investigating similarities and differences between the music played at airship terminals in various regions on Earth.

AS: And your affiliation, what institution was that, again?

GR: University of British Columbia.

AS: That where your accent's from?

GR: My accent?

AS: It just shifted. I have an ear for accents.

GR: Oh. I'm from Colony Two.

AS: Interesting. My wife was from Colony One, but I wouldn't say she sounded anything like you. How long have you been doing this?

GR: Assisting in investigations? A few years.

AS: You go to school for that? How does a person get into that line of work?

GR: Fair question. I was spinning my wheels, if we're being honest here. I had a job in hotel security. It was fine. I just stood around a hotel lobby, staring at people. But then, well, I saw an opportunity. Something came up that really interested me, in a way I'd never been interested in anything. I spent five years in training, studying linguistics and psychology and history.

AS: I understand the history part, but why psychology and linguistics?

GR: Well, linguistics because people speak differently, at different points in history, and if you're dealing with old music that has a spoken-word element, it's helpful.

AS: Makes sense. And psychology?

GR: Personal interest. It wasn't relevant. It wasn't relevant at all. I don't know why I mentioned it.

AS: Methinks the lady doth protest too much.

GR: Wait, did you just call me a lady?

AS: That was Shakespeare, son. Come on, now. Didn't you go to school?

"Smooth," Zoey said when she reviewed the recording. "Real sophisticate there."

Ephrem, who was sitting with us in her office, suppressed a smile.

"I know," I said. "Sorry."

"No, look," my sister said, "we didn't cover Shakespeare in your training."

"Zoey," I said, "Ephrem, what would happen, just theoretically, if I messed up?"

"Don't mess up." Ephrem glanced at his device. "I'm sorry," he said, "I have a meeting with my boss, but I'll see you in my office in an hour." He left us then, and I was alone with my sister.

"What were your impressions of the violinist?" Zoey asked.

"He was in his eighties," I said, "maybe even nineties. He had a slow way of talking, like his accent kind of dragged everything out. He'd done that thing to his eyes, that colour-change thing? His eyes were this strange shade of purple. Violet, I guess."

"Probably all the rage in his youth."

She looked back at the transcript, rereading something. I rose and went to the window. It was night, and the dome had gone clear. Earth was rising on the horizon, a vision in green and blue.

"Zoey," I said, "can I ask you something?"

"Of course."

I turned back to her, and she looked up from the transcript.

"Do you remember Talia Anderson from the Night City?" I asked.

"No. No, I don't think so."

"She was in my grade for a while in elementary school. Her family lived in the Olive Llewellyn house, and then I ran into her again when she hired me for that hotel security job."

"Wait," Zoey said, "are we talking about Natalia Anderson at the Grand Luna Hotel?"

"Yes."

Zoey nodded. "She was on the list of people we interviewed when you were being cleared for this position."

"How do you remember a name on a list from five years ago?"

"I don't know," she said. "I just do."

"I wish I had your brain. Anyway. She kind of warned me off coming here, to be honest."

"So did I," Zoey said.

"I guess her parents worked here," I said, ignoring this. "A long time ago. She said her dad was indiscreet."

Zoey was watching me closely. "What did she say?"

"She said, *The traveller's presence itself is a disruption*—"

"Those exact words?"

"I think so. Why?"

"That's from a classified training manual that went out of circulation ten years ago. I wonder if she's telling anyone else about it. What else did she say?"

"She said that when the Institute was done with me, it would throw me away."

Zoey looked away. "It's not always the easiest place to work," she said. "Staff turnover is high. You'll remember that I tried to dissuade you."

"You were afraid I'd get thrown away?"

She was quiet for so long that I thought she wasn't going to answer. When she spoke again, she wouldn't look at me, and her voice was strained. "I was close with someone, a long time ago, another traveller who was investigating something else. She messed up."

"What happened to her?"

Her hand drifted to the necklace she always wore. It was a simple gold chain, and I'd never really noticed it before, but from the way she touched it, I understood that the lost traveller had given it to her.

"Here's what you have to understand," she said. "You don't have to be a terrible person to intentionally try to change the time line. You just have to have a moment of weakness. Really just a moment. When I say *weakness,* I might mean something more like *humanity.*"

"And if you intentionally change the time line . . ."

"It's not difficult to deliberately lose someone in time. Frame them for a crime they didn't commit, for example, or, in less serious cases, they can just be placed somewhere with no way home."

"Wouldn't framing a traveller for a crime have, well, some repercussions for the time line?"

"The Research department maintains a list of crimes," Zoey said. "Carefully selected, carefully vetted to avoid any major repercussions."

(*"Bureaucracy exists to protect itself,"* Talia said, *gazing out over the river.*)

Zoey cleared her throat. "Big day tomorrow," she said. "Remind me where you're going first?"

"1912," I said, "to talk to Edwin St. Andrew. I'm going to pretend to be a priest and see if he'll talk to me in the church."

"Right. And then?"

"Then I'm going to January 2020," I said, "to talk to the video artist, Paul James Smith, see what we can learn about that weird footage."

She nodded. "And you talk to Olive Llewellyn the next day?"

"Yeah." By now I'd read all of her books. I hadn't especially liked any of them, but it was hard to parse whether this was the fault of the books or the fault of the dread I felt when I thought of her, given the timing of the scheduled interview.

"You know you're meeting her in the last week of her life," Zoey said. "You'll interview her in Philadelphia, and she'll die three days later in a hotel room in New York."

"I know." I felt a little sick about it.

Zoey's face softened. "Remember how Mom used to quote *Marienbad* at us when we were kids?"

I nodded, and for a moment I was transported back to the hospital, the last days of our mother, the week outside of time and space when we never left her side.

"But you'll keep it together, right?" In the way my sister looked at me, I knew she saw a previous Gaspery, a shiftless version of myself who was prone to error, who lived aimlessly and hadn't spent the past five years in training and study and research.

"Of course. I'm a professional."

I knew the facts of the life, and of the death: Olive Llewellyn died in a pandemic that began during a book tour. She died in an Atlantic Republic hotel room. But of course the thought of breaking the protocol occurred to me, then and in the morning two days later when I reported to the travel chamber, when the coordinates were entered into my device, when I stepped into the machine to meet her.

5

Last Book Tour on Earth /

2203

"LISTEN," THE JOURNALIST SAID, "I DON'T MEAN TO MAKE you uncomfortable or put you on the spot. But I'm curious if you experienced something strange in the Oklahoma City Airship Terminal."

In the quiet, Olive could hear the soft hum of the building, the sounds of ventilation and plumbing. Perhaps she wouldn't have admitted it if he hadn't caught her toward the end of the tour, if she hadn't been so tired. The journalist, Gaspery-Jacques Roberts, was watching her closely. She felt he already knew what she was about to say.

"I don't mind talking about this," she said, "but I'm afraid I'll seem too eccentric if it makes it into the final version of the interview. Could we go off the record for a moment?"

"Yes," he said.

"I was in the terminal. I was walking toward my flight, and I remember I walked by a guy playing a violin. And then all of a sudden, everything went dark and I was in a forest. Just for a second. It was . . ."

"It was exactly like you described it in the book," Gaspery said.

"Yes."

"Can you tell me anything else?"

"There's not much else. It was so fast. I had an impression . . . This is going to sound crazy, but I was in two places at once. When I say I was in a forest, I was also still in the terminal."

"I knew it," he said.

"I'm not sure . . ." Olive didn't know how to ask the question. "Does it mean something?" she asked.

He looked at her, and seemed to grapple with what to say next. "This will sound silly," he said, in tones of forced lightness, "but my editor over at *Contingencies Magazine* likes me to end interviews with a fun question."

Olive clenched her hands together and nodded.

"Okay, so," he said, "this is kind of a question about destiny, I guess?" Olive noticed that he was sweating. "Barring some kind of unforeseen catastrophe, assuming that our technology continues to advance, we'll probably have time travel in the next century. If a time traveller appeared before you and told you to drop everything and go home immediately, would you do it?"

"How would I know they were a time traveller?"

The door was opening, and Olive's publicist was coming in.

"Well, let's say there was something about the person that couldn't be reconciled."

"For example."

Gaspery leaned forward, speaking softly and quickly. "Well, for example, suppose this person were an adult," he said. "Now suppose this person, this adult in his thirties, had a name you'd made up for a book that you only published five years ago."

"How's it going in here?" Aretta asked.

"Great," Gaspery said. "Your timing's perfect."

"You could've changed your name," Olive said.

"I could have." He held her gaze. "But I didn't." His tone brightened as he rose. "Olive, thanks so much for your time. Especially that last question. I know fun questions are the worst."

"Olive, you look tired," Aretta said. "You doing okay?"

"Just tired," Olive said, parroting the explanation.

"But you're going home right after this, aren't you?" Gaspery said smoothly. "Straight from here to the airship terminal, right? Well, anyway, goodbye, thank you!"

"No, she has another— Oh," Aretta said, "yes, goodbye!" Gaspery was gone. "He's a little odd, isn't he?"

"A little," Olive said.

"What was that about going home? You have another three days on Earth."

"Something's come up."

She frowned. "But—"

But Olive had never been more certain of anything. She'd never been warned more clearly in her life. "I'm sorry," she said, "I know this causes problems for everyone, but I need to go to the airship terminal. I'm going home on the next flight."

"What?"

"Aretta," Olive said, "you should go home to your family."

It's shocking to wake up in one world and find yourself in another by nightfall, but the situation isn't actually all that unusual. You wake up married, then your spouse dies over the course of the day; you wake in peacetime and by noon your country is at war; you wake in ignorance and by evening it's clear that a pandemic is already here. You wake on a book tour with several days left to go, and by evening you're racing toward home, your suitcase abandoned in a hotel room.

Olive called her husband from the car. It was a self-driven car, for which she was grateful; there was no driver to hear her and wonder if she'd lost her mind, which was something she was wondering herself. "Dion," she said, "I'm going to ask you to do something that's going to sound kind of extreme."

"Okay," he said.

"We need to pull Sylvie out of school."

"Like, not bring her in tomorrow? I have to work."

"Could you go and pick her up now?"

"Olive, what's this about?"

Outside the window, the Philadelphia suburbs were a blur of apartment towers. You can have an excellent marriage and still be unable to tell your spouse absolutely everything. "It's about this new virus," Olive said. "I met someone at the hotel with some inside knowledge."

"What kind of inside knowledge?"

"It's bad, Dion, it's spreading out of control."

"In the colonies too?"

"How many flights are there every day between Earth and the moon?"

He drew in his breath. "Okay," he said. "Okay. I'll go get her."

"Thank you. I'm on my way home."

"What? I know it's serious if you're cutting a book tour short."

"It's serious, Dion, it seems like it's really serious," and Olive realized she was beginning to cry.

"Don't cry," he said softly. "Don't cry. I'm heading to the school now. I'll bring her home."

In the departure lounge, Olive found a corner far from anyone else and took out her device. There was no new news of the pandemic, but she ordered three months' worth of pharmaceutical supplies, then bottled water for good measure, then a mountain of new toys for Sylvie. By the time she boarded the flight she had spent a small fortune and felt mildly insane.

What it was like to leave Earth:

A rapid ascent over the green-and-blue world, then the world was blotted out all at once by clouds. The atmosphere turned thin and blue, the blue shaded into indigo, and then—it was like slipping through the skin of a bubble—there was black space. Six hours to the moon. Olive had bought a package of surgical masks at the airport—sold to travellers who'd picked up colds on the road—and she was wearing three of them, which made it difficult to breathe. She had a window seat and was all but curled around her armrest, trying to stay as far from other people as possible. The surface of the moon rose out of blackness, bright from a distance and grey up close, the opaque bubbles of Colonies One, Two, and Three gleaming in the sunlight.

Her device lit up with a soft chime. She frowned at the new

appointment alert, because she couldn't remember having scheduled a doctor's appointment, and then she understood: Dion had scheduled the appointment for her. He'd seen how much money she'd just spent on canned goods. He thought she was losing her grip.

Then the landing, so gentle after that hurtling speed between Earth and the moon. Olive put on dark glasses to hide her tears. But it wasn't unreasonable, actually, the doctor's appointment. If Dion had called from a business trip to say that a plague was coming and she should pull their child out of school, if she'd seen those massive charges go through on their shared credit account, she would've feared for his sanity too. She waited as long as possible before disembarking, in order to create some distance between herself and other people, and stayed as far away as possible from everyone in the spaceport and on the platform for the Colony Two train. In the train car she stared out the window at the passing tunnel lights, through the composite glass to the moon's bright surface. She disembarked on a platform, where she kept reaching for her suitcase and then remembering that she was never going to see it again.

Olive had a moment of passing regret for the strange star-weapon burrs that she'd pulled from her socks in the Republic of Texas—she'd looked forward to showing them to Sylvie—but beyond that there was nothing of any real value in that suitcase, she told herself. (But she felt bereft: she'd been travelling with the suitcase for years now and it was almost a friend.) The trolley arrived. Olive sat close to the doors, for increased airflow—it was all coming back to her now, all of her research into pandemics—and the trolley glided through the streets and boulevards of this city of white stone, which had never looked more beautiful to her. The bridges arching over the street were possessed of uncommon architectural grace; the trees lining the boulevards and softening the tower balconies were almost unnaturally verdant, oversaturated in their green; and then there were the countless little shops with people walking in and out—unmasked, ungloved, oblivious, blind to the imminent catastrophe—and the sight of them was too much, actually, she could bear no more but of course she had to. Olive was weeping quietly, so no one came near her.

She disembarked early, and walked the last ten blocks in the sunlight. The Colony Two dome was displaying her favourite kind of sky, white skittering clouds on a background of deep blue. What was missing was the sound of suitcase wheels on cobblestones.

Olive turned the corner and there was the complex where she lived, a line of square white buildings with staircases leading down from the second and third floors to the sidewalk. She took the stairs to the second floor with a sense of unreality. How could she be home so soon? Without her suitcase? And why, because a journalist had said something strange about time travel? She raised her hand to knock—her keys were in her suitcase, on Earth—but froze. What if the contagion were on her clothes? She took off her jacket, her shoes, and then—after only a moment of hesitation—her pants and shirt. She looked down at the street and a passerby looked quickly away.

She called Dion.

"Olive, where are you?"

"Could you unlock the door, and then take Sylvie into the bedroom, and stay in there till I come into the room?"

"Olive . . ."

"I'm afraid of the contagion," Olive said. "I'm outside the front door, but I want to take a shower before either of you hug me. It could be on my clothes." Her clothes were puddled around her feet.

"Olive," he said, and she heard the pain in his voice. He thought she was terribly, desperately unwell, but not from the approaching pandemic.

"Please."

"Okay," he said. "I'll do it."

The lock clicked open. Olive waited for a slow count of ten, then let herself in, dropped her device and underwear into a heap on the floor, and went straight to the shower room. She scrubbed herself with soap, then found the cleaning alcohol, retraced her footsteps, and disinfected every surface she'd touched, then turned on the air purifier to its highest setting and opened all the windows, then used her towel to lift her underwear from the floor and dropped both underwear and towel into the garbage disposal, then disinfected her device, then disinfected the floor where the device had been, then disinfected her hands again.

This will be our lives now, she thought dully, *memorizing which surfaces we've touched.* Olive took a deep breath, and arranged her face into a semblance of calm. She opened the door to the bedroom, naked and deranged, and her daughter flew across the room and leaped into her arms. Olive fell to her knees, tears running hot down her face and onto Sylvie's shoulder.

"Mama," Sylvie said, "why are you crying?"

Because I was supposed to die in the pandemic but I was warned by a time traveller. Because a lot of people are going to die soon and there's nothing I can do to prevent it. Because nothing makes sense and I might be insane.

"I just missed you so much," Olive said.

"You missed me so much you had to come home early?" Sylvie asked.

"Yes," Olive said. "I missed you so much I had to come home early."

A strange alarm filled the room: Dion's device was blaring with a public alert. Over Sylvie's shoulder, Olive watched Dion staring at the screen. He looked up and saw her watching him.

"You were right," he said. "I'm sorry for doubting you. The virus is here."

For the first one hundred days of lockdown, Olive closed herself into her office every morning and sat at her desk, but it was easier to stare out the window than to write. Sometimes she just took notes on the soundscape.

Siren

Quiet; birds

Siren

Another siren

A third? Overlapping, from at least two directions

All quiet

Birds

Siren

The blur of passing days: Olive woke at four a.m. to work for two hours while Sylvie slept, then Dion worked from six a.m. to noon while Olive made an attempt to be a schoolteacher and to keep their daughter reasonably sane, then Olive worked for two hours while Dion and Sylvie played, then Sylvie got an hour of hologram time while both her parents worked, then Dion worked while Olive played with Sylvie, then somehow it was time to make dinner and then dinner blurred into the bedtime hour, then by eight p.m. Sylvie was asleep and Olive went to bed not long after, then Olive's alarm rang because it was once again four a.m., etc.

"We could think of it as an opportunity," Dion said, on the seventy-third night of lockdown. Olive and Dion were sitting together in the kitchen, eating ice cream. Sylvie was sleeping.

"An opportunity for what?" Olive asked. Even on Day 73, she still felt a little stunned. There was an element of incredulity— a pandemic? *Seriously?*—that hadn't quite faded.

"To think about how to re-enter the world," Dion said, "when re-entry is possible." There were certain friends he didn't miss, he said. He was quietly applying for new jobs.

"Let's pretend this seltzer bottle is a friend," Sylvie said, at dinner on Day 85. "Make it talk to me."

"Hello, Sylvie!" Olive said. She moved the glass bottle closer to Sylvie.

"Hi, bottle," Sylvie said.

In lockdown, there was a new kind of travel, but that didn't seem the right word. There was a new kind of anti-travel. In the evenings Olive keyed a series of codes into her device, donned a headset that covered her eyes, and entered the holospace. Holographic meetings had once been hailed as the way of the future—why go to the time and expense of physical travel, when one could transport oneself into a strange silvery-blank digital room and converse there with flickering simulations of one's colleagues?—but the unreality was painfully flat. Dion's job required a great many meetings, so he was in the holospace six hours a day and was dazed with exhaustion in the evenings.

"I don't know why it's so tiring," he said. "So much more tiring than normal meetings, I mean."

"I think it's because it isn't real." It was very late, and they were standing by the living room windows together, looking down at the deserted street.

"Maybe you're right. Turns out reality is more important than we thought," Dion said.

The thing with the tour—the thing with all the tours—is that there was no moment when she wasn't grateful, but also it was always too many faces. She'd always been shy. On tour all those faces kept appearing before her, face after face after face, and most of them were kind but all of them were the wrong faces, because after a few days on the road the only people Olive wanted to see were Sylvie and Dion.

But when the world shrank to the size of the interior of the apartment, and to a population of three, the people were what she missed. Where was the driver who was writing the book about the talking rats? She'd never even known the woman's name. Where was Aretta—the out-of-office message on Aretta's device was weeks out of date, which was worrying—and the other authors she'd met on that last tour, Ibby Mohammed and Jessica Marley? Where was the driver who sang an old jazz song as they drove through Tallinn, and the woman in Buenos Aires with the tattoo?

In lockdown, Colony Two was a strange, frozen place, silent except for the ambulance sirens and the soft *whir* of passing trolleys with their freight of masked medical workers. No one was supposed to go outside except for medical appointments and essential work, but on the one-hundredth night, while Sylvie was sleeping, Olive slipped out of the kitchen door and into the outside world. She moved swiftly and silently down the stairs to the garden, where she sat on the grass, under a small tree shaped like an umbrella. She was inches from the sidewalk but hidden by leaves. Being out of the apartment was disorienting. She was certain that the air here hadn't changed, but after her time on Earth it seemed wrong to her, flat and overly filtered. She stayed outdoors for an hour, then slipped back in with a sense of revelation. After that she went out every night to sit under the umbrella tree.

It was on one of those nights that the journalist appeared. The last journalist, as she'd always think of him, Gaspery-Jacques Roberts of *Contingencies Magazine*. On the night he appeared, she was under the umbrella tree, cross-legged on the grass, trying not to think of the day's numbers—752 dead today in Colony Two, with 3,458 new cases—and trying to let go of conscious thought, when she heard soft footsteps approaching. She didn't think it could be a patrol officer—they walked in pairs—but the fines for being outside in lockdown were steep, so she stayed very still and tried to breathe as quietly as possible.

The footsteps stopped, so close that she could see the person's shadow angled over the sidewalk. Could they have sensed her? It didn't seem possible. Someone else—another set of footsteps— was approaching, from the opposite direction.

"Zoey? What are you doing here?" Olive recognized the man's voice immediately, and her breath caught in her chest.

"I could ask you the same thing," a woman said. She had his accent.

"I told you in the travel chamber five minutes ago," Gaspery said. "I want to interview a literary scholar who interviewed Olive Llewellyn. One more layer of confirmation."

"I thought it was strange that you wanted to leave again after your interview with her, on an unscheduled trip," she said.

Gaspery didn't speak for a moment. "I thought you didn't travel anymore," he said finally.

"Yes, well, I felt the circumstances warranted an exception. Gaspery, how could you?"

"I was going to just talk to her," Gaspery said. "I was going to stick to the plan, but Zoey, I couldn't do it. I couldn't just let her die."

There was a moment of silence, during which both of these incomprehensible people were, Olive imagined, staring directly into her living room window. She looked up, but from her angle she could see only patches of the living room ceiling, mostly obscured by leaves.

"It's like you warned me," he said quietly. "You said the job required a lack of humanity, and it did. It does."

"You shouldn't come back to the present," Zoey said.

What?

"Of course I'll come back to the present," Gaspery said. "I believe in facing consequences."

"But the consequences will be terrible," Zoey said. "I've seen it happen before."

There was silence then. Gaspery didn't respond.

"The Night City's beautiful in this era," he said finally.

"I know." She was crying, Olive could hear it in her voice. "It isn't the Night City yet."

"You're right," he said. "The dome lighting still works. Are we standing on cobblestones?"

"Yes," she said, "I believe we are."

"There's a patrol coming," Gaspery said suddenly, and they were gone, walking quickly away together.

Olive stayed there for a long time in the shadows, in the strangeness. She was supposed to die in the pandemic, as she understood it, but then Gaspery had saved her. Hadn't he even told her what he was? *If a time traveller appeared before you . . .*

That night she looked up Gaspery-Jacques Roberts and the results were flooded with references to her own work, the book and the screen adaptation of *Marienbad*. She looked up *Contingencies Magazine,* and found a website with a few dozen articles, but the more she searched, the more it seemed like a front. It hadn't been updated in a long time, and its social media accounts were dormant.

She heard a small noise and started, but it was only Sylvie, standing in the doorway in unicorn pyjamas.

"Oh, sweetie," Olive said, "it's the middle of the night. Let me tuck you in."

"I have an insomnia," Sylvie said.

"I'll sit with you for a bit."

Olive lifted her daughter, this warm weight in her arms, and carried her back to her bedroom. Everything in the room was blue. Olive tucked her in under an indigo duvet and sat beside her. *I was supposed to die in the pandemic.*

"Could we play Enchanted Forest?" Sylvie asked.

"Of course," Olive said. "Let's play for a few minutes, till you feel sleepy." Sylvie shivered with delight. The Enchanted Forest was a new invention: Sylvie had never gone in for imaginary friends, but in lockdown she had an entire kingdom filled with them, and she was their queen.

"When I feel sleepy we'll stop," Sylvie said agreeably. "We'll stop before I fall asleep."

"The portal door opens," Olive said, because that was how the game always began. Sylvie's bedroom was quieter than Olive's office, being at the back of the building, but Olive still heard the faint wail of an ambulance siren.

"Who comes through?" Sylvie asked.

"Magic Foxy leaps through the portal. 'Queen Sylvie,' says Magic Foxy, 'come quickly! There's a problem in the Enchanted Forest!'"

Sylvie laughed, delighted. Magic Foxy was her favourite friend. "And only I can help, Magic Foxy?"

"'Yes, Queen Sylvie,' says Magic Foxy, 'only you can help.'"

Another lecture, this one virtual. No, the same lecture, just performed now in the holospace. (In non-space. Nowhere.) Olive was a hologram in a room of holograms, a sea of dim lights flickering before her, all of them gathered in a minimalistic suggestion of a room. She gazed out at several hundred slightly luminescent facsimiles of people, their actual bodies in individual rooms all over Earth and in the colonies, and had the unhinged thought that she was speaking directly to a congregation of souls.

"An interesting question," Olive said, "which I'd like to consider in these last few minutes, is why there's been such interest in postapocalyptic literature over this past decade or so. I've had the tremendous good fortune of getting to travel a great deal in the service of *Marienbad*—"

> *Blue sky over Salt Lake City, birds wheeling overhead*
> *The rooftop of a hotel in Cape Town, lights sparkling in the trees*
> *Wind rippling over a field of long grass by a train station in northern*
> *England*
> *"Can I show you my tattoo?" the woman in Buenos Aires said*

"—which is to say I've had the opportunity to speak with a great many people about postapocalyptic literature. I've heard a great many theories about why there's such interest in the genre. One person suggested to me that it had to do with economic inequality, that in a world that can seem fundamentally unfair, perhaps we long to just blow everything up and start over—"

> *"That's just how it seems to me," the bookseller had said,*
> *in an old shop in Vancouver, while Olive admired his pink glasses*

"—and I'm not sure I agree with that, but it's an intriguing thought." The holograms shifted and stared. She liked the idea that she could still hold a room, even if now the room was just in the holospace, even if the room wasn't really a room. "Someone suggested to me that it has to do with a secret longing for heroism, which I found interesting. Perhaps we believe on some level that if the world were to end and be remade, if some unthinkable catastrophe were to occur, then perhaps we might be remade too, perhaps into better, more heroic, more honourable people."

"Doesn't it seem possible?" the librarian in Brazzaville asked,
her eyes shining, and outside on the street
someone was playing a trumpet,
"I mean, no one wants this to happen, obviously,
but think of the opportunity for heroism . . ."

"Some people have suggested to me that it's about the catastrophes on Earth, the decision to build domes over countless cities, the tragedy of being forced to abandon entire countries due to rising water or rising heat, but—"

A memory: waking in an airship between cities,
looking down at the dome over Dubai,
and believing for a wildly disorienting moment that she'd left Earth

"—that doesn't ring true to me. Our anxiety is warranted, and it's not unreasonable to suggest that we might channel that anxiety into fiction, but the problem with that theory is, our anxiety is nothing new. When have we ever believed that the world *wasn't* ending?

"I had a fascinating conversation with my mother once, where she talked about the guilt she and her friends had felt about bringing children into the universe. This was in the mid-2160s, in Colony Two. It's hard to imagine a more tranquil time or place, but they were concerned about asteroid storms, and if life on the moon became untenable, about the continued viability of life on Earth—"

> *Olive's mother drinking coffee in Olive's childhood home:*
> *yellow flowered tablecloth*
> *hands clasped around a blue coffee mug*
> *her smile*

"—and my point is, there's always something. I think, as a species, we have a desire to believe that we're living at the climax of the story. It's a kind of narcissism. We want to believe that we're uniquely important, that we're living at the end of history, that *now,* after all these millennia of false alarms, *now* is finally the worst that it's ever been, that finally we have reached the end of the world."

> *In a world that no longer exists but whose exact end date is unclear,*
> *Captain George Vancouver stands on the deck of the HMS Discovery,*
> *gazing anxiously out at a landscape with no people in it*

"But all of this raises an interesting question," Olive said. "What if it always *is* the end of the world?"

She paused for effect. Before her, the holographic audience was almost perfectly still. "Because we might reasonably think of the end of the world," Olive said, "as a continuous and never-ending process."

An hour later, Olive removed her headset and was once again alone in her office. She wasn't sure if she'd ever been so tired. She sat still for a while, absorbing the details of the physical world: the bookshelves, the framed drawings by Sylvie, the painting of a garden that her parents had given her as a wedding present, the odd piece of metal she'd once found on Earth that she'd hung on the wall because she loved the shape of it. She rose and went to the window to look out at the city. White street, white buildings, green trees, ambulance lights. It was midnight, and so the ambulances had no need of sirens. Lights flashed blue and red up the street and then receded.

I was supposed to die in the pandemic. She didn't entirely understand what that meant, and yet it was the point around which all of her thoughts revolved. A trolley passed, carrying medical workers, then another ambulance, then the stillness returned. Movement in the air: an owl flying silently through the dark.

"When we consider the question of why *now*," Olive said, before a different audience of holograms the following evening, "I mean why there's been this increased interest in postapocalyptic fiction over the past decade, I think we have to consider what's changed in the world in that timeframe, and that line of thinking leads me inevitably to our technology." A hologram in the front row was shimmering oddly, which meant the attendee had an unstable connection. "My personal belief is that we turn to postapocalyptic fiction not because we're drawn to disaster, per se, but because we're drawn to what we imagine might come next. We long secretly for a world with less technology in it."

"So I'm guessing I'm not the first to ask you what it's like to be the author of a pandemic novel during a pandemic," another journalist said.

"You might not be the very first."

Olive was standing by the window, staring up at the sky. The Colony Two dome had the same pixelations as Colonies One and Three, a shifting pattern of blue sky and clouds, but it seemed to her that there was a glitchy patch on the horizon, a section that flickered just slightly so that a square of black space showed through. It was hard to tell.

"What are you working on these days? Are you able to work?"

"I'm writing this crazy sci-fi thing," Olive said.

"Interesting. Can you tell me about it?"

"I don't know much about it myself, to be honest. I don't even know if it's a novel or a novella. It's actually kind of deranged."

"I suppose anything written this year is likely to be deranged," the journalist said, and Olive decided she liked her. "What drew you to sci-fi?"

That patch of sky had definitely just flickered. What would it look like if the dome lighting failed? It was a strange thought. She'd always taken the illusion of an atmosphere for granted.

"I've been in lockdown for one hundred and nine days," Olive said. "I think I just wanted to write something set as far away as possible from my apartment."

"Is that all it is?" the journalist asked. "Physical distance, a way of travelling during lockdown?"

"No, I guess not." An ambulance siren was approaching, and then the ambulance stopped in front of the building across the street. Olive turned her back to the window. "There's just . . . Look," Olive said, "I don't mean to be melodramatic, and I know it's like this in a lot of places now, but there's just, there is so much death. There's death all around us. I don't want to write about anything real."

The journalist was quiet.

"And I know it's like this for everyone else too. I know how fortunate I am. I know how much worse it could be. I'm not complaining. But my parents live on Earth, and I don't know if . . ." She had to stop and take a breath to compose herself. "I don't know when I'll see them again."

Two ambulances passed, one after the other, then silence. Olive looked over her shoulder. The ambulance across the street was still there.

"Are you there?" Olive asked.

"I'm sorry," the journalist said. Her voice was choked.

"What's your situation?" Olive asked softly. It occurred to her that the journalist sounded very young. She glanced at her calendar. The journalist's name was Annabel Escobar, and she worked in the city of Charlotte, which Olive dimly recalled visiting on a long-ago tour of United Carolina.

"I live alone," Annabel said. "We're not supposed to leave our houses, and it's just . . ." But she was crying now, truly weeping.

"I'm sorry," Olive said. "That sounds so lonely." She was staring out the window. The ambulance hadn't moved.

"I just haven't been in a room with anyone in a very long time," Annabel said.

On another night of searching, a centuries-old academic journal yielded a reference to a Gaspery J. Roberts. The journal had been devoted to prison reform. The hit sent Olive down a rabbit hole, at the end of which she found prison records from Earth: Gaspery J. Roberts had been sentenced to fifty years for a double homicide in Ohio in the late twentieth century. But there was no picture, so Olive couldn't be sure it was the same man.

"So, Olive," another journalist said. They were holograms in a silvery holospace room, along with two other authors who'd also written books whose plots involved pandemics. The four of them flickered like ghosts. "How many copies of *Marienbad* have you sold since the pandemic began?"

"Oh," Olive said. "I'm not sure. A lot."

"I know you've sold a lot," he said. "It's been on bestseller lists in a dozen Earth countries, all three moon colonies, and two of the three colonies on Titan. I'm asking you to be more specific."

"I'm afraid I don't have my sales numbers in front of me," Olive said. All of the holograms were staring at her.

"Really?" the journalist asked.

"It didn't occur to me to bring my royalty statements to this interview," Olive said.

An hour later, when the interview was over, she removed her headset and sat for a while with her eyes closed. She'd been home from Earth for long enough that when she opened the window, the night air of the Second Colony seemed fresh again. The air might be filtered, but there were plants, there was running water, there was a world outside her window as real as any world that anyone had ever lived in. Olive found herself thinking of Jessica Marley, for the first time in a while, and Jessica Marley's insufferable little coming-of-age-on-the-moon novel. Look, she wanted to tell her, there's no *pain in unreality* happening here. A life lived under a dome, in an artificially generated atmosphere, is still a life. A siren wailed and receded. Olive picked up her device, ran a search on Jessica's name, and discovered that she'd died two months ago in Spain.

"Mama?" Sylvie was in the doorway. "Is your interview over?"

"Hi, sweetie. Yes. It ended early." Jessica Marley was thirty-seven years old.

"Do you have another interview?"

"No." Olive knelt before her daughter, and then hugged her quickly. "No more till tomorrow."

"Then can we play Enchanted Forest?"

"Of course."

Sylvie wriggled a little in anticipation. *I was supposed to die in the pandemic.* Olive knew now that she was going to spend the rest of her life trying to understand that fact. But her effervescent five-year-old sat before her, grinning, and what she found at that moment, as the lights of yet another ambulance flickered over the ceiling, was that it was possible to smile back. This is the strange lesson of living in a pandemic: life can be tranquil in the face of death.

"Mama? Let's play Enchanted Forest."

"Okay," Olive said. "The portal door opens . . ."

6

Mirella and Vincent /

file corruption

1

Follow the evidence. In Gaspery's years of training, from the night he called Zoey to wish her a happy birthday through the present moment, that mantra had been a compass. *Present moment* was beginning to seem like a nonsensical term, but every moment can be distilled to a date, so let's call it November 30, 2203, in Colony Two, this city in the grip of a pandemic that would eventually kill 5 percent of its residents, this place that wasn't yet Gaspery's home and not yet the Night City, walking rapidly through the streets with Zoey to evade a lockdown-enforcement patrol.

"Here," Zoey said, and pulled him into a doorway. Gaspery peered through the glass door beside him, into a room of shadowy tables and chairs. This place was a restaurant, or had been. All of the restaurants in Colony Two were closed now.

They stood close together in the shadows, listening. All Gaspery could hear were sirens.

"You know you broke the most important protocol," Zoey said quietly. "Why did you do it?"

"I couldn't not warn her," Gaspery said.

"Okay," she said, "here's your situation. I've only done a preliminary analysis, but as far as I can tell, your decision to save Olive Llewellyn had no recognizable effect on the Time Institute."

"Does that mean I'll be okay?"

"No," she said, "it means you weren't immediately lost in time. It means your travel privileges haven't been revoked yet, because we sank five years of training into you and you still might be useful to the Time Institute, for at least the duration of this investigation. But if I were you, I'd get that tracker out of my arm and I wouldn't come back." She held up her device. "I have to go," she said. "Stay here, in this time, and I'll try to visit."

"Wait. Please."

She was still, watching him.

"I know you would never do what I did," he said. "But suppose you had done it. If you were in my position, Zoey, what would you do?"

"It's hard for me to imagine things that aren't real," she said.

"Can you try?"

Zoey sighed and closed her eyes. What occurred to Gaspery in that moment, watching her, was that he was her only person. Their parents were gone. She had never married. If she had friends or romantic interests, they'd never come up in conversation. He felt a fathomless guilt. Zoey opened her eyes.

"I might try to solve the anomaly," she said.

"How?"

Zoey was quiet for so long that he thought she wasn't going to answer. "Hold on," she said. "It took our best research teams a year to figure out these coordinates." She typed something into her device, and he heard his own device chime softly in his pocket.

"I sent you a new destination," Zoey said. "We don't know the time, we only know the day and the place, so you'll have to wait in the forest." She entered another code into her device and blinked out.

Gaspery was alone in the doorway, in the right city but the wrong time. He closed his eyes and considered the course of the investigation, because that was preferable to thinking about his sister, or thinking of what awaited him if he returned to his own time. He had a new destination. He entered the codes into his device, and he left.

2

He was on the beach at Caiette. He could see from the coordinates that he'd landed in the summer of 1994, but at first it seemed like a mistake, because the place hadn't changed at all over the past eight decades. He was staring at two little islands, tufts of trees across the water, and for a disorienting moment he thought he was back in 1912, dressed in the costume of an early-twentieth-century priest, preparing to meet Edwin St. Andrew in the church.

The little white church on the hillside was unchanged since the last time he'd been here—it must have recently been repainted—but the houses around it were different. He turned his back on the settlement, and his gaze fell on the ocean. The sun was rising, shades of blue and pink rippling over the water. He liked the way it moved, the gentle repetition of waves. He found himself thinking of his mother now, for the first time in a while. She'd spent time on Earth as a child. She'd kept a framed photo of an Earth ocean in the kitchen of his childhood home, a small rectangle of waves on the wall near the stove. He remembered her gazing at it while she stirred soup. And yet for himself, he realized, the ocean carried no weight in his heart, it featured in none of his childhood memories and none of the important moments of his life; it was just a place he'd seen in movies and visited for work, so he couldn't summon much feeling for it, and after a moment he turned and walked away down the beach, following the coordinates that flashed softly on his device. He walked beyond the last house, then into the forest.

Walking through this forest was easier now than when he'd been wearing a priest's robe, but he still had no talent for it. The ground was too soft; branches caught at his clothes; he felt assailed from all sides. It was a sunny afternoon, but it must have rained that morning. Ferns pulled wetly at his legs. His shoes were less waterproof than he'd thought. His device pulsed softly in his hand, with a message that he was very close to the place he sought; he let go of the branch he'd been holding to study the screen, and the branch slapped him across the face.

Here was the maple tree, eighty-two years older than the last time he'd seen it. It had gained less in height than in breadth and magnificence. The clearing around it had widened with the passage of time. He walked under the canopy of its branches, to look up at the sunlight shifting through leaves, and for the first time in memory, he felt true reverence.

When would Vincent Smith come here? There was no way to

know. Gaspery stepped just outside the clearing, and fought his way into a thicket of dense leaves, where he knelt on the cool, wet earth, and waited.

He was very still, listening. Another thing he didn't like about forests was the constant sound. It wasn't the steady white noise of the moon cities, the distant mechanicals that increased the gravity to Earth levels and kept the air inside the domes breathable and created the illusion of a breeze. There was no pattern to the white noise of a forest, and the randomness put Gaspery on edge. Time passed, hours. His muscles cramped. He was desperately thirsty. He stood a few times, to stretch, then crouched low again. It was impossible to hear anything coming, until it wasn't. A little after four in the afternoon, he heard the girl's soft footsteps on the path.

Vincent Smith at thirteen: she looked like she'd cut her own hair with blunt scissors before she'd dyed it bright blue. Her eyes were ringed in black. She radiated neglect. She walked slowly, looking through the viewfinder of her camera, and from his hiding place Gaspery recognized the scene: once he'd sat in a theatre in New York City and watched a somewhat tedious musical performance accompanied by the footage that Vincent was creating at this moment. She stopped under the tree, angled the camera upward—

—*and reality broke: Gaspery and Vincent were in the cavernous echoing cathedral of the Oklahoma City Airship Terminal, where Olive Llewellyn was walking just ahead of them and notes were rising from a nearby violin. And here too, impossibly,*

*was Edwin St. Andrew, face upturned toward the branches/the
terminal ceiling—*

Vincent staggered and all but dropped her camera. Gaspery's
hands were clasped over his mouth, because he wanted to scream,
and the terminal was gone. It's one thing to know in the abstract
that one moment might corrupt another moment; it's another to
experience both moments at once; it's something else again to
suspect what it might mean. Vincent was staring around wildly,
but Gaspery was crouched low and she didn't see him. He closed
his eyes, sank his hands into the mud, and tried to convince himself that the cold water seeping through the knees of his pants
was real.

3

But what makes a world real?

Gaspery was lying on his back in the mud, staring up at leaves silhouetted against a darkening sky, and it seemed to him that he'd been there for some time. Night was falling in the forest. Vincent was gone. He sat up, with some effort—his back was stiff; how long had he been lying there unmoving?—and sent a message through his device: *I saw it! I saw the file corruption! It's real, Zoey.*

There was no reply. He knew what he'd done, he knew he'd broken the most important rule by saving Olive Llewellyn, but he retained a sliver of hope that the message might save him.

4

Gaspery returned to the moment he'd left, to Travel Room Eight in the third sub-basement of the Time Institute, Zoey sitting before him at the control desk.

"I saw it," Gaspery said. "I saw the anomaly."

"I got your message." Zoey was staring at him, and he saw that she'd been crying. "I just spoke with Ephrem," she said. "You're being taken out of commission."

"What will happen to me?"

"Nothing good."

"I know what I did," Gaspery said. "But if I finish the investigation, maybe they'll . . ."

"I don't think there's anything you can do to save yourself now."

"But there *might* be. Look. I just want another level of confirmation, another witness. I need two more destinations." Gaspery stepped out of the machine, and handed over his device.

She looked at it and frowned. "1918?"

"I have follow-up questions for Edwin St. Andrew."

"In 1918? He experienced the anomaly in 1912. And what's in 2007?"

"A party Vincent Smith attended," he said. "Or I guess she's Vincent Alkaitis by that point. The party was on a list of secondary destinations."

"But your device and your tracker are out of commission," she said.

"Zoey," Gaspery said. "Please."

She closed her eyes for just a moment, and then took his device. She was typing something that he couldn't see, then she leaned close to the projection for an iris scan. "I'm overriding the decommissioning order," she said. Her voice was strangely flat, and he saw terror in her eyes. "Ephrem will be here any minute, probably with security forces. I won't stop you from going, Gaspery, but I can't protect you if you come back."

"I understand," he said. "Thank you."

Gaspery heard the knock on the door just as he was leaving.

5

Gaspery stepped out of a New York City men's room in the winter of 2007, into the warmth and light of a party in an art gallery. He moved slowly through the crowd, trying to orient himself. He was looking for Vincent Smith. He knew she'd be here—her presence had been entered into the historical record, because somewhere in this room was a society photographer—but what that meant, in 2007, was that Mirella Kessler was here too, and after his strange encounter with her in 2020, Gaspery hoped to avoid her.

He saw them together at the far end of the room, admiring a large-scale oil painting. He plucked a glass of red wine from a little round tray and went to stare at a different painting and plot his next move. He was utterly unnerved by the crowd. They were shaking hands, which even after all of his cultural-sensitivity training seemed like a bizarre thing to do in flu season, and kissing one another on the cheek. These people have no direct experience of pandemics, he reminded himself. None of them were old enough to remember the winter of 1918–1919; Ebola was a few years out and would mostly be confined to the other side of the Atlantic; Covid-19 would not arrive for another thirteen years. Gaspery began moving slowly around the periphery of the room, sidling toward Vincent.

In 2007, Vincent was wealthy, and possessed of a sheen of elegance and self-confidence that he wouldn't have expected of the blue-haired waif he'd just encountered in Caiette. Her arm was looped through Mirella's, and they were standing in front of a painting, but, he saw now, not really looking at it. They were speaking in a conspiratorial way. Mirella laughed softly. They had a look of inseparability that brought him close to despair. But then Vincent extricated herself to say hello to someone else, while Mirella turned to find her husband, and Gaspery saw his chance.

"Vincent?"

"Hello." She had a warm smile, and he found that he liked her immediately.

"I'm sorry to bother you. I'm conducting an investigation on behalf of an art collector, and I wondered if I might ask you a quick question about your brother Paul's videos."

He had her attention. Her eyes widened. "My brother? But I didn't think—I didn't know he did videos. He's a musician. Or a composer, I guess."

"That's my suspicion," he said. "I don't think he shot those videos. I think someone else did."

She frowned. "Can you describe them?"

"Well, there's one in particular," Gaspery said. "The videographer was walking through a forest. British Columbia, I think. It was a sunny day. Judging by the quality of the footage, I'd say probably sometime in the mid-nineties."

Her gaze softened. Gaspery had a sense of performing some kind of hypnosis. "The videographer walked along a path," he continued, "toward a maple tree."

She nodded. "I used to record on that path all the time," she said.

"On this particular video, something strange happens. There's this weird flash of something," Gaspery said, "like it all goes dark for a second, probably just some kind of glitch on the tape—"

"It seemed like a glitch," Vincent said, "but it wasn't on the tape."

"You saw it?"

"I heard these weird noises, and everything went dark."

"What did you hear?"

"Violin music. Then a noise like hydraulics. It was inexplicable." Her eyes focused suddenly. "I'm sorry," she said, "what did you say your name was?"

Her husband was moving through the crowd toward them, he was handing Vincent a glass of wine, and Gaspery took advantage of this momentary distraction to slip away from them. He felt a strange elation that was equal parts exhaustion and joy. He had a corroborating interview, recorded on his device. He had his own observations. For the first time since his interview with Olive Llewellyn, on the morning of this strange and seemingly infinite day, he felt he might not be doomed.

But Gaspery hesitated by the men's room door for a moment, watching the party, and his happiness faded. Here was the awfulness that Zoey had warned him of, the utterly miserable knowledge of how everyone else's stories would end. He looked out over the room, and for the first time in his life, Gaspery felt old.

Vincent and her husband clinked their glasses together. In fourteen months Alkaitis would be arrested for running a massive Ponzi scheme, then released on bail, at which point he would flee to Dubai—abandoning Vincent—and live out the rest of his long life in a series of hotels.

Vincent would live for another twelve years, and then disappear under mysterious circumstances from the deck of a container ship.

Nearby was Mirella, talking with her husband, Faisal. Faisal was an investor in Jonathan's fraud scheme, and when the scheme collapsed in a year he would lose everything, as would the family members who'd invested at his urging. Faisal would die of suicide.

Mirella would find the body, and the note. Then she would remain for more than a decade in New York City, until in March 2020 she would travel to Dubai for unknown reasons, arriving just in time to be stranded by the Covid-19 pandemic.

There she would meet Himesh Chiang, a guest at the same hotel where she was staying, and after some time the two of them would return to his native London, where they would survive the pandemic, marry, and live out the rest of their lives together; she would give birth to three children, have a successful career in retail management, and die of pneumonia at eighty-five, a year after her husband's death in a car accident.

But so much is inevitably left out of any biography, any accounting of any life. Before all of that, before Mirella lost Faisal, before this party in this city by the sea, she'd been a child in Ohio. Gaspery shivered. He was thinking of the way she'd looked at him in the park, in January 2020. *You were under the overpass,* she'd said to him, with terrible certainty, *in Ohio, when I was a kid*. Not just that. She'd said he was arrested there.

He'd been thinking of 1918 as his final trip. He had made every effort to save himself, and after 1918 he was going home to face the consequences. But what he realized now, watching Mirella, was that it was too late. He was going to go to 1918, but there would be one more destination after that.

7

Remittance /

1918, 1990, 2008

In 1918 Edwin had no more brothers, and only one foot. He lived with his parents on the family estate. He walked constantly, ostensibly because he was trying to improve his gait—he'd been fitted with a prosthetic and walked in a lurching way—but really because if he stopped moving, the enemy might get him. He walked at all hours of the day and night. Sleep transported him reliably back to the trenches, so he avoided sleep, which meant it ambushed him unexpectedly: while reading in the library, while sitting in the garden, once or twice at dinner.

His parents weren't sure how to speak to him, or how to look at him even. They couldn't accuse him of shiftlessness anymore, because he was a war hero but also something of an invalid. It was obvious to everyone that he wasn't well. "You've changed so much, darling," his mother said gently, and he wasn't sure whether this was a compliment, an accusation, or pure observation. He'd never been good at reading people and now he was worse.

"Well," he said, "I saw some things I wish I hadn't."

Understatement of the goddamned twentieth century.

He felt more empathy for his mother than previously, though. When Abigail floated off at the dinner table, when talk turned to the colonies and the look that her sons had once unkindly termed her British India expression came over her face, Edwin understood more vividly now that she was mourning a loss. He still found the Raj indefensible, but that didn't mean she hadn't lost an entire world. It wasn't her fault that the world she'd grown up in had ceased to exist.

Sometimes in the garden, he liked to talk to Gilbert, although Gilbert was dead. Gilbert and Niall had both died in the Battle of the Somme, a day apart, while Edwin had survived Passchendaele. No, *survived* was the wrong word. Edwin's animate body had returned from Passchendaele. He thought of his body now in strictly mechanical terms. His heart flapped deathlessly. He continued to breathe. He was in good physical health, except for the missing foot, but he was fundamentally unsound. It was difficult to be alive in the world.

"It's not uncommon," he heard the doctor say in the corridor outside his room, in the earliest weeks, when all he did was lie in bed. "The boys who went over there and wound up in the trenches, well, some of them saw things none of us should."

He hadn't entirely surrendered. He was making an effort. He rose and dressed in the mornings now, he ate the food that appeared in front of him at the table, and then, his strength exhausted, he spent most of the remaining day in the garden. He liked to sit out there on a bench under a tree and talk to Gilbert. He knew Gilbert wasn't there—he wasn't *that* far gone—but there was no one else to talk to. He'd had friends here, once, but now one friend was in China and all the others were dead.

"Now that you and Niall are dead," he confided, to Gilbert, "I'll inherit the title and the estate." He was surprised by how little he cared.

It came as an odd jolt when he walked out into the walled garden one morning and saw a man waiting on the bench. For just a heartbeat he thought it was Gilbert—at this point anything seemed possible—but then he came closer and the man's true identity was almost as strange: he was the impostor from that tiny church on the westernmost edge of British Columbia, the strange man in the clothes of a priest whom no one else in that place had ever seen or heard of.

"Please," the man said. "Sit." That same unplaceable foreign accent.

Edwin sat beside him on the bench.

"I thought you were a hallucination," Edwin said. "When I

saw Father Pike and asked him about the new priest I'd just been speaking to, Pike looked at me like I had two heads."

"My name is Gaspery-Jacques Roberts," the stranger said. "I'm afraid I only have a few minutes, but I wanted to see you."

"A few minutes until what?"

"An appointment. You'll think I'm a lunatic if I tell you the details."

"I'm afraid I'm in no position to judge anyone else's lunacy, just at present, but why are you lurking around my garden?"

Gaspery hesitated. "You were on the Western Front, weren't you?"

Mud. Cold rain. An explosion, blinding light, things raining down around him, then one of those things hit him in the chest and when he looked down he recognized his best friend's arm—

"Belgium," Edwin confirmed, through gritted teeth.

Friend wasn't really the word for what that man was to him, actually. The thing that hit his jacket and fell to his feet was the arm of his beloved. His beloved's head landed nearby in the mud, eyes still wide with amazement.

"And now you fear for your sanity," Gaspery said carefully.

"It was always a little fragile, in all honesty," Edwin said.

"Do you remember what you saw in the forest at Caiette? It was years ago now."

"Vividly, but it was a hallucination. The first of many, I'm afraid."

Gaspery was quiet for a moment. "I can't explain the mechanics here," he said. "My sister probably could, but it's still beyond me. But whatever happened to you afterward, whatever you saw in Belgium, it's possible you're saner than you think. I can assure you that what you saw in Caiette was real."

"How do I know that you're real?" Edwin asked.

Gaspery reached out his hand, and touched Edwin's shoulder. They stayed like that for a moment, Edwin staring at the hand on his shoulder, then Gaspery removed his hand and Edwin cleared his throat.

"What I experienced in Caiette couldn't possibly have been real," Edwin said. "It was a derangement of the senses."

"Was it? I believe you heard a few notes of violin music, played by a musician in an airship terminal in the year 2195."

"An airship . . . the year twenty-one-*what*?"

"Followed by a sound that must have seemed quite strange to you. A sort of *whoosh*, wasn't it?"

Edwin stared at him. "How did you know?"

"Because that's the sound that airships make," Gaspery said. "They won't be invented for some time. As for the violin music . . . a kind of lullaby, wasn't it?" He was quiet for a beat, then hummed a few notes. Edwin gripped the armrest of the bench. "The man who composed that song won't be born for another hundred and eighty-nine years."

"None of this is possible," Edwin said.

Gaspery sighed. "Think of it in terms of . . . well, in terms of corruption. Moments in time can corrupt one another. There was a derangement, but it had nothing to do with you. You're just a man who saw it. You were helpful in my investigation, and

I believe you're in a somewhat delicate state, and I thought perhaps it might ease your mind just a little to know that you might be saner than you think. At that moment, at least, you were not hallucinating. You were experiencing a moment from elsewhere in time."

Edwin's gaze drifted away from the man's face, to the mild decrepitude of the September garden. The salvias were bare now, for the most part, brown stalks and dried leaves, a few last blooms wisping blue and violet in the failing light. He was struck by an understanding of what his life could be from this moment: he could live here quietly, and care for the garden, and that might eventually be enough.

"Thank you for telling me," Edwin said.

"Don't tell anyone else." Gaspery rose, brushing a fallen leaf from his jacket. "You'll get committed to an asylum."

"Where are you going?" Edwin asked.

"I've an appointment in Ohio," Gaspery said. "Good luck."

"Ohio?"

But Gaspery was already walking away from him, disappearing around the side of the house. Edwin watched him go and then remained on his bench for a long time, hours, watching the way the garden faded into twilight.

2

Gaspery walked around the side of the house, and in the shadows at the base of a weeping willow, he stood staring at his device
for a moment. A message pulsed softly on the screen: *Return.*
He had exhausted the limits of his itinerary. The only possible
destination was home. For just a moment he entertained a wild
notion of staying here in 1918, burying his device in the garden
and cutting his tracker out of his arm, taking his chances in the
flu pandemic and trying to find some kind of life for himself in a
foreign world, but even as he thought this he was already entering the code, he was already leaving, and when he opened his
eyes in the harsh light of the Time Institute, he was unsurprised
to see the figures gathered there, the men and women in black
uniforms waiting with weapons drawn. What was surprising,
though, was that Olive Llewellyn's publicist was standing next to
Ephrem. They were the only two out of uniform.

"Aretta?"

"Hello, Gaspery," she said.

"Stay where you are, please," Ephrem said. "There's no need to leave the machine." His hands were clasped behind his back. Gaspery stayed where he was. At the back of the room—he had to crane his neck to see around the black uniforms—Zoey was being restrained by two men.

"I never guessed," Gaspery said, to Aretta.

"That's because I'm competent at my job," Aretta said. "I don't go around telling people I'm a time traveller."

"That's fair." Gaspery felt a little unhinged. "I'm sorry," he said to Zoey. "I'm sorry I tricked you." But she was already being escorted from the room, the door closing behind her.

"You tricked her?" Ephrem asked.

"I told her I was going to 1918 as part of the investigation. I was really there to try to save Edwin St. Andrew from dying in an insane asylum."

"Seriously, Gaspery? Yet another crime? Does someone have an updated bio?"

Aretta was frowning at her device. "Updated bio," she said. "Thirty-five days after Gaspery's visit, Edwin St. Andrew died in the 1918 flu pandemic."

"Isn't that the same bio?" Ephrem reached for her device, read for a moment, then handed it back with a sigh. "If you hadn't changed the time line," he said to Gaspery, "he still would've died of the flu, just forty-eight hours later and in an insane asylum. You see how *pointless* that was?"

"You're missing the point," Gaspery said.

"That's very possible." Were there tears in Ephrem's eyes? He looked tired and strained. A man who'd preferred being an arborist; a man in a difficult position, doing a difficult job. "Is there anything you'd like to say?"

"Are we at last words already, Ephrem?"

"Well, last words in this century," Ephrem said. "Last words on the moon. I'm afraid you'll be travelling some distance and not returning."

"Can you take care of my cat?" Gaspery asked.

Ephrem blinked.

"Yes, Gaspery, I'll take care of your cat."

"Thank you."

"Is there anything else?"

"I'd do it again," Gaspery said. "I wouldn't even hesitate."

Ephrem sighed. "Good to know." He'd been holding a glass bottle behind his back. He raised it now, and misted something in Gaspery's face. There was a sweet scent, a dimming of the lights, then Gaspery's legs were giving way—

3

—as he faded out, he had an impression that Ephrem had stepped into the machine behind him—

4

—Two gunshots, in quick succession—

Footsteps, a man running away—

Gaspery was in a tunnel. Light at either end, not just light but snow—

No, not a tunnel, an overpass. He could smell the exhaust of twentieth-century cars. He was very sleepy, from whatever he'd just been misted with. His back was to the embankment.

Ephrem was there too, calm and efficient in his dark suit. "I'm sorry, Gaspery," he said softly, his breath warm in Gaspery's ear. "I really am." He plucked Gaspery's device from his hand and replaced it with something hard and cold and much heavier—

A gun. Gaspery looked at it, curious, and the running man— the shooter, he realized dimly—disappeared, scrambling away and out of sight. Ephrem was gone too, a passing ghost. The air was cold.

He heard a soft groan near his feet. It was difficult for Gaspery to stay awake. His eyes kept closing. But he saw two men lying nearby, two men whose blood was seeping across the concrete, and one of them was staring directly at him. There was clear confusion in the man's stare—*Who are you? Where did you come from?*—but he'd passed beyond speaking, and as Gaspery watched, the light left his eyes. Gaspery was alone under an expressway with two dead men. He nodded off, just for a moment. When he opened his eyes, he was staring at the gun in his hand, and the pieces of the puzzle were drifting together. *It's possible to get lost in time,* Zoey had said, in a different century. Why go to the bother of incarcerating a man for life on the moon, when that man can be sent elsewhere, framed, and imprisoned at someone else's expense?

He sensed movement to his left. He turned his head, very slowly, and saw the children. Two girls, aged perhaps nine and eleven, holding hands. They'd been walking under the overpass, but now they'd stopped some distance away, staring. He saw their backpacks, and realized they were on their way home from school.

Gaspery let the gun fall from his hand, and it clattered away like a harmless thing. There were lights washing over him now, red and blue. The girls were staring at the two dead men, then the younger girl looked at him, and he recognized her.

"Mirella," he said.

5

No star burns forever. Gaspery scratched the words on a wall in prison some years later, so delicately that from any distance at all it looked like a flaw in the paint. You had to get close to see it, and you had to have lived in the twenty-second century or later to know what it meant. You had to have seen that twenty-second-century press conference, the president of China on a podium with a half-dozen of her favourite world leaders arrayed behind her, flags snapping against a brilliant blue sky.

There was time in prison, infinite time, so Gaspery spent a lot of it thinking about the past, no, the future, the point in time in which he'd walked into Zoey's office on her birthday with cupcakes and flowers, and everything that had followed. What had happened now was terrible, he was in prison in the wrong century and he was going to die here, but as months slipped into years, he found his regrets were very few. Warning Olive Llewellyn of the approaching pandemic was not, no matter how he turned the moment over in his mind, the wrong thing to do. If someone's about to drown, you have a duty to pull them from the water. His conscience was clear.

"What's that you wrote there, Roberts?" Hazelton asked. Hazelton was his cellmate, a much younger man who paced and talked incessantly. Gaspery didn't mind him.

"No star burns forever," Gaspery said.

Hazelton nodded. "I like that," he said. "Power of positive thinking, right? You're in prison, but that's not forever, because nothing is *forever,* right? Me, every time I start feeling a little down about my life, I—" He kept talking, but Gaspery stopped listening. He was calm these days, in a way he wouldn't have expected. In the early evenings Gaspery liked to sit on the farthest possible edge of his bunk, almost falling off the end, because from that angle there was a sliver of sky visible through the window, and through it he could see the moon.

8

Anomaly

1

Is this the promised end?

A line from Olive Llewellyn's novel *Marienbad,* but really a quote from Shakespeare. I found it in the prison library five or six years in, in a paperback with a missing cover.

2

No star burns forever.

3

Not long after my sixtieth birthday I developed some heart trouble, the kind of thing that could have been easily fixed in my own century but was dangerous in this time and place, and I was transferred to the prison hospital. I couldn't see the moon from my bed, so there was nothing for it now but to close my eyes and play old movies:

walking to school in the Night City, past Olive Llewellyn's childhood home
with its boarded-up front window and plaque;
standing in the church in Caiette in 1912 in my priest costume,
waiting for Edwin St. Andrew to stagger in;
chasing squirrels when I was five in the strip of wilderness
between the Night City dome and the Periphery Road;
drinking with Ephrem behind the school on an afternoon without

sunlight when we were fifteen or so, one of those afternoons that felt a
little dangerous,
even though all we were doing was getting slightly drunk and
trading dumb jokes;
holding hands and laughing with my mother on a
sunlit day in the Night City when I was six or seven,
stopping to look down at the river from a
pedestrian bridge, the river dark and sparkling below—

"Gaspery."

I felt a sharp pain in my arm. I gasped and almost cried out, but a hand was over my mouth.

"Shh," Zoey whispered. She looked like she was in her early forties, she was wearing a nurse's uniform, and she had just cut the tracker out of my arm. I stared at her, uncomprehending.

"I'm going to place this under your tongue," she said. She held it up for me to see: a new tracker, to correspond with the new device that she was pressing into my hand. She had drawn the curtain around my bed. She held her device against mine for a second or two, until the devices flashed in a quick coordinated pattern. I stared at those lights—

4

—and we were in a different room, in a different place.

I was lying on my back on a wood floor, in a bedroom, in what seemed to me to be an old-fashioned kind of house. My arm was bleeding; I held it reflexively to my chest. Sunlight poured in through a window. I sat up. There was wallpaper with roses, wooden furniture, and through a doorway I saw a room with a shower and a toilet.

"What is this place?"

"This is a farm on the outskirts of Oklahoma City," she said. "I've paid a great deal of money to the owners, and you can stay here indefinitely, as a boarder. The year is 2172."

"2172," I said. "So in twenty-three years, I'll visit Oklahoma City to interview the violinist."

"Yes."

"How are you here? Surely the Time Institute didn't approve this trip."

"I was arrested that day," she said. "The day you were sent to Ohio. I had tenure and an otherwise sterling record, so I wasn't lost in time, but I spent a year in prison and then immigrated to the Far Colonies. The Time Institute thinks they have the only functional time machine in existence. They don't."

"There's a time machine in the Far Colonies? And you just, what, get to use it?"

"I'm employed by . . . another organization there," she said.

"Even with your record?"

"Gaspery," she said, "no one's better than me at what I do." She spoke matter-of-factly; she wasn't boasting.

"You know, I still don't know what that is."

She ignored this. "I made this mission a condition of my agreeing to take the job in the Far Colonies," she said. "I'm sorry I couldn't come sooner. I mean to an earlier point in time."

"It's okay. I mean, thank you. Thank you for coming for me."

"I think it's safe here, Gaspery. I built a paper trail for you. You should settle in. Meet the neighbours."

"Zoey, I can't thank you enough."

"You'd do the same for me." (Unspoken between us: I *couldn't* do the same for her. She was of a different order from me, and always had been.) "I don't know if we'll see each other again," Zoey said.

Had we ever hugged before? I couldn't remember. She clasped me close for just a moment, stepped back, and was gone.

I was alone in the room, but *alone* wasn't a strong enough word for it. I knew no one in this century, and the fact of having been through this before did nothing to assuage my loneliness. I had a deranged moment of wondering how Hazelton was doing, then remembered that my cellmate would have died of old age by now.

I went to the window, in a daze, and looked out at a sea of green. The farm reached almost to the horizon, field upon field with agricultural robots moving slowly in the sunlight. In the far distance, I saw the spires of Oklahoma City. The sky was a dazzling blue.

The farm was owned and run by an older couple, Clara and Mariam. They were in their late eighties and had been here all their lives. They were pleased to have a well-paying boarder, they told me that first night, over a dinner of quiche and the freshest salad I'd tasted in decades, and they would ask me no questions. They respected privacy above all.

"Thank you," I said.

"Your sister left us some identity paperwork for you," Clara said. "Birth certificate and such. Shall we call you by the name on the paperwork?"

"Call me Gaspery," I said. "Please."

"Well, Gaspery," Clara said, "should you ever have need of your documents, it's all in that blue cabinet by the hallway door."

I didn't leave the farm at all those first few years, but I feared that eventually I'd have to. When Mariam fell ill, Clara drove her to the hospital, but who would drive Clara? They were nearing ninety. *My first case at the Institute involved a doppel-gänger,* Ephrem had told me once, in another, unfathomable life. *According to our best facial-recognition software, the same woman appeared in photographs and video footage taken in 1925 and 2093.* Whenever I imagined leaving the farm, I imagined surveillance cameras picking up my face and setting off alarms through the centuries, a Time Institute agent arriving to investigate, a cascade of horrors. I spoke with Clara, who made discreet inquiries with a neighbour, who had a friend with useful contacts, and a short time later I was lying on my back on the farmhouse kitchen table, undergoing laser facial resculpting and iris recolouring.

When the sedation wore off and I sat up, the surgeon was gone.

"Whisky?" Mariam asked.

"Please," I said.

"You look completely different," Clara said. She passed me a mirror, and I gasped.

I did look completely different. But I recognized my face.

6

Later that month, I found the violin. It was very old, and in a box at the very back of the hall closet; Mariam hadn't played it in years. Clara arranged for lessons from a neighbour.

"She goes by Lina," Clara said on the drive over. "She's been playing violin all her life, in my understanding. Came here in much the same manner as you, if you get my drift."

I glanced at her. She was ninety-two that year, but her profile was still strong. Her eyes were unreadable.

"I had no idea," I said. There must have been a note of reproach in this, because Clara fixed me for a beat or two in her calm gaze.

"You know I believe in privacy," she said. "So does she, by all appearances. She's barely left that farm in thirty years."

We pulled up at the neighbouring farmhouse—a grey cubist monstrosity that could have served as a hotel—and I was think-

ing of Zoey's words when she left me here, four years ago now—
You should settle in. Meet the neighbours—and wondering why
I'd never been able to properly apprehend anything she'd ever
said. I stepped out of the truck into glaring sunlight.

The front door opened, and the woman who stepped out was
around my age, early sixties.

"Good morning, Gaspery," Talia said.

7

"Your sister probably got me out just in time," Talia told me. "She came to the hotel one night, must have been right after she got out of prison, and told me the police had opened a file on me, something about repeating classified information."

"Well, in fairness, you did have a habit of repeating classified information." We were sitting on the porch of the farmhouse where she lived, our violins resting between us.

"I was reckless. Tempting fate, I suppose. She said she was about to move to the Far Colonies, and strongly suggested I come with her, but the Far Colonies have an extradition treaty with the moon, so she suggested once we got there that perhaps that shouldn't be my final destination."

"And that was thirty years ago?"

"Twenty-six."

I could see it when I looked at her, that quarter-century of living on this farm. Her skin was darkened by the sun and she had a peacefulness about her.

"What are they like?" I asked. "The Far Colonies?"

"They're beautiful," she said, "but I didn't like living underground."

We were married within a year, Talia and I, and when Clara and Mariam died, they left the farm to us.

This, I found myself thinking in the years that followed, on nights when my wife and I played the violin together, when we cooked together, when we walked in our fields watching the movements of the farm robots, when we sat on the porch watching the airships rise up like fireflies on the horizon over Oklahoma City, this is what the Time Institute never understood: if definitive proof emerges that we're living in a simulation, the correct response to that news will be *So what*. A life lived in a simulation is still a life.

9

A countdown had begun. I sensed it in the background of all my days. Sometime soon, I knew, I would move to Oklahoma City. I was scheduled to begin playing the violin in the airship terminal by 2195. I knew, because I remembered the interview, that my wife was going to die first.

10

Quietly
in the night
of an aneurysm
when she was seventy-five.

11

When Talia was gone I sat alone on the porch every night for a while, watching the airships rising over the distant city. My dog, Odie, lay beside me, head on his paws. At first I thought I was putting off moving to the city because I loved the farm, but one night it hit me: I *longed* for those lights. After all this time, I wanted to be around people again.

"I'll take you with me," I told Odie, who wagged his tail.

12

What someone—anyone!—at the Time Institute really should have caught, given how intelligent everyone was supposed to be over there, was that I was the anomaly. No, that's not fair. I *triggered* the anomaly. How did no one catch that I was interviewing myself? Because thanks to the documentation Zoey had created, on paper my name was Alan Sami and I'd been born and spent my life on a farm outside of Oklahoma City.

I watched the anomaly from the airship terminal. On an October day in 2195, I was playing the violin, my dog beside me, and I noticed two people almost at the same time.

Olive Llewellyn was walking along the corridor, pulling her silver suitcase. She didn't notice the man walking toward me a few metres ahead of her, but I did. The man had just stepped out of a utility closet.

As the man walked toward me, crossing Olive Llewellyn's path, the air seemed to ripple behind him. He didn't notice, because he was focused on me, and because he was a little anxious; this was, after all, his first interview for the Time Institute.

I kept playing, sweating now, holding on for dear life to my lullaby for Talia. The rippling intensified; the software, if that was the word for it, whatever unknowable engine kept our world intact, was struggling to reconcile the impossibility of both of us being here. But it wasn't just that the same person was in the same place twice; the engine, the intelligence, the software, whatever it was, it had detected a third Gaspery, somewhere else altogether in time and space, in the forest at Caiette, and now things were truly coming apart: this moment was corrupted, but so was *that place,* that point in the forest where in 1912 Edwin St. Andrew gazed up into the branches, where in 1994 I hid behind ferns and watched Vincent Smith. There was a strange wave of darkness behind the approaching man, light rippling away. Olive Llewellyn stopped as if struck. I saw myself kneeling in 1994, and Edwin St. Andrew in exactly the same spot—we were superimposed on one another—and nearby was Vincent Smith, thirteen years old with a camera in her hand.

An airship ascended at a nearby port, that unmistakable *whoosh,* and the spectres were gone. Time was running smoothly again. The file corruption was repairing itself, the threads of the simulation knitting into place around us, and Gaspery-Jacques Roberts, my younger self, new recruit and distressingly inept investigator for the Time Institute, had noticed none of it. It had all transpired behind his back. He did glance over his shoulder, but—I remembered the moment—chalked up his overwhelming sense of wrongness to runaway nerves.

I closed my eyes. All this time, it had been me. Vincent and Edwin had seen the anomaly because I'd been with them in the forest. I must not have been close enough to Edwin to see it myself, that first time in 1912. I finished the lullaby, and heard Gaspery's applause.

He stood before me, clapping awkwardly. I was so embarrassed for him—for me? for us?—that it was difficult to meet his eyes, but I managed it. I was grateful that my dog had slept through my younger self's incompetence.

"Hello," he said brightly, in a jarringly imperfect accent. "My name's Gaspery-Jacques Roberts. I'm conducting some research on behalf of a music historian, and I wondered if I could possibly buy you some lunch."

13

"How would I describe my life?" I repeated, stalling. "Well, son, that's a big question. I don't know what I can tell you."

"Maybe you could tell me a little about what your days are like. If you don't mind. I haven't turned the recorder on yet, by the way. This is just us talking."

I nodded. I would keep him off-balance. I would quote Shakespeare at him because I knew he didn't know his Shakespeare yet. I would call him *son* because he hated being called *son*, and his irritation would distract him. I would bring up my dead wife because he was embarrassed by his own failed marriage. I would make him feel insecure about his accent, because accents and dialects were what he'd struggled with the most in his training. But first I would lull him with the quiet of my life.

"Well," I said. "I stand there for a few hours a day, playing the violin, while my dog naps at my feet, and the commuters dash by and throw change at me. They move with inhuman speed, the commuters. It took me some time to get used to this."

"Are you from around here?" the investigator asked.

"A farm just outside the city. Lived there all my life. But listen, son, by the time I took over the farm, small-scale farming had become mostly a matter of watching. You watch the robots move over the fields. You tinker with their settings sometimes but they're well made, they adjust themselves mostly, they don't need you for much. You play your violin in the field just to keep yourself occupied. In the distance the airships rise with the speed of fireflies, but they're faster up close."

When I played my violin at the airship terminal I sometimes thought it was as if the airships were falling upward, gravity reversed. They filled with a cargo of blank-faced commuters, then fell toward the sky. The commuters glanced at me sometimes as they passed, tossed coins into my hat. I watched their ships carry them up into the early morning, to jobs in Los Angeles, Nairobi, Edinburgh, Beijing. I thought of their souls moving fast through the morning sky.

"When my wife died," I told the investigator, "I kept up the farm for another year and then thought, to hell with it."

He was nodding, feigning interest, trying not to be nervous, trying to convince himself that he was doing a good job. What I didn't tell him: I felt that without Talia I might disappear into thin air, out there by myself. Just me and the dog and the farm robots, day after day. Loneliness wasn't a strong enough word for it. All that empty space. At night I sat on the porch with my dog, avoiding the silent house. Playing that game kids play, where you squint at the moon and half-convince yourself that you can see the brighter spots of the colonies on its surface. Distant over the fields, the lights of the city.

"Is it okay if I switch on the recorder?" the investigator asked.

"Go ahead."

"Okay, it's on. Thank you for taking the time to speak with me."

"You're welcome. Thank you for lunch."

"Now, just for the benefit of my recording, you're a violinist," my earlier self said.

I followed the script. "I am," I said. "I play in the airship terminal."

When I wasn't playing my violin in the airship terminal I liked to walk my dog in the streets between the towers. In those streets everyone moved faster than me, but what they didn't know was that I had already moved too fast, too far, and wished to travel no further. I've been thinking a great deal about time and motion lately, about being a still point in the ceaseless rush.

Notes and Acknowledgments

The quote referenced on page 72, "It's a great life if you don't weaken," is from John Buchan's 1919 novel *Mr. Standfast*.

The riff on page 95 re: chickens coming home to roost—"It's never good chickens"—is paraphrased from something the American poet Kay Ryan said when we were at a literary festival together in 2015.

The quote in the same chapter from the fourth-century Roman soldier and historian Ammianus Marcellinus, re: the Antonine Plague, is from Book XXIII of his writings, which are fascinating and available online.

I'm indebted to the books *Voyages of the* Columbia (ed. Frederic W. Howay) and *Scoundrels, Dreamers and Second Sons: British Remittance Men in the Canadian West,* by Mark Zuehlke.

With thanks to my agent, Katherine Fausset, and her colleagues at Curtis Brown; my editors—Jennifer Jackson at Knopf in New York City, Sophie Jonathan at Picador in London, and Jennifer Lambert at HarperCollins Canada in Toronto—and their colleagues; my U.K. agent, Anna Webber, and her colleagues at United Agents; Kevin Mandel, Rachel Fershleiser, and Semi Chellas, for reading and commenting on early drafts of this manuscript; and Michelle Jones, my daughter's nanny, for taking care of my daughter while I wrote this book.

here to relish.' *Mail on Sunday*

'Extremely clever but, better than that, immensely entertaining.' *Oxford Times*

Arcadia

IAIN PEARS

FABER & FABER

First published in 2015
by Faber & Faber Ltd
Bloomsbury House
74–77 Great Russell Street
London WC1B 3DA

This open market paperback edition first published in 2016

Typeset by Faber & Faber Ltd
Printed by CPI Group (UK) Ltd, Croydon, CRO 4YY

A CIP record for this book
is available from the British Library

ISBN 978-0-571-30157-7

FSC
www.fsc.org
MIX
Paper from
responsible sources
FSC® C101712

To Ruth, as ever.

Imagine a landscape. Bathed in sunshine, sweet-smelling from the gentle shower that fell overnight then stopped as dawn broke. A dense grove of holm oak stands at the foot of a hill, damp with the drops of soft-sounding water which leave the ground moist but firm underfoot. In the distance a sliver of water, bright and glittering, reflects the brightness of the sky. The wide river is of a blue so translucent that it is almost indistinguishable from the heavens above. Only the vegetation marks the division between the fields and the range of low-lying hills beyond. It is warm now, but will be hot later on; there is not a cloud to be seen. Down by the river, there are the harvesters with their pitchforks, fanning out across the fields, some already at work.

A young boy looks down on them. They are far away, and he sees that they are talking quietly and seriously, eager to get on with a day's work. Over his shoulder is an empty leather bag; he is going for the water which the men will soon need when the sun rises higher. The stream is cool from the hills beyond, which mark the end of their world. He does not know what lies outside it. His entire universe is here, the few villages with their rivalries, the seasonal round of crops, animals and festivities.

He is about to leave it for ever.

His name is Jay. He is eleven years old and is an entirely normal boy apart from his tendency to bother people with questions. Why are you doing this? What is that for? What are these? His insatiable curiosity – considered unseemly by his elders and tiresome by those of his own age – means that he has few friends but, on the whole, he is, as his mother continually tells people, no trouble really.

Today the boy's mind is empty. It is too glorious, and he knows that the warmth on his back and the brilliant sunshine will not last much longer. Already the birds are gathering, preparing for their departure; he does not want to waste a moment in thought. He reaches the stream and kneels down to bathe, feeling the icy cold on his face and his neck, washing away the sweat. Then he bends over and drinks, cupping the water in his hands and slurping it up.

He sits back on his haunches, staring at the water as it reflects the sun in its path, listening to the birds and the gentle sound of the breeze in the trees on the other side of the stream. Then he hears an odd noise, low, even almost melodic. It stops, and Jay shakes his head, then unslings the leather bag to begin filling it.

The noise starts up again, the same tone, like the wind humming through a gap in a window board in winter. It is coming from the other side of a great outcrop of rock which forces the stream to curve in its path down the hill. He gets up, dusts the earth from his bare knees, and wades through the water to where he thinks the sound is coming from.

There is an overhang in the rock, and under it an indentation which forms a small cave. It is dark inside, with the faint, but not unpleasant, smell of rotting vegetation. He peers intently, but sees nothing. It is very perplexing, but no more than that. He is not afraid.

2

He remembers he has a job to do and is about to go back across the stream to the water bag when he sees a sudden slice of light inside the cave. He starts, and blinks, but he has made no mistake. The light is getting larger. Not bright, just brighter than the surrounding darkness, sufficient only to illuminate the gloom; he can see the ferns, with drops of water hanging off the fronds, the shape of the rocks at the back, the moss and lichen growing over everything.

Then he sees a figure in the light. Hazy, difficult to make out, but definitely a person of some sort. He knows all the stories about the creatures of the woods; the devils and demons, the fairies and the monsters. It is why no one goes there alone, not even in a cold winter when fuel is short. The woods are dangerous to anyone who ventures in unprotected.

Now he realises all the stories were true; his feet and legs are under a mysterious power which stops them obeying his commands to run. He tries to sing – the other way of deterring evil – but no sound comes from his mouth. It is too late.

The figure steps forward and stops. It has seen him. Jay feels he should go down on his knees and beg for mercy, but he can't do that either. He just stands, mute, trembling and helpless.

He instinctively casts his eyes down to the earth, but still sneaks a glance through his eyelashes. What he sees gives him hope. It is a fairy, that is certain. It has the form of a girl, scarcely bigger than he is, but its face is gentle – although all the world knows that could change in an instant.

He puts his fingertips together and brings them to his lips as he bows, then looks up. The fairy smiles, and he relaxes a little. He got that right, at least. Fairies are sticklers for politeness, and once you have been polite to them and they have accepted the courtesy, they are bound to be peaceable back. So he has heard.

Better still, it then repeats his gesture, and bows back to him! He almost laughs out loud in relief and astonishment, but this unexpected response gesture robs him of any notion of what to do next. So he makes a mistake, stepping out of the rules which the stories have handed down. He speaks.

'Who are you?'

The creature looks angry, and he regrets his words bitterly.

'I apologise, my lady,' he blurts out in the old language, the words of respect he has heard in tales. 'How may I serve you?'

It smiles once more, a radiant, celestial smile that brings the warmth back to his body. It raises its hands in what he takes to be a gesture of peace – and is gone.

*

Henry Lytten laid down the manuscript he had been reading and peered over his glasses at his audience. He always did that. It was an affected, donnish sort of mannerism, but nobody minded or even noticed. They all had their own affectations and they were long used to his.

'Bit of Ovid in there,' one said, screwing up his eyes and examining the ceiling. '*Amores* 3, if I recall. You're plagiarising again.' He never looked directly at people when he spoke.

'So I am,' Lytten said. 'Consider it a subtle allusion to the pastoral tradition.'

'If I must.'

'Is that all?' another asked, beer mug in one hand, pipe in the other, a trail of tobacco ash falling onto the old wooden table as he spoke. 'It's a bit short for twenty years' work.'

'No,' Lytten replied. 'Do you want more?'

'Where are the dragons? A whole chapter, and not a single dragon?'

Lytten scowled. 'There are no dragons.'

'No dragons?' said the other in mock astonishment. 'What about wizards?'

'No.'

'Trolls?'

'No. Nothing of the sort.'

'Thank God for that. Go on.'

It was a very small pub, and shortly after noon on a Saturday. The tiny windows let in little light even at the front; in the room at the back it was almost totally dark, the occasional shaft of illumination from the back door cutting a beam through the thick tobacco smoke which already filled the room. All around were bare walls decorated only with small mirrors, the once-white paint stained yellow by years of smoke. The four men occupied the entire area; occasionally someone else would stick a head through and be met with frowns. The landlord discouraged such interruptions. The group had the back room on a Saturday. They came every week for a few hours of masculine conversation, none of them even thinking of being at home with their wives and families. They were more used to the company of other men, and if asked why they had married in the first place, many of Lytten's friends and colleagues would have had difficulty coming up with an answer.

5

Lytten, who had paused so that he could make sure that the others really did want to hear what he had written and weren't just being polite, sipped his beer, then picked up his pile of paper once more. 'Very well. You can't say I didn't give you a choice. Pay attention now.'

*

Jay was trembling and in tears by the time he got back to the fields; he headed for the women working away from the men, instinctively thinking they would be more understanding. With a surge of relief, he saw his mother, the brown scarf knotted around her head to keep off the sun. He shouted and ran, buried himself into her warm and comforting body, shaking and sobbing uncontrollably.

'What is it? Jay, what's happened?'

She examined him quickly, checking for injuries. 'What is it?' She bent down level with his face and scrutinised him, holding him by the shoulders. The other women gathered round. 'Had a fright,' said an old woman there to supervise the younger ones.

Jay was sure they wouldn't believe him. Who would? They would think he was just trying to get out of work. His mother would be ashamed of him, would say he was letting the family down.

'What is it?' his mother said more urgently.

'I saw . . . I saw a . . . I don't know. I saw someone. Something. Up there. It just appeared in a cave. Out of nothing. Then vanished again.'

There was a titter of nervous laughter; his mother looked alarmed and annoyed at the same time.

'What do you mean? Where?'

He pointed back up the hill. 'Beyond the stream,' he said.

'In the woods?'

He nodded. 'I didn't mean to go there. But I heard a strange noise.'

'He's making it up,' a woman said: Dell, a gossip who never had a good word to say for anyone. She'd once been beautiful, it was said, but the hardness in her face had long since covered any loveliness. Her scorn was enough to make Jay's mother straighten up with defiance.

'We'll go and look,' she said. 'Come on, Jay. I'm sure it was just a trick of the light. You had a fright, but don't worry.'

Her kindness was reassuring and, ignoring the others who clearly now thought this was some sort of childish joke, Jay's mother took him by the hand. Only one other woman came as well, the eldest of them, who thought it her duty to be present at every disturbance, however minor. Everyone else got back to work.

Jay retraced his steps to the stream, then over it and into the woods. The old widow bowed and muttered to herself to ward off the spirits until they all stood once more, looking into the cave. There was nothing. No sound, no light, and certainly no fairy.

'It was just here. It really was,' he said, looking to see whether they were angry or dismissive. He got no hint, though; their expressions were completely unreadable.

'What did this fairy look like?'

'A girl,' Jay said. 'She had dark hair. She smiled at me. She was so beautiful.'

'How was she dressed?'

'Oh, like nothing you have ever seen! A red robe, shiny

and glittering, like it was made of rubies.'

'You've never seen a ruby,' the old widow said. 'How would you know?'

'It shone in the light, dazzlingly bright,' he insisted. 'It was wonderful. Then she just disappeared.'

The women looked at each other, then shrugged helplessly. 'Well, there's nothing here now,' his mother said. 'So I think it would be best to forget about it.'

'Listen, Jay. This is important,' said the old widow. She bent down and looked him firmly in the eyes. 'Not a word. You understand? The sooner this is forgotten the better. You don't want a reputation for being mad, or a trickster, do you?'

He shook his head.

'Good. Now, if I hear that you've been talking about this, then I'll give you the biggest beating of your life, and I'm a strong old woman. Now, get your water, and let's go back to work.'

There was an atmosphere for the rest of the day, an odd division between the men, who knew nothing, worked cheerfully and well, and the women, whose mood was subdued, almost fearful. Jay himself remained shaken; he knew, or rather he hoped, that he had not been dreaming. But he also realised that it was unlikely anyone would ever believe him.

*

Lytten glanced at his companions and smiled briefly. Most were, like him, men in their fifties; all had the care-worn, slightly shabby look of their type. None cared much for

8

elegant clothes, preferring battered tweeds and comfortable, solid shoes. The collars of their shirts were frayed, except for those whose wives turned their shirts before admitting they were beyond repair. The jackets had leather patches sewn onto the elbows to prolong their life; most had socks that had been carefully, and repeatedly, darned. They were, he supposed, his closest friends, people he had known in some cases for decades. Yet he didn't really think of them as friends, or even as colleagues. He didn't really know what they were. Just part of his life; the people he spent Saturday with, after some had been in the library and others had worked on the business of teaching for an hour or two.

All of them had a secret passion, which they hid carefully from most of the world. They liked stories. Some had a weakness for detective tales, and had volumes of green-backed Penguins stacked out of sight behind the leather-bound books on Anglo-Saxon history or classical philosophy. Others had an equally fervent and illicit love of science fiction, and adored nothing better than curling up with a tale of interstellar exploration in between lectures on the evolution and reception of the nineteenth-century Russian novel. Others preferred spy stories and adventures, whether Rider Haggard or Buchan or (for the more raffish) James Bond.

Lytten had a weakness for fantastical tales of imaginary lands, peopled (if that was the word) by dragons and trolls and goblins. It was what had drawn him, many years before, into the company of Lewis and Tolkien.

It was an enthusiasm which had taken possession of him when he was thirteen, packed off to bed for four months with measles, then mumps, then chicken pox. So he read. And read, and read. There was nothing else to do; there wasn't yet even a wireless set to listen to. While his mother kept on bringing him worthy and improving works to read, his father would smuggle in nonsense. Tales of knights and fair maidens, of gods and goddesses, of quests and adventures. He would read, then lie back and dream, improving the stories where he thought the authors had gone wrong. The dragons would become nastier, the women cleverer, the men less boringly virtuous.

Eventually he had started penning such stories himself, but was always too reticent to show them to anyone. He went to war, then became a scholar, a man of intellectual distinction, and the stories were left unfinished. Besides, it was all very well to criticise the works of others, but in fact it was quite hard, he discovered, to tell a story. His first efforts were not that much better than those he so easily faulted.

Gradually he formed a new ambition, and it was this that he was now, on a quiet Saturday in October 1960, going to reveal in all its as yet unfinished glory to his friends in the pub. He had spent years discussing the efforts of others; now, after much prodding, it was his turn.

He hoped they would be responsive; members had come and gone over the years, and the best had disappeared – Lewis sick in Cambridge, Tolkien in retirement, becoming too famous and too old to write much any more. He missed them; he would have enjoyed watching Lewis's face.

'Very well, gentlemen, if you could put your drinks down and pay attention, then I will explain.'

'About time.'

'In brief . . .'

'Surely not?'

'In brief, I am creating the world.'

He stopped and looked around. The others seemed unimpressed. 'No goblins?' one asked hopefully.

Lytten sniffed. 'No goblins,' he said. 'This is serious. I want to construct a society that works. With beliefs, laws, superstitions, customs. With an economy and politics. An entire sociology of the fantastic.'

'A story as well, I hope?'

'Naturally. But stories take place in societies, otherwise they cannot exist. The first must precede the second.'

'Don't we have one already? A society, that is.'

'I want a better one.'

'Might it not become a bit boring?' asked Thompson, briefly pulling the pipe out of his mouth to speak. This time he addressed his remarks to the mirror on the far wall. 'I mean, I suppose you are aiming at the ideal society, but perfection cannot change. How can things happen? If things cannot happen, then you have no story. Anyway, it's human nature to change, even if for the worse. Otherwise people die of boredom. If you start out perfect, there is nowhere to go but down.'

'Besides which, of course,' added Davies, 'you risk turning into Stalin. A perfect society requires perfect people. The People are always a terrible disappointment. Not up to it, you know. Damned nuisance, they are. No wonder rulers go mad and turn nasty. You have no doubt read as many Utopias as I have. How many would you want to live in?'

'True. Anterwold will be a framework for a better

society, not a perfect one, which is obviously impossible. Still, I will need your help, my friends. I will, over the next few weeks, bring you the basic outlines of my world. You will tell me whether or not you think it might work. I will modify them until it becomes strong, stable, and capable of dealing with the feeble creatures that are men without collapsing into a nightmare as bad as the one we already have.'

He smiled. 'In return, I will listen to you again. Persimmon' – he looked at the man on his left who had not yet spoken – 'I hope you are driving a coach and horses through the laws of physics? If you would care to remove that look of disapproval at my escapist frivolity, perhaps you would like to tell us what you are doing?'

*

I want a beautiful, open, empty landscape, bathed in sun-light, Lytten thought as he pedalled his old bike home a little later. Gentle rolling hills, green and dotted with sheep. The very ideal of paradise. At least for an English reader. Mountains always contain evil. They are where people die, or are attacked by wild animals or wild people. We think of mountains as beautiful, but then we can rush through them on a warm train. Our attitude would be different if we had to walk up and down them, buffeted by rain or snow.

It is easy to imagine a world where not only can few people read, few need to or want to. Serious reading can become the preserve of a small group of specialists, just as shoe-making or farming is for us. Think how much time would be saved. We send children to school and they

12

spend most of their time learning to read and then, when they leave, they never pick up another book for the rest of their lives. Reading is only important if there is something worthwhile to read. Most of it is ephemeral. That means an oral culture of tales told and remembered. People can be immensely sophisticated in thought and understanding without much writing.

Such were Lytten's thoughts as he made his way up the road back to his house. There was bread and cheese in the kitchen; he'd put the kettle on the hob to boil up some water for tea, put coke on the fire and soon enough his study would be warm. No one would disturb him. The doorbell rang rarely; only the tradesmen – the groceries being delivered, the coal man once a month, the laundry man to bring back a sack of damp washing – disturbed his peace, and they were all dealt with by Mrs Morris, who came in three mornings a week to look after him. Most evenings he ate in college, then came home to read or settle down with a record on his extremely expensive record player. An indulgence, but he had always adored music – which is why his imaginary world would place a high value on song.

He felt genuinely affectionate towards many, but needed few. Take Rosie, the girl who fed his cat, for example. Either she had adopted him, or he had adopted her. Or perhaps the cat had been the matchmaker. She came, and often enough they had long chats. He liked her company, found her views and opinions stimulating, for he had no experience of young girls, especially not those of the most recent vintage. The young were very different these days. Flatteringly, Rosie seemed to like him as well and their conversations would start off on some perfectly ordinary subject, then meander into music, or books, or politics. Much more interesting an individual than most of his students or colleagues. She was insatiably curious about everything.

Rosie Wilson breathed in the air with appreciation; she was old enough at fifteen (and a bit, she thought fondly) to recognise the first faint tang of winter. Not that she needed such evidence to know it was coming. She was long back at school, after all, and that was a more reliable indicator of the time of year than anything else.

It was Saturday, and she was free until Monday. Of course there were tasks to fill up the time she could have spent enjoying herself. Walking the next-door neighbour's dog. Doing the shopping. Peeling the vegetables and washing up after meals. Her brother never did any chores. He was at work today and on Sunday would go off with his friends to play football. That was normal. That was what boys did, and she was doing what girls did.

'I want to play with my friends too,' she had protested once. It was the wrong thing to say.

'You don't have any,' her brother had snapped back. He was two years older and already had a girlfriend and was earning good money in an ironmonger's shop. 'Brainy girls don't have friends.'

She suspected that her brother's statement was true; that was why it had hurt, and that was why he had said it. It was her own fault for passing her exams and going to a school where they taught her things. Her parents had almost refused, but she had got her way.

So she shopped, although she took her time, walking along the canal at the end of the road and strolling over the common with the dog first. It was a good dog, obedient and amiable. She tied it up outside the shops and it would wait patiently for her.

Except that now it had disappeared. She shouted, looked around, and then heard it barking, down by the river bank. 'Come here! Bad dog!' she called out, not too seriously, as she walked over to find out what it was up to.

'Come away! Stop that!' she scolded when she saw the beast, tail wagging enthusiastically as it snuffled at a bundle of old clothes. Then she looked closer. The clothes were inhabited. It was a man, lying on the ground.

Rosie cautiously walked closer; she had read in the papers of murdered bodies being discovered by people out for a walk. As she approached, though, the pile of clothes moved and let out a groan. The face of a man, pale and sick-looking, was staring up at her. He blinked and rubbed his red, bloodshot eyes. That's a relief, she thought. 'Are you all right?' she said loudly, not daring to get too near and making up for her timidity with volume.

He rolled over and squinted as he focused on the figure of the girl in her bright red coat, clutching a large bag with one hand and the animal's neck with the other. 'Back!' she said to the animal. 'Bad dog! Naughty!'

'Food,' he croaked. His mouth moved as he tried to say more but no other words would come.

'Food?' she repeated. 'Is that a good idea? You seem ill. Should I call an ambulance? A doctor?'

'Just food. Give.'

She hesitated, uncertain about what to do. Then she

opened up her bag and looked in it.

'Here,' she said. 'You can have a little cake. One won't be missed, I'm sure. It's not very nutritious, I'm afraid. Just sponge, really.'

She held it out, but he didn't move to take it, so she cautiously put it on the ground beside him, pulling the large animal away as she did so. 'Don't you dare!'

'It's a very nice cake,' she added when she saw the way he looked at it.

He concentrated hard. 'Thank you.'

'You're welcome. I must go. Sorry about Freddy here. He just wants to play. Are you sure you don't need help?'

He ignored her, and she turned, took a few steps, then came back. She peered for a moment in the bag once more, and held out her hand with a coin between two fingers.

'Get yourself some proper food if you're hungry. It's not much, but . . .'

'Go away.'

She looked at him a second or so longer, scowled in disapproval, then hurried away. She was now so late she rapidly forgot the thoughtful state walking the dog had induced in her. Still, she felt vaguely proud of herself for giving a little money to that man. It had been, she reassured herself, the right thing to do. Charitable. Kind. The sort of thing nice, friendly people did. Not that she had got many thanks for her gesture. Probably just a drunk who had staggered there after too long in the pub on Friday night, spending his week's wages. But what if he'd been really ill? Shouldn't she go back and make sure?

She thought about it, but decided against. She had done what she could, and he had told her to go away. If you really want help, you are polite. You say, help me. That sort of thing. Still . . .

The thought spoiled her sense of virtue, and now she was annoyed as well as late. The shops closed at half past twelve and would not open again until Monday. If she missed the butcher the rest of her day would be in ruins. What would they eat? Guess who would get the blame? Her dad was a man of habit. It was Saturday, so it was pork chops. And tomorrow a roast. Sometimes Rosie wondered whether they might have pork chops on a Wednesday, but that would have caused confusion. When she grew up and was married with children and a house to look after, she'd have pork chops on whatever day she wanted. If, of course, anyone would have her.

She walked swiftly along the road, trying to keep her mind on the list in her pocket. Grocer, then butcher, then greengrocer. Or perhaps the other way around. Then she'd drop off the dog and the shopping and in the afternoon go round to old Professor Lytten and feed his cat – the thruppence would come in handy now her charitable inclinations had depleted her resources.

*

Rosie liked Professor Lytten, although she knew she shouldn't call him that. 'Not a professor, my dear,' he would say gently, 'merely a fellow, toiling in the undergrowth of scholarship.' But he looked and talked as if he were one. If only her teachers at school were a little bit more like him, she was sure she would enjoy being educated so much more. Instead, she had the prospect of Sunday morning preparing for a spelling test, with her parents muttering in the background, 'Don't know why you bother with that.' And grammar. She hated grammar. 'Never say "can I be excused",' the teacher had thundered at her only the other day. She had had to stand on one leg in agony as the impromptu lesson progressed. 'We know you can, Wilson. That is obvious just from looking at you. But may you be? That depends. You are asking my permission, not enquiring about your capabilities.'

'But Miss . . .' she had interrupted desperately.

'Never start a sentence with "But". It is a conjunction, and in that position joins nothing. It is an error of the sort that marks out the ill-educated.'

When the woman had finished, Rosie had run off to the toilets so quickly she could have won a medal at the Olympics, while the rest of the class cheered derisively.

Feeding Professor Lytten's cat wasn't really a job, although only she could ever find anything remotely lovable or interesting in the beast, whose ill-humour was tempered only by laziness. Rather, she did it because every now and then the Professor would be there, and would talk to her. He knew everything.

'He is a very nice man,' Rosie had said to her mother once. 'He talks to me very seriously, you know. But sometimes he just stops, halfway through a sentence, and tells me to go away.'

Rosie was not disconcerted by this peculiar behaviour, and her mother assumed that it was the way professors were all the time. Certainly he never behaved in a manner which was, well, worrying. Quite the contrary; he addressed her gravely and carefully. She would tell him about the books she had read, or a song she had heard, and he never made fun of her or was scornful of her juvenile tastes. Nor did he seem to think that being a girl was a serious flaw.

'I am afraid I do not know any of Mr Acker Bilk's music,' he might say. 'A grave error on my part, perhaps. I will put on the radio next Saturday and expand my horizons. The clarinet, you say? A popular form of jazz, by the sound of it. It is, certainly, a most expressive instrument, in the right hands. As is the saxophone, of course . . .'

So Rosie would go home clutching records by Ella Fitzgerald or Duke Ellington – for Lytten was a great enthusiast – convinced of the sophistication of her musical tastes, and knowing rather more about both jazz and the clarinet than she had done when she arrived.

Lytten had even told her some of the stories of Anterwold, to gauge her reaction. She was the only person to know about this imaginary creation of his, apart from his colleagues in the pub and his old friend Angela Meerson. A grand idea, full of interesting characters, although, from Rosie's critical point of view, there wasn't much of a story yet. 'They don't seem to do anything,' she pointed out one day. 'Don't they fight, or have adventures? Couldn't you get someone to fall in love, or something? You need stuff like a love interest in a story.'

Lytten coughed, then frowned. 'I'm setting the context, you see, in which the story takes place.'

'Oh.'

'When that's done, then people will know how to fall in love, and what to fight about.' He paused and studied her face. 'You are not convinced, I fear.'

'It sounds just lovely,' she reassured him as he looked

crestfallen. 'Professor,' she continued cautiously, 'are apparitions real?'

'How curious you should ask that,' he said in surprise. 'I have been thinking about the same thing myself. Great minds, eh? Why do you ask?'

'Oh . . . a book. By Agatha Christie.' She was shamefaced that this was the best she could think of, as she was sure he knew nothing of books with paper covers and pictures on the front. To her surprise, Lytten's eyes lit up.

'Agatha Christie! I am very fond of her, although I fear she cheats a bit by always introducing a crucial piece of evidence right at the end. Who do you prefer, Poirot or Miss Marple?'

Rosie considered. 'Miss Marple is nicer, but Poirot goes to more interesting places. I like reading about foreign places.'

'A very judicious reply,' he said. 'Do you wish to travel, Rosie?'

'Oh! Yes!' she replied. 'Ever since I was little. I want to see everything. Cities and mountains, and strange places. Places no one else has ever seen.'

'An explorer, then?'

'Mummy says I should be a nurse.'

Lytten regarded her sympathetically. 'It is not my place to tell you to ignore your mother's advice,' he said. 'That said, in my opinion, I think you should seriously consider ignoring your mother's advice. What does Miss Christie have to say about apparitions?'

'There's a scene where a character looms out of the mist like an apparition.'

'I see. A true apparition is something which is not

physical. "An idea raised in us", as Hutcheson put it. It exists only in the mind of the person seeing it, like Beauty or Virtue. Or their opposites, of course. It is supernatural – a ghost or a fairy, or an angel – or it is an optical illusion, like a mirage, or, perhaps, the result of psychological disturbance. Those three classes, I believe, would account for all the possibilities. Would you like a slice of cake with your tea?'

Rosie digested the information, but not the cake. Her mother was strict about eating between meals. 'A fat girl will never find a good man, Rosie,' was her view, handed down to her by Great-aunt Jessie, a woman of many clichés.

'Fairies don't exist, though.'

Lytten frowned. 'Scientists would say they do not. But what do they know, eh? Believing something can make it so, I often think. If you believe in them you will never convince someone who does not. If you do not, you will never persuade someone who does. If you ever do encounter a fairy, it would probably be wise to be careful who you tell.'

'You may be right,' Rosie said.

*

The subject had become important a few days previously when Rosie had dropped in to feed Professor Jenkins.

Jenkins was old, malevolent and abominably overweight, his entire life dedicated to spreading his ancient carcass over the most comfortable piece of furniture which could accommodate it. Most of his few waking moments were spent in eating; he had long ago discovered that he could digest and sleep simultaneously. No bird or mouse had ever cause to fear his presence. Play was unknown to him, even as a kitten, although it was hard to imagine him being young.

That was the origin of his name, in fact – the beast was named after a man who had taught Lytten chemistry in his youth, a figure equally fat, unpleasant and idle. Sometimes Lytten wondered if his pet was the reincarnation of his old tormentor. There was something about the cold malice of his stare which reminded him of lessons, long ago, in an icy classroom.

Whatever the origin of his immortal soul, Jenkins would rarely allow anyone near him. But he tolerated Lytten, and almost seemed to like Rosie; she was the only person permitted to tickle his stomach.

Ordinarily, when Rosie arrived she would go upstairs, where Jenkins would be found lying flat on his back, his fat little legs sticking up into the air, the very embodiment of debauchery. Amongst his many other failings, he was slightly deaf and did not take kindly to coming downstairs and finding his food already waiting. So Rosie not only fed him but also had to wake him up, although she drew the line at actually carrying him down to the kitchen.

That day, Jenkins was not in his usual place, so Rosie had deposited her satchel in the hallway and walked from room to room, calling out to him. He was nowhere to be seen, but, as she was about to leave, she noticed that the door leading into the cellar was ajar. This was the bit of the house Lytten never used; it was really far too big for one person, although he had done his best to cram every room full of books.

Even by the standards of the rest of the house – and Lytten

was not the tidiest of men – the cellar was unpleasant. It was covered in dust, with a damp, rotting smell. It was dark as well, and, as she crept down the narrow staircase, she could just make out the piles of paper, the old cups, the few, poor pieces of furniture in what had once been the servants' kitchen. The only light came through a filthy window in a door that gave onto the overgrown back garden.

'Hello?' she called out. 'Jenkins?' She experienced a slight apprehension looking around at the squalor, even though she was rarely afraid of anything. She didn't know whether she should really be there, for one thing.

'Jenkins?' she called again, then, more sure the place was empty, more loudly. 'Jenkins, you lump.'

Maybe the deaf brute was hiding under something? Still calling out, she began peering in the cupboards and under the table. Nothing. Then she saw a rusty iron arch, the sort of thing people grow roses around, stacked in the middle of a pile of gardening equipment. She'd seen one at a country house her class had visited on a school trip the previous summer. It was odd, though, covered in cans and bits of paper and tin foil, with a thick curtain draped over it, as heavy and dark as the blackout material that was still tucked away in many houses. Rosie doubted it would be much use against atom bombs, but people kept it just in case.

She walked to the curtain, which smelled mildewed, and pulled it open to make sure Jenkins wasn't skulking behind it. She let out a cry of alarm, her hands reflexively going up to her face to cover her eyes, turning away from the dazzling light that flooded into the dingy little room.

Gradually, she opened her fingers so she could peer

through them, letting her eyes accustom themselves to the sudden brightness. It was unbelievable. The pergola – in a drab, grim house, in a drab, grim street on a drab, grim day – gave a view not of the damp stained wall beyond, but of open countryside bathed in brilliant light. Before her eyes were rolling hills, parched by the sun. She had seen such landscapes before, in the books she borrowed from the library. Mediterranean, or so it seemed to her. Dark trees which she thought might be olives, hills covered in scrub. In the distance a wide river of an extraordinary blue, reflecting the sun in a way which was almost hypnotic.

It was not a photograph – surely no photograph could be that good – because she could see movement. The sun on the water. Birds in the sky. And in the fields there were people. She stood open-mouthed. The sight was delicious, irresistible.

She stepped closer and touched the ironwork; it was cold.

She never thought of turning away; all she wanted to do was get closer. A strange shivering, tingling feeling passed through her body as she moved through the frame, almost as though someone was tickling her inside.

When she was completely through, she was hit by the warm air, shocking in contrast to the chilly dampness of the cellar.

It was beautiful; she wanted to tear off her coat – the ugly red one she had been given for her birthday – and feel the warmth on her skin. She wanted to run down to the river and bathe her face in it. She knew the feeling would be wonderful.

She stopped, feeling nervous for the first time. She

seemed to be at the entrance of a small cave or something; the walls were covered in brush and thin straggly trees that somehow managed to grow in the crevices. Suddenly she realised there was someone there.

It was a boy, younger than she was by the look of him, dressed in a rough tunic, with bare brown legs. He had fair, tousled hair and a pleasant, open expression. Or might do, if he didn't look so terrified. She looked around to see what was causing him such fright, and then realised that it must be her.

She couldn't speak; she did not know what to say. She hoped he wasn't going to attack her, or throw rocks, or something.

He took a few steps, hesitated, then stopped. He bowed to her. Cautiously, she nodded back, to show she was friendly.

He spoke, but she couldn't understand him. The warmth of the summer day was all around them, birds singing quite normally in the background, the dense heat pressing down on them. Neither noticed.

'How may I serve you?' said the boy slowly, this time in a heavily accented but just understandable English.

Rosie smiled in relief, but was so surprised that she took a step back, and tripped on a stone. She had to keep her balance by taking another step, and that took her through the light. Instantly, she was in the smelly cold cellar once more; the heat, the sound were all gone, although she could still see the boy looking frightened and confused. He had gone down on his knees now, and was touching his forehead to the ground.

The spell was broken; the wonder had gone, and all

Rosie wanted to do was escape. She pulled the curtain back into its place, rushed up the stairs and into the grey of an English morning. Jenkins would just have to go without food today, that was all there was to it.

3

As far as Jack More was concerned, the outside world, unhealthy and artificial though it might be, was a tantalising idea of freedom. So he often came to the large display screen that decorated the space leading to the conference rooms, just to stare and remember. It wasn't real; there were no windows anywhere in the complex, but it was better than nothing. At the moment, it was an imaginary but fairly realistic view of cows and hills and grass. Only the hills might still actually exist, but he liked looking at it nonetheless. In a moment it would change to empty snow-topped mountains, also imaginary as no snow had fallen anywhere in the world for at least a decade. He didn't know why it was there. Few except him had any interest in the outside world; everything of importance lay inside the huge, sealed building they lived and worked in. It was dangerous and frightening outside.

He turned as he heard voices. A little group was walking along the corridor that led to the research area, talking quietly. He scowled in annoyance. He wasn't meant to be in this part of the facility; he was meant to stay in the administrative block, and certainly he was not meant to hear anything that others might say.

Then there was an explosion of wrath from around the corner. Jack stopped in his tracks and positioned himself to observe without attracting attention. The group of scientists formed a sort of defensive gaggle, huddling together to meet the approaching threat.

The source of the noise was a mathematician by the name of Angela Meerson. She strode into sight, the look of thunder on her face contrasting strongly with the flat, compliant appearance of the others. Everything else was different as well; she was taller, dressed in vivid purple, while they wore the almost uniform grey-brown look of their type. Her hair was long, and untidy, as though she had just got out of bed. Their gestures were measured and controlled, hers free-flowing and as ill-disciplined as her hair, which had been valiantly organised into a complicated bun at some stage and then allowed to grow wild.

The researchers collectively decided to pretend she wasn't there. This was a mistake on their part. She did not take kindly to it.

'Where is he?' she bellowed at the top of her voice. Some looked shocked at her lack of respect, control and decorum. Others were merely frightened. They weren't used to such behaviour, although some had worked with her in the past and had witnessed her explosions before. They generally meant that she was working hard.

'Well? Can't you talk? Where is the devious little weasel?'

'You really should calm yourself,' said one anxiously. 'The protocols for registering dissatisfaction are clearly laid down. I can forward the documentation, if you like, I'm sure . . .'

'Oh, shut up, you moron.' She brandished a piece of paper in his face. 'Look at this.'

He read it with what looked like genuine surprise.

'You are being suspended,' he observed.

'Is that a smirk on your face?'

'Of course not,' he replied hastily. 'I didn't know anything about it. Really.'

She snorted. 'Liar,' she said.

'There's a hearing tomorrow. I'm sure everything will be explained.'

'Ha!' she cried out. 'Tomorrow? Why not today? Shall I tell you? Because he's a weasel.'

'I'm sure Dr Hanslip has the best interests of everyone in mind, and it is our duty to obey his wishes. We all have complete faith in his leadership and I don't see what you hope to achieve through such a display.'

She gave him a look of withering disgust. 'Do you not? Do you really not? Then watch me. You might learn something.'

She hurled the crumpled piece of paper at him, making him flinch, then wheeled around and marched off down the corridor, going 'Ha!' twice before she disappeared.

The group broke out into giggles of nervous relief. 'Must be tanked up again,' one said. 'She needs it to get up to full power. She'll come down again in a day or two.'

'She really is quite mad, though,' added another. 'I don't know how she's lasted this long. I wouldn't stand for it.' Then he noticed Jack watching from the sidelines. He glared and dropped his voice.

*

I very much hoped my dramatic exit impressed them all; I was certainly not feeling so very confident at that moment.

30

My relations with Hanslip had always been fragile, to say the least, but for a long time that fragility had been firmly in the domain of what you might term creative tension. He disliked me, I couldn't stand him, but we sort of needed each other. Like an old-time musical duo: Robert Hanslip on money, Angela Meerson on intelligence. We talked, as well, and his stupidity often enough made me think and consider things anew. This time, however, it was different. He had gone too far. I had just discovered a plot to steal my work and sell it to that creature Oldmanter, perhaps the foulest, most poisonous man on the planet. That was my opinion and I admit that others thought differently. But they were idiots.

What's more, I had found out that he had been working on this scheme for some time, all the while lying to my face. I'd known, of course, that he was up to something, but it was only by chance that I put the pieces together, because of a surprise visit by the sort of person I would normally have ignored.

'Lucien Grange, sales representative', it said on the daily manifest. What do I care for such people? They come and go all the time, hawking their wares. Only by chance did I notice this particular one, and then only because of a leaky pipe in a corridor, which meant that I had to take a diversion through some of the lesser passageways. Only because Lucien Grange chose that precise moment to come out of the room he had been assigned to. I remembered him; I knew I did. Somewhere in the back of my mind, I knew he was important to me, and not because of any facility he might have with toilet brushes. Eventually, in a small disused corner of my memory, I found it. Eighteen years previously, we had spent some time together at an out-of-the-way institute in the South of France, on the very fringes of the great desert that stretched from the Pyrenees right down to South Africa. I'd wanted to see more but fell ill, and spent my time in a coma instead; as soon as I began to recover they shipped me back north, and by then I was too drugged even to look out of the window of the helicopter.

I couldn't for the life of me remember why, but the memory made me feel uncomfortable. Not that it mattered; the important detail was the fact that I knew him, and I was not in the habit of knowing sales representatives. I wasn't even allowed, technically, to talk to them. It destroyed the mystique of scientific aloofness so important to us in the elite. Familiarity breeds contempt; they might see through us.

When I got to my office, I poured myself a glass of wine – medicinal purposes only, licensed and perfectly legal – then set to work. It didn't take long to track him down. Sales representative, forsooth! In fact, he was senior vice-president of Zoffany Oldmanter's prime research outfit, and a rapid look through his activities showed that he specialised in gobbling up lesser operations and binding them firmly into Oldmanter's ever-increasing empire. He was a corporate hit man, in other words; a trained scientific assassin.

Now he was here, pretending to be flogging hygienic sundries. Suddenly everything made sense. I had been on the verge of finally telling Hanslip about the little experiment that proved I was correct; I had even sent a message asking for an urgent appointment, but I realised it was too late. I now understood everything, and a powerful surge of emotions ran through me. This project was mine; he wasn't going to rip it from my arms.

I bottled it up for as long as I could, which was about ten minutes, then went to confront Grange in his room. The look of shock on his face when I walked through the door was very revealing.

'I hope you remember me. You're not taking my machine,' I announced as I slammed the door shut so he couldn't escape.

'I beg your pardon?'

Actually quite a handsome fellow; it's amazing what technology can accomplish. He must have been older than I was.

'What this facility does is low-grade garbage, except for my work; one of Oldmanter's acolytes wouldn't cross the street for any of it. If you have travelled five hundred miles to a boggy island in the north-west of Scotland, then it is because of my machine. Don't deny it. Nothing else could attract the attention of that crook.'

'I will not have Mr Oldmanter referred to in that way.'

Toady, I thought.

'Nor is it appropriate for me to discuss such matters with staff.'

Staff? Me? What was Hanslip saying about me behind my back? What role was he claiming for himself? That he had done all the work? That it was his idea? It wouldn't have surprised me.

I decided to pile on the pressure and burst into tears. Naturally, that sent him into a panic. I had learned over the past fifty years that uncontrolled displays of emotion were capable of inducing a sense of terror when released in a confined space. I was used to them; my work depended on their judicious deployment. Most people would run a mile to avoid even being in close vicinity and Grange was now obviously feeling disoriented.

'Oh, Lucien!' I sobbed. 'After all these years! You do not even remember me!' Odd; I was most certainly putting it on, but a part of me was feeling genuine distress, although I did not understand why.

I could almost see him running through the options for how to fend me off. 'Good God! I mean, ah . . .'

I collapsed on the settee and sobbed into my sleeve, taking the occasional peek to see if this was having the desired effect. Eventually, he tentatively approached. 'Of course I remember you,' he said. 'But that was a long time ago and best forgotten. Besides, I am under strict instructions. Complete the deal, then leave. There is no time for personal sentiment. Much as I would have liked . . .'

'How long are you staying?'

'I plan to wrap up tomorrow.'

'Tomorrow!' I shrieked, standing up abruptly and rounding on him. 'You are going to do a deal for my project by tomorrow? You don't even know what you're buying.'

'Of course we do. We've been studying the proposals for months.'

I must have seemed shocked, or perhaps he thought I had a slightly murderous air, and he went all official on me again. 'This is not appropriate. You must talk to your employer; you are not authorised to talk directly to me.'

It didn't matter. He had told me enough already. I swept out in tearful triumph. An hour later, I got the letter of suspension. Hanslip was one step ahead of me.

*

It goes without saying that I never had the slightest intention of turning up to his ridiculous disciplinary committee. It was pretty obvious, after all, that it was going to be filled with his creatures. He would pronounce, anything I said would be ignored, and then I would be bundled aside to clear the way for his nasty little plot. The stuffed toys he surrounded himself with would nod and agree to anything he wanted, and I would be locked out of my own work as he handed it over to Oldmanter and his team of overpaid half-wits.

So I had two priorities. The most important was to hang on to my property; the second was to prevent the entire universe being reshaped in the image of a bunch of thugs and reduced to ruin. I was on the verge of a major breakthrough in understanding. I wasn't there yet, but if I was right, then a fascinating experiment could well metamorphose into the most dangerous discovery in the history of humanity. It would be better, in my opinion, to be sure before letting other people play around with it too much. Oldmanter's lot would not be so cautious. Already I had seen alarmingly covetous looks in Hanslip's eyes as he contemplated the possibilities.

I was not thinking quite as clearly as I should have been; I'd been working long and hard in the previous few days and my brain was still befuddled with the effects of the stimulants. As they cleared out of my system, though, I began to see a way through the problem. I had no confidence that I could persuade anyone to take my doubts seriously unless I could complete the work and prove my case. For that I needed more time. So I decided the best thing would be to get hold of some. In the meantime, I had to make sure no one else fiddled around with the machine in my absence.

Going into hiding was not an option, of course. I could, perhaps, have evaded detection for a day or so, but not for much longer than that. In fact, there was only one possibility, which was to use the machine myself. I knew it worked, but it was hard to get everything ready on my own and with no one noticing.

I managed, though; I rerouted the power supply from a few generators to ensure that all trace of my destination would be erased and the data hopelessly jumbled when I left. I had built that possibility in years ago, as I had seen enough of scientific integrity by then not to trust my colleagues further than I could throw them. If Hanslip and Oldmanter wanted to experiment, then let them. They'd have to do all the work themselves from scratch. I doubted they'd get very far.

It took a long time to prepare, but at one in the morning I was ready to go. As I heard the hum in the final moments before the power engaged, I felt very pleased with myself. I was prepared to bet Hanslip hadn't anticipated my move. He worked purely in the realm of calculated rationality; I did not. In a world of chemically induced sanity, a little lunacy confers immense advantages.

Perhaps I should explain what this is about? There is a risk, I am sure, that I am giving the impression that I was petulant and egotistical, that my only concern was to bathe in the light of glory that was my due.

Very well; I admit that was a reason. But only one. There

were other issues at stake, and my desire that the whole of humanity should not be wiped out played a small part in my decision also.

It began with my unofficial experiments, which demonstrated that the fundamental assumptions underlying the entire project were wrong. Not to put too fine a point on it, I stuffed one of the cleaning staff into the machine to see what happened. He was a somewhat nervous fellow called Gunter, who needed a lot of tranquillisers to make him cooperate. Admittedly, I should not have done this, especially as I did not ask official permission first, but – there we are. I couldn't use an animal, or an inanimate object, as the chances of finding it again were non-existent. Only a human being could possibly be tracked.

He was. Alex Chang, one of the most junior people in the department and thus too insecure to snitch on me, was given the job and spotted the unfortunate cleaner in 1895. Three hundred and twenty-seven years back. It was a good piece of work on Chang's part, as he had to learn a lot of new techniques to analyse the evidence. Gunter had gone mad when he arrived and, not surprisingly, had eventually entered the priesthood. Without going into the details – what I had done was not really ethical and I knew it would be used against me – I tried to tell Hanslip that we had a problem, but he couldn't see what I was on about.

'Don't you understand?' I told him one evening. 'This whole project is based on the assumption that what we are doing is not time travel. Laws of physics. Accepted and proven for two centuries or more. All we can possibly do is transit to a parallel universe. Right?'

He nodded, looking around him to see if there was

anyone he could summon for protection in case I got too vehement.

'Wrong,' I went on. 'Wrong, wrong. It's all wrong. I know it is. Think. In theory, we should be able to access any number of universes. So why can we only seem to access one, eh? No one has thought about the implications of that. I think the whole alternative universe theory is complete nonsense. We would be moving in this universe. The only one there is. Time travel, to put it bluntly. If that is the case, we have to stop now. We need to start again. From the beginning. Immediately.'

'We can't possibly start again,' he protested. 'Think of the cost. Why are you telling me this?'

'Because I'm right. I feel it.'

At this point, you see, I could not explain properly. Still, I didn't understand why he was so keen on dismissing my concerns. He knew how I worked, and knew that my instincts were fundamental. Besides, I thought he would be happy about overturning two centuries' worth of physics. What better way of making a name for yourself?

Instead, he took refuge in pomposity, muttering about budget projections. It didn't make sense until I realised that he was negotiating to sell everything to Oldmanter. A functioning, usable device that gave the possibility of infinite space and resources at no risk was his central selling point. Quite a good one, if only what he was telling them had any truth to it.

Something too dangerous to use except for small experiments would have opened no wallets. Besides, he was terribly conservative in approach. Faced with a choice between my hunch and generations of scientific labour,

38

his only response was to demand proof. It was part of his character I never understood or appreciated. Why wouldn't he just take my word for it?

*

The summons to the emergency meeting arrived at four o'clock in the morning, an event rare enough to cause all concerned to wake, dress and move with remarkable speed. Even rarer was the way it was done; no dream to jerk the sleeper awake with images of what was needed; not even a message coming through the communications system. No; a person, an individual, actually hammered on the door, and kept hammering until the occupant on the other side was sleepily, confusedly awake.

There was no explanation for such bizarre behaviour, so the six people who arrived at the anonymous underground office were suitably worried in advance. What could possibly have happened? Some speculated about a reactor melting down; the more bureaucratically minded gloomily decided it was a test of emergency procedures launched by some over-enthusiastic zealot.

Jack More thought none of these things. He didn't think at all, and not simply because he was tired; he was the only person who had no obvious reason to be there. He was merely a security officer. He was curious, certainly, but he did not jump to conclusions. If there was any need to panic he was quite happy to let others worry themselves silly. Whatever had gone wrong couldn't possibly be his fault. It was one of the virtues of insignificance.

His presence was enough to make the others worry all

the more. They looked at him, half wanting to ask why he was there. A meeting, in person, in the middle of the night, was a good reason to think there might be something to worry about.

'Sit down, please.' Robert Hanslip had walked in. The boss who controlled the money, the individual on whose approval depended the lives and careers of every person in the room, everyone on the island. No one liked him, although whether they did or not was irrelevant. All admitted that he was very efficient. Some believed he was highly intelligent, although few would say so, lest they get a lengthy – and, recently, obsessive – diatribe from Angela Meerson on the precise size of the large hole where his intelligence should have been located. No one in the room really knew him anyway. He never mixed with people of a lower grade, and they had noted already that no senior figures were at this strange meeting.

Hanslip's weakness was a somewhat ostentatious self-presentation. He affected an old-fashioned style, and had had his metabolism tweaked so that he stabilised at about ten per cent overweight: enough to give him a more solid look without requiring frequent adjustments to the heart. Not for him either the dandyish ways of the modern or the austerity of scientific garb; he preferred the carefully crumpled look, harking back six decades to his youth when such things were briefly fashionable.

He never talked loudly, but suffered no opposition. Anyone who annoyed him would soon enough find their assistants taken away, their budget cut. All done with a smile designed to make his victim feel somehow grateful the punishment hadn't been worse.

Part of his authority lay in ensuring that everything ran smoothly, so any sort of crisis damaged him; certainly, his appearance now caused a shiver of alarm to pass through the little meeting. He looked shaken; whatever had happened, they knew the moment he walked in that it was going to be bad.

'Forgive me for disturbing your beauty sleep,' he said. 'Three hours ago a serious power surge caused electricity supplies in northern Germany, Finland, Sweden, Denmark and Scotland to fail for 0.6 of a second.'

Jack looked around him, wondering what it meant. Everyone else went suddenly still.

'How much of a surge?' one asked.

'We're still trying to get the precise figures.'

'You are going to tell us it originated with us.'

Hanslip nodded. 'I am going to tell you exactly that. The official analysis is not yet in, but I am sure it came from here. Needless to say, I have already sent out a report denying it was anything to do with us, and demanding an apology from whoever was responsible.'

'That's one hell of a lot of power,' a young man remarked, after he had goggled at the figures on the paper Hanslip handed round. He must have been fairly new, or he would have known Hanslip did not approve of any sort of swearing. 'Are you sure it was us? How could it have happened?'

'I am sure it was us. Otherwise I would not have disturbed your rest. As for what caused it, that will be your job. There is no need to find out *who* caused it. That, I fear, is obvious already.'

Hanslip's concern communicated itself to the rest of

the meeting. 'Time,' he said. 'We don't have much time.' But bureaucracies move in their own stately way, however urgent the situation. The main result of the meeting was to form a committee. Several committees, in fact; one to analyse the data to find out what the power was used for, another to investigate how someone had managed to bypass some of the most sophisticated security systems on the planet. A third took charge of destroying all evidence implicating their institute. The checks necessary to establish that their troublesome star mathematician had indeed vanished were quickly enough performed.

'A moment, Mr More,' Hanslip said as the meeting broke up. Jack had not said a word throughout the discussion, nor had anyone else even looked at him. 'I imagine you are wondering what you are doing here?'

'Yes, but I decided that you would tell me soon enough, and would ignore anything I asked until you were ready.'

'Well judged. I may need your assistance. The closure of this facility and all of us landing in jail is one of the better options open to us at the moment. A rapid and unorthodox response may be called for. That is your department.'

'What exactly is so bad about a power surge?'

Hanslip peered at him scornfully. 'It blacked out a billion people, many of whom will have had panic attacks. There will undoubtedly have been many suicides and murders as a result of the chaos. We know of two airliners which crashed because all controls and backups shut down simultaneously. The death toll already is more than two thousand and rising. More to the point, our authority rests on the efficient management of society. It is a very serious disaster, and someone is going to be blamed for it.'

'Ah.'

'There will be a search for those responsible. A public punishment for the people who have disgraced the reputation of Scientific Government. To show we care; that sort of nonsense. Now do you see?'

'I do.'

'Good. We need the culprit, together with a report saying that she suffered a mental breakdown that pushed her into an act of destructive terrorism. Something along those lines. I'm sure you know the sort of thing. Come for a walk. You will need to know a little more if you are going to help us.'

4

When the strange girl returned and left the bright, shiny coin by the food she had put on the grass beside him, Alex Chang rolled over and watched in fascination as she disappeared. Fortunately, the terrifying animal he had thought was about to savage him went as well. Had he heard of such things? Tame animals? Yes, dimly. He had hardly thought the tales could actually be true, though. Did that mean it had worked?

He was confused and dizzy. He couldn't remember who he was, let alone where. There'd been a hum; that was the first thing that came back to him. He remembered a blurring in his eyes. Then nothing. All the chatter in his head suddenly stopped, leaving him in a terrifying silence. He kept his eyes closed, trying to calm himself, then carefully started to breathe. That was all right. The air was warm, but full of strange smells, things he had never smelled before. Not unpleasant, certainly.

Then he began to sneeze; he searched around in his head for an explanation but there was nothing. Panic swept over him; it took some time to discipline himself and analyse the situation. Pollen, dust, particles of organic matter, came the answer eventually. The unfiltered air was thick with it. Some part of his mind took over, and gradually the spasms were isolated and confined, then controlled, leaving only one thought hammering away at his consciousness.

Eat. You have to eat. An odd idea, as he didn't feel hungry. Far from it. One part of his mind was urging him to eat, another part rebelled at the very notion and knew it would make him sick. Reluctantly and carefully, he reached over and picked up the thing the girl had given him. It looked disgusting. Oval, a light brown colour, squashy with a slight feel of grease oozing out as he squeezed it. He sniffed it cautiously, then recoiled, revolted. It came from an animal.

But the urging returned. Eat. Eat. Very carefully, he put it to his lips, tried not to smell it, and bit. Then again, and again, stuffing the little cake into his mouth, almost choking, and swallowing.

Immediately thoughts, memories, sensations flooded back into his mind, jumbled, confused, meaningless, but a whole range of images and recollections, so many he could not absorb or listen, or interpret anything. He concentrated, trying to pick out one as a start. History. It meant nothing. A renegade. Finally, an image of two men formed, one standing. A tall man, curly hair, powerfully built. He felt slightly afraid of this man, but also pleased. Why? More. That was the name. His name was Jack More. What about the other? A slight, cowed, timid-looking fellow. Sitting down, an air of cautious resentment. He realised he must be looking at himself. He lay back on the grass, closed his eyes and tried to relax. The scene pieced itself together, and he remembered the conversation with Jack More. Two days ago? A countless age? Or a mirage? He had no idea.

*

45

'You were one of Angela Meerson's team, I believe,' More said. 'I have been asked to interview everyone to see if they have any useful information.'

It was a few hours after Angela had vanished, and the entire place was in a state of panic. Chang knew that More had questioned many of those who had worked with her, and would be questioning many more in due course. He didn't mind; everybody had their job to do and he was perfectly polite, almost diffident in the way he put his questions. Many would have put on a show of authority to demonstrate how powerful they were.

'That's right. I am a physicist by training, although my job here is to analyse data, mainly. It doesn't really matter what it is. Often enough, I don't know myself.'

'You are low-grade, low-level.'

'Yes,' he said with the slightest hesitation.

'I see you have had an unusual career.'

Chang sighed. 'That again. I once expressed doubts about whether the organisation of society was either permanent or necessarily beneficial.'

'I'd be careful how you speak.'

'Oh, don't worry. Angela disabled all the listening devices in here. She hated eavesdropping. As I say, I expressed doubts in a vague way. It was picked up and I was offered reconditioning to sort out any latent antisocial tendencies. I refused, one thing led to another and I briefly ended up in a Retreat. That was more than thirty years ago. It is still on my file. I suppose it will be for ever.'

'Angela recruited you?'

'Two years ago. I was cheap. It was hard to get a job.'

They were sitting in Chang's cubicle in the far distant,

46

most insalubrious part of the operation, a mile or so from the centre through ever more depressing and neglected corridors, then buried three floors underground. There was a smell of stale air, and oil from the heating system, which Jack found almost insupportable.

'Can you shed any light on this mess? Where she's gone? You understand, I'm sure, that it would be a good idea to have some conspicuous display of loyalty from you at the moment.'

Chang shook his head. 'I realise that, and I am trying to come up with something. If you mean did she say or do anything that should have aroused suspicion, then the answer is no. On the contrary, she had been working hard and was looking forward to completing the next stage of the project.'

'Tell me about her. The file on her just has information. I want to know what she was like.'

'I can tell you a bit,' Chang said, 'but she was never very forthcoming about herself. Apart from working and popping stimulants, I don't think she did much. She was very obsessed.'

'How old is she?'

'Actual age is seventy-eight; biological is early twenties. She got a top-up three days ago, and there's some gone missing. I checked. If she took some with her, she might well live for another century or more.'

'Character? Is she capable of sabotage, terrorism, illegality, subversion?'

'Oh, easily; she'd love it.'

'Did you like her?'

'What a question! I never really thought about it. She

was certainly the most stimulating person I ever worked for. Once you learned how to handle her moods she could be very kind as well, although she was completely ruthless in the way she worked. So – yes. I suppose I liked her. I liked working for her, certainly.'

More grunted, then stood up to leave.

'Good luck in your hunt,' Chang said as he watched the man open the door. 'You may be wasting your time, though. You won't find her if she doesn't want you to.'

'Where do you think she'd go?'

Chang thought. 'If it was me, I'd hide out amongst the renegades. But then, it isn't me. So,' he said with a smile, 'that's not much help.'

'Then if you can think of anything . . .'

'I will certainly tell you. In fact, I do have an idea, but it is a silly one. If it comes to anything I'll let you know.'

That was it. The scene faded, a bit like a screen going dark, and he became aware of his surroundings once more. He was now sitting down, in an open space, in the open air. There was a cool breeze, which gave him pleasure.

After half an hour he tried to stand, and found he could do so easily, although he was a little unsteady at first. Then he began to walk – this was harder and more tiring, but he went slowly, stopping for a rest when his legs began to ache. He walked east; there were buildings he could see above the trees, and they might jog his memory some more. In the other direction there was nothing except wildness.

After a while he came to a street. Houses with little gardens and trees, extraordinary flowers growing every-where. More birds. Black ones, ones with red patches on their breasts, big fat grey ones. Once he jumped in fright.

There was another wild animal on a wall, furry and looking decidedly dangerous. It examined him with pale green eyes and he stopped uncertainly until he noticed that everyone else ignored it as though it was the most normal thing in the world. The beast stared with what appeared surprisingly like disdain, then looked away and began licking itself. It, at least, saw nothing unusual in him.

And the noise! People talking, different sorts of vehicle in chaotic movement. The wind in the trees, the birds singing. The smells too, floating everywhere, some sweet, most foul, alarming. There was no control to anything, no order, just random movements.

Two people walked past him, talking. Could he understand them? He followed closely, until one turned round and looked at him suspiciously. He had heard enough, though; he had understood. Could he speak? He had not been impressed by his one attempt with the girl. The idea made him feel nervous, but it seemed necessary to find out. He stood to one side, summoned his courage, and prepared. Choose your target, walk up, stop, smile. Wait for eye contact but don't stare. Polite expressions at both beginning and end of sentence. Keep your distance.

'Excuse me, dearest Madam. Would you kindly do me the great honour of informing me of the time, please?'

Then he stopped. Time. The word jogged something deep in his memory. He was short of time. Why? Again, almost like the answer to his question, thoughts began to pour back into his head, so many that he had to sit on a wall, oblivious to the passers-by, who stared nervously at the strangely dressed man rocking to and fro, head in hands.

He had wanted to show off, maybe win himself a little

praise and added job security. It had been a bad mistake. He'd contacted the security man about his ideas to show he was more important than was the case, and because More had brought up his record. More had then passed the message on to Hanslip because he also needed to show he was on top of things. He should have kept quiet.

5

The ceremony proper began at dusk; all day the senior villagers presented their dues to the Visitor, handing over wooden tablets with markings which tallied what they had produced and what they owed. Each figure was written down meticulously, and if there were any discrepancies, the elders would be called across to account for the problem. The Visitor had arrived that afternoon; the space around the great oak tree where the ceremony always took place had been carefully prepared, and the senior men of the village had dressed in their best before walking to the limits of the village territory, marked by a great stone at the side of the road.

There they had waited to greet the Visitor. It was not a grand procession – although as grand as anything the village ever witnessed. One man was on a horse, which tossed its head and neighed as its rider came to a halt. He was in his forties at least, with fair, thin hair and bright eyes; a little fat as well, and dressed in a light brown cloak of wool. On his feet were sandals of leather, another luxury. There were rules, and there were laws, which could be applied severely or gently. He did not look particularly gentle, and the villagers worried when they cast eyes on him.

Curiously, it was not he who replied to the words of welcome. Rather a much younger man on a donkey behind him dismounted and came forward. He was hesitant, almost nervous, as though he was not used to the task. This did not reassure them either; they did not want someone too inexperienced to bend the rules. Still, he had an open face, with darting eyes and a faint smile that played around his mouth; he did not appear over-impressed by himself, but everyone knew that he was as aware of the older man as they were.

'I thank you for your welcome,' he said, speaking each word with care, 'and I declare that I am the Visitor you expect. Does anybody here dispute this statement?'

No one replied. 'Then let it be accepted.' He took a step forward, over the boundary between the village and the great world outside.

That step cast the law into motion. He had been recognised as the Visitor, he had been welcomed, he had entered the village. Until he left again he was now the master of them all. Everything and everybody, every man and child, every animal, every tool and every sheaf of wheat, belonged to him. He could take what he wanted, leave them as much or as little as he pleased, guided only by custom. When he heard the complaints and arguments that had built up over the year waiting for resolution, he could punish any wrong-doing as he saw fit. His decisions were final.

For people who respected age and saw it as being little different from wisdom and authority, there was puzzlement that this man had come forward, not the older one on the horse. There was something unseemly about it. It had got the ceremony off to a bad start, and what started badly ended badly.

If the young man understood this, he did not seek to

allay their fears. He did not introduce the other man, nor even give his own name. He was the Visitor; that was all they needed to know. But he jumped to attention when the older man came down off his horse, stretched himself and rubbed his sore back.

'I would like a drink, Visitor,' he said in a pleasant voice. 'I am dusty and tired. Could that be arranged, do you think?'

'Certainly, Storyteller,' came the reply, which sent a wave of shock through the villagers. 'At once.'

*

Once the arrangements had been made, and the villagers assembled in the dip by the oak trees where the meetings were always held, then the young man, the Visitor, stood up, peered at the audience severely and began to speak in a dry, monotonous voice. The older one, the Storyteller whose presence had so alarmed everyone, stood behind him, apparently uninterested in the proceedings. Still no one knew why he was there.

'The counting took place on the fifth day of autumn, and these are the results. The settlement has in the last four seasons raised forty-two goats, sixty-seven sheep, 120 bushels of wheat and sixty-two of barley. In addition there were twenty-four pigs, 122 chickens, fifteen geese and eight oxen.'

He looked around. 'A very much better result than last year; you are all to be congratulated. It is a blessing. The tithe is therefore four goats, six sheep, twelve bushels of wheat and six of barley. In addition, during the drought of the past few years a portion of the tithe was waived. This amounts to twelve goats . . .'

A quiet groan went up from the assembled villagers. They knew this was coming, of course. It was the law, and it was fair. The Visitors had been gentle during the drought; they could easily have insisted on their rights and left them to starve. But for three years they had taken less than their due and the debt had mounted up. Now there had been a bumper harvest, and there was no reason why they should not take what was owed.

The village could have taken their surplus – once enough had been put aside for the winter – loaded it onto wagons and traded it at the market. Bought cloth and pans and tools with the result. A few luxuries. It was not to be this year. A gloom descended and they all looked up at the Visitor, who was waiting for the murmuring to subside.

He didn't look annoyed, as he had a right to be. The Visitor was not to be interrupted. Then they noticed that, if he was not actually smiling, he was at least looking faintly amused.

'It is decided, to give proper thanks to the seasons and our common good fortune, to collect this by adding a quarter of the tenth to the next four years. This will amount, this year and the following three years, to three goats, nine sheep . . .'

Another murmur, but not from despair this time. Broad grins spread over all those listening. It was better than they could possibly have hoped. Yes, they'd have to pay their debt, but they'd have something to take to market as well. The Visitor had been generous; not for the first time, there were many who counted their blessings. They'd often heard tales of what life was like elsewhere, where the Visitors were not so flexible.

Their Visitor – who was trying hard to keep a solemn expression – spread out his arms. 'The judgement is given,' he pronounced. 'The tithe will be made ready to depart after the Storyteller has spoken and the feast has been eaten.'

*

Even by nine o'clock, the air was still warm and thick with the insects which flew wildly around the lamps set to mark the boundaries of the assembly.

Only a few remembered the last time a Storyteller had come. If there was any reason for their rare appearances, no one knew what it was. But they knew that he knew everything. How the world was, how it operated, the laws of men and nature and of God. What was right, and what was wrong. Why it was that men walked the face of the earth, their past and their future. All this the Storytellers knew and kept safe.

Now he stepped forward, and waited until the Visitor – now seen as a very much lesser figure – walked to one side.

No one knew what to expect. Would it be some terrifying, awe-inspiring ceremony? Were they expected to listen on their knees, heads bowed reverentially? Could anyone listen, or were they meant to send the young away?

'Firstly,' said the old man, 'I must thank you for your good work over the past year, and say how pleased I am to be here on this wonderful evening, when the world has been smiling on us so generously.'

He had a gentle, melodious voice, and talked just like a normal person – well, less roughly, obviously, but there were no words they did not understand.

'Many of you know little about storytelling. Before I begin, let me explain. The Story is the Story of us all. If understood properly, it is of immense power. It tells you who you are, what you might expect from this life. Some believe it can foretell the future. Mastery of the Story gives you mastery over life itself. It contains precious, holy relics of the age of giants which preceded us. It tells of our rise, our glories and our occasional disgraces. It tells of our fathers and grandfathers, of the animals and the trees and the spirits, containing all the knowledge you need to please them so they will help rather than punish you.

'I am one of the guardians of this great Story. My telling is the truthful one, no matter what tales your grandmothers may have told you in the kitchen, or your grandfathers over a pint of ale, or wanderers who offer to entertain you in exchange for food and shelter. I keep the truth and you are commanded that, if you have heard differently from my account, you remember only what I say.

'So we shall begin, and afterwards I will explain the importance of what I have told you, and what it teaches us. I take my story not from the beginning, not even when God abandoned this earth, when the darkness fell and mankind was oppressed and begging for relief. Not even in the days of Exile, when cruelty stalked the lands. Now, to match the bounty of our days, I will tell a tale from the Return, when men led by Esilio came back to the places that once were theirs, and now are so again. They left a land of hardship, "of cruelty and ice, of hardship and desert", as it is said, and travelled to a place of peace and plenty . . .'

'How can you have desert and ice at the same time?'

The Storyteller looked almost as though he had been slapped in the face. The audience drew in its breath as one person. Many people felt a cold shiver running down their spine.

Someone had interrupted. Someone had queried a story. That did not happen. No one, even a madman, was so stupid that they didn't know that silence – total silence – was required. Even a cough was like a rebellion.

'Who said that?' the Storyteller said sharply. No one dared reply.

'I asked a question, and it will be answered. Someone spoke. He must identify himself immediately.'

The Storyteller, whose authority was now self-evident to everyone, stood and walked forward, surveying the crowd. He was insistent, but not angry. He seemed to have no doubts that his command would be obeyed.

'Well?'

The Storyteller was already walking towards him. He knew full well who had spoken. There was no possibility of hiding or denying it. He stood over the young boy until he reluctantly rose, then stuck his chin out defiantly.

'I did,' he said in a clear voice, which had no trace of a shake or tremor in it. He was scared witless, but at least it did not show.

The old man nodded to the two soldiers, who came forward. He nodded again, and each took him by an arm and began to lead him to the door of the tent.

Jay did not protest or resist. He knew there was no point. His mother looked on, petrified and helpless. The worst possible thing now would be if she doubled Jay's sin and made some noise or protest herself. Then the entire family would be shamed.

*

'You've done it now, boy,' one of the soldiers muttered. 'You're going to get a whipping like you wouldn't believe. If you're lucky.'

'I just wanted to know . . .'

They led him to the tent where the visitors were to sleep, which had been put up for them in the afternoon.

'Sit.'

Jay moved to obey. 'Not in there!' the soldier said as Jay bent to go through the tent entrance. 'Who do you think you are? Maybe you want a sleep in the Storyteller's bed? I'm sure he'd be happy to camp out on the floor so you can be comfortable.'

'Please forgive me.'

'Perhaps a glass of his wine? Would you like to try on his clothes?'

The soldier looked at Jay's miserable, frightened face, then relented. 'Well, we'll forget that one, shall we? Sit down, shut up and don't move. Right?'

Jay nodded. He buried his face in his hands and began to pray to the spirits of village and family for help. He was, in truth, more worried about his mother's look of sadness and fear, and what his father would do, than anything that might befall him in that tent. That he could not even imagine.

*

The Visitor and the Storyteller stood talking, muttering, to each other a few yards away from where the lad squatted on the ground, now cold, hungry and miserable. He had been sitting there, scarcely moving, for more than two hours. It was dark, and the cold was spreading through his young body. On the far side of the village, the feast was continuing despite his best efforts to ruin it; he could hear the sounds of merriment as it went on, and he thought wistfully of the food he was missing. The best food of the year, the feast that everyone looked forward to – wine and beer, fruit and bread, pork and mutton, vegetables fresh from the ground. People ate as though they had never eaten before, or never would again. The children would be given presents – little presents, certainly, but the only ones they ever got. Then they would sing and dance . . .

He was missing it all. His fear began to dissipate and be replaced by resentment. What had he done, apart from ask a question? So it was unheard of. So it was rude. But to miss the feast!

One of the soldiers walked over. 'Up,' he said. 'Follow me.'

He took him by the arm and led him towards the tent, which the Storyteller had just entered.

'Now listen,' he whispered in his ear. 'Speak when you're spoken to. Answer any questions. Don't try to be funny or smart. Understand?'

He had never been in such a thing before. The tent was almost as large as his house, and rich hangings had been draped over bars to hide the fact that it wasn't a real building. Candles – wax ones, not tallow – burned, almost a dozen of them. More hangings hid what he assumed was a sleeping area.

There was a makeshift desk, covered in cloth and laden with papers, behind which sat the Storyteller, who examined him keenly as he stood nervously by the tent flap. He had spoken for nearly an hour, telling the story, weaving it into a grand tale of entertainment and instruction, entrancing them with the sound of his voice, bringing out the melodies and meanings hidden in the words in the way that only many years of training could permit. An exhausting, draining experience because it was so important, and because no mistakes could be made. The story had to be delivered without hesitation or doubt.

'You will find a seat in the corner. Bring it and sit down.'

He obeyed, and then sat silently, as instructed, while the Storyteller looked at him carefully.

'What is your name?' he asked eventually. His voice was quiet but hoarse from his efforts.

'Jaramal, son of Antus and Antusa.'

The old man seemed almost annoyed by the response. He threw a piece of paper on the desk.

'Very well,' he said with a sort of finality.

'Everybody calls me Jay, though.'

The Storyteller snapped round as he finished delivering this entirely useless piece of information. Jay cursed himself. Speak when you are spoken to. Answer the questions.

The Storyteller had been about to get up and let him go. Jay was sure of it. Now he was infuriated, perhaps confused.

Maybe not, though. More a look of caution, worry. Not

anger. Jay longed to ask; the questions were almost bursting out of him.

'Did you work in the fields yesterday, Jay?'

Jay nodded, and said nothing, just to be safe.

'Did you leave the fields at any time? To get water, for example?'

Jay nodded once more, but very cautiously.

'Describe it.'

'I went up the hill, filled the bag and came down again.' Jay was scared, and he knew it showed. He knew nothing about the world, or its laws. But if he could get into trouble for having asked a question, what could happen to him if he told the truth? He couldn't lie, though. He was clever enough to know that, if he were found out, then the punishment would be severe indeed.

'I see. Anything else?'

Jay kept silent.

'You didn't, for example, bathe your face in the water?'

'I . . . I . . . yes. Maybe.' How did he know that? He hadn't even told his mother that.

'It was a hot day, of course you would have done. Perhaps you heard something? You are a curious boy; everyone I have talked to in the past hour says that your nosiness knows no bounds. If you heard a noise, you would have gone to investigate, no? Don't lie to me. I have talked to your mother, and others. Now I want to hear it from you. You alone were there.'

The old widow, Jay thought. He knew his mother would lie to save him, knew the old widow would tell the truth to get him into trouble. He was trapped. He didn't know what to do. He stayed silent still.

'It would be best if you told me exactly what you did. Every single thing. I am not angry, Jay. You will not be punished for telling me the truth. The truth is sacred, you know that. Even murderers have their punishment reduced if they tell the truth.'

It was strange. His tone of speaking hadn't changed. His expression was still the same. He hadn't moved, but something about him was reassuring. Not very; but enough. Jay began to speak. He told how he had indeed heard a noise, how he had walked round an outcrop of rock and seen a light, and then the fairy. The Storyteller listened passively, not saying anything until Jay stuttered to a halt.

'Do you say now that it must have been an illusion? That perhaps you fell asleep and dreamed it? Are you prepared to admit that you made it all up?'

'No,' Jay said stoutly. 'No. I'm not. She was there. As solid as you are.'

'But a little thinner, I hope?'

'Oh, yes, much.' Jay had done it again.

The Storyteller looked at the ceiling and recited quietly, '"It smiled once more, a radiant, celestial smile that brought the warmth back to his body. It raised its hands in what Jay took to be a gesture of peace, then took a step back and was gone." Would that be a reasonable account?'

Jay closed his eyes to avoid meeting the man's gaze. 'How do you know that?'

'How indeed? A good question, although I am sure you were told to ask none. Obedience and silence are not your strongest characteristics. But what are we to do with you now, eh?'

62

'You said I wouldn't be punished. You promised.'

'Did I?' He stood up, walked to the tent entrance and summoned the soldier guarding it. 'This boy must stay here tonight. I have to discuss matters with his family. Make sure he does not leave this tent. Oh – and could you get him some food? I imagine he is hungry.'

Jay got up, numbed and shaken. He had been lied to. He had trusted the Storyteller – trusted the sound of his voice – and had been betrayed.

'Jay.'

He turned round. The Storyteller was standing over him, but was not frightening now. 'Why did you interrupt me?'

'I . . . I just wanted to know the answer. I had to know.'

'You asked how something could be ice and desert at the same time?'

Jay nodded.

'It is a good question. Do you want a correct answer or a truthful one? The two are not always the same.'

'I want a truthful one.'

'Then I will tell you. I do not know.'

Jay stared at him, puzzled.

'There are many questions in this life, and few answers. Would you like to help me find some?'

*

The next morning, before dawn, Jay – who had slept on the ground, wrapped in a thick blanket given to him by the soldier – was roughly awoken by the toe of a boot.

'Up. We're leaving. So keep quiet.'

'Where are we going?'

'Never you mind.'

'What about my mother? My family?'

'You will not see them again. Not for many years.'

6

After he put the final full stop to his writing that evening, Lytten laid down his pen and leaned back in his chair. This he did with great ceremony; not for him a hastily scribbled note, or the vulgarities of a ballpoint pen. He used an ancient Parker with a gold nib which had belonged to his grandfather, with a peculiar purple-brown ink that he mixed himself. His handwriting was florid, almost ostentatious, the down strokes broad, the letters elegant. Each piece of paper was carefully blotted before he turned the page. In neat stacks on the leather-topped desk – his father's, once – were his notebooks, jottings of thought and information stretching back to his youth. In them, Anterwold had formed in fragments, and now he was drawing those together into a world. He had sent Jay to Ossenfud, and brought in village life, the importance of the Story.

As he considered the visitation scene he had written a few days previously, he realised what he had done. He had taken a scene from Lewis and inverted it – presented it from the point of view of the person who sees the vision, not of the person mistaken for one. He had also disposed of Lewis's annoying tendency to make everything so terribly suburban.

Lytten believed he had a somewhat better approach. Anyone encountering the supernatural would be terrified, aghast, awe-struck. Bernadette of Lourdes reacted like that, as indeed did most people who were predisposed to believe in things they had never actually seen for themselves, be they gods or flying saucers.

The trouble was, of course, that Lewis operated in a simple world where, oddly, the supernatural was banished except for that bloody bore of a lion of his, perhaps the most humourless creation in all literature. It was all so unsatisfactory. If a rat started talking, (despite grossly inadequate vocal arrangements and brain pan which did not allow for anything other than squeaks) his characters did not seem even briefly surprised. If a beaver offered you tea, your only reaction was to specify how many lumps of sugar you wanted. Lewis tried to invent an entire world, and created only a middle-class English suburb with a few swords.

However, if Lytten had just written about an apparition to show how an ordinary person would react if suddenly confronted with a mere fairy, he had to admit he had constructed a problem for himself. What was he going to do with it now? Writing something down because it popped into your head was one thing, but he suspected it would have to come out again later. Unless he could make it into a general point about religion and its place in societies of all sorts. It could stay until he made up his mind, but he was certain of one thing. No fairies in his story. Not real ones, anyway.

The darkness of an English autumn was falling; summer had put up a reasonable struggle this year, but was now surrendering to the inevitable. Outside there was the chill of night already tinged with the more serious cold of winter;

it was the time of day and year when all good people pull the curtains shut and block out the world until morning comes again. A moment of comfort and tea, and of little sponge cakes which were his evening treat on a Saturday, made for him especially by Mrs Morris, who had for some reason taken on the task a few years ago.

In truth, he did not care for the damp fingers of sponge with their thin layer of strawberry jam in the middle. They made Mrs Morris happy, though, and she would be hurt if he did not eat them. So he would sip his tea in the battered armchair by the fire, and only occasionally give way to temptation and hide the cakes under the settee until she had gone home and he could safely throw them away.

He was mildly surprised by what he had written so far; it certainly had not been his intention to stray into mystical meanderings, at least not so early on. He had put in a vision, and that smacked of religion. While he knew he would have to grapple with beliefs at some stage he didn't want it taking over a major part of his narrative.

He realised where it had come from. Rosie had asked – with a strange intensity, as though it was important – about apparitions, and the girl's question had made him reflect on the question, especially as he had already jotted down a passage about a vision to establish the idea of the scholars as authority figures. All societies held supernatural beliefs, but the nature of the apparitions told you a great deal about the people who saw them. A mechanical society feared mechanical things, a spiritual society feared spiritual things. The beliefs of Anterwold would have to be sculpted carefully.

Rosie, bless her, was still – just – in that innocent state

which found room in her imagination for ghosts and fairies. It wouldn't last long, no doubt. Soon she would be worrying about her clothes and boyfriends. Indeed, there were alarming signs of that already.

He liked the girl, who had such great spirit and such drab parents. Rosie had introduced them when they met on the street once. Her mother was a silly, fussy woman; her father dull and conventional. How on earth they had produced a girl like her was quite beyond him. He could only assume there had been some mix-up in the hospital where she was born, and they had come home with the wrong infant. They all look pretty much the same at that age, so he understood. A mistake could easily have been made.

The Wilsons lived in the next street, across one of those invisible but powerful divides which criss-cross most English towns. Lytten owned a shabby Victorian house which had a small front garden in a street with trees lining the pavement. Rosie's family was in a shabby Victorian house with neither. One street was the preserve of academics, lawyers and men of business; the other was inhabited by shopkeepers and bank clerks. Neither would ever dream of crossing over into the other's territory to live. It wasn't done, and England was a place where what wasn't done had a force greater than any statute.

Every now and then a group of boys would pass Lytten's house on their way to the parks to play football and, on one occasion, Rosie's utterly uninteresting elder brother had kicked a ball into his garden. He had been too afraid to come himself and Rosie had been sent to get it back. Lytten handed it over gravely and they had talked for some time about the weather, purely for the pleasure in making the boys wait.

They greeted each other in the street a few days later and talked again; she saw Professor Jenkins stretched out by an open window – a rare concession on his part to fresh air – and stroked him. He warned her that the cat could get nasty, but Jenkins had stood up and become almost flirtatious. Gradually she took to dropping in and, bit by bit, they became as good friends as a fifteen-year-old girl and a fifty-year-old man with little in common can become. Rosie took charge of Jenkins periodically, and Lytten slipped her a little money by way of thanks. He knew she got no pocket money.

He had given his apparition her coat and face. She was a pretty girl, and her face could be that of a fairy, had it not been for the ridiculous way she had cut her hair. Dreadful coat, though. Red plastic and shiny. Adolescent fashion.

*

Lytten's speciality was Sir Philip Sidney, favourite of Queen Elizabeth, courtier, scholar, poet and man of action. Indeed, he died fighting the Spanish in 1586. A romantic figure; dashing, handsome, well connected, even if his abilities were never as great as he imagined. He desired a fine role in the government but Elizabeth, wise old bird that she was, kept him at arm's length. The great queen was highly suspicious of extravagance from anyone but herself.

He compensated for this by writing (or at least starting – he never quite finished anything) the greatest romance in the English language. Almost no one has even heard of it now, which is a pity, because if modern sensibilities are suspended – if you do not care about plot, action, events, morality, structure or pace, if you are not bothered by absurd coincidence or unlikely motivations, if irrelevant digressions of immense length do not weary you – then his *Arcadia* has many fine qualities. His characters do not do much, it must be admitted; the only event of any real note in the entire book is a seduction, but Sidney cut this out in a later rewriting for fear of being considered vulgar.

What is left is a rudimentary plot of such absurdity it is best ignored – aristocrats dressed up as peasants when they are not disguising themselves as women, falling in love with other peasants who are also aristocrats in disguise for reasons which really don't matter too much. Many of Shakespeare's plots are similar, if a little shorter.

Besides, for Sidney the plot is only a vehicle for talk. Rather than doing anything, the characters talk in language which is so beautiful that it is difficult to resist. The words create an imaginary landscape of perfection, a soft dream of warm evenings with chuckling streams and dappled sunlight playing through the leaves of a forest.

Death and threat are there, but only to highlight the perfection of the present. Others have created a similar effect – the scene in *Le Grand Meaulnes*, where Meaulnes wanders into a Watteau-esque party and goes in a daze around an elegant estate, full of beautiful women in silk and men in Pierrot costume. The Venice Carnevale, when all reality is suspended and dreams take over the entire city. All these images and impressions had lodged in Lytten's youthful mind, a hidden refuge from the reality of a grey industrial land, full of strife and surrounded by the darkening clouds of another war.

Lytten never allowed his imaginings to overwhelm reality. Sidney was a man he studied; Meaulnes a character in a book; Venice a city he visited. Still, over the years, his recollections and studies slowly reorganised themselves in his mind to the point where the land of Anterwold began to take shape, particularly the domain of Willdon, which was the central point from which the whole story emerged, just as Sidney's world emerged from his sister's possessions as Countess of Pembroke.

7

Until the soldier – the same one who had shown him kindness – pulled back the covering and gestured to him, Jay travelled in near darkness. Not a single person had so much as said a word to him. Competing emotions had beset him throughout the journey. Fear, of course. Boredom. Resentment. Finally, a burning, desperate curiosity. Just on the other side of the canvas were wonders such as he had never seen before. Forests, woods, houses, mountains – who knew what was there to be looked at? He tried to pull up a piece of the covering so he could see out, but it was too thick and strong. He dreamed of a daring escape, but it was pointless even to try.

Then he emerged into the fading light of an early evening, with a fresh wind in contrast to the smelly, sweltering heat of the wagon, which he had endured in glum silence.

'Come and sit by me, and keep your mouth shut,' the soldier said. Jay hurried to obey in case he changed his mind, and squeezed himself down besides the man's impressive bulk. He looked around and gasped. Not in astonishment or wonder, but in surprise. There was nothing much to see that was very different from his home.

'Where are we?' he began.

The soldier shook his head. 'I said shut up. It means be quiet. Keep your mouth closed. Say nothing. Silence. Do you understand?'

Jay nodded.

'I will talk. You will not. Agreed?'

Jay nodded again.

'That's good. Because there is not much time. We will arrive in an hour or so. Are you frightened?'

Jay opened his mouth to speak, saw the look on the soldier's face, then nodded for a third time.

'Do you know what is going to happen to you?'

He shook his head.

'Thought not. It seems a shame to be scared for no reason. So I'll tell you what I've heard. Okay?'

Another nod.

The soldier grunted. 'You see? You can do it when you try. Right then. You are going to Ossenfud to be a student.'

Jay looked at him curiously.

'You don't even know what that is? Very well. A student is someone who learns. What you learn depends on your teacher, but it takes years and years, and the best become Storytellers.'

Jay could no longer contain himself. 'A Storyteller! Me?'

'I said the best. Storytellers need years of discipline and immense knowledge and intelligence. They must commit everything to memory and be able to summon it all as required. They are the custodians of the past and the shapers of the future. Does that sound like you?'

Jay shook his head.

'Precisely. You may become a keeper of accounts, or something like that. Lower, but still important. That's more like it. The thing is, you were chosen. By that Storyteller himself. Henary, his name is. That's very unusual.'

'Why?'

'That's not how it's done, usually. As the Visitors and Storytellers go around the country, they keep an eye open for people. Young, trainable. Generally they are recommended. Someone exceptionally smart. They'll be noticed by a mayor or a chief. They'll be questioned, tested. Then chosen. That's not the way it was with you. Something you must have said or done – and don't ask me what, because I would have just given you a good thrashing and sent you back to your mother – must have persuaded Henary that you were just such a kid.'

'But I can't do anything. I know a bit about blacksmithing.'

'You will be taught. Don't think it will be fun. Long hours, hard work, sitting at a desk all day every day. You'll wish you were back in the fields. Most people couldn't stand it. I certainly couldn't. You can have the power and the glory if you have to become a wizened, half-blind creature with a bent back to get it. Not for me.'

'Who are you? I'm sorry, but I really don't know much.'

'Just a soldier. I come from Willdon, about three days' march from here. Every settlement sends soldiers to act as guards to the scholars, for a while. I'll be done soon, and then I'll go back to work in the forests again. It's too complicated to explain. You'll know in due course. You'll know more than me, and I'll be asking you questions.'

'I doubt it.'

'I doubt you'll answer.'

'Why?'

'Because you don't. You people.'

You people. Jay found it confusing. Until three days ago, someone like the soldier sitting beside him would have

74

been impossibly grand and powerful. Someone Jay would naturally have addressed as 'sir', with a bow. Yet here he was, talking almost as though they were equals. Already he could feel an even greater change; but what it meant his young mind could not begin to grasp.

'I'll answer you. What's your name?'

'Callan. Son of Perel.'

'Callan Perelson, then. When we meet, whoever I become, you will be my friend, and I will answer your questions.'

Callan looked touched by this naivety. 'Thank you. You will forgive me if I say I don't believe you.'

'No,' said Jay a little sadly. 'No, I won't forgive you.'

*

Jay had never seen a town before, and the city of Ossenfud, where the scholars lived, was fairly large. About six thousand souls lived there most of the year, although this number fluctuated according to the seasons. It was settled on a river, and was approached by four roads, one coming from each of the points of the compass. Unusually, outlying buildings were scattered along these roads, up to a mile away from the city proper.

So many houses, so many people, the clattering of the cart over roads paved with stones, everything made Jay tremble with excitement. Even more alarming was when they stopped outside a vast building of unimaginable magnificence.

'Here we are, then,' Callan said cheerfully. 'Home, sweet home. East College, where Scholar Henary is, and where you will be until either you are finished or they throw you out.'

He eased himself down to the ground and waited. 'If you think I'm going to carry your bag for you, you're mistaken,' he called up.

Jay searched for the pathetic little sack which contained everything he owned in the world: two shirts, two pairs of trousers, one pair of clogs and one pair of shoes, his pride and joy. Also a piece of carved wood his uncle had once given him. Nothing else. At least the bag was light.

Then he, too, jumped down and found that Callan was talking to a young man who had stopped to watch. Jay wondered whether it was good manners to go up and join them, and decided to play safe. He listened intently, nonetheless.

'I'm surprised to see you here,' Callan was saying.

'Oh, domain business. Someone had to come and I offered. A little change, you know.' He pointed at Jay. 'What's that you've got there?'

'Henary found him. Asked me to deliver him here.'

The young man crooked his finger, so Jay obediently approached.

'A find by Scholar Henary? You are a lucky boy. I hope you realise that?'

He was a tall and finely dressed young man, perhaps ten years or so older than Jay was, but decades away in manner and self-possession. Jay noticed that he talked to the grizzled soldier with familiarity, even amusement, as though he was doing him some sort of favour. Jay was now even more confused.

'Well, I will not keep you. I hope your service will end soon and you will return to your old place, Callan Perelson. Our trees miss you badly.'

'I miss them. I will return soon enough.'

The young man nodded and walked away. Callan grunted.

'Who was that?'

'The nephew of Lord Thenald. A grand fellow, don't you think? Actually, not a bad young man, but a little too aware of his name. Still, he has a sense of fairness and decency, which is valuable in these days.'

Jay understood not one word, and Callan laughed at his puzzlement. 'You're going to have to disguise your ignorance better, young man. Remember: scholars know everything, even when they know nothing. Merchants are honest, even when they are crooks, and domain holders are just, even when they are total bastards.'

'What about foresters?'

'Splendid fellows all,' he said. 'Come on. Grit your teeth, calm your nerves and follow me.'

Jay did as instructed, and the next day began his new life.

8

Henary's negotiations with Jay's parents had been easy enough; not only were they proud at the idea of having a student in the family, his father in particular was quite glad to see the back of him. Henary was doing everyone a favour; the lad was the sort who could get himself into trouble without a suitable outlet, and this Henary could provide. He would spend the next few years of his life working harder than he ever dreamed possible.

Once Henary had packed the boy off with the soldiers and the wagon, he and the Visitor mounted their horses and left. Both were exhausted. Henary wished his companion didn't feel the need to converse all the way. The young man, one of his students, had been a Visitor for the first time. He had been nervous, and Henary had decided to hold his hand, guide him through. Now he was exhilarated from relief that it had passed off without disaster. He had a tendency to be over-eager, to show off. Henary had been there to calm him. 'Easy, my boy. What do they care about precedents? They will trust you. You don't have to give them a lecture as well. Their lives are quite hard enough as it is.'

He'd done well, grown into his role. After only three weeks, he was already much more confident, much less likely to glance at Henary to seek advice or take refuge in pomposity. He'd proved himself to be judicious and generous as well. Henary was pleased.

'I have space for a student, and he tickled my fancy,' Henary said when the young man asked about Jay. 'If he's no good, then I will know before the six months' probation is up, and I'll send him home again.'

Eventually, the talk petered out. Henary didn't really want to explain and further possibility of discussion was ended by a small delegation standing in the middle of the road as they came round a sharp bend. Henary groaned. 'Oh, no. Please, no!' he said. 'I've had enough.'

Duties were duties. The pair stopped to hear what they had to say. They were worried. A hermit named Jaqui had turned up some months back. He had been delirious, raving, and they had nursed him back to health. He had retreated a mile or so out of the village, where he had taken over an old hut. A few children had assisted him and he had paid them by telling wonderful stories. He had helped with the harvest and had some skill in healing. When someone was ill he would visit and his presence could fend off the demons which cluster around the seriously sick. He would attend births and his touch was helpful.

'So what do you want from us?'

Because Jaqui could read and write, the villagers knew he had to have been a scholar or student, and they wanted to be certain they were not harbouring an outcast.

Henary sighed.

'I'll go,' his student offered.

'No, no. I'll do it. You've worked hard enough these few weeks. You go on. I'll have a look, stay the night and then branch off to Willdon.'

Very grumpily, he turned his horse and wearily allowed

79

the villagers to lead him to the east. When he arrived at the village of Hooke he was welcomed, then given directions over the fields.

'Ho there!' he called when he came to the hut. 'I seek Jaqui, hermit.'

'You are looking in the wrong place,' came a voice from behind him.

Henary turned and saw a man standing a few feet away, leaning on a stick. He was unkempt, with long, greasy hair; his eyes were strangely formed and wild. He looked as though he could be dangerous.

'I have been asked to talk to you. I am a Storyteller from Ossenfud.'

'I have done no harm.' He spoke with a strange accent.

'The villagers are concerned, that is all. They mean you no trouble, and nor do I.'

Jaqui was an unusual hermit. He was strong, for a start. Not too old, either, nor did he have the extravagant speech which many of his ilk affected. An odd face, though, which Henary found himself examining closely.

'Where are you from? Your place and family?'

'I have no place and no family.'

'I am told you can read and write.'

'I have nothing to read, except what I write. Perhaps they are just scribbles on a page.'

'Show me and I will tell you.'

'Ah, no, Storyteller. That I cannot do. Perhaps you will find they are meaningless, and disappoint me. Why don't you go away? I do not trespass on your stories. I have no interest in them, and you have no interest in mine. I know that already.'

'How do you know that?'

'I talked to a scholar once, one like you. He asked me questions. I told him things, what I knew and thought, but he wasn't interested.'

'What was the name of this man?'

'Etheran. You know him?'

'He was my teacher. The man I revered above all others. He died a month ago.'

Jaqui nodded slowly. 'I am sorry for that. He was a good man. I had hopes for him.'

'You are insolent.'

Jaqui laughed.

'I think we have talked enough,' Henary went on. 'You do not seem very dangerous to me. But I counsel you to be careful about what you say.'

'Who are you, scholar? You know my name, I do not know yours.'

'My name is Henary, son of Henary.'

'What are you doing here? Am I now so famous that a Storyteller comes all the way from Ossenfud to visit? Did Etheran talk of me to you?'

'Hardly,' Henary said. 'I am on my way to Willdon for the festivity.'

'What is that?'

'A celebration of the seventh year of Thenald's rule. I am a friend to his wife.'

'I am flattered you spend your time with me, then. I'm sure the lord and lady would not.'

'Probably Thenald would not,' Henary said, 'although if I know Lady Catherine, she might well welcome you. You judge too easily.'

He considered this as though it was some weighty, important statement. 'Well, perhaps I do. But as I am a hermit in a hut, I can do as I please. Now, will you leave me be?'

*

That expedition was the last time Henary ventured out of Ossenfud on a formal Visitation for many years. He had his studies and his teaching, and when Thenald died, shortly after he had met Jay, he found himself travelling to Willdon far more often to give advice to his widow. He liked his life, apart from the interruptions. His new student was introduced into Ossenfud and learned enough to pass through the probation period without too many difficulties.

Eventually, Henary also began writing the story of Etheran, dutiful student that he was, doing what his master never had time for, setting down his memorial to be lodged in the Story Hall of Ossenfud along with that of every other scholar. Etheran's death had shaken everyone; the most brilliant man he had ever known. An austere teacher, who never drank alcohol, never ate too much, slept on a straw pallet like the least student. Who rose at dawn and read until night had fallen, without a break. He had been the most generous man as well, able to turn the dullest passage into magic through his enthusiasm and skill.

Then he died. Quietly, one night, he went out of his little house and was found the next morning, dead in a field. There were enquiries, but not too many, as people were afraid to know, lest his memory be tarnished. Henary's own wife had examined his body. 'Let us just say that he had a broken heart,' she said. 'There is no more to it than that . . .'

Henary took on the task of preserving the memory of his teacher and friend, knowing that if he did not then his wisdom and knowledge would be lost as well.

He had loved the man and wished to do a proper job, teasing out the sense and the value even in his later work, when he became wild and unbalanced in his assertions. It meant trying to find out all those things which he had never known, and then crafting them into a narrative which summed up his life. The good and the bad had to be there; the scholarly achievements, greater than he knew; the final death, sadder than he feared.

Etheran had gone mad, he thought. He had begun to question the Story, but without knowing how to answer his questions. Loyalty and curiosity came into murderous conflict, and his heart broke under the strain. So his tribute was also an exploration and an apology, for Henary had grown apart from Etheran in his last year. He had accused his teacher of becoming foolish and indulgent, giving credence to the irrational, lending support to those who disdained intellectual rigour. Henary thought it was irresponsible.

A terrible lesson, and as he wrote – taking his time, for the dead are in no hurry – he often thought of Jay, who resembled Etheran in some ways, as he was also incapable of restraining his questions and was tempted to stray into dangerous areas. Often Jay was disciplined and punished, but it never made any difference. There was a structure to argument: thesis; evidence from the story, preferably examples separated by several Levels; counter-argument, similarly backed up; and conclusion, where the most important quotations and examples were deployed. Simple enough, surely?

It was for most people, but not for Jay, who seemed to see it as a surrender. He was a good student, and Henary was pleased to see how he learned quickly and developed a real feel for the Story. In all respects except one he demonstrated time and again that Henary had chosen well. The exception, however, was troublesome, for Jay found it difficult, even painful, to conform to the styles of disquisition that marked out the true scholar. How do you prove iron wheels were not as good as wooden ones? It was a simple task, set to all students after five years of study when they had mastered the language and scripts. All he had to do was cite the example of Yadrel, in Level 1, the cartwright who built the wagons which brought the travellers south, and who hewed yew trees and seasoned them and cut them to make wheels strong and pliant. What more was needed?

Jay ignored the tale of Yadrel, because he had gone mushroom hunting in the woods when he should have been at a lecture on the subject. Instead, he went and talked to a wheelwright and a blacksmith, and wrote about the way iron could shatter under strain. Right conclusion, wrong argument. His teacher (not Henary on this occasion) had hardly known where to start.

'Jay, just stick to the texts next time,' Henary said wearily after he had spent an hour listening to the teacher's complaints. 'Everything is to be found in the Story. Go and do it again.'

Look where that sort of thing led Etheran, he could have added. But he was loyal to the memory of his master, and loyal to the potential of Jay. Both had a spark which promised wonders and threatened disaster. So he used Etheran's story to present the case for such wildness and equally the need to discipline it. To gather evidence for his case, he took himself off to the Story Hall, where Etheran's papers had been stored, trying to understand how his mind had developed, and why it had then broken down.

There he came across the hermit Jaqui once more.

This encounter happened one evening, when anyone watching the main square of Ossenfud might have glimpsed a curious sight. A shadow passed across, and, hugging the walls of the buildings, made its way around the central area where markets were held every second Tuesday. The shadow paused by an opening in the great wall that formed one of the massive sides of the Story Hall and there was the lightest clinking of metal, the faintest scrape of a key turning in a lock.

Henary was at that moment breaking any number of rules. Against being out after dark, which was frowned upon even for senior scholars. Against going into the Story Hall out of hours. Against taking a light in without someone else to guard against accident or fire. Luckily, he was much too grand a figure to be questioned, and when he entered he paused in the semi-dark, savouring the smell and atmosphere of this most wonderful place, the quiet, the banks of boxes climbing the whitewashed walls, each containing their precious scroll or book. The whole world was there; Henary was conscious that he was standing in the very centre of the entire universe, and it gave him, as usual, a profound sense of humility and peace.

The papers he sought were grouped in five bundles and he made his discovery in the third: scraps of paper in a very different hand that stood out amongst his old master's appalling scrawl, which, on its own, was almost enough to ensure that his thought remained forever hidden.

There were two letters only; Henary tucked them into the pocket of his thick cloak, carefully replaced the manuscripts, blew the dust off the table so no one would suspect he had been there, and then, as quietly and surely as he had arrived, slipped across the great echoing hall, through the little side door and back into the alleyway.

*

The letters described the encounter between Etheran and Jaqui, although as only half of the correspondence was there, it gave the impression that his poor teacher submitted silently to a torrent of meaningless abuse.

'You tell me that the Story contains everything, and I reply that you are a fool, Etheran the Wise. You don't think, and prefer silly tales and blind belief. How is it that someone like you is considered intelligent? What must your colleagues be like if a dunderhead like you is acclaimed?

'How can this Story of yours contain everything? Ah, you say, only in potential, and its meaning will not be understood until Esilio returns and brings it to its end. Obscure nonsense. Meaningless babbling.

'What do you mean by containing everything? Every bird and leaf and insect? What pathetic creatures you are! You await your end like cattle, and it will come, believe me. You will vanish as if you had never existed; it's all you deserve.

'Everything is something to do with the giants. But who were they? You don't know. You are here because of the great Return from Exile. What was that? You don't

86

care. All you do is compare this tale to that tale; see that a certain phrase in one part of the Story is used in another part; discover that one dead scholar generations back contradicted another dead scholar generations back. You call this learning?

'"When the Story is finished, it will fold into the world and each will extinguish the other." One of your quotations. When? How? Anyone can come up with grandiose and meaningless phrases. I can too. How about this: "The world will end on the fifth day of the fifth year." Is it any more nonsense than the sort of thing you recite with such reverence? No. Except that what I say is true. Wait and see.'

There was no notion of what prompted this lunatic outburst because Etheran had not made copies of his own letters. Henary could guess, though. In his last year, Etheran had been preoccupied with stories of the End, when the god returns to judge his creation. Silly stories, ignored by serious scholars, but Etheran had become alarmingly fascinated by them. It had been the cause of Henary's disaffection from his master.

What astonished Henary was not just the content, but the fluency and ease of these letters. An interesting lunatic, he thought. None of it made sense, though, and he thought no more of Jaqui the hermit until the time came for Jay to consider his thesis.

9

The key problem I was working on derived from a computer simulation that was ordered by Hanslip in one of his fits of caution. It was carefully designed to do two things: firstly to establish the degree to which the course of history would be altered by changing an event, and secondly to test various theories of the nature of historical evolution. This was supposed to be a preliminary investigation into the practicality of altering parallel universes to create suitable conditions for exploitation.

The trouble was that events were simplified in order to make the calculations possible within a reasonable time-frame and budget; Hanslip was always parsimonious. It was also anonymised; the assessment programme was unaware which of the scenarios was real, in case natural prejudice on its part influenced its decisions.

The first scenario posited that the presidential election in the United States in 1960 was won by the Republican nominee, Richard Nixon, who defeated his Democratic opponent, a man called John Kennedy. Nixon's much greater depth and knowledge came through and he won the election by a small margin. The result was inevitable; while Nixon had a good track record and gravitas, Kennedy had little knowledge of government and a reputation (fiercely exposed in the campaign and confirmed in a bitter divorce in 1965) as a playboy. Nixon's greater experience led him to quash a foolish attempt to invade Cuba in 1961. However, this allowed his enemies to accuse him of weakness, which he tried to counter by ordering troops to Vietnam the following year.

Nixon won the 1964 election, defeating Lyndon Johnson, but by that stage was committed to an all-out war. In 1968 he was replaced by Johnson, who died of appendicitis in 1971 and was replaced in turn by Jimmy Carter, who ended up in jail for gross misconduct. Ultimately the actor Ronald Reagan, Nixon's vice-president for his second term and by then a man of great experience, became president in 1980.

So far so good. Then the computer programme turned its attention to the second scenario, in which the 1960 election was won by Kennedy, not Nixon. The result, it opined, was narrow but inevitable because of Nixon's reputation for dishonesty. Kennedy was dashing, young, handsome and fresh. This came across in a television debate in which Kennedy was bright and confident, Nixon unshaven, scruffy and hesitant.

Kennedy's true potential is unknown, due to his assassination in 1963. He made a badly bungled attempt to invade Cuba in 1961, but redeemed this by defusing the Cuban missile crisis in 1962. After his murder he was succeeded by Lyndon Johnson, who destroyed his presidency by ordering, then losing, a full-scale war in Vietnam. Johnson was replaced by Nixon at a time of political turmoil following the murder of Kennedy's brother and other high-profile figures. Nixon also destroyed his presidency, this time through illegal activities. There followed Gerald Ford, who declined to run when he could have won, then Jimmy Carter, who destroyed his presidency with another ill-thought-out foreign venture. Finally, Reagan was elected in 1980.

Hanslip was a bit despondent at this, as the simulation suggested very strongly that, although individuals and small events did affect the course of historical development, the influence of even major figures was strictly limited. In the long term, it appeared exceptionally difficult to alter the past except through massive intervention. If any individual was not born, for example, they seemed to be replaced by someone similar.

Even here, though, warning signs should have been spotted by the people running the experiment. For example, the programme changed the parameters of its task all on its own in order to achieve what it called dramatic credibility. It also restructured events to take account of the results it was getting, as it was set up to disregard coincidence. So it changed Nixon's reputation for decency, based on his Quaker upbringing, to one for duplicity and ruthlessness. It married Kennedy to a dowdy, pious woman rather than a charming and beautiful one, in order to explain his otherwise incomprehensible womanising.

*

My objection – set out forcefully in a memorandum which was completely ignored – was that the fundamental problem stemmed from Hanslip's penny-pinching. The programme was instructed to take into account only internal political dynamics. External actions – such as decisions taken by other countries, for example – were ignored, which struck me as unwise, even if it was cheaper.

A clear sign that something was badly wrong came from a small control that had been built in. For the sake of objectivity, the programme analysed both histories – real and alternative – without being informed which was which. It concluded that the second, actual sequence of events was statistically so improbable that it could not possibly happen.

Specifically, it reasoned that there were too many random events whose only purpose seemed to be to get history back on track. History returned to what the programme thought should be its normal path by 1980 only through what it sneeringly referred to as plot devices which even a novelist of the period would have rejected as ludicrously far-fetched.

I quote the conclusion: 'We are required to believe a) that a drug-addled, womanising, inexperienced Catholic with strong links to criminal organisations could defeat the most experienced politician in the country, and that his dire medical condition and dubious character could be kept secret. Also that he could conduct exceptionally successful diplomacy in 1962 while being as high as a kite on a cocktail of painkillers and stimulants;

b) that a president, his brother and several others could all be murdered in a short space of time, by insane gunmen, each acting alone, for no discernible reason. Also that Kennedy could be shot by someone with known links to the Soviet Union without there being any consequences;

c) that Nixon in office would sanction a pointless burglary, during an election campaign he was bound to win anyway, and that a man of such experience would fail to control the very minor political scandal that resulted;

d) that in 1980 the United States would elect as president

an ageing actor with little experience and dyed orange hair.

None of these make any sense whatsoever. In fact the second scenario would have resulted in a nuclear war at some stage in the period covered, in which case history would most certainly not have returned to normal by 1980.'

The only product of merit from this otherwise worthless experiment was the one which was dismissed as a programming error. The implication that, under certain circumstances, not only the future but also the past could and must rearrange itself to fit available events was an extraordinary conclusion, which stuck in my mind simply because of its sheer improbability.

*

That simulation was run just a week before I left, and I have no doubt whatsoever that no one paid the slightest attention to my objections. The response – that if history could not be changed in small ways, then it might be necessary to explore bigger ones – demonstrated how weak my position already was and strengthened my conviction that flight was the only real option. So that is what I did. I cleared everyone out of the section, locked myself in and set to work.

That didn't mean I was happy about having to leave, not least because I arrived in Germany in 1936. It was hardly the best time or place, what with one thing and another. But my departure was hurried and, in the circumstances, I think I did pretty well, although it was unfortunate that I hadn't loaded up the newspapers for the period. I took them for 1960 onwards only, as I thought that would be all

I'd need. I didn't have that much space in my head.

For the first nine months it didn't matter, as I spent the time in a lunatic asylum. This was not the best introduction to my new world, although if you really want to understand any society, looking at it through the eyes of the mentally deranged is remarkably illuminating. One thing I learned was that the transmission process plays merry hell with your brain, although I suspected this was due to the effects of cerebral implants rather than an inevitable consequence of the shift. Even more unfortunately, I had popped a few hallucinogens before I left, to ramp up my performance; many of the settings I had to do manually, so I needed all the help I could get. As I say, I did pretty well, but I emerged the other end raving and incoherent. Even the little sense I could talk merely convinced people that I was completely nuts.

I had been aiming for San Francisco in 1972; hitting a small village three miles south of Munich in 1936 was pretty good. I will not here describe the experience of landing in a world so foreign to my experience, so brutal and so intoxicating in many ways. Suffice it to say that it is a most peculiar business. The new reality is so overwhelming that you quickly forget your own past circumstances: I found that I spent little time thinking about my previous life, which very speedily took on the nature of a dream, dissociated from my current existence.

That didn't make it any easier, mind you; even when I returned to sanity, the chances of making mistakes and attracting attention were enormous. Social mores were very different, for a start. Getting money was a strange business and quite how you were supposed to behave with others – depending on your age, sex, wealth, education, location and beliefs – was incomparably complex. I was, in fact, quite glad I had a long time to get used to it all. I was convalescing, so I thought I might as well make it pleasant. I had set my heart on a surfboard and a Thunderbird but, once I moved to France in 1937, I found there were more than enough pleasures to fill my days for a while.

I had left with a full suite of implants which made my life very much easier. I could speak German fluently, for example, and could manage just as well in twenty-three other languages. I had the expertise to be a highly successful lawyer or surgeon; I could have won the Nobel Prize many times over simply by printing other people's work a little ahead of them. By the standards of the day, I was also quite remarkably beautiful and healthy, and could easily have become a major film star. I did none of that, of course, as I did not want to attract any attention, just in case.

The lack of newspapers was a nuisance, though; I remembered that a war was going to start, for example, and knew more or less who would win it, but I had no more idea what the following day would bring than anyone else. Foolish, no doubt, but I was a psychomathematician whose speciality was time; events were mere epiphenomena which interested me not at all. I was briefly worried that the lack of stock market reports (I wanted a simple life, but not a poor simple life) might doom me to poverty, but soon enough realised that calculating asset price movements was absurdly easy. Rudimentary mathematical ability and a simple star chart were the only things needed.

So I spent several months in Paris amassing some seed money in the most enjoyable way women could in those days, and also worked out the formula for predicting the markets. I then sorted out my finances once and for all and settled in a quiet location in the countryside where a studied eccentricity – my behaviour was, in fact, very bizarre, and it took years to learn how to behave properly and inconspicuously – protected me from prying eyes until I felt able to blend in.

Only during the war did I emerge, as not doing anything would have been more noticeable than actually taking part. I also relocated to England, as France didn't promise to be so very entertaining. Then I was free to get on with my work. Oddly I found that my greatest advantage was having no assistance whatsoever. My mind could roam freely and, unshackled from the limits of standard procedure, could approach the problem from entirely new directions. It was wonderful.

10

As the years passed, Jay worked, learned and grew. By the time he was nearly seventeen, he had become a young man who was more self-confident and somewhat better at hiding his natural tendency to doubt authority, query orders and try to do things in the way he thought best. He had his friends, although he was not known as one of the wild and sociable students. He was still difficult to manage but, on the whole, this was confined to his work and only rarely affected his behaviour, which was polite and considerate. It was true that he was often chastised for missing lectures, but the talks he missed tended to be judiciously chosen. Only the most tedious had reason to complain that he had not turned up again. Jay considered an afternoon sitting by the river staring at the sky with a dreamy look on his face to be more valuable and instructive and often enough Henary found it difficult to disagree.

He progressed through the levels of studentship well and without major incident; his knowledge grew, his understanding grew much faster. Only the indiscipline remained; sooner or later the frustration at the unasked question would burst forth. Some of his contemporaries nicknamed him 'Master Yesbut'.

'You know,' Henary had said after one lesson, 'that part of your training is to write your own thesis?'

Jay nodded. He also knew that soon enough he would have to appear before a committee and say what his subject would be. Most chose some old scholar, their work unread for generations, who was disinterred from the shelves and analysed. Then put back and forgotten again.

'Do you have any ideas?'

'I've thought of many. But they are all so . . .'

'Boring?' Henary said lightly. Jay blushed. 'You are quite right. Many of the commentaries are entirely useless, except to lull you to sleep late at night. Besides, all the really good ones have been gone over again and again.'

'Laszlo and the weather,' Jay said despondently.

'A fine body of work, and very useful for sailors. What is there to say apart from that?'

'Fered on theft?'

'Then you would end up as a lawyer. A worthy trade, no doubt, but not what you are ideally suited to do with your life. You are not nearly precise enough.'

'What I would like to do is something on the Shrine of Esilio. You know, collect writings on the subject and compare them. I've read a lot about it.'

'A bit sophisticated for one of your age.'

'Then what? Who?'

'I have an idea. You do not have to take it, but if you do, it will mean a little travel for you. You might also care to render me a small service and go and meet someone.'

'Who?'

'A man called Jaqui. A hermit.'

*

Two days after their conversation, and armed with a letter of introduction for the elders of Hooke, Jay took leave of absence from his lessons and walked out of Ossenfud on the Great West Road. It led, so he knew, to the towns and settlements that were scattered throughout Anterwold, curling down to the sea in the south, and west into the mountains. It was itself a tributary, so to speak, of other roads: Garlden had mapped them many generations back and tried to explain why they were as they were, although his account was so amateurish that no one ever read it. But the maps – annotated and corrected as travellers found errors – were the best available.

According to Garlden, he had a twenty-mile walk on the road, then had to branch off to the north for about twenty-five miles to the village of Hooke.

When Henary had made the suggestion, Jay had looked almost scornful. 'A hermit?'

'Yes. A very strange man. I assume he's still alive. He is an intriguing character. I think you might consider writing your dissertation on the subject of painting. It is an interesting topic, in my opinion. We always think of the Story in terms of words, but there are countless times when a drawing or illustration has been added. A map, or a plan, or a scribble in the margin. No one has ever looked at how they contribute to the Story as a whole. You will find a fascinating example of storytelling through pictures at Hooke.'

'What's that got to do with hermits?'

'Nothing. That's a job for me. Before you go, you should read Lardley on hermits. An obscure and little-read text, but rather good. He tackled the problem of knowledge. Hermits are often known for their wisdom; yet all wisdom

98

is contained in the Story, of which they know nothing. A conundrum, you see. Unfortunately, Lardley never bothered actually to talk to a hermit.'

'So it is not much use.'

Henary peered at him. 'Ah . . . no. I suppose not. But it might help when you meet Jaqui.'

'Why do you want me to do that?'

'Well, you see,' said the older man, 'Jaqui is a curious fellow. He is uneducated, but he can write. I want to know what he writes, and how he writes. I want you to bring back some of his scripts.'

'Will he give them to me?'

'I have no idea. I won't blame you if you fail. It'll give you something to do, and may win favours from your tutor. That's me, by the way, and I'm sure you realise keeping me happy is of the utmost importance.'

*

It wasn't a hugely successful trip, in the sense that the meeting with the hermit never happened. When Jay arrived at Hooke, he knocked at the gate of the village, stated his business and was led to the collection of buildings that comprised the communal section. There he was told to wait while the gatekeeper went to fetch someone for him to talk to. Eventually a woman appeared, who introduced herself as a member of the village council and the keeper of the settlement's stories.

'Your name, young man?' she asked; she seemed quite intrigued by the arrival of a student in their midst. Jay introduced himself and explained his interest in painting.

'I wish also to see a man called Jaqui, a hermit who lives near you.'

'I'm afraid you are too late. Jaqui left us a little while ago. We do not know why. He had everything he needed and wanted.'

'That is a great shame.'

'He often disappeared for short periods, but this time he said he would not return.'

'My master met him some years ago. He wanted me to question him.'

'That will be Scholar Henary? I remember his visit well. He was a man who brought credit to himself and our village.'

'I trust I will also. If not, then I hope you will tell me, that I might amend what I say and do.'

'Well said, young man. Alas, I'm afraid you have had a wasted journey. But at least we can show you our hall.'

'Thank you,' Jay said gloomily. He knew he would have to stand in a dark chilly building while listening to a long lecture about village history, full of names he had never heard of and events he cared nothing for. Important for the village, of course, but the few nuggets of importance would inevitably be left out in favour of long tales of families and fields.

He followed dutifully as the woman led him around the wooden buildings to the Story Hall. Jay said the right things when he glimpsed it. 'A fine building, made with love,' he said. 'I congratulate your village on its devotion.'

'Thank you. We are proud of it. It took many years to build, and the tales say we used no outside hands. It was all from our own labour and sweat and ingenuity.'

Jay had seen worse by this stage, but he had also seen better. It was nowhere near as grand as the great halls of Ossenfud, for example, but nor was it a mean hut of painted wood such as he had seen in some places. It was of dark brown stone, roughly put together and circular in shape, some forty feet in diameter and rising up two storeys in height to a conical roof covered in tiles. It resembled a huge dovecote, except that there were only four small openings at the very top to allow air to circulate and light to enter. Set apart was another small structure which contained the everlasting fire.

Inside, however, was a revelation, and Jay exclaimed in surprise when he walked in and his eyes adjusted. The keeper smiled broadly at him.

'It is . . . charming. Delightful,' he said.

Indeed it was. The floor was of multi-coloured stones laid out in a pattern that matched the timbering of the roof, so that one echoed the other. The walls were whitewashed and a thick band was left uncovered by story boxes at about eye height. This was covered in paintings of the life of the village, a joyful and extraordinary depiction of men and women and fields and birds.

'Good heavens! Isn't that remarkable? So that's what Henary wanted me to look at.'

'It is old,' she replied with pride. 'We repair it when we have to.'

'I'm glad to hear it. It must be unique in the world. At least, I have never heard of such a thing before. Many halls have floors, often elaborate ones, and I know that some have paintings. But I have never heard of anything so lovely. I'm glad I came now. Can you tell me what the pictures are?'

She was now in an exceptionally good mood, delighted with Jay's delight, and proud to have impressed a student of Ossenfud. 'It begins here, with the foundation of the village. You see these figures? They are the first families, from whom all descend. Then here we have the division of the land, and the building of the first Story Hall – it burned down, so the earliest stories were lost, except for those that were remembered and could be written down again. The second Story Hall, here . . .'

Jay stared, entranced. 'Who painted it?'

'We do not know,' she said. 'A traveller who wanted food. He listened to us talking round the fire and sketched out a picture of a tale, so it is said. He painted one small picture in exchange for lodging, and then the council offered to let him stay if he painted some more. It is said he stayed for a year, then moved on.'

'When was this?'

'Generations back. I do not know.'

'So is he in the stories from that period?'

'There may be mention of him.'

'What was his name?'

'I do not know. He was known as Fortune, as people thought he brought good luck.'

'I would like to know more about him. If I got permission and came back . . . ?'

'We would have to put it to the council, but with my recommendation I am sure you would be received as an honoured guest.'

Then Jay remembered the task of keeping Henary happy. 'First I will have to go back to Ossenfud and report my failure to find Jaqui.'

'Some time ago,' she began quietly, looking at him to see his reaction, 'Jaqui came to me and asked a favour. He asked to leave something in the Story Hall.'

Clearly he had just passed some sort of test. 'Really? He wrote his story? Was he ill?'

'No, but he thought it of importance and was afraid that it might become damaged or lost. It was unusual, but he had recently assisted my eldest daughter through a difficult childbirth. I owed him a favour in return, and this was what he asked for.

'It was a packet, wrapped up in strong paper and tied firmly. He said it would belong to the person who could make use of it. I doubt it is of any real value or importance. Jaqui was touched, you know. We learned to ignore these periods, but he would rave and talk in voices, fall on the floor and weep. He did not become violent, but he suffered badly and made no sense. I believe that he wrote at these times.'

'In which case the writings would make no sense either.'

'Perhaps not.'

'May I see, at least?'

'Please sit at the desk, and I will prepare the package for you.'

So Jay sat and composed himself until the woman returned and put the package on the desk in front of him, then backed away. Jay ignored her, for it was wrong to speak in the presence of another's memories.

Slowly he undid the rough string that held the package together and opened it. Inside was a book, covered in leather, of beautiful design and manufacture.

On top was a piece of paper, written in a script that was

103

perfectly legible, and all the more shocking for being so.

'Read if you can, and a curse on him who will not understand. May he have my misfortune.'

Jay let out a cry of terror that echoed around the beautiful hall.

'Do not approach,' he said to the woman as she came running over. 'The package is cursed.'

She retreated swiftly. 'Are you all right?'

'So far.'

'What are you going to do?'

'I don't know.'

He read the curse again and considered its wording. 'Read if you can . . .' Well, he could read, although a curse which could not be understood was of little power. A curse if you will not understand. Did that mean a curse if you do not understand, or a curse if you refuse to understand? What if he simply could not understand, because the script was meaningless? He would not understand, but not because he refused to do so. Besides, the curse might apply to the text he had just read, not to the content of the book. That he had read and understood, he thought, in all its possible meanings.

Jay thought, weighed the options, then reached for the book. 'It is all right,' he called out. 'I have disarmed the curse. It can do me no harm.'

'I think,' he added in an undertone as he opened it.

The book was some forty pages long, written on both sides of the paper with a fine black ink which had not faded in any way, although it was difficult to tell the age. He peered at it carefully; evidently it was made up of letters, but few made any sense to him. He flipped through the pages one after the other, hoping that somewhere it would turn into something recognisable, but the manuscript refused to cooperate. Nor was there any explanation which would allow him to unravel the meaning. He needed to take it to Henary. He might understand it.

'What's all that stuff downstairs, Professor?' Rosie asked after an absence of several days when, unaccountably as far as he was concerned, she had failed to drop in for tea and a chat.

'Eh? Oh, that all belongs to Mrs Meerson,' he said. 'Why do you ask?'

'Just wondering. I went down there to look for Jenkins. Who is she? A friend of yours?'

'Angela? A very old friend, yes. She mainly lives in France, and is storing all of that stuff until she takes it there, although she never seems to get around to it. I inherited it from Tolkien when he retired and needed space for his library.'

'Who is he?'

'Another friend. She was keeping it in his garage, and didn't know what to do with it all when he moved, so I said she could have the cellar. It's not as if I ever use it.'

Lytten looked at Rosie curiously, but did not press the matter. 'Now, what are we going to do about Professor Jenkins? I confess I am quite worried about him.'

The Mysterious Affair of the Missing Cat was indeed a concern. It was most unusual behaviour. Even how he had got out of the house was unknown.

'A locked room mystery,' Lytten pronounced. 'Someone broke in and stole the cat, carefully locking the door as they left, in which case – why no ransom note? Or the cat has learned to fly, and escaped up the chimney on its own. Or – and here I fix you with my piercing gaze and force a confession out of you – it was you, Rosalind Wilson, who stole the cat, constructing an elaborate story to throw me off the scent. Means, opportunity.'

'But no motive,' the girl said. 'I mean, Professor, really. Who on earth would want your cat?'

'Very true. No one in their right mind would want Professor Jenkins. That's what comes of taking your plots from books. Life, alas, is always new and different and rather more complicated. We must be looking for a lunatic. Or, of course, the idiot animal just wandered off, got confused and is now hopelessly wedged under a piece of furniture, too fat to move, too lazy to cry out, like Winnie the Pooh in the rabbit hole. It will no doubt wait until I am fast asleep and then start yowling until I rescue it, foul night-waking cat.'

'Pardon?'

'Shakespeare, my dear. *The Rape of Lucrece*.'

Rosie blushed.

'A fine poem, although not his best. Based on the Roman legend. Do you know the story? It is very famous as a tale of the consequences when the powerful abuse their position . . .'

This gave Lytten an opportunity to discourse while he made the girl some tea, ranging from Ovid right the way through Shakespeare and Hogarth, then on to a recent opera he had seen and thoroughly disliked.

'We are our past, my dear, and if you want to know the future you have to know what has already taken place. The past is everywhere in us. Even in little things, like names. Take yours, for example.'

'What about it?' Rosie did not like her name. It was the sort of name grandmothers had. She wanted a modern name. Like Sandra.

'You are named – accidentally or on purpose I could not say – after the most perfect character in all of English literature.'

'Really?'

'You are. Rosalind, in *As You Like It*, is by far the finest of Shakespeare's inventions. She is bold, witty, intelligent, kind, beautiful and not at all soppy. Often enough his women are either silly or murderous. Rosalind is magnificent in all respects, so much so that I am sure she must have been based on someone he knew and admired greatly. So, my dear, you were once Shakespeare's beloved. Not many young girls can boast of such a thing.'

'I should say not,' she replied, greatly impressed.

*

When Rosie received a message a few days later saying that Lytten had been unexpectedly called away and asking her to keep an eye open for Jenkins in his absence, she was delighted. She was worried about the cat, but excited because it meant she would have a free run of his cellar for a while. She had had a very bad fright in Lytten's house. She did not like to be frightened; it happened only very rarely, and she was now suffering from an overwhelming, burning curiosity. She had lain awake at night, thinking. Dancing in her head as she stared at the ceiling were the jumbled memories of the cellar, the dank, gloomy squalor, the smell, the dust. Then the birds, the soft wind, the beauty . . .

The more she thought, the more she doubted her own sanity. Psychological disturbance, the Professor had called it. How could it have happened, after all? She was a reasonable girl, and had tried to come up with an explanation, although she was hampered by a reluctance to tell anyone what she had seen.

The only thing she could think of that made any sense was that Lytten had in his basement – or this Mrs Meerson had – a new and terribly clever cinema machine, or a new type of television. But she was pretty certain that neither had mastered the art of making you feel the wind, or smell pine needles in the heat, let alone creating young boys who offer to serve you.

No. It was either a delusion or it was real. The former might mean she was insane, which would distress her parents, so she felt obliged, for their sake, to establish the truth. As Poirot himself was fond of saying, she needed more evidence before the mystery could be solved.

The first opportunity came a couple of days after the delivery of Lytten's note. She told her mother she planned to stay on for an extra choir rehearsal, which was entirely believable. Rosie sang well, and this year they were going to perform *Zadok the Priest* with (as a concession to what teachers considered modernity) some catchy numbers from *The King and I* for afters. Rosie – whose burgeoning tastes were beginning to drift far from Broadway musicals but who could still appreciate a good tune – was quite happy to sing anything. Ordinarily rehearsals took place on

Thursday, but an extra one would not be queried. This gave her a blank couple of hours in which to settle the matter of the cellar once and for all.

The amount of time she had spent reading detective stories now proved its worth. She did not have to break in, as she already had the key, but she did have to establish that the basement was empty and set up a warning system in case the mysterious Mrs Meerson appeared. She raided Professor Lytten's kitchen for a length of string and some empty cans. These she strung together and tied at ankle height across the doorway, invisible in the darkness. No one could get in without tripping over them and making a noise. Rosie would have a couple of minutes' notice, she thought, if anyone did come back to the house.

Her preparations made, she opened the door to the cellar and tiptoed down the stairs. She checked that the place was indeed deserted, and went over to the rusting piece of ironwork in the corner. It was most certainly there; at least she hadn't invented that. She did not know what she wanted to happen next. It might, after all, be safer if she was deluded. That at least could be explained. There'd be nothing except a couple of old spades and a metal bucket. She would laugh, feel stupid, then go home, glad she hadn't mentioned it to anyone.

But she didn't really want to be wrong. She didn't want to spend her time wondering if she was seeing things every time she noticed something slightly unusual or unexpected.

She stepped to the curtain, shut her eyes against the disappointment, and pulled it back.

A sudden light penetrating her closed eyelids was all she needed to be reassured about her sanity. While before there had been a glorious view across a valley bathed in sunlight, now there was a wooded landscape; clumps of trees and brushwood mainly, no river and no valley. It did look sunny, though; she could see small white clouds in an otherwise perfectly blue sky. There was only the slightest wind, judging by the way the branches and leaves were moving.

She took a deep breath and walked through.

It felt like a spring afternoon, but much warmer and drier than she was used to. The leaves on the trees were young and not all properly opened. There was a thick mass of bluebells in a patch a few hundred feet away, and she knew that meant spring, even if she didn't know much about plants.

So what now? She had established that this was real. Now if she were sensible she would go straight back through the iron thing – which on this side was merely a faint patch of light, rather like looking through a window that had slightly steamed up. You could see through it perfectly well, but the image beyond was a little blurred. She should do exactly as she had done last time, take a look around, then get back to safety. She was a cautious, sensible girl, she told herself.

The smell of that dank kitchen, the cold of the autumn weather and the prospect of a shepherd's pie for dinner, followed by English homework and a list of French irregular verbs did not appeal, though. Who would want to learn another speech from *Julius Caesar* when she had a sunny wood to explore? Who could not want to know where this place was, and what it was? It was not as if it looked dangerous, or anything like that.

'What I'll do,' she said to herself, 'is just have a look around.' Being a practical girl, she took off her coat and draped it over a bush, so she would be able to find the way back easily. She reached in her pocket and brought out a supply of sweets. Theseus in the labyrinth, she thought. Drop the sweets and leave a trail back to safety. Doubly secure and cautious.

'Now,' she continued in a conversational vein, speaking to no one. 'Where am I? In a wood, obviously. But it's not just a wood. It's warm, for a start. And it's in Professor Lytten's cellar. Perhaps it's magic?'

This was a tricky question. Had it been posed a year or two earlier, Rosie would, undoubtedly, have said yes; it would have been the first explanation to come into her head. Had it been asked a year later, she would have scornfully refused even to contemplate such a silly idea. But she was in between these two blessed states of certainty, so she left the question unanswered.

To her right was a gap which, if not exactly a path, at least offered the possibility that she might squeeze through without getting her legs scratched by brambles. She walked off, turning back when she got to the line of trees to make sure she could see her coat. It was still there, hanging on the branch, looking a little peculiar in its surroundings. She had read about forests in her childhood. Little Red Riding Hood had a red cloak, too, and look what nearly happened to her. Rosie walked as quietly as possible, cursing her refusal to join the Girl Guides. She was sure that tracking and approaching things unobtrusively was part of the training. But the uniform! All those dreadful songs! Never.

The path did a sharp left-hand turn and opened out into

another clearing, much larger than the first.

Rosie stopped dead, suddenly cautious and quiet in her alarm.

In the middle of the clearing there was a low stone wall enclosing a broad oval patch of rough grass. At the far end was a stone structure that looked like one of the bigger graves in the cemetery where she had to go once a year, when her mother put flowers on her grandfather's grave. That was not the cause of Rosie's caution, however. She stopped, her heart pounding, because a young man was leaning over it, tracing the letters written on the side with his finger. One foot was on a lump of rock and in his other hand he rested his weight on a long pole. His clothes were the most striking thing about him; he was wearing a light blue cloak, although it was quite old-looking and threadbare, some form of shorts underneath and a tunic, with sandals of a sort Rosie had never seen before, a flat sole laced up and over the feet, then up the ankle to keep them in place.

He didn't look dangerous but still, he was so odd in appearance . . . Rosie moved, ever so slightly, to get a better view, and the foolishness of failing to join the Girl Guides was amply demonstrated. She stood on a twig, which broke in two with a sharp crack.

The young man looked up at the noise, and saw her.

12

Henry Lytten, the man who dutifully taught his students and whose reputation, such as it was, centred on a deep knowledge of Elizabethan pastoral, had once had a more turbulent life. He was, after all, one of those rare people with a facility for languages and the analysis of texts. He had mastered French and Italian with ease at an early age; another accomplishment of his months in bed as a child was a decent knowledge of German, which he taught himself with only a dictionary, a grammar and his father's copy of Schiller to practise on.

School taught him little except the art of survival, but an encouraging father sent him off regularly as he approached manhood to travel through Europe. There his conversational skills were honed and he learned much about the people whose languages he was coming to know perfectly.

Such abilities were rare, and in 1939 they saved Lytten from some of the more obvious miseries of war. They were too valuable to be shot at; once he was called up he was rapidly transferred to Intelligence – something of a misnomer at the start of hostilities – where initially he spent his time interpreting intercepted communications which flooded in over the airwaves. Eventually he began to do more, and was sent to France, parachuting into the Corrèze to liaise with the scattered Resistance movements.

Then, his work done there, he was attached once more to the army as it moved into Germany itself, and stayed there for several years.

He left all of this as soon as he could; what he saw and did in those years confirmed his disenchantment with reality, and he escaped back to his books the moment he was allowed to do so. But he was too valuable to be let go entirely. Not only did he know many people who remained in the Service, he retained also a quite extraordinary instinct for documents – what they said, what they meant, and what they implied about their authors and recipients. It was part of his past, and so remained part of his present. Several times he had decided to have no more of it; every time he would be summoned by Portmore, now the head of the Service. 'We need you still, Henry,' he'd say in that regretful way he had. 'Your duty.'

He could never refuse. Portmore was one of those people whose patriotism and self-sacrifice was so exceptional everyone else seemed slightly mean in comparison. He had taken on the most dangerous of missions in the war, been wounded, captured, tortured, and come back for more. He couldn't understand anyone who would not want to give their entire life to their country, who did not relish the game of cat-and-mouse with worthy adversaries, be they German, Russian or – as he saw it – American. Portmore had recruited Lytten in the first place, trained, advised, guided and protected him. He was a father figure, a model and an inspiration. The only person Henry was in awe of, but he was at least in good company. The man was accepted by all as the Service's greatest asset, able to operate with the same skill and success in Whitehall as in the Balkans; the only worry was what would happen when he finally retired and left them all leaderless. He knew from old contacts that others were wondering the same thing, and discreetly positioning themselves accordingly.

So Henry never refused a request, always obliged; Portmore had this strange ability to make everyone feel indispensable, as though the future of the Empire – what was left of it – depended on them alone. Every now and then someone would show up at his door, or the telephone would ring and a familiar voice would summon him to lunch in London. 'Just a small job, if you could see your way to helping us out . . .'

Lytten would reluctantly put aside his life, vowing it would be for the last time. Every now and then he would, also, suggest to a promising student that they have a little chat with a friend of his who worked for the government. He never really understood why he offered up sacrifices of young men to a life which he had so hated himself.

He never talked of this to anyone, of course. Of the three regular drinking companions who still remained to meet in the pub, all had had what was termed 'a war'; that is, they had done and seen things which would traumatise most generations of men. They had done their best to pack the experience away in a corner of their memory and forget it. It had no importance for their lives now and, besides, these were people brought up to control their emotions, not to explore them. Lytten had gone into the war cheerful, extroverted, optimistic. He came out of it locked in himself. Only a few people noticed, and they never mentioned it. It was not their business.

The past can be hidden, but never entirely forgotten,

Lytten knew this too. Indeed, his story as it evolved depended on it. 'We are our past,' so he had said to Rosie. Sooner or later it returns. That was why the only unexpected thing about the ring at the doorbell at ten in the evening a few days after that conversation was its timing. Certainly, Lytten gave no sign of surprise when he opened the door and saw the heavily muffled figure, covered in a dark overcoat with a hat pulled down over his face in the gloomy light of the porch.

'What are you doing here?'

'Dinner at high table. I couldn't stand the prospect of pudding, so I thought I'd just drop in. Catch up with an old friend, you know. I hope you weren't off to bed?'

'That is just where I was about to go,' Lytten said. 'Go away.'

'Good. I'd hate to disturb you. I'm soaking and cold. Do you have any brandy?'

Sam Wind took off his coat, folded it over Lytten's arm as though he were a coat rack and walked briskly through to the little table by the fire in the study, on which stood two glass decanters.

He poured himself a generous measure, swept Lytten's unmarked essays from the spare armchair and sat down on it with a sigh, stretching his long legs towards the fire and twiddling his toes to warm them up. He was an angular man with a mop of greying hair and a melancholic face that these days was set in a permanent expression of disappointment. He had delicate hands with bony fingers which he cracked alarmingly when he made a point, and his clothes were expensive but scruffy, with hand-made shoes that hadn't been polished in weeks.

'It's bloody awful out there,' he remarked. 'It's not meant to be winter yet. I hate this country.'

'I thought you were in the business of loving it, reverencing it and defending it with all your heart and soul?'

'Only between the hours of nine and five, Monday to Friday. Rest of the time I am free to detest the grubby little dump.'

'It is good to see you, Sam,' Lytten said, 'but I really was going to bed.'

'I'm sure you were. But you know me well enough to realise I do not walk a mile on a cold night just to visit you.'

He picked up the battered brown briefcase he'd put beside the armchair, pulled out a sealed envelope and tossed it over.

'What's this?'

'How should I know? That's your job, it seems. Orders from on high, from God himself. I'm just the messenger boy.'

'How is Portmore these days?'

'Flourishing, flourishing. How he does it, I do not know. He has this annoying habit of seeming to get younger and more vigorous as the years go by, unlike the rest of us. He sends his best and requests that you do yours. Read, figure it all out, tell us what you think.'

'What if I don't want to?'

Sam looked at him doubtfully. 'Next week some time would be appreciated.'

'Very well, Sam. As you command.'

13

Going outside with Hanslip and heading to the thin sliver of sand that separated the island of Mull from the sea was not a sign of intimacy or favour. Reality was very different from the balmy scene projected inside the building. It was freezing cold, for one thing, which was why Jack More normally took exercise only when it was warmer and when the wind had thinned the thick smog which habitually covered the globe. He felt cold as they walked along; Hanslip, who started shivering within minutes despite being encased in protective gear, was clearly not there for the pleasure of it. At least it wasn't wet, though; he had seen from the news reports that it had been raining without a break for the past three weeks, and the ground – those bits which hadn't been covered in protective concrete – was sodden and muddy, giving off a foul smell of rotting vegetation.

'This is one of the few places where I can be sure I will not be overheard,' Hanslip said as they left the double gateway and stepped into the air. 'It's the wind, mainly, but also a strange effect of the chemicals coming off the sea which disrupts the circuitry. We must put up with the unpleasantness.'

'Being inside all the time makes me feel ill.'

'So I gather. I suppose that's a result of your energetic past.'

'Probably.'

'You never felt like having it fixed? Why is that?'

'I suppose I assume that sooner or later I will leave here and go back to a normal life. What I think of as normal, anyway. I don't want to have it fixed.'

The remarks exhausted Hanslip's interest in the subject. They walked silently for a while, Jack looking at the sea and Hanslip studiously ignoring it, until the older man decided they had gone far enough.

'What do you know about us?'

Jack tried to formulate a sensible reply. 'I know this institute is of middling stature, that it is financially fairly secure, and that it employs a disproportionate number of people of doubtful quality.'

'Doubtful quality? What do you mean by that?'

'Some have been tagged as uncooperative and a few as borderline renegade. They are not the people a top-rank operation, or one engaged in sensitive research, would employ.'

'We must be insignificant as we get the dregs no one else wants, is that what you mean?'

'Well . . .'

'Of course it is. You are quite right. A very second-rate organisation we are.' Hanslip smiled. 'Stuck on this revolting island on the fringes of nowhere. Nobody thinks we're of the slightest importance and nobody pays much attention to what we are doing. Which is why it is so very annoying that this has happened.'

'Then what are you doing?'

'We are unlocking the deepest mysteries of the universe. Gaining access to worlds beyond the imagination, even beyond the power of science itself. We are conquering what does not exist.'

Jack considered this portentous remark. 'Would you care to tell me what that means?'

'Yes, although I must remind you of the need for secrecy. If you are to look for Angela Meerson, you need to know, if only to give you a sense of how important this is, and how urgent it is that you find her.'

Hanslip skirted round a solitary pile of seaweed, giving it a glance of distaste.

'You know as well as I do that my contract here requires the highest level of discretion and loyalty. It is what you pay me for.'

'Indeed. We have discovered a means of accessing parallel universes. Only one, at the moment, but once we understand the process properly, then potentially an infinite number. The space and resources that might become available to humanity would be stunning. It is also, of course, a scientific discovery of extraordinary importance.'

There didn't seem much to say to this, so Jack contented himself with: 'Really?'

'Is that the best you can do?'

'Congratulations, then.'

'Officially, as you say, we are a minor little operation trying to eke out a few efficiencies in power transmission. In the last few years we have been quietly devoting ourselves to this other project. Angela noted a strange anomaly while running an experiment. We kept on getting more energy out than we were putting in. On its own it is a fabulous discovery: with the right equipment, a single watt of electricity could in theory power an entire city of millions. Since then we have refined the technology and discovered that if we do this in a tightly controlled space, then we can actually shift physical objects.'

'How do you get from there to assuming the existence of parallel universes?'

'That's probably beyond your ability to understand,' Hanslip replied in a slightly superior tone. 'We transmit the matter – we began with electrons and have built up to more complex objects – then recover it. Analysis proves it has been gone for longer than it has been gone, if you see what I mean. The only scientifically valid explanation is that the matter has existed in a different state of reality. Another universe, in effect.'

'Can you get to it, though? Electrons are one thing, but . . .'

'We can. We have. There are now three machines. The first has been operational for four years and is capable of dealing with little more than molecules. The second was completed six months ago and can take up to two hundred kilograms; this has provided all the confirmation we need.'

'What about the third?'

'Still under development. It will take up to fifteen tonnes. It is designed to be able to move metal. Its power consumption will be colossal, though; far more than we can afford at the moment, and even more than Angela used up.'

Jack could see what the man meant by a discovery of extraordinary importance. He remained sceptical, however. What were the chances of a small, unimportant organisation making such a gigantic leap forward when others hadn't even come near?

'I hope you're not suggesting that this mathematician of yours might have decided, in a carefree way, to go off and hide in a different universe? That would be suicidal lunacy, wouldn't it?'

'Quite. And although Angela is a lunatic, she is not suicidal. That's why I am sure she has done nothing of the sort.'

'So . . . ?'

'Angela is a psychomathematician,' Hanslip said. 'She works by harnessing emotions to power her calculations, and further enhancing these through the use of powerful stimulants. It is a highly specialised technique, but people established centuries ago that many people could do maths by associating complex calculations with things like shapes or colours. It is a sort of controlled insanity and in the right hands it can outperform any computer in intuition. Angela's intuitions then have to be converted into orthodox calculations, of course, but she has done extraordinary work. Unfortunately, the process makes her emotionally unstable. In the last few months she was obsessively advancing a theory so outlandish it could not possibly be true, and fell in love with it to the point that she became capable of irrational actions to defend it.'

'She is nuts, then?'

'Sometimes. Her response to her calculations is like a mother defending a child, literally so. When she is in one of these states she would die, or kill, to protect whatever she is working on. She had come up with a new idea and wanted to stop the entire programme to explore it. She would not take no for an answer, and was incapable of listening to reason.'

'Why does she work like that?'

Hanslip considered how to answer, coughing occasionally

from the pollution in the air. 'She was always exceptionally talented, but to enhance this she was subjected to a procedure some eighteen years ago. That is, she was put into an artificial coma, and a pregnancy was induced. The complex emotional responses were then captured and harnessed.'

'How revolting. Was it voluntary?'

'No,' Hanslip said flatly, 'and it was nothing to do with me. It was years before she came to work here. The procedure worked in that it greatly augmented her abilities, but it also made her so wayward that she became almost unemployable.'

'Why are you telling me this?'

'You've got to find her, and you'll need to take account of her unpredictability. Besides, one of the people involved in that experiment arrived here yesterday. It may be that he triggered some response and sent her into a panic.'

'It couldn't just be that she is suicidal?'

'I doubt that. She would not risk depriving humanity of anything as important as herself.'

'She's that vain?'

Hanslip nodded. 'Oh, yes. Personally I always thought it the best proof of the existence of multiple universes. One isn't nearly big enough to contain her vanity.'

'Anything else?'

'Perhaps. I refused to reconfigure the experiment as she wished, but she went ahead and did it anyway. She began diverting time and resources away from the official programme to her own activities.'

'Was that why you suspended her?'

'I had no choice, but for Angela it may have been like having a newborn infant ripped from her arms. I had to ensure she could do no damage, either to the experiment or to herself. You must understand that this programme is way beyond our resources. Potentially it could be the largest research project ever undertaken. It is now getting to the stage where we need a more formal arrangement with a better resourced partner.'

'Who?'

'Oldmanter.'

Jack whistled.

'Zoffany Oldmanter controls the most important and powerful institutions on the planet. He has the resources to develop this properly, in a way we could not. It is a sensible and necessary move. The negotiations were going very well indeed, until I found out that Angela had been misappropriating resources. I knew she would be likely to spread false rumours about the project in order to destroy any possibility of a partnership.'

'I see. Did she know of this?'

'It might help explain her actions. The point is that we must find her. For all her difficulties, she is exceptionally able and the only person who truly understands the deep science behind this. I do not want her going off to a rival, and I don't want her scaring people with half-baked theories. Also . . .' He paused with evident reluctance at having to admit the scale of the disaster the woman had unleashed. 'Also, she seems to have erased all the data before she left.'

'What data?'

'Everything concerning the project, going back six years. All the prime documentation, all the copies, backups. Unless we retrieve it, it will set us back a decade or more, perhaps even kill the project altogether. The machine can be used twice more. Then it will need to be recalibrated, which we cannot now do.'

'Why?'

'It's very sensitive. A prototype which requires constant maintenance, otherwise it becomes dangerously unreliable. Angela was working on how to stabilise it, but that is information that disappeared with her. So unless we get the data back, or Angela back, then it is dead.'

'Where might she have gone?'

'Our predictions are ninety-seven per cent that she has gone into hiding, probably amongst renegades. That, I understand, was your area of expertise before you came here.'

Jack nodded. 'I was in the Social Protection Service. I monitored the activity of Retreats.'

'There is a 2.94 per cent chance that she did indeed go off her head and use the machine, in which case she will be beyond our reach. The idea that she may have been converted into a thousand trillion particles scattered across multiple universes is appealing, but not necessarily true just because it would give me pleasure.'

Jack did a quick calculation. 'What about the remaining 0.06 per cent? What's that?'

'A generous overstatement. That is the chance that she is right.'

'About what?'

Hanslip waved his hand dismissively. 'She couldn't be. So go and find her.'

*

Hanslip's main task was to stem the possibility of any leak and there was one huge, obvious hole in the institute's defences, wandering around the place with a bland look on his face. This was Lucien Grange, sent by the great Zoffany Oldmanter to negotiate the partnership to exploit Angela's discovery. Hanslip was uncomfortably aware that the man's unexpected arrival could well have been what had pushed Angela over the edge. That had badly harmed his negotiating position; thanks to Angela, he no longer had the tight grip on the technology he needed. He had the machine, certainly. But only Angela really understood it.

His first task was to ensure that Grange did not realise this, and that no link could be established between the institute and the cataclysm that had spread over northern Europe. The news kept getting worse; Hanslip stopped looking when the death toll reached nine thousand and the public calls to find the perpetrators became shrill and hysterical. Luckily, everyone's first instinct was to assume it was the work of terrorists, renegades dedicated to sabotaging the smooth running of society. Punishment was promised, violently backed up by messages from Hanslip, pointing out that the surge had caused considerable damage to delicate instrumentation in his institute and demanding compensation. It would work for a while, but not for long.

He was furious that Grange had shown up now. He had known that Angela would be difficult, but he had been certain that he could bring her round to the idea of collaborating with Oldmanter eventually. Grange's arrival had been discreet by Oldmanter's standards – none of the usual helicopters, armed guards, let alone the motorcades that announced the arrival of a scientist of importance – but was still hardly secret. Angela, he knew, was quite likely to have noticed.

The trouble was that she was so impractical. She was into purity, the elegance of the research. She didn't care that the money was draining away or that it was getting harder and harder to keep supplies flowing in. She wasn't bothered that in six months' time they would be out of funds completely. When that happened, he would have no choice but to take whatever terms he could get. So he had delicately courted Oldmanter, tempting him with hints and suggestions, letting him see some of the work, grasp the possibilities. He knew everything – except how it worked.

The worst of it was that Oldmanter was interested and excited, and the greater his interest, the more coy Hanslip had become. He had talked of perhaps not needing a partner. Of talking to others. He had played (in his opinion) a poor hand brilliantly.

His ace was Angela. She alone truly understood the science, and as long as he controlled access to her, he would be indispensable. He had to keep her quiet and out of the way until the deal was done and he had the time to persuade her to accept the situation. Now she had not only ruined his careful plans, she threatened to bring the entire institute down around their heads.

If Grange figured out where the surge had come from, then the security forces would arrive within twenty-four hours. So, first things first. First Grange, then Angela. Then he would have space to manoeuvre.

*

Two hours later, a furious Grange was brought into Hanslip's office under escort. There were security guards on his door, he said as he sat down. He had not been allowed out, been forbidden to communicate with the outside world. It was an outrage. Was this the way to build the trust necessary for a working relationship?

Hanslip eyed him carefully as he waited for the expressions of indignation to subside. He was no more impressed now than he had been during their meetings of the past few days. The anger seemed artificial and unnatural, an act put on to intimidate.

'Terrible error,' he said. 'I can't imagine what security thought it was doing. Naturally, I offer my full apologies.'

'You realise what sort of message this could send?'

Hanslip nodded. 'Of course. We have a crisis here, as you may have noticed, and the security system got a little jumpy. It concluded that there was too close a coincidence between your arrival and the disappearance of Angela Meerson, and so . . .'

'I heard about that.'

'I know. We are investigating the possibility that you were responsible for her flight. Did you have any encounter with her?'

'A brief one. She sought me out.'

'So she remembered you?'

'Perhaps.'

'You understand why I am asking? She has an inflated view of her own importance. She considers this technology to be her own; she will not allow anyone to take it, and will never leave it. Maternal protectiveness. You should know; you put it there. I have spent years carefully cosseting her, and then you turn up, and within twelve hours she has become unbalanced and disappeared. Naturally, our main concern is that she may seek protection from one of our rivals.'

'Then perhaps we should move a little faster? If we can finalise an arrangement quickly, then we can take legal ownership before anyone else does. Another organisation might think it could ignore your claims, but I doubt anyone would be foolish enough to take us on.'

'Legal ownership?'

'I have come with a draft proposal. We believe it requires much more investment than you suggest. As the funds for this will come from us, we will naturally require a higher stake.'

'How much higher?'

'Eighty-five per cent.'

'We had agreed a fifty–fifty split,' Hanslip protested.

'That was last week,' Grange said with a smile. 'Before you had a security breach, before you lost your prime researcher, before you killed nearly ten thousand people and caused nearly seventy billion dollars' worth of damage, and before you engaged in a criminal conspiracy to conceal your involvement.'

'I'm sure I do not understand what you are talking about.'

'I am equally sure that you do. You will sign whatever agreement I choose to put before you, and you will do it by the time I leave this evening.' He smiled and stood up. 'We will proceed with or without your mathematician.'

'You will find that difficult.'

'We'll manage. That is the end of the discussion. I'm

afraid you must take it, or take the consequences of refusal. This is a cruel world in which to be without friends, and with powerful enemies.

'Now,' he went on brightly, 'as this Meerson woman is no longer around, I imagine that you are not quite so desperate to keep me out of the laboratory where she worked. So I would like to see this machine of yours. If you will show it to me, then we can sign these papers, and I will be on my way.'

*

When Hanslip was angry he did not, like Angela, shout, turn red or throw things. Over many years he had learned to focus the anger. He entered a state of calm. As he walked with Lucien Grange to the laboratory, he was very angry indeed.

Grange's brutal exposition of the facts brought him to the point where he knew he only had two rational choices: submit or resist. He knew, also, that his thinking was far from rational. He was tired, for one thing, and very shaken. He had supported and sustained Angela for years. His reward had been a comprehensive, total betrayal, with Grange now preparing to administer the final blow. Were they in it together? Had Angela been bought by Oldmanter? Was she already setting up her new laboratory in one of his research facilities? Unlikely, but Hanslip was able to consider any possibility now, as long as it was unpleasant.

He could sign or refuse to sign. Or he could behave rather as Angela would in the same position. It was not a reasoned calculation that made him decide, as he opened the doors into the laboratory, to go for the third option. He simply rebelled at the idea of being bullied.

The machine was all fired up, ready for a simulation to try and duplicate what Angela might have done. Hanslip showed Grange around, pointing out the control room and concentrating on the translucent sphere in the middle of the carefully shielded room. He tried to be ingratiating, preserving what little dignity defeat had left him.

'That's the actual transmitter. Small, I know, but you can just get a person in it. We have completed a much bigger one, but it is not yet ready to be used. This one isn't really intended for people, you see. Mainly objects. The new one will have a much greater capacity.'

'What's it made of?'

'It's just a shape created by magnetic fields. If you get into it and lie flat, you float a few inches above the floor. It gives a very peculiar feeling, almost like weightlessness. We were thinking at one stage that we could market it as a recreational tool of some sort, or maybe a bed. Do try, if you want. It is extraordinarily comfortable and perfectly safe.'

Lucien crawled in and stretched out. 'Yes,' he said in a muffled voice, 'very pleasant.'

'Some volunteers have found it so calming they drop off to sleep.'

'How do I get out?'

'You have to release the fields surrounding you. That can only be done from the outside, or through the power shutting down automatically.'

'Very interesting and, as you say, quite calming,' he called out. 'Still, I've had enough, so could you let me out?'

'I'm afraid not.'

Hanslip, Grange noticed by twisting his body round to see more clearly, was now alone in the room with him. The two technicians had vanished. The director squatted down, so that their faces were at the same level.

'I do not take kindly to being bullied and threatened.'

'Don't be ridiculous,' Grange said. 'Business is business, and you need our protection. Let me out now.'

Hanslip smiled. 'Very well. Just a moment.'

He left Lucien floating oddly in mid-air in the half-darkened room and strolled next door to the control room. Everything was running; setting up required many people but once all the systems were on automatic they were no longer necessary. He placed the palm of his hand on the matt black surface and felt the information he needed coursing up his nerves and into his brain. With twenty seconds to go he cancelled the original programme; then he summoned up the reserve power he needed and spun the dial to increase massively the scale of the transmission. Then the control panel froze as the automated transmission sequence took over.

A fraction of a second later and it was done. It was always a disappointing moment. Nothing changed, nothing happened. According to Angela, that was because nothing did change. The matter was still in the chamber, sort of. Only when the field dissolved would reality coalesce. Until then the contents were both there and not there. They would remain in a state of latent non-existence for ever.

Hanslip briefly considered this option, but decided it was a bad idea. It was too extreme. Besides, he needed the machine.

He ran a little routine to erase the records and overlay data to demonstrate that they had merely been testing the equipment. He made sure that it was impossible to unravel what had happened, then summoned the technicians back to wind the operation down.

'Thank you, gentlemen,' he said. 'Our visitor has gone off in a state of high excitement. You should have seen the look on his face.'

14

Alex Chang wandered around the streets of Oxford in a reverie of overpowering sensations. He now had only one thing in his head. He needed, wanted, to sleep. He was more tired than he could believe. Whatever had happened to him had been exhausting. Or perhaps he just hadn't slept for a long time?

Where could he sleep? It was already getting colder, the sky was darkening. What was he to do? He searched in his memory for guidance, but there was nothing. He had to lie down, that was all.

He stumbled around for a few more hours, trying to stimulate some sort of response, but to no avail. Eventually he could do no more. He was going to fall over, hurt himself, or get killed by one of the vehicles that passed by, belching smoke only inches from where unprotected people walked. They seemed used to it; they would just walk out into the path of the oncoming traffic and get to the other side perfectly safely. Their sense of timing was extraordinary. He stood watching this reckless display of skill from young and old, men and women for a long time.

He settled in a doorway down a little alley. It was quiet; the streets were almost deserted, and that solitude was enough to scare him on its own. He had figured out enough to realise that sleeping outside was unusual and possibly dangerous. It required either immense trust or utter desperation. He hid himself as far back as possible, where he hoped he would not be noticed, and drew his knees up to his chest. It was cold and uncomfortable. He'd never manage to fall . . .

The memories flooded back in his dreams as he slept and the sheer quantity of information that coursed through his head was overwhelming. Too much or too little; it was always the same. Why can't they ever get the settings right? Who are they, though? He knew enough to realise that he hadn't pieced everything together yet but when he woke up several hours later – stiff, cold and hungry – he felt at least he was making progress. He knew who he was; he knew where he was. Now he had to establish when he was.

He stood up, stretched and walked from his hiding place into the street. Rubbish of all sorts was thrown onto the ground in this place, or into bins with little thought of the health considerations. Paper was used in vast quantities. He scuffled through one of the bins, unaware of the few passers-by who glanced disapprovingly at him as they passed. He found something of use. A large piece of paper with what he decided was a greasy piece of fried potato stuck to it, and a heavy smell of what he analysed as vinegar. There was writing on it. *Daily Herald*, it said. Below it a date. October 18th, 1960.

Instantly, another memory arrived, like some sort of reward. Evidently his memory was working by association. When a new stimulus matched some preordained trigger, the appropriate bit of memory was pulled into his awareness to fill in another gap. 'If all has gone according to plan,' came the voice in his head, 'you are now in Oxford, some time in 1960.'

So it seems, he thought.

There was a flippant tone to it which he found annoying. He wished whoever it was would stick to the facts and cut out the commentary. He wasn't in the mood for idle chatter.

'Apart from paranoia and a great deal of fear, it is a time with little to complain about; even the poor are cared for, more or less. In this part of the world, at least, no one has starved to death for some time. The same cannot be said for other parts of the world, but the local population is able to show a remarkable lack of interest in anyone but themselves. They pay for it eventually, but you may be able to avoid the worst . . .'

Very interesting, he thought. How does that help me get something to eat? I'm starving.

'Glad you asked. Try a cafe. But you need some money first.'

The domain of Willdon lay some three days' travel to the south and west of Ossenfud, in a series of river valleys noted for their fertility and lushness. A domain was a particular thing; entirely independent, but containing no town or main settlement. Rather, it was a whole series of farms big and small, of villages and hamlets and one great house which gave the entire area its name. All were the possession of the domain, and the domain was the possession of one person.

This was Catherine, the widow who had come to her role on the death of her husband, Thenald. Such a thing was unusual; the desire for strict family rights would ordinarily have meant that it would have passed to a member of the family by blood. But one was disqualified by his character, the other by his position. For Thenald had been brutally murdered by his heir, Pamarchon, who had fled and left the scholar Gontal as the next in line.

Nobody, except Gontal, regarded this prospect as anything but a disaster. Joining the wealth of Willdon to the authority of Ossenfud would have unsettled the whole land, creating a power which could not be resisted. Henary had been the one who had deflected the threat.

He had been at Willdon when the catastrophe happened, so naturally his advice had been sought. The death of Thenald, he said, was a monstrosity without parallel.

Perhaps it was merely the start. Perhaps at this moment outlaws were gathered in the forest, planning their attack on a leaderless, confused domain. Willdon needed a leader quickly. It had to choose now.

And Gontal? Henary had said what the man should have thought. Gontal was a scholar, he pointed out. Would he give up such honour for mere wealth and power? The people of Willdon had considered his remarks, and an hour later had elected Catherine, who knew the domain, who had run it already and who was, in any case, already more popular than her husband had ever been. They chose well.

Only Gontal was displeased when he arrived, too late, the next day.

'My dear friend,' Henary had said, 'I naturally assumed . . . Did I do wrong?'

'Of course not,' he said through gritted teeth. 'Just what I would have said myself.'

＊

As she was one of the most powerful people in the land, and both unmarried and childless, it was important to know the state of Lady Catherine's mind and so scholars were constantly finding reasons to pay her a visit, beyond the usual ones that their duties prescribed. All were after the same information: what would happen to Willdon should she die?

Catherine found this both amusing and exasperating. She once remarked to a visiting scholar of particular dullness that it might be easier for everyone if she merely wrote a weekly letter detailing her health and marital status. That would spare them the trouble of having to travel so far. She intended to hold on to her lands until her death, and she was in no hurry to discover whether or not the narratives of the Afterlife were true or should properly be interpreted as allegories. As for marriage . . . there were stories about her affections, but anyone who became close to her was much too discreet to talk of it.

Under her rule, the domain had prospered greatly. It had always been wealthy, but now it was, in addition, content. It needed nothing from the outside world; the land provided everything in abundance, fruit and flowers, crops of all sorts. There was fresh water in a multitude of brooks and rivers; good grazing land for cows and sheep; clay for tiles, stone for buildings. Great woods were as well stocked with deer as the lakes and rivers were filled with fish, and the skies with pheasant, doves and partridge. So Henary – waxing a little poetical – explained to Jay when they were about two hours away.

For Jay, this was an immense adventure. Henary had extracted him suddenly from his lessons without explanation and told him to pack a bag. Jay was delighted; very few students ever left Ossenfud except at harvest time, and fewer still were taken on official visits like this. He could scarcely contain his excitement and had been pestering Henary with questions throughout the journey.

'It is a delightful place, although mainly because of the character of the Lady Catherine herself. "She is the sun which keeps the land fertile and content. Her smile makes the flowers bloom, her frown brings the rain."'

Jay racked his memory. 'Level 1, 17?'

'Close. Level 2, 14. The same theme, though. She is an

exceptionally able woman, far more so than her dolt of a husband, who would have brought the domain to ruin had she not restrained him – and had he not so conveniently died. Don't look so shocked, boy. I speak only the truth. A pity you will not meet her. Or even see the Shrine of Esilio, which is certainly the most remarkable thing in the domain.'

'What? I thought . . .'

'She dislikes uninvited guests. Well, she tolerates scholars, of course. As you are only a student, I fear you will have to stay outside.'

'Why did you bring me then?' Jay cried.

'I hate travelling on my own. It is so tiring.'

'That's very unfair.'

Henary looked almost puzzled, although he was more occupied with not showing his amusement. 'Unfair? Why? I give the orders, you obey them. Where is there room for unfairness in that?'

'It is unfair because you made me look forward to something you knew I was not to get.'

'I gave you information and my company. What more could you want?'

Jay wanted to snort with derision, but could not, so fell into a sulky silence instead.

*

When they arrived, Henary left him just outside the borders. On either side of the little track was a stone pillar, each about three feet high, with a bird carved into every side. This, Henary explained, was the sign of her lands, and had been for longer than anyone could remember. Once crossed all but scholars were subject to her laws, and anyone who crossed uninvited – here he looked severely at Jay – could be declared a trespasser.

'You know what that means,' he said. 'Disgrace and servitude. So you have been warned. Busy yourself with pitching the tent over there by that stream, and get back to the fourth theme. You may have forgotten, but I have not, that you have to deliver an oration in two weeks' time. You may embarrass yourself if you wish, but you will not embarrass me.'

He mounted his little horse, saluted his young charge and soon enough disappeared into the woods which lay just ahead of the stone markers.

Jay watched him go. There was one follower only, borrowed from the kitchens for the occasion, as there was no need to maintain the dignity of the college. Nor was Jay yet senior enough to get someone else to do all the work. Had he tried, he would just have got a look of sullen refusal, together with a bad reputation when he returned. Besides, he had no sense of his own place. It never occurred to him not to help out.

'Come on then, let's get the tent up. Then you can start preparing the food and I'll get some firewood.'

His plan was already formed. He knew – everybody knew – about the Shrine, where Esilio had been buried after leading them back from exile countless generations ago. He had read about it; the passages where the old man's body was laid to rest were some of the most beautiful and touching in the entire Story. To come so close and be denied such an experience was too much. He simply had to see it for himself. Besides, it was work, he told himself: to compare the description and the reality. No one would know, no one would see him; Henary would never suspect.

He and the kitchen boy – who was no older than ten at most – put up the tent, and one part of Jay was looking forward to the great luxury of spending the night alone in it. For the first time he was going to have a proper bed, and covers, and everything a young man might desire in the way of comfort. Once, that is, he had done a little exploring. Really, if Henary had been trying to rouse his curiosity he could not have done much better. Still, he would have to be discreet. He did not want the kitchen boy to get into trouble, or to get into trouble himself.

He had fetched wood while the boy prepared the food but deliberately picked up only a very little, just enough for the cooking. By morning, it would all have gone. They could do without, of course; generally few but the most fastidious had anything but cold water to wash in and breakfast was, in any case, just bread or perhaps some cold porridge. Still, they would need more wood for when Henary returned.

'I'll go,' said the lad.

'No. I insist. It was my fault.'

The boy did not argue; he was quite happy to settle down on the ground and dream of whatever ten-year-olds dream of.

So Jay strolled off, going left and staying out of the domain until he could not be seen from the tent. Then, briefly glancing back so he could be sure he was not observed, he veered sharply to the right and walked over the invisible line which divided the domain of the Lady Catherine of Willdon from the common lands outside.

It was completely unremarkable, although he didn't really know what he was expecting. He walked for ten minutes or so straight into the woods, and found them to be perfectly ordinary woods. He crossed a stream, which was a perfectly ordinary stream, and if there were indeed lots of birds they were, for the most part, perfectly ordinary ones. There was little point in continuing to trespass – and risk who knew what punishment – just for the limited pleasure of looking at trees. He decided to go a little further, then turn back. Another ten minutes later, however, he came to a clearing which made him change his mind.

It was a few hundred feet long, covered in soft grass with the trees rising up all around so that they formed a natural circle. Presumably animals came to graze here, and to drink at the stream that cut straight across, tinkling and chortling as it fell through stones and dropped a few feet through a natural, if miniature, waterfall.

Other things in the clearing gave him pause, however. A second, smaller circle was formed by stones set in the middle, each one shaped and covered in moss and lichen. Within this circle were half a dozen tall round columns. His curiosity was aroused and he was, in truth, a bit scared. Were these put there by the hands of giants, those mythical creatures who never existed except in firelight tales?

Then, of course, he realised: this was it, the Shrine of Esilio, the great glory of Willdon. But how very un-impressive it was! It was peaceful and pretty, certainly, but he had imagined something grand, something which overwhelmed with its holiness and majesty. Instead it was

144

just a clearing, surrounded by a circle of stones. What he now realised was the tomb of the Leader was no more than a plain and untended stone oblong. It was one of the most famous places in the whole of Anterwold and he could easily have walked straight across it without giving it a second thought.

He walked around the perimeter for some time, not daring to cross into it for fear of enchantment, but eventually his curiosity could no longer be denied. He put first a hand, then his arm over the boundary. Nothing happened, so he stepped over and ventured further towards the centre.

He wished Henary had been with him; he would be punished for his disobedience, no doubt, but it would be worth it to hear Henary's explanation, for he knew his teacher would have grand tales to tell about the place.

But enough was enough. He had satisfied his curiosity and quelled that irritated feeling deep inside which began to niggle at his soul whenever he was prevented from doing something. He had entered Willdon, seen the Shrine, and now it was time to go back. With one last look at the circle, he began walking down the path that would take him back to the boundary. There was nothing in his mind; just a feeling of contentment to be out in the sun, and satisfaction at having seen something interesting. He paid no attention to anything; didn't hear the twigs breaking behind him, or the rustle of leaves ahead of him. He noticed nothing, in fact, until he went round a gentle bend and saw three armed men standing in the middle of the path. They were tall and strong, and did not look happy to see him.

'Trespasser. You are under arrest, and your freedom is forfeit. Give yourself up peacefully,' one called.

Jay's stomach churned. The trees grew thickly to the path; there was no chance of breaking through the dense undergrowth and getting away. He looked back, but two more soldiers had quietly slipped into view; they must have been following him all along. There was no possibility of escaping, even if the man with the bow proved to be a poor shot. He did not intend to find out.

Instead, he lifted his chin and replied defiantly. 'Who do you call trespasser? I am a student of Ossenfud. I do no harm here.'

'You could be the greatest scholar in the land, and you would still have no right to enter the Lady's domains without her permission. You will give yourself up – peacefully or not, it makes no difference to us.'

'To what end?'

'To what end?' came the mocking reply. 'To the end, young student, of being taken to the tribunal. You have violated the circle, the most precious part of her domain. You have entered the land without her permission. You will be punished for it.'

Jay knew that already; Henary had gone out of his way to explain it. The magnitude of his foolishness now swept over him. Nothing could save him from – what? Henary would be humiliated; to have a student fall from grace in such a spectacular fashion would be a blot on his reputation that would never be forgotten. Jay's own name would be erased from the college roll, his story obliterated from memory. How could he have done anything so stupid?

In the time he took to think this, one of the soldiers had walked up to him and whipped out a rope, which he fastened around his neck – not tightly, but impossible to throw off rapidly. No chance of making a dash for freedom now.

'Right. Two ways of doing this. Peaceful and helpful, or kicking and screaming. Which do you prefer?'

'I'll be peaceful,' Jay said. 'I'm not afraid. When my master hears about this . . .'

'You'll get the worst beating of your life,' the soldier completed for him.

'Then you'll go to the tribunal,' added another.

'Stop the talking,' called the man who was, Jay presumed, the sergeant in charge of the little platoon. 'We've got the other one to catch as well.'

'What other one?' Jay asked. 'There isn't anyone else. I'm quite alone. I left my servant by our camp, outside the domain. You may not touch him.'

'Quiet. You two' – he gestured at the two soldiers who had appeared behind Jay – 'back to your places. Whistle when you hear something.'

Ten minutes later, the whistle floated softly through the trees.

16

A day after Angela's disappearance, Hanslip's various damage limitation committees presented their findings. Some progress had been made in wiping out all suggestions that the damaging power surge had originated with them. None, however, had been made in analysing Angela's machine and establishing if it had been used in earnest.

'Why the hell not?' Hanslip snapped. The strain of the last day was beginning to take a toll. It was so rare for him to display any emotion that the unfortunate target of his frustration fell silent.

'That was the point of the surge,' another said tentatively. The electricity had coursed through their systems, burned through their defences and not only erased all the data but also wiped out any trace of whether the machine had been used. Before it could actually damage the machine itself, it had been diverted into the outside world, where it had caused havoc.

'There is one other thing,' this second man said. 'I spent half a day checking the records in the computing department. It seems that all the data was copied out at noon the previous lunchtime. So presumably a copy of it does still exist somewhere.'

'Why would she do that? She had the information in her head already.'

There was no answer. Hanslip turned away from them

in disgust. 'So now we know what we are dealing with. This is terrorism on a huge scale. Perhaps someone here has something helpful to say? Mr More? Have you found her?'

'I am limited by the fact that you do not wish anyone to know we are looking,' Jack replied. 'Unless you change your orders, I cannot put out a general alert, or search records to see if she checked in anywhere or bought anything. I can't examine surveillance material. If I could do that . . .'

'No. The fewer people who know the better.'

'Then I will have to go the slow way round. I intend to travel south, so I can contact old friends in security and make unofficial enquiries. I plan to leave as soon as possible.'

Hanslip nodded. At least someone was taking the initiative. 'Anything else?'

'Yes,' Jack said, handing over the piece of paper Angela's assistant had pushed into his hand as he was heading for the meeting. 'I was asked to give you this by Mr Chang. He was unable to make an appointment, as he is insufficiently senior to talk to you directly.'

Hanslip looked curiously at him, then unfolded it.

1960, it said.

*

Hanslip summoned Chang the moment the meeting broke up; he had to wait outside until everyone else had gone and only Jack More remained. The director waved the piece of paper at him: 'Well? What does this mean?'

'There is a trace in the historical records for 1960 which

matches Angela Meerson. So I thought it important to tell you.' He had the tone of a man who thought he was perhaps making an enormous mistake. In truth, he was somewhat overawed by being in the same room as the man he had only ever seen before from a distance.

'Did anyone ask you to make such a search?'

Chang blushed a little. 'Mr More here asked me to see if I could think of anything. Data analysis is my speciality, you see, and the techniques are as easily applied to historical records as anything else. So I thought . . .'

'I see. How did you come to this conclusion?'

'Conclusion might be too strong,' he replied. 'I was just experimenting. I know of the theories – her theories, if you see what I mean – and just wanted to check. You know, see if she really had gone to a parallel universe. If she turned up somewhere I could find her, then obviously she hadn't.'

'And?'

'Well, I began by assuming that she does not change her name; I had to start somewhere. So I ran a search for every record with someone of that name in the period after 1700.'

'Why then?'

'It's when the records became good enough. I identified 1,639 individuals. After 2034, when global biological identification became compulsory, it was easy enough to prove that no one recorded was her. I eliminated all those who died before the age of twenty-five, as well as women who had children, as this was a capability she had removed eighteen years ago, and finally took out those who died of a communicable disease she could not have contracted, and I was left with twenty-one people.

'One of these stands out. In 1960, there is a footnote

in an article which states simply, 'My thanks, as usual, to Angela Meerson for her help with translations.' That is all, but the languages referred to are Serbo-Croat, Finnish and Sinhalese, which is a very unusual combination. Angela took a full language suite with her, including those three.

'Significantly, in my opinion, there is no other trace of this individual. There is no birth or death certificate. No parents or siblings. She never fell ill. Never went to school, never paid tax. She may have changed her name to keep out of sight, but there is no trace of her marrying – women then used to adopt their husband's name.'

'Why?'

'No idea. The point is that there ought to be abundant traces. Now, it seems that some personal papers of the man who referred to her still exist, so I would recommend examining them. I haven't had the time to be completely certain.'

'I don't have time either,' Hanslip interrupted. 'This is nonsense. You are peddling this rubbish about time travel that she was obsessing about. You know full well that Angela is not to be listened to when she is in one of her states. Did she tell you to undermine me and sow doubt? Is that what's going on here?'

'Of course not.'

Hanslip glared at him, then relaxed. 'I will consider what you say,' he said in a more even tone. 'Come to my office in an hour.'

*

More was waiting in the corridor when a very frightened Chang presented himself as instructed. He was not pleased. It was obvious to him that efforts to cover up the debacle of Angela's disappearance were becoming increasingly illegal and risky. He did not greatly appreciate being drawn into other people's disasters.

'A second-grade security officer and a junior researcher with a blot on his file,' Chang observed. 'Things must be bad.'

'If anything goes wrong, then it will be useful to blame people like us. How do you fancy global notoriety as a terrorist ringleader?'

'That makes me feel better.'

'It is amazing how the heresy of individualism resurfaces when there is a jail sentence in prospect.'

'Don't worry, gentlemen.' Hanslip's voice echoed around them as the man himself came strolling down the corridor. 'You are both much too useful to be thrown away at the moment. You may have to fill that role eventually, but not yet.'

He led the way into his office and asked them to sit. 'Thank you for your efforts, both of you. I'm afraid I do not know you very well, Mr Chang,' he continued, as though this was somehow the researcher's fault. 'You have been here for about a year, is that correct?'

'Yes. I was a . . .'

'Just answer the questions. In your time as a renegade you spent long periods cut off from all electronic assistance?'

'Yes. It was very strange, to start off with.'

'You experienced no unfortunate consequences? No insanity, no delirium? No mental instability?'

'I was certainly disoriented. It's a most peculiar feeling to be without the chatter in your head, to sleep without adverts popping up in your dreams all the time. Once you get used to it, it can be quite pleasant.'

'What about you, Mr More?'

'Once. When I suffered an injury. I did not enjoy the experience.'

'I see. Now, Mr Chang. You base your conclusion on one solitary line of print, is that correct?'

Alex nodded. 'In an article written by a man called Henry Lytten, who lived in Oxford. He was born in 1910, died in 1979. I now have a copy of the document, if you wish to look at it. As I said, it was published in 1960.'

'There is no other evidence?'

'You must bear in mind that quite a lot of documentation from that period was lost. Finding this was remarkably good fortune.'

'So it would seem,' Hanslip said drily. 'What was the article?'

'I haven't read it yet. It was called "Rosalind as the Universal Ideal: *As You Like It* in the Wider World".'

Hanslip looked at him blankly.

'I have no idea either,' Chang said. 'However, Shakespeare was quite well known.'

Hanslip cut him off. 'Then we must investigate your lead, must we not? We are hardly spoiled for other options.'

'Certainly. I thought that if I went to the Depository . . .'

'Mr More can do that. But only visual confirmation will settle the matter conclusively.'

There was a long silence after this, as both men tried to figure out what he was saying.

'Solid proof,' Hanslip explained. 'Someone must go and check.'

'What? Who?'

'You, of course. Who else?'

'Me?' Chang said, his voice louder and with a touch of panic in it. 'How?'

'The same method you seem to imply she used. The machine. Or do you now want to withdraw your findings?'

'Well, no. I mean, the reference is there.'

'Good. I like a man who stands by his opinion, whatever the consequences.'

'Making a suggestion is one thing –'

'Besides, I'm not asking. I have decided and I have the authority to dispose of you as I see fit. You worked with her, she may well trust you. If indeed this reference is to her, then you are the best person to find and approach her.'

Chang scarcely reacted; Jack studied him carefully as Hanslip talked. He was not frightened, although that, surely, would have been justified. He seemed more alarmed at having to talk to Hanslip than he was at the prospect of being used in such a way. He said nothing, so Hanslip, the matter settled as far as he was concerned, passed on to the next topic. 'You have an appointment in implants in an hour. We will make sure you are properly equipped. Don't worry about that.'

*

After the meeting, Jack continued his investigations into Angela's disappearance and spent the afternoon in his little office, going through old files and records. It was dull and profitless work, and in the evening he took a break and went to find Alex Chang once more. He found him in implant maintenance, sitting on a table looking delirious.

'Are you all right?' he asked.

Chang had an asinine smile on his face from the anaesthetics used when they drilled a tiny hole in his skull. '*Assez bien, mais j'ai pas dormi*,' he began, then stopped.

'I beg your pardon?' Jack asked as a look of alarm passed over the man's face. He opened his mouth, then shut it again.

'New additions,' a technician standing behind him whispered. 'Not properly absorbed yet.'

'Oh. I see. Do you have a sort of buzzing in your head? I remember that from when I had my legal codes updated.'

'*Ja, es ist sehr ärgerlich*.'

'That's the briefings, probably,' the technician continued. 'We loaded everything we had. Bit of a rush job, though. It may give you a few headaches until it settles in,' he said in a loud voice in Chang's ear. 'We gave you a full set of European languages, and you'll have to learn to control them. Try to speak in English. Otherwise you'll just hop from one language to another at random.'

'That's what's wrong, is it?'

'We've given you news reports, maps, guidebooks, various technical manuals. Not a comprehensive selection, I'm afraid, but there should be enough to help you out. All put into your memory so it can be recalled at will. Just think of a question, and the answer will appear. I think. We didn't have time to test it properly.'

Chang shook his head. 'I'm all confused,' he said. 'It's a very odd feeling, this. What was it? It was important.'

'Well?'

'Give me an hour. It may be my head will clear by then. I needed to talk to – what's his name? The man in charge.'

'Hanslip?'

'That's the one.' Chang pursed his lips in determination. 'That's right. I need to see him. I found something else. It's important. I mean, this whole idea . . .'

'One more thing,' the technician said. 'When we send you, you are likely to be disoriented. At least, the bluebottles we've experimented on went completely crazy for a while, and simulations suggest a high likelihood of memory loss, confusion, even temporary madness. So we have linked some of your more important memories to another part of your brain to ensure you can remember who you are and why you are there. All you have to do is find them. The memories are associated with food. So when you arrive, the first thing you will need to do is eat something. All right?'

*

Two hours later, Chang got his third meeting with Hanslip in twenty-four hours and launched immediately into his final argument. 'The thing is,' he said with an air of desperation, 'that I got hold of as many of this man Lytten's publications as I could find, to see if there were any other references to Angela Meerson. I thought that if I could find something, then you would see that I wasn't trying to deceive you.'

'Were there?' Hanslip asked.

'Ah, no. There weren't.'

'What a surprise.'

'What there was, however, was an article entitled "The Devil's Handwriting", published in 1959. It's about an ancient manuscript, supposedly medieval although the author, this man Lytten, decided it was a fake. The story is that a man named Ludovico Spoletano summoned the devil and asked him to respond, in writing, to a question. The pen was taken by "an invisible power which suspended it in air".'

Hanslip gazed balefully at him, so Chang hurried on before his patience was exhausted. 'This manuscript was impossible to read, hence the attribution. Various people suggested that it was an Old Iberic script.'

'Mr Chang?' Hanslip prompted. 'You are beginning to weary me.'

'The point is that there's an illustration.'

Chang fumbled in the folder he was gripping tightly in his hand, pulled out a few sheets and handed them nervously to Hanslip, who glanced at them, then bowed his head and studied them much more closely.

'How fascinating,' Hanslip said softly when he finished.

'May I?' Jack interrupted.

Hanslip handed over the papers. 'The script,' he explained. 'You may not recognise it, but it is three lines of mathematics in the Tsou notation.'

'What's that?'

'A method of compressing information, not unlike the way Chinese characters managed to squeeze multi-syllabic words into a couple of strokes. Each symbol is made up of many different elements, and can be unbundled to produce more orthodox notation.'

'That's interesting.'

'The point that Mr Chang is trying to make, I am sure,

is that Tsou was only developed sixty years ago. The article in which this illustration was published supposedly dates back more than two hundred.' Hanslip peered at Chang. 'Is that correct?'

'Yes. The reference to Angela appeared in 1960; the article including the Tsou notation was published in 1959.'

'Supposedly,' Hanslip added.

'So what does that mean?' Jack asked.

'Well, that is a very good question. What indeed? Either this is genuinely old, or it is an elaborate hoax designed to make us think it is. Another attempt to throw us off the scent, so to speak.'

'Now I think,' Chang continued earnestly, 'that it would surely be better if I concentrated on this, rather than going after Angela Meerson.'

Hanslip peered enquiringly. 'Go on.'

'The text says the complete manuscript is in the author's possession. Henry Lytten, that is. I have discovered that his papers are supposed to be in the National Depository. The obvious thing would be to go and look first of all. Genuine or fake, if this document is there you will be able to recover the data you have lost, and finding Angela Meerson won't be so important.'

'Oh, I see! You are trying to disobey my orders,' Hanslip said theatrically. 'No chance of that, I'm afraid. I have no doubt that if I let you out, then you would abscond back to the renegades and I'd never see you or the data ever again, even if it exists. Sorry, Mr Chang. You are insufficiently trustworthy for such a task. Mr More here can follow your very useful lead. Your orders stand. Please don't think I'm not appreciative.'

'But what am I meant to do?'

'You will see if you can find Angela, then get her to come back.'

'How can she do that? She doesn't have a machine . . .'

Hanslip peered at him. 'When you have known her for as long as I have,' he said, 'you will know never, ever, to underestimate her. It will be your only route back as well, so you can think of it as an incentive to do as you're told. Besides, I have given you a message to relay to her.'

'What is it?'

'It will come back to you if you meet her.'

*

Apart from the lab technicians, Jack was the only person to see Chang off when he was helped – rather pale and anxious, but calm because of the sedatives that had been poured in to stop him causing trouble – into the sphere of electricity. He had wished the strange, now rather pathetic man luck. He would, surely, need it.

'I still don't know how I'm meant to do this,' he said as he sat in what they all hoped was period costume in the waiting room next door.

'Find Angela Meerson, if she is to be found,' Jack said. 'Get her to return, if it is possible. Or let us know somehow.'

Chang seemed doubtful. 'I suppose I could take out an advert in a newspaper that will survive. But that is assuming that she's right about where I'm going. Make sure you look.'

'Why did Hanslip get so annoyed by your idea? I thought he'd be pleased she might have been found.'

'He thinks I'm undermining him. If the standard theory is correct, I am about to go to an alternative universe, and there can be no communication between us and it except by using the machine. If Angela is correct, then the machine may simply move us to a different moment of the same universe. Time travel, in fact. It's what they were fighting about. He is desperate for Angela to be wrong. If I find her and manage to tell you about it, that means she is right.'

'I know you scientists get worked up about such things, but . . .'

'It's not abstract,' Chang said. 'Hanslip sees himself as a sort of conquistador, finding new worlds to colonise. But if Angela is correct, then the machine would be too dangerous to use, as it would be impossible to control its effects. So Hanslip's dreams of power and glory would have to be abandoned, or at least they would become prohibitively expensive. More to the point, no one would invest in it. That was Angela's argument, and Hanslip evidently thought I was taking her side.'

'Were you?'

'No. I'm nowhere near good enough to have any opinion.'

'You seem remarkably relaxed about all this, if I may say so.'

Chang smiled briefly as the technician approached.

'Ready for you, sir,' he said.

'That's the first time anyone here has ever called me sir,' Chang said in a weak voice. 'That's really worrying.'

*

Jack reported personally to Hanslip that wherever Chang now was, he wasn't in the sphere.

Hanslip ignored him until he had finished the report he was reading. 'Thank you, Mr More.'

'May I ask what you think his chances of success are?'

Hanslip frowned in puzzlement. 'None whatsoever,' he said.

'So why send him?'

'What business is that of yours?'

'It would help to know what exactly I am doing, and why. At the moment I am very confused.'

'Oh, very well. Mr Chang's conclusions are undoubtedly as faked as Angela's disappearance. The way he presented them is proof of that.'

'How so?'

'Firstly he made an immensely difficult search through a vast number of records with no experience of how to do it, and produced a result within a few hours, which is extraordinary to the point of being suspicious. Secondly, he claimed to have found a trace of Angela when, in fact, nearly two centuries of scientific work has established that it is impossible. Thirdly, when I said I planned to send him in the machine, he immediately produced yet another piece of evidence designed to make that unnecessary. Angela may have hidden the data amongst old historical documents. You will check, but I am certain that she will be found hiding out amongst the renegades. That's why your main task will be to seek out her daughter.'

'Her what?' Jack asked in genuine astonishment.

'The procedure to enhance her abilities produced a child as a by-product. A daughter, to be precise, who now goes under the name of Emily Strang. She is highly intelligent as well but proved herself to be unsuited for membership of the elite. She was assigned to the appropriate level of education for her considerable potential, but walked out at the age of fifteen after a long period of being uncooperative and disruptive. Even heavy doses of drugs made no difference to her attitude and eventually the system washed its hands of her. She became a renegade and now lives in a Retreat in the south.'

'Was there some relationship with Angela?'

'Not that I know of. Angela knows she exists, but the procedure diverted all her affective abilities onto her work. She doesn't feel anything for the girl. Or she didn't. It may be that recent difficulties unbalanced her. If so, there is a possibility that she formed a link between her work and her daughter. At least, that's what the psychiatrists tell me; I've been consulting our in-house specialists. They think that there is a good chance you will find her by going through the child.'

'What about that document with the Tsou notation that Chang produced?'

'It is a very small extract of her work,' Hanslip said.

'So surely finding the rest should be our main priority?'

'I suspect that if you find one, you will find the other. Again, the daughter is the key. She is what is termed a historian. They dabble in the occult, these renegades, as I am sure you are aware; they all have some pointless obsession to which they attribute mystical importance. Emily Strang's is the study of the past. Now, do you not think it a remarkable coincidence that this document is supposed to be hidden in the National Depository, when she is one of the few people who might be able to find it? I do not believe in coincidences, Mr More.'

Hanslip waved a hand to dismiss him. 'Find out. If the daughter knows anything, have her arrested and brought here.'

Jack stood up to leave.

'Here,' Hanslip added. 'New documentation for you. Until you are done, you are now a scientist, first class. The identity gives you full privileges. You may go anywhere, talk to anyone, without hindrance. You have access to our central funding. You need answer to no one except superiors in rank, and there aren't many of those.'

Jack looked carefully at the documents Hanslip gave him, the qualifications, the educational profile, the psychometric test results, all showing that he was a very impressive character.

'These look genuine.'

'That's because they are. Like most organisations, we keep a few ghosts on the payroll.'

Jack stood up. 'One more thing,' he said. 'Chang made me concerned, just before he was transmitted.'

'Well?'

'He wasn't worried. He was about to be put in an untested machine and potentially vaporised and he wasn't worried.'

'He was drugged, presumably.'

'Not that much. I think he knew it worked. Has it been used before?'

'Not with people.'

'Are you sure?'

Hanslip considered this remark for some time. 'I will

investigate while you are away. Now, there is one other thing you should know. I have broken off negotiations with Oldmanter, as it was not possible to reach a suitable agreement at the moment. It is quite possible that he will attempt to obtain the technology by other means.'

'Does he know what has happened here?'

'No. I do not wish him to find out, either. It could easily be made to look bad.'

'Yes. It could.'

'No one must know what you are doing when you leave. Should things become unpleasant, then possession of this technology will be our main defence. Be careful who you talk to and what you say, and do not fail. Is that understood?'

17

In the dark years that followed his meeting with Callan Perelson and the young student on the streets of Ossenfud, Pamarchon often thought back to that day, almost the last time when he had felt carefree and safe. Within three months he had become a fugitive, hunted for the murder of his own uncle.

From being a source of pride, his name became a death sentence, and he had to become a wanderer, a person of no name. He had travelled in search of safety, and had found it, but never any peace. His fall weighed heavily on him. Bit by bit others, all outcasts, men and women with grievances, or those who could not settle, came to join him. All societies produce their injustices, and those who will not accept those injustices. So around Pamarchon there gathered the men forced into crime, the young and wild, the bold and adventurous, the women who yearned for something different, though they rarely knew what.

They could not live among other men, so they travelled in bands, living out in the forests, occupying part of the vast emptiness which covered the landscape. Few ever noticed them and those who did could not find them. Many no longer wanted to hide and be fearful, or to have to move at regular intervals. Others wished to keep on moving for ever.

Pamarchon became their leader because he understood both, and sympathised with both, although he pondered how long that uneasy state could continue. He could settle their disputes, persuade them to stay together and learn how to help each other. They relied on him, and he came to rely on them as well. With such people he found a comradeship he had never discovered in his days of wealth and ease. Eventually their wanderings brought them back almost to where he had started his long journey, to the place of his fall. They settled in the forests to the south of Willdon, pitching camp, clearing spaces, setting up the areas for cooking, sending out scouts to guard and hunters to find food. Then, as was their custom, they blended into the trees and waited, to see if their arrival had been noticed. No one came. It was as if they were not there. They began to relax and to live their lives once more.

Pamarchon was busy in those first days, supervising the setting of the camps, making sure everyone was provided for, discussing the best places for guards, making rotas of duties. Then, one fine morning, he realised he had nothing left to do. He could leave the camp to Antros, his closest friend, and wander off by himself to think and consider.

It was always his delight and his greatest pleasure to walk through the great trees, listening to the never-ending song of the birds. He knew he was hiding his intentions even from himself, though. He was going back to Willdon. He would go to the Shrine of Esilio and leave a prayer. He would go to the circle and hope that a dream would come to him which would clarify everything and that he would know, finally, what to do.

It took several hours, as he went by a circuitous route, but eventually he came to the clearing, surrounded by stones overgrown with plants all in flower. It was deserted.

So he stood up and stepped over the stone surrounds and went up to the monument. He knew that you had to trace your fingers over the scratching on the side as you made your wish. 'Grant us all peace and safety, and do not let ill come from my desires,' he said quietly as he bent over and performed the simple ritual. 'You know what I am, and what I have done, and not done. Grant me what I deserve, whatever that might be. Come and help me in my hour of need.'

He closed his eyes to concentrate, so his words would have more force, then stopped suddenly. A noise behind him. He had let his guard down and had paid the price. There was nothing to be done; he had a knife but no other means of defending himself. He took a deep breath, straightened and turned to meet his foe.

Before him was a young girl, mouth open in surprise, looking at him with an intensity which was instantly unsettling. She was strangely dressed, a creature such as he had never seen before. But her face was lovely. Magical-looking. He felt that his heart would burst, just from looking at her.

He did not know what to do. Her costume was exotic and disturbing, as was the perplexed look on her face as she studied him equally intently. Then she moved, but only because a fly was buzzing round her head; she made an instinctive movement to swat it away.

That broke the spell; a fairy or other supernatural being was not going to be disturbed by a fly in her ear, after all. The fly changed an apparition into something real in a split second, and Pamarchon felt himself relaxing, just a little. He stepped away from the stone block and approached. The girl was still frozen to the spot. She didn't look frightened, merely confused.

For a long time each examined the other. The girl bit her lip nervously. He brushed the hair from his forehead, she entwined her fingers, then let her arms fall to her side. He put down his staff, dropping it on the ground without even looking where it fell.

He came closer and she looked up at his face.

'Hello.' It was not much of a start, but at least she began.

He felt frightened for a brief moment, but then he replied: 'Hello.'

Both relapsed into silence, as though their powers of conversation were quite exhausted by the effort.

'Who are you?' Difficult though it was for her to talk to a strange, half-clad man much older than herself, it was easier than he found the task of addressing her.

'My name is Pamarchon,' he said. 'Who are you?' He spoke slowly, as though he was unsure of what he was saying.

'Rosie. That's my name. Rosie – Rosalind – Wilson.'

'You don't look like the son of anyone,' he said gravely.

'What?'

He reached forward and touched her cheek. Rosie recoiled in alarm.

'Forgive me.'

She reached up and touched his also. His cheek tingled as her finger stroked down it. 'We're both real, then,' she whispered, half to herself. 'That's a bit of a relief.' She was unclear whether she was reassuring herself or him.

'At least, you seem to be,' she added. 'It might still be a very complicated dream. I think I fell asleep. It was a long day. We had lots of lessons, you see. And hockey. In the rain. I hate hockey. Have you ever played it?'

He had no idea what she was talking about. 'Are you a messenger? Have you a complaint?'

The question was reasonable, as it was commonplace for spirits of the dead with unfinished business on earth to come back to complain, or give information, even if the girl's clothing and solidity hardly fitted any tale of visitation. Nor did her words.

Rosie, however, understood him no better than he understood her. 'I don't think so, although I am a bit lost.' She paused, still fascinated. 'I'd better go,' she said. 'I'll be late for tea. Mummy's always cross when I'm late.'

She walked a few steps, then looked back. 'Why don't you come too? I'm sure you could share my shepherd's pie and it'll be bread-and-butter pudding for afters. It always is.'

'Stop! Don't go. Tell me, are you part of the Lady's household?' A foolish question, spoken just to make sure she didn't leave him.

She giggled. 'I don't know that anyone has ever called Mummy a lady. She's quite nice, though. And I suppose you could say I'm part of the household.'

The more they said, the less each understood. So Pamarchon, not wanting to let her go, fell in alongside her as she began to retrace her steps into the woods.

'Along here,' she said, 'then through Mrs Meerson's pagoda thing. It will only take a few minutes. You're not really dressed properly, though. You'll be dreadfully cold, but I'm sure you can borrow Professor Lytten's old coat.'

He stopped suddenly. 'Did you hear that?'

'What?'

'A noise. There is someone near.' He listened some more. 'Is this a trap?'

'What?' She knew she was saying this rather often.

'False woman,' he hissed suddenly.

He turned and ran, disappearing into the forest as though he had never existed.

*

Rosie stared in astonishment as the lithe figure slipped silently away into the trees after being so suddenly rude to her. She was now completely shaken, not just by the whole experience of being in a forest in Professor Lytten's cellar – curiously, this was almost the least of the things on her mind – but more by the feelings which had passed through her when she had met this strange young man. His touch had felt like an electric shock on her skin; her hand – she had noticed it quite distinctly – had been shaking when she reached out and touched him. She had felt breathless, confused, upset and elated. She had never felt anything quite like it before.

She thought for a moment of calling after him, maybe giving chase, but common sense prevailed. The last thing she needed was to get lost. She had been very careful to make sure she knew exactly where she was. All she had to do was follow the line of sweets and she could go home. She had once gone on a school trip in some woods and had got lost. She remembered the humiliation of being found, crying and afraid. It had made a great impression on her, and the memory now flushed all thought of further adventure from her mind. It was time – more than time – to get back home.

She kept walking, eyes on the ground, following the Smarties, picking them up and – waste not, want not – eating them as she went. The crunch as she bit through the coating and the taste of chocolate inside reassured her. This place, whatever it was, had unsettled her. The contrast with the Smarties, familiar and known, could not have been greater. She would go back, walk down to the corner shop and buy another tube. Maybe some wine gums, to settle her nerves. A reward for not being so silly. She wasn't going to come back here again. It was just a forest, after all, however odd its location. She was even beginning to look forward to her English homework.

She spotted the last of the Smarties, popped it into her mouth and pushed her way through the bracken to the place where the light waited for her. She knew she was in the right place. She saw her coat, hanging on the branch where she had left it.

Except that the light wasn't there. She waved her hand around in the precise place where she was certain it must be, walked, then ran forwards and backwards, trying to find it, summon it into existence. There was nothing, and she was stuck. She had no way back home.

She stopped and stood in disbelief, unable to credit what had happened, or even to start thinking what it meant.

She was so absorbed she didn't even hear the soft whistle coming from a hundred yards away, off in the undergrowth. Nor did she pay any attention to the growing sound of footsteps as they crashed through the forest towards her.

The armed men who burst noisily through the trees, swords at the ready, naturally assumed that the arrest would be as straightforward as their earlier success had been. It was only a young girl, after all, who would certainly be terrified. They were rapidly disabused of this notion. Far from submitting meekly to their superior strength and authority, their new quarry completely ignored them. Then, when one shouted at her, she came out of her reverie and turned on them with fury.

'What have you done?' she demanded, stamping her foot for emphasis. 'Where is it?' They didn't answer. 'Well,' she went on, 'don't you have tongues in your heads? Answer me. What have you done?'

The look of shock – and what could easily have passed for fright – on the faces of the soldiers almost made her giggle. In the circumstances, no one thought it strange that only the boy they had captured and held secure with the rope around his neck managed to speak.

'Forgive us, my lady, but what do you mean?' The others were impressed and grateful in equal measure that he could speak to her. They could not understand a word she had said.

The two stared at each other.

'You!' they both cried out simultaneously.

'What has happened to you? You look older. Or maybe you have a younger brother? It is you, isn't it?'

He nodded cautiously. 'You haven't changed in the slightest, even though it is more than five years since I saw you. You must be a fairy.'

'I am not a fairy. Don't be stupid. I'm Rosie. And it was last week, not five years ago. Who are you? And who,' she continued, waving her hand contemptuously at the soldiers, 'are these idiots?'

'My name is Jay. These are soldiers who—'

'Very well,' she interrupted. 'What have you done to my light, Jay?'

Jay understood the words but not the meaning. His fairy was, it seemed, a bit crazy.

The sergeant decided it was high time to reassert his waning authority, even though he felt thoroughly diminished by the girl's reaction.

'What's he saying?' Rosie asked. 'Who are these people?'

'He is saying you are under arrest as a trespasser.'

'I most certainly am not. And you can tell them from me that if they want to arrest me, they can do it in English.'

Another exchange of words. 'They are instructed to take you to their Lady, and you are under arrest. As am I, in fact.'

'We'll see about that,' Rosie said. 'Keep your hands off me!' she said, wagging her finger disapprovingly as one soldier approached her. 'I know my rights. Touch me and I shall write to my MP.'

'You seem to have frightened them. Which is more than I managed. But they are determined to obey their orders and it would be best to do as they say. They are the ones with the swords.'

Rosie sniffed contemptuously. She examined the soldiers once more – they were getting back their self-confidence after the initial shock – and took a deep breath.

'Oh, if I must,' she said grumpily.

A man was waiting for them as they walked out of the woods and onto a straight path which led over a low hill in the middle distance. It was warm, all were hot and the soldiers were silent and unresponsive. Rosie's behaviour had unnerved them. She was meant to be frightened, apologetic, begging for mercy. Tears would have been satisfactory. Instead she had given them a dressing down and had done it in the old language. They had not known what she said, but they had all too well understood what that meant. The girl was very much more important than they had been told.

They slowed as they saw the man in the middle of the path, carrying a white stick in his right hand. He approached and bowed deeply to them.

'Most honoured guest, I welcome you in the name of the Lady Catherine of this domain. May you enter, and take your pleasure here.'

It was the highest level of greeting in a land which graded these things very meticulously; even a scholar generally received a lesser welcome. The soldiers looked at the Chamberlain, then at their prisoners, and wondered if they had made some terrible error. They also noted, as did Jay, that the address was in the singular, with the gestures in the female form. Rosie was most honoured. Jay wasn't even noticed. The Chamberlain's face gave no clues either as he snapped his fingers to dismiss them. 'Her thanks for your assistance,' he said reassuringly. 'You may go.'

'Please,' he said, turning to Rosie and Jay, 'would you be so kind as to accompany me? The entertainments are preparing, and the Lady wishes to greet you herself.'

'We cannot possibly . . . I mean, we are not dressed,' said Jay, who was now more frightened than when he had thought himself under arrest.

'Do not concern yourself. Your master awaits you, and there are clothes and baths prepared.'

'Is there any chance of something to eat?' asked Rosie. 'I haven't had so much as a bite since breakfast.'

'Of course,' replied the Chamberlain after a long moment of thought. 'Whatever you wish.' He spoke as though the words were foreign to him.

'Golly.'

They fell in step behind the Chamberlain, who walked quickly ahead, rapping his staff on the ground every few paces. The noise alerted people nearby. Men working in fields stopped, removed their caps. Women passing by put down anything they were carrying and curtsied. Their children stared.

'Jay,' whispered Rosie. 'What is this? Where am I? What's going on?'

'I don't know,' he murmured back. 'I was threatened with dreadful punishment until you showed up. So I think it must be something to do with you.'

'Why would anyone do this for me? How does anyone even know I'm here? What is this place? Who is this Lady?'

'I'll tell you later. But she is not someone to annoy.'

'Who is this master of yours?'

Jay hushed her. 'I don't know. I don't know anything. We'll just have to wait and see.'

They entered the grounds in procession, passing through small courtyards, then bigger, and finally into the great house itself. At each stage, people Rosie thought must be servants were present, and bowed deeply to the new arrivals. Jay bowed back to each group; Rosie thought she ought to follow suit. This was greeted with a faint snort from Jay.

'What's wrong?'

'Curtsy. They'll think you're making fun of them.'

'I don't know how to curtsy. I've never done it. Not in anger, so to speak.'

'Watch everyone else. Bend your knees, extend your arms and incline your head.'

She did her best, and by the fourth courtyard was, in her opinion, getting quite good at it. Jay, however, was looking increasingly ill at ease.

'Am I doing it wrong?'

He shook his head and did not answer.

They were led into the building itself, a room with entirely white walls and a floor of multi-coloured stone. It was cool and dark in comparison to the outside; the blue-framed windows were small and let in only a little of the brilliant sunshine.

More bowing, more silent greetings; then a double door was opened with great ceremony, and they passed through. Then another, and another, with each room more furnished, with lamps hanging from the ceiling and tapestries on the wall. Rosie looked at them; she couldn't make out what they were about.

In the third room, Jay let out a groan of misery. This time there were four servants standing on one side of the room – they bowed and curtsied – and on the other a solitary man, dressed in cream robes.

'Professor!' Rosie cried with pleasure. 'I'm so happy to see you! Why are you in those ridiculous clothes?' She rushed up to him, ready to give him a hug.

The reaction was extraordinary. At once, two servants stepped in front of her to bar her passage; the man looked shocked, and Jay let out a strangled cry of alarm.

'Perhaps you should introduce us?'

Jay recovered himself, bowing quickly although a little indiscriminately. 'Of course. Certainly. It is my very great pleasure, and an honour to me and to my family, to present these two distinguished people to each other for the first time, and to be the agent of their meeting. I present to you' – here he bowed to Rosie, then turned back – 'Henary, son of Henary, Scholar of East College in Ossenfud, Storyteller of the first level, and my master.'

Henary in turn bowed to Jay, and then to Rosie. Jay then repeated the process in reverse.

'It is my very great pleasure, and an honour to me and to my family, to present to you, Master, Rosie,' here he paused, and a look of alarm spread over his face. Henary's darkened. 'Rosie, daughter of . . . ah . . .'

Rosie's mouth twitched almost uncontrollably as she tried not to burst out laughing. She succeeded. But only just. 'I'm afraid we did not have time to introduce ourselves properly,' she said, 'as we were arrested by soldiers and Jay here had a rope around his neck. It does cut politeness short a bit, don't you think?'

Henary's face had a look of the utmost astonishment on it as she spoke.

'My name is Rosalind Wilson. I am very pleased to meet you. At least, I think I am.'

Henary glanced enquiringly at Jay and then bowed to her. 'It is a great pleasure to make the acquaintance of a woman of such refinement and education, Lady Rosalind.'

'Well, that's jolly nice of you,' Rosie said.

'I think you and I need to talk, Jay. Do you not agree?'

Jay nodded silently. Rosie could see from his face that he wasn't looking forward to it. She wasn't sure what, exactly, Jay had done – it was one of the very many things she wasn't sure of – but it must have been pretty bad.

She watched helplessly as Jay was led off. Then the procession began again.

18

All events displace in both temporal directions simultaneously and equally. The magnitude of displacement is in direct proportion to the mass of the event – Meerson's second law.

I formulated this in a library in 1949, the Bibliothèque Mazarine in Paris, rather a pleasant place to sit and read. I had worked out some of the mathematics before I left but it was highly speculative and didn't make much sense, even to me. While I was still stymied, I had little to do, so I spent many years reading – really reading, I mean, in libraries at a wooden desk, or curled up on a settee with a little light, holding the book in my hands, turning the pages, glass of brandy, warm fire, all of that. Anyway, I was reading *La Cousine Bette* by Balzac (which I also recommend) and was struck by how convincing were both the characters and the situations he described. I wondered whether Balzac had taken them from personal observation and simply amended real people and circumstance to serve his purpose.

Then it dawned on me in a moment of such excitement I can remember it perfectly well to this day. Of course he had done that; he had transferred reality into his imagination. But – and this was my great insight – he must, at the same time, have transferred his imagination into reality. Clearly, in an infinite universe every possibility must exist, including Balzac's. Imagining Cousin Bette called her into being, although only potentially. The universe is merely a quantity of information; imagining a fictional character does not add to that quantity – it cannot do so by definition – but does reorganise it slightly. The Bette-ish universe has no material existence, but the initial idea in Balzac's brandy-soaked brain then spreads outwards: not only to those who read his books, but also, by implication, backwards and forwards. Imagining Cousin Bette also creates, in potential, her ancestors and descendants, friends, enemies, acquaintances, her thoughts and actions and those of everybody else in her universe.

I settled down for a long night of home-brewed LSD and (in homage to Balzac) coffee and brandy. A fabulous mixture, and the result was pure joy, although I paid a price with a headache of monumental proportions when the effects wore off. So very simple. It was merely a question of turning my insights into mathematics and much of that was there already, just not in a coherent form. I felt drained and exhausted when I finished after five days of delirium, but more satisfied than at any time in my life.

It was gorgeous. Elegant, stylish and so obviously correct that my one regret was that there was no one to tell. No one could possibly understand it. Many generations of physicists and mathematicians would have to do their work before anyone could even begin to grasp what I had accomplished. It would have been as if Einstein had laid out his work in the Middle Ages. Out of context, without the background of another couple of centuries of other people's labour, even the notation was meaningless. That was a pity, as a little applause and admiration would have been most welcome.

My insight marked the point where orthodoxy and I diverged for ever. The standard model, current for several centuries by my time, assumes that all pasts, presents and futures exist, and that time does as well; out of that came Hanslip's insistence that travel through time is impossible. If we change events in the past, and the past is fixed, then we cannot be changing our past, but must be moving to the universe where what we do takes place. QED. He even stole my phrase for it: 'What was, is.'

Cute. But wrong. 'What was, is. Until it isn't.' Not as elegant, I admit, but more accurate. The universe is not wasteful: why have lots of universes, when one will do perfectly well? It is simpler to assume an infinite number of potential universes, than an infinite number of actual ones. So, a universe with Cousin Bette in it could exist, but doesn't. If it did, then a universe without her – like ours – could not. One or the other. Take your pick.

What was more, I had already proven it before I left. I just didn't understand the proof. It was the bluebottle experiment that nailed it, an attempt to examine the hoary old paradox-of-time business that has so annoyed anyone who has dealt with the issue. It got no funding, as no one took it seriously; only a very lowly researcher was assigned to it as a training exercise and so, naturally, no one paid any attention to the result.

What if you go back and shoot your grandmother before you are born, so that you are not born and can't shoot her? Dealing with this logical impossibility gave birth to the alternative universe theory: you can shoot your grannie, but not in your own universe, so that in one you exist as a murderer but are not subsequently born, and in the other you are born, but disappear when you transit to a different one to commit your crime.

Experimental simulations were carried out to test the hypothesis, but were subsequently abandoned because there were so many errors. The idea was simple: a bluebottle was persuaded to eat its own egg. This was difficult, as it was assumed this had to take place within the confines of the machine and the technicians kept on making mistakes. The results were confusing and meaningless; sometimes the bluebottle simply refused to eat its own egg, which prevented a paradox; sometimes the controlling programme altered the present so that, if the insect did eat the egg presented to it, then it was subsequently discovered that the wrong egg had been sent and again no paradox occurred. But occasionally the right egg was sent and the bluebottle happily ate itself without any consequences.

Nobody could understand how such a simple thing could be so badly handled and the poor researcher was fired as a result. But, much later, I began to wonder what explanation could be offered if you assumed that everything had, in fact, been done perfectly. The answer was that if everything was done perfectly to create a paradox, then both past and future had to change simultaneously. Clearly, this was difficult to prove, because not only would all documentary evidence be re-formed, all memories would be as well – the researchers could not remember having done the experiment properly because, the moment the fly dug its nasty little choppers into its own egg, then everything changed so that, in fact, it hadn't been. The point being that the re-formation of events took place subsequent to the paradox; at neither point, past or future, were paradoxical actions prevented.

Let me put it this way. We accept easily the idea that the future is the consequence of events in the past. With a bit of an effort, we can wrap our heads round the idea that the past is the consequence of events in the future. What this suggested was that neither of these was quite true; rather both are simultaneously dependent on the other. An event which we consider to be in the future is not happening after, or as a sole consequence of, events in the past. Remove that illusion, and the whole business becomes understandable.

People are naturally so fond of themselves that they assume the past must lead to them. They have egos of such size that they cannot imagine it doing otherwise. Rather like biologists of the past imagining the whole of evolution leading to Homo sapiens, so that we almost become the point of evolution, or religious types assuming that the world was created to give us somewhere nice to live, so those who concern themselves with time assume that the only purpose of the past is to produce the present, with us as the lead characters. This desire is so strong we wilfully ignore all evidence to the contrary.

The central point is that while all variants of the universe exist in latent form, only one is actualised. A simple metaphor will suffice; say that reality is a piece of string on a flat surface. Birth at one end, death at the other. Big Bang to Big Crunch, if you prefer. 'Now' is at any point between the two. The piece of string can, in theory, move anywhere on the surface, but can only be in one place at a time.

Now, if you push it at any one place, the string on both sides of your finger will change position a little – in temporal terms, both before and after will adjust. Next, move the end – create a different future. Again, the rest of the string will move. There are an infinite number of places where the string can be, but only one where it actually is.

Now add another illustration. Say that the relationship of future and past is also like a pair of scales: events in one balance the other; 'now' is merely the fulcrum. A change in the relationship between the two alters the balance. Either side can instigate that change or it can even take place from outside the balance, but the sides respond equally.

The more strongly an alternative world is imagined, the more it becomes a viable candidate as a successor to our present. Then events become merely probabilistic. Historical evolution will naturally tend to the easiest destination, a bit like water finding the easiest route down a hill. The point is that there is nothing special about my future, except in terms of probability. Nor (by extension) is there anything particularly special about my past. The trouble was that the computer simulation had already established that, in terms of probability, my own history was both highly unlikely and very unstable. If it was knocked off course, it would tend to flow in a different direction very easily. I should have paid more attention to that than I did.

In theory, therefore, all I had to do was come up with an algorithm which made it more likely for, say, Hanslip not to exist and the laws of probability would take care of the rest. Past and present would re-form to flow in a new direction to reach the easier destination. The computer simulation had demonstrated (even if it had otherwise been useless) that this is difficult – history follows definite, if broad, rules. The more dramatically different the future, the more dramatically different the past must become. But all I wanted was a simple tweak to take care of my little difficulties.

Time travel has nothing to do with either travel or time. The term is a sort of unfortunate hangover. When I went to 1936, I was not travelling 'through' time in any real sense; this has no meaning. Rather, I was making small adjustments to the totality of information that makes up the universe. It was like cutting a block of text from a manuscript and inserting it at an earlier point, which causes everything else to shift to make room. 'I' am simply a particular block of information within a much larger whole which, as far as I am concerned, seems like a different time and place. The version of 1936 without me faded out, and the version with me came into existence. I moved the string, to use my metaphor again, or, if you prefer, slightly changed the disposition of events on the scales.

Now I wanted to experiment with more deliberation to see if it would be possible to reconstruct my own point of origin, but with certain improvements. If I was going to go back, then there was no point in returning simply to be arrested and locked up, as I was sure would happen. The calculations for that, however, were way beyond my current abilities. I wanted to experiment with a grosser construct first of all to amass the data. So I needed a world so outlandish that the likelihood of it seriously challenging my own line of reality would be too slight to be worth worrying about. I didn't want a nasty accident.

Fairly simple in theory. Very optimistic in practice.

*

My decision to go to England for the war was not merely a desire for self-preservation. By that stage, I had given

185

up worrying too much about pursuit; I had assumed that Hanslip would at least try to send someone after me but no one showed up. It was true that I had disguised my destination and there was little juice left in the machine, but I had assumed that he would be able to do something. That he didn't suggested he was much dumber than even I thought.

I began to relax. I had been more or less living the life of a hermit; I had only casual acquaintances, no one who might (for example) refer to me in a diary or letter that stood a chance of surviving, just in case. I avoided important or notable people and steered clear of officialdom as much as possible. I was stuck, however, with my name. The psychiatrists got it out of me in my delirium, and it was too late to change.

Two years in, though, and I felt much safer and began to explore the mysteries of friendship. The world had many attractions, and I was missing most of them. I was also becoming a little complacent and rash. What possible danger could I face in Europe in 1939?

One day that spring, while driving into Collioure, I stopped to get some petrol and water for the radiator at a small village. I loved that part of the world, not least because the first time I had seen it the whole area had been a barren, scorched wasteland. To see it in its glory – the pine trees, the vegetation, the olives, the vines, the sea still blue and alive – was glorious beyond words. I settled there, mainly because the place had lodged in my mind as being important.

This time, rather than watching with interest as the man slowly filled the tank and the radiator and washed the windscreen, I crossed over to the bar for a drink for myself. It was just over the road from the railway station.

I ordered a cold glass of local white wine with some bread and, when it was delivered, took a sip and looked around me.

There, at the only other table in this dusty little bar, was Lucien Grange, reading a newspaper.

My cry of shock must have been quite loud; if not, then the way I suddenly stood up, knocked over the chair and table and sent the bowl of rather tasty sausage spinning across the floor may have been what attracted attention. Either way, I was noticed. He saw my distress and himself got up.

'Is anything the matter, madam?' he asked in perfect French.

'No, thank you so much,' I said, still trembling. I examined him carefully, then began to relax. It was close. The same nose, the same eyes, the same mouth. But it wasn't him. The moment I could collect myself enough and be calm I knew it wasn't him. The voice was different, the shape similar, but not similar enough . . .

'Forgive me,' I said, as the waiter came over, grumbled and began repairing the damage I had caused. 'You so greatly resembled someone I knew.'

'I'm afraid it cannot be,' he replied. 'I could never have forgotten meeting you.'

Charmed? Of course I was; it was delivered handsomely, and I was unused to such rhetorical devices.

'You must have thought me terribly clumsy.'

'On the contrary. It brightened up a tedious time waiting for my train. May I offer you a replacement for your drink?'

Of course he might. He did.

'May I introduce myself?' he said once it was delivered. 'My name is Henry Lytten.'

I suppose it was Henry who took the full force of my desire to explore the nature of human interactions, and the fact that (I suspected) he was the ancestor of someone I knew made me cling to him in a way I had never experienced before. I didn't exactly kidnap him, but very nearly: I took him back to my little house in the hills, and he stayed with me for three weeks. By the end we were firm friends. He was a kind, gentle fellow, and put up with me: not easy considering the huge outpouring of entirely raw and uncontrolled emotions that erupted from me in those days. When I was angry I was murderous; when affectionate, then such love had never been felt before by any human being. My hunger was insatiable, my thirst unquenchable and I once laughed so hard I had to go into hospital for three days because of the torn muscles. I learned to avoid Walt Disney cartoons, as the despair at watching the cruelty inflicted on Snow White by that horrid Witch was so great it took me weeks to recover. As for *Romeo and Juliet* . . . Henry took me to see it in Stratford in 1941, with Margaretta Scott as Juliet; I nearly expired from sheer anguish. I was quite sophisticated by that stage, but was hard pressed not to leap onto the stage, grab the knife and kill myself in order to spare her. Only the thought of Henry's embarrassment made me stop myself.

What I mean is that it took a lot of practice to get these emotions under control, and Henry, dear man, taught me more than anyone, with patience and kindness. Do you know, I even thought of marrying him? But how could I have possibly done such a thing? I still planned to go home one day and we were ageing at different rates. I had habits (drink, drugs and work, mainly) which he could not understand. Great friends make bad spouses. I cannot easily say how much I regretted it. I almost abandoned everything, just for the sake of happiness. It was the first time in my life I had ever loved anybody. The realisation that I could, and the extraordinary impact on me in comparison to the chemically induced emotions I was used to, made me think deeply. Did I really want to go back to a place where such things were illegal, where people conducted themselves only in a narrow range of efficient civility?

I fear I hurt poor Henry, but I think that even he realised that I would have been a difficult partner; he had certainly seen enough to know that I would be, at best, an uncertain companion who would not easily fit into the quiet contemplative life he had in mind. On the other hand, he never found anyone to take my place. I regret that too; had I not come into his life then perhaps he would not have become the slightly reclusive figure of later years, although considering the polite and distant way most of his contemporaries dealt with their marital relationships I am not sure he was missing so very much.

We spent a great deal of time in each other's company until the war started, and afterwards, when I went back to France, he would come and visit almost every vacation. We drove around France and Italy, staying in little hotels, eating in restaurants, enjoying ourselves as the world recovered from its trauma. He taught me about Christmas and birthdays, how to give gifts and pay compliments. I still smile when I think of that period.

He was a great talker as well. We would sit until late

at night and I would question him remorselessly about everything – life, family, work, education. About his country, the books he liked, those he didn't. About music, theatre, poetry and the cinema. About the French and the Germans, the Italians, Americans and the Spanish. About politics and religion. About manners, customs, habits. I absorbed it all and came back for more. He taught me the art of conversation, of being in company for no purpose. The pleasure of wasting time.

It was not that I didn't know the facts. I knew many of them better than he did. I just didn't know what they meant, how they fitted together. Henry didn't provide all the answers, but he was a good start, and his generosity and kindness was the greatest lesson of all. He changed me irrevocably, and certainly for the better. I fear that I was not able to do the same for him. But from that moment, I began to question many things I had previously taken for granted.

*

It was because of Henry that I came to England and again because of him that I spent much of the next five years doing my bit for British Intelligence, although in a very much more lowly capacity than his. He came to rescue me in France in early 1940, which was terribly chivalrous of him, and whisked me off to safety. I had already decided this was the best option, but Henry's assistance and then recommendation was useful in getting me employment to pass the time. If this sounds both grand and unlikely, then it was not. The country was desperate for expertise of all sorts and my quite phenomenal ability at languages was useful. My somewhat greater skill at mathematics remained unknown, however; properly tanked up, I could have done all of Bletchley Park's work for it over a cup of tea, but that would have been hard to explain. Besides, I didn't really want to do it; I rather thought it would have been pleasant to be a land girl, ploughing the fields and growing vegetables for the war effort. Dawn, fresh air, the nobility of physical labour, all that stuff. The camaraderie of a common purpose, getting drunk in pubs on days off. Lots of sex. I had a particularly romantic notion of working in a factory, joining a union, complaining about the oppression of the capitalist classes.

But no: because of Henry, I worked for Intelligence, ploughing through Polish, German, Norwegian, Swedish, Bulgarian, Serbian, Greek and Russian texts with a speed which was considered by my superiors to be extraordinarily impressive. Boring work, for the most part. I wouldn't have minded being parachuted into France and shooting people as Henry got to do, as it sounded quite fun, except that I was extraneous to history and so there was no guarantee I would survive. The moral considerations were complex, as well; I would hardly be murdering people, as from my point of view they were long dead anyway, but I would be shortening their lives, and I would have had to calculate the potential consequences for each target. Too much work. I still think I would have been quite good at it, though. I did think of offering myself as a sort of Mata Hari, seducing German officers, combining business with pleasure, but Henry's superior, the saintly Portmore, was rather prudish and thought it a bit unladylike and un-English. Pointing out that I was neither a lady nor English did not persuade him.

Later in the war, though, such scruples were abandoned.

It had its moments, although in my case the drama was a little spoiled by knowing the outcome. I didn't share the frisson of fear at the thought of defeat, nor the remarkable uplift at the realisation of likely survival. I only let my guard slip once, in 1941, with Henry's friend Sam Wind, a man I never liked much. I had just about figured out relationships between the sexes; male friendship was quite beyond me, at least the very peculiar English variety of it. I was being cheerful – don't worry, I'm sure it will all be fine – and Wind had snapped back that I didn't know what I was talking about. Once Germany had defeated the Soviet Union and could turn back to us . . .

'No,' I said with a cheery wave of the hand. We were in a pub and I had been sampling the whisky. 'After Pearl Harbor and Stalingrad . . .'

Then, of course, I remembered it was only October. Some time to go before either of those. And the Germans were doing jolly well at that moment.

Sam, who was supercilious and superior at the best of times, gave me one of his finest sniffs of disdain, but as the news of the Japanese surprise attack began to come through in December, I remember him looking at me in a funny sort of way. All I can say is that it was the only time I ever made a mistake like that.

19

The file of papers Wind had given Lytten lay unopened in a drawer until Monday evening. Lytten had, in the past, been both flexible and adaptable, but he had never considered either to be a virtue and now he lived quite strictly to an orderly regime. That included not doing any work on a Sunday. He went to church in the morning at ten thirty, not because he was religious but because he found it a calming experience, and, what was more, the thing one should do on a Sunday morning. He liked the music, the architecture and the rhythm of ceremony. Then he walked home and had lunch. Cold meat, cold boiled potatoes, some bread and cheese. Occasionally he would accept an invitation for dinner. Otherwise, in the afternoon he would read or sometimes write, although never anything to do with his academic duties, and never at the behest of Samuel Wind.

He had known Wind for much of his life; like many male English friendships it was based on faint disdain mixed with longevity. That is, he had disliked the man for such a long time that he no longer minded the way he tended to talk primarily about himself, the way he dismissed any concerns but his own, the drawling contempt that he affected for almost everyone and everything. Life had conspired to throw them together far too often; they had, briefly, attended the same school, then the same university. When Portmore brought Lytten into Intelligence, Wind somehow found a way of joining him. He was able, he was ambitious but . . . what? Lytten never bothered to figure it out. He was too pleased with himself, and was always there.

Eventually he submitted; he made a sandwich, stacked the fire and drew the curtains, then picked up, at last, the little folder of papers.

It didn't take long to read it. There were a few East German briefing papers of only mild interest. The rest were gibberish, padding, random bits of paper swept off someone's desk with no meaning. Only one sheet mattered, and on that there was only one sentence, suitably meaningless.

'I will see the Storyteller in Paradise.'

Underneath was a date and a time. Here we go, he thought.

*

He was distracted for the rest of the evening, trying to make notes for his tale but more often staring emptily, a faint smile only occasionally playing over his face as he thought about the Storyteller. The idea had been woven through his life so much it was now embedded in his imagination as well. Was that why it had come to him when he searched for the centrepiece that would hold Anterwold together? He did not want to write about priests or kings, let alone talking lions or wizards, but all societies need authority figures. So he had come up with the Storytellers, on the grounds that they had a chance of being more peaceful than generals and more benevolent than politicians. They had popped into his mind quite on their own, so he had thought, but now he realised they had been there all along, waiting for him.

He had been the Storyteller, of course; it was a nickname given to him in 1946. When he followed the invading armies as they crossed first France, then the Rhine and into Germany, his job had not been to fight, but to interrogate captured Germans left behind as their armies retreated without them. Then he spent a year and a half living in the ruins of Berlin, surrounded by a depressed and frightened population. He was nominally a liaison officer, a messenger boy talking to the French in French, the Germans in German. He knew many of his opposite numbers well, and there he became known as the Storyteller. It might have been because, one night, at an impromptu dinner in one of the few buildings not ruined, the group of half a dozen had begun to tell each other stories. It had been his idea; he had mentioned the *Canterbury Tales*, how Chaucer's pilgrims entertained each other on their long road with anecdotes, and how Boccaccio's characters whiled away the time when hiding from the plague. They should do the same, he suggested. Tell us your stories. Truth or fiction; each man could choose.

He was the impresario of these strange evenings, the comradeship of people who knew that they would soon be enemies. After the Russian had talked of how he had learned German, and the Frenchman of life in a prison camp, and the American of his parents' route to the US from Europe, and his travels all the way back again, then Lytten told his tale, about kings and battles, the fantastical tales of Britain and the myths of the Mediterranean, putting in enough of each so that at various times each man nodded into his drink in melancholy recognition, for they were all quite drunk by the time he started, and even drunker by the time he finished.

If that was not the reason someone might remember him as the Storyteller, then other reasons, less admirable, might be responsible. For the silent war of East and West was already beginning and Lytten was there to sow uncertainty and distrust. He had done a good job, until he gave up in disgust at his task and at himself.

Now he was being summoned back to that world. He would meet this man in Paradise. Besides, he had little enough to do at the moment and he was curious as to how it would turn out. Then he could wash his hands of it all.

He would ask Rosie to look in to see if Professor Jenkins had returned – if he ever did the animal was bound to be ill-humoured, demanding and hungry. Then he would take the morning train to London, consult with the powers that be, and get this tiresome business under way.

*

Whenever Lytten went to London he avoided the nine-thirty train, as it was generally full of people he knew and he could sometimes not avoid being dragged into a conversation with someone whose name he could not remember. Most observed the unwritten rules; you would nod, smile, exchange a few words, then ignore each other totally for the rest of the journey. Occasionally, though, there would be someone who did not understand that morning train journeys were for the purposes of contemplation, not idle chatter. Just in case, Lytten always took the ten o'clock. Now he had to go twice in two days, and he was annoyed at the waste of time.

The first day he went to see Portmore, an occasion which always made him feel slightly like an eager schoolboy hoping for praise. The old man wanted to know every last detail, and Lytten thought it best to clear the little operation with him. So he discreetly went and listened carefully as Portmore, ever more garrulous as he aged, ranged over missions great and small, recent and ancient, and in the end told him to go ahead.

'Then I will leave for Paris tomorrow,' Lytten said.

'What is the meaning of this mysterious message?'

'I believe it is from a man I once knew.'

'What does he want, do you think?'

'I've no idea. A chat about old times? A job offer?'

Portmore smiled thinly. 'Why would the Soviets want any more employees here? They've got enough already. How are your enquiries?'

'I have been through the records of seven of the eight people you think are most likely to be traitors. All can be cleared.'

'That leaves Sam, does it? You left him to last?'

Lytten hesitated, then nodded. 'If there really is a traitor, as you seem to think. Are you sure you are correct?'

'Every time we get a defector, he is arrested and shot first. Every time we run an operation, our people are picked up or watched. Our contacts in Hungary are in prison. The Americans won't tell us anything any more. I am sure, as you must be.'

Portmore leaned back in his chair and stretched. 'I

am constantly being told it is time to retire, hand over to someone else. They are right. But I do not wish to leave the Service in this state. I've spent my entire life working for it, and I will not risk handing it over to a traitor. There is one, Henry, and I need you to keep looking until he is found. If we are not trusted, then we cannot work.'

'What if I do not succeed?'

'Then I will have to bypass all the most obvious candidates, just in case. Go for someone else. I have someone in mind who would suit. He's not ideal, but I cannot take the risk.'

Lytten nodded. It was a distasteful business, and he hated every moment of it. But who else could do it? Only he knew enough, and only he was above suspicion because he had left so many years back.

'Very well.'

'Keep me informed, if you will. I shall sit here and wait. You go off to Paris and have a good time. I hardly need to remind you how important this might be.'

Lytten thought about that meeting a great deal, as he lumbered back on the train, ate breakfast the next morning, and locked the house to go off yet again. So much so he didn't even notice the man standing on the pavement watching him as he heaved his bike round and began to push it towards the street.

*

Lytten stopped, uncertainly, as he saw the curious fellow standing there, staring at him, in the middle of the drive-way. He looked frightened to death.

'Can I help you?' he asked.

No reply. Just a slightly crazy stare, which faded suddenly as the eyes focused on him.

'No!' he almost shouted. 'Of course not! Why should you?'

'Well then . . . would you mind getting out of my way?'

'Oh, sorry! So sorry.' He jumped sideways, looking red in the face and flustered. Then he opened and shut his mouth several times and eventually blurted out: 'Are you Henry Lytten?'

'Yes,' Lytten said. 'Can I help you?'

'Ha!' he exclaimed, turned on his heel and ran up the road, as fast as his legs could carry him.

*

Lytten dismissed the incident from his mind. Oxford was, after all, full of strange folk whose grasp of the social niceties was often tenuous. The man had been no more awkward, rude or deranged than many of his colleagues who would twitch in embarrassment when meeting someone. Persimmon, for example.

On the boat train to Paris, because he knew it would put him to sleep, Lytten read the man's latest instalment. What better way of casting off dull care? Just about anything, in fact, but he had promised. Chapter 12 of Persimmon's lengthy diatribe extolling the virtues of Modern Scientific Management. Or rather, his work of science fiction, which seemed, in fact, to have little science and no fiction in it. Rather Persimmon, whose enthusiasm for Central Planning made him such a danger at the dinner table, and whose swivel-eyed intensity made him such an uncomfortable part of the Saturday conversations in the pub, was writing a story of such indescribable tedium that anyone who read it would feel like killing themselves. If he was correct that the future of humanity lay in carefully organised scientific efficiency, then killing yourself now would probably be a good idea.

Persimmon was a youngish man, thin, gawky, severe in appearance, who did everything in annoying moderation. He never ate too much or drank too much. He never laughed, and smiling sometimes seemed painful to him. His thin lips had trouble parting far enough to let words out, or food in. For the most part he would sit through dinners silently, eyes flickering over colleagues, and, even if he did speak, it was so quietly that only the grim precision of his enunciation made anything he said comprehensible. His colleagues put up with him but no one thought he was the greatest asset to the place and some wondered why on earth they had ever elected him. Since when was politics a subject anyway? The new generation of serious folk seemed to have an inferiority complex about never having been in a war and so made up for it with radical politics, reluctant to accept that their parents had made the world a better place. Maybe not; maybe that was just Lytten feeling old and jaded.

Letting him join the Saturday group had been a mistake. Previously it had been a group of like-minded, easy-going men who would drink their beer and smoke their pipes, comfortable in their common experiences and outlook. Persimmon changed it all. He wanted to introduce rules, set the agenda in advance, ensure everyone had an equal chance of speaking. He wanted a chairman to run what had been a random conversation and turn it into a meeting. Soon he would want a secretary and minutes written up, no doubt. Persimmon had started coming on Saturdays, clutching ever more pages fresh from the typewriter. Lytten didn't really know why; it was not as if he could abide any criticism. He was there to teach them, not to learn something from their responses. It was pure cowardice on their part – cowardice masquerading as politeness – that they did not tell him to go away and leave them in peace.

Occasionally Lytten's dutiful politeness created such inner tension that he could not avoid taking revenge. When he was feeling impishly malicious, it was irresistibly easy to goad Persimmon.

'How is the science fiction?' he might ask innocently.

'We do not say that. We say speculative fiction.'

Off he would go, bathing Lytten in a sea of censorious severity, lecturing him about fiction at the service of education, exploring human potential. Think of satellites, first dreamed of in a short story . . .

'Why write a novel then?'

'It is a way of educating the masses,' Persimmon would reply. 'To make great thought available in ways they can understand. Fiction does not interest me. As a didactic vehicle, however, it has its uses.'

'You are not afraid your readers might see what you are doing and prefer something which doesn't want to teach them a lesson?'

'No. Eventually it will be required reading in schools.'

'Will there not always be rebels and outlaws, poets and dreamers?'

'I intend to put such people in so the contrast between

antisocial disruptivism and constructive behaviour is clear. They will come to a nasty end. We have tamed the outside world through science. Why cannot we tame the inner one as well?'

'Then what of beauty and madness? Would you eliminate them as well?'

'Most certainly. Madness will be eliminated in our lifetime by drugs.'

'I suppose Plato would agree with you. I always thought his world sounded quite dreadful. I will just have to hope that we blow ourselves up before we get to your state of perfection.'

Persimmon permitted himself a smile. 'That is why the control of technology must rest with those who understand it.'

'Not politicians, then?'

'They will be swept aside and replaced by a meritocracy, chosen for ability and dedicated to achieving the best for society.'

*

He slept a little on the boat train, lulled to sleep by Persimmon's prose. In some ways it was flattering, although annoyingly so. Persimmon had listened to Lytten's careful exposition about creating Anterwold from the ground up and had decided to do the same. But, through an extraordinary feat of imagination, he had taken the very worst of communism and the very worst of capitalism and fused them together into a monstrous whole. Lytten plodded through, hoping for even the faintest glimmer of a story, a joke, a bit of whimsy, but there was nothing. How he pitied the man's students.

This occupied him until the bed in the sleeping compartment of the train was prepared and he lay down on the fresh linen sheets and drifted off to sleep. In the morning he took the Métro to the centre of the city, having his ticket clipped by the old lady who had been in the same position the last time he had come to Paris. Then onto the ancient wooden train, thick with the pungent smells of garlic, sweat and Gitanes.

Considering the circumstances, it was strange that he thought neither of his purpose nor his surroundings. Paris was a grimy place; the buildings crumbling and black from neglect, the streets dirty. Sometimes you could see the skeleton of a once fine building, a glimpse of a splendid vista, but by and large it was sad and neglected, somewhat like London, which also showed the signs of decrepitude on every soot-covered wall.

The meeting place was a dingy room in the Hotel du Paradis in another bedraggled part of the city near the Place des Vosges, its former grandeur now ruined and derelict. Lytten approached it carefully, old habits coming back to him reluctantly and without pleasure. He was not happy to remember how to avoid being noticed, how to check the way ahead and the path behind. He took no pride in his skill, rather as one takes no pride in the ability to breathe or to walk. It was just a way of life and a way of staying alive.

Why had he introduced an apparition into his story, and why did that continue to bother him? He must be getting old, and lazy. The thought was even in his mind as he walked, quietly and with ears alert for any unusual sound, up the two flights of cold, damp stairs to the room. No sound of footsteps in another room, nothing obviously out of place or strange. The concierge had given no look that was out of the ordinary.

*

Lytten knew who he was meeting, of course; it was going to be the man who had told tales of wolves and forests, and who had listened intently as he had spun his yarns in turn. Why? Because a dreaminess in his eyes made him a good choice, that was all. The others had been too steadfast, too rooted in the ground. Only the man known as Volkov would have conceived of calling a meeting with the Storyteller. Once Lytten had talked to him of Paris, of magnificence and decay, of grand hotels like the Ritz, and seedy, squalid ones, like the Paradis. The name had appealed to him. He had chuckled appreciatively at the idea of Paradise being filled with prostitutes. If only, he had said with a laugh. If only.

Volkov opened the door not with hesitation, but normally and calmly. Foolish; he should be more careful. What if it had not been Lytten? What if instead of a book in his hand he had had something more dangerous?

He stood there, a cautious smile on his face, very different from the man Lytten remembered with his fair, cropped hair, the short stocky stature, the sad eyes that would fix you intently, then dart away. His face was unlined, almost fresh, as though he had led a life without concern. Lytten remembered also the impish grin, the other Volkov, jolly and exuberant, the caricature Russian. He gestured for

Lytten to come in, throwing the door wide to show there was no one else there.

It is an important Russian who can go out alone in a western city. A trusted one; the only other people around – apart from the raddled women smoking away their loneliness in every arch of the crumbling square – were those shadows Lytten had sensed as he walked from his hotel; sensed but never seen or heard. There were no Russian minders, but . . .

He gestured for Lytten to sit on the rickety chair.

'Shall we begin?'

'By all means.'

'Then,' he said, screwing up his eyes and almost reciting, saying words he had practised often, 'I wish to come and live in your country, with a job and safety. I ask for your help.'

He paused, then grinned broadly at Lytten. 'How was that for a start?'

'Very good,' Lytten replied.

*

Volkov asked for no assurances and set no conditions. They would talk properly when they were back in England. Until then it was better to say nothing. A sensible precaution; the conversation was carefully arranged just in case someone had put microphones in the room. Unlikely, but possible.

So they did not discuss why he wished to defect, to abandon country and family and the high position of a colonel in the Soviet secret services. 'Let's just say that

205

I want to see Salisbury Cathedral,' he said. It was a poor explanation, said with a faint smile, but it was good enough. Her Majesty's government was to be presented with its latest Intelligence coup because of the power of the English language. Volkov knew England was not like Thomas Hardy's Wessex, but he was attracted by a country that could produce such works. He was attracted by an illusion, a fugitive from reality, rather like Lytten was himself.

Getting him to England was not, in principle, difficult. Except that Henry had noticed another shadow on the wall as he looked out of the window, and remembered now that he had heard a footstep, a very faint scuffling, as he walked through the street that led to the hotel. Then he wondered about the strange man who had stared at him outside his own house the previous day.

'I think we may have been noticed,' he said quietly as he studied the street below some more.

'I saw no one,' Volkov said.

'Maybe not.'

'I have told no one,' he added.

'Hmm.' Lytten again drew back the curtain very slightly. Again he saw the faintest movement under an archway; one of the girls glanced to one side and moved away. It was enough; all he needed.

'Let us be cautious, though. Just to be on the safe side.'

*

What was supposed to be simple had now become complex, but he had done more, and worse, in the past. It was not so difficult to lose those following him. Just after eleven,

206

he and Volkov slipped out the back of the hotel, across a courtyard, and took the Métro to the Gare Saint-Lazare, travelling by an indirect route, waiting on platforms to study passers-by, getting on trains then getting off again at the last moment. Neither saw anything to give cause for concern. Then they boarded a small commuter train which went only into the suburbs, and found a hotel for commercial travellers behind the station. The next morning, Lytten got him on a bus to Rennes, then another to Granville. A tiny port, filled only with fishing boats. Lytten found one that was setting out that evening; it would deliver post and food to Jersey late at night, then head for the open waters of the western Channel the next morning. With the help of a suitable inducement, the captain agreed to take them. Ports in Jersey rarely bothered to check the passports of fishermen coming from France, and ports in England rarely checked boats coming from Jersey either.

By Thursday – and Lytten was aware that he had been away much longer than he had intended – they arrived in Weymouth, then took the stopping train to Salisbury. Here they stayed the night with an old friend from school, a clergyman who had never had any contact with the Intelligence services. A good friend, who lived in the Close in a very cold, very badly looked-after house which had a large number of unused bedrooms. Here Volkov could stay until Lytten decided what to do with him.

Lytten was satisfied with him, but would he convince Sam Wind? Would he be assessed as a fraud, a plant or a treasure? That was out of his hands. The Very Reverend Horace Williams (MA Oxon) agreed to act as host and so, after extracting a firm promise that he would stay in the house and behave himself, Lytten left Volkov behind and took the train home. Unorthodox, possibly even rash, but it was an unusual situation. He could not tell anyone of his prize for fear of spoiling things. Now, he thought as he walked alone to the railway station, a little peace at last.

20

After Henary left an ill-humoured Jay by the side of the road outside Willdon, he went off on his donkey feeling strangely downcast. He hoped he was doing the right thing. He didn't even know what outcome he wanted. Did he want just to spend an evening with the Lady Catherine, discuss pleasant matters and return the next morning to find Jay there, still in a bad mood?

If that was what happened, it would be an immense weight off his shoulders, certainly. The alternative promised difficulties and heartache. He had spent much of the last five years working on the problem; he had constructed an entire intellectual edifice of speculation which now rested entirely on Jay being disobedient. But what would that really mean?

He could share his ideas with only a few people, but fortunately the Lady of Willdon was one of them. He had taught her informally before her marriage and continued to do so afterwards. He had advised her after Thenald's death, taught her much of what she needed to know about rule and authority. While few outside the world of the scholars had much taught knowledge, some grandees were educated to a fairly high degree. None would use it for practical purposes, but many studied the stories and loved lengthy discussions about their meanings. Some, by their own efforts, came to a level of understanding that approached that of the scholars themselves. Catherine was one such.

Several of the domains scattered around were of immense age and possessed treasures of great antiquity. In theory, written material was meant to be given to the scholars to be copied and protected. A copy was always presented to the original owners when this had been done, to make it worth their while. It was understood that every scrap which might elucidate or expand the Story should be known, catalogued and made available. Except, of course, that human beings often fall below the standards expected of them and there were still many documents and manuscripts the scholars knew nothing about. Henary had found some at Willdon.

The manuscripts were old but exceptionally well preserved. Half a dozen fragments and scraps written in scripts which took immense labour to decipher. Even now, after many years of study, he had only managed some thirty lines of text.

It was all but meaningless, yet that suggested its meaning was deeper than anything Henary had ever come across before. Words were magic; he who unravelled them took possession of their power. Properly deciphered, even these few lines of scribbles might shed light on the darkness, the forgotten times. He who understood the darkness would also understand the Return, for the beginning and the end were one and the same.

His colleagues would have been violently critical of him for keeping it to himself. There was a reason nothing was known of the darkness and that was, mainly, that people did not want to know. The exiles returned, settled, and history began. Men believed two things simultaneously: that there was no before, and that it was the age of giants.

Instead, the scholars focused on the Story, which began with the Return. All else was myth and allegory, which was left to the mystics, the hermits, the seers and the insane. There were many of them, the believers in prophecies and signs and hidden meanings. It was a constant struggle to stop them from whipping up people with silly ideas, of gods and disasters. The world will end; a Herald will come and summon the emissary of the divine. He will judge Anterwold and either forgive it or destroy it. It took a perverse mind to read such stuff into the texts, unless you deliberately quoted them out of context. By concealing the document, he had saved it from being hidden in an archive or from being an encouragement for the foolish.

He had found it when Catherine, then the dutiful wife, was sorting out the muniments room to restore some order in it after the neglect of her husband. Mainly legal documents, the memorial stories of long-dead members of the domain, records of crop yields and so on, dusty unrewarding work that had taken weeks to complete with a handful of assistants. The manuscripts were in a lead box, inside a wooden, iron-clad chest.

'Do you wish to take them?' Catherine had asked.

He had shaken his head. 'Not yet. Not until I know what they are.'

'How can you know, if you can't read them?'

'Work, my Lady,' he said with a smile. 'The sweat of my brow, the labour of the years. Persistence and effort. If I can't read it, no one else can. So I'm hardly depriving the scholarship of anything.'

'Arrogant man!' she said. 'Even if you are truthful. Tell me why it is so important.'

He had done so, and she had listened with fascination. 'Where did we come from? Who are we? Who were the giants? I doubt this will provide an answer, but it may offer clues.'

'This will tell you?'

He smiled ruefully. 'How should I know? All I've unpicked so far is a few short sentences. It speaks of a young boy who has a vision on a hilltop. His name is Jay. The longest passage reads, "It smiled once more, a radiant, celestial smile that brought the warmth back to his body. It raised its hands in what Jay took to be a gesture of peace, then took a step back and was gone."'

'What do you think is the meaning of it?'

'It makes no sense to me. It is obviously of a deep religious significance; the balancing of the celestial with warmth in the sentence suggests linkages between heaven and comfort. Note the words "what Jay took", which imply doubt and hidden threat. But it is only a passage from a larger text, which remains hidden to me. Then there is another, longer one which I cannot read.'

There the matter had rested until one day, some months later, Henary had gone on a Visitation and had been interrupted by a questioning child. When he had interrogated the family about the boy, he had got the shock of his life.

'Please forgive him, please. He's not been himself. He had a shock today, on the hillside . . .'

'. . . says he saw a girl. Don't we all . . . ?'

'. . . makes things up. Sees a fairy. Then the fairy vanishes

212

before anyone else can see it. Of course it does.'

But the name was wrong. Until he questioned the boy himself – 'everyone calls me Jay.'

Henary had not slept that night. How could it be? What did it mean? How could a child have relived so precisely a sentence of such antiquity?

*

He had to know the truth but Jay knew nothing. So Henary had taken the boy and begun his education. He had responded well; indeed he was a very able student who had bolstered Henary's reputation. This Henary carefully hid from his pupil. Jay knew, certainly, that he was quite clever, but Henary did not wish him to become proud, for 'pride dulls the mind, and blunts the spirit.' All the while he waited, and whenever he went to Willdon he took out the manuscript and worked on it some more. The girl and the boy would meet again, the words told him eventually.

Henary was annoyed by this, and the temptation it represented. He was trying to unravel the document as a light into the past, and here it was, offering the very different temptations of prophecy.

He had spent his entire career attacking such stuff. All the mystical nonsense babbled by his feeble-minded colleagues he would dismiss, and methodically pick apart their musings, subjecting them and the texts to the cold light of reason. The Story was the truth, but it was not always direct in communicating it. It certainly contained no magic and no prophecies. It concerned what was, not what will be.

But in his last months even Etheran had begun to wonder whether there was something in the utterances of hermits and the interpretations of mystics. Now here was this manuscript, which had foretold Jay and his encounter on the hillside, presenting a new, unrivalled opportunity to test the power of such things. Jay would, one day, trespass in the forest and the girl would appear once more, near the Shrine of the Leader. That was the prediction.

Much was uncertain, there were so many passages and words he could not understand or decipher, but the outline was clear. So he would bring Jay to Willdon and see what happened. He would prove to his satisfaction that this manuscript was not, in fact, magical. It was not prophetic. He would present his case at Ossenfud in a blast against all those who took such things seriously.

'Why do you pursue this?' Catherine asked him.

'Because I need to know. This is undoubtedly a manuscript of high importance. I do not want it diminished by becoming the plaything of soothsayers. It may contain great wisdom. I do not want that lost because it gets tangled up in superstitious babbling.'

'You really think an apparition will show up in the Shrine?'

'Of course not.'

'And if one did?'

'That would be awkward.'

'Does your student know any of this?'

'Not a word.'

*

There was no guide in the manuscript about when, or how. If the girl did not appear, then sceptics would argue that it was because the manuscript was a fraud, and mystics would respond that he should have brought Jay to the outskirts of Willdon the year before, or six months later. He had worried for long months, checked and rechecked. Then he had decided. Not doing anything would certainly produce no result. He took Jay to Willdon, left him outside and told him not to dare set foot inside the domain. Then he had gone to wait.

'Is everything ready, Lady Catherine?'

'I believe so. Your directions are so very poor I have had to use almost every man I have at my disposal. But if your boy enters my land, he will be seen and followed.'

'You won't frighten him? I feel as though I am deceiving him, and don't want him to suffer for my foolishness.'

'Not a hair on his head will be so much as ruffled.'

Henary was sitting opposite her at a table. He closed his eyes and put his fingers to his lips, uttering a silent prayer, then looked up at her. Truly, she was a remarkable woman.

'Do not think, by the way, that I am unaware of the gravity of what we are doing,' she said. 'I know full well that if this goes wrong and it becomes public then my reputation will be damaged. Gontal would be delighted to have evidence that I believe in summoning spirits and such nonsense.'

'Then why are you helping me? Goading me on, indeed?'

'Because you have fascinated me. Also, if the great Henary is about to make a complete fool of himself, I want to watch. Don't worry, though; the realisation will be my private pleasure. There is some knowledge which is best kept secret.'

She leaned back in her seat – higher than his; she liked these little demonstrations of her authority. 'Are you sure this manuscript is as old as you say?'

'I have no idea how old it is, but it is certainly ancient. I could prove it if you wanted, by showing you how the passage I am working on employs certain symbols, certain grammatical forms, uses words that are otherwise unknown. This manuscript, in other words, may tell us about the age of giants. If it does, then the Story itself may become simply part of a much greater story, perhaps not even the major part of it. If there is any power in it, then that is where it lies.'

'Yet Jay saw a fairy.'

'Coincidence, I'm sure. If it happened again, of course...'

'It would eat away at the foundations of all custom and authority,' Lady Catherine said softly. 'Who would listen to you scholars when they could listen to prophets instead?'

There was a long silence as each stared thoughtfully at the other. 'Dangerous things indeed, Scholar Henary. We must discuss them later,' she said briskly. 'There is one thing, though.'

'What?'

'What on earth do we do if someone does show up?'

'I suppose you will have an honoured guest on your hands.'

Catherine stood up and clapped her hands. 'You will excuse me,' she said as a servant appeared in response. 'I must prepare.'

For nearly three hours, Henary had to wait in an agony of hope, despair, anticipation. Several times he reassured himself that nothing was going to happen. Bit by bit, news came in which raised his hopes, then dashed them again. Jay was in his tent. He had wandered off. The lad accompanying him was primed to send signals. Henary's heart skipped a beat, but he had only gone to get some wood for the fire. Nothing more. His spirits rose, then fell once more as the message came through that he hadn't returned. Then that he had crossed the boundary into the domain.

Henary rocked back and forward with impatience and anxiety. The soldiers waiting in the forest had not found him. An hour. Nothing. Catherine came in to see how he was, and he snapped at her.

Soldiers had found him. He was under arrest. 'And?' Henary said to the runner who had sped in with the message. 'Anyone else?'

'No one else,' came the reply, and he sighed in relief. The manuscript had lied.

Then one more messenger. The last one. He was brought in by Catherine, who propelled him forward. He stood there nervous and breathless. 'Well?' Henary said. 'What is it?'

'A girl. She turned up out of nowhere.'

Henary felt his stomach turning over in panic. It could not possibly have happened. Was it a joke organised by Catherine to make fun of him? One glance at her face convinced him it was not.

'Who is she? What's her name? What does she have to say for herself?'

'I don't know, sir. But she speaks the old tongue.'

'What about Jay? How did he react?'

'He seemed to recognise her, sir.'

As the messenger departed, he went over to Catherine. He wrapped his arms around her and squeezed her tight. 'My God,' he said. 'What have I done?'

'Congratulations, Scholar Henary, wisest of the wise,' she said, pulling away and giving him a little curtsy. 'Who would have thought?'

Henary shook his head. He could think of no words to even hint at what he thought or felt.

'So, we have a new guest,' Catherine went on in a practical tone. 'I think I should give her a proper welcome, don't you? It's not often an emissary from the gods shows up. Is she the Herald of the last days? That would be so tiresome. You go and sit down and contemplate your own genius for a bit, and come through when you think you can stand straight.'

Henary grunted, but knew she was talking sense. He composed himself, reminding himself that he was a scholar of the first rank, a man of authority and the greatest learning. That he deserved respect and honour. It was hard.

When he was indeed ready, he walked through to the hallway and stood to one side, so that he would not ruin Catherine's welcome. His heart was beating hard when the doors opened and the welcoming procession came in. He saw the Chamberlain, then Jay, and finally the girl he had thought about for so long, whom he had seen in his mind thousands of times.

He was disappointed. What to make of her? No spirit or fairy, certainly. Jay's description had been a good one. She had short hair, a pretty face and a look of bemusement or even irritation. But he expected – what? What was a celestial being meant to look like? There was nothing special about her, except for her strange clothes.

The moment of study didn't last long. The girl looked around the hall and her eyes lit on him. She grinned broadly and came bounding over. He didn't catch the first words, they meant nothing to him, but the rest he understood. She spoke with absolute fluency and ease, as though she wasn't even trying. 'I'm so happy to see you! Why are you in those ridiculous clothes?'

21

Using the information available, Chang got some money and then a room in a hotel for the night. The operation shredded his nerves but he was desperate by that stage. He needed rest and shelter. He could not risk eating in public again until he had a chance of keeping the food down. He could not go into any public place if the inhalation of tobacco was going to make his head spin.

What did he need? Somewhere to sleep and eat and clean his clothes; cigarettes; wine, beer and whisky so that he could practise. Illustrated magazines and journals so that he could see how people dressed, moved and talked.

He also bought a local newspaper, which advertised accommodation to rent and in which, in due course, he could place a notice himself disclosing whether he had found Angela Meerson or not. He examined it carefully. Paper, print; he imagined men laying it all out by hand, huge presses rolling around, the paper being cut and folded, put on lorries in great stacks, taken to shops, then exchanged for money. With the money then moving back from buyer to shopkeeper, to the company, then to the workers, who went out and bought . . .

Extraordinary system. All that effort so that he could discover that two rooms (with bathroom available – hot water five shillings extra) were available at twenty-five shillings a week. He had no idea whether that was expensive or not, but it seemed to be well within his means now he had tested the theory of crime on the collection box of St Margaret's Church and placed the result on Fire Boy at eighty to one in the 2.30 at Doncaster. The voice in his head told him it was a sure thing.

So he set off the following morning. He was less frightened now by the disorder of life. Everything – roads, buildings, cars and bicycles – fascinated him. He went slowly, taking an indirect route, until he came to the run-down house with a garden that looked as though it had not been tended for years. The windows were filthy, the paintwork peeling off, and it had a general air of poverty that was most evocative.

He was tired. He was unused to walking long distances, while all around people were striding along or pedalled past on bicycles. There were hundreds of them, thousands. Much of the town was on the move, and most were on bikes. Already Chang was beginning to pick out distinctions – soft caps and rough brown coats meant workers of some sort. Dark material and hard hats meant the richer sort.

Big old houses needed to be cared for, and that cost money, so many of the occupants rented out rooms. His prospective landlady was one of these. Being alone and lonely, she liked to talk. That he had not bargained for. Within a few minutes of knocking, he was deep in a conversation. His first real one, and a terrifying experience it was.

It was exceptionally difficult, not least because it became clear that different things were communicated simultaneously – negotiating the rental of a room, obviously, but also who and what you were, whether you were honest and pleasant. Were you the sort of person who could be called on to change a light bulb? What were your interests, background, tastes? Were you – and this was the most important – respectable, itself a concept that was so complicated it was impossible to define.

The subject of the room did not crop up for some time; much of it was spent telling him things he did not see why he needed to know. She showed him pictures of her grandchildren. He had, he told her, been travelling abroad after a recent illness.

'Oh, dear! Nothing serious, I hope?'

'No, no,' he said casually. 'Brain tumour.'

The stunned look on her face showed him he had made another mistake. 'Only a little one,' he added hastily. 'Hardly anything, really.'

'You must tell me all about it,' she said brightly, and his heart sank at the very idea. 'Perhaps you want to see your room?'

Chang nodded eagerly, anything to bring his ordeal to an end, and she led him upstairs, then upstairs again. As he followed her frail form, he eagerly drank in every detail – the brown paint, the wallpaper peeling charmingly off the wall, the smell of damp exuding from the carpet. The aroma of old food hanging in the air . . .

There was a bed, a desk, a little heating device, a couple of chairs with the stuffing coming out of them, dirty yellow linoleum on the floor.

'I should have it all painted, I suppose . . .'

'It is perfect. Perfect. Just what I wanted.'

She seemed quite surprised by his response. 'Well, if you're sure . . . ?'

*

Chang sat on the old bed, his feet tapping on the cold lino-leum. He found it helped him think. He could feel a thin gust of wind coming in through the ill-fitting sash window, and he was cold. He sat perfectly still for many hours, digesting and sorting information, occasionally getting up and distracting himself by switching on and off the taps in the small cracked ceramic sink on the wall.

He was fairly confident that everything he needed had now been restored; the transmission had wiped his memory, and it had taken time for the information to seep back to a place he could access. He was fully himself again, and he even knew what he needed to do.

His job was to find Angela Meerson, and he had to do that by finding Henry Lytten. His secondary task was to find and recover the manuscript known as the Devil's Handwriting. Then . . . what? He had no idea.

He did some breathing exercises to achieve a measure of concentration and slowly wrote down a list on a piece of paper. He could not yet rely on being able to remember efficiently. As fast as his memories had come back, he had jotted down notes. Angela. Henry Lytten. Rosalind in that article. Not much, as he found writing incredibly hard, but enough to help him recall the details.

Then he went shopping, which took much of the afternoon because every item was sold in a different shop, and in each one he had to wait his turn. He returned home with three pounds of carrots, some bread, a packet of sugar and some baby food. Not perfect, by any means, but not bad for a first go. He also bought a bottle of whisky, one of beer, one of gin, two cigars and a packet of cigarettes. The baby food was delicious.

*

Well, he said to his memory, tell me. What do I do now?

There was a long silence until the response came back. 'You might as well get on with finding this Henry Lytten.'

'How do I do that?'

'Ask your landlady if she has a phone book, and look him up. Then I can give you directions. Will you want the pretty route or the quick one?'

Did he want to go home? he thought as he walked cautiously down the street the next morning. Could he survive here? Perhaps he could use the knowledge he had in his head to make some money, settle down. He could blend in. Get married, join a darts club or play snooker on a Friday. Buy a car, and wash it on a Saturday morning. Have children and worry about them. Go on holiday to the seaside every August. Could be worse.

He crossed the road (narrowly being missed by a bus) then, with increasing confidence, walked north until he came to Polstead Road, where the directory said Lytten, Dr H., lived. He was red-faced and puffing from the effort, but walked until he stood outside what was supposed to be the house. Now what? Should he just ring the bell? Was that allowed without an appointment? The idea frightened him. What would he say? He stood in the entrance to the scruffy little front garden as he thought through all the options. As he stood, the door opened and a man came out. Chang stared, fascinated. He was of middling height, with thinning hair, a portly look about him. Perfectly ordinary face. He wore those strange trousers with a ribbed effect and a green checked jacket. Chang watched as he bent down and put on a pair of bicycle clips, then grabbed a bike and, with a mighty push, began to wheel it towards the road, and towards him. He spoke, but Chang was too flustered to understand.

'Are you Henry Lytten?'

'Yes. Can I help you?'

Chang panicked and ran.

22

For all its gloomy side, I found the Second World War immensely useful. By keeping quiet, watching and listening, I perfected the art of being a middle-class lady of uncertain antecedents. Indeed, I learned how to be quite English in my general appearance, and devoted myself to growing flowers and wearing tweed. When I was in England, that is; I left all of that behind when I went back in 1946 to my little house in the south-west of France, where I spent much of the next few years growing vegetables and cooking.

In France (which I preferred for the food and the weather) I cultivated a generally bohemian air which satisfactorily disguised my occasional lapses. I also set up as a sculptor. Not because I wished to express my creativity in a three-dimensional plasticity, exploring the multi-faceted tactility of the solid form, you understand. I was rather more used to expressing myself in eleven dimensions and found a mere three a little puerile. But in the 1950s I started to build the new, improved version of my machine and, as it resembled a piece of abstract modernism, I decided that I might as well explain it as such to anyone who saw it and asked.

Once I had thought about it for a decade, I realised that the machine itself was not that difficult to construct; the version I had overseen for Hanslip had been over-designed because it passed through so many committees that it ended up being far more complex, expensive and cumbersome than was necessary. I needed no materials that weren't easily available and I realised that the amount of power required could be greatly reduced with only a few modifications. Until I worked that out (in about 1957) I had the problem of potentially needing the output of an entire power station to get it to function. After serious thought I reduced that requirement to a quantity I could get out of an ordinary plug socket, which meant I could finally start building properly, rather than just playing around.

I used an iron pergola as the basis for it – a piece of nineteenth-century garden furniture that you were meant to grow roses over. It was quite pretty in a rusty, decrepit sort of way. This became the framework for a matrix of carefully placed and shaped materials – from aluminium to zinc – arranged so the various elements in the body would be recognised and transposed in the correct order. Ideally I would have used refined aluminium, but I had to use aluminium foil in its place. Instead of sheets of pure graphite, I used lead pencils and old newspapers. Other requirements were satisfied by using patent medicines containing iron, potassium, sodium and all the rest as needed. Not quite as efficient, but a damn sight cheaper.

The result was most peculiar, and it took a lot of work to get it laid out properly, but first tests were satisfactory. I called it 'Momentum' and told anyone who saw it that it was a biting critique of modernity, representing how the culture of the past (the pergola) was contaminated and overwhelmed by the detritus of consumerist industrialism that was covering over the elegance of civilisation with mass-produced conformity. It was thus both a radical critique of capitalism and a nostalgic vision of traditional society. The essence of the concept lay in the inherent tension that existed between the two competing visions. The explanation, which sounded a lot better in French, was generally met with a look of panic and a rapid change of subject, which was just what I wanted.

*

I set up a base in Oxford in 1959. My work had advanced greatly by then, and I was ready to begin trials. I was pleased, but I needed to run tests to see if the theory held up.

My new habits of caution had not dissipated. I wanted no accidents. To be on the safe side, I aimed initially to create something so far removed from the actual future that it could not possibly become a viable alternative. For that, I decided a fantastical world would be ideal, so I could check the machinery and complete all the theoretical calculations without fear of any unpleasantness. Even that would be difficult enough at this early stage, but I could always shut it down in an emergency.

I should explain how my device worked. It operated by manipulating the ether, that non-existent substance which physicists had rationalised out of their theories on the usual grounds that if it could not be converted into one of their little numbers it could not possibly be there. Einstein's biggest mistake. This assumption was what stopped the advance of human knowledge in its tracks for the better part of a century and a half. The collected material I converted into complex algorithms and then projected them into a static, neutral space which was as abstracted as it was artificial.

Particularly, I wanted to monitor the way imagination distorted the ether (which is really just an archaic term for the universal totality of information flows). Once properly processed I could (in theory) bring a universe to life by taking an imaginative invention, projecting the information it represented into a confined space and then allowing it to extend far beyond its original size by logical progression. For this I needed a robust but simple outline, a world of the imagination which, however incomplete, was coherent, structured and – most of all – possible. Not only that, it had to be different enough from the current strand that variations could be measured and contamination avoided. Put enough information in (and what are we all but information in peculiar packaging?) and the universe would construct itself in a sort of chain reaction. Simple.

I found nothing in France which met my requirements. There was almost no one with the fanciful, whimsical sense of invention that I needed. Modern French novels were either too rooted in a rather grim reality or increasingly obsessed with sober meditations on the pointlessness of existence. The few writers of science fiction knew little science, and children's books for the most part involved an awful lot of cooking. I considered seeing what would happen if I projected a world full of talking elephants, but decided that the improbability of success did not merit the effort.

The English were a different matter. As their lives were so dreary and constrained, the fanciful exuberance of the human spirit was forced to take refuge in the imagination, which was the only place it could exist without attracting disapproval. There it flourished like a wild flower in spring. Even so, my task was hard and frustrating until Henry introduced me to his friend Tolkien. One day when he and his family were out, I set up sensors in his house. The information they slowly harvested was then processed and decanted into the device to see what happened.

Alas, quite a lot. I nearly killed myself.

*

It took a long time before I could figure out what went wrong, but every time I tried, the whole thing shut down. I thought initially that it was the magic, the population of dragons, orcs, trolls and all those beasts that he used. So I edited them out, but it still did not work – every time I ran the test, the universe would come into existence, work seemingly well, and then suddenly the entire cosmos would implode, leaving nothing but a void.

Once I thought I had succeeded. I had decided that the problem was with his wizards, who every now and then exhibit magical powers. So I reprogrammed those passages to make them ordinary people with funny hats. A world without rings, hobbits, dwarfs, dragons, elves, wizards and very large eagles became more boring, but I was desperate by this time, and finally what I hoped was Middle Earth flickered into existence. Through the entry into the controlled space I could see a seaport set into a cove, with tall, ancient buildings shrouded in mist so thick they were scarcely discernible, climbing the hills. I could see a single strange sailing ship, of a sort which fitted the style of the book but which was nowhere described in the actual text. I was excited. The device had taken the parameters of the story and extended them outside its own limits. In order to create that ship, it must also have assumed a history of shipbuilding, of carpentry, of seafaring, of past generations who had evolved the necessary techniques. It wasn't perfect, though – the buildings were fog-bound because they were still ill-defined.

Still, it was there and was sturdy enough to prove that my work had been correct in most particulars. I left it running for a few days to go off and celebrate, and it both grew and remained stable. So I foolishly gave way to temptation, decided to take a closer look and very carefully stepped through.

Much about it was satisfactory. It was indeed real – there was air, wind, land, the smells of vegetation, a sun in the sky. The ground was firm and clearly defined. But there were no animals – no birds, no sign of any fish. That worried me. Such a world cannot be stable: someone had built the ship. If people did not exist, then the ship could not have been built, which was obviously a dangerous inconsistency.

I was right to be worried. As I stood there, I felt the temperature of the wind changing, from mild to freezing cold, then hot in a way that nature, no matter how constructed, could not possibly emulate. I saw the sun change colour, then seemingly begin to melt in the sky. The buildings turned into something resembling mud and slid down into a sea that was no longer made of water but was sticky and glutinous, shining with a light that came from deep underneath. Even the hills themselves began to turn fuzzy and smudged round the edges.

I ran. Luckily I had ventured in just a few paces, but even so I had only seconds to spare. I got through, back into the safety of the Tolkiens' garage on Sandfield Road, and looked back just in time to see an entire universe collapse into chaos, then nothingness, before my very eyes.

*

I had worked hard for years, and the only thing to show for it was a universe that lasted a few hours. I had little choice – I shut down all the machinery, stashed it into a safe lock-away in a small village to the north of Oxford, and disappeared back to France to do a lot of work. It took me the better part of a year before I thought I'd worked out the difficulty. A whole series of issues had combined to make the creation of a universe derived from Tolkien's imagination impossible. Luckily they had done so, because each of them was enough to create something unstable enough to collapse eventually. I was fortunate that it had done so speedily.

The first problem was with Tolkien's world itself. In it he plays something of a trick with religion. For the most part, the tale unfolds without the divine, yet at the same time it is part of real history. As a human tale, of course this is normal. The Bible is both myth and history, and we do not know whether the ancient Greeks believed in the gods of Olympus or saw them merely as stories. Human beings can believe and disbelieve at the same time. Physics, alas, cannot, and faced with Tolkien's indecision on the matter my machinery tried to summon the gods into existence. This was a little beyond its power; it could create a belief in them, but not the actual gods. So my world was empty. As long as I did no more than observe it from the outside, all was well, but the moment I entered, it was forced to confront the contradiction and shut down.

Another problem was that it needed to be located (theoretically at least) on the line which ran from the Big Bang to the Big Crunch through Oxford 1959. Before or after did not matter, but it had to be somewhere. Tolkien's world was neither in our past nor in our future. Either it or the present had to go for the universe to be coherent. Oxford 1959 could not vanish as the machine controlling it was there, so Tolkien's world had to.

The failure convinced me that this model was too much trouble and I abandoned it, although with the greatest reluctance. That was why I thought of Henry, once he told me of his reawakened passion for fantastical tales. I realised instantly that because of his reluctance to do more than sketch out notes, his Anterwold would be perfect for my purposes.

*

Henry had returned to academia after the war and buried himself in an ideal past of words. Poetry became his reality, the people who wrote it his gallery of saints. His knowledge and imagination mingled to produce Anterwold. To the outside world, this might sound sad, even pathetic, but it was not so unusual. Many people nurse their own passions, which are the more valuable because of their privacy. In that time, some read novels or painted; still more dug their gardens or went fishing. All such activities were useless, if you define them in a purely utilitarian way. But they were also a form of contemplation in one of the last moments of humanity's existence when people were allowed time to think. 'A poor life this if, full of care, we have no time to stand and stare.' A poem Henry recited to me once to explain a line of fishermen, sitting morosely in the rain, their lines dangled into a filthy and self-evidently lifeless canal. I pointed out there was no chance of them catching any fish, and it would be quicker to get them at the fishmonger; he pointed out that they didn't want to catch anything. That wasn't why they were there.

His story would never be completed, never published, never read. His hiding place would be snatched away if it ever was. Its purpose for him was to be forever malleable, evolving in his mind and in the innumerable notebooks in which he jotted thoughts and ideas. He wasn't, in any case, trying to write anything as banal as a novel, nor was he trying to please anyone but himself. Rather, he wished to construct a world that worked, rather like some people labour away in their attics building model railways that are better (certainly cleaner and more punctual) than the real thing.

His withdrawal from active life was hardly monastic, though. Although he never referred to it directly, I gathered that he still dabbled, when asked, in the mucky ponds of Intelligence work. He taught, attended dinner parties, went to the pub. These Saturday meetings became crucial, for they guided him, steered his mind away from unlikely fantasies, added layer upon layer of human knowledge and history so that his conception became ever richer and stronger.

When I was certain that Henry was doing something to bring all the notes and jottings that he had been making for nearly twenty years into a usable form, I persuaded him to let me store my equipment in his cellar. He had no idea what it was, of course, and I rarely went to check on it. I wasn't particularly afraid of it being tampered with; it was of such a design that no one could even recognise it as a piece of machinery.

This time I planned a very cautious development. Once I got going – I finished the tests and switched the machine to autonomous operation in April 1960 – I spent weeks simply waiting for the ground to form; I didn't anticipate anything like animals or people for months, if not years. My timetable was to have a perfectly static empty world in twelve months, evidence for the existence of people in about eighteen, and then – only then – would I risk venturing in to see how solid it was. But only for a few seconds, at the most, and I thought that sending in an animal on a lead might be a good start. I had my eye on that snarling, spitting abomination of Henry's which had scratched my leg very nastily once. Exposing it to the dangers of cosmic annihilation seemed only fair.

*

My mistake – and it was a big mistake – was to omit to set the machine for a global prohibition. Henry had almost no visitors, and certainly no one who ever stayed overnight. I discounted the possibility of a stray burglar as it was an era of exceptionally low crime, and he simply never mentioned the existence of the young girl who had begun to visit him and feed his cat. Besides, for the first few months nothing happened. The damn thing just sat there, occasionally humming to itself, but otherwise entirely inert.

Then, all of a sudden, the device switched from absorption to production. A vacant universe (so I assumed) began to take form and develop at remarkable speed.

I was immensely excited by this and didn't worry too much about why it had suddenly got a move on. I assumed initially that the preparation had somehow reached a tipping point, a bit like a kettle coming to the boil after a long period of heating up. It was only when I settled down and reviewed progress properly that I realised something far more dangerous had taken place.

Anterwold had been entered, long before I would have considered it safe to do so, and it had not only remained stable, it had begun to grow magnificently as a consequence. Whereas my entry into Middle Earth had realised its impossibilities, this time the opposite had happened.

When I reviewed the security systems I had installed – not very good ones, admittedly – I spotted a girl coming down into the cellar, pulling aside the curtain that I had thrown over the pergola, staring for a while, then stepping through and, a fraction of a second later, stumbling back and running up the stairs in panic.

Over the next few days, I had some hard thinking and working to do. It had never occurred to me until then that such a powerful reaction could take place, and I needed to know how it had happened. I had an acute moral dilemma as well. Either I could guard against any risk of harm coming to the girl – for if she went through again there was no certainty she would be so lucky second time round – and shut down the machinery for a while, or I could permit her to go through, and monitor very much more carefully what happened when she did.

I decided to be responsible. Believe me when I say I had to overcome a powerful temptation; it showed how the non-utilitarian moralism of the twentieth century had affected me. Back home, the potential sacrifice of one girl for the sake of so much knowledge would not even have been worth worrying about. I went to Henry's house and closed down the machine, took a more thorough output of readings and returned home to go through them. Even the few seconds the girl had been in Anterwold had generated a rich stream of data, and I was eager to begin analysing it. It was the better part of a day before I spotted the anomaly that made me realise, with a shock, that I was too late. She had already gone back through. And I had locked her in.

*

Naturally, the first thing I thought of was restarting the machine so that the girl could come back, but that wasn't so easy; it would reset itself, as it had done last time. According to my calculations, after I briefly closed it down in order to take the readings it had reopened some eighty kilometres to the south-east, and five years and two months later. This was mainly because I hadn't been paying any attention; I wasn't trying to get it close to its previous location. I could do better, although only with a lot of work. Even then, it still wouldn't be precise, so how could the girl possibly find it?

Although I didn't mind in theory someone going into a universe created from Henry's head, there were obvious issues. I didn't know the effect of forging such a strong link between the two universes, but it was most certainly too early to find out. This was meant to be an informal experiment, just to see what happened, little more than calibrating the machinery. The trouble was, when I closed down the machine and opened it up again later, Anterwold was still there. I suspected that as long as that girl was inside it, I would not be able to shut it down. Because she was observing it as an external figure, it would continue to exist. I would have to wait until she came back, and if she didn't come back on her own, then someone would have to go and get her.

At no stage, I must be clear, did I ever even hint to Henry what I was up to. Quite apart from the clichéd responses I would get – derived no doubt from the trashy novels and films that he liked to consume while no one was looking – there wasn't much chance he would understand. Equally, there was the slight possibility that he might be offended that I had helped myself to the contents of his head without asking.

Even worse, he might believe me and demand to go and see for himself. Not many people, I suppose, have even the remotest chance of seeing their literary creation in the flesh. Henry is convinced that Shakespeare knew his Rosalind personally in some guise, but that is quite rare. I am sure Dickens would have jumped at the chance of some time in the pub with Mr Pickwick. No doubt Jane Austen would have got on like a house on fire with Mr Darcy, and what about Bram Stoker spending an evening chatting away to Count Dracula over a cup of cocoa? The dangers of Henry's imagination ending up inside itself are so evident they hardly need to be stated. Henry would know everything about the world he was in; his thoughts and Anterwold would be the same. He would be, in effect, a god. No; better he did not know.

*

The first thing I had to do was to head to Henry's house and get all the information I could – check on the stability of the whole thing, see how big it had become, do basic tests for growth and resilience. Once that was done, I could perhaps start thinking about who I might persuade to go through and search for Rosie if she didn't return. For the longer she stayed there, the stronger Anterwold would become. To anthropomorphise again, it would start getting ideas above its station; it would start sending out feelers to try and connect with its past and future, adjusting each to justify and confirm its existence.

I apologise; that's not what it would do. That suggests a degree of eventfulness, of discrete existence which is not real. It is just that I do not know how to express it in any more accurate a fashion. To put it as crudely as possible, the longer it continued, the more it would try to shunt my future (or past, or wherever it was) out of the way and take its place. I was fairly confident this would not happen but it worried me, because then everything would be down to probability. As I had no idea what Henry's universe was, then I could not calculate whether it was more or less likely than my reality.

The one thing I hoped was that his house would be empty when I arrived, as I was anxious to have an uninterrupted hour in his cellar. It was about lunchtime, and the middle of the week, so I didn't think Henry would be there. I parked in a side street nearby, walked round and, unfortunately, spotted his bike outside the front door. What a nuisance. Lovely man. But not at the moment.

23

Rosie was led through the final door – she was convinced they had gone round in circles, they had passed through so many rooms – and into a huge hall. There was a large fireplace; the windows were not merely open, they seemed to have been actually removed so that it was light and airy, with what could only be described as a throne on a plinth at the far end. The servants halted at a little wooden balustrade that ran across the room with only a small gap. Rosie stopped as well, but one inclined his head to show that she was meant to go through. She did so – feeling nervous, as if she was being ushered into some form of court room – and the servants began stamping their feet on the broad wooden planks of the floor.

She was clearly meant to continue, so she started walking again. They started clapping, adding to the noise. She kept going, and they started shouting, ululating like African tribesmen she had seen once on television. From outside, she could hear others as well, joining in the noise, all shouting and stamping as loudly as they could.

Then – silence. Rosie was now confused and alarmed. A door opened and a woman walked – glided really – through it, and placed her hands together against her mouth, and bowed to her.

'Greetings to you, and peace be with you through all your days, traveller,' she said in a melodious voice which was so quiet Rosie could hardly make it out. 'You are welcome to the hospitality of my house, as welcome as if it were your own. May you be comfortable and happy here.'

Rosie realised that this was a very formal, polite sort of greeting which presumably required an equally formal and polite reply. She didn't know what it was, but 'Hello' didn't seem right.

'I thank you for your great kindness,' she said, hoping this would do for a start, 'and for the hospitality of your great house. May it know peace and happiness all the days it stands.'

Not bad. Not bad at all. It was evidently not what she ought to have said – the slightly perplexed look on the woman's face showed that very clearly – but it seemed to be acceptable, if unorthodox.

The woman clapped her hands and immediately the others in the room began filing out. The last one closed the great doors, leaving them alone.

'Good,' she said in a warm voice. 'Now come with me. You need some care and attention before the Festivity begins.'

She came close to Rosie and studied her carefully with her deep blue eyes. Rosie did the same in return. She was a beautiful woman, with a delicate face and a way of standing that – to Rosie – made her seem like a queen with her long fair hair under a tiara of glittering stones. She was dressed all in white with a blue sash around her waist. She wore no shoes, but had a ring of gold on every toe. Rosie thought that looked rather good.

'Forgive me for asking,' she said, 'but who are you?'

'I am called Catherine, widow of Thenald, Lord

and Lady both of the domain of Willdon,' she replied. 'Although the conventions of etiquette insist that I am never introduced to anyone.'

'Why not?'

She thought. 'Probably because I should not need to be.'

'You're the one Jay is so frightened of?'

'I very much hope so,' she said with a light laugh.

'I don't see what he has done which is so terrible.'

'Ah, but you seem to know very little. Young Jay has disobeyed the direct command of his master. He has trespassed on my lands and ventured unbidden into the Shrine of the Leader. For the first he could be dismissed from his calling, for the second he could become my property, and his children and his children's children, for seventy and seven harvests. For the last, he could be cast out of human society for ever.'

'That's ridiculous.'

'It is. His master will scold him, then forgive him. As for the second, it is a law which has not been enforced in my time and I do not intend to revive it for Master Jay. Nonetheless, he has not covered himself in glory.'

'He'll be all right, then?'

'Oh, certainly. Apart from burning ears, he will be returned to you in almost perfect condition. Now, through this door here . . .'

Lady Catherine led Rosie through a door into a much smaller room which was lined with the most curious shelves the girl had ever seen: lots of square wooden boxes filled with rolls of paper. It smelled of wax and dust and flowers. It was a bit like an office, like her father's little study, except that it had big windows that opened directly onto the courtyard beyond and was bathed in light, while her father's was always dark and smelled of stale pipe smoke. 'What a nice room,' she said.

'Thank you. It is where the story of Willdon is kept.'

She said this in a way which weighed the words down with meaning, although Rosie didn't see what the meaning was. It didn't seem that serious a business, after all, to have stories. But she nodded as though she understood, and tried to look impressed.

*

While the mysterious visitor was becoming acquainted with Lady Catherine, Jay was being reminded how fearsome his master could be when in a bad mood. He had caused offence in so many different ways it was difficult to know which was going to be the most serious. Making a mess of the introduction was merely the last straw, but what could he do? The girl said her name was Rosie Wilson, and if he had said that, everyone would have burst out laughing. But to introduce her merely as Rosie made her seem like a servant, someone who had only one name. So he had stumbled and invented. So be it. He'd done his best; it was not as if he had time to prepare and besides, the welcome given them had been so unexpected he felt quite proud he had managed to say anything. He'd expected to be thrown into jail; instead they had been progressed through so many levels of greeting – six for himself, the number a scholar might expect, and Rosie was getting even more. Actually to go into the house – that was the sort of thing that only the greatest might expect.

Henary led him into a small room with a chair and a desk and closed the door.

'Well,' he said. 'Where should I begin?'

Jay shook his head and opened his mouth to reply, but Henary held up his hand to silence him.

'Just for once, Jay . . .' he said.

Henary rested his head in his hands. 'You really seem quite incapable of doing anything you are told. I cannot tell you how distressed I am that I am unable to punish you over the matter.'

Jay peered at him carefully.

'The Lady of Willdon has prepared a great festival to mark the fifth anniversary of her accession, part of which will now also be to honour the guest you discovered. As the first person to encounter her, you will continue as her escort for the occasion. Please do not smile, speak or show any sign of pleasure, or you will provoke me beyond endurance.'

Jay sat completely immobile.

'When we get back to Ossenfud I will have dreamed up a punishment which will be time-consuming, difficult and acutely unpleasant for you. Until then, I propose to say no more on the matter, although I trust you will do me the honour of not thinking that I am so addled that I will forget something which will be as satisfying to me as it will be miserable for you.'

Jay, who could not believe his good fortune and could not understand it either, nodded mutely.

'Now, you have a few hours to prepare yourself, so you will go, bathe and dress in clothes which do not bring disgrace either on East College or on me.'

'But Master . . .'

'Well done. Well done indeed. I believe you have kept quiet for nearly two minutes. That must be a record. If you wish to speak, you can answer questions instead, not ask them. This girl. Her name is Rosalind?'

'Yes.'

'Where does she come from? Who is she?'

'I don't know. She talked a little about herself, but I couldn't make sense of it. We didn't have much time. She said she wanted to go home, and kept talking about a light which wasn't there any more.'

'What do you mean?'

'She just said a light,' Jay replied helplessly.

'A light? In the woods?'

'That wasn't there.'

'Are you – or is she – playing some sort of elaborate joke?'

'Believe me, I would not dare at the moment.'

'A credible answer.'

'As for her – I don't know. I don't think so. She seemed very worried, and annoyed. You should ask her. She was very willing to answer the few questions I put to her. I just didn't understand the answers.'

'I will certainly do so. Meanwhile she must be treated with the utmost care.'

'Why?' A question. Henary raised an eyebrow.

'Because, young man, she may well be the key to knowledge of immense importance. We must not frighten her and must not lose her. Your job – and the reason your punishment is to be postponed temporarily – is to make sure my wishes in this matter are respected. You know her already. Did she like you?'

Jay blushed.

'Perhaps she did. Perhaps she trusts you. You must live up to that trust. Watch over her carefully.'

'If she has to be protected and kept from others, why display her at a festival?'

'The festival, not a festival. The grand ceremony to confirm the rule of the domain holder. The etiquette is complicated and precise. Believe me, I would keep her locked away if I could, safe from prying eyes. If that is understood, you may go and prepare yourself, and I will go and meet your fairy.'

*

'Ah! Henary,' Catherine said, turning as the door opened. 'How was that?'

'Most enjoyable,' Henary said with a smile.

'Good. Now, you two know each other already, so there is no need to go through that. Henary has asked to speak with you alone for a while. I trust that is acceptable?'

'Um ... yes. Why not?' Rosie said. 'As long as you haven't been mean to Jay. If you have, I won't say a word to you.'

Henary appeared to find this answer highly pleasing. He rubbed his hands together in satisfaction. 'We are the very best of friends,' he assured her. 'All his limbs and bodily organs are exactly where they should be, and I have packed him off for a long bath.'

'That's all right, then. What do you want to know?' she asked. Catherine nodded to them both and slipped quietly out of the room.

'Well,' Henary replied, as he gestured for her to sit,

waited until she had done so, then sat himself, 'I would like you to answer a question. How do you speak so well?'

Rosie did her best. 'Mummy tried sending me to elocution lessons, because she thinks ladies should speak properly, and of course we have to recite poetry at school, you know. I never win, but I do well enough.'

'So you are a scholar?'

'A what? Oh, a scholar, I suppose you mean.' She was perplexed by the way he pronounced the word for a moment. 'Oh! No. Everyone knows I'm not clever enough for that. Are you a foreigner? I suppose that explains why you talk so oddly.'

'I've always been told my enunciation of the values of the speech is perfect,' he said stiffly. 'Skoo-LAIR. Short, then long, emphasis on the second syllable.'

'It isn't said like that,' Rosie said. 'It's SKOL-ur. Short o, emphasis on the first. Hard ch.' She looked at him suspiciously. 'Are you French?'

The conversation was not going as Henary intended. He walked to a large box in the corner and brought out a manuscript, which he lovingly removed from its protective casing. 'Would you come over here, please?' Rosie obediently did as he asked. 'Now tell me, can you read this?'

She reached out to take it, but Henary grabbed her hand. 'Careful!'

He was so obviously and genuinely alarmed that Rosie instantly apologised, although she could not see what she was really meant to be apologising for. She craned her neck and peered over his arm.

'What is it?'

'A fragment from a document I have been working on for many years.'

'I'll give it a whirl. "In the autumn of his life," she read swiftly, "'Esilio gathered all his followers, and spoke. 'My friends, my journey is at an end. You must continue without me, knowing that for you, also, an end is near. This place belongs to all men, all women equal. I will see you no more, until we meet again at the end of time.' The old man lay down his head and died. He was an hundred and twenty, yet his eye was not dim, nor his force abated." Well,' Rosie said, looking up at the reverent face of Henary, 'that's a bit odd. All women equal? His eye not dim? It should be "all women equally" and "eye not dimmed". It must have been written down in a real hurry.'

She noticed to her very great surprise that Henary was looking at her with disbelief. 'What's the matter?'

'Do you know what that is?'

'Not the faintest idea. Sounds a bit like the Bible. You know, Moses and the Promised Land. We get that at Sunday School. It's the same idea, surely? Old man, leading his flock to a new land and dying just as he gets there.'

'Yet you read it and find fault.'

'It's not hard. The handwriting's terrible though.'

Henary smiled bravely. 'We must talk some more,' he said. 'Alas, it is now time for you to prepare for the evening.' There was a slight tremor in his voice.

*

The next few hours were, in Rosie's opinion, the most wonderful of her life. Lady Catherine returned and led her into a room – a whole series of rooms, in fact – which were full of all sorts of delightful things. Baths, thick cloths, bottles of strange substances; it was warm and comfortable there, with a thick pall of steam from hot water coming from one of the rooms, heavy smells of perfume coming from others.

'Here I will leave you again,' she said. 'You will be in good hands.'

'What are they going to do to me?' Rosie asked in alarm.

'Prepare you for the festivity. We cannot have an honoured guest looking like . . . well, you are not dressed quite properly. You will be washed, and prepared, and dressed.'

'You make me sound like a chicken,' Rosie said. 'You're not a witch, are you? I mean, like *Hansel and Gretel*?'

'Like who?'

'You know. The story. The boy and a girl who get captured by a witch, and she fattens them up to eat them, then they push her in the oven and escape.'

'Why do you want a witch? Are you ill? I could summon one from the village if there is something which ails you.'

'Oh, no,' Rosie said quickly. 'No. Not in the slightest. Forget I said it.'

'Very well.' She clapped her hands and two women appeared, one scarcely older than Rosie and one about the same age as her mother. They went through the ritual of greeting once more.

'We will meet again at dusk. Until then you must relax and cleanse your mind and body of all wearisome things.'

She left, and they began.

In the back of Rosie's mind was still the thought that this might be an elaborate trap – although it seemed a lot of trouble to go to. It might be they were preparing her to become a human sacrifice – she had read about that. Or that they planned to eat her. Or something equally horrible and unpleasant.

But they were so nice and once it was clear they had no intention of listening to her protests – I've been doing my own bath since I was six, thank you very much – Rosie accepted that she had no choice but to give in.

Conversation was not very good – Rosie tried to ask them questions, but they just blushed and giggled when she did – so communication was limited to requests and instructions, delivered in a strange accent, very much as though they were speaking a foreign language which they knew only poorly. 'If you would have the goodness to stand while we remove . . . ?'

They did this, and were much less perturbed by Rosie standing there with nothing on than she was; then they bathed her, and led her to a table where she received her first massage, which she enjoyed greatly once she got used to it, although at the beginning she was still thinking actively about cannibalism. By the end – pummelled as she was – she was so relaxed she didn't care. Let them eat her! She didn't mind.

Then another long soapy bath, after which she was dried and anointed again with oil from head to toe. Next they wrapped her in thick towels and began on her feet, which elicited a tutting of disapproval. These they scraped and rubbed, then painted her toenails a bright red and slipped rings over her toes. One gold and two silver on each foot. Her hands were treated similarly.

Finally, they applied themselves to her head. Her hair

was brushed like it had never been brushed before, with sweet-smelling liquids massaged into her scalp so it tingled. They cut it – how on earth would she explain that when she got home? If she ever did – and bound it up in a complicated arrangement which somehow stayed in place when they had finished. It never did when she tried it in her bedroom.

Rosie was almost asleep from the surfeit of sensations by this time, so she made no objection when they began on her face. This was again rubbed and massaged, her eyebrows plucked, her teeth violently cleaned, before they began on the make-up. Her mother had never allowed even the slightest hint of paint – though other girls her age were experimenting – so she would have become excited had she not been so relaxed. Lips, cheeks, eyelashes, eyebrows, nose, ears were all given full attention until Rosie could no longer even grasp what they were doing to her. Later she realised that they had not only cut her hair, they had dyed it as well. Oh, am I going to be in trouble, she thought. Finally they brought an extraordinary wig, long and golden, quite unlike her own hair, and carefully put it on her head, tucking her hair out of the way. It was surprisingly comfortable.

Then they were finished and – tentatively, nervously – held up a mirror for her to see herself.

Rosie gasped in utter astonishment. In the glass there stared back at her, wide-eyed with wonder, the face of an undeniably, amazingly, fabulously, magnificently beautiful young woman, the like of which she had never seen in a mirror before. 'Lordy!' she said reverently. 'Just look at that!'

The servants smiled nervously, realised it was approval and then grinned broadly.

*

When she was finally ready, Rosie was taken to Lady Catherine's private suite in the house, shown through the door and left alone with her.

She was so bewildered by this stage she had stopped thinking altogether. Nothing made sense. She could, of course, have behaved normally – stamped her feet, burst into tears and demanded to be taken home – but she suspected that would achieve nothing. This was all too elaborate to be some joke. Too solid to be a dream. Too strange to be anything other than real. She was dressed, manicured and coiffed more elaborately than any debutante or film star, being treated like some form of royalty and had no choice but to play her role. That might, at least, allow her to find out what all this was about. Meanwhile, she might as well enjoy herself. Worrying wasn't going to make any difference.

Her idea of courtly behaviour came mainly from the novels of Jean Plaidy and the lesser Hollywood epics she saw on a Saturday morning at the Odeon. Not much, but in all of these silence and slow movement seemed to be the foundation of grace. The first was not her strong suit, but she had, often enough, practised being presented at court in the privacy of her little bedroom. She could do what was necessary.

To her vague disappointment, it wasn't required, at least not yet. In her rooms Lady Catherine was relieved of her duties as Lady of the domain. There – and there alone – she could be herself. It was where she received Henary, for example, when she wanted a proper argument with him. Where she received those she trusted and liked, when she did not need the protection of her position. By Rosie's standards she was still formal, but certainly less scary or strange.

'Sit, Rosalind, please do.'

Lady Catherine was also transformed for the Festivity. She wore what Rosie guessed was a cloth-of-gold robe and had rings on every finger, one of gold, one of silver on each and all with stones in them. Her fair hair – which Rosie now realised was a wig as well – had been brushed with gold paint, so that it sparkled in the light. Around her were belts, several of them, across her chest, stomach and hips. The effect was very peculiar but, Rosie conceded, very attractive also. 'You look very nice,' she said.

Lady Catherine smiled. 'Thank you,' she said. 'You also look quite different.'

'Don't I just! Who would have thought! If Mummy could see me at the moment, she'd have a heart attack, I think.'

'I do hope not. Is your mother ill?'

'Oh, no. Fit as a flea, but she's not one for dressing up, if you see what I mean. Especially me. She thinks I'm too young.'

'Too young? You must be – what, fifteen?'

'And a quarter.'

'You are not married?'

'Of course not.'

'Betrothed, then?'

Rosie laughed. 'Don't be daft,' she said. 'Oh, I do beg your pardon. It's just a saying. No. I am not. People don't get married until they are in their twenties at least. Normally, I mean.' She decided not to go into the example of Amy, who had had to leave school suddenly last year.

'You come from a long way away, don't you?' came the suddenly serious question.

Rosie nodded. 'I think I must.'

'Do you know anything of Anterwold?'

Rosie looked at her, open-mouthed. 'Did you say Anterwold?' she asked incredulously. 'Anterwold?'

'Yes. That is what this land is called. Did you not know that?'

'Oh. No,' the girl replied, properly flustered for the first time. 'I know nothing. I don't know where I am or how I got here. I don't know how I'm going to get home. I'm going to be in real trouble when I do. I mean, not perpetual slavery. But a lot of detentions. Anterwold? Are you serious?'

'Hush, my dear, don't worry. We wish to help you. It may be you will be able to help us as well. We shall see. I must tell you that at the moment there is nothing we can do. We don't know how you got here either. But Henary . . .'

'Yes. Him. He seems terribly nice.'

'He is the wisest and most learned man in the land. If anyone can help you, he can. You must trust him, for he means only well. Can you do so?'

'I will ask Jay.'

Lady Catherine raised an eyebrow. 'You trust the opinion of a student over mine?'

'Certainly,' Rosie said. She smiled apologetically for her cheek.

'In that case, you must ask him. He will be your escort for the Festivity. I hope that does not offend you.'

'Oh no! Why should it? Who is he, anyway?'

'Henary says he is one of the most gifted students he has ever had, although apparently he is quite unaware of that, so please do not tell him. Pride gets in the way of learning. One day – if he learns to obey rules and follow orders, which at the moment seems unlikely – he may be a very great Storyteller.'

'Is that good?'

Catherine looked at the girl, who was evidently serious.

'Yes,' she said. 'There is no higher achievement or honour in the world.'

'In that case, it must be a very different world from mine,' Rosie replied.

*

In contrast to Rosie, Jay received no special treatment, for which he was deeply grateful. Any attention he might have received would certainly have been unpleasant, and he still could not believe his good fortune in escaping unscathed, at least temporarily.

Moreover, he had questions of his own to ask. For example, when he left Henary, he was met by a servant, carrying his best robes. By the elevated standards of Willdon, they were poor enough, what he had to wear on high days at college, but they were a great deal better than his normal clothes. Henary had brought them with him, but how had he known in advance that Jay would disobey his orders to stay outside the domain? Had he been determined to overlook the fault even before it had been committed?

An imponderable question, with no answer that he could see. Oddly, mysterious though it was, it was not the thought that filled his mind as he found his way to the bathhouse (the communal one – no one was going to celebrate his presence) and began to prepare himself for the night.

No; his mind was full to bursting with the strange girl who had reappeared before him. So many questions floated in his head, he could not fix on any one long enough to make sense of it. Who was she? Where was she from? Why the unusual name, appearance, clothes, words, behaviour? Why was he given the job of being her guide for the evening? (Henary's explanation made no sense.) Why such a welcome for her? Who (he repeated for the tenth time) was she?

When he met her once more, just as dusk was beginning to fall, he did not recognise her. He was standing in the first courtyard, wondering how the evening would unfold, when he saw two figures approaching him. Both were of unmatched beauty and elegance, one tall and fair, the other shorter, and with long golden hair. Both wore the finest clothes he had ever seen in his life; over their faces they already wore the glittering, elaborately painted masks which gave both an air of mystery. They were, he thought, nothing to do with him; his role was merely to stand in the corner, watch them go by and admire from a distance.

But they walked towards him and the shorter woman smiled. It was the smile that jolted him into realising who she was, and also that the creature next to her must be the Lady Catherine. He went down onto one knee with a deep reverence.

'Stand up, Master Jay,' said Lady Catherine. 'I do not intend to eat you this evening. Breakfast tomorrow, perhaps?'

Jay returned to his feet but could not look into her eyes, so shy and abashed was he.

'Or perhaps I should leave that to your master. What do you think?' she added.

'Shall I do the introductions?' Rosie asked. 'Now, let me see; I'd like to get it right. It seems so important here. "It is my very great pleasure, and an honour to me and my family . . ."'

'Only a pleasure,' Jay corrected. 'Only a master should be introduced with very great pleasure. In fact, in my case, you should probably say "It is my duty".'

'For this evening, we grant you very great pleasure,' Catherine said. 'In fact, we might dispense with it altogether, as the Festivity starts so soon. You are Jaramal, son of Antus and Antusa, and are known as Jay.'

He nodded.

'Then that is what I will call you also. I welcome you to my home, Jay Antusson; may you be happy here, as if it were your own.'

Jay was speechless, which was, for once, not good. He was expected to say something in return. Luckily Rosie did not realise this and interrupted.

'Jay!' she said. 'Isn't this just fantastic? There's going to be a party, and you are to be my escort. Lady Catherine says it will last all night. I've never been up all night. Except once on New Year's, but that was only because I sneaked out of bed when everyone was downstairs.'

'It will be my very great honour . . .'

'Oh, do stop all that, please, or you'll be no fun. As I'm stuck here, I have decided to enjoy myself, and I can't do that if you keep on bowing at me and looking as though you've just swallowed the soap.'

Lady Catherine laughed. 'Well said, Lady Rosalind. Jay, I command you to obey her wishes, and those of your master.'

With that she withdrew, leaving them alone.

Jay scarcely noticed her going; instead he was gazing at Rosalind.

'What? What is it? What's wrong? What have I done now?'

'Nothing. I just think you look beautiful.'

She blushed mightily at the compliment. No one had ever said anything like that to her before. The closest she had ever come was when Colin in year two had said she was quite pretty, he supposed. This was a great improvement and she didn't know how to reply. So she just said, 'Do you mean it? Or is that just what you're meant to say?'

'I mean it. Every word.' Then he held out his arm and she linked hers in it. He adjusted it so that her hand was gently resting on his forearm, and said, 'Would you care to walk around the Festivity?'

The guests had been arriving in the far courtyard for some time and were spreading out around the gardens. All were in their finest clothes, all talked softly. Only the occasional sound of laughter rose above the gentle murmur of voices. Then a loud trumpet sounded from an open window on the second floor of the house and a great cheer rose up, with applause and cries of 'Well sounded, trumpeter! Sleep well! May you sleep through dawn!'

'We've begun,' Jay said. 'Now all is permitted until dawn.'

'Anything?'

'Yes.'

'So go and ask Lady Catherine – or should I call her Katie? – for a dance.'

'You should not call her Katie. It may be permitted but that does not mean it is wise.'

'Coward.'

'I admit it. Besides, I want nothing more than to talk to you. "I would not want to choose for wealth and not for perfect love."'

It was a quotation, of course, but not entirely spoiled by the fact that Rosie didn't notice. In fact, Jay realised with a start, it was just as well she didn't. The story was of the starving man given a choice between a pig and a beautiful but foolish woman. In the end, after much anguish, he chooses the pig to feed his family, uttering the words as he sends the woman away. Not the best of compliments.

'What's this party in aid of? This Festivity, I mean.'

'It is the fifth Festivity of the rule of Lady Catherine. It marks her accession.'

'She has it every year?'

'She should, but Henary tells me that for the last two years she cancelled it. The harvests were bad, and she said it would be better to leave the food with those who needed it.'

'Good for her.'

'Not everyone thought so. Some considered it a scandalous break of tradition. Gontal made a fuss about it.'

'Did you think it scandalous?'

'I know nothing about it. Only what Henary told me an

260

hour ago. Anyway, the music will begin soon. Let us walk until then.'

'What about food? I'm starving.'

'Later.'

*

The Festivity was magical beyond imagining. Much of the grounds had been taken over and the paths were lit with torches which cast a soft, reassuring light over the hedges and bushes. All around were gaily coloured pavilions and tents, which contained food and drink or music and dancing. Some were put up by guests, for it was a grand thing to have your own tent for such an occasion. At one point a tall masked man bowed deeply to Rosie, leaving her confused about how to respond.

'Should I have done something there?' she asked when they had walked past.

'You should have curtsied back,' Jay said. 'It is safe to do so for a while longer. As you did not, he undoubtedly thinks you are haughty and proud. You have humiliated him, and the only good thing to say about it is that there was no one around to watch.'

'Oh, I'm so sorry! Let's go back and I'll apologise. It's just that he reminded me a little of that horrid man I met in the forest.'

'That would make things worse. What man?'

'Before I came across you. There was this man. I said hello and we talked, but then he ran off. It wasn't important, I suppose, but he was really rude. I didn't like him in the slightest. Do you know how sometimes you can dislike someone the moment you meet them? And what do you mean, young Jay, when you say "safe to do so for a while longer"?'

'After night has properly fallen and the stars are out, if you curtsy back to a man you become his companion for the next hour.'

'Goodness. What for?'

'To do whatever you wish to do. It's not a promise of marriage or anything, if that's what's worrying you.'

'I'm glad to hear it.'

'Best to forget about it now. Explaining why you didn't respond might take all night. Besides, I am supposed to keep you close.'

'Are you indeed?'

'Yes. Henary gave me strict instructions.'

'Did he? Then you can tell Henary from me that I don't want him choosing my companions any more. I suppose if it wasn't for that you would be off with someone else. I'm sorry you have to spend time with me. You must find it a terrible imposition.'

'No, no, no. Dear Rosalind, I can think of nothing better. I am the luckiest man in the world. Do you think I would be able to accompany a woman of such beauty otherwise?'

She grunted, slightly mollified by the completeness of his apology. 'I'm sorry. I am a long way from home. Please remember that every time I make a mistake.'

They walked without speaking for a while, until Jay said softly, glad to be able to move on to a new subject, 'Look, we are at the lake. Shall we take a boat?'

They had indeed arrived at a small jetty which jutted out into a broad lake that had been illuminated by torches on tall poles in the water. On the lake already were half a dozen boats, drifting or being rowed slowly towards the centre. They had lanterns in the rear and were covered in brilliantly coloured cloths.

'Would you join us, young couple?' cried a man standing upright in one of the boats. 'We have space for two more, and I'd welcome another pair of hands.'

'Gladly, sir, thank you,' Jay said, and he steered Rosie towards the water. 'Do you mind?' he whispered. She shook her head and allowed herself to be handed into the boat, where she sat next to a large woman at the front.

'The best evening to you,' said this woman cheerfully. 'What a splendid occasion this is. I present myself as Renata from Cister. That is my husband, Beltan. Are you comfortable? I do hope your young man is better with boats than mine is. Otherwise we are going to go round in circles and get seasick. Do you care to introduce yourself, my dear?'

All this was delivered in a torrent of good humour that rather reminded Rosie of Mrs Hamilton, the old lady who ran the bed and breakfast for students down the road. She also would begin a conversation with about twenty questions.

'My name is Rosalind,' she said, aware of the fact that she was beginning to think of it as her proper name. That reminded her of the young man in the forest again. Of his look, his eyes, and the tingled confusion in her stomach. 'This is Jay,' she added.

'Excellent! Young, tall and strong. That's the way I like 'em. Master Jay! Pick up that pole and pay the price of youth, if you please.'

Jay laughed and did as instructed, or tried to. In truth,

he wasn't very good. Rosie, who had been taken punting once or twice and had watched students from the river bank, wanted to jump up and show him how it should be done, but it would ruin her clothes and might not be the right thing to do. 'Make sure the pole goes down fast and straight,' she called out. 'Otherwise you'll push us sideways.'

Jay flushed. 'It's just that I've seen it done before,' she said, as she worried that she had humiliated him in front of strangers. 'Try it.'

Annoyed he might have been, but he followed her advice and soon the little boat was skimming across the surface, with both Renata and Beltan applauding loudly from their cushion-covered seats. 'Bravo, young man,' they said. 'Now could you manage to stop?'

Jay figured it out eventually, and they took up a position close by a sort of pontoon floating in the water. On it was a solitary man and a jumble of what were obviously musical instruments.

'Just in time,' someone from another boat called. 'The music begins in a few moments.'

'Who is singing?'

'Aliena, the student of Rambert.'

Beltan gave a laugh of astonishment and delight. 'Is that the truth, now? This is wonderful, wonderful!' he cried. 'We may just have time for some food as well. Tie up the boat, young man, and come and sit with us.'

He patted the seat beside him and then leaned forward to open the hamper beside his legs. 'Chicken! "Bread, wine, fruit and sweetmeats! Come one and all, and eat your fill!"' he cackled.

'Level 3, 47?' Jay suggested.

'Perhaps. A student, are you? I thought you had the look of one. Boating skills as well.'

Jay made a face. 'And you, sir?'

'My uncle, now long dead, was a student. He used to quote things at us all the time, and some stuck in my memory. He didn't become a Storyteller, though. We've never had one in our family, as far as I know. Now you, beautiful Lady Rosalind, are you also a student?'

'A sort of student,' she said. 'It's complicated.'

Fortunately, she was pressed no further on the subject, although she was quite pleased with herself. By concentrating hard she had managed to make out enough of what the couple had said, and had ventured a reply, which had been understood. They seemed, she thought, to be talking a sort of English after all. It was very simple, though, almost the way an infant might speak.

The older couple settled back in their cushions with a look of contentment on their faces. Rosie noticed that the old man slyly took hold of his wife's chubby hand and gave it a squeeze. With the other, she brought out rolls and chicken and strange-looking sausages.

Their boat was moored to a gaily coloured pole topped with a lantern that spread its light on the ripples of the lake. Beyond the shore, stretching into the distance, were rolling uplands, covered in fields and woodland, still just visible in the rapidly fading light. Twenty or thirty other boats were moored around them, each lit by lanterns, and the murmur of voices, subdued by the beauty of the scenery, echoed across the water. Although night was falling, the air was still warm and even the water, as Rosie pulled her hand through it, was pleasant to the touch.

She lay back and looked up at the stars, which were beginning to shine more brilliantly than she had ever seen them before. She recognised some. She didn't know much about the stars, but she knew enough to realise that, wherever she was, the stars were the same. She listened carefully, but there was no sound, no background rumbling of traffic. Only the noise of the water against the side of the boat, the distant sound of crickets on the banks, the occasional screech from some passing bird.

'Here they come,' Jay said, disturbing her peace. 'Here comes Aliena. Just look at her!'

A heavy boat was being driven purposefully through the water. In it were six people, four rowing, two sitting idly, one at each end. The man at the front leapt out onto the pontoon when the boat nudged alongside and tied it up. Then the rowers followed, and, last of all, the small figure in the back walked delicately forwards and was handed up onto the floating stage. Another boat, unlit, rowed by a single hunched figure followed, then rowed off to rest in isolation away from the audience.

She was dressed in a robe of deep red, which was all the more striking for being lit only by dim candlelight, and stood straight and still, facing the boats and ignoring the men behind her as they took their places, picked up their instruments and began to tune them.

'Isn't she lovely?' Beltan said with a tone of awe.

'Oh, she is,' Jay said with too much appreciation in his voice for Rosie's taste.

'You wait till she sings,' his wife added. 'From all I've heard, at any rate.'

The sound of tuning died away, and, after a moment's

silence, Aliena held up one hand and began to sing.

It was the strangest singing Rosie had ever heard in her life, and it took some time to get used to it. It wasn't a song, exactly, nor an opera; indeed, she couldn't quite make out what it was, but it went on for a very long time. Sometimes it was recognisably tuneful, but this never lasted long. It wasn't like the sort of song Rosie knew, where the tune would be repeated three or four times. Rather it was sung once and then the singer changed it, bit by bit, so it slowly disappeared or turned into another tune altogether. There were parts which were like chanting, others almost speaking, but always there was some brief fragment of a melody, so short Rosie's mind could only just notice it before it was snatched away again. Sometimes the musicians would echo what she was singing, other times they would seem to be playing something entirely different.

Above all, there was the voice of the diminutive but commanding figure standing before them, gently responding with her body to the sounds she was making. It was like liquid gold, rich, amber, resonant. Rosie thought of the songs which Professor Lytten had played her, the sort of singing where the music isn't so important, a voice which can make anything sound beautiful. This Aliena, although she must surely be very young, had a voice like that. When this was joined to the hypnotic music, Rosie – along with everyone else in the audience – soon fell into a sort of trance.

Even the words were strange. No be my baby, let alone rocking around the clock. This instead was a most peculiar story about people coming to some place and making a fire and having a dinner. That was about it, really, but the singing put emphasis on certain parts – the taste of the first food produced a lovely (if brief) tune. When everyone went to sleep afterwards there was another, which Rosie was sure she had heard before.

Then it came to an end. The musicians faded out, leaving the girl to sing alone for the last couple of minutes, until her voice also disappeared into the sounds of the water and wind, leaving nothing behind her except what even Rosie was beginning to think of as the real world. There was no applause; the people in the boats showed their appreciation by beating their hands firmly against their breasts. Aliena responded by clasping her hands together and looking down for as long as the noise continued. One by one, the punts occupied by the audience were untied and they began to drift back towards the shore, trailing the yellow torchlight behind them. Only Jay noticed the single boatman also rowing off, in a different direction. He saw Aliena glance at him, then toss her head in anger.

*

'Well, young students, have you ever heard the like before?'

It was Renata who spoke as Jay punted slowly back to the shore. Her husband was incapable of speech. The tears had run down his face for most of the performance, and he was still dabbing a handkerchief against his eyes and snuffling occasionally.

'She was wonderful,' Jay agreed enthusiastically. Too much so, in Rosie's opinion.

'You must tell her, then. I'm told she gets offended if

people fail to compliment her. She does deserve all the compliments we might proffer.'

For this was the true applause. The singer had taken up her position at the very end of the jetty, and one by one the audience got out of the boats, approached her, bowed and spoke a few words. It was, Rosie realised, going to be another of those terribly formal moments where what was said was prescribed down to the last breath.

'Jay,' she whispered urgently. 'What should I say?'

He looked panicked. 'I don't know. I know what a man must say to a female singer. I know what a woman must say to a male singer. When one or the other is older or younger. But I don't know the words for a woman to a woman when they are the same age and both under the age of maturity. Renata?'

She also looked apologetic. 'It is most unusual for a girl of your age to go to such performances. And even more unusual for a girl of her age to sing at them. I'd just say the usual, if I were you, my dear.'

That didn't help, of course, and now it was too late. The punt was alongside and Beltan had recovered himself enough to get out and hand up his wife, then Rosie. Jay followed and they were then in the queue to give greetings to their singer.

Although hardly older than Rosie was herself, she looked terribly mature and grown up. Her stance was almost imperious, her expression frigid and cold; only her short stature diminished the effect. She received the enthusiastic thanks and congratulations like an empress, nodding only and scarcely looking at the person addressing her. Beltan and Renata got the same treatment, and so did

Jay, who was evidently star struck, almost trembling with excitement.

That annoyed Rosie greatly, as did the realisation that all these silly rules were going to make her feel like a fool again. In her opinion, she was doing her best in very difficult circumstances. Indeed, when had anyone been in more difficult circumstances?

So when her turn came, the fearful mood had been replaced by one of defiance. 'I'm a foreigner,' she announced. 'I don't know the words, and I don't know what I am meant to say, but that was beautiful. Utterly wonderful and I have never heard anything like it before. And your clothes are just amazing.'

Aliena flinched, then broke into a broad grin. 'Do you like them?' she said. 'I was told they looked coarse.'

'Heavens no! You look like a queen. It suits you perfectly. Velvet, isn't it?'

'Yes. It's more expensive than . . . well. It was expensive.'

'I can imagine. Who made it?'

'I made it myself, but I couldn't get the seam right.' She lifted the sash around the waist and Rosie saw how the join of two bits of cloth was rumpled and untidy. Very amateurish.

She made a face. 'You need to cut little darts right the way around,' she said. 'My mum showed me how to do that. I could fix it easily.'

'Really? Could you really?'

'Of course.'

'Then you will. You must. Will you?'

'It would be my pleasure. A practical gesture of thanks for the delight you have given me this evening.'

Aliena laughed. 'That is a better way of putting it than many I have heard. Did you like my ending? I put it in just to annoy Rambert.'

'Who?'

'Rambert. My teacher. He was the one alone in the boat with a sour look on his face. We had a real fight this afternoon, so I thought I'd put in something unorthodox to annoy him. We'll have another fight about it later, I suppose.'

'I thought it was lovely.' Then Rosie remembered where she had heard it. Just a snatch of a tune, scarcely recognisable. '*Casablanca*,' she said. 'That's what it was. You know. Although I suppose you don't,' she added a little lamely.

Rosie started humming 'As Time Goes By', then began to sing.

'You know this melody? What are those words?'

'Of course I know it. I can't sing well, though.'

'No. You can't. I am astonished you know this. Do you know any others?'

'Lots.'

'Sing me one.'

This was enough to make Rosie's mind go blank. In desperation, she thought of what made people of her parents' age look happy. 'I know. There's this one. You'll like this.' She sang a bit of 'Fly Me to the Moon'. 'Professor Lytten played me that. Peggy Lee. Good, isn't it?'

Aliena sang it herself, the same tune but very different words. 'That's one of the oldest lines of melody there is,' she said. 'So Rambert tells me. It is used only for the most beautiful and poignant of passages.'

Rosie felt confused. She was sure it wasn't that old. 'We don't do songs like that,' she said. 'Any old words will do, normally. Doo-wop, be-bop. That sort of thing.'

'That's disgusting. For prancing peasants.'

'I'm sorry if I have offended you.'

'You are a foreigner, so I will overlook it. This time.'

'Do you still want me to fix your dress?'

Aliena was torn between her dignity and her clothes sense. 'Yes,' she said finally.

Rosie waited expectantly.

'Please.'

'It will be a pleasure.'

Rosie left her there, and saw that Jay was still bewitched by the young singer. It would have been inaccurate to say that his mouth was actually hanging open but, in her opinion, he was not behaving in quite the way a companion of hers should behave.

She sniffed disdainfully and walked up the bank of the lake on her own and then saw, standing on the narrow pathway, the tall man she had accidentally insulted earlier in the evening. He had a look of contempt on his face, or what could be seen of it under the mask.

With an exaggerated gesture of ironic distaste, he bowed deeply to her once again.

Rosie flushed, glanced briefly at Jay, who was still staring goggle-eyed at Aliena, and, with an equally exaggerated movement, curtsied deeply back.

24

Jack More was travelling back into a world which was familiar, even comforting, after the sterile, dead and entirely regimented institute that sprawled over the Island of Mull. He talked to no one as he took the old ferry across to the mainland with the workers, then the link to the transport hub fifty miles inland. He sat as inconspicuously as possible, trying to lose himself in the mass of reeking humanity which was, like him, travelling south for work, into the sprawling metropolis which extended for some two hundred miles and contained so many people that no one was even sure how many there were. Most could not move, bound for life to their factories or jobs so that production would never cease. They got up, worked, went home and thought themselves happy. Some, though, like the people now surrounding him, were floating workers, assigned to one task or another as needed; others, he suspected, had run away, hoping to hide themselves and not be noticed. He realised he had become separated from them, even felt superior to them despite being born one of them, in a housing unit of twenty thousand attached to a food processing plant where his family had worked for generations. Jack had hated it, and volunteered for military service simply to escape. Then he had gone into security, to avoid being sent back. Was his time in an institute having an effect on him? Was he getting used to the small privileges that he now possessed? How hard would he try to hang on to them, if he ever had to choose?

It was, after all, most peculiar behaviour for someone like him – someone as he was now pretending to be – to use mass transport and to travel to the grubby, dingy suburbs of the south. He was also going alone, without the usual panoply of security detail and aides which someone of his supposed rank would have insisted upon to give protection from the envious and dangerous populace.

He studied the wan reflections of his travelling companions in the coach, the lined faces, the signs of hunger, the weariness and wariness of their expressions. All were insignificant, consumers not producers, there to be controlled and monitored and to work for the greater good, even if they never knew what it was. He did not examine them directly, but rather in the window of the compartment, half steamed up from the heavy rain lashing down outside. He studied his own face and knew why they looked at him cautiously, a little suspiciously. He was too healthy, too exercised and self-confident, not like those all around him.

Some people did look at him more closely, then glanced away. He did not think any of them were excessively interested, nor did anyone follow him when he arrived at his destination. But then why should they? Cameras were following his every move anyway. He was banking on no one bothering to look at them.

*

For the next two days he went back to his old business, call-ing on former colleagues and friends who, unlike him, had remained in the front line of security and policing when he had left in disgust. He could no longer see the point of harassing and monitoring, of travelling into the heart of vast housing complexes to pick up people for trivial offences. The arrests, the interrogations, the forced re-education programmes had no purpose other than to remind people of the power of their guardians. People like him were meant to find and neutralise renegades, criminals and troublemakers, convert them into useful citizens serving the good of all. He had increasingly come to the view that it was a waste of time. Most were incorrigible, and increasingly he doubted that they were much of a threat in any case. They arrested a few to intimidate everyone else and to reassure the masses they were looked after and kept secure. Working for Hanslip was hardly exciting, in contrast, but until a couple of days ago it hadn't required him to pretend he was doing something useful.

But his old life had at least provided the comradeship he no longer had, and he was almost nostalgic when he walked in through the doors to be greeted by the sense of purposeful activity. The building was just as run-down and decrepit as it had been the day he left, three years previously; the same mountains of files, paint peeling from the walls, overflowing rubbish bins, probably even the same dust over the stained floors. Many of the inhabitants were the same as well; he recognised several but it was strange – and annoying – to realise how easily he had been forgotten. One man, whom he had worked with on a complicated case of smuggling years back, walked past him in the corridor, stared at him with a puzzled expression, then said, 'Hello, Jack. Been on nights?'

Others – young and new – simply had no idea who he was.

So, in a bad mood that only a sense of irrelevance can bring on, Jack wandered through the building until he came to the office which had once been his own. In fact, he had shared it with six others, all undercover operators. These were wilder, less disciplined, more irreverent, less enamoured of rules. They knew how to keep their opinions to themselves, and made fun of the authorities behind their backs even as they served them loyally. They had to understand those they lived with, and often enough came to sympathise with them. Their job was to catch subversives; frequently they ended up protecting them as well.

He spent an hour in there, talking about old times, asking after old acquaintances before getting down to business. He needed a favour, he said. A missing woman. Nothing official. No public announcements, no broadcasts of the have-you-seen-this-woman variety. Discreet. Not a word.

'Urgent?'

'Very.'

'Explanation?'

He shook his head. 'Not yet.'

They did not query, bargain, set conditions. Of course they would help. Jack handed over Angela's basic information – all identifying qualities, numbers and back history, financial information, health data.

'Photo?'

He handed it over.

'Cute.'

'She's seventy-eight, and a psychomathematician.'

'Ah. A nutter.'

'So it seems, but a very intelligent one. During her training she never once scored less than 99.9 per cent on any exam. Also extravagant, emotional and high-risk. She has never held a job for more than two years, until she ended up in this institute on Mull, where she has been placated and perhaps sedated enough to function.'

'Criminal activities?'

'None that we know of. No history of violence beyond once threatening her employer with a broken bottle, although, from what I know of him, that might well have been entirely justifiable. She's gone missing, and she won't be easily found. There may be a connection to renegade groupings. Retreats. Leave that to me. Don't go near them or alarm them. I do want the current inventory of people in Retreats near here, though.'

'Why?'

'Just in case something strikes me.'

'Then you might as well do the work yourself. You know where the files are. Most haven't even been touched since you left.'

*

He read carefully for four hours, both the dossier on Emily Strang and the reports on the Retreat where she was registered. It was routine stuff, for the most part. The Retreat was about thirty years old, a breakaway from another one because of internal faction fighting. They probably split into warring fragments, he thought, over the best way of baking bread or something like that. Few Retreats lasted for very long before they broke into pieces over some minor dispute. It was one reason why they were tolerated – you see what freedom of expression gets you? Chaos. You want to be like these people, wasting your energies in pointless argument over trivia?

What this one did was not mentioned, as any activities the inmates were likely to indulge in were, almost by definition, pointless. The only question was whether they were dangerous in any way. In this case the answer was no. No more needed to be said, which was a pity; it would have been useful to have had some idea of their internal philosophy before he approached.

The inmates were the usual collection of misfits. Some had been born in Retreats and scarcely knew what they were missing; others had gone there of their own accord after some display of egotistical individuality – refusing drugs, venturing opinions, discontent or semi-criminal activity. To Jack's practised eye, none seemed either remarkable or difficult to deal with. Merely people who thought their opinion was better than the collective wisdom of the best scientific minds on the planet. The nominal head, Sylvia Glass, was a woman with the prospect of a great career in administration until, one day, she simply walked out when disciplined for singing to herself. A few others had been promising scientists or managers. All had rebelled and been isolated and barred from contact with others in case they spread the infection.

As for Emily Strang, the record was much too simple to be convincing. If she was indeed the daughter of Angela Meerson, then someone had evidently doctored the records very carefully. She appeared as the child of two renegades, flagged as unremarkable but – and this was the interesting bit – given the highest rating at the assessment all infants were subjected to at the age of six weeks. It was, so they said, an infallible way of determining intelligence and future usefulness to society. Emily was assessed at level one, which would ordinarily have meant instant acceptance into the elite training system. She would have been taken off and put into special schools, given every comfort and resource to develop her mind and skills. Jack had been assessed at level six and he knew – because he had looked – that even Hanslip himself had been assigned only level two status. But there she was in a Retreat, and nothing in the dossier suggested this was in any way remarkable.

Jack finished reading in the comfort of his room, as he had decided that he would stay in the sort of accommodation suitable to his new rank, just to see what it was like. The journey from the police headquarters through the filthy streets, never-ending in their squalor, took nearly an hour, until he got to the heavily guarded outer perimeter of the compound and was allowed through after a detailed check of his credentials. They worked flawlessly.

The room he was given was grand. He was impressed; he had never been in such a place before. The luxury was extraordinary. He could go out into the open, under the huge glass dome which stretched as far as he could see, and breathe in the carefully filtered and cleaned air almost as though it was natural. He could walk without protection and have no fear of being shot or kidnapped. There wasn't even any overhead surveillance. The security guards were placed discreetly so they wouldn't be seen, and there were no billboards or loudspeakers to encourage loyalty and effort. There was grass, and a tree. Most wouldn't care for trees, but they symbolised space and luxury and safety. There was a lot to be said for making it into the elite. He wasn't sure whether the security was to protect the guests or to make sure that the outside world had no idea how well their masters lived.

He ordered a meal, showered and relaxed. He decided against signalling his intentions of going to the National Depository, just in case someone was listening in, and finished his evening by reading about the place instead.

The chances of finding anything in there without specialised knowledge was minimal. It only existed because of a dispute between various committees of scientists; one wanted to destroy all records of the past entirely on the grounds of redundancy, the other wished to preserve them for the same reason that plants were preserved, in case future generations found a use for the information.

When all libraries and archives and museums had been forcibly closed eighty years ago, their contents had been transferred to a single building twenty miles long, four wide and twelve storeys high. It had been promoted as a demonstration of how much the government cared about the cultural heritage of the world, while the real reason was to keep it under guard. It was said to contain every piece of paper, every book, every painting or print that still existed in what had been known as the British Isles. Almost no one wanted to go there, only a few renegades, and even they were now banned from the place. Many thought that keeping it was a waste of resources and wanted to burn the Depository to the ground. No doubt in due course that would happen. It would be easy to set a fire, blame it on terrorists and sweep them all up. There had been a proposal to do just that a few years ago; the plans had been laid out and Jack and his comrades had even been sent off for training in how to round up so many people quickly and efficiently. The internment camps were prepared, courts readied to give them mass trials and find them guilty.

It had all faded away, as the more cynical of his comrades said it would. Budget cuts and lack of interest, a game of politics won and lost. In the last few months, though, it had suddenly been revived; this time, some said, the authorities were serious.

25

Once both Chang and More had been dispatched, Hanslip walked slowly up to his private viewing platform, which gave him a clear panorama of his domain, and considered his options. Doing nothing and simply hoping for the best was not one of them. Sooner or later, the source of the power surge would be traced. There was also a certainty that, sooner or later, someone would start looking for Lucien Grange.

The four hundred acres of the institute stretching to the water's edge; the tower blocks of accommodation where his employees lived entirely protected from the outside world; the antennae on top of the bare, useless mountains which monitored everything that approached in case of attack; the missile sites to guard against anything unauthorised that might come near. All belonged to him. Nothing so grand, he thought. Not like some other places he had visited.

The island of Mull was exile, pure and simple, but being out of the way has its uses. He was a lesser baron of scientific research and now he had his own fortress. He had spent the last fifteen years building this place and the last five hiding what it was doing from the outside world. He would never be Newton or Einstein. He might, though, be the person under whom such a figure flourished. Besides, it wasn't Einstein who built the bomb.

For years he had schemed and manoeuvred: taking

Angela when Oldmanter decided the experiment to enhance her abilities had rendered her useless; providing a safe environment for her to work, finding the money and the people. He was nearly there, had almost got to the point where he had a technology so powerful that he could command whatever resources he needed. With it would come power as well; a place on the World Council, the supreme body of technocrats and scientists which exercised authority over the entire globe. It would be his by right, if he delivered this opportunity to a society which needed it so badly. He might even challenge Oldmanter himself; the old man's day was done, and it was time his power was transferred to someone with new ideas.

Then a programme of colonisation, moving the world's surplus population to universes cleared of inhabitants. There would be no limit on expansion or on resources. He did not know yet how to do this; initially, he had thought of finding worlds sufficiently distant that they were uninhabited, but this had proven difficult; so far they had managed to access only one world, and he was hoping that Angela would come up with both an explanation and a solution. In the meantime, he had considered accessing a world so far in the past that humanity had not yet developed, but going back two hundred thousand years presented its own problems because of the amount of energy required.

That was why he had contacted Emily Strang. He knew nothing of history, and he had persuaded her to teach him. He had kept it secret, as he had no desire to have any public connection to a renegade, but had found the encounters useful.

They would talk for an hour or two every month and

she was deliberately provocative, asking him questions designed to make him argue rather than simply state conclusions.

'Why should the world be organised efficiently as a first priority?'

'If the government of the world is so benevolent, why does it need such vast armies to keep people under control?'

'What do you mean by a happy life, anyway? Merely more goods and services?'

'Why do you think this society will last for ever? I can tell you of many that have destroyed themselves through their own violence. For example . . .'

She had even written a paper for him on the subject. Total extinction would require possession of the means of destruction and the willingness to use them. The best examples were the various crises which erupted during the Cold War, when the United States and the Soviet Union challenged each other with nuclear weapons. At any stage, an accident or a misinterpreted piece of evidence could have set off a chain reaction of consequences.

Hanslip had been sufficiently intrigued to run his own checks. He had ordered a computer simulation to see whether or not what Emily said was true. The world had indeed come close to disaster but the simulation suggested that tipping it over the edge would not have been easy. Change events, and very rapidly history returns to its proper path. It would take a very large shift indeed to significantly alter the course of history.

The more he thought about it, the more he was repelled by the very idea. Even if not strictly aimed at real people, it involved a level of violence that he could not readily contemplate. There was, he was sure, a better way which would turn up in due course, one which did not involve wholesale destruction. He rejected the concept as both unworthy and impractical, and stowed her report and his thoughts away.

It had been a fascinating period of speculation, but now it was over. Angela had ruined it. Hanslip had tried desperately to keep her focused, but to no avail. He had tried to dismiss her concerns, but knew her too well to do so without reservation. Then Jack More had mentioned that Chang hadn't been worried, almost as if he knew the machine worked. It concerned him. He needed to check all the possibilities.

It took over a day before he found what he was afraid of. Every scrap of paper in Angela's room, every piece of data that remained on the computers – not much, as she had done a good job of erasing it – was brought to his office, and Hanslip settled down to read through every last syllable. It was a measure of his thoroughness that he noticed the sliver of information when he read it, for it consisted only of four names, with a tick beside one of them. Gunter. That was all.

It meant nothing until he checked the lists of employees. First the scientists, then the administrators, then the support staff and finally everyone else who came and went. The only reference he could find to anyone called Gunter was to a cleaner who had walked off the job some six months ago. Curiously, the records suggested he had vanished while on the island; there was a flaw in the security system so that his last journey from Mull back to the mainland hadn't been logged. This had caused – Hanslip now remembered – an enquiry into the monitoring systems, which had revealed no errors or malfunctions.

Now here was a piece of paper in Angela's room with his name on it. It took six hours of interviews to get to the bottom of it, and by the end Hanslip was exhausted, worried and deeply angry.

The third technician he had brought to his office had told him everything he needed to know, after being subjected to the most severe threats. Angela, he said in a trembling voice, almost choking in fear, had conducted experiments on her own without registering them or having them approved and certainly without notifying anyone. She had brooked no interference or criticism and had refused to listen to any objections. She had selected someone from the ancillary staff who had no family or connections and who would not be missed. She had drugged him and transmitted him in her machine to see what happened.

It was getting worse and worse. 'Did this man know what was happening to him?'

'I don't think so.'

'What did she think she was doing?'

'She wanted proof that her theories were correct. The idea was to transmit him a week back and a few yards away to see if he turned up in our universe or vanished. The settings were all done wrong, though. It was an accident. He was never seen again, but she got Chang to search the records and he found a possible match in the 1890s. It took some time, but Chang thought he might have become a priest deep in the Pyrenees. Angela packed him off to find out – without official permission or clearance – six months ago. Chang found the man's grave and tested the bones.

They were a perfect match. The bones were really old. Do you want to see his report?'

'He wrote a report as well? No one thought of giving it to me?'

The man nodded nervously and handed over some sheets of paper. Hanslip warned him of dire consequences if he said so much as a word to anyone else, waited until the door was shut, took a deep breath and began to read.

*

By the time he finished reading, his strategy for coping with the nightmare Angela had concocted for him was in tatters, as were his dreams for the future. He spent hours going through the evidence and could find no hole in it. The conclusion was unavoidable: bones, as the man said, did not lie. The cleaner had indeed ended up in the late nineteenth century, had died there and been buried there. Angela had been right. She had single-handedly over-turned all the laws of physics and demonstrated that the multiple universe theory, accepted convention for nearly two hundred years, was wrong. Time travel – true time travel, not a transition to a copy – was possible. Hanslip thought carefully, then took every scrap of paper referring to the missing cleaner and incinerated them. The last thing he needed was more evidence of illegality if a search was ever made.

Why had she not said anything about this? Presumably because she thought that the experiment on the cleaner would have been used against her. Which it would have been, until Hanslip himself had disposed of Oldmanter's most trusted aide in the same way. Although maybe she had been going to tell him; she had made an appointment, saying it was vital and urgent, the day before she vanished. Just before she'd come across Grange, in fact.

That made him stop and think. Surely that was the answer, then, to the Devil's Handwriting? Not some bizarre and incomprehensible act of deceit; rather it must have been Grange. A further hour's work in what remained of the computer's records confirmed this one as well. Grange had not come to sign a collaboration agreement but to steal it. He had broken into the computer system and helped himself. He had then gone on to offer terms he knew Hanslip could not accept.

The machine was too dangerous to use, and the data to operate it or build another one was out there, somewhere. It might be found by anyone unless More managed to fulfil his orders to the letter. If Hanslip had realised how much depended on More's success, he would never have sent him alone. The loyalty requirement built into his contract was immensely strong, but nothing was unbreakable.

Pamarchon's encounter with the peculiar girl in the forest that afternoon had been short, inconclusive and disturbing, but at least his instincts had not let him down. The soldiers – more likely rangers – were good, quiet and knew their business, but his senses were better. The faintest crack of a twig, and he had known instantly that it was not an animal or the effect of the wind on an old branch. He had known exactly where it was coming from, how little time he had to escape and hide.

Had it been a trap set for him? Did it mean someone knew his band had arrived, and that they would now have to pack and leave? Who was that young woman who spoke so flawlessly, with an ease and assurance that suggested many years' training? Why had she said such strange things? She had sounded like someone prepared to say anything to distract him and keep his attention while the soldiers circled.

No. It was possible, but not convincing. She was so very unusual. So oddly dressed . . .

Pamarchon circled back and watched as she stopped and picked things off the ground which she popped into her mouth, then came to a small clearing and let out a little cry of what sounded like disappointment. Saw her turn as the soldiers slipped in behind her. Five of them with a youth who was, perhaps, their quarry, as he was evidently a prisoner. Watched in bemusement as she berated them, gave them such a talking to in the old language that, rather than frightening her, they seemed cowed instead. Heard the captive take over the conversation. Saw her eventually walk off with them. Noted how none of the soldiers dared touch her.

He followed until he was certain she was being taken to the great house, then peeled off and hurried swiftly back into the deep forest on his horse. He had much to think about on his way back to the camp. When he arrived, he immediately sought out Antros. They had known each other for years, ever since they had lived together as children at the grand southern estates of the chieftain of Cormell, both sent there by their families for their education and training. Antros was the younger by two years, but both felt lost and alone in their new, frightening life.

Pamarchon was the better-born; Antros the son of a bookkeeper, a man who had trained to be a scholar and won some advancement until he realised he was unsuited to the life and began work on his own in a town where there were many merchants and traders. Pamarchon appointed himself the boy's protector, beginning a friendship which had lasted years, so that when Pamarchon's time of hardship came and he was accused of murdering his uncle, Antros without hesitation stood by him.

So he headed straight for his old friend. Pamarchon was not a reverent man, but old habits and the training of years gone by had remained and moulded him. As a boy, he had played at being the heroes of the stories, re-enacted the tales in the hills of Cormell, listened at night as their old teacher recited to them before bed, sung the songs of great deeds and terrible adventures. The words were in his soul, both for their beauty and for their association with beatings received when he had misspoken a phrase, or placed the wrong value on a word.

Now he had witnessed a girl speaking with a fluency and skill which he knew he would never be able to attain, not even with years of hard labour and the best of teachers.

He described the encounter to his friend, who listened carefully. Ordinarily Antros was of a sunny disposition, prone to making jokes about everything, especially the most serious of subjects, but he was also a man of great kindness, a sympathetic listener and consoling presence.

'What did she look like?'

'Ah, she was beautiful, lovely beyond words.'

'I meant, how old?' Antros said. 'Was she a stranger? How was she dressed?'

'She talked of things I didn't understand. She seemed to know little about where she was. Clearly Lady Catherine knew of her arrival, but why greet her with armed men?'

'You have set many riddles. I can't solve them for you.'

Pamarchon stood up and stretched himself. 'I know. I just wanted to make sure it would make no more sense to you than it did to me. I need to know more, and there is only one way of finding out, I think.'

'Do you want to find the answer, or do you want to find the girl?'

Pamarchon sniffed disdainfully at the very idea, and Antros laughed and pointed his finger. 'Aha!' he said mockingly.

'Not at all. I need to know precisely what is going on before we can move to take back Willdon. But I admit freely she was the most radiant creature I ever beheld in my life.'

'Why not ask Lady Catherine herself what it is all about?'

'I may do that. It is the day of the Festivity, remember. I think I will go to the river and bathe. Then I will find my mask.'

*

Once he was bathed, Pamarchon retired to his tent and opened the rarely touched trunk which contained his treasures. There was no money, no gold, nothing like that. Like most people in Anterwold, he had little use for such things. Rather the case contained his scrolls, the extracts of the story which were particularly attached to his family line.

For Pamarchon could trace his lineage back to the travellers themselves, those people who had accompanied the leaders on the Great March which led to the foundation of Anterwold. Everybody could do so in theory, of course, but few had a documented line of succession, from mother to mother, back so many generations. Such families could be numbered on the fingers of two hands and they occupied a high place as a result.

Position did not confer either power or wealth. Members of such families could be found in every strand of life, high and low. Some were scholars and magistrates and lawmakers, and it is true that they were disproportionately successful in gaining such places. There were also many who were artisans or labourers or tradesmen, important only because they confirmed human continuity and the Story's truth.

The first cycle covered the leaving of the northern lands and the long journey to Anterwold, ending with the great battle that enabled the travellers to settle. Pamarchon's ancestor Isenwar was the man who counselled that the journey continue after a difficult winter had sapped spirits and health. Many wanted to go back, but Isenwar denounced their cowardice and promised that he and his family would go on alone, bringing shame on all who did not have the courage of his four-year-old daughter, who would willingly die rather than return to a land which loved them not.

Pamarchon unwrapped the text and read it once again, seeking the same courage to continue. He wanted to return to his place as the true descendant of such a man, to be no longer a nameless outcast. It was his duty to act, as Isenwar had. Willdon was his by right; he had been deprived by subterfuge. It was time to make his response, and he had waited long enough.

He dressed in a way which would make him inconspicuous, neither too elegant nor too dowdy, and tied the mask around his neck so that it could be pulled up when needed. Then, quietly, he collected his beloved horse, which he would leave half an hour's walk outside Willdon, and began the long journey. It would, he knew, take at least a couple of hours even by a direct route. He would risk it, for no one would query too closely a well-dressed and mounted man who was obviously going to Lady Catherine's Festivity.

It would be a simple thing to mingle with the crowd and the moment he found out enough to satisfy his curiosity about the current state of the domain, he would slip away again, find his horse and return.

So he told himself. Nothing to do with the girl.

When he arrived at Willdon he slipped in unnoticed and slowed to an elegant saunter, mask in place, and strolled around for some time, studying the guests. He sighted a couple who were walking along the path. The young man was assiduously courting his companion, but clearly had little hope. He smiled; he remembered being like that himself. She was obviously far beyond her companion; he in the robes of a student and she clearly of immense position, beautiful, elegant, poised. Her long fair wig fell down her shoulders, her mask glittered with precious stones in the candlelight and her dress was a masterpiece of the dressmaker's art. She didn't even respond to Pamarchon's bow, but rather stared haughtily at him through her mask, as though astonished at his presumption. He snorted. How he detested such people now, even though he had once been one of them.

He spent the next hour walking through the festivities, eating a little, exchanging toasts with strangers, making light but meaningless conversation. All was as it should be; he bowed to a lady who curtsied back, and became her companion for an hour, much to the relief of her escort. He could see why; the woman was the wife of an apothecary in the nearby town, and never stopped talking. About her husband, his business, his family, her children, the way Lady Catherine had bowed at her. So many words, but Pamarchon sensed a kindness and decency underneath.

'Have you greeted her yet? Oh, you should see her! So beautiful! The only woman who can rival her is her guest, who must be from a great family.'

294

'What guest is this?'

'Now then,' said his companion, who was delighted to be able to retell gossip. 'No one knows, do they? All anyone knows is that she was given the highest ceremony of welcome, that she has been kept close in the house ever since, and that she speaks the old language so perfectly that she has astonished everyone who has had the privilege of greeting her.'

'That includes you, I hope?'

'Oh, no.' The woman blushed. 'I had little education. I know much, of course, but not the language. That I do not know.'

She looked sad. 'You regret that you bowed to me, I imagine. You are a man of education, and now you have to spend an hour with me.'

He smiled at her with sympathy, for he liked her, despite the chatter. 'No,' he said. 'I do not regret it. Not for a second. At the risk of insulting you with my learning, I offer you a quotation as a gift. "For the highest are the lowest and the lowest are the highest, when kindness is placed in the balance."'

She bowed her head. 'Thank you, sir,' she said.

Then the moment was broken; her companion returned, the hour was over and it was his duty to reclaim his prize. Pamarchon bowed to him, and then to the woman. She curtsied back, gave one final glance and disappeared into the night.

He wandered on, considering the fragments of gossip the woman had passed on to him. Clearly this important guest had to be the same as the girl he had come across. She had not been arrested after all, it seemed. Or else Lady Catherine had made a bad mistake – which was most unlike her.

So where was this paragon of learning? Such a prize would not be wandering around unattended, that was for sure. She would rather be receiving, probably in a specially decorated part of the house or a great tent erected for her sole use. There would be people milling around, waiting to pay court and pretending they were there by accident. He walked around the courtyards and the gardens but could find no obvious signs of such a thing.

Eventually he noticed a trickle of people walking up a small hill, back to the refreshments, talking excitedly. His curiosity was piqued, so he strolled down to see what he had been missing. He arrived at the lake and admired the clever way it was illuminated, picking out the patterns in the lanterns, how they reflected the stars flickering above. A dozen or so boats, now empty, were tied up and the last of the people were leaving.

Only one couple remained, talking to a woman who, he guessed, must be a singer. He realised with shock that one was the woman who had disdained him so contemptuously earlier in the evening. Clearly she was not so frosty with everyone; her gestures were animated, her laughter echoed softly over the water. All were entranced by her.

As he was watching, she turned and saw him. He bowed deeply to her a second time, giving her the opportunity to repulse him once more, to show he did not care.

To his astonishment she paused, glanced briefly at her companion and curtsied deeply back.

The two looked at each other, one defiant and the other scarcely able to conceal his surprise. The only sound came from her young escort, who let out a strangled cry of what sounded like alarm when he noticed what had happened. Both ignored him.

The man held out his arm and his new companion, after a moment's hesitation, placed her hand lightly on it. 'Let us walk,' he said, 'for the hour we have in each other's company is only a short moment.'

He looked back at the boy he had just replaced, then led her away.

'It is an honour to make your acquaintance,' he began.

'Well,' she replied. 'As for whether it is an honour to make yours, that I will have to decide later. If I remember correctly – and I am sure I do, as I have a very good memory – you said the most horrid things to me earlier. And you ran off leaving me to the tender mercies of a bunch of soldiers. You can hardly be annoyed if I gave you a nasty look. It was my very best nasty look, you know, even if I didn't know it was you. I have practised it many times for just such an occasion.'

He studied her face, as far as it could be seen because of the mask; next her long golden hair, her clothes. Then he realised it was the girl who called herself Rosalind. No wonder Lady Catherine was so keen to get hold of her. Her mere presence would adorn Willdon. 'My apologies. I was in grave error.'

'You gave me a very unpleasant fright. I come from a long way away, you see, and it wasn't a good way to begin. Everything is so strange to me.'

'What is?'

'Everything. Why people are making such a fuss of me, for a start. Why they are so polite and formal all the time. Why you speak as though English was a foreign language.

It's so easy to insult people or say the wrong thing. I don't suppose I'll ever get it right.'

'I'm sure you will learn very quickly if you stay here. Are you going to?'

'I hope not. I'm meant to be back at school. My parents will be frantic. Oh! Don't let's talk about that. I'll get so worried, and there is nothing I can do about it. You should either do something or not do something. Worrying is a waste of time. Don't you agree?'

'It sounds very sensible.'

'Besides, I'm having such a lovely evening. As long as I don't think too much about how very odd it all is.'

'Is Lady Catherine being welcoming?' Pamarchon asked.

'Yes! Isn't she lovely! Such a kind woman. Do you know her well?'

'Not really.'

'Oh.' Rosie paused. 'So why are you here?'

'To meet you again, of course,' he replied with a smile.

'Me?' She frowned. 'You see? That's what I mean. Why me? Why me all the time?'

'I was hoping you would tell me that. You are a stranger, and strangers are rare here. You were received with the greatest honour by Lady Catherine, which is even rarer. You speak the language with exceptional ability, which is rarer still. What is more, you are most certainly the most beautiful woman I have ever met in my life.'

There was a pause, as Rosie felt her entire universe give way. She had often wondered, in the privacy of her bedroom, what it would be like if – when, she had determined – some boy paid her a real compliment. Or even noticed her.

Now two had done so in the space of scarcely an hour. The first had pleased her, but a similar remark from this man nearly made her faint. She stared at the ground, hoping that her blushing red cheeks, deep breathing and worrying air of dizziness would clear before he noticed.

'Are you well, fair lady?' Pamarchon cried. 'Have I offended you in some way?'

'Oh, oh yes. I mean, no. Not at all. I am quite well, thank you.'

Rosie was sure that the conversation was supposed to continue; she had seen her parents valiantly trying to make small talk at functions and she knew that saying anything in these circumstances was better than nothing. But there was so much swirling around her head that she could not fix on anything to say. There was the party, the music, the soft touch of this man's hand resting lightly on her arm, all making it hard to concentrate.

'Do you come here often?' she asked desperately. 'Where do you live? Is it a nice house like this?'

He laughed. 'Oh, no. Very few people live in a house like this. Certainly not me. I live quite a long way away, and it is a difficult place to find without a guide.'

'Where, though? In a village? A nearby town?'

'No. None of those. I live in the forest, under the shade of melancholy boughs.'

'Why melancholy?'

'Because you do not dwell there with me,' he replied with a smile, which made Rosie blush bright red once more.

'That was a quotation. Do not distress yourself. I live many hours' walk from here, where the rivers meet and the land gives everything a man might need for happiness.'

'Another quotation?'

'Yes, but a tolerably accurate description as well. Tell me, how do you speak so well, yet know so little?'

'Everyone keeps asking me that. It's just because – it's the way I speak. That's all. Everybody speaks their own language. This is mine.'

'But nobody speaks it.'

'That's just silly,' she said. 'Don't you see? It's silly. We do. Lots of people do.'

'Not here. It is the language only of the most educated and refined.'

'If you say so.'

'What does Lady Catherine want with you?'

'I didn't know she wanted anything.'

'In that case,' Pamarchon said, 'you do not know her. Who else have you met here?'

'Well,' said Rosie. 'There is Jay, of course. He's the boy I was with just now. Henary wants him to escort me for the evening. I've known him for some time, it seems.'

'What do you mean?'

'I met him a week or so ago, the first time I came here, but he was only eleven then. Now he's nearly seventeen.' She smiled apologetically. 'I'm not making much sense, I know. I'm sorry.'

'Smile at me again, and I will forgive you.'

She did, and their eyes met. Rosie was quite sure that the breath had suddenly been sucked out of her body.

'Do you like to dance, Lady? Will you now speak your name once more? It is music on your lips.'

Rosie took a deep breath. 'Rosalind,' she said. 'Just Rosalind.'

*

Dancing was no simple matter of draping an arm around your partner and then moving more or (as with her parents) less in time with the music. The music played was, even she could discern, much rougher and less sophisticated than the singing she had just heard on the lake. But it was still very complicated, the rhythms and speeds changing seemingly at random. Pamarchon knew what he was doing, however, and did his best to guide her, but on several occasions even he stopped and burst out laughing as she once again stood on his foot.

'I just can't get the hang of this.'

The phrase puzzled him, but he got the meaning.

'Alas, our hour is up, in any case. Now we must part.'

'Oh no!'

'Does that displease you, Lady Rosalind?'

'Yes, yes. Very much.'

'Thank you. I am honoured.'

'What happens now?'

'Now? You return to your escort, and I return home. Any other entertainment will be a poor thing after your company.'

Rosalind stamped her foot. 'That's not fair!' she said. 'That's just not fair! Why do you have so many rules for everything?'

'You are too severe. "It is as it is, and must always be."'

'Well, that sounds clever. But it isn't.'

'It comes from the Story.'

'It must be a very stupid story then, if it stops you doing what you want so often.'

It was as though she had slapped him in the face. His expression instantly hardened.

'As you say, my Lady,' he said stiffly. He bowed, then turned on his heel and walked off swiftly into the crowd.

*

Rosalind was horrified. She had done it again. What was it about her? Every time she started talking to someone, sooner or later they took offence. She knew quite well that it wasn't only in this weird place that things like that happened. Not many people liked her at school either. She had few friends. Everyone thought she was horrid.

And she wasn't. She really wasn't. Why was it that no one ever saw how hard she was trying all the time? How much she wanted people to like her? She had loved the last couple of hours, because she had thought that finally she was getting it right. Then she had ruined it, and he was so nice. So tall. So . . .

She would apologise. She would run after him and explain. Make him like her again.

She hurried after him. But he had vanished.

Five minutes later she was quite lost. She had marched off with determination in the right direction and left the golden, illuminated area in which the Festivity was set. It was now dark, and she could scarcely see, but she thought she could make out a narrow track, a slightly lighter grey on the ground. She waited until her eyes were more used to the gloom – trying the trick her uncle had told her about, of looking out of the corner of her eyes so she could see better. It must, she decided, be the way Pamarchon had gone. She would follow. She took a few steps, tripped, then stopped. There was no possibility of walking any proper distance in those shoes. She paused and took them off, then picked up the long flowing dress so it wouldn't get dirty and – looking no doubt a bit ridiculous – strode off in the direction of the woods, looming up dark and a little menacing, a few hundred yards ahead of her.

She walked for about twenty minutes, her resolution slowly ebbing away. It was not that she was frightened of the woods, but it was getting colder and her determination to find the tall young man who had held her so nicely dimmed as the memory of him also faded. So much had happened in the past few hours, it was difficult to believe that it wasn't some sort of dream. A dream inside a dream, in fact. But can you dream of dreaming?

An interesting if useless thought, and minor in comparison to the realisation that she was lost. Apart from the moon glimmering through the overhanging trees it was pitch black. There was no sound except the hooting of owls in the distance and the more worrying rustles in the undergrowth. She didn't know whether to go on or turn back or even which was which. Her dress – her beautiful dress, which wasn't even hers – kept snagging on brambles.

Get a grip, she told herself. Think. She tried that, but nothing came except a slow curiosity as she dimly noticed, a little way to her left, a faint, unusual noise. Forgetting about the dress, she crashed through the trees in the right direction. The noise got louder and louder until, just in front of a large oak tree, she saw a hazy rectangular area that was slightly lighter than the surrounding darkness. It was the way home.

Of course she should rush straight through; it might disappear. But to leave this wonderful place where people thought she was so interesting? To go back to the rain and the cold and the pork chops and homework? Could she not just wait, just another hour or so?

Oh, she was tempted. But before she could make up her mind she heard a sad, plaintive noise. She recognised it, or thought she did.

'Jenkins?' she called out in amazement. 'Jenkins? Is that you?'

Another yowl came from the bushes, and she tiptoed over. 'Jenkins?'

It was Professor Lytten's cat, but how transformed from the last time she had seen him! Only the malevolent gaze reassured her that it was indeed Jenkins, who rushed towards her like a long-lost friend, curling himself around her ankles with every sign of relief. He even purred. Rosalind bent down and picked the beast up, cradling him in her arms as he erupted into a positive symphony of delight. 'How you've changed! You've lost so much weight. Don't worry, you're safe now.'

Except that he wasn't, any more than she was. Jenkins's sudden appearance made up her mind. She had a duty to get him back home. For some reason it seemed more important than to get back herself. At least he wouldn't be shouted at.

Still cradling the cat, she walked up to the thin light, took a deep breath and stepped through.

27

As he rattled up Walton Street on his way back from the railway station, Henry Lytten wanted nothing more than to get home, draw the curtains and shut out the entire world. He propped the old bike against the wall beside the house, picked the little bag out of the pannier at the front and gratefully, blessedly, opened his front door. Then, dropping everything into a pile on the floor of the dingy entrance, he went into his study. There he found Rosie, sitting in his armchair, looking at him.

'Good heavens! You made me jump,' he said. 'What on earth are you doing here?'

'I found Jenkins,' she said. 'I thought you'd like to know.'

He thought about that, then went into the kitchen to put the kettle on and came back again.

'Have you been eating in my kitchen?'

'I was hungry,' she said, 'and I didn't want to go home.'

'Why not?'

'Look at me.'

Lytten obeyed; he rarely looked closely at women, and then he realised with a jolt that that was exactly what he was looking at. When he had left four days earlier, Rosie had been a gawky, awkward, girlish creature. What on earth had happened to her? Her hair was shorter and darker, her eyebrows . . . had they been plucked? Her nails were painted, her skin looked as though it had been polished.

Even the way she sat and moved had changed.

'I see what you mean,' he said.

'I'm going to get absolute hell from my parents, so I've sort of run away for a bit. This is the only place I could think of coming. And you should see Jenkins,' she added. 'He looks as though he has been on a long walking holiday in the mountains. I almost didn't recognise him.'

Lytten grunted. 'You'd better show me.'

Rosie led the way up to the spare bedroom, the one rarely used except as Jenkins's morning boudoir. It was obvious that she had also used it last night.

On the bed lay a fine figure of a feline stretched out contentedly and snoring. 'God bless my soul!' Lytten exclaimed when he saw it. Jenkins was indeed transformed. Thin, sleek, healthy-looking, everything a cat should be and Jenkins never had been. His cat, he thought, had been born obese. 'How on earth did that happen? Are you sure it's him?' He went over to inspect the beast, which rolled over in its sleep and hissed unpleasantly. 'Yes, that's him. Extraordinary. What do you think happened? More importantly, what has happened to you?'

Then the doorbell went again. Really, life was simply too much sometimes.

He opened the door, an air of distracted thought about him that was mingled only with a slight impatience at being disturbed by the tweedy but still quite beautiful lady standing there with a shopping bag by her feet.

'How lovely to see you! I was just passing,' she said. 'Thought I'd drop in.'

'Angela. How nice.'

'You don't sound pleased to see me.'

'I am. Of course.'

He tried to indicate that this wasn't a good time but she paid no attention, picked up the bag and advanced through his door.

'You don't have any milk in there, do you?' he asked. 'I've been away for a few days.'

'I do wish you'd learn to look after yourself better, Henry. You'd starve to death if you didn't have people to help you. I do have some milk in here somewhere. You can have some if you give me a cup of tea in exchange. I have some buns as well.'

She swept past him and headed for the grim little kitchen.

'I need some things from the cellar, if that's all right,' she called over her shoulder. 'How are you, my dear?'

'Well enough. I had to go to Paris.'

'That's nice.'

'Not really.'

He turned as he heard a movement behind him. 'Ah!' he said. 'Have you two met? No; of course, you haven't.'

Girl and woman regarded each other with what Lytten thought was a strange expression. Somewhat egotistically, he decided it must be a sort of possessiveness. Both wanted to talk to him and neither wanted the other there. He felt briefly rather pleased to have such a magnetic effect.

'Rosie, this is Mrs Meerson.'

'Angela, dear. Call me Angela.'

'Miss Rosalind Wilson, who has just restored my cat to me in a quite inexplicable state of health.'

'Cats do wander,' Angela said wisely.

'Not this one,' Rosie replied. 'As far as I can see, it must have been here all the time, locked in the cellar. It's strange that it looks like a beast that has been wandering for months in the wilds, don't you think?'

'Yes, what have you got down there, Angela? Some sort of feline exercise bike?' Lytten asked heartily.

'Just bits and bobs.'

They chatted inconsequentially for the next half hour, both visitors blithely ignoring Lytten's obvious desire that they should go away as quickly as possible. Eventually he gave up and took his bag upstairs to wash and get changed. When he got back, he found the two still sitting opposite each other, looking uncomfortable.

'Henry,' Angela said, following him into the kitchen. 'We have a little problem. Rosie here is not here.'

Lytten scratched his freshly shaved chin. 'Why not?'

'There are things,' she continued mysteriously, 'that you have no need to know. Things which concern women. I'm sure you understand.'

Lytten smiled nervously. 'I do hope you are not going to give details.'

'Good man!' she said. 'You have not seen Rosie. You have no idea where she is or who she might be with. She has a few things that need to be sorted out before she can be returned to her parents.'

Lytten began thinking about the Cold War.

'It is very important,' she went on. 'I will deal with the situation, but I must have a little time to do so. Otherwise Rosie will be in considerable trouble. Her parents, her reputation, you know . . .' she concluded airily.

'I don't know and I don't want to know. You two do whatever you need.'

'Thank you. So you give me your word? Even if her parents come round, friends, the police? Anybody at all. You haven't seen her. Is that agreed?'

'Well . . .'

'Henry!'

'Very well, if you insist. But you will have to do something in return. A sort of friend is coming in the next few days. Tomorrow, probably. Russian. I was wondering if you'd do a spot of translating.'

'"A sort of friend",' she echoed. 'Is this old business, dear?'

Lytten nodded.

'Happy to oblige then. Let me know when and where.'

Angela dusted the crumbs off her dress, disappeared downstairs for whatever she had come for and then left, taking Rosie with her.

*

If Lytten thought that the disappearance of his two visitors meant that he would finally get some time to recover himself, then he was wrong. Scarcely half an hour later the doorbell rang again, and he stumped to the door once more.

'What?' he asked crossly. 'I don't want anything.'

A terrible thing, this country, he thought to himself underneath his annoyance. For he knew the man standing on his porch. Didn't know him, of course, but could place the cheap, ill-fitting suit, the unhealthy complexion, the poorly cut hair, the way of standing.

Life is full of surprises. The man pulled out a small badge and showed it to him. Detective Sergeant Allan

Maltby. 'Would you mind if I came in, sir?'

Lytten cursed. Not that he took the police so very seriously, but it was a complication. A promise was a promise, however annoying.

'By all means,' he said, opening the door a little wider, adopting what he hoped was an air of mystification.

'A report of a missing girl, sir,' Sergeant Maltby continued, 'called Rosie Wilson. No reason to think that it's anything other than youthful irresponsibility at the moment.'

'Could you tell me what has happened?'

'Well, not much, frankly, sir. It seems she has been misbehaving, and had a row with her parents and stormed out. She hasn't been seen since yesterday, and the parents called us. More to punish her than because they are really worried, I suspect. You know her, I believe?'

'She looks after my cat sometimes. I have been away in France since Monday, and got back about an hour ago.'

'So you haven't seen her?'

'No,' he said baldly. He thought of some circumlocution to preserve the appearance of truth, but decided against. Years of experience had inured him to the rigours of bare-faced lies. 'I am sure she is fine, though. She's a good, sensible girl. She is probably just off with friends. They are like that at fifteen nowadays, I believe.'

'Indeed they are, sir. Can I ask you to let us know?'

'Of course. If she rings the doorbell, I will either call you or march her straight home.'

'Kind of you, sir. I understand, by the way . . .'

Here the policeman – Lytten had not allowed him out of the little hallway, not because of rudeness but because Rosie had left her schoolbag in his study – hesitated with a certain air of knowingness.

'Yes?'

'I understand you work for the government, sir,' he said.

'Do I?'

'I'm temporarily assigned to Special Branch, you see. One day a week. Great opportunity for me. Very exciting.'

'Of course. You get to harass trade unionists, that sort of thing. Subversion and spies. Not much of that around here, I imagine.'

'Not really, no,' he said regretfully. 'You are on our list, you see.'

'How annoying. What list?'

'Not as a subversive, sir, of course not. Wouldn't say if you were. If you ever contact us, we look you up and know that you are to be listened to.'

'There really shouldn't be any such list, you know,' Lytten said. 'Sometimes I wonder which term is most inappropriate, "secret" or "intelligence". Sometimes neither seems to be in evidence.'

'Quite, sir. But if you ever need anything, if you see what I mean?'

'I will ask for you specially, Sergeant Maltby. If it will help in any way, I will say what a splendid fellow you are as well.'

'Oh, that would be kind, sir.'

'In fact,' he said, an idea suddenly coming into his head, 'I may have something for you. I hope I can trust to your discretion. Shortly before I left England, I noticed a man watching my house. I saw him again as I let you in just now. If you would care to look through this window here . . .'

Lytten flicked the curtains back a little and peered out.

'Aha!' said Maltby, bending down to look through the narrow gap. 'Six foot, dark hair, no glasses, overcoat on his arm. A bit foreign-looking. That the one?'

'That's the one. It may be nothing, but he concerns me. Would you oblige me and find out who he is, please?'

28

The light worked for Jenkins, but not for Rosalind. When she walked through the patch of light she felt an uncomfortable sensation, rather like something hard and metallic being dragged through her entire body. It was so unpleasant that she lost her concentration, staggered and stubbed her foot on an old root sticking out from the ground. With a cry of distress and confusion she pitched forward, through the light and onto the earth. She lay on the ground, breathing in the sweet soft smell of decaying leaves. She was still in Anterwold. The light no longer worked. She was stuck.

But Jenkins had vanished and she noticed that the light was now much dimmer, flickering like a light bulb that was about to blow. Through it she could just see a faint outline of someone. She let out a cry of alarm and got up, desperate to try again, but before she could get anywhere near, the light flickered out completely.

It was gone. No light. No Jenkins. Now she was really in trouble.

She sank to the ground. Once she had taken the decision to go home, she realised she desperately wanted to see her mum and dad and even her brother. She even wanted to go back to school.

So now what was she going to do?

A strange sound brought her back to reality; if that was

what it really was. A little like a howl, or a roar, or a screech. Certainly a person, but it sounded more like rage and fury than pain or distress, coming from behind a small group of trees. Rosalind considered, then decided she must find out. Whoever it was might know something about the light. Or at least how to get back to the party. Anything was better than being stuck alone in the middle of this forest.

She tiptoed as quietly as she could towards the sound and came to a small clearing. There was not much to see except for the sort of glimmer you get from a candle, coming from the general direction of the noise. In the background she thought she could just make out a hut, but she wasn't sure.

'Hello?' she called out. 'Is anyone there?'

The sobbing and howling stopped instantly; there was a pause and then a rustle of clothes as a hunched figure on the ground rose up in the gloom and approached. A lantern was thrust close to her face. Then there was a loud sniff.

It was Aliena. Rosalind recognised the voice immediately, but she was no longer the confident, self-possessed star of the concert. She was now just an upset girl, even if less upset than Rosalind, who instantly felt sympathetic.

'What's the matter?'

Another strangled noise. 'Rambert. My teacher. I think he's dead.'

'Goodness. What happened?'

'He was furious at me. About my singing.'

'Why? It was lovely.'

'It was. Yes, indeed it was. I was expecting congratulations.' She snorted bitterly. 'But he didn't like my intonation at the end of one passage, thought my variation in another wasn't proper. He never said "well done", or "that was really good". Straight into the criticisms. How I'd never be good enough . . .'

'I'm sorry.'

'So I hit him. He hasn't moved since. I think he may be dead.'

'Don't you think you should find out?'

'I'm too frightened.'

'What did you hit him with?'

'A frying pan.'

Rosalind began to laugh nervously. Aliena looked at her, then laughed herself. 'He went down like an old bottle. You should have seen the look on his face.'

'Still, if you've killed him . . . I mean, that's serious.'

'Will you go and have a look? I really don't want to go back in there.'

Rosalind wasn't overjoyed at the prospect of seeing a dead body either, but she nodded. Aliena led the way, occasionally telling her to be careful, pointing out the steps and the thin wooden door.

'Do you live here?' Rosalind asked, trying to disguise her surprise at how bare and primitive it was.

'Yes,' Aliena replied. 'Lovely, isn't it?' She handed over the lamp and pointed. 'Go on.'

Rosalind cautiously stepped over the threshold and held the lamp high above her head. There, slumped on the ground, was a body, weedy and small, looking very dead indeed. Rosalind glanced back at Aliena, then gingerly approached, kneeling down beside the corpse, which let out a loud belch, exuding a miasma of alcohol fumes into her face. 'Oh, goodness!' Rosalind said, leaning backwards so quickly she almost toppled over. 'You didn't kill him.

He's blind drunk. He reminds me of Uncle Charlie.'

An emboldened diva walked over, disguising her relief. 'What a pity. Shall I have another go?'

'No. It's not a pity. You know it's not. You've given him a nasty bruise, though.'

'That's something for him to remember me by, then. I've had enough. I'm leaving.'

'Where will you go?'

Aliena evidently hadn't thought of that. 'It doesn't matter,' she said eventually. 'What about you? What are you doing here?'

'I'm looking for someone.' No point making explanations complicated, she thought.

'Who?'

'I don't know, really. I danced with him. He's very – well, he's very nice.'

'Very nice?' Aliena said, mimicking her voice a bit too well. 'So very nice you chase him into the forest at night wearing your finest clothes? That sort of very nice?'

Rosalind blushed.

'Ah-ha!'

'I liked him.'

'Did he like you?'

Rosalind's face fell.

'Where does he come from?'

It fell further. 'He said he lived over there,' she gestured vaguely, 'in the forest.'

'Nobody lives in the forest. That's why it's called the forest. Otherwise it would be a wood. Do you even know his name?'

'Pamarchon.'

Aliena stopped dead. 'Pamarchon? You have fallen in love with Pamarchon?'

'What's wrong with that?'

'You don't know who he is?'

'Of course I don't.'

'Then let me tell you. Pamarchon, son of Isenwar, is the most dangerous and wanted criminal in the whole land. He murdered his uncle to steal Willdon, then became a fugitive and now leads a band of cutthroats and murderers.'

'Surely not!' Rosalind said. 'He has such a nice smile. Most of the time. He's very . . .'

'Nice, I know. You said. Don't start making up romantic ideas about him. If he is really Pamarchon, then he's dangerous.'

'He has such kind eyes, and gentle manners.'

'A man of great contradictions, then. But what if you find him and discover he is really just a short, dumpy little fellow with bad breath and a liking for slitting people's throats? That all this romance was made by the light and the music and the Festivity? When did you meet him?'

'The moment I arrived this afternoon, and again at the Festivity. I was terribly rude to him, it seems. Then after you had sung . . .'

'Ah!' exclaimed Aliena smugly. 'It is my doing, then. My singing does indeed make the old seem young, the ugly beautiful and the mean charming. It is a special ability I have,' she confided.

'Along with modesty?'

Aliena glared, but not seriously. She was in a remarkably good mood now that she knew she was not a murderer. 'Along with that, yes. Do you really want to find him?'

Rosalind thought. 'Yes,' she said. 'I do. I can't possibly have been that wrong. There must be some mistake. Besides, if people mistake him for some murderer, he might be in danger. He needs to be warned and saved . . .'

Aliena rolled her eyes. 'Heaven save me!' she said. 'This isn't going to end well. Still, if that's what you want, we can go together.'

'Where?'

'To the forest, dearest Rosalind. You wish to find the man of your dreams, I wish to escape the man of my nightmares.'

'Just a moment,' Rosalind said. 'I don't know that I should. I mean, it would be rude just to leave without saying goodbye. Besides, I have to get home.'

'I thought you wanted to find this man?'

'I do.'

'Then go and find him. You can come back easily enough when you discover you don't like him after all. Or he doesn't like you.'

'Well . . .' Rosalind was astonished by herself. Why was she even listening to this girl?

'We both need to leave this place, and I was a little worried about being on my own,' Aliena said. 'But with my dearest, oldest friend with me, what harm could possibly come to either of us?'

'You said the forest was full of criminals and outlaws.'

'Oh, no. Hardly any. Please come with me. We can sleep under the stars, pick fruit from the trees and mushrooms from the ground. "For the land cares for the virtuous, and ever will."'

'Is that another one of your quotations?'

'Of course.'

'And you'll really help me?'

'Naturally.'

Rosalind glanced back into the trees to the place where she had seen the light; there was nothing there and, she realised, it hadn't been in the place where she had arrived anyway. What was the point of staying here? If she really wanted to find her way home, she was as likely to find it in the forest as she was here. In fact, it was better to assume that she wouldn't find it. That she was, barring a miracle of some sort, stuck. If that was the case, she was, for the first time in her life, not only free to do whatever she wanted, but obliged to look after herself. She wasn't certain if that was frightening or wonderful, but it was surely different. On the other hand . . .

'I'd love to,' she said, gesturing at her dress. 'But I can hardly go wandering through the forest like this.'

'Of course you can't! Besides, if you're wrong about him, then you might not get a friendly welcome. It's said they kidnap people and hold them to ransom. You don't want that. Take off the wig and the mask and I will find you something.'

'You're a bit short.'

Aliena thought, then smiled and pointed at the now snoring form on the floor. 'That is true. But Rambert is pretty much the same size as you, I think. His clean clothes are in the corner. I know; I have to wash them. You won't look elegant, but you'll be comfortable and by the time I'm done, no one will know who you are, and that's the important thing.'

29

Lady Catherine had gone to find Henary immediately after delivering Rosalind to the bathhouse. 'How do your theories stand up, Storyteller?' she asked him.

'I am devastated,' he said. 'I planned to give cast-iron proof of the foolishness of prophecy, and I have accomplished the opposite.'

'Oh, poor you,' she said unsympathetically, 'you so hate being wrong.'

'It's not funny. It is her,' he said. 'Her name, or rather names, are as they are in the manuscript. She is a girl of some fifteen years. She is dressed strangely, but the descriptions fit as well. I am overwhelmed by what has happened. I can still scarcely credit it. What do you think?'

'She seems perfectly sweet.'

Henary grimaced. He had just witnessed a girl reading from the manuscript he had spent several years trying to decipher. She had shown it to be one of the most significant passages in the Story, but far older than the Story itself. How could that be? She had done it perfectly, as though it was nothing. Then she had not only tackled its meaning but even casually pointed out a couple of mistakes and offered corrections.

'It is impossible,' he told Catherine. 'Adults who have studied for years could not do that. I would rate her skill far above mine, for example.'

'Do you have an explanation?'

Henary spread his hands wide in something approaching despair. 'She was as astonished at the idea it was difficult as I was at the idea it was easy.'

'Tomorrow we will sit her down and question her properly. It is not as if she is unwilling to talk. She doesn't stop once she gets going.'

'We will find out who she is and where she comes from. Then we will return to Ossenfud and I will take her into the restricted room, show her the Shelf of Perplexities. Can you even begin to imagine what we might learn from her if she can read everything that is in there? What she can tell us? What we are on the brink of discovering? If only you didn't have your Festivity. Would it really matter if . . .'

'Yes, it would. You know that perfectly well. If troops can make her safe, then she will be so.'

'I hope she will be protected by something much stronger than swords.'

'What is that?'

'Her heart,' Henary said. 'If this manuscript really is magical, it states it clearly. "Both find themselves breathing through their mouths, almost panting although they are quite unaware of the warmth of the day; each is fascinated by the other . . ." There is more I cannot decipher, but it is quite plain. The manuscript foretells she falls in love with the young man she meets in the forest. Jay will have his hands full.'

*

It was unendurably hard for Henary to let go and trust the manuscript which he had spent the last few years trying to demonstrate contained nothing but false prophecies. Everything about him wanted not to let her out of his sight until he understood what was happening. He knew that was the wrong course to take, though. Girl and boy meet and fall in love. She cannot be away from him. Thus it was said. As the manuscript had demonstrated its powers so clearly, he had to trust it.

Truly, it was terrifying. It had foretold a girl would appear to a young boy called Jay on a hillside, and the girl had appeared. It had told that she would appear again many years later, and would be exactly the same age – in itself an impossibility. She had done so. That she would speak the language with staggering fluency, and she did. She had glanced at that manuscript he had been struggling with for years, looked at the most unreadable passage and read it without thinking. What could persuade her to assist him? What might he learn and understand?

He had often been tempted to raise the subject of the manuscript at Ossenfud but every time had bitten his tongue. He knew the reaction would be distrust from those who refused to countenance anything which claimed to be before the Story and enthusiastic support from those who believed in magic. He would be condemned by association with the most idiotic and dim-witted.

So tomorrow he would question the girl anew, get her to read that manuscript in its entirety. Find out who she was and where she was from. He would wait until he had the sort of proof that would convince even the most rigid and doctrinaire of traditionalists. He would proceed carefully and build his case.

Until then, he decided to pass the time as best he could. It was a beautiful evening, he had been welcomed with open arms and was to be entertained magnificently, and he had already had the sort of success that most men could only ever dream about. Of course he was nervous; but then, who would not be?

The girl had appeared, and he had calculated that from an old manuscript. Come, my sceptical friends! How do you explain that? he said to himself as he took a glass of cold white wine – a fine vintage from Lady Catherine's famous vineyard – and sipped appreciatively.

He beamed at an old man who was eyeing him warily, awed, no doubt, by his scholar's robes. 'Good evening, sir!' he said, and was soon lost in a conversation which normally he would have found perfectly tedious but which that particular evening he found curiously comforting.

His carefully tended good humour lasted all evening, until he saw the look on Jay's face as he came into the courtyard.

*

The emotions which coursed through Jay as he watched Rosalind take the arm of the tall, masked stranger were many and unfamiliar. Had he had greater experience, he would have been more adept at picking them apart. The first was guilt; he knew quite well it wouldn't have happened had he been able to take his eyes off Aliena, who, he thought, had smiled at him quite encouragingly. The second was surprise; he had not noticed the man standing behind them, and when he did, he had quickly assumed that he would never be so rude as to repeat an invitation which had already been rejected. The third was panic. He had been instructed to keep Rosalind close, implicitly to guard her. She was to be fed and entertained then delivered back to Lady Catherine and Henary for safe-keeping.

It would all be fine, he told himself. No need to raise the alarm unnecessarily. Why court a reprimand for no reason? It was a bad decision, he vaguely knew.

Jay followed carefully after the couple as they walked, but there were so many people milling around. The laughter bore in on him like an insult; the music annoyed him, the sounds of happiness and diversion he wanted to swat away like an annoying plague of flies.

And he lost them.

What was he to do now? Except wait and hope – a reasonable hope, after all. A sensible hope, in fact, that after the hour was up Rosalind would reappear and the masked man would be seen, and spoken of, no more. A frightening dream only.

After nearly an hour and a half had passed, even Jay realised it was no dream and it was time to hand matters over to his betters. Reluctantly he went in search of his master, nervousness mounting as he went from courtyard to courtyard until he heard a familiar voice holding forth. He gathered up the tattered remains of his courage and approached.

'I did my best, I really did. But she's gone.'

Henary greeted this with silence: what was there to say, after all?

'A man bowed to her. She curtsied back and they walked

off together. There was nothing I could do to stop that.'

'I suppose not. You couldn't cause a scandal.'

'I tried to follow them at a reasonable distance, just to make sure everything was all right, but I wasn't worried. She was under the protection of Willdon, after all.'

'Keep going.'

'I can't find them. I've looked everywhere. He was meant to bring her back to the place where they began but he didn't. The hour was up ages ago.'

The full import of his failure was borne in on Jay by the look on Henary's face.

'Ages ago?'

'At least three quarters of an hour now. I've been going around. I've asked many people if they have seen them. She's just vanished.'

'Was she upset or distressed when she left you? Had you said anything to annoy her? Do you think she decided to get back to this light she was talking about?'

'We were having a lovely time, I thought.'

'How was her attitude to you? Please answer carefully. This is of immense importance.'

'She was perfectly friendly.'

'Friendly? Only friendly?'

'Yes. I mean, she was . . . friendly. I liked her a lot and she seemed to like me. I mean, she didn't think I was rude to her. Not like the other one.'

'What other one?'

'The one she met in the forest before me. Kept on telling me how horrid he had been to her. She didn't like him, and kept on saying how much she didn't like him.'

'Let me get this straight,' Henary said. 'She met someone

in the forest before you? Before you saw her?'

'Yes. I was jumped by the soldiers and arrested, and a short time later she came into the clearing where they'd found me. She'd met this man who ran off when he heard us coming.'

*

Jay discovered the first details about what had happened to Rosalind by presenting such a woebegone, miserable face to the world that it drew the attention of his punting companions of the previous evening. Dawn was coming on, the dream world conjured up by Lady Catherine was fading. Candles were guttering out and the air of melancholy which always attends such endings was beginning to fall over those who still remained. In the tents and courtyards, villagers were feasting, consuming the drink and food set apart for their pleasure. They were, in turn, paying for the kindness with raucous songs and dancing, jokes and tumbling, dissipating the refinement of the previous night. Through the gateway of ribald amusement, the guests passed back into normal life, where the last would drift off to sleep. Only Jay stood out from the crowd, a fact remarked upon by Renata, who waddled towards him with a happy greeting that swiftly enough changed to concern.

'Why, whatever is the matter? You look so sad.'

'Have you seen my companion anywhere? I cannot find her.'

'Ah!' she said. 'A good cause of sadness, if ever there was one. I'm sure you will find her, mind.'

'I've been everywhere,' Jay replied. 'I don't know where

she might be hiding. I've searched every pavilion, every part of the gardens.'

'She is not in the gardens,' Renata said. 'Or at least, she may not be.'

'What makes you think that?'

'I saw her walking down that little track over there ages ago.'

Jay grabbed her by the arm. 'Are you sure?'

'Of course. Who could mistake such a figure, such clothes? It was most certainly her.'

'She didn't say where she was going?'

'We didn't talk. I didn't pay much attention really. I just noticed it.'

Jay pointed. 'Down that path?'

'That's the one,' she said. 'She was with a man who walked off and left her standing there. A few minutes later she followed him.'

'He didn't force her to go? She wasn't going against her will?'

'Oh no. She was definitely following him.'

This made Jay feel even worse. 'Thank you,' he said.

'Don't aim too high, young student,' she said in a kind voice. 'Remember the tale of Gagary, who wanted to touch the stars, but fell to earth in a ball of fire.'

Jay did not hear her warning. He was already walking in the direction she had indicated.

30

Jack More was tired and ill-humoured by the time he arrived at the Retreat where Emily Strang lived. It was a mistake to go so soon; he should have waited to see if the hunt for Angela Meerson bore any fruit first of all. But he was mindful of Hanslip's insistence on speed, so he decided a more direct approach was necessary. He would question the girl; if she was uncooperative, he could arrest her and interrogate her properly. His old colleagues would provide the space, and tell no tales afterwards.

It was a dangerous walk for the last mile or so; the Retreat occupied a strip of land only a few hundred yards wide and perhaps half a mile long, in between two accommodation sectors. One was evidently high-level, as the searchlights pointed outwards from the guard towers around the perimeter wall, watching for intruders rather than trying to spot criminal activity within. The other settlement was very different; the constant racket of helicopters flying over it, the thick barbed wire stretching along the top of the walls, the watchful guards patrolling outside were all signs of a low-grade unit, offering the most basic accommodation for those of the lowest value. They had to be watched lest they try to take more than their due, which was, as Jack knew, little enough.

The Retreat looked, if anything, even worse, scarcely fit for human habitation at all. A wall of concrete blocks stretched round it and the rusty steel door rattled from the impact of his fist when he hammered on it. With a bit of effort he probably could have pushed it in with his shoulder. A dog barked in response, then another. He bashed on it again, only stopping when he heard footsteps on the other side.

'Who is it?' The door didn't open.

'Just open up, will you?'

A light shone down on him from the top of the wall, ten feet above his head. 'Only one,' came a voice from behind it.

The door creaked open and another bright light shone directly into Jack's face. 'Put that down,' he snapped, holding his arms up to shield his eyes.

He walked over the threshold and the door was shut again immediately. A young man clattered down a metal ladder and stood in front of him. 'Your name?'

'None of your business,' Jack replied.

'It is my business. No one comes in unless they are registered. It is against the law and it is not one worth breaking.'

He'd forgotten that. Reluctantly he took out his identification and handed it over. The young man glanced at it without interest. 'Now, what do you want?'

'I want to see your leader. Do not ask why, as I do not intend to tell you.'

The man, who had long unkempt hair and looked as though he had not shaved for days, grinned at him. 'I will say you are here. If she says no, then you go away again. Understood?'

Jack nodded.

'Now, come with me.'

He led the way in silence to one of the buildings, pushed on the door to get into it and stood at the bottom of an old damp-smelling concrete stairwell. The compound had once been a street of shops, or something like that, when shops still existed. It was probably scheduled for final demolition, to build more accommodation blocks for the ever-increasing population, but had been illegally taken over until the diggers moved in. When that happened, they would be evicted and go somewhere else. Until then, they lived and planted flowers and had even painted the buildings in bright colours. Pointless, but it kept them busy.

'Sylvia!' the young man bellowed. 'Visitor! We're coming up!'

He started marching up the stairs. 'No lift,' he said over his shoulder. 'We don't have them.'

'I'll manage.'

They walked up three flights of stairs, and then Jack was ushered into the most extraordinary room he had ever been in.

It was large, about twenty feet long and wide, much greater than any usual living space for anyone but the elite. There was no furniture, only a floor covered in multi-coloured and patterned fabrics and cushions that were almost dizzying in their abundance. The walls had more material hanging down them, covering every square inch of space. The whole was illuminated by candles in glass bowls, dozens of them at different levels which gave off a yellow, flickering light, so that the room was at moments in darkness, at others perfectly clear. From them came strange scents, sweet and spicy, the like of which he had not smelled for years. He took a deep, appreciative breath.

'Your implants do not work in here,' came a quiet voice from the far end of the room. 'You are quite alone now.'

It wasn't a threatening voice; on the contrary, it was soft and mellow, pleasant almost in its tonal range.

Jack heard a rustling of clothes and feet walking across the floor. An old but handsome woman loomed out of the darkness. She was short, with close-cropped white hair – white from age, not fashion – and looked carefully at him.

'I wasn't trying to connect. I was sniffing.'

'You are wet. Come and sit by the fire to dry.'

'I prefer to stand.'

'I prefer you to sit.'

Sylvia stared dreamily at the fire and ignored Jack. She had patience, more than he had. Reluctantly, Jack sat down. Or tried to; he had not sat on the floor for a long time, and it was painful to take up the required position. He felt absurd, ungainly, while she was peaceful and composed. It was stuffy in the room; he stopped shivering and began to feel the heat penetrating his clothes.

'Thank you,' she said. 'I do not like people such as yourself standing over me. You may find that foolish, but then I find some of your ways foolish also. Perhaps you can now explain yourself?'

'I have come to ask for your assistance.'

'That is very surprising. You know that we do not take part in the affairs of your world.'

'Of course. I will not ask for something you will not freely give. I merely ask that you lend me the expertise of a young woman called Emily Strang. I am told that she knows something about history, old documents. I need to find one.'

'Do you offer anything in return?'

'I am afraid I am in no position to offer anything precise at present, although I can assure you that any assistance will be properly rewarded.'

'Not very tempting. You are aware, no doubt, that there is a renewed campaign of persecution against us. Hundreds have been arrested, dozens of Retreats closed down.'

'That is nothing to do with the people I work for. In fact, I may be able to offer some small protection.'

'We will listen. I advise you to hold nothing back and tell no falsehoods. I will go and find Emily. She will decide whether she wishes to help you or not.'

*

He had visited such places in the past, sometimes to arrest people but more often to conduct inspections and searches, and had never felt comfortable in them. Sometimes the inmates were hostile or fearful, though they were often indulgent even when he arrived armed with both weapons and official powers. Frequently they acted as if they felt sorry for him and answered his questions readily, as though they were trying to make his life that little bit easier.

Try as he might, he had found himself almost liking some, which was ridiculous. They were the self-appointed custodians of ideas and practices which had no purpose or function. They set themselves against the whole of society, weakening it by ignoring it. They refused to be happy, preferring their own misery; they refused to be comfortable, preferring the squalor of their own making, and they refused to be healthy, preferring what they decided were the natural processes of ageing and decay. The woman called Sylvia was no more than fifty; just a quick course of pills and she would be a young girl again. Why would anyone not want that? In his time he had found out a great deal about the Retreats, how they operated, what they wanted. Much was impenetrable, although whether that was because it was hidden, or because he simply could not understand, he did not know.

He did know, however, that many were believers in what they termed the preservation of the past, holding that what had gone before had some value. No one else agreed, at least not until Angela had come along.

He was businesslike, planning to lay out his requirements and to compel their acquiescence either by inducement or by threat, whichever was necessary. He did not really care which, as long as he got what he needed. He prepared to start when the door opened and the head of the Retreat returned with a young woman of striking appearance. It had to be Angela's daughter, the girl Emily. The resemblance was obvious once he looked, but it required an effort to see the similarities. She was as tall as Angela, with the same bone structure, but, like most of her sort, her hair was cut close to her scalp without style or care, and the identity rings in her ears, so she could be easily spotted as dangerous by the authorities, were ugly. Nor did she wear any decoration of the sort that most adopted to enhance their appeal. Her skin was clear and her eyes bright, but dark patches under them suggested both lack of sleep and the absence of the medications most would use to hide blemishes. Finally there were the clothes, rough and coarse, shapeless and drab; only with the greatest effort could Jack see what she could have looked like had she taken a little more care, or had she lived in different surroundings.

Still, there was something about her face which made him wonder if he was interpreting her correctly. While Angela always seemed tense and in the grip of powerful emotions, this one was utterly calm and peaceful as she walked gracefully across the carpeted floor, then sat cross-legged beside Sylvia, back straight, regarding him not with apprehension but with an open and fearless curiosity.

'This is Emily,' Sylvia explained briefly.

Emily nodded but did not speak, waiting for him to say what he had come to say and then, presumably, go away and leave them in peace once more.

'Let me begin by asking you if you know the identity of your mother,' he said.

Whatever they might have anticipated, it was not that. Jack could sense the watchfulness and caution that greeted his question. Sylvia's face was unreadable, while the girl recoiled slightly in surprise.

'Why do you ask?'

'It is important.'

'I do know,' she said. 'She is a scientist and her name is Angela Meerson. Sylvia told me when I came here. We have never met.'

'She has disappeared. I need your help to find her.'

'Why do you think I could be of any help? I know nothing of her. Nor do I want to.'

'Nonetheless, it is possible she may try to contact you. I take it she has not done so already?'

'No. Why are you telling me this?'

'She works for an institute which operates on an island

334

called Mull in the north-west of Scotland,' Jack said. 'You would consider it fairly harmless, I think. Most of its research is on energy transmission. It owns the rights to few people, is largely unarmed. It avoids participation in public affairs and has no position on treatment of renegades such as yourself. I am sure you would not feel comfortable taking my word for it, but I am equally sure you could easily enough confirm what I have said.

'Your mother seems to have made a discovery of some importance. A few days ago she vanished, destroying all the data on her project before she left. I need to find her before someone else does. As yet her disappearance is not common knowledge, but when it gets out there are many people who will wish to gain her services and some of them are not pleasant people. I have come partly to obtain your assistance and partly to warn you. If my employer can consider the possibility that the route to Angela might lie through you, then others may do so as well, and they will not be as kindly as us. Have you noticed any sign of increased surveillance in the past couple of days?'

'No.'

Jack stopped to see how he was doing. It was impossible to say. Neither of the people sitting opposite betrayed the slightest emotion. He rather hoped they would do or say something, anything, so that he could get some clue whether his approach – honesty, if not total openness – was the correct one to take.

'Thank you for your warning, Dr More,' Sylvia said. 'We will take such precautions as we think necessary. Do you have anything else you wish to tell us?'

'I do. We believe Emily's mother may have hidden a

335

copy of the data before she vanished. It is possible that she wanted Emily to find it.'

Finally he got a reaction, although only a small one. Emily looked surprised and then sceptical at the very idea.

'Explain.'

'We believe it may be hidden in the National Depository.'

'Why on earth would she hide something there?'

'Why indeed? If I could find it, or find your mother, I might be able to give you an answer. My employer came up with two possibilities. One is that you are in league with her and that you hid it.'

'I've already told you . . .'

'The other is that a person with your skills is one of the few who could find it. I don't know. It may be a false lead entirely, but it is the only one we have at the moment, and so it is there that I wish to begin my search. Your assistance would be very well rewarded.'

'Surely you people normally just swoop down with helicopters and assault troops and take whatever you want?' Emily's words were hostile, but her voice was not; it was merely enquiring.

Jack smiled reassuringly. 'We do not have an army, and the security force is little more than a dozen people.'

'The police?'

'Then it becomes public. We prefer to recover this information before anyone even knows it is missing. Someone who knows their way around the place would be a great help.'

'You are aware that people like us are now banned from the building? I have not been into it for a year.'

'I have the authority to enter.'

336

'So you want to go in, get the documents if they are there and – what then? Anything?'

'Then I can concentrate on finding your mother.'

'You must realise,' Sylvia said, 'that while people in your world concentrate on numbers and facts, we deal in words and emotions. We are as expert in our field as you are in yours. We listen far more carefully than you do. You are not lying to us, but you leave out far too much for us to trust you at the moment.'

'I have tried to say all that is relevant.'

'This is not about making the trains run more efficiently, is it?'

'No. In the wrong hands this data could be exceptionally dangerous for the entire planet. This is not about making money.'

'When did Angela Meerson disappear?'

'About three days ago now.'

'That was when the power failures killed so many people?'

'I believe so.'

'A coincidence, I'm sure, but you will understand our caution. People are already blaming us, trying to pretend it was terrorism rather than incompetence.'

'I can say nothing useful about that. I have come here with a simple task and a straightforward request. Will you assist me, as I ask?'

'We will discuss this in private, Dr More, when you have gone.'

'Does it need discussion?'

'Here everything needs discussion,' she replied with a faint smile. 'Be at the main entrance to the Depository tomorrow at nine. If we will help, then Emily will meet you there. If not . . .'

'Yes?'

'Then she will not meet you there, and we will not wish you to come here again.'

*

That was that. Jack realised he could do nothing now except wait and hope his appeal would have some effect. So he went back to the residence, ordered himself some food and settled down for a quiet night.

His peace did not last very long, however. Less than half an hour after he had arrived, there was a knock on the door. He had taken another indirect route back and arrived tired, and dirty and wet from the grime-filled rain that had been coming down in torrents all day. He wanted a long shower and an even longer sleep. He was annoyed that he had spent so much time on his journey thinking of the girl. Dare he access the files once more to find out about her? Risky. He wanted no direct contact linking him to her, or to her Retreat. But there was no reason he could not send the request through one of his old colleagues to muddy the trail. He had just sent one off when the door lit up to indicate visitors.

He knew exactly who, or rather what, the two men were when he opened the door and saw them standing there. The size, the sureness, the watchful eyes assessing him. The look of faint surprise to see someone who was so unlike most members of the elite they had ever met. More like them, in fact.

'Dr More?'

'Yes.'

'Come with us, please.'

Well – polite, Jack thought, but it would have been interesting to discover how they would respond if he refused. 'I am just about to get into the shower.'

'Sorry, sir. Orders.'

'Under whose authority?'

'You will be given an explanation in due course. It is a necessary security precaution, I'm afraid.'

Jack liked that 'I'm afraid' bit. Conciliatory, regretful, as spoken to a superior. Despite their appearance they weren't about to beat him up.

'Oh, very well,' he said. 'I don't want to make your life difficult. Come in though. Give me five minutes. Fix yourselves a drink while I make myself presentable. I'm sure whoever is responsible for all this must be terribly important. I wouldn't want to appear scruffy.'

Experience. He knew exactly how to make them relax. Cooperate, make their job easy, get something in return. That's the way it worked. Always had and always would.

'Hope I've not been too long,' he said when he emerged. 'Shall we go?'

But they still wouldn't tell him who he was going to see, or why.

31

When they left Lytten's house, Rosie and Angela walked for some way along the road together. 'Where are you heading?' the older woman asked after a while.

'I have to go home and face the music, I suppose. My parents won't let me out again for months. What do you want with me? Why did the Professor agree to do what you asked?'

'I assume he believes you have been spending the last few days in an orgy of depravity. So, naturally, he wouldn't want to know anything about it. But mainly because he likes you and trusts me. I thought you might like to have lunch, so we could get to know each other.'

'I see.' Rosie reflected; it was strange, she rather liked the idea of being suspected of some terrible vice. What was really strange, though, was that Professor Lytten found it credible.

They walked on a while further before Rosie finally plucked up courage. 'Jenkins. He looks like that because of that thing in the cellar.'

Angela gave a light laugh. 'Oh, surely not.'

'Fiddlesticks. The Professor wasn't interested, but the moment I mentioned it, you shot off down to the cellar to have a look. Then you started questioning me.'

'You were very evasive. Not an attractive characteristic in a young woman.'

'There was a forest behind the curtain. And people, and rivers, and men with swords. And an extraordinary party. And they cut my hair and dressed me up. How do you think I came to look like this?'

'What an imagination you have.'

Rosie reached into her bag and pulled out a golden wig. She handed it to Angela. Then she sat on the wall of the house they were passing and took off a shoe, showing the three gleaming rings on her middle toes.

'You know perfectly well it is nothing to do with my imagination.'

There was a pause. 'You were wearing those rings? When you came back?'

'So now you believe me?'

'But not when you went through?'

'No. What's the matter?'

'Are they metal?'

'Gold and silver, I think. I feel terribly guilty about them.'

'When you came back, was it the same as the last time?' Angela's tone had changed dramatically.

'What do you mean?'

'Did it feel the same? Happen in the same way?'

'Oh, I see.' Rosie thought. 'No. The first time it was like just stepping through a door. A bit tickly, but nothing much. This time it started off like that but then got harder, like trying to wade through water. As though it was thicker, if you see what I mean.'

'You didn't get stuck?'

'No. It was just much harder. I had this odd feeling for a moment that I got frozen. Not cold, you understand. Just like I stopped for the tiniest moment. Then I came through and everything was just fine. The odd thing was that when I stepped through there was no one near me, but when I looked back I could see someone.'

'Who?'

'I don't know. It was night. I could just make out a shadow.'

'Ah,' said Angela softly. 'How very interesting.'

'What is going on? I've worried you about something.'

'That is really very difficult to explain,' she said. 'Not least because I doubt you could understand it.'

'Try.'

'Listen, will you trust me?'

Rosie laughed. 'I doubt it.'

*

How does a universe come into existence? An odd question, certainly, and not one which – to my knowledge – anyone has ever answered before. All worlds exist, but only one is actualised at any point; another might take concrete form only if some external force acts upon it. The world projected from Tolkien's thoughts existed in potential only, and did so before I opened it up. As long as I merely observed through the pergola, only that part of it which came to my view was actualised. When I stepped through, it began to coalesce and immediately came up against its own inherent contradictions. The essential laws of physics took over and it began cancelling itself out, with nearly fatal consequences for me.

Anterwold was more stable, but it was very lucky that

this was so, as instead of being realised in slow increments, each small addition tested for stability, it became concrete at a breakneck pace. The fine human detail was generated by Rosie on her two irruptions: whatever she had done, whoever she had seen or talked to, instantly meant that these people, their friends and family, customers, possessions, ancestors – and indeed their descendants – sprang from a latent into an actualised state of existence.

Time started moving. Lytten had sketched out the basics of a functioning alternative society and created something frozen, unchanging and immoveable; I had built in limits so that this state would continue just in case of accidents, but the irruption of Rosie threatened to break through those limits and set everything in motion. From the moment she stepped into Anterwold, both past and future started to adjust to fit.

This could be a serious problem. The experiment was at risk of spinning totally out of control, as I discovered when I tried to shut it down and found it would not respond. In theory, now that Rosie (and the cat) were out, then it should have been possible. I couldn't understand it, until I saw those rings on her toes and she mentioned the shadow. I talked to her with one part of my mind, set up a few rapid calculations in the background and, with what little mental space I had left over, I began to worry.

*

Angela led Rosie to the side street where she had parked her car. 'I'm starving, and we might as well talk over food. Have you ever been to the Randolph?'

Rosie hadn't. She had, in fact, never been anywhere really, except, of course, to Lytten's cellar. Angela knew this perfectly well, which was why she made the invitation. She reasoned that the girl would be in a much more pliable state if she formed an attachment, or if she had a couple of drinks inside her. So she drove into the centre of town and led Rosie into the hotel, where she requested a table for two in a corner.

'I suppose,' she said once they were sitting comfortably and she had lit her cigarette, 'I may not offer you a sherry.'

'I don't think so,' Rosie replied, 'but I would like one.' She sat perfectly still and glanced around her. 'It might be good for me. It's very nice here.'

'Yes, all appearance and little substance, I'm afraid. The food,' she confided, 'is quite dreadful. I would have liked to give you a good meal, but that is not possible in England at the moment. We will have to settle for a charming one instead.'

'Have you travelled much?'

'You could say that.'

'Tell me about it.'

So Angela did, and warmed to the girl as she saw the misty look of longing pass over her eyes while she told of mountains, of little restaurants in village squares, of warmth and sun and blue skies, and of all the sorts of food that were to be had.

'Ah, that sounds just lovely,' Rosie said.

'Have you ever been abroad?'

'I don't know,' Rosie replied cautiously. 'I suppose that is why we are here. So you can be nice to me until I answer all your questions. Oh, I don't mean to be rude,' she added hurriedly when she saw the look of surprise on Angela's face.

'No, no. You are quite right. It is I who have been rude. I have been treating you like a silly girl, and you clearly are not. Not any longer, at least. I think a sherry would be a very good idea. And a large gin for me. Very large. I'm so glad they haven't introduced drink-driving laws yet.'

They drank and conversed of little until the pea soup arrived, ladled into their plates from a grand silver-plated tureen. They got a great deal of attention from the waiter, as they were the only people in the place.

'Now, which of us is going to start?' Angela said, once she had tasted the soup, grimaced and then doggedly drunk a small portion of it. 'Are you going to tell me what happened on the other side of the pergola? Or am I going to tell you what it is? I would prefer the first. Then I can explain the second much better. You must understand that I don't really know what is there. I give you a solemn promise that I will fulfil my side of the bargain.'

Rosie drank a spoonful of soup. 'Just answer one question first,' she said. 'Is that a time machine?'

'Good guess,' Angela said. 'But not exactly. It moved you somewhere. Relatively past or future I do not know. But not our past or future, I hope.'

'There are lots of pasts and futures?'

'No. Only one. That is the problem. One of the two I've noticed, at least.'

'What's the other one?'

Angela dabbed her lips. 'Well, you were sticky coming back, you were wearing rings and you saw a shadow.'

'What does that mean?'

'I don't know. I'm working on it; it's why I am not going to hide anything from you. I need your help. I have to figure out what has happened. Rather more is at stake than your current status with your parents, serious matter though that is. Besides, it's not as if you can tell anyone else. So, what were you doing in that cellar? The first time, I mean.'

'I was looking for Jenkins. I thought he might have got himself stuck there. I pulled back the old curtain in case he was behind it.'

'I see. Then you went through.'

'Just for a moment. I saw this boy, and he bowed at me, and then I came back. That was all, really.'

'This was Jay?'

'So I discovered later. How did you know that?'

'Then you went through again. When? On Thursday?'

'Wednesday. This time I was there until late at night, but I seem to have been away until dawn here.'

'Ah!' Angela seemed very interested in that. 'Go on. What did you see this time?'

'Wonderful things! Everybody was so nice to me. They acted as if I was terribly important. There was a super party, and I was a sort of guest of honour.'

'Who was your host?'

'Lady Catherine. She is the Lady of Willdon, and awfully rich.' Rosie peered at her over the table. 'She looked a bit like you, except that she was younger, and wore a wig. She was beautiful.'

'I'm flattered.'

'It was odd, though. Everybody made a fuss of her house, but it was really very simple. Pretty and big, but simple. And they were all in awe of things like her cups and

346

glasses, but they were old and scratched and a lot of them looked as though they'd come from Woolworth's. We've got nicer ones at school.'

'Tell me about the party.'

'There was food, which they thought was terribly grand but was quite simple as well. And everyone asked why I wasn't married. I heard some of the oddest music I have ever come across. And I met this really handsome man called Pamarchon.'

'You're blushing.'

'And everyone called me Lady Rosalind and acted as though being able to read and speak English was amazing.'

'What did they speak?'

'The ones I talked to most spoke English, although like it was a foreign language. The others . . . I don't know. I began to recognise a few words after a while, and even managed to say a few things. It's quite basic, you know. Not like French or Latin. It sounded a bit like English put through a mangle, if you see what I mean. Or a badly tuned radio where you can almost make out what is being said.'

'You seem to have had an interesting evening.'

'It was magical. Wonderful. I danced, and everybody admired me, and it was lovely.'

'I'm glad you had a good time. I'm surprised you came back.'

'I was going into the forest after Pamarchon. I'd upset him, although I don't know how I did it, and I wanted to apologise. I got a bit lost, and then I found Jenkins and saw the light. Saw the light. That sounds silly. But you know what I mean. I thought I'd better take the chance while it was there. Last time it had vanished.'

'That was my fault. I'm sorry about that. I shut it down to stop anyone going through. I didn't know you already had. Anyway, you decided to abandon your lover for the sake of your homework. Faithless mistress you are!'

Rosie blushed scarlet. 'Oh, don't say that! Please! Whatever will people think? Was that a quotation, by the way?'

'You sound worried.'

'They're always quoting things. It is a bit annoying.'

'What do they quote?'

'The Story. It seems to be a bit like a cross between the Bible and the *Encyclopaedia Britannica*. The thing which really worried me is that they call the place Anterwold.'

'Well, they would.'

'But that's what Professor Lytten . . .'

'Indeed. I built it out of his head.'

'Seriously?'

'Seriously.'

Rosie digested this surprising statement for a few moments. 'Go on, then. What is that thing? I mean, really?'

'It is a machine which I invented, designed and built. It is a way of gaining access to a variety of realities. As I say, at the moment it leads to a world created from Henry's imagination.'

'Does he know?'

'No, and I'd prefer it if you didn't tell him. He might be offended.'

'What do you mean by variety of realities?'

'It means that for any given state of the universe, there are an infinite number of other possibilities. For example, we came to this restaurant and you ordered chicken. You could have ordered fish. A universe where you did order fish is a viable alternative to this one. One where you ordered roast Brontosaurus is more distant and more difficult to access.'

Rosie's eyes narrowed. 'So?'

'Anterwold is one of those variants. A very distant one, I hope. To get to it, the number of different events must be gigantic. That was why I chose it. I didn't want any confusion with the line of events which leads from here to my future. Otherwise it would be difficult to study properly. Are you confused?'

'Very. Especially the "my future" part. Do you mean that?'

'Yes. I am born – you notice I don't say "I will be born"; it is an important distinction – in a little over two hundred years' time. I do hope you are not going to say that I am mad.'

'I've been into your invention,' Rosie pointed out. 'But I don't rate your chances with anyone else.'

'You may be correct. That's why I don't want you to mention any of this to Henry. Girls' secret. It will be a lot easier if you simply take my word for it. Just as the future is determined by the past, so the past is determined by the future. Where I come from is the future and I want it to stay like that. What Anterwold is I do not yet know.'

'So what is now? The present.'

'Ah,' said Angela airily, waving her fork in the air. 'Nothing.'

'Nothing?'

'Mathematically speaking. An abstract concept. Now is just what lies between yesterday and today, just as zero lies between minus one and one. From the point of view of the future, the present is the past. From the point of . . .'

'Yes. I get the idea,' Rosie interrupted. 'But it's not nothing. It really is now.'

'So is Monday morning and Saturday evening.'

'Now I am eating a piece of chicken. Monday morning I overslept, and Saturday evening – heaven knows what I'll be doing.'

'You are still doing those things. Unless something changes so that last Monday you do not oversleep and now you are somewhere else. If, for example, you decide not to come back . . .'

'But I did.'

'Yes. You did. But will you?'

'You're really annoying, you know.'

'No. I'm not. Existence is. It's not my fault.'

Angela poured herself a glass of the not very good red wine she had ordered after her gin and sipped thoughtfully. It was curious talking to this girl. She had, after all, had to keep it to herself for nearly thirty years. Now she was explaining in simple language, the simplest language, to a young girl who listened with great seriousness to what she was saying. The only person in the world she could talk to, because she knew at least that it worked.

'Now, let me make everything clear. I am a sort of mathematician, and I got myself into a situation where I had to do many years' work in a couple of days. The only way of doing that was to step out of time, so to speak. So I came here. I arrived in 1936.'

Rosie seemed to cope with that very well.

'And now you're stuck, and want to go home again.'

'Sort of. I need to make a few modifications before I do.

I wanted to discover something fundamental about reality. My boss wanted – or wants – to make lots of money, in ways which I think are dangerous. I have to stop him.'

'Is it really dangerous?'

'Yes. It is the most dangerous thing anyone has ever invented. Nuclear bombs can destroy the present. This can destroy the past and the future as well. Which, if you see my point, I think is a bad idea.'

Rosie chewed a piece of chicken. 'Is it really true that in the future we all have lots of money, and no one works because machines do everything, and everyone is happy? I saw that on the television.'

'Never underestimate the ability of humanity to mess things up. There are thirty-five billion people in the world, and most live lives which I consider miserable and pointless. Or I used to think that. Now I'm not so sure. Everything is run by a small elite of specially selected experts. Much of the planet is uninhabitable. All animals except us and things we eat have been sent into extinction. Democracy has been abolished as inefficient, everyone is automatically tracked every second of their lives, and dreams have been replaced by advertising. Most people are happy, though. The drugs in their food make certain of that, except for the few people who refuse to take them. They're really miserable. We call them renegades and lock them up occasionally.'

'For not being happy?'

'A crime against Society. They occasionally go on marches shouting slogans like "Glad to be grumpy". They get locked up or have their brains wiped.'

'That's not what we've been promised,' Rosie protested. 'What were you?'

'I was one of the elite.'

'You should be ashamed of yourself, then.'

'I am increasingly so. It didn't occur to me that it was anything other than natural at the time, and there was not much I could have done about it in any case. One person cannot change the world. Except, of course, that now I can.'

'What do you mean?'

'Once my tests are done and I am confident it will work, I think I can alter a few things. Then I can safely go back and take my knowledge with me. Immensely complicated; it'll take at least another decade.'

'Won't you be a bit old by then?'

Angela looked puzzled. 'I'm good for another eighty years at least,' she said stiffly, 'once I take another shot of treatment. I'm only ninety-three.'

'My grandmother's ninety-three. You don't look like her.'

'I should hope not.'

'What about Anterwold?'

'Oh, that's just to calibrate the machinery.'

'So what happens to it?'

'In due course, I will shut it down. I'll need the machine and there can't be two universes existing simultaneously for ever.'

'What about all my friends? Jay, and Pamarchon, and Aliena? What about Lady Catherine and Henary?'

'They'll just be as they were before. In a latent state.'

'They'll vanish? Be eradicated?'

'Anterwold only exists inside the confines of the machinery, you know. It's not real, and it had better not become real, either.'

'It seems rather nicer than where you come from.'

'You have seen just a small part of it. I have no idea what it is really like. Not that it matters. There is no chance of it achieving permanence.'

'Why not?'

'Because . . . Because I say so.'

Rosie studied her suspiciously. 'That's what my mum says when she doesn't know what she's talking about. Are you sure you know what you're doing?'

'It is a little complicated at the moment. I couldn't shut it down because you were in it. That locked it into a sort of fake permanence.'

'Good,' Rosie said.

'It wasn't good, and it was all your fault.'

'You didn't put up a sign saying No Entry. What did you think would happen if someone saw a forest in Professor Lytten's cellar?'

'I certainly didn't think anyone would sneak around someone else's house, look through their possessions, then go and join a party they hadn't been invited to. It was very nosy of you.'

'You were careless and now you are proposing to snuff out my friends. I don't have many.'

'Please don't start to be self-pitying. It's unbecoming. You must have friends here.'

Rosie shook her head. 'Not really.'

'I'm clever, but not that clever. If people in Anterwold think you are wonderful, then it must be because you are. Which means that there is no reason why you shouldn't be pursued as ardently here as Pamarchon was pursuing you there.'

353

'He was running away from me. I was pursuing him.'

'A minor detail.'

'Listen. Does this place exist or not?'

Angela sighed. 'That is a meaningless question. As I say, it depends on your viewpoint.'

'You said you couldn't switch it off because I was in it.'

'True.'

'I'm here now.'

'True.'

'When you went into the cellar an hour ago, did you manage to switch it off then?'

Angela looked a bit shifty. 'No,' she admitted.

'Aha!' Rosie said in triumph.

Angela put down her glass. 'You're annoying me.'

'You don't know what is going on.'

'I am going to take you home, settle down to a night's thinking and find out. In the morning I will go back to Henry's house and have another go. I'm meant to be going to help him with something anyway.'

*

Once I had taken Rosie back home – and she walked through the door like one of Dante's sinners heading for punishment – I felt free to get to work. Firstly, of course, I needed all the information I could possibly gather together. I had ideas, my intuition was working just fine; it was the context, the overall framework that was lacking.

I could guess, but I didn't like doing that for long; it always made me feel a little unbalanced. But all I could do practically at the moment was go back to the machinery and run some tests to get the basic information I needed. Then settle down, figure out what was wrong and work out a way to pull the plug. It was fortunate that I had promised to help Henry out the next day with his translation. What was that about? I did very much hope that he wasn't frittering away his time on nonsense when he had a fantasy to dream about.

The trouble was, I knew already what was going on. My instincts were good enough for that. There was still a foreign body in Anterwold that had originated here. It had to be that; there could be no other access to it, and no other reason why it was locked into existence. Only the cat and Rosie had been in there, and both had come back, so by a process of elimination there could be only one, bizarre, explanation.

Bizarre but not impossible. Transmission did not mean the actual physical movement of all the molecules and atoms and electrons which constitute matter. It was the transmission of information only, which was used to reorganise ever so slightly the universe at the point of arrival. As anyone who has ever used a computer knows, there are few simpler tasks than copying data. On transmission, the body is converted into information which the machine stores – a very great deal of it, admittedly, but in principle a simple task. This is then projected outwards into the new destination. A copy is kept, however, for the return, as it is simpler and quicker to modify a given set of information than it is to reproduce it entirely. The machine was set up to reject any body of matter which did not have that copy in store, to prevent people from Anterwold coming through to Henry's cellar. I'd instructed it to ignore clothes and other insubstantial material, otherwise a bit of fluff might have caused problems, but not anything else. What I suspected was that Rosie, on her return, had confused the machinery because of those rings. It rejected her, and kept her in Anterwold, because it did not recognise her. At the same time, it let her through, because it did.

The result had been a duplication. If I was right, there were now two Rosies, and in that case I had one massive headache. I was concerned and, much to my surprise, the main focus of my concern was for Rosie herself. I should have paid more attention to that. I felt protective. I had enjoyed her company, her questions, her cheek and her criticisms. I was far fonder of her than I should have been, considering that I had only known her for a couple of hours and she had already given me grief.

32

Discovering what must have happened to Rosalind after she disappeared was not that difficult; the path led through the decorative woods, tended and trimmed, which formed the outer part of the Willdon gardens. It twisted and turned so that occasionally the walker was presented with a handsome vista, back towards the house or outwards to the hills beyond. It was very pleasing and carefully thought out; indeed, it was part of a much grander plan which encircled the house entirely, each punctuation point of column, fountain or grotto arranged in a symbolic pattern lauding the resilience of the domain and its necessity to the unfolding of the Story.

Not that Jay had any time or patience for such things, even had he noticed them. As far as he was concerned it was a path, no more nor less, which led past a small tumbledown cottage, on the steps of which was an old man sitting slumped over with his head in his hands.

'Ho there!' Jay called. 'Good morning, sir.'

The man slowly lifted his head and looked at Jay with such a pained expression that Jay wondered whether he was a madman. It was customary for great owners to give room to such people; villages did so as well with hermits like Jaqui. The foolish and the weak-headed deserved charity, and it was a goodness to give them care.

'It is not a good morning to me,' he said. 'I have never known a worse.'

'You are injured! What has happened to you?'

It was true. The old man – not that old, perhaps, but he had such an air of weariness that it was easy to think him ancient – was naturally cadaverous; his hands bony, his hair lank and greasy. His face had the yellow pallor of ill-health and poor eating, and that, more than anything, set off and highlighted the large purple-black bruise on his left cheek, so prominent and striking that it dominated his face entirely.

'You need assistance,' Jay said. 'Tell me where there is some water and a cloth.'

He didn't reply, but Jay was not to be deflected. He found a cloth and drew some cold fresh water from the well, then settled down to apply it to the man's cheek. He winced and gritted his teeth at the pressure, but did not complain.

'I know you!' Jay said as he worked. 'I saw you last night in a boat on the lake. Your name is Rambert, no?'

'That's right. I was there, listening to that hell-cat of mine murder music in the way only she can manage.'

'Do you mean Aliena? She was wonderful, I thought.'

'No doubt. You have the look of stupidity about you.'

'What was wrong with it?' Jay asked, determined not to take offence. In truth, Rambert was no worse than some of the teachers he'd had in the past few years.

'Oh, it was lovely,' said Rambert bitterly. 'They adored her, didn't they? Such soaring tones, such a beautiful voice. So tender and moving. I imagine a few of the weak-minded were almost in tears.'

'Well . . . yes.'

'She can never resist playing to an audience. As if that mattered. She destroys, ignores tradition. She mangles the beauties of the forms, which reflect the heavens and cannot be changed. She is so full of herself she thinks rules are for other people. She, the great Aliena, can do as she pleases. So she makes her cheap effects, and weak, ill-educated people like you applaud and encourage her, and the great fabric of music is shredded. Every time she opens her mouth it becomes a smaller thing, more like peasant entertainment. But all she wants is the applause and the adoration. She doesn't care what damage she causes to get it.'

He looked at Jay, one eye closed from the pain of his bruise. 'You're a student. How do you feel about people changing a story just because the listeners might like it better? Eh? That's what she does.'

He was so despairing that Jay could not think of anything cheering to say.

'How did you get that bruise?'

'I fell.'

'I don't think so. Who attacked you?'

'That I couldn't say,' he replied. He seemed hesitant, shifty even. 'It was dark, and I was very tired.'

'It must have been a hefty blow,' Jay observed. 'Has anything been stolen?'

'How would I know? I doubt it. I don't have anything.'

Jay got up from the step and walked into the little cottage, which was dirty and untidy. All around were piles of music and musical instruments – very valuable for those who could play them – but he could see no signs that anything had been taken. The cottage's main room had a table and some chairs and a large fireplace for heat and cooking. A small cupboard contained such pots and pans as Rambert possessed. Nothing appeared to have been disturbed, although it was so disorganised it was difficult to tell.

A small door led through to a chamber which had on the floor Rambert's cotton-stuffed mattress. At the foot was another, smaller one which presumably was used by Aliena. Jay felt his skin prickle.

Thrown across the bed was a dress of incomparable beauty and richness, golden blue and glistening in the shards of light cutting through the gaps in the shuttered window. There could be no doubt. It was the dress that Rosalind had worn the night before.

*

The discovery gave the pursuit a sense of urgency, as the circumstances that Jay related suggested she could be in considerable danger. The young man – still afraid of punishment but knowing that he had at least been of some use now – had run to the house carrying the evidence and found Henary and Lady Catherine deep in conversation. He held the dress out before him.

'Where did you get that?' Lady Catherine asked.

'In a cottage in the woods. Rambert lives there. He was attacked there last night. There's no sign of Rosalind, though. Someone saw her walking into the woods after the man she had partnered.'

Henary and Lady Catherine exchanged glances.

'This dress was taken off quite roughly,' Catherine said. 'See – it's torn down the side. Not greatly, but it was evidently removed in a hurry. You would expect greater care for something so valuable. Are you sure Rambert was telling the truth? Did he describe his attacker?'

'He said he didn't see anyone. I think he was too drunk. As for the dress, he said he had no idea how it got there.'

'How do you estimate his account?'

'I didn't think he was telling me everything,' Jay said. 'But he was not obviously lying. He was more interested in his pupil than anyone else. She's vanished as well.'

Lady Catherine – who had, Jay noted, taken control of the conversation, with Henary standing quietly at the side – pursed her lips. 'So we either have a mysterious stranger attacking Rambert and perhaps Rosalind, or maybe Rambert attacking her.'

'Or maybe neither,' Henary added. 'All we have is a sequence of events. We know they must be connected, but we do not know how. It is very worrying, nonetheless.'

'Extremely.'

'We must move quickly. Now I must recommend a proper search party, and I think it would be best to detain Rambert for a while. I would be distressed indeed if a man of his distinction had committed an abominable crime, but all things are possible.'

'No. No one must go into the forest for two days except me.'

'But Lady Catherine . . .'

'You know the reason.'

Henary seemed for a moment as though he was about to argue. Then his shoulders sagged a little. 'I wish we could pursue them further, though.'

'That is out of my hands. I must go to the Abasement.'

'But we must do something. She may be in danger,' Jay said once a very disappointed Henary had left. In truth he did not understand what had happened, but he knew that, for whatever reason, the immediate pursuit of Rosalind had been postponed. 'The trail is still fresh. If we wait even an hour . . .'

For the first time, Jay was alone with the Lady of Willdon and his worry overwhelmed his discretion. She was staring out of the window thoughtfully, watching as a small group went around packing away the tables and collecting the bowls and plates and glasses from the night before. Jay knew he had no right to say anything, but he was astonished by the lack of urgency. Lady Catherine regarded him coolly.

'When I say it is not possible, I mean just that. The matter is closed.'

Jay realised he had overstepped the mark, but still could not restrain himself. 'Why?' he said. 'Surely it is better . . .'

'It is the day of Abasement,' she said. 'Did you not realise that was the purpose of all the festivities yesterday?'

Jay shook his head. He had not the slightest idea what she was talking about.

'Walk with me,' she said, and Jay, knowing a command when he heard one, fell cautiously in line with her as she led him out of the building and towards a little area of fruit trees – damson and peach and plum and apple – with a path that led through into the far garden.

'I am the Lord and Lady of Willdon. My position is one of high authority and great power. You, for example. You trespassed on my lands. Once you were caught I could have had you declared a slave. I could have flogged you. I could have cut off your hands or your head. I need consult no one for such a decision, and answer to no one after it.'

Jay thought it wise to remain silent.

'Ordinarily, such decisions and punishments I pass to a court of men and women chosen from the locality. Three men, three women. Is that how it works with you?'

'Not really. In my village, the old men judge the women, the old women judge the men and any serious crime is passed to the Visitor. In Ossenfud each college deals with its own.'

'Well, here all authority derives from me. The courts decide my justice and mercy. Only I can overrule their decision. Not that I do.'

Jay did not see what the point of this was, but he nodded. It was interesting, and he had never met anyone who could order the death of another. Nor had he expected that such a person would look like Lady Catherine.

'Do you know where my power comes from?'

He shook his head. She was going to tell him so there wasn't much point in guessing.

'It comes from the people I judge. They give me all authority, I hand it to my courts. A heady thing, don't you think? There is much more, of course. My authority determines the level of taxes, adjudicates inheritance, apportions vacant lands, looks after the domain's relations with the outside world, decides which roads need to be repaired, which streams cleansed. I own the mills on behalf of all, and the granaries and the farming equipment. It would be easy to become drunk on so much power, no?'

'I really do not know, my Lady. I have never had any power.'

'Believe me, then. It would need only a brief moment of weakness for any man or woman to think this power is theirs by right and that they are better than the people they rule. That way lies tyranny, and we have seen it in the stories many times. You have studied them, no?'

'A few.'

'What year of studies are you in?'

'My sixth.'

'Then you haven't studied them.'

'Well, no.'

'Never lie like that to me, Jay. I forgive ignorance but not vanity. If you do not know something, then admit it freely. Has Henary never told you that?'

Jay nodded. 'Many times. He will tell you, if you ask. But I have read many of these stories on my own account, even if I have not yet formally studied them.'

'And now?'

'My Lady, I am a poor boy from a farm. A student who knows that he knows little. In the last day I have narrowly escaped slavery, met a fairy, been to a festivity of wonderment, heard music such as I have never heard before, lost a girl whose importance I do not understand, and now am walking in the sunshine with a woman reputedly the most powerful and beautiful in Anterwold. I am doing my best.'

Lady Catherine burst out in a peal of laughter. 'Yes, you are. It may be that Henary is right about you. I have not been kind to you and I apologise. Shall we start again and be friends?'

Jay smiled bravely.

'Then let me continue with my lengthy and tedious account,' she went on, resuming her way down the alley of trees.

'My predecessors here knew full well the folly of

mankind, their infinite capacity for self-importance. So they constructed reminders to make the people of this land recall that they were not slaves, and the rulers that they were not masters. Did you know that the least of labourers on my estate can have me hurled from my office?'

He shook his head.

'They can. In theory. They can lodge a complaint against me with my own court, and that court can summon me for a hearing. If my failing is serious enough they can call a meeting of every council in the domain and strip me of my power and authority. It has never happened. After all, they'd just have to replace the ruler with someone else. But every few years there is a ceremony of reminder that it is possible. It begins in an hour.'

'What happens?'

'It is best if you see for yourself. I am telling you this because I have a use for you. I need someone with me from noon to dusk, to dusk and to dusk. Two days and a half. To watch and report that I bear my humiliation with dignity, and that the humiliation is within the bounds of tradition. That person has to be independent of me and independent of the people. Often enough the task goes to a Storyteller, but Henary has rather too much to do today.'

Jay could almost feel the panic flowing over him.

'So I want you to take up the task. Will you, Jay, witness the ceremony of Abasement?'

'I wouldn't have the faintest idea what to do.'

'Oh, it's nothing. You watch. Make sure everyone behaves themselves. Smile sweetly and look grave at the appropriate moments. Now I must go and dress.'

33

Over the next couple of days, Chang tried to summon the courage needed for another approach to Henry Lytten. Several times he walked down the road and gazed at the house. Once, heart pounding, he even rang the doorbell. No answer, though. On another occasion he thought he saw a curtain twitch but, if the windows fitted as badly as they did in his own house, then that meant nothing.

All the while he was getting used to his new situation and even began to feel tolerably optimistic. That was possibly because he was also starting to sleep properly, undisturbed by nightmares or worries generated by the sheer strangeness of it all. When he got out of bed, he would sit at the little table next to the sink while he waited for the kettle on the hob to boil. Then he would spoon some Nescafé into a mug, add the water, and listen to the sounds of life outside the window, trying to pin down each one and identify it.

It was early, no more than seven, but there were the noises from the room underneath, where the spotty young man who worked in the haberdasher's was getting up. He heard the padding of feet as he went to the bathroom at the end of the corridor, wrapped in his dressing gown. The clopping of horses' hooves from the milkman in the street; the tinkle of bicycle bells as the first people pedalled off to work in town.

Then came an unaccustomed noise. A doorbell; the front door opening and shutting; the sound of feet – heavy feet, clumping up the stairs; a pause outside his door; a hard, repeated knock, one which could not be ignored.

He put on his dressing gown and walked to the door. He wasn't expecting anything, as he didn't know what to expect: he had no friends, no associates; no one knew where he lived, or cared; no one had cause to visit him at any hour, let alone at seven in the morning.

'Yes?'

'Would you come with us, please?'

Two men came into the room. One was large and burly, far larger than Chang; the other was slighter. He was the one who seemed to be in charge.

'Who are you?' he asked the quiet one.

'Detective Sergeant Maltby. Special Branch.'

'Does that mean you're a policeman?'

'No. I'm the window cleaner.'

'That's good. The windows are really dirty. I can hardly see out of . . .'

'Very funny. Now if you'd come with us?'

'But if you are window cleaners, then . . .'

Maltby held up his hand. 'Just stop there, please. Don't make my life more difficult. We don't wish to make a fuss if this turns out to be a misunderstanding.'

Chang scanned his memory but there were no briefings which allowed him to interpret what was going on. He knew, of course, of accounts about knocks on doors but he had been told that was associated with an earlier period, or different countries. He knew about police forces, but they wore uniforms, he thought.

'What is this about?'

'We will explain later.'

They didn't seem threatening. That is, they didn't behave like people who were about to kill him or attack him or anything like that, but Chang had too little information to come to a reasoned conclusion. He was simply not yet prepared for any interaction as complex as this one. He began to feel anxious, and knew the policeman had noticed.

So he made an effort. 'Super!' he said as brightly as possible. 'Will you give me some breakfast?'

'Just get dressed, sir.' They stood and watched as he did so, then, one in front and one behind, they trooped down the stairs.

*

'Your name?'

'Alexander Chang.'

'Date and place of birth?'

'Ah . . . 28th June 1930, Uganda.'

'Where did you go to school?'

He hesitated again; he had been prepared for casual conversation, but not for a detailed interrogation. If this Maltby man was going to take him through his entire life – his supposed life – it wasn't going to be difficult to find huge gaping holes. His memory had quickly prepped him on his biography and briefed him on interrogations during the short trip to the police station and the result wasn't encouraging.

'A mission school run by my father.'

'Where?'

'It moved around with him.'

'Where?'

'I don't remember.'

'You don't remember where you lived when you were fourteen? Fifteen?'

'No.'

'Did you go to university?'

'No.'

'When did you come to England?'

'I arrived about a week ago.' That was true, at any rate.

'How?'

A pause. 'By boat.'

'Which one?'

'I don't remember.'

'What port did you arrive at?'

'Ah . . . Liverpool.'

'Which port did you leave from?'

'The main port. You know . . .'

'The main port of Uganda?'

'Yes.'

'I find that surprising.'

'Why?'

'Uganda has no coastline.'

'Why are you asking me all this?'

They were sitting in a small, grey room in the police station. Chang had been led down the stairs and put into a car. Under normal circumstances, he would have been excited: he had never been in a car, and was fascinated by the experience.

'A Rover, no?' he said. There was no reply. 'P80 straight-4 overhead valve engine. Designed by Gordon Bashford.

African walnut dashboard. Not a great success, I believe. Twenty-three point five miles to the gallon, nought to sixty in twenty-two seconds. Fewer than six thousand produced before it was cancelled.'

'They've only just been introduced.'

He lapsed into a chastened silence. So much for small talk. Never volunteer information, never take the initiative. His head was full of information that he could call on at will. He could, had it been needed, give the complete specifications of the car, compare it to other models, recite newspaper articles reviewing its performance.

All this he knew. What he didn't know was much about his own history. There hadn't been time. He knew quite well that what he said was riddled with contradictions and outright absurdity. Even a seven-year-old child would have been suspicious of a man who did not know precisely where he was born or where he went to school, was decidedly hazy about his work and could not name a single friend, acquaintance or family member who might vouch for him. How did he get into the country without a passport? A good – no, an excellent – question. Why had he been standing outside Lytten's house the previous evening? Another good question.

The two policemen went to get him a cup of tea, which was nice of them, he thought. In their brief absence, he scanned through his briefing papers. 'Lying,' he said out loud, hoping no one would hear. 'I need to lie. Teach me, quickly.'

I wouldn't if I were you, came the response. For a start, it's a variable concept here. You are in a culture where ambiguity has been raised to a high level. Let me give an example: depending on phrasing, circumstance, expression, body movement, intonation and context, the statement 'I love you' can mean I love you; I don't love you; I hate you; I want to have sex with you; I do, in fact, love your sister; I don't love you any more; leave me alone, I'm tired, or I'm sorry I forgot your birthday. The person being talked to would instantly understand the meaning but might choose to attribute an entirely different meaning to the statement. Lying is a social act and the nature and import of the lie depends in effect on an unspoken agreement between the parties concerned. Please note that this description does not even begin to explore the concept of deep lies, in which the speaker simultaneously says something he knows to be untrue and genuinely believes it nonetheless: politicians are particularly adept at this.

What I am trying to say is that lying is a linguistic exercise of extraordinary complexity. It is better at your stage to tell the truth, although this may also have unintended consequences.

There we are, it concluded after its recitation was done. Does that help?

No, he thought.

As Chang sat trying to find something useful in the torrent of information, Maltby returned with the tea, handed it to him and sat down opposite him. They were interrupted by a man who brought in a large envelope. 'That's all,' he said, and left.

Maltby pulled out the contents and Chang saw that they were bits of paper from his room, mainly his efforts at handwriting, which he still found difficult. He had spent many a long hour clutching a pen tightly in his hand, scrawling on the paper, trying to acquire the sort of ease, fluency and legibility that most people around him could manage as second nature. He had tried English, and Cyrillic and Arabic. He found the Cyrillic easiest and had begun to take notes to fix his still erratic memory. That, he thought, might not be good.

'There are several words of Russian here,' the man observed. 'Why is that?'

'Just notes,' he replied.

'You speak Russian?'

'Oh yes.'

'Really? Now how did the son of an African missionary learn to speak Russian?'

'I taught myself.'

'Why were you watching the house of Henry Lytten?'

Chang began to sweat. 'I wasn't.'

'Then would you care to explain this, sir?'

Maltby held up a piece of paper that had been collected from Chang's little desk. On it were written three names. Henry Lytten. Angela Meerson. Rosalind.

'Lytten. You have been watching his house. Meerson? Who is she? Then there is Rosalind. A young girl called Rosalind briefly disappeared two days ago. Her parents are convinced she's been seduced by an older man. She's only fifteen. A serious crime, that would be.'

Chang's mind went into panic.

'Anyway,' Maltby continued. 'We're done with you here.'

'Really? Thank heavens for that!'

Maltby smiled in a cold sort of way. An hour later, Chang was put back into the car and driven to Henry Lytten's house.

34

Henry was out when I arrived at his house, but I had a key and let myself in. I put on the kettle and then went downstairs to visit my machine. It was reassuringly quiet, looking gratifyingly like a rusty old pergola covered in bits of tinfoil, and I had a brief burst of hope that, suddenly and miraculously, my little problem had resolved itself. I carefully went through the routines required to activate it and watched as the electricity began to flow through it, crossing my fingers in a perfectly unscientific fashion as I waited.

No luck. Slowly the scene resolved itself; the grim view of the bare grey wall beyond faded and was replaced by the rather more beautiful sight of a coastline from the top of a hill, stretching down to the sea. Birds flew overhead and the waves were breaking on the shore of enticingly clean white sand.

Why wouldn't the damned thing just go away? I had had an idea during the night; a recommendation had arrived in my mind when the calculations were nearly complete. Why don't you set it back to before the girl first stepped through? Reset to before she met the boy for the first time and that might unblock it.

Worth a try. So I closed it, recalibrated for about six months before the moment I thought Rosie had first gone in, and went through the start-up procedure once more.

Please, I thought to myself. Please don't work . . .

Another view took shape and solidified, a river landscape this time. With ducks. For some reason the ducks really annoyed me. They were unnecessary, almost a gratuitous insult.

Then the phone rang. I left the machine running, in the vain hope it would correct itself, and ran upstairs to answer. An earnest voice with a Midlands accent asking for Henry. Detective Sergeant Maltby, he said his name was. I announced myself as his associate and said he could speak freely. 'I have full authorisation and clearance in all matters,' I reassured him in my grandest manner.

'It's about the man watching his house,' Maltby said. 'We've arrested him.'

'Really?' I replied. 'That was good work. What do you think?' Nothing like vague questions to find out what on earth someone is talking about.

'He's a queer one, no doubt about it. One of the worst liars I've ever come across. Foreign, obviously, and speaks Russian. I think he may be . . . you know.'

'Describe him.'

'Looks early thirties. Brown eyes. Average height. Healthy-looking, pale complexion. A bit Chinese-looking, but he says he isn't. His name is Alexander Chang, so he says.'

'Is that so?' I said in what I hoped was a distant, uninterested tone.

'The thing is, we found papers saying he wanted to get something from Professor Lytten, and needing to find someone called Angela Meerson. There is also a possible reference to a girl who briefly went missing. We don't know what it means, but it doesn't sound good. Does the name Angela Meerson mean anything to you?'

'Nothing,' I replied.

'What should I do with him?'

'I'd just shoot him, if I were you.'

'Ah . . . no. Not one for the police, that.'

'Tell you what,' I said. 'Could you bring him here at, say, eleven o'clock? We can ask him questions and get to the bottom of it. We're good at that sort of thing.'

I put down the phone. Alexander Chang? The man who tracked down the cleaner in my experiment? After all this time? Talk about inconvenient. Perhaps a coincidence. I made myself a cup of tea and went back downstairs again until Lytten arrived in a taxi with a man whom I assumed must be his visitor. They were soon followed by a taller one I had not seen for nearly fifteen years. 'Sam Wind!' I said, giving him a warm embrace. 'How simply lovely to see you again!' I'd never liked him.

'Angela, a long time,' said Sam Wind. 'So kind of you to help out. Odd circumstances. How's your Russian?'

'Good as ever. How's yours?'

'I've no idea. Not met him yet. Henry found him,' Wind replied. 'I was only told this morning. I was planning to do some gardening. Ah, well. The things we do for our country, eh? With your assistance, we might find out what Henry has dredged up.'

'I didn't know he still did this sort of thing. I thought he'd given up years ago.'

'He did, but this man wouldn't trust anyone else. They knew each other during the war, apparently. So the old warhorse came clumping out of retirement to help. He's

375

in rather a bad mood about it. Not the man I knew once.'

'We all change.'

'You don't. You look disgracefully well-preserved for a woman of your years. You should be ashamed of yourself. Shall we begin? We can chat afterwards, no doubt. Lot of water under the bridge and so on.'

We all went in and sat down, and the interrogation of Dimitri Volkov could begin.

*

I had done translating on many occasions; it was why initially I had been brought into this world of Henry's and Wind's. I had been really good at it; it reached the point where the people I worked for would deliberately look for messages in obscure languages, just to try and find one I didn't know. Careful experimentation established that I knew few Asian or African languages and my Icelandic was patchy, but apart from that, I could manage nearly all that came my way.

Portmore had asked me to stay on after the war but I had refused even to consider the idea. I'd done my bit, I pointed out, and I was desperate for some peace and quiet. Besides, I wanted to get back to a decent climate and I suspected my little garden in the South of France was so overgrown that, unless I gave it some urgent attention, my house might disappear for ever into the forest.

It would be strange, though, to see Henry shift back to his old self, no longer the tweedy, slightly abstracted academic, but once more the incisive interrogator, asking carefully thought-out questions, preparing traps several moves ahead, mentally noting every word and gesture, giving as much weight to the unsaid as the said. He had been a natural. His students must be terrified of him.

*

A very obedient Volkov had arrived at Oxford station accompanied by his host, who was visibly glad to see the back of him. Lytten was there to collect him; he had very carefully made sure not to tell anyone when he was arriving or where.

He took a taxi back to his house. Volkov sat quietly beside him as the taxi turned into Beaumont Street, then went north.

'Who am I going to meet?'

'A man called Sam Wind. Are you ready for this?'

He didn't seem nervous at the prospect; perfectly calm, in fact. Lytten wasn't. 'Be at my house at ten,' he had told Wind. 'I have something for you.'

'Really? What?'

'You may find it interesting.'

But he had said no more. Only to Portmore had he been forthcoming. 'I'll bring him to my house for a preliminary interrogation and then hand him over to you.'

'Why not send him straight here?'

'I'm going to ask Sam to come, just to see how he reacts. Kill two birds, if you see what I mean.'

'I see. Then be careful how you proceed.'

*

Wind was delighted when he arrived and Lytten gave him a quick summary. 'How wonderful! I'm looking forward to this. If he's what he says he is then it will be a serious success. Do you have any idea,' he said, 'how long it is since we had a decent defector? We just get the dregs these days.'

'Do you want me to stay with you, or would you prefer to talk to him by yourself?'

'Certainly you must be there. He's yours, after all.'

Lytten nodded. 'Bear in mind the problem of understanding him. We talk in German, but that is hardly one of your skills, and not really one of his either. I have asked Angela Meerson to come along to help.'

'Oh, good God! That lunatic.'

'I thought she'd be useful.'

'She always made me feel a bit uncomfortable. What does she do now?'

'Nothing. She lives a simple life. She amuses herself in the usual sort of arty way that women find to pass the hours, I think. Collects all sorts of odd things; some seem to have found a permanent storage place in my cellar. For the most part she lives in France. It is lucky I could get hold of her.'

Wind glanced around the dingy hallway. 'Do you never get bored living up here?'

'Oh, no,' Lytten replied with a smile. A slightly sad smile. 'Why should I? I have my colleagues and my students to keep me entertained, and my friends to keep me on my toes. I know exactly what I will be doing on every day, weeks in advance. All around me is calm and predictable, unless you show up. What more can any man ask? You concern yourself with Armageddon and revolution. I concern myself with whether Hetherington will manage a decent second, and with a few curious lines in *As You Like It*. I believe firmly that my work is the more important.'

'You've changed a great deal, you know.'

'No,' Henry said. 'I'm the same. It is the world that has changed. I might put the same point to you. You know this is all a foolish game. I had a policeman here yesterday, Special Branch, all fired up about finding subversives down in the Morris factory. There aren't any. Even if there were they'd be too incompetent to do anything. So what's it for?'

'Bombs are real.'

'They are, and will be used or not, whether I do something or sit quietly reading my books. Shall we begin?'

*

'I think we should start with your telling us the story of your life. Just to get the ball rolling, so to speak ...' That was Wind talking. They were in Lytten's study, the big room at the front of the house, the room which, had it been a family abode, would have been the drawing room, with its large bay windows, high ceilings and elaborate Victorian fireplace. And books, nearly every wall covered in them, huge piles on the floor and the furniture, disguising the fact that the room had been neither painted nor properly cleaned for many a long year.

Volkov's English seemed poor, his German tolerably good, but conversational when precision was badly needed. Angela's occasional contributions, in contrast, were clipped, efficient and faultless; somehow she managed to provide a translation so well and quickly the others almost forgot she was there.

'I was born on 23rd April 1917 in North Ossetia and I am – or was, rather – a full-time officer in the GRU. I wish to apply for asylum, and I am willing to pay for it with such information as I possess.'

'Why us? Why not the Americans?'

'I approached the Americans last year. I never received any response. I imagine that the crudeness of my approach convinced them that it must have been some sort of trap. So I decided I would have to go through someone who knew me.'

'You will understand, I am sure, that we will assume the same as the Americans.'

'I am quite content to be considered more cunning than I actually am.'

'We will, you realise, become very much more specific later on. For the time being I see no reason why we cannot treat this as a conversation between colleagues.'

'As you wish. I have many stories. Which do you want?'

'The truth.'

'They are all true.'

'Then tell us them all.'

'Very well. The first is that my career has stalled. So I am defecting out of bitterness and angst. I should have been promoted many times over, to a much higher level than colonel, but have been bested at office politics by people less able than I am. I will, at the appropriate moment, give you the names of those I know in the GRU hierarchy, what they do and how they do it, in order to have my revenge.'

'That is a good reason.'

'No. It is not,' Volkov said. 'Many people are in that position, no? I imagine even MI6 has office politics, with winners and losers. Do you worry every time someone is promoted that the losers will run off to the Soviet Union? Of course not. That is no reason. Anyone who came to you with such a story would either be a fool or a liar.'

'Give us another one.'

'Love. In the 1930s I fell in love with a beautiful woman, funny, intelligent, delightful. She was everything to me. We were to be married. Except that one day she said the wrong thing to the wrong person. She disappeared. I had to pretend not to know her. I married someone else, but I have never forgiven them.'

'I see.'

'No you don't. That happened nearly twenty years ago. Who would wait such a long time? A third reason, then. I have lost faith. I do not believe in the onward inevitability of history. I do not believe that the proletariat will triumph. To put it another way, if the Soviet Union is the ultimate expression of mankind's future, then I want no part of it.'

He smiled faintly. 'A good reason, no? One which appeals to you, as patriotic Englishmen? You may take that one, then. It is true, after all. So is this: I am getting old, I wish to do something worthwhile, so the world, if it remembers me, will think favourably of me. I have no God and no beliefs. I can only serve the future. I wish to give a gift to the future. You are the only people who can make use of it.'

He leaned forward. 'There is danger coming. I know. Time is short.'

'Go on. Astonish us.'

Volkov pointed at Angela. 'Not with her in the room. You I trust, Henry, and you, Wind, I must trust. But not this woman. I do not know her.'

'Angela?' Wind asked. 'Would you mind stepping out? If you could stay in the house, though, in case we get ourselves into a tangle?'

'Certainly,' she replied, and stood up. 'Mr Volkov. Such a pleasure. Delighted to meet you. I do hope you settle down nicely here.' She turned to the two Englishmen. 'I'll be in the kitchen making sandwiches if you need me. And,' she said cocking her head as the doorbell rang, 'answering the door for you. What a busy life you lead, Henry.'

*

When she had left the room, Volkov smiled and tapped the side of his head with an exaggerated gesture. 'In here, my friends. In here, I have such secrets.'

'Feel free to share some,' Wind said.

They kept talking for an hour in a mixture of poor German and halting English, then took a break. Wind and Lytten left Volkov and retreated into Lytten's dingy hallway.

'Well?' Lytten said, after Wind had gone quickly into the kitchen to see if he could get Angela to make him some tea. 'What do you think?'

'If what he says is true, then we have a major coup and everyone else has a major crisis. True or false, the best thing would be to pass this on to the Americans and let them get on with it. They're in charge, after all,' he said gloomily.

For an hour Wind had lounged on the armchair, looking

382

slightly bored, occasionally interrupting with a vague or sarcastic question. For the most part, though, he had left the questioning to Lytten. But the moment the door of the sitting room had closed, the air of studied disinterest vanished, to be replaced by a thoughtful, alert look.

Calmly, giving details and dates, names and places, Volkov had blown the West's strategic thinking out of the water. Everything, he said, was wrong. The Soviet Union was not far behind in the development of ballistic missiles, as was thought. The Soviet high command did not assume the West intended no hostile move. They were frightened and had decided to hit out first. All that was needed was to complete their preparations – complete, Volkov said; he was very insistent on this point. A few weeks, he said. In a few weeks' time they would be ready.

'Could the Americans have got it all so wrong?' Lytten asked.

'It wouldn't be the first time,' Wind said. 'It can be checked, easily enough. It's the rest which bothered me.'

Lytten could see his point. Once Angela had left the room, Volkov had leaned forward in his chair. 'There is a traitor among you,' he said with a sly smile. 'Do you want to know who it is? I can tell you.'

Then he had refused to say any more. Knowledge has its price, he had said. How much did they want to know? Make an offer, and then he would tell them all they needed. All in good time.

'Do you think he's a fake?'

'Of course he's a fake,' Wind replied, although Lytten could hear the doubt in his voice. 'Trying to get a nice pension off us. Trying to make us look ridiculous to the Americans.

Or he's a plant, a walking piece of disinformation.'

Wind looked suddenly haggard. 'I'd better have him anyway. Cart him off and give him a good going over, and perhaps suggest to the Americans that we may have a problem of one sort or another. Either what Volkov says is true, which is catastrophic, or the Russians are playing a game which is so clever I can't even understand the rules.' He sighed. 'Who was at the door?'

'No idea.'

'I'll get my people ready to take Volkov away. I'll call the van. I'll tell Angela we won't be wanting the tea after all.'

35

There are many ceremonies at Ossenfud, and Jay had taken part in a good proportion of them. For the dead time, the start of the year, the start and end of study each day, the arrival of food. Ceremonies for each season, and for the harvest. Each college had its own rituals and the town had still more.

But he had never witnessed anything quite as strange as the one he observed that day in Willdon. Shortly before noon Jay was summoned by a messenger and instructed to present himself at the entrance to the great courtyard. He took up his position just in time to see the huge doors leading into the grand chamber being thrown open. Henary was there already. A procession, gaudy and ostentatious, slowly emerged, consisting of all the people who lived and worked in the house, some of them carrying Lady Catherine on an elaborate gilt chair. Trumpets sounded, the watchers stamped their feet. It was, for Jay, a fascinating display of power and wealth, not least because Lady Catherine herself was dressed with all the magnificence of her position, covered in jewels from head to foot, wearing the richest garments imaginable and her finest wig.

They proceeded to the edge of the gardens, with Jay, Henary and many others following. Waiting for them was a small party, roughly dressed and looking decidedly uncomfortable and nervous. The jumpiest was a man carrying a large axe, who was dressed in brown working clothes, with heavy leather boots.

'Who are you?' he called out in a loud voice, once he had been elbowed in the ribs by a companion as a prompt.

The procession stopped and the golden chair was laid on the ground. Lady Catherine stood up and walked a few steps forward as her entourage fell back to make way for her.

'I am Lady Catherine, Lord and Lady of the domain of Willdon by right, and I command your obedience.' She spoke imperiously, disdainfully.

'That is the wrong answer.'

Two of the other men with him stepped forward and began taking off the jewellery, starting with the huge tiara she wore on her head, then her necklaces, the encrusted belts, the rings on fingers and toes, until she wore no decoration at all. She stood there passively and allowed all this to happen. Each article was handed carefully to an attendant, who placed them carefully in a large wooden box.

'Who are you?' The question came again.

'I am Lady Catherine of Willdon, and I demand your obedience.'

'That is the wrong answer.'

Again the three men stepped forward, and this time started taking off the wig, the multi-coloured velvets and cloths which adorned her body, until she was standing in a simple dress.

'Who are you?' came the question for the third time.

'I am Lady Catherine of Willdon.'

'That is the wrong answer.'

For a third time the men stepped forward. They removed her dress, so that she was wearing only the least of undergarments. Then they pushed her down so she was kneeling on the bare ground, her head bowed.

'No man or woman is above any man or woman. Three times you have denied this.'

The man with the axe, now trembling, stepped forward, carrying a length of leather. He walked up to her and, biting his lip, swung the strap down onto her back, so that the impact could be heard all over the glade. He did not do it so very hard, however. Jay noticed that he attempted to make the lash as light as possible. Still, he repeated the operation twice, and there were three distinct red lines across her back when he had finished. Lady Catherine did not flinch.

'Who are you?'

'I am Kate.'

'That is the right answer. What do you have?'

'Nothing.'

'What do you want?'

'I want to live.'

'What will you give in return?'

'What I am asked.'

'Then you will be the least of people, until you have earned the right to be more. Do you accept this?'

'I do.'

'Then stand up, Kate, and follow me.'

She stood and dusted herself down, and Jay could see the broad man whispering anxiously into her ear. He didn't hear it, but he thought he was asking – was that all right? She nodded briefly, and a second man came forward and dressed her in the rough clothes of a labourer, and gave her a pair of hard shoes with wooden soles.

'Anyone who wishes to see that I obey the laws and customs of Willdon should step forward now,' the man said.

There was a silence, apart from a rustling of clothes as the assembled multitude looked around expectantly. Then Jay realised Lady Catherine was looking at him. He stepped forward.

'I wish to see,' he said.

'Then you will be my guest and companion.'

At which point the ceremony was at an end. Those who were gathered around burst into enthusiastic applause, and Jay could feel the tension seep away. Then the procession re-formed, the empty chair was lifted high and the members of the household withdrew.

The large man, Jay and Lady Catherine were now alone. 'So, for the next two days I am your servant Kate. This is Jay, presently at Ossenfud, who has generously offered to see everything is done properly. That is to say, you will show me no favour or special treatment, nor will you be cruel or harsh undeservedly. Have you done anything like this before?'

'No. I have not.'

'Well, I have, but you will get no advice from me. What's your name, by the way?'

'I am called Callan, my La—'

'What do you have planned?'

'Wood cutting and collecting. It'll be hard work, and tiring. We will go into the forest and chop logs. Or at least, I will. Your job will be to collect and stack them. If we have time, I want to make a fire for charcoal. You will cook and clean the pots, make my bed and sleep on the leaves.'

'What am I meant to do?' Jay asked.

'Nothing. You just watch.'

'Oh, must I?' Jay said. 'I used to burn charcoal with my uncle when I was little. I loved it. Do let me do something useful.'

Callan looked at his earnest young face and laughed. 'A lady and a scholar,' he said. 'What more could any forester need? Lord, but this is going to be hard work!'

*

Callan followed the rules very carefully, showing neither of them any favour. He marched off and took them deep into the forest, walking for nearly three hours without stopping for food or rest, keeping up a swift pace. Even Jay, who got a great deal of exercise in the college's fields around Ossenfud, was tired, and he was concerned that Lady Catherine – Kate, he reminded himself – was quite unused to such exertion. Already her bare legs were scratched from the brambles, her short hair was tangled, her hands were dirty. She didn't seem to mind, and bore it all with good heart.

'You thought I had forgotten you, didn't you, Callan Perelson?' Jay said after a while.

Callan smiled. 'I did.'

'I remember you very well. You were kind to me.'

'No more than a frightened little boy deserved.'

'I thought you were a soldier.'

'Me? No. I was just doing my service. Three years I spent marching around, standing guard, doing nothing of importance. That was enough. I missed my forest. Being in towns made me ill. All those people . . .'

'So now you're happy again?'

'Not today I'm not.' He jerked his head in the direction of Kate, who was walking dutifully behind them. 'I could do without this.'

'So why are you doing it?'

'Chosen by lot. It's not as if anyone in their right mind would volunteer.'

'What are the rules?'

'She does as I say. She works. If she refuses, she gets beaten.'

'You are going to beat the Lady of Willdon?'

'I hope not. If I do, then no one will ever know. She cannot say what happens to her. Nor can I, and you can only speak if one or other of us breaks the rules. You know that, don't you?'

Jay shook his head. 'No. I don't know anything.'

'You've not changed, then.'

They walked on some more, then Callan dropped his backpack on the ground. 'Time for a rest,' he said, 'and some food. Kate! In the bag you'll find some bread and cheese. Set it out for us.'

Kate came, and bowed, and set to work.

*

Jay had forgotten how hard it was to lift and carry logs, stacking them in a neat pile for collection. They didn't even begin until their long march through the forest had come to its end. By then they must have been twelve miles away from Willdon, and had been passing through never-ending trees, crossing brooks and rivers and occasionally little meadows cleared for sheep and goats. Once they spent a few minutes up a broad oak tree; Callan thought he had heard a wild boar. He stood guard at the bottom while Jay and Kate – neither much good in a fight, he reckoned – scuttled up the tree and hung on to the branches.

'Think ahead,' Jay whispered to Kate. 'The boar comes, kills Callan and eats him. It then settles down for a sleep. Its family comes and joins in. We're stuck up here. What do we do then?'

'Are you always so cheerful?'

No such disaster occurred. Jay reckoned this was down to him, on the grounds that a disaster anticipated never happens. It is only the things you don't think of which come to pass. Kate declined to give him much credit, but was at least grateful for the ten minutes' rest they had lying on the branches before Callan told them they could come down.

'Wouldn't have minded some meat for dinner,' he said. 'Next time, Jay, you go ahead and make a noise to attract it.'

'As long as you tell Henary how his student died.'

'I could do that,' Kate said. 'He would understand and bear his loss. Henary is not a man to do without food.'

It was a good-natured march. Callan treated Kate rather as a kind master treats a servant and she, in turn, played her part well. Jay, whose respect had previously clouded his vision, found himself considering things he would never have dared allow himself to think about the Lady of Willdon. Stripped of authority and of finery, she remained a lovely woman, much younger-looking now that her body was not bound and cosseted. Her face, perhaps, showed a few lines around the eyes, but her skin was clear and fresh, her eyes bright. Nor did her luxurious life mean she was unfit; she walked strongly and, when it came to work, lifted and stacked logs with steady effort.

It was dark by the time Callan called a halt for the day. He and Jay settled down on a blanket while Kate built a fire, which Callan, as master, lit. Then she began to prepare their food.

'Forgive me for asking, but can you cook?' Jay enquired.

'Of course I can cook,' she said crossly. 'I used to enjoy it. I can do fresh perch in a cream and sorrel sauce. Calf's head in honey and vinegar. Jams and preserves of all sorts. What do we have?'

'Bread, cheese, beer, some pickled meats as a treat and porridge for breakfast,' Callan said with an amused snort.

'What about tomorrow?'

'Bread, cheese, beer, some pickled meats as a treat and porridge for breakfast,' Callan said again.

'That's easy enough, then.'

She could drink as well, and felt she deserved to, as she had been the one who had carried the two heavy jars of strong beer. Once the food was ready, Callan made the blessing over it and poured the beer into three earthenware pots. 'It may be against the rules,' he said, 'but in my village, servants eat with the family. So sit you down, servant Kate, and join our meal.'

He raised his glass when they were all around the fire. 'To the health and lasting life of two of the worst woodsmen I have ever encountered.'

They cheered this and drank; Jay watched as the beer spilled down Kate's chin, her neck and her body. He forced himself to think of other things.

'Your turn, Master Scholar!' Callan said when they had eaten part of their meal.

'I would like a toast to the weather,' Jay said. 'Neither too hot, which would be bad for working, nor cold and wet, which would be miserable. May it be as generous tomorrow and ever after.'

Another cheer, and another drink.

'Now you, servant Kate. You are one of us this evening, and you must make a toast as well,' Callan said.

Kate, who was lying propped up on one arm, chewing an apple, straightened herself and picked up her mug. She peered into it with one eye closed to make sure there was still some beer in it.

'I,' she began, then stopped, and thought. 'I,' she resumed after a while, 'would like to toast those who take the good in the Story and shun the bad. Who stray never from kindness, and who know where lies true contentment. I would like to toast kind masters and good friends.' She saluted the other two and drank deeply. They followed her lead, then clapped enthusiastically.

'Bravo, servant!' said Callan. 'As a reward you may clear the plates and prepare the beds. After you are done, it seems a pity to waste the opportunity of having a Storyteller with us.'

'But I am not a Storyteller,' Jay said. 'I've never told one in public.'

'Nonsense,' Kate said, momentarily reverting to her true self before remembering. 'Sorry. Slipped.'

'She is right,' Callan added. 'You may not have told a story, but what better start could there be, under the warm

393

night sky, with an appreciative and' – here he glanced at Kate – 'slightly drunk audience? What better place and time could you have? Besides, no word of this interlude must ever be spoken, so if you make an idiot of yourself then no one will ever know.'

'Except us,' Kate pointed out happily.

'Come along, Jay,' Callan said. 'Please do. Remember, you owe me a kindness. While you prepare, this excellent servant will clean up, and I will stack some more logs on the fire, and when you are done, we will sleep.'

While they worked, Jay calmed himself down with the breathing exercises he had been taught, sitting still and loosening his muscles, gaining control of his diaphragm, then putting his hands together and bowing his head to empty it of extraneous thought.

When he was as prepared as he could be, he began.

*

There was once a Storyteller who was known as the wisest man of his generation. He was kind to his students, careful in his judgements. His reasoning was so powerful, his use of argument so great that all naturally accepted his word. For twenty years he had gone on the regular circle of visits, listening, considering and deciding. In that time there was not one appeal against his verdicts, and his relations with those who went with him were perfect.

Often, when travelling through the countryside, he would stop on a hilltop at evening and stare at the beauty of the valley below. Or he would pause as he passed a ruin of great antiquity and wonder aloud what its history was.

Later, one remembered him in a library, running his fingers over the leather of an old manuscript, looking at it in a way that was not easy to interpret.

One day he went to a town where there was a difficult dispute to resolve. The mayor had married his daughter to a lord ten miles away. The marriage had been settled, the dowry agreement signed, but then an argument had erupted. The lord said the girl was bad-tempered, lazy and offensive. He would not repudiate her, but demanded more money to keep her. The mayor refused, saying the agreement had been freely made. So the lord sent her back, but kept the dowry, as she was still his wife.

The dispute caused ill-feeling between the town, which was angry at the insult, and the lands around. Blows were exchanged, local farmers assaulted as they came into market. So it was the scholar's first duty to resolve the matter when he arrived. He listened (as was his habit) to those involved, and many who were not. He asked penetrating questions and decided that all were equally at fault. Such was his reputation and his secret pride that he did not listen to his fellow who was with him, but reached his decisions alone.

Here was the judgement: the girl was indeed rude and offensive to her husband, but this was because he was a dolt, well-meaning but stupid. The girl's father had filled her with vanity at her beauty and importance, so had made her unwilling to see the good in others. And the lord was incapable of seeing what a lovely creature he had, although unworthily, been allotted as his wife.

All should apologise. The father should pay the extra dowry, but give it to the poor of the lands around, and the husband should give an equal amount.

The mayor of the town was a cunning fellow. He pretended to accept the judgement, with fine words of praise for the scholar's wisdom, but secretly he was furious. He invited the scholar to his house and gave him food and wine. Then he brought out a great treasure, a small picture of ageless antiquity. It was his, and had been in his family for longer than anyone could remember, he said.

The scholar wondered at the object, which was more beautiful than anything made by the hand of man that he had ever seen, and the mayor knew that the scholar coveted the beautiful thing for himself.

'It is yours, as thanks for your wisdom,' said the mayor. 'Or rather, it would have been. For now I have to pay the extra dowry for my daughter I will be a poor man, and will have to sell it to the highest bidder for whatever I can get for it.'

The next day the scholar gave his judgement. He found in favour of the mayor and condemned the lord for his actions. He took the little picture, wrapped it in his baggage and left the town.

But it was not the mayor's to give. It was the most precious possession of the town, and as soon as its loss was discovered there was much unhappiness. The townspeople searched the baggage of the scholar's clerk, found the picture and arrested him.

The scholar immediately returned and confessed what had happened. He said his clerk had been innocent, and that he had taken the picture as a gift.

Then he left the town and went wandering, no longer a scholar, but a beggar until his dying day.

Jay had chosen well; at the end, it took some time before his audience – small but appreciative – came out of the reverie the words had induced in them. Rather than showing off, he had taken a simple tale, one which had been translated into the spoken language so that Callan could understand it. This was not the place for a virtuoso display. It was not a first-level telling, nor a second, nor even a third; indeed, it fitted no proper category that he knew of.

It was not as he had imagined his first telling. He had thought it would be in a formal setting, after weeks of preparation and coaching and rehearsal, to make sure every vowel, every weighting, every intonation was correct, that the movements of his hands and body fitted the words he spoke, emphasising but not distracting. It was to have been in a grand hall, advertised in advance, witnessed by his friends, his teachers – and those who were there to sit in judgement. On it his future reputation would have depended. Many failed through nerves, many more were sick beforehand and collapsed afterwards. It was said to be the single most terrifying event any man could endure.

It could not have been more different. He sat, rather than stood; his audience was two people, rather than two hundred. They wanted to hear the story, not to spot his mistakes. At the end, they didn't even need to applaud. He loved it, once the nervousness passed. He adopted a tone that was conversational rather than declamatory, only rarely raising his voice, sometimes almost whispering the words. Occasionally he did drop in a few sentences of the old language, for emphasis, but only when the meaning was obvious. They loved the words, loved the story, loved him. For the first time in his life, Jay felt what it was to be respected, to use his skill to obliterate the loneliness of life. He became the story, and through it he merged with his audience, by instinctively responding to them.

Neither spoke for a long time after he finished, but just stared dreamily at the fire, smiling occasionally as they recalled passages. Then, roughly, Callan pulled himself together.

'Sleep, my friends,' he said. 'We have a hard day's work tomorrow, and I intend to make you remember just what hard work is.'

'I will sit awhile, if you don't mind,' Jay said. 'I will sleep soon enough.'

Kate had pitched Callan's little tent some way off; he didn't like sleeping by fires, he had said, and never felt the cold. He went, leaving the warmth to the soft house dwellers. Jay scarcely noticed him going. Nor did he pay much attention when he felt her settle down beside him and gently knead his shoulders. She said nothing, but laid her head on his shoulder so he could feel her hair against his neck.

'Now I understand what Henary sees in you.'

'What do you mean?'

'It doesn't matter tonight. Now you must rest. We are all transformed by the forest, no? I the servant, you the Storyteller, Callan the master. Soon enough I will again be the great lady, and you will be a simple student, and he will be but a forester once more. The magic will fade. Then we must talk. But not now. Now your servant Kate will soothe you to sleep. So lie down, my master Jay, and rest.'

He lay down, and Kate folded him in her arms and held him close, stroking his hair and kissing his forehead until the oblivion of sleep took him over.

36

The three people standing in Lytten's porch were a mismatched bunch, and none of them looked particularly comfortable, despite the effusive welcome they received.

'Do come in! So lovely to see you!'

'Are you the lady I talked to on the phone?'

'I am indeed. You must be Sergeant Maltby?'

'Yes, ma'am. This is the man here.'

'You don't mind waiting while we have a chat with him?'

'Ah, no. Glad to help.'

She nodded at her new visitor, who was staring at her in a way which many would have considered rude. She led him to the kitchen at the back of the house, shut the door, gestured for him to sit down and then sat herself on the other side of the table, cupped her face in her hands and studied him calmly.

'Well, well, well,' she said. 'Alexander Chang. What a surprise! After such a long time, too. What brings you here?'

She could see that he was still in a state of shock. He recognised her, but she was so much older; he hadn't taken that into account.

'To find you, of course, Dr Meerson,' he said.

'Call me Angela. No point standing on ceremony here, eh?'

'Do you have any idea the trouble you're in?'

'Nothing like the trouble you're in.'

'What do you mean?'

'You have been arrested as a suspected Soviet spy,' she said, shaking her head in barely suppressed delight. 'When did you get here?'

'About a week ago.'

'What have you been doing since?'

'Getting my mind back. I didn't realise . . .'

'Yes, nasty, isn't it? I was off my head for the better part of a year. It's the implants. Without them, you'd be fine. So why now? I got fed up waiting years ago.'

'Why would anyone think I'm a Soviet spy?'

'You've just been exceptionally unlucky. No point explaining it; you wouldn't understand the complications. At the moment they are wondering whether to lock you up, accidentally push you under a train, or send you back to the Soviet Union. This would, no doubt, be a great surprise to the Russians, who might just shoot you themselves to be on the safe side. Answer my question. Why now?'

'It was the only link we could find. The reference in that article.'

'What article?'

'The one Lytten wrote on Shakespeare.'

'I didn't know anything about that,' Angela said.

'I was sent to check. It has implications for how they use your machine.'

'Use my machine?' she said. 'They can't use it.'

'They can if they figure out where you hid the data.'

Angela thought for a long time. 'I think we need to have a little understanding here.'

'What?'

'A little help for you, a little help for me.'

401

'You scratch my backside, I'll scratch yours,' he said proudly.

'Not quite,' she said.

*

The door opened and Lytten came in. He glanced at the new arrival, then grunted and ignored him. 'Half an hour,' he said to her. 'Then they'll be coming to take him away. So we won't need tea.'

Chang looked worried as Lytten disappeared once more.

'Interrogation.' Angela smiled, and shook her head sympathetically.

'That sounds bad.'

'Torture, beatings. Possibly a painful execution. Have you ever been in unbearable agony for days on end?'

'No.'

'The dark side of the age,' she explained. 'They can't just fiddle with people's brains, so they have to be more crude. Electrodes on sensitive bits of the body, that sort of thing. Pliers. We don't have much time, so we need to get going. Use my machine, you say. They can't. I wiped everything.'

'You blacked out most of Europe and killed nearly ten thousand people.'

'Did I? I didn't mean to. I was in a hurry.'

'You don't sound very upset.'

'What can I do? I will fix it in due course.'

'Can you?'

'I think so. Not that it matters at the moment. They can't use the machine. As I said, I erased the data.'

'No.'

'Yes.'

'No. I found two pages of your work in the Tsou script. A security man has been sent off to try and recover the rest of it.'

'That's simply not possible.'

Chang smiled. 'Got you worried, eh? It's true. It was buried in an article by this man Lytten, published last year. That and the reference to you in the article I found . . .'

'That's absurd.'

'Here I am. And you, too.'

'You say it may still exist?'

'Yes. Hanslip assumed it was some devious fraud on your part. He still thinks that you are hiding with renegades and have concealed the data somewhere. I've been sent here just to make sure, and a security man called Jack More has been sent after the data.'

'More? I remember him. Tall, strong, out of place. All dark and dangerous. I'm not convinced, though.'

'The article says that the document was known as the Devil's Handwriting and dates from the eighteenth century. There is a possibility that it is in Lytten's papers, which went to some library on his death.'

'When does he die?'

'1979.'

'Oh, poor Henry! At least he will miss Mrs Thatcher. He'd hate her.' She thought for a moment about what she had heard so far. 'Have they used the machine? Apart from sending you.'

'I don't think so. I don't think they can. Someone said they'd have to recalibrate it after sending me, and couldn't without the data.'

'I wonder,' she said after a moment, 'if that is connected to the difficulties I am having with the universe in the cellar.'

'The what?'

'I've made a universe in the cellar,' she said with a modest blush. 'A prototype, little more than an outline, really, but a jolly good one. Except that I can't shut it down. I was assuming it was a glitch, but maybe not.'

She now looked pointedly at her watch. 'Oh, dear, time's nearly up. They start with fingernails, you see,' she explained kindly. 'That's what the pliers are for. It's not very nice, but much better than what follows.'

'Dr Meerson . . .'

'Angela,' she reminded him. 'Or you can hide in Anterwold.'

'What's that?'

'My universe. I really need someone to find out what it is. Perhaps to get a girl back as well. You could keep out of the way for a bit; until the coast is clear, as they say here.'

Chang's mouth sagged. 'I can't go through that again,' he said. 'Not so soon. I just can't. Don't even suggest it.'

'Rusty,' Angela said. 'The pliers they use, I mean. It will only be for a few hours. By the time here, I mean. You'll be a bit longer there. Besides, remember: you work for me.'

'What exactly do you want?'

'I need to know the connection between Anterwold and here. What lies between them, historically speaking. What it is.' She glanced at the clock again in a meaningful fashion.

'Then what?'

'I also need to know if the defences are holding. I built it to be static. Nothing should happen, because any event has a cause and a consequence. So I placed limits on them.

404

I need to know if these still work, or whether the girl has broken them.'

'What girl? What are you talking about?'

'Rosie. A friend of Henry's. She accidentally went into it and is still there. Sort of. It's terribly interesting. She's why I know you'll be perfectly safe.'

'You want me to get her back?'

'I doubt you'll have the chance. The machine's set for a few years earlier at the moment, and I don't have time to change it. You don't want to stay for long, I imagine?'

'Certainly not.'

'So go, examine, come back. I can't shut it down until we get Rosie out, but we can deal with her later. You can still work for me, if you like. I'll need help. You can't imagine how much fun it can be here, once you get the hang of the place. What on earth is the matter with you?'

Chang suddenly looked as though he was about to be sick. His face turned white, then red and blotchy, and he was breathing hard.

'I . . .' he began in a strange voice, rather like someone who had swallowed something too big for him. Then his voice changed completely. 'Angela,' he said. 'Robert Hanslip here. You really must come back. I fear Oldmanter will make Emily pay a heavy price if you refuse. I'm sure you know what that means.'

Then he stopped and his face recovered its colour. 'I'm sorry. My mind was wandering.'

'What did you just say?'

'I said I didn't want to stay long.'

Angela sat very still for a few moments. 'You just spoke like Hanslip,' she said.

405

Chang wrinkled his nose in slight distaste. 'Did I? He said he was sending a message to you. It was meant to appear if I found you. Maybe that was it. Was it useful?'

'No.'

There was a short silence as Angela – for once seeming quite unsettled – disappeared into herself.

'Well, it doesn't change anything,' she said eventually. 'I still have to find out what it is, and you still need somewhere to hide. It's very simple, not like the other machine. Say you need the toilet, go downstairs. You'll see an iron pergola against the far wall. Just walk through. I'll reopen it in the same place in six days' time. Your time, not the time here. Be back where you arrived without fail. If something goes wrong . . .'

'Such as?'

'I don't know. I'm just being careful. I don't want to lose another person in there. If you do miss it, go to the Circle of Esilio at Willdon. That gives me a place. Timing is more difficult. Aim for the evening of the fifth day of the fifth-year festival at Willdon. I've already done the calculations for that.'

'I don't know what that means.'

'There are festivals to mark the accession of the rulers there. There's no better way of calculating dates that I know of. They don't have any rational or fixed system for counting time. Henry never devised one and I used the absence to keep it secure. Their attitude to time is one thing I need you to check.'

Chang opened his mouth to ask more questions, but she was spared the difficulty of answering by the door opening once more.

Wind peered round at the two people. 'Who are you?' he said to the unknown man. 'Oh, it doesn't matter. I just thought I'd tell you that the van will be here any moment now. I'll be off as well.'

He glanced briefly at the other person in the room, who had raised a hand like a naughty schoolboy.

'I need to, ah . . .'

'Ah what?'

'To go to the toilet.'

Wind grunted. 'Good for you,' he said. 'I believe it's on the half landing, if that's what you want to know.'

'Shouldn't you go with him?' Angela asked loudly.

'Why on earth would I want to do that?'

'I just thought . . . oh, no reason,' she said. 'Up to you, of course. I'm sorry.'

Wind stared at her. Odd woman, he thought to himself as he heard the sound of footsteps going towards Lytten's cellar.

37

By late morning the next day, a passing fox might have paused, sniffed the air cautiously, then quietly changed its course to avoid a small copse of trees deep in the forest of Willdon. It would have known by the faintest of smells that something unusual lurked there. An inquisitive beast would have found, curled up in the perfect blanket of dry leaves left over from the previous autumn, two recumbent forms, lying in each other's arms in a pose of complete friendship. One, the shorter, snored gently. The other, the taller, grunted in her sleep as she relived in her dreams the remarkable events of the previous twenty-four hours.

As the sun rose in the sky, a large fly settled on the nose of the taller figure, and slowly, after a moment's careful thought, decided to investigate the possibilities of food up the left nostril. The intrusion provoked a response. The girl sat up and slapped her own nose with her hand, causing her to cry out in pain and surprise. The sound made her companion roll over and groan, then open an eye.

'I'm sleeping,' she said.

Rosalind did not answer; instead she was too occupied trying to make sure that whatever it was that had crawled up her nose was gone. By the time she was satisfied, she was fully awake and standing up. Only then did she realise that, if she had been dreaming, then the dream, quite against all custom, was continuing to run its course. She was, indeed, dressed as a man, having evidently spent the night sleeping in a wood with a singer she had met, in some entirely unlikely land which was as real as the fly up her nose. The shock was so great that the alternative – that she should be in double French – never even crossed her mind. Instead, she sat down heavily and burst into tears.

Her companion was more perplexed than sympathetic, although she too was beginning to realise the enormous consequences of her presence there. She had fled from her master after trying to murder him. Fights and physical violence were one thing; laying him out cold was quite another. This time she had gone too far. Curiously, though, she did not regret it in the slightest. What possibly could happen to someone as beautiful and as gifted as she was? She had lost her master. She would find another. She would never starve and now she could sing as she wanted, not as Rambert said she must. She was free.

She was also hungry. As, indeed, was Rosalind when, after five minutes of constant crying, her companion had done nothing whatsoever to comfort her.

'Are you finished?' Aliena asked when the sobbing finally came to an end.

She nodded.

'Good. Horrible noise.'

'I'm upset. Don't you see?'

'Of course I see. But what do you want me to do about it?'

'You're meant to cheer me up.'

'Very well. Cheer up.'

Aliena brushed the leaves off her clothing and stood up, then stretched herself.

'I want my breakfast.'

'So do I.'

It was at this precise point that the shepherd – looking for a stray ewe and curious about the sounds of life coming from the little copse – discovered them.

He was a good-looking man in his way, with an open face hard and tanned from life in the fresh air, gnarled hands and strong chest and arms. He approached, saw the pair sitting on the ground and, after a few moments' contemplation of the scene, smiled broadly.

'Ah, young lovers! Good morning to you both, good sir and young lady. It is a fine day to awake so.'

'What?' Rosalind said in utter astonishment, not least because for the first time she found she could understand much of what he said.

The shepherd winked. 'You'll have been at the Lady's Festivity, I'll be bound,' he said, '"where love blossoms and fair affections thrive," as they say.'

Rosalind stared open-mouthed. She understood that wink. It was left to Aliena to reply.

'Indeed, but as it is said also, "love does not always welcome the light, nor the eyes of strangers."'

'That is certainly true, young lady. But what is hidden is often the most valuable.'

Aliena nodded appreciatively. 'You are a very learned shepherd.'

'And you are a lady of refinement, but what of your silent companion here? Is he so exhausted from his night's labours he cannot even talk?' He winked again, which Rosalind found offensive. Aliena, however, seemed to be enjoying herself.

'Ah, good shepherd, "his virtues do not lie in his words,"' she said, at which the man laughed heartily.

'"He who labours, hungers after,"' he responded. 'In that case, you must allow me to offer you the sustenance you require, you and your young man. I have a poor abode, small and rough, but it is comfortable and welcoming to those of good heart. In it there is porridge and milk fresh from the ewe; bread and butter, honey from the hive. All that man or woman could desire. Or almost all,' he added with another wink.

'Lead on, then, good man,' Aliena said with a curtsy, 'and let us be honoured by your hospitality.'

'As my house will be honoured by your presence,' came the reply.

He whistled to his dog, which bounded up and sniffed around the newcomers, then walked off. Aliena dug Rosalind in the ribs. 'Wasn't that lucky?'

Rosalind, however, was still in a state of indignation. 'But he thought . . . he thought . . . He winked at me.'

'You are dressed as a man, you know. Your hair is short, and those clothes cover up your shape very effectively. So of course he winked. Don't you find it funny?'

'No.'

'Oh, dearest Rosalind, don't be cross! It is a beautiful morning, we are in the forest, we are going to eat. What more could woman (or man, in your case) want?'

'You have no idea,' Rosalind said.

'We can talk about that later. In the meantime, we must eat, and pay for our food.'

'How are we going to do that? I have no money.'

'Nor I. We must pay in entertainment. We must give

you a new name, to go with your manhood.'

'Why?'

'How are we going to cross his threshold if we are not presented to the house spirits?'

'Oh. Silly me,' Rosalind said.

*

She found the meal in the forest cottage even more enchanting than the world of the grand house. Unlike the squalid abode of Aliena's teacher, it was fresh and clean and airy, more a shelter than a house, open to the elements, with a table outside under a little awning of creeper from which hung delicate purple flowers that gave off a faint but agreeable scent. They were presented to the house as Mistress Aliena and Master Ganimed – this a name that Aliena came up with on the spur of the moment – and breakfast was served, although this was marred a little for Rosalind by the frequent toasts from the shepherd that the fruit of her loins be sturdy. But the food was all simple and delicious.

'How do you do all this?' she asked when they had finished eating. 'All this food? Where does it come from?'

'Why, my friends give it, in exchange for looking after their flocks, of course. I have a deep cool hole to keep it fresh; the milk I get myself, the fruit I pick myself. The water comes cold from the stream. What more could I desire, which nature does not provide?'

For a moment she agreed, and then Rosalind thought of her mother's new washing machine, the comfy new sofa, the iron, the radio . . . there was no point even mentioning such things, though. She would have to explain how they worked, for a start.

'Isn't it cold in winter?'

'Oh, I don't stay here in winter, young sir. I take my flocks back to their owners and rest myself with them, one after the other, until spring comes again. It is only in the snow months that it is truly difficult to be in the open.'

'What if you get ill, or something like that?'

'Then I get better again. If I do not, then I die,' he said simply. 'How else could it be?'

Rosalind had no answer to that one, although she felt instinctively that there should be more to say on the topic, so she lapsed into silence while Aliena carried on the conversation. She was beginning to get the hang of how the ordinary people spoke, but it was still an effort to understand, and an even greater one to say anything. She let her mind drift and watched the shadows dance on the ground, feeling the warmth of the air. It was going to be hot today. She should be tired, but her senses were so alive she felt no fatigue, just a sort of dreamy state where she was aware of everything, but only as a bystander. She even stopped wondering where on earth she was. If, indeed, she was on earth.

She came to as she heard Aliena saying that it was time to move on, that they had trespassed on his hospitality for long enough. The shepherd was in no rush, though; Rosalind got the feeling that he didn't have much company, alone in the woods, and was grateful for the diversion.

'Where are you going?'

'We don't really know,' Aliena said. 'Into the forest. We need . . . time. And privacy.' Here she glanced archly at him.

He nodded knowingly. 'I understand. I was young

myself once. It is natural that you wish to know each other first. But you cannot go into the forest. It is dangerous if you do not know it. A good friend to those it accepts, but not safe for anyone else.'

'We don't have much choice.'

'Have my cottage.'

'We can't!' Rosalind said, and instantly regretted it. The man's face fell, the disappointment clearly marked.

'You must forgive him,' Aliena interrupted quickly. 'He is a stranger and does not know our ways. He thinks only of the inconvenience to you, and of our unworthiness for such kindness. Not that your cottage is unacceptable to us.' She gave Rosalind a look.

The man's face brightened. 'There is no inconvenience, as today I lead my flock up into the hills to settle them for the summer, and will not return for several weeks. As for your unworthiness, then mine is the greater.'

'We will not fight over such things,' Aliena replied. 'We both accept your kindness with the greatest of pleasure and honour. Don't we, Ganimed?'

'Oh . . . yes. Of course, honoured. Very,' Rosalind said.

*

For two days and nights, then, Rosalind and Aliena lived in perfect happiness in the cottage, cooking, sleeping and talking. Rosalind was delighted; she had never had a proper girlfriend before, someone to talk to without restraint, to gossip and speculate with. Aliena was like her in one thing: she was still at an age when all is believable, if explained by a friend.

So Rosalind told her of her home and her life. Of the pergola in Lytten's basement. Of her bemusement and slightly giddy feeling about being in a world which Aliena took for granted.

'The thing is,' she said, 'you call it Anterwold.'

'That's its name.'

'Yes, but it's so very like what someone told me once. In fact, all of this could almost be his story . . .'

'. . . What's a school?' Aliena interrupted. 'Do you mean a college?'

'. . . Hockey?'

'. . . A gas cooker?'

Aliena listened, questioned and doubted nothing.

'I wish I'd brought a record player,' Rosalind said wistfully. 'There's my grandmother's in the loft. It's a wind-up one, so it would have worked. We could have given a party, invited everyone.'

She started to sing 'I Could Have Danced All Night', and Aliena listened carefully, then, after a couple of verses, joined in. Together the two girls sat on the porch of the shepherd's cottage, carolling their way through the Broadway classics.

'Oh, Rambert is going to get such a surprise when he hears me again,' Aliena said happily. 'He will disown me, cast me out. He will die of a heart attack from shock and despair. Let's sing that last one again.' And they did.

'Tell me about that boy Jay. Is he married?'

'I should hope not. That would be very deceitful of him. Why?'

'Oh, just wondering.'

'Did you like him?'

415

'Of course not.'

Only very slowly did they acknowledge that this blessed interlude was just that – an interlude. They had run off into the forest without much of a thought. Now they had to decide what they were doing there. The second morning, Aliena stood up. 'We should go and get a little kindling and some fresh water. If you want to eat today, that is. So, come, my strange friend from another world, if that is what you really are, let us walk. I'll get the water, you get the sticks. Then we must talk about what to do next.'

*

A few hundred yards into the deep forest, the two girls split up, Aliena going to the right towards the stream with two large leather buckets, Rosalind to the left with a canvas bag, open at both ends so that it could store sticks of varying length. She needed dry, short branches but there weren't many to be found; forests, she was learning, did not just mean close-packed trees.

She walked on, keeping a careful watch, until she saw ahead of her a large, handsome grove, almost perfectly circular, of tall broad oak trees standing isolated amongst low-lying scrub. It seemed almost impenetrable because of the bushes growing all around it, but the next group of trees was some way away and she didn't feel like carrying heavy wood unnecessarily. So she circled it in the hope that there was some gap or hole she could squeeze through.

On the far side she found one, although it gave her pause when she came to it. It was, quite obviously, deliberately shaped. There was a distinct, clearly maintained hole in the undergrowth, and outside were two stone columns, one on either side. A pathway passed between them and on either side of the track was a large amount of mouldy food, which had been picked at and scattered by birds and wild animals. Although the columns gave it a sort of grandeur, the debris and mess cancelled that out, as it made the area around look more like a rubbish tip. Bones stuck out from rotting meat and the half-chewed carcasses of chickens and small animals. Vegetables and fruit lay in sticky piles, covered in flies and ants.

Rosalind crouched down and peered into the dark hole that led inside, but could see nothing. She was suddenly in a quandary. She wanted wood, and this was the best place to get it. She was curious about all the food scattered around, but she also had a profound sense of apprehension.

There was no sign saying Keep Out, no barrier or fence, but it didn't seem like a good idea nonetheless. On the other hand, it was just a clump of trees and it would undoubtedly provide the firewood she needed. Besides, monsters didn't exist.

Rosalind advanced, passed the two columns and listened. Nothing beyond the usual sounds of woodland. She took another few steps and paused again. No tell-tale snaps of twigs as someone followed her. No slithering of snakes. No growls of predators. She relaxed a little, then took a few more steps.

'Such a silly I am,' she said to herself. 'Why shouldn't I get wood here? There's no one around. It's entirely safe.'

She bent down and picked up her first stick, which she put in the shepherd's pannier, then saw another a few steps ahead and picked up that one as well. It would only take a few minutes and she'd have as much as she could carry. Eyes to the ground, she picked her way forward, deeper into the copse, quite forgetting her nervousness of a few moments ago.

Then she got to a dark clearing in its centre and stepped forward to pick up the last twigs, just perfect for kindling. That done, she straightened up.

And screamed. And screamed and screamed before she dropped her pannier of carefully collected wood and ran, tripping over wood and briars, until she burst sobbing into the outside world again.

38

It occurred to Jack, as he walked along the corridors accompanied by the two men, that if someone like Emily had been there, she might have given him a lengthy lecture on ceremonial through the ages. She could have described the various ways popes, emperors, kings and presidents had used ritual to inspire awe, turn equals into inferiors and the courageous into trembling supplicants. Whether it was a throne room or an oval office, a cavalcade or a motorcade, the object was to win any argument by psychological intimidation before it had even started.

The great elite of science was no different. The entire top floor of the residence had been taken over; security men were placed every few steps; Jack passed through room after room, being examined or merely ignored by ever more important-looking people. Eventually he came to the holy of holies, the inner sanctum, laid out in an old-fashioned style with comfortable chairs and settees and huge windows, the curtains drawn to keep out the light.

The door shut behind him, leaving Jack in what he at first thought was an empty room. Only as his eyes got accustomed to the dim light did he realise he was wrong. A tiny man, frail and almost elf-like, was perched on a chair. He did not move, but sat with his hands clasped on his lap, looking at him curiously, judging how he reacted to these strange circumstances.

'Please sit down. You are Dr More, I believe.' Jack started in surprise; he expected a voice to match the appearance, as thin and wispy as the man's body, but instead it was a deep baritone, clear and precise.

'Yes. Who are you?'

He looked mildly puzzled. 'Did they not say? Oh, they do like their mystery, no? Forgive me. My name is Zoffany Oldmanter. Please sit down. I do not like looking up at people.'

He should have realised. But Oldmanter was so different from anything he might have expected that he sat himself down opposite the man, so fearsome in reputation, so harmless in appearance, and studied him with renewed interest. It was no surprise that he had not recognised him; there were no photographs. Oldmanter never appeared in public; no one outside an inner circle had seen him for years, decades. He was his reputation, and his unimaginable power. He was very old. He had spent a lifetime accumulating his resources of countless companies, huge lands and hundreds of millions of people, all serving his laboratories and controlled with an iron grip. He had never taken his rightful place on any of the governing councils, preferring to get whatever he wanted by informal means – a request here, an attack there. His army was said to be the best equipped in the world, the most ruthless when let loose on anyone who opposed him.

Now he was sitting, alone and unguarded, opposite him. Jack could lean over and break his neck with one simple movement.

'But you are not going to,' Oldmanter said, almost apologetically.

'I beg your pardon?'

'Break my neck, or whatever it was passing through your head.'

'You read minds?'

'I don't need to. I suspect it would be very tedious. No; everybody thinks the same when they meet me for the first time.' He smiled wanly. 'I used to find it annoying.'

'What am I doing here?'

'You did not say how honoured you are to be in my presence,' he noted.

Jack shrugged.

'Good. I hate obsequiousness. It is perfectly simple. I want an explanation of the lamentable chaos that seems to be overwhelming Hanslip's laboratories. Let me list the things that concern me,' Oldmanter said. 'One of my advisers has gone missing. Dr Hanslip is refusing to respond to any communications. There was a catastrophic accident last week that resulted in widespread disturbance and Hanslip is ostentatiously trying to blame it all on renegades. He has also, I learn, lost his star mathematician.'

He paused. 'I do not care too much about any of that, but I am very concerned about the state of Dr Hanslip's project.'

'I'm sure that I don't know . . .'

'I am sure that you do.'

'I am bound by my oath of confidentiality.'

'I am well aware of where your loyalties lie, and I honour you for that. Nonetheless, circumstances have changed. Hanslip's operation will soon enough belong to us, as will all the information it owns.'

'In which case surely it would be better to wait until then?'

'I would, if I was confident that the situation wasn't going to degenerate further. What are you looking for?'

Jack hesitated for a moment. 'Why do you think I am looking for something?'

'In the middle of a crisis you suddenly leave and travel south. You try to ensure that you cannot be tracked from the moment you get to the mainland to the moment you arrive here. Naturally we have your institute watched. It is standard procedure when we are negotiating to acquire something.'

As the man seemed to know a great deal, there was little to be gained by pretending otherwise. 'We were subject to attempted sabotage and theft. I was sent to make enquiries. My main task is to track down Angela Meerson, who, as you say, has vanished.'

'Theft of . . . ?'

'Some data.'

'Have you succeeded?'

'I have scarcely started.'

'I see. You understand that with the resources I have at my disposal I could track Meerson down very much faster than you could.'

'I doubt that. You would make a great deal of noise and put her on the alert. She is, as perhaps you know, very intelligent and almost paranoid in her lack of trust in others.'

'You have a low opinion of our skills.'

'I do. I have learned over the years that the bigger the organisation, the clumsier it is. I will find her faster and more efficiently than you can.'

Oldmanter considered this remark for a moment and

then said: 'You are not telling me the entire truth, of course.'

'Of course not,' Jack replied with a smile. 'It is the truth, nonetheless.'

'Very well. Bear in mind that I wish to secure control of this technology for the good of humanity. Hanslip has neither the vision nor the resources to develop it properly. I do. Your assistance will be valued and rewarded, if and when it is forthcoming.'

'I have nothing useful to offer you at the moment.'

'Then I would urge you to remember my words when you do.'

*

Jack moved swiftly when he left Oldmanter's quarters. The first task was to escape the residence unnoticed. For this he assumed he had an advantage; if Oldmanter truly thought that he was a high-ranking scientist, and the polite way he talked suggested he did, then no one would assume he had the skills necessary to evade them. With luck, he could disappear thoroughly before they even noticed he had gone.

Signing out, he decided, he could do without. Instead, he left through the doors that led to the service area, full of the sort of people that Oldmanter scarcely knew existed, the cooks and cleaners who toiled unseen in the bowels of the building. There he ducked and weaved through the corridors, borrowing at one stage a floor sweeper's brown coat and cap that he found hanging on a peg by a cupboard. Then he went to the loading bay, where the food came in and the rubbish went out. It was not hard to hitch a lift in one of the trucks, and he was certain he could rely on the suspicion and surliness of such people for protection. Did you see anyone unusual this morning? No. Not a soul . . . Many a time he had been faced with such obstruction. It was the first and often enough the last response to any question.

He got out at a busy intersection where there were only multiple lanes of transports but no pedestrians. No one paid any attention to him as he slipped out, thanking the driver with a clap on the shoulder as he slid to the ground. The man never even looked at him, just grunted as he slammed the door. Then he spent the next hour criss-crossing the area, a commercial zone full of factories and processing plants, surrounded by massive high-rise blocks for the workers who kept them going, ducking into buildings and out the back, walking, then doubling back. He left his wallet with his money card in it on a bench where he knew it would be found and, inevitably, stolen. Once it was used, his location would be tracked wherever it went, and his followers would go off on a wild goose chase, convinced they knew exactly where he was.

He hadn't really believed Hanslip when he had told him to be careful just before he left. But if Oldmanter in person was intervening, then it was serious indeed; this was not a man who occupied himself with details. He had tens of thousands of people who could have come and interviewed him. Now he knew the institute was being monitored, and Oldmanter considered Angela's technology to be so important that it required him to get involved personally. This was no longer tidying up after a security lapse and an embarrassing accident.

He now had the entire night to pass before he could get

into the Depository. It was cold, it was wet and he had no money. All of a sudden, life was much less pleasant.

*

The moment he arrived the following morning at the daunting steel gates which led to the main entrance, he realised that, if Emily did not show up, there was not a chance he could find anything on his own. It was huge. A vast building, so tall and long that the edges were lost in the fog, the windowless walls in grimy concrete, bleak and unwelcoming, surrounded by barbed-wire fencing. It would be like looking for a piece of paper in a city, even if the place was well organised, and he suspected strongly that it would not be.

That was all he needed. He was cold and miserable from having been on the streets the entire night. There was nowhere to sit by the road, which was covered in rubbish and filth, and nowhere to get anything to eat or drink, even if he had had any money, just a bleak, broad multi-lane highway which led nowhere. He began to feel his spirits sag, and to wonder what he would do if Emily Strang did not turn up. Why should she, after all?

Then there was a shout from behind him. As he turned his heart lightened, and not just because it was now possible that he might succeed in his task. The sight of her walking along, in a thick coat, bag over her shoulder, smiling as she waved, revived his spirits. Still, there was nothing that remarkable about her, he reminded himself. Just a renegade, who showed her nature in the loose way she walked, the ostentatious scruffiness of her clothes.

'I'm late. Sorry about that,' she said cheerfully. 'Dear God! What's happened to you? You look as though you slept on a bench all night.'

'I was on a bench, but I didn't sleep. I had a meeting last night. I thought it would be a good idea to make myself scarce.'

'Why?'

'I met the great Zoffany Oldmanter. In the flesh.'

'Aren't you important then.'

Even she had heard of him. But of course she had. Oldmanter was the instigator of the current campaign against the renegades.

'If he finds out I went to your Retreat yesterday, it won't take long for him to figure out who I came to visit.'

'Then I might get to meet him as well?'

'A few of his rougher people, more like.'

'I see. I am beginning to wish I had never met you, Dr More.'

'It would be best to make him lose interest in you. Are you sure you have had no contact with your mother?'

'I've already told you. I'm not protecting her. It's not as if I owe her anything.'

'Can we go in? I'm freezing out here. How well do you know this place?'

'Fairly well. I've been here often. Are you sure you don't want to get some food or something? You really do look a fright.'

'It's not the first time.'

'Hmm,' she said thoughtfully. 'What an unusual scientist you are, to be sure. Well, if you're certain, let's go in. It is a complete mess in there, and huge amounts of material get lost or destroyed, but what still exists is in there, somewhere. If I know where to look, I might find what you're after. You will have to give me a hint.'

'We found an electronic reference to what was supposedly an article published in 1959. The copy we obtained contained some script called the Devil's Handwriting. It was in fact in something called the Tsou notation, which was only invented half a century ago. It appears to be a fragment of your mother's work. The complete document is said to be in the papers of an academic who died in 1979, which were lodged in here.'

'Are you serious?'

'Yes,' he said, a little ruffled by her tone of disdain. 'Why?'

'It's just that I have never heard such a ridiculous story in my life.'

'It's the best we have.'

'You are desperate, then.'

'What are the chances that this man's papers are in there?'

'I have no idea,' she said. 'If they ever existed then I don't imagine anyone has looked at them, and it's the things which are consulted which get destroyed. Nobody can be bothered putting them back again. Finding them may take some time, but the only way to tell is to go and look.'

'Then let us begin,' he said.

*

They spent all day on it and despite Emily's skill and knowledge they came up empty. Jack doubted whether

427

anyone else could ever find it, even if they tore the place to bits. How she did it, by what process of logic she went from one underground level to another, marching what seemed like miles through anonymous, half-lit ranks of files, occasionally pulling out a flashlight, examining a shelf, then grunting and moving on, he did not know. Still, she gave the impression that she knew what she was doing, and the more he trailed after her, the more confident he became. There was something about her competence which re-assured him.

Even when a deafening siren went off after many hours and she cursed noisily he did not feel too disheartened.

'Chucking-out time,' she said with a sniff of disapproval. 'We'll have to stop and come back tomorrow.'

'Have you found anything?'

'Well,' she said, 'I have established that the papers still existed fifty years ago, which is pretty good. I have even narrowed down where they might be. So we have made progress. One thing puzzles me, though.'

'And that is?'

They were walking swiftly towards the exit, feet clattering on the cold concrete floors. Jack was looking forward to being outside once more; the weather wasn't good, but the clammy feeling inside the building was even worse.

'There is no trace of anyone ever having consulted them. In order for someone to have hidden something among the papers, they would have had to find them first. In that case there would be a record that they had been looked at. It would really be a great help to know more,' she said.

'I'm afraid I . . .'

'Great secrets, my renegade ears unsuited to hear?'

'That sort of thing. Also, the less you know, the safer you are.'

There was a long pause, with each feeling offended at the way the other was speaking. Jack was the first to make amends.

'Can I offer you some food? A meal? There must be somewhere round here.'

'I thought you had no money,' she pointed out.

'True.'

'We can offer you hospitality, if you wish to accept it. It will not be as comfortable or hygienic as you are used to, but you don't look as if you can afford to be too fussy. You smell a bit, as well.'

*

He accepted the invitation; he had no real choice as he didn't fancy the idea of another night sleeping in the open. In summer he might not have minded, but at this time of year it was far too cold. Besides, he was tired and worried. He felt half dead by the time he was led into a bare chamber furnished only with a rough bed, after a quick but surprisingly enjoyable meal. He collapsed onto the bed before Emily had even left him alone in the room. As he sank into oblivion, he was sure he heard a faint titter of amusement. He didn't care, as long as everyone let him be.

When he did finally surface, he was bathed in sweat and couldn't immediately remember where he was, why he was there. Only the smell from the pillow, used no doubt by many people before him and without even a sterilised cover, jolted him back to understanding. Slowly, desperately, he levered himself up and sat on the edge of the bed for a while before going to find the shower.

The bathing facilities were primitive beyond belief; just a tube with a nozzle which rained hot water down on him. At least it took his mind off his thoughts, forming and half-forming uncontrollably as he dried himself.

The clothes they had found for him were a different matter; they reminded him of his past too much. He had to dress like one of the people he was more used to watching and controlling. Trousers, cream top and a light blue jacket. There was a mirror in the washing room, and he examined himself thoughtfully when he was done. He had not shaved, and in the clothes he looked very different. No longer the sleek member of the elite, but not convincingly anything else yet either. He looked ridiculous.

Emily didn't agree. 'Much better. You don't look quite so full of yourself.'

'Thank you. I'll take that as a compliment.'

It was only six in the morning, but the trip back to the Depository was a long one, especially as Jack insisted on a roundabout route and walking the last mile. He wasn't even entirely certain why he was bothering, but Emily seemed quite optimistic and he didn't have any other ideas at the moment.

'It was a long shot, you know,' he said as he padded after her down yet another dimly lit corridor made of stacks of rotting cardboard boxes.

'Thrill of the hunt,' she said, craning her neck to stare up twenty feet into the gloom. 'This place has never defeated me yet, and it is not going to today.'

So, when she finally gave a cry of triumph and clambered up a ladder, then pulled out an old box which cascaded dust onto his head, he was surprised, and relieved. Above all, he was quite proud of the fact that he had gone to the trouble of finding her. He doubted anyone else could have made their way through this hell-hole of antiquity so effectively.

She gently carried the box down and blew even more dust off the top. 'Look.'

He could just make out the writing on an old label, nearly detached and yellow with age. 'Lytten, Henry. Papers. 1982/3346.'

'What are the numbers?'

'An old and now entirely useless filing system. We're lucky. If the label had fallen off I would never have found it.'

'Well done. Now let's have a look and leave.'

She laughed. 'Oh, dear me, it's not that easy.'

'What do you mean?'

'There are another eight boxes up there. It could be in any one of them. Still, the longest journey starts with a single step,' she added cheerfully, taking him over to a desk in a dark corner. 'You look through this one and I'll start getting the rest down. Now, what are we looking for?'

'It could be an electronic data holder. Or a paper printout. That's the most likely.'

'Off you go, then.'

He did as instructed. Piece by piece, he took the papers out of the boxes and settled down and tried to read, if only because Emily had begun to do the same. He didn't want her to realise that he found reading difficult, that he was long out of practice. It was made tolerable only by the fact that he would occasionally sneak a glance at the young woman now sitting opposite doing the same, a frown of concentration on her forehead somehow making her dusty face oddly attractive.

It had an almost hypnotic effect on him, to concentrate absolutely on something. He even began to have a faint glimmer of understanding of these people and their insistence on the virtues of pointless activity.

Alongside that was a sense of growing frustration. What was all this stuff, these boxes of old, dank notebooks and crumbling envelopes? Everything was written by hand, and he had never seen that before, except in a museum. He was impressed by the effort, but he had to struggle through every word, and even then they meant very little to him.

There were dozens of notebooks, folders, packets of paper, some covered with writing, others with only a few illegible scribbles. He spent half an hour on an old, yellowed, fragile sheet, carefully analysing each letter, adding them together then extracting the sentence, but it meant nothing. 'I will see the storyteller next Wednesday' had so far lost any context that there was no hope of understanding its significance, if it had ever had any. Another scrap, which was written on a primitive writing machine and so was much easier to read, was equally problematic – 'Mr Williams' work over the past three years has ranged from the incompetent to the fatuous. He is ideally suited to a career in your bank.'

After three hours Emily found it, but only because she ignored his instructions and went through everything. The prize was not what he had anticipated. No little sliver of plastic or metal. No freshly printed sheets of symbols.

Instead, it was buried at the bottom of a large box of papers, and it did not look new or fresh. It was scarcely larger than his hand and consisted of about fifteen pages that were bound in leather. The dust as he opened it made him sneeze. Inside was page after page of the bizarre script which meant nothing to him and which, Hanslip had said, only a machine could understand.

He studied it closely. It was written by hand, in an ink which had not faded. Only the first page was in normal characters. It read, 'The Devil's Handwriting'. There was a stuck-down piece of paper with 'Tudmore Court' printed on it in black.

'That must be it,' he said. 'Well done!'

'Not what you expected?'

'No. Tell me, does this look as if it was recently put there?' It seemed more than ever like a bizarrely complicated way of hiding something. The box and its contents looked as though they had been undisturbed for a very long time indeed: the dust, the smell of decay, the mouse droppings all appeared as though they had never been touched.

'If it was, then it was hidden by someone who knew what they were doing. I would have said it had been there for a while. Look,' Emily said as she picked up another book. 'You see the mark here? It's the outline of the notebook. The cover has stained it a little. That only happens over a long period. And it was slightly stuck to the papers above it. That again normally takes years.'

She took it from his hands, examined it closely, then held it to her face and sniffed. 'If you want my opinion, then it seems like the real thing to me. Genuinely eighteenth-century.'

433

'What do you mean? Eighteenth-century?' he asked sharply. 'Not twentieth?'

'No. The paper, the handwriting, the smell . . .'

'That's not possible.'

'Then we will have to go through the entire lot carefully. See if there are any other references, to give it a context. Faking one document is hard, but faking several of them would be almost impossible. We can run some tests on the paper and ink.'

'Let me try something else, first of all. Could you call the man in charge?'

Emily ran up the stairs and came back a few minutes later with the caretaker, the old man who had waved his hand dismissively when they had arrived and allowed them to wander around at will.

'Has anyone else ever asked for these papers?' Jack asked him. 'I know there are no official records. But unofficially?'

'These? Why do you ask?'

'Answer the question.'

'No one has been to look at them. Officially or unofficially.'

He glanced sideways, very slightly, but in a way which put Jack on the alert. Taking Emily by the arm, he pulled her close.

'I think we should get out of here quickly,' he said. 'Not through the main gate. Is there another exit?'

She nodded. 'Follow me.'

39

Jay woke up alone the next morning; Kate was already preparing breakfast, and Callan was sharpening his spade so that the earth could be dug and stacked into a mound over the burning twigs to make the charcoal. They would set it going, then leave it; the charcoal burner would be along later to tend it for the next three days.

He was peaceful and happy until a flood of memories burst into his head. Was all of that true? Surely not, but every single recollection was crystal clear. The memory of her warm body against his, mixed with images of Henary's dark countenance as he heard the news. The pleasure he had felt in telling the story mingled with a vision announcing that he would never be allowed to tell a story again. That, in turn, faded as he recalled how her hair had felt as she rested her head on his chest.

Maybe it was all a fantasy. No one else was behaving any differently. Callan was whistling, Kate was busy stirring a pot, her hair now held up with a short length of vine so it would not fall into her eyes. He got up cautiously. They both greeted him. Nothing in their words or expressions suggested anything amiss.

As they ate, Callan laid out the plan for the day. Make the fire, stack more wood, walk halfway back to Willdon, stopping to mend a bridge over the river which was in poor repair. Then one more night in the forest.

Work began; Kate prepared the sticks, he and Callan stacked them in triangles, about three feet high, then stacked longer ones around and on top, leaving only a small hole for the smoke to escape. Next the wooden structure was packed with leaves and turf to make it airtight, and finally covered with earth. Once this was done, they were ready to drop the burning embers of the fire into the hole to set the structure alight, and finally seal it so that it would burn slowly, combusting the wood but not consuming it. That was the tricky part, which needed the charcoal burner's skill.

The memory of his young days spent sitting all night with his uncle in the woods near his village made Jay forget more recent events. He lost himself in the work and was pleased to see how much he remembered, cutting short logs and sticks so they fitted perfectly, sealing the structure and making sure as much wood as possible would be burned.

Only towards the end did he get a reminder. They were nearly ready for the embers when Callan stood up and stretched himself.

'That was a good morning's work, young student,' he said. 'I'm surprised.'

Jay smiled.

'She is good as well. I thought she'd just go through the motions, but she's worked hard and well. Look at her! She even looks like a farmer's girl now. If I could have her for a few months I'd turn her into a proper forester.'

'I think she's enjoyed herself. It must be oppressive, being so powerful.'

'Well, maybe, but she'll go back to her real life quick enough, I think.'

Jay knew instantly what was passing through the soldier's mind.

'When she does, everything else will go back to normal as well. You know that, don't you, young Jay?' He smiled in a kindly way.

Then he sank to his knees, a surprised look on his face, and pitched over onto the grass.

Jay backed away in horror as he saw the thick arrow that had gone straight through Callan and out the other side. The blood was already flowing copiously from both wounds, and he was transfixed by the sight until he heard a scream from the woods. It was Kate, who was struggling with two men who had grabbed her. Ignoring all danger, she shook off her attackers and hurried towards Callan, going down on her knees to examine the damage. Stony-faced with fury, she stood to face the three men who came running up, swords and bows at the ready.

'What have you done?' she spat. 'Why did you do that? Fetch me some water, quickly.'

They slowed as she spoke but did not seem inclined to heed her words until one man – tall and massive, who looked as though he could pick her up with one hand – grunted. 'Do as she says,' he said in a thick, almost incomprehensible voice. 'Find me something to use as a bandage.'

He glared at one man in particular, who was carrying a bow.

'You. Go back to the camp. I don't need you here. You've done enough harm.'

The huge man sank down beside the twitching, moaning form of Callan and bent over him. 'You've been injured. I'm going to have to take the arrow out, otherwise you'll die. Do you understand? It'll hurt, but I know what I'm doing.'

Callan nodded, his teeth gritted in pain. The man bent over once more and, with great force, took the arrow in both hands and snapped off the head as easily as Jay would have snapped a twig. Then, holding him with astonishing gentleness, he rolled him over. 'Pull out the arrow,' he said gently. 'Can you do that?'

Kate bit her lip with nervousness. 'One swift pull, evenly and straight. It's the only way. Are you ready?'

She prepared herself, taking hold of the arrow with both hands, closed her eyes and, with a mighty tug, pulled. It came out in one go, and Callan's screams echoed through the forest, making the birds fly off in fright.

'Do you know how to bind wounds?'

She nodded silently.

'Then I will hold him still. Bathe the openings with cold water and we will patch him up. Then we'll take him to the camp and get him proper treatment.'

'Will he live?' Jay asked in a trembling voice.

'I don't know. He will if I have anything to do with it.'

As they walked through the forest, the mood of the little group was sombre. Even though he was a big man, Callan was borne in the arms of the giant who had tended him as though he weighed nothing. There was no time for a stretcher, he had said, and it wasn't far.

It was Jay's task now, his task alone, to protect the Lady of Willdon, who had fallen into the hands of a band of marauders. What could he do against swords and bows and knives? The only flicker of hope was that at least they did not see the magnitude of their prize. They had captured a scholar and his servant. If that deception could be made to hold up, then they had some small chance, perhaps. Otherwise they could demand any price for her return. If her absence was prolonged, the domain of Willdon could fall into chaos, sucking in the outside world with it. Willdon was the balancing force in the land; it had fulfilled this role for generations, and its glory was that it never sought to impose its power on anyone else. But what would happen if it was vacant?

He glanced at her as she walked dutifully beside him, her head down as a servant's should be. In her small body, on her frail shoulders, rested the peace of Anterwold. At least she now looked like a servant with her bedraggled hair and ill-fitting dress, her bare feet. 'She even looks like a farmer's girl.' So Callan had said, just before . . .

'You will have to be Kate a little longer,' he said quietly. 'Do you know who these people are?'

'I hope not. Are you prepared to be the hostage in my stead?'

'Of course. I would die for you.'

'Let us hope that will not be necessary. But thank you.'

'Stop talking,' called one of their captors, the man who had fired the arrow.

'Why?' Jay replied. 'What's it to you?'

'Because . . .'

'Leave him be,' said the huge man, breathless from carrying Callan but trying not to show his tiredness. They were short with each other. Jay could see quite easily that this had not been planned.

'Where are you taking us?'

'To our leader. He will decide what to do with you.'

'Why should you do anything with us? We were walking in the forest.'

'Why? This is our territory. Our forest. Our land. And you come scouting and spying.'

'We were not.'

'A scholar as well. What is going on? Is there to be an alliance? Are the scholars going to rouse up Willdon against us? Is that what this is about?'

'No,' said Jay in genuine astonishment. 'If it was, no one would ever tell me about it. I'm just a student.'

'Students don't have servants.'

'She's not actually my servant,' Jay said quickly. 'She belongs to my master. Can't you just let her go? She's not important.'

'She can work. We'll treat her well. Besides, she could bring the Lady's soldiers here. We're not ready for them yet.'

*

Pamarchon was going around the outer perimeter of the camp to check it was secure, examining weapons, counting the stocks of arrows, ensuring there were enough bandages and medicines for the inevitable injuries that must come soon if he took his decision to launch the long-planned, often-delayed attack. When he came back, he discovered that there were captives, newly brought into the camp. One had been injured. He listened in fury to the account of how it had happened. It was exactly the sort of thing he always tried to prevent. Their existence and safety depended on the good will of those they encountered. A reputation

440

for violence and brutality would lead to betrayal, sooner or later. It was not the first time this particular man had lacked the self-control he had tried over the years to instil in them all.

'You,' he said, pointing to the sallow-faced, resentful man who had fired. 'You don't leave the camp again, unless you're with others and unarmed. How does this keep on happening? How often do I have to tell people . . . ? How badly is he injured?'

'Badly. But he might live,' said the huge man.

'I will go and see him. What about the others?'

'A young lad and a servant. The lad says he's from Ossenfud.'

'Bring him to me.'

*

'Right, then, scholar. Our leader wants you. Get up.'

Jay was sitting on the ground, waiting. He was alone; when they had arrived at the camp, he had been taken to the very centre of it and told to stay put. They had pointed out how far he would have to run to escape, pointed out also how many people carried weapons. You wouldn't stand a chance, was the message. He took their advice.

He sat for an hour until he was taken to a large tent, square and fully open on one side to let in the light. The floor was covered in cloth and cushions; there was a rough trestle table in one corner and a rolled-up mattress on the other side. Otherwise, the only furniture was a wooden chest. It was simple and not very comfortable.

He caught his breath, though, when he saw the tall man

sitting on the floor. It was the man who had taken Rosalind away at the Festivity. Jay knew quite well that he had been recognised too.

'Leave us alone, then,' the tall man said, and gestured for Jay to sit down.

'The world seems to be an astonishingly small place these days,' he began.

Jay's face twitched in a sort of half-smile.

'When I was told that they had captured some of the Lady's scouts in the forest, I hardly thought it would be you, Master Jay. It is Jay, is it not?'

He nodded. 'I'm not a scout. Nor was Callan. You shouldn't have hurt him. He is a good man, and my friend.'

'Callan, you say? The forester?'

'Yes.'

He bowed his head. 'Then I am truly sorry. I knew him once and liked him well. He is a good man. Had I been there it would not have happened. I will make my peace with him and, if necessary, with his family. He will get the best treatment and care we can offer. If he can be saved, he will be.'

'Who are you?'

'My name is Pamarchon, son of Isenwar, son of Isenwar.'

'Isenwar?'

'Yes. I trace my lineage back to the first level. Have you not heard of me?'

'No. Why is your name not Isenwar as well?'

'My brother bore that name, but he died. My children will bear it again, so it will continue.'

'May your wishes be granted.'

He nodded. 'Thank you.'

'Why do you live here? A name like yours . . .'

'You come from Willdon and you do not know of the evil Pamarchon and his foul deeds? I am surprised, although perhaps you would not. I am sure my name has been erased for its infamy.'

'I know nothing,' Jay said. 'I do not even know why you want me as your prisoner. Or my servant.'

'What servant?'

'Well, maybe not mine. She works for my master but I am responsible for her. He'll be very annoyed if any harm comes to her.'

'Your master is . . . ?'

'Henary, son of Henary, scholar of the first rank.'

'That remarkable young woman, Rosalind,' Pamarchon said, changing the subject abruptly. 'Who is she? I was her companion for more than an hour, and I knew little more of her when we parted than when we met.'

'You are not the only one,' Jay said. 'I have no idea who – or what – she is. You may form your own opinion of her beauty and charm. Where she comes from I do not know.'

'Henary does?'

'Perhaps. If so, he did not share his knowledge with me.'

'He did with Lady Catherine, no doubt.'

'I am not privy to their conversations. Why do you speak of her in such a tone?'

'The Lord and Lady both? In what tone do I speak?'

'Hostility and dislike.'

'I suppose you find her charming and gracious.'

'Yes.'

'Perhaps I know her better.'

Jay looked uncomprehending. 'Surely . . .'

'I do not wish to discuss this. I want to know your reasons for being in the forest. Looking for us? Spying?'

'Look at me,' Jay said. 'Am I your idea of a spy?'

'You are not telling me the truth.'

'I am. I met Callan the day I was selected. I am preparing my disquisition, which concerns a passage on the relationship between man and the forest. Henary arranged for me to spend a few days with him.'

'Which passage?'

'Level 3, upper 60s.'

Pamarchon's eyes narrowed. 'Those are monster stories. An unusual choice, surely?'

'I'm impressed by your knowledge.'

'You went into the forest to meet monsters . . .'

'And met you,' Jay finished coldly.

Pamarchon stood up. 'Do as you are told, don't be foolish and you will come to no harm.' He went to the tent entrance. 'I'm sorry for Callan,' he said. 'I mean that. You may visit him as you will, and you may have your servant back. You will be responsible for her good behaviour as well as her safety. You will be free to move around, if you give your word that you will not escape. Otherwise I am afraid you will have to be placed somewhere you cannot escape. Do you agree to that?'

Jay was so pleased that he didn't hesitate. 'Of course.'

*

Kate was peeling potatoes when Jay found her again and, considering the circumstances, was doing quite well. Still, she was exhausted from the effort of caring for Callan, and

444

was in shock at what had happened. Nor did she know much about peeling potatoes. Now she sat, frown on face, knife in hand, beside a huge pile of freshly dug, earth-covered potatoes large enough to feed everyone in the camp for days to come. She threw one into the pot beside her and stretched, rubbing her back to ease the pain that came from sitting too long in the same position.

'You'll be glad to know I have recovered my servant,' Jay said as he approached and sat down next to her. 'Your job once more is to look after my every need. And Callan, as much as you can and wish. No one suspects you.'

'That's good,' she said.

'So leave those and come with me.'

'No. I'm going to finish.'

'You don't have to.'

'I started, so I'll finish. It is quite an art, you know. Why don't you grab a knife and help? Then I will finish quicker and we can talk undisturbed. I find it calming after everything that has happened.'

It was a good idea in all respects except for the potatoes, but for the next hour they laboured together, earning the curious and not unappreciative glances of those who passed by.

Jay had pressed her for details of Callan's state. Not well, she said. The injury was bad. As long as he didn't develop a fever, though, he might survive.

'Well? What is going on?' she asked.

'I could ask you the same question,' he replied. 'Our captor is called Pamarchon and he is the man I told you was at your Festivity. He talks as though he knows you well and doesn't like you. I fear you would be in some difficulty

445

if he learned who you are. Why does he hate you?'

Kate finished a potato, then tossed it in the pot. 'Quite simple. He murdered my husband,' she said. 'I'm sure he would have killed me as well, given the chance. Did you not know this?'

'I knew your husband had died. Henary didn't tell me anything else at all.'

'Unusually discreet of him. Pamarchon is – or rather was – my husband's cousin. The second son of his eldest sister, actually, and his closest living relation. He was nominated as heir to Willdon and expected to inherit, until Thenald married me, with the prospect of producing an heir. Pamarchon acted first. Thenald was stabbed to death in the forest and Pamarchon proved his own guilt by fleeing. Willdon chose me quickly for fear he was planning to attack. I was the best available.'

'So what is he doing here?'

'What is he doing here? With a bitter heart, a tendency to violence and what seems like several hundred armed followers, scarcely a few days' march from Willdon?'

Jay sucked in his breath. 'Did you know about this?'

'I knew there was movement. I didn't know who or why, or that there were anything like as many people as this.'

'Then you were very unwise to put yourself at risk.'

There was a brief flash of Lady Catherine in her face, but it passed quickly. 'Perhaps you are right. But I am in no present danger, and I am better informed than I was. I need to get back to Willdon though, and soon. It seems I will have to prepare our defences.'

40

When Sam Wind was told that, while they had been talking in the study with Volkov, the police had brought a suspected Soviet spy to the house and that he had now vanished, he was both furious and in a high state of panic. Volkov was bundled out of the door into the van Sam had summoned and driven off at high speed. Sam himself stayed behind, his habitual mask of insouciance completely gone.

'How the hell did that happen? Whose idea was that?'

'I assumed that Henry wanted him,' Angela said meekly. 'The policeman said they had picked him up, and what were they to do with him now? I didn't know anything about it, and didn't want to interrupt . . .'

'So you gave him tea in the kitchen? Tea?'

'He didn't want coffee. Besides, what else was I supposed to do with him? I thought you must have known all about it.'

'What did he say? Who was he?'

'He didn't say very much.'

'How did he escape?'

'He went to the toilet and never came back. How should I know?'

Wind grunted and stumped downstairs into Lytten's cellar. Lytten and Angela followed.

'What is all this rubbish?' Wind said as he surveyed the dust-covered junk and peered scornfully at a rusty iron structure against the wall covered in old cans and bits of tinfoil.

'That is called "Momentum",' Angela said. 'It's a sculpture I've been making. I'm rather proud of it. It is a re-evaluation of traditional mores as metamorphosed under the incessant impact of consumerist . . .'

'What?'

'Really it's just a Victorian iron pergola. French, so I suppose not Victorian really. Fin de siècle, if you prefer, although I can't date it precisely. You put it in your garden and grow roses over it. I keep meaning to take it back to France. But somehow . . .'

Her voice trailed off. Not that Wind cared. All he cared about was who that man was. How he had escaped. What it all meant. To those questions, he found no answer in the gloomy and damp cellar.

'Who was he, Henry?' Wind asked 'Why were you interested in him?'

'He was watching the house. I thought it worth pursuing.'

'What do you mean by watching?'

'What most people mean by watching. The first time he was standing in the middle of my driveway with his mouth hanging open. Then he was walking up and down the street. Another time he stood on the other side of the road. He was trying to look nonchalant, but didn't do it very well. The last time was yesterday. I pointed him out to the policeman who came about the missing girl.'

'What missing girl?'

'She's not missing,' Lytten said shortly.

'Nothing for you to worry about,' Angela added.

'Can we stay on the subject, please?' Wind said. 'If he

was a Russian, then they must know Volkov is here.' He took a deep breath. 'It does indicate that Volkov is the real thing, of course. Why the hell did you let him go?'

'I didn't let him go,' Angela said tartly. 'He went to the toilet.'

*

'That was exciting,' Angela said, once Sam had finally given up and only she and Lytten remained in the house. 'Sam Wind agitated. I've never seen that before. I am sorry, by the way, if I did something wrong.'

Lytten was on the phone and not paying her any attention. 'Oh, I think so, Portmore,' he was saying. 'Volkov says he has information to identify the man you are after. No, he won't say yet. They left half an hour ago. They'll take him to the usual place . . . It does, doesn't it . . .

'It's not your fault,' he reassured Angela when he put the phone down. 'You weren't to know. You may recall that Sam is overly concerned with not looking bad. Potentially compromising a defector does look bad. In fact, if the Americans ever hear about it they will laugh themselves silly. That won't make any difference to me, but Sam will spend the next day or so rushing around trying to find someone else to blame. He wants so desperately to get the top job, and this might torpedo his chances.'

'Oh, you boys,' Angela said. 'You never grow up, do you?'

'It seems not. In the circumstances, I think a glass of whisky would be a good idea.'

He got two glasses, blew into them to make sure there

was no dust and poured two generous measures before sitting in his old armchair. 'Did that man really say nothing of interest?' he asked Angela, who had returned to the settee. 'Did he have a name, by the way?'

'He said his name was Alexander Chang.'

'Chinese?'

'Not by the look of him. A little, maybe. But not much. He was very flustered,' she said. 'Most of the time he talked what you would consider nonsense. By the way, did you ever thank me in some article you wrote a year or so back?'

Lytten blinked in confusion. She did sometimes have trouble keeping on the subject, but this was bizarre even by her standards. 'An article on *As You Like It*. I believe I thanked you for your help. The translations, you know. Could we keep on the point?'

'This man mentioned it to prove he was some scholar interested in your work. His story was that he was plucking up courage to ask you a question about the Devil's Handwriting. Do you know what he meant?'

'I assume he meant a little article I published last year. It was about a manuscript bought by one of my ancestors. I was convinced that not a single person ever read it, judging by the lack of impact it had. Mind you, it was a very little thing.'

'What is it?'

'The Devil's Handwriting? Something written in an incomprehensible script that people thought in the eighteenth century was the work of the devil. I argued that it was a rather bad fake.'

'Where is it now?'

'Tudmore; what is grandly called the family seat. It's a

bit of a ruin, but my great-aunt still lives there. I constantly worry about what will happen when the old girl dies. I'm sure I've mentioned it to you before.'

'Who bought it?'

'You seem remarkably interested, if I may say so. It was acquired by Charles Lytten, the Founding Father. He was the only one with any drive and he seems to have used up the family supply of initiative for the next three centuries. Have I never shown you the painting of him?'

Angela shook her head.

'Come and have a look, if you want. It's in the spare bedroom. No one else wanted it.'

*

I followed him upstairs into the spartan back bedroom. A tarnished brass bed, a side table, bare floors and thin, dirty curtains completely inadequate to the task of keeping out either light or cold. I never understood why the English went out of their way to be uncomfortable. Something to do with the schools, I think.

I was still in a state of shock. Suddenly hearing Hanslip's voice, coming out of Chang's mouth in that way, had been decidedly spooky. The message was spookier still. Why would he think that would influence me? I knew who he meant, of course. I hadn't given my daughter a moment's thought for years until I met Grange and he tripped my memory, and now there was this. I knew Hanslip well. He wouldn't have put such effort into delivering that message unless he was pretty certain it would have an effect. So how was I meant to react? Was I reacting? All I knew was that

451

I was thoroughly unsettled by the whole thing.

On top of it all, there he was in front of me; the man responsible in a distant sort of way, although much changed from the man I remembered. There was no doubt, once I was able to ignore the powdered wig and silly clothes. It was Lucien Grange, aged about seventy. Henry was his descendant, not his ancestor. I'd never even thought of that possibility. Even so, I remained just a little sceptical until I studied the portrait with greater care.

'Not very good, is it?' Henry said, peering at it over my shoulder. 'I don't keep it for its artistic value. In fact, I don't know why I keep it.'

He answered my questions with an air of surprise that I should take any interest. This Charles had been, he said, a proper paterfamilias. He had insisted on his children having a serious education (the girls as well as the boys) and had held exceptionally advanced views on religion and politics. 'A woman without a brain is like a sandwich without a filling,' was his apparent response to one possible marriage partner. That was a clue, when I checked the etymology of the word 'sandwich'. He was also exceptionally long-lived, which was another clue. He outlived his children, two wives and some of his grandchildren, finally succumbing in 1753 at what was thought to be an age of some 107 years, when he was run over by a horse and cart in Piccadilly.

Then I got an even bigger surprise. The picture was a standard eighteenth-century portrait, terribly stylised, and, as was often the case, the sitter had been painted to look properly serious and educated. He was in a chair, looking learnedly at a piece of paper – this to disguise the fact that he had, in reality, made his fortune by becoming a developer of jerry-built properties for an expanding London. I peered carefully at the writing on the paper and caught my breath.

'Henry!' I called out. 'What's this?'

'*Qui moderatur tempus intelligit omnia*. Family motto. Even more pointless than most, I think. No one has the faintest idea what it is supposed to mean.'

'What does it mean?' Latin was one of the few languages I hadn't brought with me. I didn't think I'd need it. The only word I recognised was the third.

'He who controls time understands everything.'

'Golly,' I said.

'I think he must have had a weakness for metaphysical poetry. I once tried to figure out where it came from. It must be some tag from a classical author, but I never tracked it down.'

I stared at Lucien carefully as Henry pottered off downstairs again. 'Well, that's complicated everything, hasn't it?'

*

Sam Wind returned with another man, as anonymous as Wind was noticeable, late that evening. 'Henry,' they said as they walked straight into his study and poured themselves more of his whisky, then both settled themselves down on the settee.

'Do come in. Would you like a drink?' Lytten had not had a good day. He had only just managed to get Angela out of the door and was looking forward to some peace.

'Sarcasm is most unbecoming. Volkov is in hospital.'

'What? Whatever happened to him?'

'Someone took a pot shot at him. We were taking him to the usual place near Yeovil. The van was going round the bend just outside the village, you remember how dangerous it is, so it slowed down a lot. And – pop. One shot.'

'How badly was he hurt?'

'He'll live. Just. It hit him in the chest, but the driver – with commendable aplomb, I must say – pulled him down and slammed his foot on the accelerator. But for that, I'm sure there would have been another shot.'

Lytten fell silent. This was bad. Unexpected. This should not have happened. He examined Wind's expression carefully, then looked away. Until now it had been almost a game. He had never really thought . . .

'Where is he now?'

'He's being taken to an army hospital on Salisbury Plain. He'll have half a tank regiment guarding him, so he should be safe.'

'Poor fellow! We should have done better for him. What about the attacker?'

'Not even a cartridge left behind.'

'Someone who knew what they were doing.'

'Yes. The point is . . .'

'The point is that someone wanted to shut him up. Someone knew he would be in a van, slowing down and turning the corner. Is that what you are saying, Sam?'

'Yes.'

'I would like to ask a few questions, if you don't mind.' It was the other man, dark-haired, serious, looking slightly nervous.

'Who are you?'

'Forgive my companion,' Wind drawled from the side.

'He does have a name. Some county or other. Dorset? Devon? Somewhere like that. Careful what you say to him though.' Wind looked annoyingly fake-conspiratorial for a moment. 'I've seen him, scribbling away when he thinks no one will notice. You'll probably turn up as a character in some thriller one day.'

'Very interesting, but why is he here?'

'Oh. He's some junior diplomat, temporarily assigned to our new, ever-so-keen counter-intelligence department. Just temporary. I take him out for a walk every now and then to stop him going mad with frustration. Now. This man. This morning. The man who never was.'

'Angela and I decided he was probably a foreign academic. He told her he was interested in an obscure manuscript in my family.'

'I very much doubt that. The police evidence is quite clear. He was foreign, certainly, but he had no passport and no account of how he got here. Spoke fluent Russian. He knew Angela Meerson and wanted to find you.'

'She doesn't seem to have known him.'

'So she says. How well do you know her, really?'

'Angela? As well as I know anyone.'

'Who were her parents?'

'I don't know. She's never mentioned them.'

'What is her nationality? By birth?'

'English? French?'

'Precisely. When did you first meet her?'

'1939. In France.'

'Ah yes. Near the Spanish border, which was, at the time, infested with Republicans, aided by the Soviet Union. Then, through you, she came to England and got a job with us.'

'Only as a translator. She was brilliant at it. You know that.'

'She was. Impeccable. Remarkably so.'

'What do you mean?'

'I remember one conversation with her. I was despondent about the war. She brushed it aside, and said that because of Pearl Harbor, all would be well.'

'She was right.'

'She was. Except that she said it three months beforehand.'

'Who knew about Volkov, Dr Lytten?' It was the young man who spoke again. Very polite. He'd probably been through some training course. 'Did you tell Angela Meerson about him coming?'

'No. I asked her to come and translate only the day before. I didn't say why.'

'Did you tell her you were going away to France?'

'No. No need. She has her own key if she wants to get something from the cellar.'

'Was she ever in your house alone after Mr Wind delivered that package to you?'

'Perhaps.'

'Yes or no?'

'"Perhaps" is a common English word used to express uncertainty. If I knew I would have used a different term.' He stood up to pour another drink. Old technique. Take command of the momentum. Enforce your own rhythm. Also a handy way of getting some time to think.

'Let me sum up,' Lytten said when he was back in his chair. 'See if I get the drift of your questions properly. You are now convinced that Volkov is the real thing. You think that this man was a Russian sent to find him.

456

You are beginning to think that the conduit between them was Angela. Which would mean that she is a long-term agent of the Soviet Union, who used me as a way of manoeuvring herself into a position where she could spy on us during the war. She discovered the papers on my desk, realised what they meant and tipped off her masters. They dispatched this strange man, who disappears and later takes a shot at Volkov.'

He gazed balefully at the pair of them. 'Balderdash. Pure gibberish. Sam? You don't really think this nonsense, do you? You're clutching at straws to avoid looking like an idiot.'

'At least she needs to answer some questions. Clear things up.'

'You're getting spooked by nothing.'

'Volkov is in hospital with a bullet in him. It's not nothing.'

*

When I left Henry I made my way to my little home in Barton, where I had lived since relocating my activities to England. It was a charming place, newly built in a burst of post-war social engineering, with a tiny garden, delightfully picturesque neighbours and never-ending interest, especially after the pubs closed on a Friday night. I had carefully furnished it, using adverts in magazines as models, and it was very 1960 in its aesthetic tone. Lots of linoleum and Formica and brightly patterned curtains. I was hugely pleased with it, and used to sit at my Danish Moderne dining-room table, admiring the general effect.

I had two beds, one in each bedroom, one for sleeping and the other for work; I always found that separating activities was important. It was the second I planned to use that evening, for I had a great deal of hard mental labour to get through, building the sudden irruption of Chang, Grange and Emily into my calculations. The number of variables had suddenly increased dramatically and I was, of course, hampered by the fact that I had no way of knowing what Hanslip would try to do. To my already complex calculations I also had to factor in the unknown and unknowable.

I was looking forward to my night of entertainment, and if that sounds peculiar, then I should explain how this was so. Once people got over their obsession with mechanical calculators and developed a better and more efficient way of doing things, such abilities were built in through a few small implants and by rerouting parts of the brain that otherwise were underemployed in daily life. Many experiments were done to establish the best sites for this; some people had the enhancements attached to the sectors of the brain which controlled physical exercise, for example, so that to perform work they would have to go on long walks to generate the required stimulation. Others, rather more peculiarly, had it attached to their sense of humour, and would be heard wandering around giggling insanely as they did complex calculations.

In my case my natural ability was so great that it could not be attached to such a limited area. Instead, I opted to have my skills powered by the zones of my brain which responded to pleasure. Later a further development had also built in maternal longing, on the grounds that it is the most powerful force in the human psyche. Without going into the more lurid details, I am sure you can see the possibilities of the first. When I was still in France, grappling with a particularly complex problem, I found that the best solution was to set up the calculation, then go to a local restaurant (the Dôme in Montparnasse was very productive) and smile in a particular fashion at one of the young single men who used to frequent the place. Not only did I get my work done, I also often got a free meal into the bargain.

I did not use the additional enhancements very often; the emotional aftershocks of doing so were too great. Instead I kept a distance from that side of my personality and did not dwell on the fact that I had a child. So what? That was my normal response when I thought of the subject. More than two decades of living in a world where emotions were permitted changed that somewhat; my response to Rosie had been far more emotional and affectionate than her existence warranted. I felt protective towards her, the first time I had ever felt such an emotion. To my surprise, it was quite pleasant.

Now I needed to unleash that unused part of my abilities fully if I was going to have any chance whatsoever of understanding the complications that now bedevilled me. I prepared myself thoroughly, summoning all the information I had stored away on my daughter to see what I was dealing with. Then I added her to the calculations as well.

*

One of the things I found myself thinking about was Wind's panic. It drove home the point that the humble coincidence could be a powerful factor in the evolution of events. If Chang hadn't turned up just at that moment . . .

Which brought me back to my worry. Why had he turned up just then? Why at that precise moment? Why not the day before or after, for example? Was it just random, or was there an underlying pattern I couldn't yet see? Shakespeare, you understand, as interpreted by Henry Lytten. The greater the coincidence, the greater the importance of the hidden causation.

My concern was that I had been around now for many years, and in all probability would be around for another seventy or so. And Chang shows up just as my tests were running out of control. Clearly there was absolutely no way that he, or anyone else, could have known about this. So my fundamental query was: did the fact that the test was out of control cause him to turn up? Or did his turning up in some way send the test out of control? Did his arrival cause Rosalind to visit Henry's cellar and put Anterwold on steroids? Or the other way round? Or was there some other factor I knew nothing of? Was it simply a coincidence that today was the first time I heard of Henry's ancestor, and saw his portrait, and was reminded of the girl he had brought into existence? I felt that if I could figure that one out, I could figure out everything else as well.

I needed to work on my machine, and I needed help. There was only one person who could provide that, so, with some trepidation, I went to Rosie's house and knocked on the door. I suspected she would be confined to her room in disgrace, or something like that. Certainly the sour look on her mother's face when I'd glimpsed her as I dropped Rosie off the previous day did not make me expect that all would be joyful in the Wilson household. On the other hand, it did explain why the girl found Anterwold so appealing.

41

Antros was on the verge of finally killing the deer that he had been patiently tracking for more than an hour. It had stopped to drink at a narrow stream and he had a clear shot at it. Only fifty feet or so, an easy target that he could not possibly miss. The arrow was in place, and slowly he pulled back on the string until he could feel the feather against his ear. Very carefully, he took aim, held his breath – and watched helplessly as the deer started, ducked, swerved and disappeared into the bushes, disturbed by the blood-curdling scream that echoed through the forest.

He cursed and cursed again. The despair and terror in that scream frightened him as much as it had the deer. More, perhaps, as he knew that it was a human voice that had produced it. He jumped to his feet – his knee aching from resting on the ground for such a long time – and listened again. Swiftly but carefully, he ran lightly toward the noise. He kept his bow close, the arrow still in place. He might very well need it.

There was nothing dangerous that he could see. In the middle of the scrub there was a figure, a slight boy sitting on the ground, hunched over. Injured? It didn't seem so, but the sound of sobbing suggested he was in some distress.

Antros did not hurry. He had lived in the forest long enough to be cautious. The boy wasn't dying. Antros lowered himself behind a bush and watched. There seemed to be no trap, no one else nearby. There was the Copse, but no one would dare hide in that. There were no untoward sounds, no movements that made him alert.

He stood up and skirted round so that he could approach the boy from behind; he didn't seem dangerous but men died in the forest from not being careful. When he got within a few feet he pulled on the bowstring once more, so that the arrow was pointing straight at the boy's back, and spoke.

'Who are you?'

Slowly the boy lifted his head, and Antros could see the pallor of his face, the tears running down his cheeks. He relaxed and loosened the string of his bow.

'What's the matter with you, young fellow?' he asked. 'Seen a ghost?'

The boy looked at him for a long time, lips trembling.

'What's your name?' he asked more gently. 'Don't be afraid.'

'My name is . . . My name is Ganimed.'

'Why are you so frightened? Are you lost? Where are your parents, your people?'

'I don't know. I'm alone here. I went into those trees and . . . and . . .'

'You went into the Copse? Why? What for? Don't you know what is in there?'

'No. But it's horrible. Horrible.'

'It is a terribly dangerous, foolish thing to do. Were you attacked?'

'There was no one there.'

'I didn't mean by people. Stand up. Let me look at you.'

Antros began to examine him, peering into his eyes and ears, then took a step back. 'You seem all right,' he said. 'Who are you? Where are you from?'

A shake of the head. 'Please don't ask me any questions. Please don't.'

Antros felt his heart softening, but he didn't let it show. There were many questions left to be answered before the lad deserved sympathy. Instead he said gruffly, 'Best come with me then.'

'No, no. I can't.'

'You must. You have to get away from here. It's dangerous for you. We have to leave now. Come, boy. Do as you are told.'

'I most certainly will not.' He peered at him.

'Do as I ask, then.'

The boy gave in. 'Very well.'

*

Rosalind was in some disarray as she padded alongside the young man who had rescued her and taken command of the situation. What was she supposed to have done? She didn't know who he was, what he wanted. She was all alone in the world and didn't have any protection. She could have refused to go with him, but didn't want to risk provoking him, just in case he wasn't as benevolent as his voice made him sound. She had been warned at school about strange men. Not, admittedly, about walking through deserted forests with strange men armed with a bow and arrow, but she was sure that the general principle was sound. If she was in some sort of danger, she didn't want Aliena to be caught up in it as well. Rosalind was sure she could find her own way back to the shepherd's hut. She hoped so, at least.

Her rambling train of thought brought her back to the moment when she had walked so carelessly into the centre of that copse of oak trees. The moment she had looked up she had realised what all the shapes were, half-hidden in the gloom, covered in leaves, and what the sweet smell was.

It was filled with dead bodies, half-consumed, rotting, torn to pieces by birds and animals, decayed by damp and covered in flies and insects. There were dozens if not hundreds of them, strewn over the ground. Before she began to run, she noticed the corpse of a young child, scarcely more than a baby. Its skin was green, its body eaten away, and there was a clump of mushrooms growing out of one eye. Then the smell began to overwhelm her, sweet and not unpleasant until you knew what it was; the sounds, the innocent sounds of woodlands, until you know why they were so loud and insistent.

She sank to the ground and began heaving. She vomited, violently and terribly, all of her breakfast, everything in her stomach welling out of her as those smells and images and sounds crowded into her brain. She clutched her stomach in pain and heaved again, then for a third time.

She was panting and exhausted from the involuntary effort, feeling the prickly sweat on her back and in her hair from the violence, the foul taste in her mouth which was at least better than her memories. She rolled over in the grass and closed her eyes, feeling the warmth of the midday sun on her. Even so, she was shivering in shock and distress.

Her companion swept the distant treeline until he was satisfied they were alone, then sat down a few feet away from her. When she stopped heaving and opened her eyes again he proffered a flask of water.

'Rinse out your mouth a few times; get rid of the taste. If there are any spirits left inside you it should help flush them out.'

She did as she was told, then wiped her forehead with the sleeve of her jacket.

'Thank you,' she said.

'They let you off lightly. You cannot have had a bad intent.'

'Who let me off?'

'The spirits. You shouldn't have gone in there. It is not a place for the living. You were an intruder. You were lucky they didn't possess you, or send you mad.'

Rosalind sniffed. 'I don't think they needed to. I think I'm mad already. What is that place, anyway?'

'Do you really not know . . . ?'

'No!' she shouted. 'I really do not know. I don't. Nothing. Do you understand? Can't you just answer a perfectly straightforward question?'

Antros took a step back in surprise at this outburst, especially as, instead of being apologetic, she glared at him defiantly, daring him to reprimand her.

'Well,' he said. 'Yes.'

'Yes what?'

'Yes, I can answer a perfectly straightforward question. That is the place of the dead. One of them, at least. For the people of Willdon. When someone dies, their body is laid there, to be returned to the forest. It is a sacred place, under the protection of the spirits. The living do not go into it without good reason. You trespassed and so the spirits entered you and made you ill. I hope that is all they intend.'

'That was adrenalin.'

'We do not name them,' he said. 'To us they are just the spirits of the forest.'

Rosalind sighed. 'Whatever you say.'

'You must be cleansed. I will take you to Pamarchon. He will know what to do.'

'Pamarchon?' she said, looking up at him suddenly.

'Don't be afraid. He is not as you may have heard. Now I must insist that you come with me.'

'Oh,' she replied, her mood changing suddenly. 'If you insist.'

Antros was caught off balance again. He had expected to have to force the lad against his will.

'Good. This way. Please.'

*

They walked for an hour – or maybe it was ten minutes; she wasn't paying attention. After a while she heard voices in the distance. The smell of smoke drifted into her nose, and then the aromas of food being cooked. She heard laughter – a good sign. Happy people don't get too rough.

A camp site, but quite unlike anything she had seen before. Not that she had ever been camping. Her parents didn't like that sort of thing. She loved her parents, she really did. But they knew nothing about being young. Rosalind suspected, in fact, that they never had been young. Still, she knew what camp sites were like – identical brown or grey canvas tents, a camp fire, another canvas construction for the toilets. Neat orderly rows. Washing on a line.

This was nothing like that. It was chaotic, for a start, with tents pitched everywhere. If you could call them tents. Some were made of bits of material, true enough. But others were made out of tree branches covered in soil and grass. Some were big, some small. Some rested on the ground, others were dug into a sort of ditch. Some were even constructed out of stone, piled high and resting on logs. All around was disorderly as well. Children ran about screaming, weaving in and out among the adults, playing and chasing each other. Women criss-crossed the ground with jugs of water or washing on their heads. In the far corner some men were having a sword fight, elsewhere others were chopping wood. Everywhere people talked, loudly and cheerfully, while cows and sheep and chickens wandered about, ignored by the numerous dogs and cats equally.

She took in the scene then stopped, open-mouthed. With a rush of amazement she recognised Jay, who was standing about twenty yards away, talking to a woman who was sitting cross-legged on the ground, peeling potatoes and throwing them into a large metal pot beside her. She was about to go over or call a greeting when Antros came back and took her by the arm. 'Prisoners,' he said. 'Don't go near them.'

42

When Chang stepped through the ironwork in the cellar into the world on the other side, it was not that time stopped; he was aware of its passage, but simply did not know what it meant. He no longer knew anything of himself or his surroundings; he was hungry but had no idea how to feed himself; he was thirsty but it took days before the idea of drinking occurred to him. He crawled in a delirium, with no personality or memories or sense of himself. He stumbled around thoughtlessly, falling and tripping, often lying on the ground in puddles or in bracken so his skin was scratched and bloodied, his clothes torn and made filthy.

He heard a murmur of voices but could not understand what was being said. He felt himself being picked up, manhandled onto the back of a cart. He stared upwards into the blue of the sky as the cart lumbered along, not knowing where he was going or why. He should have been afraid, but he couldn't even manage that.

They took him somewhere, laid him down. Someone removed his clothes and bathed him. Fed him water and some sort of broth; nursed him. He slept, for days and days. As he slept, his memories once more returned, but only partially. Now there were just dislocated and meaningless fragments.

*

After a very long time, Chang realised how great was the damage he had suffered. The effect, he realised, must be cumulative, a disruption on top of a disruption. The only thing he could do – and even that was an effort – was to shut down all the higher functions, the ones fed by the various implants, and operate more or less as nature had provided, by guesswork, memory and intuition. It was desperately hard.

This was Anterwold, then, Angela's invention, and as he slowly came round and began to observe it, he had to admit her achievement was extraordinarily impressive. Not for the first time, he was awestruck by her abilities. Every leaf and twig and insect seemed to be perfect. The climate fitted in logically with the vegetation, the vegetation with the wildlife, the wildlife with the society that had grown up inside it. He didn't like it, this primitive, dirty place with its simple bovine pleasures, its lack of movement and incurious approach to everything, but it undeniably worked.

He had no choice but to stay with the people who had found him. They gave him a name, Jaqui; they called him that because, apparently, he reminded them of some character in a story. They, not he, decided he was a hermit. He was expected to speak semi-nonsense and they were ready to interpret his mumbling confusion as wisdom. People began to ask him things, and nodded knowingly at his meaningless answers. Occasionally he saw some obvious stupidity and he could not help himself. He would, very briefly, access his memory to diagnose an illness and then say what should be done about it. He paid for that with splitting headaches but this infirmity, also, was seen as something almost holy. Others asked for advice:

should they get married? Would their child be healthy? Always he threw the question back: what do you want to do? This gained him a reputation for wisdom, which he did not deserve, and kindness, which he did not want. He wanted to be left alone, so he moved out of the village into an abandoned shepherd's hut where he wouldn't be so bothered. But still they came to ask questions and, in return, they fed him and looked after him. Slowly he realised how fortunate he was. He had permission to act strangely; it was expected. He wasn't going to starve or be locked up.

But he had to escape; weeks went by before he could reconstruct that last conversation with Angela and realise that his best chance of returning was long past. Six days, she had given him. He had missed it. Nor did he know where he had arrived, so he couldn't even go back there in the hope that, perhaps, the light would be there.

His one remaining chance was the emergency fallback. The fifth day of the fifth year at Willdon. What in God's name did that mean? They had heard of Willdon, but not what her instruction meant. But when it passed, Angela was going to try to shut the whole thing down. In theory, that could not be done if he and this girl were still in it, but he knew her well enough not to underestimate her. She might find a way. He did not want to be in here if she did.

*

Chang came across the scholar Etheran after he had been there for three months. He had left the village of Hooke which had adopted him as its mascot and gone wandering to try and find out what Anterwold was. He met Etheran

471

as he stopped at a wayside inn to beg for somewhere to sleep. The scholar watched as the landlord shook his head reluctantly. 'No room,' he said. 'Sorry.'

'May I beg you to reconsider?' the scholar said. 'He looks in need of rest.'

The kindness warmed him, and he answered the questions that followed. Where are you from? Why are you a hermit? He was unlike any person Chang had yet met in this static, unchanging place. There was a flicker of autonomy there and he knew he had to investigate it. Soon he became the one asking questions, pressing to see if Angela's defences had held up. Could Etheran begin to change, think, develop new ideas?

He probed for answers and found the man alarmingly responsive. He was stick-thin, with long arms and fingers, and he stroked his chin methodically as he listened. But his eyes shone with interest; he laughed with delight when he could not answer something. He seemed to enjoy the encounter.

Etheran even sought him out after he returned to Hooke. Chang deliberately tried to provoke him, to see how far he would go. But even when confronted with his ignorance, even when Chang made him feel like a fool, Etheran came back with questions of his own, and fumbling, confused answers.

It was a very peculiar experience; Etheran was educated and intelligent, but there were many things he simply could not understand, rather like a colour-blind person being told about the blue of the sky. What happened to send people into this exile everyone in Anterwold saw as the beginning of time? Why did they come back? When was this? A look of puzzlement, first at the questions, then at the realisation that they had never occurred to him before.

Etheran was overwhelmed at the thought that there was useful information that existed outside the great Story of Ossenfud. That the stones and rooftops of buildings could say something it could not. The look on his face would have been comical if Chang had not had some inkling of the sheer effort involved, and of the danger if he began to throw off the shackles of immobility.

He left it there that day, but over the next few weeks and months Chang talked to him some more, then wrote him letters, cajoling and encouraging, bitter and frustrated by turns, deliberately trying to push him to breaking point.

Eventually Etheran started coming up with ideas of his own. 'Could it be,' he said, 'that you could add together the rules of the domain holders, use them to date events? In the third year, or the twentieth year, of a person's rule?'

Once the idea had taken hold it grew in him. Surely you could also use records of birth, of marriage, all sorts of things? Just think what that might tell you . . . That was his last visit. Two days later Etheran left, his head brimming over with new ideas. But the effort was too much for him. Just as he was getting to the point of understanding, he died suddenly and alone and all his ideas were lost.

Angela's defences had held. Chang learned this from another scholar. This man, Henary, was brought in by the people of Hooke to look him over and see if he was dangerous. A curious encounter; the scholar did his duty, asked questions, but was clearly not very interested. He did not want to cause the hermit any difficulties, and Chang did not wish to experiment with him as well; Etheran had given him all the information he needed. So he kept him at arm's length, not least because he could discern little of Etheran's curiosity. Henary was a more sombre, less readable character altogether.

The encounter passed off without significance, until Henary told him of Etheran's death. Chang was sad and relieved at the same time. He had almost grown fond of the thin, eager figure, admired the immense efforts he made to break through into a new world of understanding. But it could not be done. Etheran's heart had given way, rather than allow him to take the next step. That was good, but Chang felt a stab of responsibility, almost as if Etheran had been a real person.

Only at the end did Henary give him something to think about. He was off to Willdon, he said. The seventh Festivity of Thenald . . .

*

After a few days, Chang left to investigate. He was lucky; after a day, a passing cart gave him a lift most of the way, exchanging the journey for company. The driver, whose name was Callan, was on his way back home.

'Tell me about this place.'

Willdon, Callan assured him, was the best, most beautiful, most fertile spot in the world. The trees were greener, the crops healthier, the birds fatter, than anywhere else. Only when the subject of the Lord of the domain came up did his face darken. 'Well,' he said, 'Thenald's a proud man. I suppose he has something to be proud of.'

'Perhaps he will die of old age?'

474

'Not him. Young and healthy, built like an ox.'

'Mellowed by children?'

'May such blessings be given him, but he's been married a year and no sign as yet. A lovely woman, cleverer than he is, I reckon.'

Chang pondered this as he slept on the floor of the soldier's hut that evening. What to do? The opportunity to go back would appear on the fifth day of the fifth year of the ruler of Willdon, that was what Angela said, and the current ruler was already in his seventh year and would remain in office until he died. So did he have to wait until then, then wait another five years after that? What if this Thenald lived for another twenty years?

He considered it some more when he first saw Thenald from a distance and realised how strong and healthy he was. He sat and meditated on his options, revolted by one, despairing at the other.

43

The Abasement had been particular to Willdon, and it was both impressive and strangely moving. Other places had similar things, of course, but none were so complete, brutal even, in their display. Henary stood lost in thought as the little party disappeared into the woods, and, though he knew perfectly well why they had left, he still allowed himself a flicker of frustration. Couldn't it have waited a day? Or even a few hours until they established what had happened to Rosalind? Well, no. It had to be on the precise day, at the precise hour, that Lady Catherine had ascended into her position as ruler of Willdon. Saying it wasn't convenient, that there were more important things, would have been noted and resented. It would have sapped her power, undermined her position.

At least, before she vanished into the forest, she had set in motion a thorough search. Her retainers and servants were scouring the grounds but Henary had few hopes that they would find anything. The ancient manuscript told him. The girl had fallen in love, and he was certain she had gone after the man whose affections she sought. She had not been coerced or forced. She had not been kidnapped. He almost wished she had been.

Would searching accomplish anything? The manuscript did not say. The fragments he had translated spoke of her; the rest was too difficult for him.

What to do now? He had no right to interfere in the affairs of Willdon; now she was stripped of her authority, Catherine's power lay in the hands of her Chamberlain. Until she returned, she was as good as dead, and her return would be greeted as a rebirth. But that would be in two days' time.

Henary had only spoken to the Chamberlain once or twice and had found him too – even. Too careful to say exactly what was required. Efficient, and loyal, no doubt; the nephew of Gontal, who was, in turn, the man who was most likely to inherit the domain if she did die.

'How is authority?' Henary asked as he walked back to the main house with him after the ceremony.

'I do as I am bidden,' was his only reply. 'As we all must do who serve.'

Witty conversation was not his strong point. 'Well, if you need any assistance. The disappearance of this girl . . .'

'Is a matter for Willdon. Not for visitors. Scholars must keep their minds on higher things, I'm sure you agree. I will endeavour to ensure that your thoughts are undisturbed.'

Mind your own business, in other words.

'You have the Story Hall at your complete disposal. Now, I must attend to domain business. Do excuse me . . .'

With a bow he walked off, giving Henary his due as a scholar by taking the first few steps backwards, but with an empty expression which undermined any pretence of deference. The Chamberlain did not want him there. Well, perhaps he had a point, Henary reflected as he turned obediently to go to work.

At least the suggestion that he keep out of the way was a good one. Henary spent the next few hours doing what he

477

loved most in the world, which was reading, slowly trying to decipher the document which was his obsession. He had many other things to look at; in the bag he had brought with him were the papers concerning Etheran which he had taken from the Story Hall and copied down, and the book which Jay had brought from Hooke. They were all, in their way, rebukes; they were all taunts, reminding him how flimsy his knowledge was. For the ones he could read made no sense, and the rest he could not read. But even ignorance and perplexity have their own peace.

*

On the next two mornings, Henary arose later than usual and ate quietly as he prepared himself for work. He had an empty time ahead of him until the return of Catherine and Jay, when life would get back to its normal course. There would be a ceremony to welcome her back – a blessedly short one this time, he hoped – and Catherine would be installed once more by acclaim. What else was taking place eluded him; there was no sign of the missing girl, or, if some news had been discovered, then it had been kept from him.

So he worked peacefully, if fruitlessly, until the time came to go down again to the point where garden and forest met, to await her return. A small party gathered and a larger group of servants and labourers, their families and friends, came together at a discreet distance, where they would watch the arrival, thrill to the sound of the trumpets and then take their share of wine and cake.

'Should be any moment now,' Henary said to the Chamberlain.

'Indeed, scholar,' he replied. 'A stickler for detail is Lady Catherine. If she were so much as a second late I would be worried. But I must say I would be just as surprised if she were a second early.'

'I suppose we are not allowed to eat or drink anything until she does appear?' Henary asked. He had worked long and hard, and was hungry.

'Oh, certainly. Go and help yourself. You are merely an observer. By all means, eat and drink your fill.'

So Henary passed the few remaining moments with a fine cake of nuts and honey in one hand and a glass of wine in the other. But no one came. Still, he thought, noon is a hazy notion. A few moments either way. It must be difficult to be precise when you are surrounded by trees.

After a while he walked back to the Chamberlain. 'Should they not be here by now?'

'I'm sure there is an explanation. Don't worry.'

'I am not. But you are. I can see it on your face.'

'No, no. Is that . . . ?'

But it wasn't; just a breath of wind blowing through the undergrowth.

The minutes passed. Then, when still nothing had happened, Henary spoke again. 'And now?'

'In theory or in practice?'

'Both.'

'In practice, we keep on waiting until she returns to us. In theory . . . Well, that is a little more serious.'

'How so?'

'The ceremony fills the vacancy in the lordship. Lady Catherine arrives, and I ask if she wishes to have the post. She signals her assent. I ask if any challenge her. There

479

should be silence. Then I declare her Lord and Lady of Willdon both by acclaim. If she is not here, then by midnight at the very latest I have to ask the question nonetheless. If none answer, then we must proceed to the person closest in blood to the family, and invite them to present themselves.'

'Oh, what a nuisance. Still, she will show up, I'm sure. Even if she doesn't, then she will be the next in line.'

'She will not. It is the closest in blood to the dead husband. She is not related by blood. She became Lord five years ago because of the exceptional circumstances. The closest in blood is Gontal, as you know, but you declined on his behalf when Thenald died. If he were to accept this time, then he would be the successor, not her. In a very short time now I will have to say so, in public.'

*

Sometimes, if you fear the worst, then the worst is summoned. At midnight, neither Lady Catherine nor Jay had appeared and the Chamberlain – who acted with extraordinary calm, going through the prescribed routine without emotion – did as he said he had to do. He declared the lordship vacant and announced that it was to be filled with the next in line to the family of Willdon. The new Lord, he said in a loud voice which had only the slightest tremor in it, was Gontal, scholar of Ossenfud, should he choose to accept. That he should present himself; that he should announce his wishes; and that the domain should, on his arrival, acclaim him as their Lord.

Henary could not sleep. Events had moved so fast, so disastrously, that he could scarcely take them in. The catastrophe would shake the whole of Anterwold. If Ossenfud took possession of Willdon, then it would become the dominant power in the land. Henary liked Gontal, oddly. But only when he was powerless, a complaining voice on the sidelines, forever bemoaning the slackness of others. Possessed of the ability to do something about his complaints, he might not be such an easy colleague.

There must be a way through. Everything that had happened had followed a script, a reading of the laws as laid down. He was certain of that. But laws have loopholes, exceptions and alternative interpretations. He had to find those, and quickly. He had to win Catherine some time.

He searched for many hours. Before dawn, as sleep would not come, he was at his seat, occasionally going over to the boxes lining the walls and taking down books and scrolls of precedents and customs, trying to find something in the long history of Willdon which would serve. He worked in the way he had always worked, with the discipline of the years. The only difference this time was that his concentration was total. Nothing interrupted the way his mind played on the problem.

But even he could not shut out everything. By mid-afternoon he was hungry and thirsty. He arose and went for some bread and water, and was eating when he heard a noise in the courtyard which presented Willdon's main face to the outside world, where the two sweeping arms of buildings reached forward, funnelling newcomers towards the main entrance and making all noise echo from wall to wall, louder than it actually was.

Henary walked over to the window. There in the courtyard was a large group of soldiers and others on horses, surrounding a single carriage. A grand carriage, of the sort you rarely see; Henary recognised it. The door opened, and Gontal got out and stretched himself. He had come to take possession with unseemly speed.

More to the point, how had he done it? Willdon was a good two days' journey from Ossenfud. Gontal must have set out with his troupe of followers long before news of Catherine's disappearance could possibly have reached him.

'I was on my way to the south, when we came across a messenger,' Gontal explained when Henary posed this very question. 'So we came straight here.'

'Is there some insurrection in the south that you are travelling with a bodyguard of – how many do you have there? – twenty people?'

'Well, you know. There are tales of outlaws in the forest . . .'

He went off to consult with the Chamberlain, leaving Henary standing, worried and disturbed.

But worry mixes no ink, as the old saying went. Soon enough, he returned to his work. He now had until midnight before the process began. That wasn't long.

Shortly before the appointed hour, Henary levered himself up and walked down to the courtyard for the ceremony. All was ready. The Chamberlain stood by the door through which the new Lord would enter. Below the shallow flight of stone steps leading up to it was the little group of people around Gontal, who was ready and prepared. He had waited for this for many years and now he was on the brink. He must be a happy man, Henary thought as he looked at the fat, unthreatening figure illuminated by the torches. You don't have to look dangerous to be so, of course.

Then a bell sounded and the small crowd stiffened in anticipation.

'Be it known to all that the lordship of Willdon must be filled for the good of all,' the Chamberlain announced, speaking the prescribed words perfectly. 'There is no Lord, and what must be done, shall be done. Only one person is of the family of Willdon, only one shall be Lord. If my statements do not conform to custom, then speak. If they do not conform to the truth, then speak. If my statements do not conform to the needs of all, then speak.'

There was a pause and a rustle of expectation from the crowd. The Chamberlain looked around, but had no chance to begin the next stage of the ceremony.

'I wish to speak,' said Henary in the loud voice that was reserved for the most thunderous moments of storytelling. 'I will say you do not speak the truth. You do not conform to custom, and you do not conform to the needs of all.'

There was silence, absolute and shocked. Henary dimly saw Gontal with a look of stunned fury on his face. Whatever happened, he had just thrown away years of distant friendship.

'You do not speak the truth, because the man here is not the closest in blood. You do not speak the truth, because there are other precedents which make this ceremony unjust. You do not speak the truth, because you are attacking the purity of the Story and undermining it with the temptations of power.'

That last was the most shocking of his statements, but Henary knew that it was the least substantial. This was not going to be a battle in which the good of all was going to be important. He had to hold the line on the law. He didn't have much. But he was fairly certain he had enough to overwhelm the Chamberlain for a while.

'If this man is not the closest, then who is?'

Henary paused. 'Pamarchon, son of Isenwar, son of Isenwar. Convicted murderer and outcast, but never punished, and so never divested of his rights nor expelled from his family. Until that is done, he is the rightful heir, unless an assembly choose another, as they did five years ago. Pamarchon has the better claim, and you may not appoint anyone to the position by right except him. Should you do so, then you will become an abomination. You will bring disgrace to all if you ignore my words, for I speak as a scholar of the first rank, and this is my judgement.'

No going back now, Henary thought to himself.

*

Once the ceremony had collapsed into chaos, Gontal's fury would have been overwhelming had not Henary been his superior in every way, and had Gontal not been well aware of this.

'What do you think you are doing?' he said in an icy tone when the two scholars confronted each other. 'My rights are clear and absolute. You dare not challenge them. I am the rightful Lord . . .'

'You are not,' Henary said. 'The case is clear, not your rights. I have spent all night reviewing the law. You would not be secure and you would be open to challenge and to discontent.'

'How so? I have already—'

'Already investigated? Just on the off-chance that this might happen?'

'Of course not. As the long-standing heir, naturally I investigated my position.'

'Naturally. I am sure you read the rules well. But you did not take into account mood. People. Life.'

'What does that have to do with anything? I don't know what you mean.'

'We must assume that although she is missing, Lady Catherine—'

'Catherine. Her name is Catherine. She has no position and so no title.'

'We must assume that she is not dead. But you cite rules for the death of the incumbent. Moreover, two people have to assure themselves that she is dead. As far as I am aware, no one has even sent out a search party. She is liked and respected, and if you use a technicality to supplant her it will earn you the distrust of all here. You may not care about that, but you should. It is important.

'Secondly, my statement was correct. Until he is expelled from his family, Pamarchon is the heir. He cannot be expelled until sentence is carried out. As long as he is alive and uncaptured, then your claim is invalid. You may in due course do as Catherine herself did, and be selected by the assembly. But you cannot take it by right and any presumption on your part would be challenged.'

'By you, I suppose?'

'By anyone who chooses to do so. Be patient. You must present yourself for election, as can anyone else. Besides, there is no alternative now I have spoken. Remember, I outrank you. My judgement is stronger than yours.'

Gontal's face was a picture of frustrated rage, of confusion, and of calculation. Eventually he smiled grimly. 'Well, Scholar Henary, you do always seem to be around to make my life that bit more difficult. Let us do as you say. Let us send out search parties. Let us call an assembly. Let us do everything properly so that you are satisfied. But bear in mind, when I am Master of Willdon, as I will be, I will remember this. The assembly will be in two days' time, as it has to be on the fifth day after the vacancy is declared. I can wait until then.'

The fifth day, Henary thought. And Catherine had been ruler of Willdon for five years.

44

When Jack More left, Oldmanter sat alone, his mind turning over the little he had learned. It was certainly most unfortunate. The loss of Angela Meerson was a great setback. He had known of her for more than half a century, and had spotted her when she was still young. He had seen the extraordinary potential there, but also noticed the lack of discipline. He had doubted then whether he could bring out the best in her, especially when her abilities had been artificially enhanced. The intervention, which he had paid for, had worked well but had made her even more ungovernable. Once he had made an approach to recruit her, but she had refused absolutely. His reputation, for once, had been a disadvantage.

Instead, she had gone from second-rate organisations to third-rate ones, always creating some dispute and walking out, on one occasion resigning before she had even arrived to take up her position. Maybe she was a genius, but most people had long since concluded that she would never deliver anything of worth, that she would be one of the might-have-beens of science.

Perhaps so; but Oldmanter, whose success rested mainly on his attention to detail, tracked her erratic progress until she ended up in Hanslip's outfit. A poor end indeed. Hanslip was never better than mediocre. He lacked the skill, the vision, the determination ever to create anything more than a minor operation. Only his vanity was larger than average.

Yet, somehow, he had allowed Meerson to flourish. He had left her alone and slowly news of her efforts began to be picked up by Oldmanter's vast intelligence operation. The work on energy transmission, the early experiments. The theoretical underpinnings. They never got hold of much fine detail, but gathered enough to guess that something truly interesting was taking place on the island of Mull. Then Hanslip himself had approached and explained exactly what Meerson had done. He wanted a partnership, and thought his possession of the technology would match Oldmanter's resources.

Hardly. Oldmanter had no partners, no collaborators. Hanslip's audacity on its own was enough to merit a sharp lesson to remind the world who was truly in charge. Hanslip would, one way or another, hand over the technology. He would take what he was given in return, and that might not be much.

Still, what the man laid out was breathtaking in its ambition. Much of science now was dedicated to squeezing out extra resources, finding marginal improvements and efficiencies. Man could not go to the stars. Several centuries of effort and human ingenuity had got nowhere. Space was just too big, and no one wanted to set off on a journey so that their great-great-grandchildren could reap the dubious reward of life on some dead lump of rock a billion miles away.

On top of that, the idiots of the early period of exploration had filled near space with so much debris that they had created a new asteroid belt, all but impossible to get through.

Mankind locked itself onto its own planet through sheer untidiness. Meanwhile, nothing stopped the constant expansion of humanity. Wars slowed things down a bit every now and then. Starvation, mass executions, birth control, all had been tried and had failed. As the amount of space to live in shrank, as the earth became exhausted, so the population continued to grow; now there were more than thirty billion people crammed onto a world which only supported and fed them through the constant, never-ending efforts of the elite, who organised and controlled everything with efficiency in mind. It had to be like that, otherwise chaos and collapse would result. Often enough programmes had been advanced to eliminate the useless population; sometimes they were even put into effect. They never worked. All that happened was that discontent rose, the renegades attracted more sympathisers and civil unrest increased to the point that the rulers' control threatened to slip.

As Hanslip explained it, Meerson had swept all of this away with a simple question – why squeeze out more from what we have? Why not just get more of everything? She opened up a vista of infinity and eternity. Billions of years and billions of universes there for the taking. Even Oldmanter, used to vast power, could not have imagined something of such grandeur. Now that she had done so, he knew that he alone could make proper use of it. He wanted it, and so he decided to take it.

Besides, so his reasoning went, what if it fell into the wrong hands? There were millions of renegades in the world, whose appetite for destruction was insatiable. He had argued long and often that they should be dealt with once and for all, but still they flourished like weeds, and few really seemed to care. They were the ones who removed themselves and criticised from the sidelines, doubting and scorning the efforts of their superiors, exploiting every disaster or failing in order to undermine the well-being of the world's society. They were the ones behind the riots, the terrorism, the strikes, the ones who sabotaged the factories to make some self-destructive point about liberty and freedom. As if people really wanted to be free and hungry.

What if they got hold of this technology? What if they withheld access to it until their demands were met? Worse still, what if they spread their stupidity like some virus across the universes? This discovery needed to be kept in the right hands. Colonists would have to be screened for obedience. If that was done, then Oldmanter could see in his mind the immense possibilities of world after world, each with vast untapped resources, trading with each other through channels which his organisation would control and tax. Each would specialise, each would produce efficiently and in unlimited quantities. But only if they were ruled by the best, and only if the populations did as they were told. Keeping control would be hard. Security would be the hardest task of all, and would require a huge investment.

He wished to give a last, great gift to humanity. He had worked and schemed for years, decades, to maintain order, to ensure that even those who could not see or understand their best interests were nonetheless governed by them. Sometimes, in councils and meetings, he operated through persuasion. At other times, with rivals and the masses, he used more direct methods.

He did not always get his way, of course not. But he was rarely defeated for ever. Thirty years ago he had proposed to end the toleration of renegades and dissidents. A single and thorough policy of elimination to dispose of people who produced little, contributed less and consumed far too much administrative time. For the benefit of the majority, the minority would have to go. He was defeated; one of his rare reverses. Now he wished to revisit the issue. All critics and dissidents would have to be removed before this new opportunity could be exploited safely, otherwise nothing would happen. There would be objections, proposals to amend his plans, claims that others should have their say.

*

When reports came in that Angela's programme was getting close to the testing phase, Oldmanter had started to manoeuvre his way into winning control of the technology and found, to his surprise, that it was barely necessary. Hanslip actually came to him, dropping hints and proposals, talking of other interested parties, rival bidders. Well, let him convince himself of his genius at negotiation, if it pleased him and made him more malleable. The only thing that mattered was the result, and that was slowly dropping into his lap. He submitted to endless meetings but eventually lost patience and summoned Lucien Grange.

'Go to Mull and wrap this one up, if you please. I can't stand listening to that man any more.'

'What do you want?'

'Everything. The entire institute. That way we can hide what we are really interested in until we are ready. I don't want the World Council demanding a say in how it is developed. I want to be sure that by the time anyone hears about it, it will be too late to challenge me. There's a woman there called Meerson. You may remember her. Steer clear but make sure you secure her services, willingly given or not. She's vital. Keep her team, get rid of everyone else.'

'What about the terms? You've been talking about a fifty–fifty split. Is that still the case?'

'Certainly not. Give Hanslip nothing if you can; that will teach him not to waste my time. You have the information needed to access the computers; copy the relevant documentation, get legal possession, then kick him out.'

*

That was the last anyone heard of Lucien Grange, apart from a brief message a week later saying that he had acquired the data and would be back the following day. The next thing Oldmanter knew was that there had been an almighty power surge across northern Europe that had caused chaos. In the outrage and confusion that followed, none had been more outraged and confused than Hanslip, who put out a furious demand with surprising speed that the people responsible be caught and punished immediately. Curious. Oldmanter tried to get hold of Grange to see what was going on but – nothing. He did not reply to messages, could not be tracked, and when Oldmanter asked Hanslip's institute, he was told only that Grange had left the island of Mull and was no longer their responsibility. After that his calls went unanswered.

The tracking devices suggested that Grange had not left the island but, at the same time, there was no evidence he was still on it. They had simply stopped functioning, which could not happen. That made no sense, so Oldmanter sent some people to keep the island under surveillance. They picked up More leaving and hurrying south. More then confirmed that Angela was missing, and that data had been lost. So he watched, and saw More go to the Retreat. It didn't take much investigation to work out why. He was going to contact Angela Meerson's child, the result of the enhancement Oldmanter had organised for her eighteen years ago.

Oldmanter had only the faintest outline of what it meant, but he had enough to realise it was time to take command of the situation. He announced that Hanslip was a suspect in the power surge case, hinted strongly that he was in league with terrorist renegades and demanded that he surrender control of his institute. He gave him three hours to comply and mobilised his troops, which he placed at the disposal of the world community to eradicate the danger that had suddenly sprouted in their midst. What if, he said to his colleagues on the Council who contacted him, the attack on northern Europe was merely the first in a wave of attacks? A trial run before the real assault began?

At the same time he put out an alert for Jack More as the link between the institute and the terrorists. He had uncovered a monstrous plot of treachery and vowed to take the lead in punishing those responsible. If anyone had doubted the need to wipe out the Retreats, surely this hideous crime should sweep such qualms aside once and for all.

45

'It seems the domain of Willdon is flooding us with surplus people. I have found you another unwanted guest, I'm afraid,' Antros said to Pamarchon when he returned to the camp with the lost boy in tow.

'Another one? Who is it this time?' Pamarchon was agitated. The arrival of the prisoners, the shooting of one of them, made him feel his grip was not as tight as it needed to be. If he could not trust his men to obey orders, act carefully and sensibly . . .

'A strange one. He speaks as well as you say this lady spoke. I think it probable that he knows her.'

'Really?' he said with quickening interest. 'Did he say so?'

'No. He was in shock, and I did not question him. He was wandering lost in the forest, and had ventured into a copse of the dead.'

Pamarchon grimaced.

'He had no idea it was forbidden,' Antros said. 'I thought I should bring him here.'

'Yes. You did exactly right.' He sighed. 'Antros, dear friend, I must tell you something.'

'What?'

'I am in love.'

'Oh,' Antros said in relief. 'That. I noticed. I thought you were going to cancel our plans, or something serious.'

'This is serious. Did you really notice?'

'I'm afraid so.'

'Please don't laugh. I was struck the moment I saw her. I could barely speak, couldn't even see closely, I was trembling so much. I have never felt like it before. Since the Festivity, I find that Rosalind is all I can think of. I know I should be worrying about other things, but I haven't slept or eaten since then. I worry that she bewitched me or cursed me.'

'Do you think so?'

'No, it is only my own foolishness, but I cannot shake it off. What am I to do?'

'I have absolutely no idea,' Antros said, trying hard not to laugh. 'What are you meant to do? You could kill yourself, like Vatel in Level 3. Or wander the land dressed in rags, like Hipergal. Or you could rush in and carry her off, like . . .'

Pamarchon held up his hand. 'Stop! I am a desperate man, and do not need to be made fun of as well. I can cope with danger and condemnation. I can live off my wits and lead men into a fight. But I have no idea what to do about this.'

Antros thought. 'Talk to the boy about it,' he said. 'If you are in love, as you say, it would be best to find out who you are in love with, no?'

*

As Pamarchon went off to check the night watch, Antros told the peculiar youth that he was to eat with their chieftain that evening, so that he might be welcomed and questioned. He thought it might distract his friend, at least.

He loved nothing better than to converse with the educated and there was little possibility of that at the camp. He had gathered good, stout people around him, but their conversation rarely rose above the simplest levels.

So, as the sun was setting, he led the boy Ganimed to the area which Pamarchon reserved for himself, where their leader's awning stretched down from a huge old oak tree, and a clearing in front was set with the low table brought from inside and rough cushions to sit on. The food was already laid out and lanterns had been placed around to provide faint illumination. The student's servant was there too, to pour the drink and serve the food. It was a measure of the boy's strangeness that initially he talked to her as though she were a guest as well.

Pamarchon made the lad sit on the cushion opposite him while they talked, every now and then being interrupted as one or other of the other outlaws – Pamarchon's closest companions – came up.

'This is Djon,' he said, introducing the vast man who had carried the injured Callan back to the camp. 'A good heart, and good man,' he added as Djon clasped the boy's hand in his huge paw.

For some reason the boy looked sceptical. 'And your real name is Robin Hood, I suppose.'

'No. Why do you think that?'

'Oh, it doesn't matter.'

'This woman, this Rosalind,' he said, bringing the topic of conversation around to her as soon as he possibly could. 'You must know her. Are you part of her entourage? A relation? I confess there is a likeness between you, though she is more beautiful by far.'

The boy frowned as though he didn't know what to say to this, and kept silent.

'Come, my lad! Don't be shy! You are amongst friends here, and if you are indeed one of the Lady Rosalind's then you are doubly safe, for I would willingly die to save you for her sake, were you in any danger.'

The boy opened his mouth, shut it again and finally said, with some hesitation, 'I am certainly connected to her. A relation, indeed. I might even say her closest confidant. As near to a brother as she has.'

'Wonderful!' Pamarchon said. 'Then did she mention that we met at the Festivity of Willdon?'

'She mentioned many people. She met so many she could not possibly remember them all.'

'I spent an hour with her, as her escort.'

'Ah! Then she did mention you. Briefly.'

'Did she speak well of me?'

'Not so much.'

'No?'

'She found your manners a little rough, sir. Queer, if you like. So naturally she could not be well disposed to you. You left her abruptly and insulted her. I believe it was the second time you had turned your back on her.'

'That pains me greatly,' the outlaw said.

'I fear you got no measure of her,' his guest replied sadly. 'Her manners and customs are very different, and if you do not know them, then certainly she will choose one of her other suitors.'

'She will choose? What about her family?'

'They will have no say in the matter. She is headstrong and will have no interference in anything which concerns

497

her happiness and fortune. She may choose no one, and have lovers instead.'

There was a brief noise as the servant dropped a plate on the ground. 'I am so sorry, my Lord,' she said, her head bowed in evident shame so that her hair covered her face.

Pamarchon had forgotten she was there. 'Go away now. You may return to clear up later. And don't call me "my Lord". I am not so.'

Then he turned back to his guest. 'Pray continue, young man,' he said as the servant withdrew. 'I must ask you frankly, how may I win her?'

*

Once the servant had risen and left, Pamarchon reclined on the cushion behind him so that he could stare up at the stars. The boy moved closer to the fire and shivered slightly.

'Would you like a cloak?'

'No. I'm fine.'

'Now we are really alone, I wish you to speak freely.'

The boy poked the fire with a stick. 'How may you win her? What a question,' he said after a while. 'It depends what you mean by win, really. Going to one such as she and saying – come and live in a tent in the forest for the rest of your life? I mean, that isn't going to go down very well, is it now?'

Pamarchon did not reply.

'She is used to courteous behaviour, and you live as an outlaw, taking prisoners, holding people against their will. You are surrounded by some sort of army. This is not so appealing.'

'I live according to my circumstances, as I must.'

'That woman who served your food, for example. Who is she?'

'I do not know. The servant of the student we found wandering in the forest.'

'Are they here of their own free will?'

'No. I suspect they are spying for the Lady of Willdon.'

'So they are prisoners?'

'For the time being. They will come to no harm, as long as they behave themselves.'

'You still go about imprisoning anyone who takes your fancy, for whatever reason you choose. That's not very nice of you.'

'It is necessary. I do not do it from choice.'

'That is the second time you have said that your life is not your fault. Perhaps someone who is in charge of their own life might be more appealing. To her you are just a rough outlaw. Perhaps a criminal, a liar, a cheat. Maybe cruel and violent. Why would anyone want such a person? However handsome,' he added.

Pamarchon was looking distressed.

'Yes, she thinks you handsome. You do not face an impossible task. All is not lost. Far from it. I would say that you could win her, if you wished.'

'I do! More than anything in the world.'

'Then you must explain yourself to me. What are you doing living here, like this? Tell me all and I will give my advice. I do not promise anything. Talk to me as if you were talking to her, remembering that she can scent a lie at a great distance. If you can win me over, you may be able to win her over as well.'

'You want a tale? Very well. You shall have one.'

His guest held up a hand. 'That's a bad start. You're supposed to be talking to a lady you love more than life itself. You shouldn't sound so grumpy about it. Try again.'

'Well,' he said, 'I live in the forest because five years ago I was falsely accused of a terrible crime. It was said that I murdered my uncle, Thenald, Lord of Willdon, in order to gain his land and position. It was completely false, but there was nothing I could do; the verdict was swiftly given, and I was to be killed. I escaped, and since then have wandered the land as a vagrant and outlaw. Others have gathered around me, and now I am strong enough to win justice for myself and for the people who place their trust in me. That is why, in a short time, I hope to be able to offer Lady Rosalind everything that a woman of her position would require. In addition, I will add my loyalty and devotion, and if that is in doubt you may query anyone here, for I have helped and nurtured them all.'

'You speak with defiance. That is not unattractive. Indeed, I am sure that any woman would find it beguiling, even hard to resist. Almost impossible, I would say. Until she considers this: what trust can be put in your words? I imagine this land has courts and laws. You were found guilty in them. Becoming rich is often enough considered a reason for murder. That is in many books I have read. Can you prove you are innocent?'

Pamarchon reached out and took the boy by the hand. 'I cannot, at present. All I can do at the moment is this,' he said, coming closer. 'Hold her hand and swear to her on my life that everything I say is true, that I would die rather than lie to her. I would beg her to trust me, for without her trust life would have no value to me. But are you all right? You are trembling.'

'I'm . . . chilly,' said the boy breathlessly. 'Just cold, that is all. The night air, you know. Nothing else, I assure you.'

'In that case, sit nearer the fire. Better now?'

'Much, thank you,' he said, swallowing hard. 'Why don't you just sit there, further away . . . further than that . . . and tell me what happened?'

Pamarchon ensured that the boy was well wrapped up in a blanket, and began once more. 'Very well. The entire story, if you wish. As I say, my uncle was the Lord of Willdon, who married the Lady Catherine only a little before my troubles began. Until then I was his only heir. I was a happy enough boy, and had been taught by the Lord of Cormell. I finished there at the age of sixteen.'

'So you are how old now?'

'Twenty-four years.'

'Twenty-four! That is a good age. A very good age. Lady Rosalind is much younger, though. You do not think that a problem?'

'How old is she?'

'Fifteen.'

'Well past the age of marrying. It would be sad if she became an old maid.'

'Ah. Anyway, you were saying?'

'I was able to read and write, ride a horse, converse well with many people, do all the things I needed to do. I was, dare I say it, popular with my contemporaries and had few cares in this world.

'Then, as my parents were both dead, I went to Willdon to live with my uncle and learn the business of being domain holder. I was dutiful; I learned about crops and people, animals and buildings, although I had little taste for these things. My only difficulty was Thenald, who was a cruel man. They were dark days for all; he was unflinching in the application of his rights, and diligent only in seeking out new ones. He discovered taxes long forgotten and imposed them without mercy. He taxed those who wished to marry; taxed again those wishing to grind corn. He found reasons to expel people from their holdings. He was suspicious and vengeful. He feared being attacked by those he had wronged. He hired more and more soldiers to defend himself, and so had to raise ever more money to pay them. The soldiers were billeted in every village and hamlet, at their expense, and he found the most brutal people to do his bidding.

'I did what I could, but I knew that if I crossed him then he would dispossess me and I would be unable to give even the small amount of assistance I could offer by staying put. There was always the chance that he would die, and then I would be able to heal the wounds he had inflicted. So I kept quiet, which was a mistake. I should have challenged him, but he had the scholars of Ossenfud behind him.'

'Why?'

'Because he gave them money. So I thought, at least. In fact, he had no intention of passing the domain to me. He was going to give it to one of the colleges. They would continue the work of despoiling the land to enrich themselves, and extend their power further across the whole of Anterwold.'

'Now, you see,' the boy interrupted, 'that is quite different from everything I have heard. I got the impression that these scholars were sort of peaceable folk, who didn't hold with money, dedicated to learning . . .'

'I suppose there are some like that, but only because they are kept in check by the domains and towns. Many are greedy for power. Gontal, Thenald's cousin, is such a man.

'My uncle could not talk to someone without betraying him. He promised Willdon to me, and to Gontal, and then he married Catherine. She is, as you noticed, beautiful and intelligent, but she proved herself to be ambitious and ruthless also. Thenald was bewitched by her, although I doubt she ever had any regard for him. I thought that she would at least be a dutiful wife and provide him with children, but I underestimated her. Within a few months my uncle was dead, murdered in the forest.'

'Stop. How was he murdered?'

'He went out hunting and was found a few hours later, stabbed to death.'

'No chance it was an accident?'

'It's hard to stab a man on a horse by accident.'

'So it is.'

'Within the hour there was a cry after me, and all were saying I had done it. So I went into hiding.'

'And you didn't do it?'

'I was nowhere near the spot, although I could not prove it. If I had been, I would surely have saved his life, even at the cost of my own. I did not like him, but he was one of my people, my family. I could no more have killed him than myself.'

'So you were suspected because you stood to get Willdon, if you waited then Lady Catherine might have a baby, and you didn't like him. These are all good reasons for thinking you guilty.'

He nodded. 'Good enough for them to begin a court hearing, and find me so without even hearing my story.'

'I imagine they decided that your disappearance was proof of your guilt.'

'They were determined to find me guilty. The funny thing was that I did not want Willdon. It was never my dream. Gathering taxes and attending weddings and funerals. Listening to petty squabbles and complaints. Who would want such a thing who had any life in them? I would have done it, it was my duty, but I also wished my uncle a long life, for his life was my freedom.'

'What did you want to do? Run around and play games?'

'No.' Here he smiled sadly and looked almost embarrassed. 'I wanted to be a voyager. To see things no one had ever seen before. To go places, cross the seas even. To discover strange lands and unknown peoples. To find out who they are and how they live. You think I am foolish.'

'On the contrary. I . . . I mean, my Lady Rosalind thinks exactly the same.'

'Does she? Really?'

'Oh, yes. Ever since she was a little girl, she has wanted to go on long sea voyages. To America and India. See the pyramids, the lions of Africa, the Great Barrier Reef. To watch the sun set into the Pacific Ocean, see the snows of the Himalayas . . .'

'I have never heard of these places. But oh, dear young boy! You make me feel even worse. You make me love her more.'

'Tell me what you would do. If she decided to have you, that is.'

'I would gather a band of fellows. Good, stout men I could

rely on. I would fit out a ship and we would set sail. She and I and them. Then south, looking out for settlements on the land which lies that way. We would see if there is a sea beyond that, and sail into it. We would stop every night and pitch our tents on a sandy beach. Talk to anyone we found. We would take someone who knows about drawing, to make sketches of the buildings and people we saw. We'd bathe in the sea and feast on the shore.'

'And when you were done? What then?'

'We'd never be done! Do you think the world is so small? We would go on and on, into the sunrise and back to the sunset, until we were too old to travel any more. We would grow old together, she and I, free of duties and obligations.'

'Now we're on to Ulysses.'

'What?'

The boy let out a long sigh. 'Nothing. It does sound lovely! What about monsters? Hostile natives?'

'I'd kill the first, befriend the second.'

'Food and clothing?'

'We'd take what we could, buy what we needed. I would have money, you see. If only . . .'

Here his face fell once more. 'If only I wasn't a fugitive, penniless and hunted.'

'You think Lady Catherine was responsible.'

'Who else? She won the most powerful domain in Anterwold on my ruin.'

'What are you going to do now?'

'I want my name back. It will not be given, so it must be taken.'

'That doesn't sound good.'

'It is as it will be.'

'And that sounds meaningless.'

He glared disapprovingly, then softened his expression. 'You do not understand, I think. Nor will you tonight. It is late. I wish to sleep, and you are yawning. Come, stay with me and share my bed.'

'What? Absolutely not.'

'Whatever is the matter?'

'I couldn't. No. That is a terribly bad idea. Really, it is. Terribly bad. I wouldn't sleep a wink.'

Pamarchon looked bemused. 'As you wish,' he said. 'In that case I will summon the servant to find you something else.'

*

'This is my honoured guest,' Pamarchon said when the servant returned. 'You will look after him as you would me, or your own master. Better, in fact. He deserves the greatest courtesy, young though he is. Take him to a place where he can sleep peacefully.'

'Where would that be?'

'I'd forgotten. You do not know the camp. I'm afraid I must ask you to share with our other visitor. We will make better arrangements for you tomorrow.'

The servant bowed. 'This way, young master. Goodnight, sir. Do you wish me to return?'

Pamarchon smiled. 'No, woman. It is late, and you have been wearied enough at my hands today. Go and sleep yourself. May both of you have dreams which bring you delight and rest.'

When the dinner was over, Pamarchon knew he would not be able to sleep. The discussion had put his spirit into turmoil. He had been a coward; he knew the moment she sat down who this boy Ganimed really was. It was understandable that Antros had not realised; he had never met her and her manner of dress disguised her well. But the moment he set eyes on her, he had felt that now familiar leaping in his heart.

He had kept up the pretence because he doubted he could have spoken to her so well and openly if she had frankly confessed who she was. So he had poured out his heart, asking if there was any chance that she could look favourably on him.

She had said that there was. She had said she could love him, maybe. For a moment, Pamarchon allowed himself to hope, and imagined himself with her, standing at the front of a great ship as it sailed the seas . . .

Then he returned to earth. He was, as she had said, an outlaw, skulking on the fringes of society. She was right; this had gone on too long. It was time to act.

He walked quietly over to Antros's tent and poked his head inside. 'Antros, my friend,' he said. 'I have decided. We start tomorrow. Warn the men we need, and get them ready to receive their instructions in the morning. Djon will be in charge; he will take three others. They are to go to Ossenfud and conceal themselves there. If this is not settled here by then, in five days they will carry out our plan for the Story Hall.'

46

Angela's explanation at lunch left Rosie feeling distressed. Shut Anterwold down? She made it sound no more than switching off a television, except they were real people in that television, living and breathing. What would happen to them? For the first time, she began to feel overwhelmed by the immense complexity of her situation. What would her own responsibility be if she stood aside and let it all happen? Accessory to murder on a huge scale?

Why couldn't Anterwold be left in peace? It wasn't as if it was doing anyone any harm. Was she wise, really, to put quite so much trust in this woman? She assumed Angela was telling the truth about bouncing back from the future, because that was the best way of explaining the unusual contents of Professor Lytten's cellar. But her tale of having to run from bad people . . . was that so believable? What if Angela was the bad one and the people chasing her were the good ones? What if she was placing her trust in a dangerous criminal? Even a total lunatic? How was she meant to tell the difference? What sort of person could talk so calmly about wiping out an entire universe?

What did she, Rosie Wilson, want? It was curious. When she had been in Anterwold it had seemed entirely natural, while life at home had become like a vague dream. Now she was back, this seemed the only solid thing. Anterwold was now like a faint memory of a summer holiday. Lying on her lumpy bed at home, she could no more imagine spending the rest of her life there than she could imagine spending it on the beach in Devon. Pamarchon was like – what? – a holiday romance, knowing it would only be for a week or so. You exchange addresses, promise to write, and never do.

*

Coming back from holiday can be a bit of a shock, though, and Rosie realised she would have to pay a high price for her pleasures. There'd be detention at school, for a start, and she'd be lucky she wasn't expelled for lying about the choir rehearsal when in fact she had been off with some boy. She hadn't been, not really, but it was the most likely way of accounting for her brief disappearance. Then her parents; with them she didn't have to guess their reaction. The moment she had come through the door – plucked, manicured and groomed – they had gone through the roof. The screaming of her mother, the threats of the belt from her father. Even her brother – no loyal ally he – had stepped in on her behalf, the first time he had ever done such a thing.

For the first time also, Rosie stood her ground. She refused absolutely to say where she had been. She threatened dire consequences if anyone so much as laid a finger on her. She scorned their lack of trust, their willingness to believe the worst. They shouted, Rosie shouted back. They advanced menacingly, she wagged her finger and threw a plate. They were aghast at the way she stood up to them and gave as good as she got, and it finished with her parents making grim predictions about the likely course of her life. Rosie replied that, whatever her life became, it wasn't going to be as boring as theirs, a comment which set the entire argument going again.

At the end she commanded the room in triumph, while her parents retreated into the kitchen to wash dishes and mutter about how she hadn't heard the end of it.

Of course not; they had already called the police, reported her missing, set off a search. Now they wanted the police to come round and frighten her with talk of reformatories for fallen women. Unfortunately, the policeman had been fairly relaxed about it when he finally turned up the next morning. Rosie had come back eventually, he pointed out, and it was obvious that she had not been in any real trouble.

'She seems quite unharmed,' Sergeant Maltby had said reassuringly. 'They often do things like this, you know. Young people are not what they were. I will make enquiries to see if she has been up to something, if you like, but I suggest you leave her be until she is ready to talk.'

Although if I had parents like that, he thought, I wouldn't say a word to them.

*

Rosie was quite invigorated by the fight with her parents and the unforeseen victory. Although she was distressed to have upset them, she told herself that she had done nothing wrong whatsoever and, in any case, there was no point in explaining. That didn't mean that she was keen to have another fight, so she was not pleased when the doorbell rang the next morning and her mother let in Angela Meerson.

She tried to keep the visitor out, saying that Rosie was indisposed and could not be disturbed, but Angela brushed her aside.

'That is completely irrelevant,' she said loftily. 'I need to interview her.'

'You can't. It's quite impossible.'

'In that case I will call the police.'

That did the trick. Rosie's mother blanched at the thought of yet another police car arriving, of Rosie being dragged off in full view of the entire street.

'It's a serious matter,' Angela went on. 'Now, go and get her.'

Five minutes later, a deeply suspicious-looking, tired and sullen Rosie appeared, very different from the confident young woman she had taken for lunch the previous day.

'Miss Wilson, I am instructed under the authority of the Official Secrets Act to take you away for assessment as pertaining to your condition thereof.'

'What?'

'You are coming with me.'

'I don't want to. I've had enough.'

'That doesn't matter. Your assistance is vital. Matters of state. Highest importance.'

Rosie scowled, then nodded.

'Good. Come along, then.'

As they left, Angela nodded at her mother, who had a strange look on her face.

'I do hope you are not under any misapprehension here,' she said sternly. 'You look disapproving and censorious, and it does nothing for your appearance, which is poor enough already. MI6 has great admiration for this fine young woman, whose service to her country is known to those who matter. Judging by your sour expression, you seem to be imagining all sorts of ridiculous things. So let me make it clear. This is a matter of the highest secrecy, Rosie will not discuss it with you and you will not question her. You do not have her level of clearance. Is that understood?'

*

'I am most terribly sorry if you are in any trouble with your parents,' Angela said after a while. 'I assume you are. You could have cut the atmosphere with a knife in there. I'm sure it is all my fault, apart from the problems caused by your own reckless curiosity.'

'That's not much of an apology.'

'I don't get much practice. But I did my best to help.'

'Mummy did look a bit stunned. It was the idea of a grateful nation which got her.'

'I suggest that if they do ask, you look secretive, tap your nose knowingly and mutter something about need to know. Now, I need your help.'

'I'm not sure I want to give it. I'm not upset about my parents. I'm upset about you.'

'Why?'

'You want to shut Anterwold down. That's what you said. I think that's a horrid thing to do.'

Angela groaned. 'Oh, really! Rosie, there is no time for this. Something bad is happening, and I may have to go in myself to sort it out.'

'Can I come?'

'No. You are already there. That's what I mean.'

'But I'm here.'

'Yes. And there. Probably.'

Rosie squinted at her. 'Both at the same time?'

'Indeed.'

'I hope you noticed how calmly I responded to that?'

'You are doing very well. What I have realised is that when you came back, the rings you were wearing confused the machinery, as your profile did not match the one you had when you went through. It didn't know whether to allow you back or block you, so it did both. Which was lucky, as if it had done neither, heaven only knows what would have happened to you. That was the sticky feeling you had. At that moment it duplicated you. One version – you – came back. The other stayed in Anterwold. As long as you are there, I cannot shut it down.'

'Good.'

'It is not good. I still don't know what Anterwold is but eventually a logical sequence of events will connect it to now. Here. When that happens, all sorts of unpleasant consequences might follow.'

'Why not pleasant ones?'

'An entire universe rampaging around like a bull in a china shop is unlikely to be pleasant. Anything which doesn't fit will be erased.'

'You told me you knew what you were doing.'

'I may have been a little optimistic,' she said with the greatest reluctance. 'I didn't put you into my calculations. Or several other things either. How much do you know about Anterwold's origins? Where it came from?'

'Nothing. The people there talk about the giants. But they never really refer to anything before the return from exile, and I don't know what that was or where they came from.'

'It was an idea Henry got from the Dorian Greeks, I think. They didn't know where they came from either. Or care.'

'There might be clues in the Story. Jay says his teacher, Henary, is the wisest of the wise, so you could ask him. Or, of course, you could just ask Professor Lytten. It's his thing, after all.'

Angela stopped. 'Do you know, that idea never occurred to me? Thank you.'

'What do you need to know, anyway?'

'The first thing is whether it is in the future or the past relative to here.'

'Well, that's easy,' Rosie said. 'The future, of course.'

'How do you know?'

'*Casablanca*. They think of that song in *Casablanca* as being ancient beyond belief, and the Professor told me it was made twenty years ago. It's the same with other songs too.'

'You might have mentioned this earlier.'

'You never asked. I still don't see what would be so terrible if Anterwold survives.'

'It would be catastrophic.'

'Why?'

'Well, I wouldn't be born, for one thing.'

Rosie stared. 'Wow,' she said.

'What?'

'I have heard of vanity, but never on that scale before.'

'I didn't mean . . .' Angela began in a flustered tone. 'At least I don't think that material existence would be improved if there were two of me.'

'Good. One of you has made quite enough mess. Think what two would do.'

'Stupid girl.'

'I am not,' Rosie responded stoutly, 'and don't you dare talk to me like that. Don't you dare.'

'Keep a civil tongue in your head.'

'I am.'

The two glared at each other.

'You turn up and decide to meddle with the whole of history just because you want to teach someone a lesson?'

'It's not like that.'

'Well, it sounds like it. And you go and say that a lot of really nice people are going to be snuffed out because you feel like it?'

'You don't understand. I didn't ask you to go nosing around down there.'

'You don't understand either. You don't know what's happened, or what will happen, or why it's happened. Do you? Go on. Tell me you do.'

Angela scowled at her. No one had talked to her like that for a long time, and she did not enjoy the experience.

'I knew it!' Rosie said triumphantly. 'You haven't got a clue.'

'No. I don't know,' she said. 'I am simply afraid.'

'That's the only reason? I don't know what happens next either. No one does. You're not meant to.'

'As you wish. But still, there can only be one future. Either Henry's story or reality will have to go.'

'How do you know yours is reality? Maybe it's just a story as well?'

Angela ignored the remark and walked on. After a few

515

steps she realised she was on her own. Rosie was standing still in the middle of the pavement.

'What is it now?'

'All those people, they're just puppets? Acting out the Professor's book?'

'Unfortunately not. If they were I wouldn't be so worried. They all have perfectly free will, as much as anyone does. It's all a bit Calvinist, if you like. Just because your choice is predetermined does not mean you do not have a free choice before you take it. In the case of your friends there, for example, they react to you in the way they wish.'

'It would be interesting to meet me.'

'That is a bad idea. Besides, what if you thought of yourself as you think of yourself? I would hate this to be resolved by one of you murdering the other. How would you divide up your boyfriend in there? I don't think Henry built bigamy into his world view. You'd have to put up with someone else having him. Just think what a difficult position that would put him in.

'One more thing. The reason I'm worried is that they shouldn't be doing anything. Henry hasn't written a story, only notes. He never finishes anything. Anterwold was meant to be a snapshot. I designed it so that nothing could happen. No causes, no effects, no consequences. But it has started moving because of you, and I don't know where it is going.

'And,' she said finally, 'if it makes you feel any better, I don't know that my world isn't just a story as well. If you knew the hideous complications that might involve, you wouldn't be looking quite so smug. Now, come along.'

*

Angela opened the front door to Lytten's house and walked into the hallway, then stood there listening for any sign that he was in.

'Good,' she said quietly when she was reassured that they were alone, and she walked softly down the old stairs into the cellar.

'Right then,' she said as she took off her coat. 'With luck this will all be easy. Now, if you'll excuse me, I will tune the machinery.'

It was very peculiar, Rosie thought. She had imagined whirling dials and plugs and buttons. Angela, in contrast, shut her eyes, hummed and twirled around a couple of times before waving her hands about in a florid, extravagant motion. Then she stopped and peered at the pergola.

'Damn,' she said, and bit her lip for a moment as she thought. 'Silly me.'

She tilted her head to one side and blinked rapidly four times. A soft glow slowly grew on the other side of the room, rays of light filtering from the sides of the curtain.

'Ha!' she said in triumph, then stepped forward and pulled off the curtain.

'Hell and damnation,' she added, after she had twitched her hands and seen the light go off.

'What's wrong?'

'He wasn't there. Something must have happened to him.'

'Who wasn't?'

'Long story.' She took a deep breath. 'Why is everything so difficult these days?'

'What was that rigmarole anyway?'

'The movements set off particular brain patterns which the machine interprets as instructions.'

'That's clever.'

'Quite routine. Now, I also put you into it and I want you to do the next one, to see if it will respond to your brain properly. Just in case I have to go through and get him. The kettle sets the year and month, the saucepans fix the day and hour and the two tea mugs set the location. It's not precise enough for minutes. Here.' She handed Rosie a piece of paper.

'"Kneel down on the floor . . ."'

'You have to do it, not read it. The two require different parts of the brain.'

Rosie looked at her doubtfully, then, concentrating hard, she knelt down on the floor and counted to six. Next she went to the window and made a humming sound with her mouth closed. Then she turned round three times, holding her left hand out parallel to her chest, span the kettle round six times and, finally, scratched her right knee.

Instantly the light came on and then faded off again.

'Did I do it wrong?'

'Oh, no. That was brilliant. It was just a test. Really good. You are a natural. It must be because you are so young. Your brain hasn't become clogged up.'

'Thank you,' Rosie said, pleased with the compliment.

'So now we get Mr Chang back.'

'What?'

'I persuaded someone to go through and investigate the place. He was meant to be there for six days, and it's time to get him back.' She took over again, made some adjustments and the light returned and this time stayed on. It was grey and cold-looking on the other side.

'It's raining,' Rosie said. They both looked intently, hoping for some sort of clue, but apart from establishing that it was about midday, there was no further progress to be made. Eventually Angela grunted. 'I might have to step in after all. There's no Chang, unfortunately. I do hope he's not got into any difficulties. I'd better try the fallback.'

She went through her bizarre routine again and the image dissolved, then slowly re-formed. It was strange to watch. The scenery emerged out of nothing; first there was just a grey light and then, bit by bit, shapes formed, became more solid and changed colour. For some time the image was sludgy and blurred, but eventually it cleared to show grass, trees and sky.

'Oh look!' Rosie said. 'It's the tomb of Esilio. You see? At the far end. That lump of stone.'

'You recognise it?'

'It's close to where I arrived.'

'Excellent. That's what I was aiming at; I'm getting quite good at this. So now we know where. When, though? That's the problem. It's meant to be five days after you went there. Oh dear!'

They both saw the movement on the left at the same moment. First one shape, still not clearly defined, then more of them. The machinery started to clear the image, making the outlines firmer, giving them colour and substance, until Rosie let out a cry of delight.

'Look! It's Henary. You know, the scholar.'

Angela studied him. 'He looks like Henry himself. The old egotist.'

'And Jay and – oh look! There's Pamarchon and . . .'

'Out of the way. Quickly. Move!' Angela changed instantly from lady with teapot and roughly pushed Rosie aside. She was very alarmed, and with good reason. For there, standing in the middle of the image, was Rosalind herself.

'Keep out of the way. She doesn't know you exist, and it will upset my calculations if she does.'

Then the two of them heard a shout from upstairs in the hallway. 'Angela? Are you down there?'

Angela rolled her eyes. 'Oh, not now, Henry, please,' she muttered. 'For heaven's sake! Don't I ever get any peace? What's he doing here?'

'It is his house, you know.'

'Angela? Would you come up here, please?'

'We'll just have to get rid of him. Come on.'

She switched off the pergola, let Rosie go first, then climbed the rickety stairs after her.

47

Dawn was long gone the next morning when servant Kate walked into the woods to the stream so that she could bathe the sleep out of her eyes. She had asked where to go, and made sure that people knew she was on an innocent errand; she didn't want an arrow in her back because of a misunderstanding. She sat on a boulder, washing her blackened, filthy feet first, watching the mud and earth which caked them dissolve in the icy water and float away, then she bent over and let her hands feel it rippling over them.

'Good morning,' said a voice from behind her. It was Pamarchon; he had crept up so quietly she had heard nothing until he spoke.

'It's obvious you are a house dweller,' he said. 'I was making as much noise as a charging pig.'

'Then I would like to see you be quiet one day.'

'Maybe you will. It is a small skill, but one I am proud of.'

He sat down a few feet away from her. 'I fear I did not thank you for your service last night. That was rude of me. So – thank you, Kate.'

Kate frowned in surprise. 'That's quite all right,' she said. 'I obey as I am commanded. What else could I have done?'

He laughed lightly. 'You could have said no. We have no servants here. I admit I omitted to tell you that.'

'In that case, ask me again tonight, and I will turn you down flat, if you wish.'

'I will do no such thing. Rather, I wish to invite you to be my guest. It is my family day in a few days' time.'

'You celebrate that? After what you have done?'

'What was that, pray?'

'You know as well as I do. I have heard the stories.'

'I know what I am said to have done. I live only because of the hope that one day I will be seen as the good and honest son of my fathers that I know myself to be. So I do celebrate. I have the right, even though my family has shown me nothing but cruelty. There will be a feast to honour what they should be, and you are invited as my guest. Will you come?'

'Family days must be celebrated in the family house. At Willdon.'

'Indeed,' he said. 'That is what I intend.'

She studied him evenly. 'If I should tell Lady Catherine of this?'

'How?'

'I could simply disappear into the forest. I could have done so, you know, if I hadn't been worried about getting lost.'

'You would have died. This encampment is carefully guarded and no one goes in or out without being seen. Even if you had managed to get through the guards because one had fallen asleep – which does happen – then your chances in the forest would have been very small. It is dangerous for people who do not know it.'

'Good reasons,' Kate said.

'Besides,' he continued, 'your master gave his word of

honour that you would not seek to escape, in exchange for not being imprisoned. Why do you think you are free to move about as you please? Did he not tell you?'

'No,' she said through gritted teeth. 'He did not.'

'Well, he did. His word is more binding than any rope or guard. So, servant Kate, forget your woes and thoughts of home for a while. It is a beautiful morning. Don't spoil it with glum looks and dark thoughts.'

*

Rosalind was woken by the noise, and the absence of noise. Jay was a fine fellow but snored abominably. Only the fact that she was so tired had permitted any sleep, and only when the dull, snuffling rumble punctuated by high whistles and snorts stopped was she disturbed. That and the sunlight on the thin cover of the tent, the sound of people bashing pots and pans, the singing and loud conversation. The birds making an extraordinary din. All of these, finally, made her roll over and open her eyes.

No; still not a dream. She groaned and rolled over again. The place next to her was empty, and in the place of Jay was an earthenware pot, evidently for her. She touched it; it was warm and she slowly levered herself up. Leaves. In boiled water. Tea! she thought. No again. Mint. Quite foul. She would have preferred a cup of hot chocolate. Cadbury's. With a spoonful of sugar and a lot of milk. With Rice Krispies, sitting at the little table in the kitchen, her mother in attendance, her brother late for work, her father hiding behind the *Daily Express*, in his shirt and braces, smelling of soap and Brylcreem.

Why had she ever felt so bad about that scene, wanted something different? Was it her fault? Had she been granted some wish like you read about in books? The ones where you ask for immortality, then get older and older. Or huge wealth, and starve to death because everything you touch turns to gold. Had she made a wish and not constructed it carefully, not read the small print? All she'd ever asked for was a life that was a little more interesting. But this was too much; as she had walked to the tent last night, Catherine had told her everything that had happened, about fights and captives and ceremonies. She hadn't known how to respond, she was too befuddled and exhausted. Instead, she'd told her to leave her alone till morning and had laid her head on the ground hoping it would go away. It hadn't.

She put down the mint tea – she appreciated the gesture, if not the taste – and reluctantly stirred herself, getting onto her hands and knees and crawling out of the tent. There, sitting on the ground a few feet away, were Jay and Kate.

'Do you know what this fool has done?' Kate snapped as she came towards them.

'And good morning to you, too,' she replied. 'Of course I don't know. Jay! What's the matter? You look as though you're about to cry.'

Jay was indeed fighting back the tears. 'What have you said to him?' Rosalind demanded, rounding on Kate.

'He has given his word that we will not try to escape.'

'So?'

'He had no right to pledge me.'

'Wouldn't it be better to keep your voice down?' Rosalind said. 'I don't know what you're talking about. It's not as if he meant it.'

'Of course he meant it. He had to mean it. If I escape, his life will be forfeit.'

'So both of you go.'

'And live with the dishonour of being an oath breaker?'

'Well . . . yes. I mean, there are worse things, surely?'

'Stupid girl.'

'I am not,' Rosalind responded stoutly. 'Don't you dare talk to me like that. Don't you dare.'

The two women glared at each other.

'She's right,' Jay mumbled into the gap.

'Oh, shut up, Jay,' Rosalind said. 'Keep out of it.'

'She's right,' Kate added. 'You've caused enough trouble already.'

Jay subsided into an outnumbered silence, and the two faced each other again.

'What's so terrible? Don't give me that Lady of Willdon nonsense. You may be terribly grand here, but not where I come from. Not here either, at the moment, as far as I can see. I couldn't care less. In fact, I've had enough of all of you.'

'Everything depends on your honour. Don't you understand that?'

Rosalind shook her head. 'Your husband was murdered, I understand. Either you or Pamarchon was responsible. Each of you would cheerfully kill the other but you get upset over a promise? Are you totally mad?'

'Let me explain,' Jay said. 'You see, it all goes back to the first Level of the Story . . .'

'I don't care about the Story,' Rosalind interrupted. 'I do not care. I care so little it almost hurts. Dear God, you people! Constantly referring everything back to a set of

525

fairy tales. No wonder you all live in little huts with muddy roads and no central heating. I want a hot bath and some toast. Is there a story for that? No. So I can't have it. I want white sliced bread with butter on it and some strawberry jam, and a proper cup of tea, and all I get is people telling me what's done and not done, and what the Story says and doesn't say. Can't you grow up?'

She stopped, leaving Jay open-mouthed; Kate seemed shocked into silence.

'Look,' Rosalind began once more in a more conciliatory tone. 'I know it's important for you, but it doesn't mean anything to me. All I see is that you are stuck here, presumably in considerable danger, and you won't do anything about it. And I am stuck here as well and I want to go home. And I can't. And all you worry about is what is proper. You're worse than my mother.'

Stifling her own tears as best she could, Rosalind strode off.

*

Had she been a little more self-aware, she would have noticed that the first thing she had thought of when she woke up was Pamarchon. When she got into an argument, in the back of her mind, she had thought that Pamarchon would understand. When she felt desperate, the person she thought of turning to for help was not Jay, or Kate, but the outlaw who had confessed his love the night before. Pamarchon. Tall and handsome, with kind eyes and elegant, gracious step. Whose gentle laughter at her dreadful dancing had been so kindly, whose sincerity she did not doubt. She remembered when he had touched her cheek in the forest, as though it was the first time she had been alive; her excitement when he held her as they danced, her distress as he had walked off and left her. She remembered the giddy feeling as he said how much he loved Lady Rosalind . . .

She stumbled into the woods, not wishing anyone to see her tears and confusion, sensible enough to get out of hearing distance before she collapsed onto a dead tree trunk and began to cry her eyes out, until her chest hurt with sobbing.

What now? In her mind, she thought someone – well, preferably Pamarchon – should come along, see her and ask what the problem was. Sympathy, understanding. That's what happened in all the books she had read. She stopped sniffling and looked around. No one. If this really did have something to do with Professor Lytten's story, she wished he'd got around to the bits about people falling in love.

She could either sit here, feeling sorry for herself, with a lump of bark sticking into her rear, or she could stand up, dry her eyes and do something. Rosalind watched a beetle trying to drag a piece of twig around. What was the point of that? But it kept on going, poor beast, with a dogged determination that made her feel slightly ashamed. It may not have had much in its head, that beetle, but it knew what it wanted.

She stood up, dusted herself down and marched back into the camp.

*

Pamarchon was deep in conversation with Antros when his guest of the previous evening walked in. He smiled at the sight.

'Would you mind waiting, my . . . boy? I will only be a very short while.'

'I do mind waiting. In fact, I will not. I have something to say to you, and it will not wait. Please ask your friend to leave.'

Both men looked up in astonishment.

'Now.'

Pamarchon opened his mouth to reply, then changed his mind. 'Antros? Perhaps we can continue this later?'

Once the young lieutenant had left, Pamarchon eyed the unkempt, unwashed but determined-looking youth who stood before him. 'You have your wish. Pray tell me how your sleep went? I hope it was kindly, and full of . . .'

'Oh, do stop that nonsense. I slept perfectly well. Whether it was kind or not I could not say. I am here to talk about the one you call Lady Rosalind. Were you saying the truth last night, or was it just the sort of guff you people always seem to spout?'

'Guff? Spout?'

'Do you love her?'

'As my life. Do not doubt me for an instant. I have never loved anyone or anything—'

'Enough. I'm glad to hear it. I have an offer.'

'Which is?'

'You can have her.'

Pamarchon stared.

'Lost for words, for once. I'm glad. By have, I mean to marry. To have and to hold, in sickness and in health, for richer or for poorer, for ever and ever. Worship her with your body, if you see what I mean. Are you interested?'

'I . . . of course. It is more than my dreams—'

'Leave the dreams out of it. Will you love and cherish, be faithful and all the rest? No doubts, hesitations or backsliding. No fancy stuff when no one is looking. Nights at the pub where you get carried away. No coming home drunk and bad-tempered.'

'I don't really know what you are talking about, but I will make her the happiest woman in the world.'

'Even if she turned out to be penniless?'

'Especially so. We would then be equal, she and I.'

'Good answer.'

She smiled hesitantly at first, then more broadly.

'I knew who you were, you know,' he said.

'I thought you did.'

Then he went down on his knees and took her hand in his.

'Oh, that's really nice,' Rosalind said. 'But do stand up. I'll start blushing again.'

He did and they looked at each other nervously awhile, until Rosalind remembered why she had come.

'That will have to wait,' she said with renewed purpose. 'Call Jay, if you please, and that servant of his. I want witnesses.'

'What for?'

'Do as you are told. Oh, and get that Antros chap back as well. He might as well hear this too. The more the merrier. Can I have this bit of bread? I'm starving.'

*

Within half an hour the area outside Pamarchon's tent had four people sitting on the ground and one standing up in front of them. The seated ones were watchful, the one standing looked like someone having second thoughts about the wisdom of an undertaking begun in haste.

'Right,' Rosalind said, addressing the others. 'This is the problem. Pamarchon here wants to marry me. It seems like a good idea if I am stuck here, but I don't want to spend my life skulking in a forest. I will not marry a murderer, and he cannot marry someone properly if he is under the accusation of murder. It seems that either he or Catherine of Willdon murdered Thenald. Each believes the other to be the person at fault. Have I summarised the situation properly?'

Pamarchon nodded cautiously. The others did not move.

'You all seem terribly keen on oaths and words of honour here. That's why I want the audience. Pamarchon. Answer a few questions. Do you love me?'

'You know I do. I love you like—'

'Yes or no will do. If I ask a favour, will you grant it?'

'Anything.'

'If I ask you to protect someone with your life, will you do it?'

'Anyone who is a friend of yours, I will gladly help.'

'Look after them as well as you look after me?'

'Yes,' he said, a little impatiently now.

'In that case, I want you to swear before everyone here that you will look after servant Kate. You will in no way molest her, harm her, or cause or allow anyone else to harm her. You will treat her as an honoured guest and protect her with your life.'

'Very well,' he said, puzzled.

'You swear?'

'Yes. I swear on all my ancestors and on the Story itself.'

'That's a good swear, is it?'

He smiled despite himself. 'The strongest there is.'

'Excellent. Now we will see how strong.' She took a deep breath. 'Stand up, please, Lady Catherine. Do we need more introductions?'

*

Pamarchon felt both humiliated and confused about what he should do next. Jay was terrified at the possible consequences. Catherine felt betrayed.

The only common point was that all were furious at Rosalind.

'Stop!' she shouted after a few minutes' denunciation. She had heard enough. All this 'false traitor' nonsense. She wasn't having it.

'Stop it,' she repeated. 'Pamarchon. There she is. What are you going to do? Remember what you stand to lose.'

He stared at Lady Catherine with utter loathing, then spat out the words: 'I protect you with my life and offer you the hospitality of my house.'

'Bravo!' Rosalind said. 'That wasn't so hard. Now then. This was getting too complicated, so I decided it was time to simplify things. I take it both of you insist you are innocent?'

'I am,' they both replied.

'How do you know someone else didn't kill him?'

'Like who?' Catherine asked disdainfully.

'How should I know? You need a proper investigation and trial. Go through all the evidence, take statements, investigate the scene of the crime. That sort of thing.'

'There's been a trial already,' she said.

'You must have appeals. To see if it was done properly.'

'No.'

'There must be some way of deciding. Obviously you are not both guilty and you can't both be Lord of Willdon.'

'At the moment, neither of us is,' Catherine said.

Rosalind glanced at her. 'Why not?'

'You don't understand anything, do you? This is the period of Abasement. I am stripped of my rank for three days, then reinstated. That passed yesterday. There is now a vacancy, and the natural successor is Gontal unless I get back quickly. The thing Henary and I were trying to avoid when this man murdered his uncle has come to pass.'

'I didn't murder him,' Pamarchon said, but everyone ignored him.

'What thing?'

'Anterwold is carefully balanced between the towns, the domains and the scholars, traders and farmers. None is powerful enough to dominate the others. But Gontal is heir to Willdon and head of the council of colleges. He will fuse the two together, and that will overwhelm the whole land. It is the disaster people have long feared. That's why I needed to escape. It was another reason we moved so quickly when Thenald died.'

'There you are!' Rosalind said. 'Prime suspect, if you ask me. Gontal would be the obvious person who stood to benefit from your husband's death if Pamarchon was got out of the way.'

'No one ever suspected Gontal. He is a scholar of the highest reputation.'

'All the more reason. It's always the unlikely ones. Trust me. How much time do you have?'

'The vacancy would have been declared last night. I assume it will take Gontal a few days to hear the news. He will hurry, though. There is no time for any nonsense like a trial. I have to leave immediately.'

'Hospitality has its limits,' Pamarchon said. 'I cannot possibly allow you to return to power, even at the risk of Gontal taking over. At the moment we are equals. If you were reinstated, you would command any appeal.'

'There must be some way of clearing this up fairly,' Rosalind said.

'Not unless one or the other of us confesses. Which I will not do,' Pamarchon said.

'Nor I,' added Catherine.

'Well,' said Rosalind, 'you'll just have to sit and grouch at each other while your world goes up in flames, then. What?'

Jay was waving his hand nervously like a schoolboy in class.

'Not now, Jay,' Catherine said.

But Jay, evidently, had had enough of being ignored. 'I want to say something. You're all talking but going nowhere. None of you knows what to do.'

'Do you?'

'Yes. This bickering is a waste of time. Rosalind is right there, but she doesn't know anything about us. She just dismisses everything and says it is all silly. It's not. The Story provides everything we need, if we understand it properly.'

533

'So how does it help here?' asked Rosalind in a somewhat offended tone.

'Esilio,' Jay replied. 'His shrine is in the woods near Willdon.'

'I've seen it. So?'

'I've studied it, in old parts of the Story that very few people know much about. There is one tale of two men with a dispute over a horse. They cannot agree, so they ask for the wisdom of Esilio to decide. They go to his shrine, and as they talk to the people, setting out their case, a wild horse wanders into the stone circle. They see it is a gift from the gods; both now have a horse, so there is nothing to argue about and the dispute is settled.'

'I don't see how that helps.'

'It sets a precedent. It is set out in the Story. Anyone with a grievance not satisfied in any other way can appeal to his judgement. I do not know if it has ever been used.'

'Not in my time,' Catherine said, 'but there is no reason it could not be, if the two sides agree.'

'Then what?' Rosalind asked. 'You wait for some message from on high, or something?'

'Each would make their case,' Jay said. 'Then the wisdom of Esilio offers a solution. That's what the story says.'

'You're sure of that?' Rosalind asked.

'It would have to take the form of a disputation,' Catherine said. 'The wisdom would flow through the will of the audience.'

'You mean they vote on it? Anyone?'

'Anyone present. It is an ingenious idea. The trouble is that it would give me the advantage Pamarchon is so afraid of. It would be my people there. Pamarchon would never agree.'

'Of course he wouldn't,' Antros said. 'Nobody but a fool would.'

'Then I am a fool,' Pamarchon said. 'If I wait, then Gontal gets Willdon and my hopes will be gone for ever. He will hunt me to death, or I him. I have always been prepared to fight if I must, but will not do so if there is even the smallest alternative. Besides,' he smiled at Catherine, 'they are not your people at the moment. Perhaps the wisdom of Esilio is already at work.'

So it was settled. An hour later, they left for Willdon.

48

'I must have been followed to the Depository,' Jack said. 'They may well know by now why we were there, and why Emily was with me. Do you have somewhere we can go?'

He was talking to Sylvia at the communal food hall, which daily saw to the nutrition of tens of thousands of workers. It was easy to go unnoticed in the vast, smoke-filled room and the noise made it impossible for anyone to overhear. In general, people came in, ate and left within ten minutes. Jack and Emily had had to wait for nearly an hour before Sylvia showed up in response to their urgent message.

'There are many such places,' she said calmly, 'but you never said you were doing anything illegal. You know how precarious our position is. We cannot afford the slightest—'

'It's not illegal,' he interrupted. 'This document is valuable. Invaluable, I might say. I am trying to get it back to its rightful owner. Others wish to take it for themselves.'

'What others?'

'Zoffany Oldmanter, I believe.'

'Would this be connected to the sudden renewal of the campaign against us? The accusations of terrorism?' She seemed neither surprised nor perturbed by his statement.

'It's possible,' he said after a moment's hesitation. 'If so, then possession of this document might help in blunting the attack on you. If I get it back to Hanslip, it will give him a powerful bargaining chip.'

'That may help him. What will it do for us?'

'He will abide by any assurance I give you. He is a decent enough man, so I have found. For what it is worth, you have my word on that.'

'I'm afraid it is not worth much. We will help you, but only if we keep possession of this document Emily found for you, as a guarantee.'

'I was going to say she would have to come anyway. Association with me, with her mother, with the document. That is more than enough reason to arrest her.'

'No. We have done enough for you.'

'But you must understand—'

'Well, that's the problem,' Sylvia interrupted. 'We don't understand, because you refuse to explain. You come to our Retreat, get our help, and we find ourselves attracting the attention of Zoffany Oldmanter. Yet we do not know why, or what this is about.'

She spoke quietly, so that Jack had to lean forward across the table to hear what she was saying. He looked around to make sure that no one was listening, but the people sitting nearby were intent only on their food, shovelling it down, occasionally pausing to take a drink.

'Angela Meerson,' he began, 'Emily's mother, seems to have discovered a way of accessing parallel universes, although there is a dispute over what that means exactly. She disappeared, destroying her data before she left. Such a discovery could obviously be of immense importance. The person who controls it might become powerful beyond words, and the world might gain access to unlimited resources. That's a simple summary.'

'So the rightful owner of this data is Angela Meerson? Should it not be given to her?'

'I have no idea. If I could find her, then I would ask, but I have had people searching for some time now, and there has been nothing. You know better than most that evading detection even for more than an hour is difficult. The moment you walk down a street, buy something, touch something, it leaves a trace. She has vanished completely. Meanwhile Oldmanter wants this badly. There isn't time to worry about the finer points of legal ownership. If he gets it, they will all become irrelevant anyway, and the people I work for and with will be arrested, as, most probably, will you be.'

'I see. This booklet you discovered today. That is the data?'

'Probably. If it is, then you and Hanslip can pretty much name your price.'

'Is this discovery of Angela Meerson's practical or just theoretical?'

'She built machines to test it, but they are at an early stage of development.'

'This dispute. Why did it cause her to disappear?'

'She thinks her discovery allows travel through time, not to parallel worlds. This document will enable her invention to be used and if it's old – I mean, really old – it may also answer the question of whether she's right. As far as I understand it, if she is correct, then it may be too dangerous to use.'

Sylvia glanced at Emily, but all she did was pick at her piece of bread and stare dreamily across the hall as though this was nothing to do with her.

'In that case,' Sylvia said, 'I think we had better find out. Emily? Would you take Mr More to Wales to see Kendred?'

*

Jack and Emily waited on the street outside until an ancient transporter, rusty and noisy, drew up alongside them and then lumbered through the streets at an agonisingly slow pace. For the first half hour Emily kept an eye on the other vehicles passing them, while Jack periodically wound down the windows to gaze up into the sky.

'I think we are in the clear,' he said after a while. 'Had there been anyone, they would have picked us up the moment we walked out of the door.'

'Are you sure?'

'Yes.'

Her leg occasionally brushed against his. It was hard to concentrate on anything else.

'You're not one of the elite, are you?' she said. 'You know too much about surveillance, don't mind sleeping on benches, weren't shocked when you first arrived at the Retreat. You also seem to know nothing about science. So who are you?'

'Do you really want to know?'

'No secrets. They are bad things to have between friends.'

'I used to be in the police. Undercover. I became contaminated, and rather than go through the cleansing process needed to keep my position, I resigned.'

'Background?'

'Level five intelligence. I was put down low as there is a trace of disobedience in my make-up. One of my

539

grandparents was executed for disobedience, and it will be another two generations before my strain is considered safe.'

'What do you mean by contaminated?'

'It is the difficulty of sending people out into the world of the masses. You end up liking the people you are supposed to be monitoring; you come to understand, sympathise, make excuses for them. In my case, I was in a unit charged with monitoring renegade groups and assessing the level of threat they posed. I decided they posed no threat, but that wasn't what anyone wanted to hear. I was told to have my opinions changed, I refused and – there we are. End of story. I ended up on the island of Mull, watching out for people stealing office pens. The pay's good, though.'

'How could you have done something like that?'

'How can you keep order in a disorderly world? You are the one who knows history, how many people have been killed over the centuries, how much inefficiency and waste there has been. Don't you think it is worthwhile to try and contain the natural tendency of people to violence?'

'What about this man Oldmanter's natural tendency to violence?'

'He acts within the law.'

'That's easy if you write the law.'

She had moved so she was no longer touching him.

*

They arrived late at night, after walking through waste-land, scrub and then hills, ever higher. Emily went easily and with determination, even though she was carrying a heavy pack. Jack struggled to keep up. He was fit but had never been called on to walk such distances before. Emily also drained his energies. She was perfectly polite but cold. He found that strangely disturbing. He wanted her to like him.

So he was glad, but also apprehensive when she came the next morning into the cold room where he had been sleeping. 'Thought I heard you. Are you all right?'

He nodded.

'You look exhausted. You don't get enough exercise.'

'I know.'

'I'm sorry,' she said suddenly. 'I was rude yesterday. I like what I see of you. I'm not so wild about what I know of you. That's all.'

'I suppose that is reasonable.'

'Here,' she said. 'Drink this. It'll help.'

He slowly and painfully sat up. Every muscle in his body ached. It annoyed him, especially as she seemed perfectly fine.

'Old remedy,' she said. 'Try it. It'll give you a buzz for a while, but it's good for the nerves. I'll come back in half an hour to see how you're doing.'

*

When he had woken properly and dressed, he found her sitting outside in the cold morning air with a mug of something hot in her hand. It was brilliantly sunny for once, even though there was a trace of frost on the ground, and she had her back against a whitewashed wall, eyes closed and head tilted back. She looked very peaceful, and even happy. When she heard him, she opened her eyes and smiled.

'Now you look a little more human,' she said. 'Come and meet Kendred.'

She led him down a corridor to the eating room, which was empty except for an old, square, muscular man with a thick neck and bald head who was, incongruously, wearing a striped apron.

'This is Kendred,' Emily said as he stretched out his hand in greeting. 'He is the moralist and cook here. Also a chemist in a previous incarnation.'

Jack raised an eyebrow.

'All I was ever allowed to do was follow orders,' he said. 'I wanted to investigate all sorts of things but could never get permission. It was why scientific discovery has almost stopped, in my opinion. It's controlled by people who are only interested in confirming their own work. Here I am an irrelevant outcast, but I can at least do as I please.

'My cooking,' he continued, 'is only mediocre, as you will discover. But as I can think and peel vegetables at the same time, it makes me highly efficient.'

'Think about what?'

'How to do things, whether it is right to do things. For example, at the moment there is uncertainty about whether we should hand you over to the authorities, as we are legally obliged to do.'

'Why would you do that?'

'Did Emily not tell you? There is an arrest warrant out for you. Armed and dangerous, terrorism, the usual sort of thing. You look fairly harmless to me, but we would get a tasty reward for handing you over, and might be able to buy immunity for the Retreat. You must see how that would be tempting, especially at the moment. Another two thousand people were sent to internment camps yesterday.'

'And you decide what to do?'

'It is my task to pose the questions, not to answer them, fortunately.'

'Assuming you don't have me arrested, how can you help me?'

'I know the tests for assessing the age of objects. Including paper. I should be able to tell you how old this document of yours really is, more or less. Now, I think we may be short of time, so if you would like to hand it over, I will begin work. I won't damage it in any way, I assure you.'

Jack hesitated, then reached inside the bag and took out the thin package. He watched as the old man studied it, sniffed it cautiously, his head held to one side almost as though he was listening to it, then opened it.

'Oh, my goodness,' he said with delight. 'Just look at this! How interesting! This will take some work. I've never seen anything like it before.' He looked up at Jack. 'Tsou?'

Jack nodded.

'Handwritten, do you see? I cannot imagine why anyone would do such a thing. It must have taken years.'

'Can you decipher it?'

'Not me. You need a very specialised mathematician for that.'

He shuffled out of the room, and Jack noticed that there was a slightly more energetic air to his movements.

'You've made his day,' Emily said with a smile. 'He tries to fit in, but he just loves messing around with test tubes.'

She led him back outside, where he took a deep appreciative breath. 'Corrupted, eh?' she said.

'I'm afraid so,' he said. 'I try to spend as much time

outside as I can. I am considered very peculiar because of it.'

'Then let us pass the time by walking.'

They strolled round an area planted out with vegetables, the awnings drawn over to protect them from the frost. The Retreat was a ramshackle assembly of buildings, but very much more appealing than the one where Emily lived. In its way – with the vegetation growing everywhere, the cracked old windows open to let in air, the crumbling stone that had been found and stuck together in a bizarre random pattern to make the walls – it was strangely peaceful.

'So what are you doing?' he asked. 'Sitting in Retreats, reading old books, waiting to be rounded up. You are level one. You had the best of everything on offer in this world.'

'It didn't suit me. I didn't want it. I wanted something I could not have, no matter how great my privileges.'

'What was that?'

'Freedom to do nothing, if I wished. To say whatever I wanted without consequence. To think how I pleased. As she must be like me in many ways, I don't know how my mother survived without going mad.'

'It is possible that she did. But what's the point of freedom? Do you think that you can change anything?'

'Of course not. We are waiting.'

'For what?'

'Until the world changes on its own. That is the one truth of history. Everything ends. Civilisations, empires, however powerful and strong. They all end, sooner or later. When it does we will be there, with all the old ideas and thoughts, preserved and ready to blossom. We're not subversives. We do nothing to bring it about, although some are more impatient. Unfortunately the authorities do not bother to make the distinction. For someone like Oldmanter, merely believing society will collapse is a crime in itself.'

'It will be a long wait.'

'Yes. Many generations. Unless someone finds a short cut.' She stopped for a moment before continuing. 'Sooner or later the machines will stop, your ideas will fail, and men will have to start again. Meanwhile we are content to survive and remember.'

'Remember what?'

'Everything. We all remember things. Each person has a task, of memorising some important, vital, vulnerable field of knowledge. To keep them alive and safe. Each generation passes it on to the next. Ideas of music and poetry, of freedom and happiness. History, philosophy, even stories. Everything that has been written about and thought about. They will have their chance again, one day. We keep it safe, as we are sure that one day the depositories and libraries will be destroyed. Many have been already. Only what is in the minds of men will survive, passed on by word of mouth.'

'How does your interest in history fit into that?'

'Anything which is forbidden is important, and the study of the past has been banned for a century, except under licence. They do not want anyone to think there might be an alternative to the way things are.'

'Quite right. Why study the follies of the past?'

'It teaches you to recognise weakness. Would a truly confident, strong society worry about such things? Would it persecute people who were so obviously wrong? All these institutions and governments overlapping in their

545

authority will fight each other for supremacy sooner or later. It is always the case and it will be again. The great edifice of authority is convinced it cannot err. It will destroy itself as a result. That is what history teaches us. Thanks to my mother, it may be that the past will become important again.'

She sat down in the shade of a high wall, mixed of crumbling stone and brick like a patchwork, and gestured for him to join her. He didn't know how to reply, so said nothing. She was deluded, of course, but he found her certainty impressive nonetheless. It was so strange to have someone patiently waiting for something which, if it ever happened, would only take place long after they were dead.

'What if you are wrong?'

'Then we would have tried.'

'You know they may have decided to wipe you out entirely this time?'

'Of course. If not this time, then next time. We have known it was coming for many years. It won't succeed, any more than past campaigns did. We have prepared, as you see. We will vanish from sight, hide away and wait. When they lose interest again, we will emerge once more. Are they really so fragile a few hundred thousand like me can bring their world to its knees? I wish we could.'

'That is why they pursue you.'

'Come along. Let's get to work.'

'Doing what?'

She smiled. 'Digging carrots, of course. Do you think we offer hospitality for free?'

*

A few hours later Emily took a break, leaving a red-faced and aching Jack to lean on his shovel and get his breath back, then returned looking pleased with herself.

'We have managed to establish contact with Dr Hanslip for you. We thought it might be useful.'

Jack followed her to the main building and politely took off the boots he had borrowed so that he would not get mud all over the brilliantly shiny stone floor of the entrance. Then he surreptitiously paused by the big fireplace for a moment to warm his hands.

Emily pointed accusingly and laughed. 'Weak and feeble man!' she said, but with a tone of what sounded almost like affection in her voice.

When he was ready, she led him along a dark corridor to another room. 'You, no doubt, would sneer if I told you this was our communications centre,' she said, as she opened the door and gestured for him to go in.

'Perhaps,' he said.

There was nothing in it except a chair, a desk and a couple of antique machines that looked as though they had been salvaged from a scrap heap.

'Well, it is,' she said. 'So sneer away.'

'What's that?' he said, pointing at what was on the desk.

'That is a telephone. We discovered long ago that the whole of Britain – the whole world, probably – was covered in copper cables before technology made them redundant. It was too expensive to dig them up, so they were left underground and forgotten. We patiently mapped out where they were and worked out which ones were still serviceable and how to use them. They're not monitored, because they haven't been used for so long. Fortunately, at the moment we can use more conventional means. While the telephone has a romantic air to it, it doesn't actually work very well.'

She laughed as she saw the relief crossing his face, then pulled out a perfectly ordinary communicator and handed it to him.

'There you are.'

'Hello?' Jack said tentatively once he had taken it from her.

'Yes. More?' came the crackly but distinct voice of Hanslip at the other end. 'Where are you?'

'It would perhaps be better if I did not say,' Jack replied. 'I am being pursued by Oldmanter, I believe.'

'I am aware of that. We have been surrounded up here and warrants issued for my arrest.'

'What charges?'

'Does it matter? He is more impatient than I thought. We cannot possibly hold out for long if he decides to attack.'

'Has there been any fighting?'

'Not yet. Just threats, but that won't last. I need that data, Mr More. It is the only defence which might offer some protection.'

'In that case, I have good news. I've found it.'

There was a sigh of relief from the other end.

'I am having it examined at the moment. It was disguised exceptionally well. If I can figure out how it was done, I might be able to find out who helped to do it—'

'Don't bother.'

'Why not?'

'You will discover it really is as old as it looks. It pains me to say it, but I am afraid Angela was correct. The phenomenon we have discovered is indeed time travel, not transit.'

'So what do you want me to do with it now?'

'If it wasn't for the fact that my life and freedom depended on it, I'd tell you to stick it on a fire.'

'Do you want me to bring it to you?'

'You'd never make it through Oldmanter's forces. Keep it safe and hidden. I will come to you. Just make absolutely certain that it does not fall into Oldmanter's hands. That is the most important thing of all. If he uses it . . .'

'Why would he, if it's as dangerous as you say?'

'Orthodoxy says it is impossible.'

'We have evidence.'

'Do we? The more evidence we produce, the more he will take it as proof only of fraud. I can't blame him. I did the same.'

Then he was gone.

'Well, well. After all that.'

'What?' Emily asked; she had discreetly stood outside during the conversation.

'He nearly told me just to burn it.'

'So what are we meant to do with it?'

'Hide it, keep it safe.' He stretched and looked out of the window. 'There are places I can go where no one will find me, and you will not have to be associated with whatever crime Oldmanter decides I have committed.'

She nodded. 'It's a bit late to set off now. Stay tonight and leave in the morning. We can take you part of the way, if you wish.'

49

When they were all prepared to leave and make their way to Willdon, the little group stood at the edge of the camp to make their farewells. Rosalind and Antros – who had offered to go as hostage in exchange for Catherine – were to be accompanied by Pamarchon, who said he wanted to make sure they were safe on the journey.

'Well,' he said to Jay, who had come to wish them luck, 'when you arrived I did not think that you would play such an important part in my life,' he said. 'I congratulate you on your intervention. It showed learning and wisdom in equal measure.'

'Thank you, but I now think it is a lunatic scheme. It can't possibly work.'

'It is worth trying. From my point of view I gain nothing if Gontal becomes the new Lord. So I will throw the dice. I have naught to lose except my life, which I value little, but if I win, I win . . .'

'Willdon.'

'No! No, young student, a thousand times no! That is worth even less to me. I was going to say that I win back my name and my liberty, except that now I want a prize more valuable still.'

'Do you really mean to tell me you wouldn't grasp Willdon in both hands if you could?'

'I can think of nothing I want less. It is beautiful, but

nothing to me. I never had happiness there, nor do I have fond memories of it. If there was someone – good, reliable, true – who would take it from me, I would hand it over readily and be the happiest man in the world.' He smiled. 'You will not believe me, I am sure. So I will say no more. I will return probably tomorrow afternoon. Then I will have to prepare myself for whatever is to come.'

*

Antros and two others acted as scouts as they walked, while Rosalind and Pamarchon fell back, talking so intensely that they almost forgot where they were going. Several times Antros had to turn and gesture for them to be quiet, as their voices and laughter threatened discovery. Both were in a state of enchantment. They had never talked to each other properly before, not openly and honestly. They loved each other – the way their hearts fluttered demonstrated that – but did not know each other. For once Pamarchon, who had learned to be cautious and guarded, spoke freely in a way he could not do even with Antros. And Rosalind responded, no longer afraid of saying the wrong thing or of not being liked.

'I wish this could go on for ever,' she said. 'Walking through the forest, just like this.'

'I'll see what I can arrange,' he replied with a smile.

'What do you do here? How do you live? There seem to be a lot of you in that camp.'

'There's about six hundred,' Pamarchon said, 'if you include the very young and the very old. Fewer than two hundred would be useful in a battle. As for living – we live. The forest provides much of what we need. There are farms around . . .'

'You steal food?'

'No. That's what they say, but we do not. We buy it. In exchange for gold, or deer or boar, or even our work. We do not steal. I do not permit it.'

'What sort of work?'

'We hunt wolves, or protect from interlopers and thieves. We help in the fields sometimes, herd animals, hunt.'

'You never steal?'

'Only from people who have more than they need. Some have too little. We borrow, for a while.'

'It'll be *The Wind in the Willows* next,' Rosalind muttered under her breath.

'You must understand that we are all entitled to our plot of land. Others have taken it from us and make use of it. We take what would have been ours had we not been expelled. No more than that. When we get what is ours back, then we will be satisfied.'

'Now, that is what I was going to ask. How do you plan to get it back?'

'By agreement or by force. We will take it in the way that a good band of men with determination and weapons can take it, when no other possibilities are open to them. Willdon will either accept our claims or it will not.'

'I don't think Lady Catherine will just say – fair enough, I'll leave.'

'We will see.'

'I assume that she also can call on men with weapons.'

'She can call on the whole of Anterwold to come to her assistance. Many more people than we have.'

Rosalind kicked some leaves as she considered this. 'I don't rate your chances then. I imagine that Willdon can be defended, and from my history lessons I always thought you needed more men if you are going to be the attacker.'

'Whoever said anything about attacking Willdon?'

'You did.'

'I did not. That would involve many people, and many deaths. I can win my victory with only a handful of people. It is a question of daring and skill. That plan is already laid, although I will not need it if I win my case.'

'Can you?'

'I don't know. Certainly not without an advocate, which I do not have yet.'

'Where can you get one?'

'That would be something you can do for me. Ask at Willdon. Get the best available, because without one there will be no point turning up.'

*

'We will stop here,' Pamarchon said once night was falling and they could no longer see the path. 'We are very close. In the morning, Rosalind and Antros will go on alone and I will return to the camp.'

The two men decided that it was too risky to light a fire which might attract attention, so they ate from the packs they had brought with them. They ate quietly, finishing off everything except for the few morsels that Antros – always careful – insisted be put aside for the morning.

'Now we sleep. It will be best to wake early and start quickly. Although if you would spare me a few moments ...'

He looked at Antros to hint that he should go to prepare the beds for them, to lay out the blankets, for they would be sleeping without tents or covering.

'I am placing a great deal of trust in you, Rosalind. Am I right to do so? Not for me, you understand, but Antros is my best and closest friend.'

'I plan to find Jay's master, Henary. From what Jay says, he will have the authority to protect us both. Besides, I have a lot at stake as well.'

'What?'

'You, of course. I lost my heart the moment I first saw you. You could ask anything of me and I would give it to you.'

Pamarchon's eyes searched hers.

'I have watched you, Pamarchon. The way you treat your fellows, your captives. I have listened to the way you talk. I can find nothing bad in you. Will you swear that you are as you seem?'

'I do. I am. Believe me.'

'Then go and find your sleeping place. But remember, I know nothing, no matter how I appear. Everything I have told you is a lie, really.'

He said no more, but rose, and she watched as he walked slowly off to a place that was private. Rosalind's heart was beating hard. She scarcely believed what she was doing, or what she was thinking of. But she never, not for a moment, considered changing her mind. She felt as though she would burst with longing. 'Please,' she said to herself, or to anyone who might listen and help, though she spoke so quietly not even the moths could possibly hear. 'Please let this be the right thing to do.'

There was no guidance, no voice in her head telling her not to be so silly, that it was shameful what she wanted so badly. The thudding inside her chest just got worse, and her mind focused more and more on that need that was vague and clear at the same time.

Legs trembling with fear, her whole body shaking with nerves, she resigned herself to her fate. She walked quietly over to where Pamarchon lay on the ground. He looked up at her and held out his hand.

50

Henary watched the search parties when they left; all, he noted, were men Gontal had brought with him. Few even knew what Catherine looked like, and none knew much about the forest. Neither Gontal nor the Chamberlain was mounting a serious hunt. They were not going to try to find her. They were going to make as sure as possible that they did not.

But where was she? She was fully aware of the importance of a timely return. Something terrible must have happened, and if it had happened to her, then Jay also was somewhere in the vast forest, dead or injured. If he had breath in his body, he knew the boy would come back to him.

There was nothing more he could do. He had bought her time, at a high price to himself. Now he had to wait and, while he was waiting, he might as well begin to construct his arguments. Win or lose, Gontal would lay a complaint against him. He had to have his arguments ready. He could start by reviewing the case of Pamarchon and the murdered Lord of Willdon to make sure that his interpretation of the criminal's conviction was correct.

He laboured hard until mid-morning, when a servant – one he trusted as utterly devoted to Catherine – approached him.

'The Lady Rosalind. She has come back in the company of an outlaw. She is insistent that she must speak to you. We have not told Scholar Gontal of her appearance, but he will undoubtedly find out soon enough.'

Henary stood up in a hurry.

'Well done. Thank you. How is she?'

'Dirty, scruffy and looking – I don't know how to put it exactly.'

'Try.'

'Radiant.'

Henary examined the man curiously, wondering about his peculiar choice of words.

'In that case, take me to her immediately.'

The servant led the way swiftly across the house, through little rooms that Henary had never visited before. The route made it less likely, so he said, that anyone would notice their passage.

'She's in here,' he said when they got to the door which led into the room where Henary had once shouted at Jay. He remembered, felt briefly guilty, and went in.

Standing by the window looking out over the gardens was the slim, short figure of the girl. She did indeed look a mess. Her hair was all over the place; she was wearing men's clothes and shoes but, as she smiled in recognition, Henary realised that the servant's description was accurate. Radiant was a good word. More than that. In the few days since he had last seen her she had changed completely. Just the set of her body, the easier way she moved. She was more assured, more – what? Commanding, perhaps. Something about her reminded him of Catherine.

The thought brought him back to reality.

'Where is she? Where is Jay? Are they well? Are they safe?' he asked the moment the door had shut.

'I am well. I am safe, thank you for asking. Tell me, is it Mr Henary? Professor Henary? Scholar Henary?'

'Just Henary,' came the reply, 'and I accept your rebuke, but I can see that you are alive and in rude health. Catherine and Jay, on the other hand . . .'

'They are both fine, although when I last saw Lady Catherine she was very grumpy.'

'Oh, thank goodness!' he said, and collapsed heavily onto a stool. Then he held his head in his hands and breathed deeply, trying to hold back the sobs of relief so she wouldn't notice. 'You have relieved me of all the burdens of life,' he said eventually. 'Thank you, dear lady. A thousand times thank you.'

'You are most welcome,' she replied. 'They have been in some considerable danger but at present are in none whatsoever. I have guaranteed their safety, and so no one will dare harm them.'

'Then why are they not with you?'

'Well, now,' she said, 'that is really quite a story. Do you want to hear it?'

'Naturally.'

'The long version or the short one?'

'The long one, of course, but first tell me where they are, and why they are not here.'

'They are both deep in the forest and are the captives of Pamarchon, chief of the forest dwellers.'

'Oh, good heavens! You think they are not in danger? I'm surprised he hasn't slit her throat already.'

'That's very judgemental of you. You'd better stop being so mean about him, considering.'

'Considering what?'

'As I say, it is a long story. She will be back tomorrow morning, so have no fear.'

Henary paused. 'I do fear. A great deal. Already the situation is dangerous.'

'I know. Listen to what we have decided. But first, tell me your news.'

So Henary began to explain how the lordship of Willdon had been declared vacant and been immediately claimed by Gontal, who had arrived very swiftly.

'We knew all that, except for the last bit. This Gontal. He's already here?'

'Yes. I was suspicious for a moment. Alas, his story was true. He really was on the way elsewhere. Very bad luck indeed. He should have been immediately installed but I managed to delay it,' Henary said gloomily, 'by pointing out that the real heir is Pamarchon until his sentence is carried out. Gontal is calling an assembly to overturn my opinion. He is likely to succeed unless Catherine returns and offers herself as candidate. We have until tomorrow, at dusk.'

Rosalind listened carefully to this, asking questions about details and events.

'How complicated,' she said, when Henary came to a stop.

'Indeed. My argument was unusual and I was lucky to get away with it. I can find nothing else in the precedent books that will help. Now, why are you so calm when Catherine is in such danger?'

'Because she is under the protection of a good man. Who is also to be my husband.'

'Who?'

'Pamarchon. So she is quite safe.'

'The man is a murderer!' Henary exclaimed. 'How could you be so foolish?'

'I don't know about this place, but where I come from the normal thing is to offer congratulations when one announces one's engagement,' Rosalind said primly. '"When's the happy day?" "What do you want as a present?" That sort of thing.'

Henary tried hard to come up with something suitable but found nothing. Rosalind felt quite sorry for him.

'As I understand it,' she said, 'everyone is worried Gontal will get Willdon and join it to the power of the scholars. Right?'

'Everybody but Gontal is terrified of the prospect,' Henary said. 'However virtuous the man . . .'

'Yes, yes. It is clear he must not have it. Even Pamarchon and Catherine agree on that. The trouble is that Pamarchon cannot have it because of his little difficulty with the law, and Catherine cannot because Pamarchon won't let her leave until his name is cleared. Unless they stop squabbling, it will go to Gontal by default. So they have agreed to a retrial, or appeal, or something. Both will come to the Shrine of Esilio tomorrow and they seem convinced that somehow or other that will settle the matter.'

'Whose idea was that?'

'That was Jay's. Everybody thought it was very clever of him.'

Henary had been doing quite well up to that point, listening carefully and nodding respectfully. This last piece of information floored him completely, though. 'Dearest heaven!' he said. 'That is extraordinary!'

Rosalind was surprised and wanted to ask what he was getting so agitated about, but he suddenly held up his hand for silence, went to the door and glanced down the corridor.

'We are about to be interrupted,' he said. 'Gontal is coming, with an entourage. He is playing the Lord already. He must have heard you're here and undoubtedly wants to examine you. When you meet him you will see why I am worried about Willdon falling into his hands. Do you think you could put on a show for him?'

'A what?'

'Seem grand beyond measure. Quote things he has never heard of. Unsettle him with the power and extent of your learning, rather as you do me.'

'I unsettle you?'

'Certainly you do.'

Rosalind shook her head. 'I will do what I can to help, of course. But I am hardly dressed properly for impressing people.'

*

As Henary predicted, Gontal made an entrance. Opening the door and walking through it was not good enough; rather two servants entered first, opened both sides of the double doors and stood until he had progressed through in silence. Then they walked backwards, closing the doors as they left and leaving him alone with Henary and Rosalind. He regarded her with curiosity and some suspicion. She responded with what she hoped was indifference.

Gontal was short and fat; what little hair he had was lank and his face was red and shiny. He walked with short steps that gave an air of absurdity to his attempt at grandeur.

'I have heard much about you in the past day, young lady,' he said with an avuncular smile as he sat on a chair, 'and it is a pleasure—'

'I have heard nothing of you. Pray, introduce yourself in the proper fashion,' Rosalind interrupted, raising a disdainful eyebrow, 'and I do not recall that I gave you permission to sit.'

With a fine mixture of surprise and annoyance, Gontal hesitated, then reluctantly levered himself up and spent the next few minutes going through the appropriate introductions.

Rosalind inclined her head at the end. 'I am pleased to see you are fat,' she said absently, addressing the mirror on the wall. 'For, as Caesar said, "Let me have men about me that are fat; sleek-headed men think too much: such men are dangerous." You know your Shakespeare, of course? Act 1, scene 2?'

'Certainly,' he said quickly, 'naturally I do.'

'Good,' she said. 'There are many who neither appreciate the beauty of his poetry nor yet the force of his morality. I look forward to a discussion with you at some stage. On Hamlet, perhaps, or Elvis.'

'It will be a pleasure to have a conversation with a lady of so great knowledge,' he replied nervously. 'But I came simply to welcome you to Willdon, and alas have no time for such discussions now. I do hope I can excuse myself, as I have a meeting I have to go to.'

'Ah,' she replied, wagging her finger at him disapprovingly. 'You must never begin a sentence with "But". It is a conjunction, don't you know. As such, it must join two parts of a sentence. It cannot, therefore, start one, for if it does then it fails to fulfil its proper function. Nor should you say "I hope I can excuse myself". You are asking my permission, not stating your capabilities. It should be "I hope I may be allowed", employing "may" as an auxiliary verb, followed by an infinitive. Finally, you should never end a sentence or other statement with a participle. That is vulgar. You must say "I have a meeting to which I must go." For, as Great-aunt Jessie said, "A place for everything, and everything in its place." That applies to grammar as well as life. As you have legs, I imagine you can go and, as far as I am concerned, you may do so.'

When the chastened Gontal had retreated through the door and the two were alone once more, there was a long silence before Henary said, 'When I said unsettle him, I didn't mean frighten him to death, poor fellow.'

'Don't be silly. I was talking nonsense. I'm sure I got that quote wrong too.'

'Who are you, Rosalind? Where are you from?'

Rosalind looked at him seriously. 'It's more where you are from that concerns me,' she replied. 'Let me try to explain. Jay says that you are the wisest man he has ever known, the most thoughtful, the most reasonable and the kindest. Catherine says the same.'

'That is generous of them both, although the sort of thing one would expect from a student about his teacher.'

'No. He really thinks it, and I know he's right. So I will tell you a story which will knock your socks off.'

'I beg your pardon?'

'Which you will not believe, is what I mean. Nonetheless, I want you to understand that I am going to tell you the truth.

The absolute, total, complete truth. Now, are you capable of believing me? Tell me truly, because it is really important.'

'I will do my best.'

'Good. Well,' she said, taking a deep breath. 'Here goes. I do not come from this world.'

'I know that,' Henary said. 'You must have journeyed far . . .'

'No. I don't mean that. I don't know I've travelled at all. I mean what I say. I live in a town which has fifty thousand people living in it. The city of London has eight million. We travel by car, or train. Some people fly through the air in aeroplanes, travelling at hundreds of miles an hour. Soldiers have guns, not swords. We buy our food in shops, all sealed in tins. We have a queen and a prime minister. We watch the television and listen to the radio. We have Christmas and birthdays and the North Pole. The weather is rotten. We have bicycles. We have French prep and the cotton industry is centred in Manchester. We don't have a Story. Don't you see? It's a different world, and I got here by walking through a lump of old iron in someone's cellar. And if you think that's bad, I haven't even started yet.'

'Then continue.'

'All this place here, this place you call Anterwold. It all seems to come from someone's head. Professor Lytten. He's a friend of mine. I think he invented this. He made it up out of books he's read, and here it is. There's a bit of Robin Hood and a bit of Ulysses, and heaven only knows what else. You know when I turned up when Jay was eleven, and he thought I was a fairy?'

'Yes.'

'Professor Lytten wrote that. He put it in his story, and

564

then it went and happened. Maybe the other way round. And Willdon. He dreamed it up. And you. I know Jay is right about you. I know you are wise and thoughtful. Do you know how? Because Professor Lytten needed a wise man to understand better than the others. So he wrote in his notebook: "Henary. The greatest scholar of his generation." He invented you. Probably after a few hours in the pub with his friends. You even look like him. Let me put it bluntly. You are all just characters in a story.'

Rosalind stopped there, quite breathless, to see what effect she had had. As she spoke, the creeping feeling had come over her that this was no way to win friends. How would she feel if someone told her something like that?

To her astonishment, Henary went down onto his knees, covered his face with his thick, heavy hands and began weeping so hard that his body shook.

'I am so sorry!' she exclaimed. 'That was terribly rude of me.'

Henary dried his eyes and slowly recovered himself. Once he trusted himself to speak once more, he swallowed hard and recited, '"When the Herald reveals the Story, the Story is near its end."'

'Eh?'

'It comes from the Tales of Perplexity, parts of the narrative which no one has ever been able to understand and so are excluded from the canon of truth. Mystical, prophetic or simple lunacy, no one knows, though there are many opinions.'

Henary was talking like a man who had just had the worst shock of his life. 'The trouble is, I never believed any of it, you see; all my life I have set myself against the idea of prophecy. But I found this manuscript which describes a boy seeing a fairy. The one I got you to look at. I thought it merely curious until I came across Jay and realised his account fitted it exactly. Then it talked of you appearing again, and you did.

'I was excited, of course I was. I thought you would help me unlock the most ancient secrets. I now fear I may have set in motion the end of the world. The prophecies are coming true.'

'Oooh,' Rosalind reassured him. 'I doubt that. Why would you think such a thing?'

'Silly, meaningless stuff, which no man of sense or education pays any attention to.' He paused. 'Should that be "to which no man pays any attention"?'

'I believe so. But it is a bit off the point.'

'"The end time is presaged by the arrival of the Herald." A tale collected by Etheran.'

'Herald of what?'

'Of the god who created then abandoned us. He returns and judges his creation. If we are found wanting, then the world is brought to an end. All stories must end eventually. He returns and closes the book. That is why Willdon is so important. This is where the end will begin.'

'It all sounds very unlikely to me. I mean, it's just the Professor trying to add a bit of mystery to things. It's not real, you know.'

'The Herald has now revealed the Story,' Henary continued.

'Who?'

'You, dear lady.'

'Fiddlesticks and stuff.'

'There is more. A prophecy by a hermit. The world ends on the fifth day of the fifth year. Catherine is in the fifth year of her rule. The fifth day is tomorrow. The day when we now have to be in the Shrine of Esilio, and call his spirit forth to judge . . .'

'Well then,' said Rosalind matter-of-factly, 'I must say I don't hold with prophecies and fairies. Having been one myself, I know what I am talking about, as well. Nor does it make any difference. *Que sera, sera*. Bet you don't know that one.'

'No.'

She sang a bit of it. 'It means, whatever happens, happens. It doesn't matter. You have to go on as if the sun will rise and the world won't end. As far as I can see, you have a day to sort everything out.'

'Me?'

'Yes. You're the wisest, remember. So forget all of this for the time being. It's not as if you can do anything about it. There's a lot to do. You have a speech to prepare as well. Pamarchon only agreed to this on condition that he had the best advocate available. That's obviously you.'

Henary shook his head. 'I cannot do that.'

'You are just going to have to. Too late now. It would be breaking the agreement, he won't come and they'll start killing each other.'

'But who will defend Catherine?'

'She said she'd take care of it. You just have to put up with her decision. So, as Julius Caesar so eloquently put it in my last Latin lesson, *alea iacta est*.'

'I beg your pardon?'

'Too late now. Get on with it.'

51

For once books failed to distract him. Every time Lytten's concentration slipped, his mind drifted back to the doubts sown by Sam Wind. Could he have overlooked something? Could Angela have deceived him for so long, so completely? Could Wind's sudden suspicions have any substance to them?

Of course they could. Think of old Sowerby, the classics don. Married for forty years and discovers that his wife had not one but three lovers all at the same time, and had slept with most of Oxford over a period of decades. Did the poor fellow ever suspect? Not a thing. Sowerby had spent more time with his wife than Lytten had ever spent with Angela. How she had had the energy, mind you . . . Such a quiet woman.

It is easy to deceive others. Telling them the truth is harder. He thought of Angela, all those queer things about her that, for some reason, he had never thought about. The strangeness when he had first met her. The way she had questioned him incessantly about England and life in general, as though she knew nothing of it. The frequent faux pas when she clearly could not see simple signals – like saying hello to people properly, not noticing when someone was being kind or dismissive or interested. Constantly getting it wrong. The bizarre opinions that sometimes had come out of her mouth. The extraordinary ignorance – like the time when it became clear she genuinely did not realise that most people stayed married until they died, or left their possessions to their children.

She always seemed out of place, wherever she was. Never at home, always disappearing for long periods. He had paid little attention, and thought only that she was wonderfully strange. He was fascinated by her. He was carefree, without responsibilities. Even if she had said she was a communist spy, he wouldn't have minded. It would have been an additional attraction, back then. Everyone with any sense or humanity sympathised. There was a choice. Russia or Germany. But could she possibly be such a person still? Prepared to have a man shot to preserve her secret? Could she really have kept up a pretence for nearly thirty years, quietly, persistently, anonymously serving her country, betraying all around her?

Balderdash, he repeated. Angela was perhaps the most ill-disciplined, badly organised person he had ever met. Her inability to control her emotions was almost total. Her knowledge of, and interest in, technology was non-existent. She didn't even really understand how to use a telephone, and she was supposed to be masterminding the theft of our greatest secrets? Besides, one thing he was certain of: Angela couldn't keep a secret to save her life.

He only had to voice the idea in his head to know that it was nonsense. He had taken on the job of finding the spy in their midst, and here was Sam Wind pointing the finger at Angela, sowing confusion by constructing impossibly arcane theories.

Sam Wind was the last candidate on Portmore's list. Someone had known about Volkov; someone had arranged for him to be followed to Paris. Someone had been watching his house. Someone had shot the poor fellow.

Add it together. The conclusion, whatever it was to be, was coming ever closer.

*

To get it out of his mind, Lytten hid himself in Anterwold, or rather, in his notebooks, concerning himself with matters of imperfection. As he had said to Persimmon, human nature is immutable. Would Anterwold be strong enough to deal with laziness, deceit, violence, selfishness and all the other little oddities that make up mankind? As far as he could see, Persimmon dealt with the problem by simply killing everyone who made a nuisance of themselves. Those he put in charge of his ideal world could simply say they were acting in the best interests of humanity and eliminate anyone who disagreed. Lytten wanted something a little bit better than that.

Years ago he had sketched out a legal code and a system of criminal justice which would work as well as it had in eighteenth-century England, before the anonymity of large cities required a professional police force. No Maltbys for him. Speakers would specialise as advocates, and the laws would be embedded in the storyline, in the way precedents lay hidden in old English court cases.

Would the poor always be among them? Probably so, but as the rich would not be so very rich, they would be less noticeable. Still, there would always be the criminally minded, the mad and the lazy; so would there be liars and cheats. Should he deal with such people harshly, or with generosity? Could Anterwold afford the latter? After all, most societies execute criminals because keeping them locked up is so expensive. Although he supposed that their own lands could be appropriated to provide for their incarceration.

But how should traitors be treated? Should they be understood, forgiven or punished severely? What was the price of betrayal, in this world or in Anterwold? Of course Sam was the most likely candidate. It was why Lytten had left him to last, not wanting to find the answer. What traitor would so obviously advertise his distaste for his country, his job and his colleagues? Or would say loudly how much he admired enemies and detested friends? At the same time, what traitor would work so selflessly for his country, putting his life at risk so often? A very good one, perhaps.

Yet Lytten sat at his desk, working on social arrangements for something which did not exist and never would. It was filling in the time, a confession of his inadequacy and helplessness. He had to wait now, to see how it all played out. Sooner or later, Sam would have to make the move that would take this miserable business to its natural end.

*

He read until dawn, and only then fell properly unconscious for a few hours before incessant, confused thoughts brought him round again.

So he got up, put on his dressing gown – a long, red flannel one which Angela, for reasons best known to herself, had bought him for Christmas – and ran a bath.

Then, as the water was never hot enough, he went to boil the kettle so he could shave properly.

He made himself some coffee and carried it back to the bathroom, then slid luxuriously into the water. He stayed there peacefully until he heard a noise from downstairs. Someone was in the house. Sam must be back, he thought glumly. Ah well. He can wait until I'm ready.

He stayed for another fifteen minutes, reluctant to leave the warmth and comfort for something that was likely to be very much less pleasant, until the doorbell rang. He ignored it and it rang again, and again. So he dried himself, put the dressing gown back on and walked downstairs to find out who it was. Again.

*

The street outside was different since the last time he'd looked. Six police cars were parked along it, for one thing. About a dozen uniformed policemen were standing there in positions which would make it very difficult for anyone to run up or down it and get away. Two large vans of the sort Sam Wind used to transport his ogres, those troglodyte characters who for some reason he allowed to carry guns, were stopped right across the road, blocking cars, bicycles and even pedestrians from walking past.

On the doorstep stood Sam Wind, Sergeant Maltby and the young one from counter-intelligence.

Henry gazed around, then bent down and picked up the milk bottle left on the step.

'Morning, Sam. What can I do for you?'

'We have come for Angela Meerson.'

'She's not here.'

'Yes she is. She came in about twenty minutes ago. With a girl.'

'Really? I was in the bath. Bit rude of them not to knock.'

'Henry, you will just have to stand aside and let us do this, you know. We need to talk to her.'

Lytten scratched his still damp scalp. 'Oh, very well, Sam. Do your worst.'

He opened the door wide and watched as the three filed through. 'Is that all? You don't think you need the Parachute Regiment in here as well, just to be on the safe side? Do wipe your feet. They're muddy, and the cleaning lady won't be here until tomorrow.'

'Where is she?'

'Angela? I have no idea.'

He walked to the bottom of the stairs and shouted, 'Angela? Are you down there? Would you come up here, please?'

There was a sound of bumping from below, then a muffled voice came drifting up from the cellar.

'Just a sec. I'll be right with you.'

Henry smiled grimly. 'You see? All you have to do is ask.'

52

'Quickly! Bring me something to write with!'

Jay burst out of the tent where the forester lay, a look of panic and distress on his face. He had spent much of his time there, keeping his old friend company. In between Catherine went in and sat next to him, saw to the changing of his dressings and bathed his head. The old man was weakening though, despite their attention, and the fever they had all feared had gripped him.

'That bad?' It was Catherine who understood first what he was saying.

'He has asked me to take his story.'

'Go back inside and stay with him. I will see that everything is brought to you. Do you know how to do this?'

'No. Not really. I mean, I know I have to take down his words, then write them properly later. Apart from that . . .'

'You let him decide. I have had to witness it many times. You listen. You don't interrogate or demand answers to anything. You must not be shocked or upset by anything he says.'

'What if his words aren't clear?'

'You can ask questions, but you cannot press him. This will be how he wants to be remembered. You are just the agent of his wishes.'

'Anything else?'

'If he stops, you stop. If he keeps on going, so do you,

for as long as he speaks. It is your judgement about what goes into the final version. I think that many leave out embarrassing or shameful details spoken in delirium but that is for you to decide.'

'Anything else?'

'Have a drink of water. You're not allowed to eat or drink while taking the story. It could go on for a long time, and you have to sit until he's finished. When you're sure he's done, then call me. I'll sit with him if his end is near.'

'I'd like to do that.'

'No. That's not your job. What you have to do is far more important. Oh – and, Jay . . .'

'Yes?'

'It will be hard for you, but you must not show it. If there is a chance, please ask him to forgive me.'

'For what?'

'He knows.'

Jay nodded and turned to go back into the tent. He was doing too many new things, too quickly. He hoped he could do this one correctly.

A few minutes later, a writing table, paper, pen and ink were brought to him. He set them up carefully and took a deep breath.

'Callan, son of Perel. You believe you are nearing the end of your life, and you have asked to tell your story, that it may remain behind you and the memory of your life be preserved. Am I acceptable as the recorder of your story for others to read?'

'You are, young Jay.' Callan's voice was thin and rasping; Jay had to lean over to hear what he was saying. 'I could wish for no one better.'

'Then I am ready, and you may begin to speak.'

The forester reached out to grasp his hand. 'Don't worry. I know how this is done. Relax,' he said with a watery smile. 'This may be worse for me than you.'

Nearly five hours later, Jay emerged. Callan had spoken for so long, he had exhausted himself and collapsed into unconsciousness. Jay wished only that he could do the same. He found that Catherine had stayed nearby throughout. Now she rose, stiff from sitting so long, to ask how they both were.

'He's asleep. You are not needed yet.'

'Are you all right?'

'Of course. It was an honour to do it. He was kind to me.'

'Then that kindness will live for ever,' Catherine replied. 'That's no consolation, is it?'

He shook his head.

'Callan has played his part in the story, and you will play yours for a long time to come. Do not worry for him. He will soon be relieved of care, although he is incredibly strong. He may well live awhile yet. You will have to bear the burdens of life for much longer.'

'I know all the words. I just don't believe any of them at the moment.'

'You have done well, Jay. Henary would be proud of you. Will be proud, I can say. You kept my secret from Pamarchon until Rosalind decided to intervene – although quite how we got away with that one I cannot say. You will be a great Storyteller. You have played your part for Callan, and it was your idea to approach Esilio to avoid bloodshed. You have done more than enough.'

He glanced at her. 'I fear I cannot finish yet.'

'Why not?'

'I need to be your advocate at the Shrine.'

'You are not trained,' she said with vehemence. 'You don't know the facts, and might well have to oppose someone who does. It's a specialised calling. You can't just stand up and speak, you know that. For a village theft, maybe. Not when lives are at stake, and the entire fate of Willdon.'

'You see, Callan told me that—'

'No! You must not say. You know you must not, not while he is alive. It would be a terrible breach of confidence.'

'Then I must simply say it again. Appoint me to be your advocate. Tell me everything you can in confidence,' Jay said eventually. 'I will be able to discharge the duty Callan laid on me without revealing anything which may cast you in a bad light. Do you understand what I am saying?'

She hesitated for a long while before she spoke again. 'You have thought this through?'

'I have.'

'Then I must trust you and place myself in your hands. Are you ready to listen to my story?'

'I am.'

'All I ask is that you do not judge me until the end.'

*

'I am, as you know, Catherine of Willdon, widow of Thenald, who was my equal in birth and dignity,' she began. 'I won Willdon on his death because of my status. Someone of my background could be trusted, it was felt, to

577

represent the domain and look after it until it returned to the family line, as it would on my death.

'I have not displeased. My rule was confirmed at the first Abasement. I went away, returned and was restored by universal acclaim, so much so that now Gontal doesn't even bother to show up. In all things, in all ways, I have done my people honour in my behaviour.'

She paused and looked at him carefully as he nodded.

'Unfortunately,' she continued, 'that is all a complete lie. I was not the equal of my husband in birth or family. I obtained my husband, and Willdon, through fraud.'

There was a very long silence as Jay digested this.

'You are known throughout the land as the finest woman in Anterwold,' he said. 'Nothing I have seen in the past few days has done anything to contradict that.'

'I am touched by the compliment, but it is true, nonetheless. I will not dwell on my birth and upbringing, but I came from a poor place, a long way away. For many years I lived a hard life, with hard people. I lived as they did, hand to mouth, with never-ending labour. There was a sort of pestilence on the land. Cruel people commanded us, and few had the spirit to protest. It happens, more often than you think.

'I left as soon as I could, and went without saying farewell. I came to richer and kinder lands and did what was necessary: I stole, slept rough, worked for shelter and clothes, met other wanderers, formed friendships for the first time. I listened to their stories and was captivated. I watched others, boys and girls from much better families. I kept quiet and absorbed everything. I learned about people, how to persuade and cajole, how to settle disputes and keep the peace. Above all I learned how to listen, to go through what people say to what they mean. It is now my greatest talent. One boy I met was going to be a student, and he was full of Ossenfud and the scholars. So I followed him there. I was already donning my disguise, becoming the mysterious, beautiful Catherine.

'Henary found me out. He was curious about the young woman sitting in rapt attention as he spoke, who seemed to live nowhere, know no one. I was twenty by then; hardened and experienced from my life, but never, ever showing it. He questioned me, befriended me and gradually instructed me. I impressed him; I had taught myself much, and had not found it difficult in the slightest. He wanted me to become a student, but I could not; your family has to be entered into the rolls; you have to inform them of the great honour done to their name. So I said no and, one night, I told him what I am now telling you.

'The reason I love Henary is that it did not matter to him. "I thought you were an intelligent, thoughtful and beautiful woman who had made the best of the many advantages that a good family had bestowed on her," he told me. "Now I think you are even more remarkable, for you make your own advantage." It made him appreciate me all the more, but he did accept that few would agree. We were thinking about it when I decided to go on a pilgrimage to Esilio's grave at Willdon. There I met Thenald, and he fell in love with me.'

'You do not say that you fell in love with him.'

'Because I did not. He was a refuge for me. To me he was not a bad man, because he was entranced by me, but gradually I saw that to all others he was not good. He was a great believer in his rights and others' duties. All must be as all had ever been and ever would be. Any deviation he found dangerous, and he reacted to it with violence. He was often heartless when a little kindness would have resolved an issue. He thought only in terms of whether people were below him or above him in family, and there were few above him, so he seemed impossibly proud. He wasn't really. Just frightened.

'He was also lazy, which was his best quality. I easily took over running the household, tempered his harshness, and was beginning to know how to run the domain. I would have tamed him eventually, but he found out who I was.'

'Did he?'

She nodded. 'He wanted to contact my family, of course he did, but I put him off for a long time. Before we married he sent Callan without telling me, but Callan lied for me and said my family had gone on pilgrimage and could not be contacted for worldly matters. But Thenald got the truth from him. He discovered that I had lied; I was nothing. He said he was going to divorce me and make sure that I was cast out utterly and in shame.

'He was murdered instead, the next day. Instead of being cast out, I was chosen to rule Willdon.'

'Henary knows this?'

'Yes. He never once questioned me or doubted me.'

'Anyone else?'

'Callan. Did he not say any of this when you took his story?'

'I cannot say. You know that. But tell me now; I want to hear it from your mouth. Did you murder Thenald?'

'No,' she said firmly and without hesitation. 'I did not.'

'Forgive me for asking an impertinent question, but why not?'

She burst out laughing. 'Oh, Jay! Why not? A good question, but not one I have ever considered. Because I believe in . . . what would you call it? Fate, if you like. How much would you have me do to safeguard myself? Kill Thenald, then overturn the whole of Anterwold? I could invade the grave of Esilio, cart Pamarchon away and just kill him. I could silence Henary, and you and Callan, for ever. My people would follow me. I could then take on the might of Ossenfud and subdue that, if it were necessary; it is hardly well defended. But I don't want to; once this starts, it never ends.'

'Do you think Pamarchon killed him, then?'

'I used to. I was convinced, genuinely convinced, that he was responsible. I never questioned it. Now – having watched him for three days? Seen him with Rosalind? Now I am not so sure.'

53

'Hello, Professor,' Rosie said as she appeared at the top of the stairs and saw that Lytten was not alone. 'Who are these people?'

Then Angela. 'Sam!' she called out. 'How nice to see you again. Sergeant Maltby too! And who are you, young man?'

'This is not the time, Angela, I'm afraid,' Sam Wind said, sounding oddly apologetic. 'We need to ask you some questions.'

'By all means. Go ahead.'

'Not here.'

'I'm a bit busy today, I'm afraid. What with one thing and another.'

'I must insist.'

'And I must decline, Sam Wind. I said I'm busy.'

Wind nodded at Maltby. 'If you would do the honours, Sergeant . . . ?'

'Angela Meerson, I am arresting you on suspicion of offences under the Official Secrets Act.'

Angela stopped, her mouth half open in surprise. 'Really? What simply extraordinary timing. Are you sure you can't come back tomorrow?'

'No. This is not a joke. Please come with us without making a fuss. It will be much easier.'

'I'm sure. What offences? Henry? Has Sam here lost his wits at last?'

'If you want my opinion, I think he may have done,' he replied. 'But he has a small army out there and so it would be best if you did as instructed. It's nothing to worry about. It happens to all of us sooner or later, if that's any consolation. I was taken off and interrogated for three days back in . . . when was it, Sam?'

'1954, I think.'

'That's right.'

'I wish I had your confidence.' Angela turned to Rosie, who was standing with an air of astonishment behind her. 'More interesting than being at school, eh?'

She nodded.

'I fear I must ask you to take over for a while. A little show and tell with Henry. Do you know what I mean? Then you have to open it at dusk. Six turns of the little saucepan from where we are. It's really important. Dusk. Are you up to it? Can you remember?'

'I think so,' she said quietly.

'Good. Rosie is an extraordinary girl, Henry. I want you to listen to her. When she is finished, I will need to see you. At your earliest convenience, please.'

She smiled at Wind. 'Lead on, Sam Wind. If it makes you feel better.'

'Professor Lytten, what have you done?' Rosie exclaimed after she had watched Angela, head high, being led to a police car, put into the back and driven off. One by one the other cars and vans followed, and in a few minutes the street was its usual self once more, apart from the faces trying hard not to be noticed in the windows of every neighbouring house.

'Rosie, you must go to school, or something. I have no

time to talk to you at the moment, and it is certainly none of your business.' Lytten seemed weary and perplexed by what had happened. She had never seen him like that before.

'I have to show you something. It's very important.'

'No, Rosie. I'm sorry. Please go. You know how much I like you, but you shouldn't be here in the first place, and I do not wish to discuss the matter.'

'I do want to discuss it.'

'Go away.'

'No.'

'I will begin to get very angry indeed with you if you—'

He didn't get to finish what would undoubtedly have been a very pompous sentence. Rosie pressed her lips together and poked him in the chest with her finger.

'Do not lecture me,' she said in a furious voice. 'This is all your fault, and Angela is trying to put it right. So you will listen.'

'I will do no—'

'Downstairs. Now,' she said in a loud, authoritative voice. Lytten had not heard the like since the terrifying Miss Barton in primary school and so, naturally, he fell silent and obeyed.

'Keep going. Right down to the bottom.'

He would give her three minutes, he thought, then he'd bring this nonsense to an end. He liked the girl but he would have to forbid her from coming to his house any more. Jenkins would miss her.

'Right, Henry Lytten. I am going to show you something. Something Angela built. Then I will explain what it is.'

She started a sort of ridiculous dance, going down on

one knee and spinning around and playing with the old kettle.

'Rosie. Stop this now.'

'Oh!' she said. 'You've broken my concentration. I'll have to start again. Just shut up for a few seconds, will you?'

Giving him a ferocious glare, she began again, twirling round, kneeling down and chanting. Then she peered behind him and smiled. 'Ha!'

'Very funny,' said Lytten.

'Look,' she said, and pointed.

Lytten scowled, turned around and stopped dead.

In front of him was the rusty old pergola that Angela had claimed was a sculpture. Except that the inside of it had started glowing, and he couldn't see where the light was coming from. Even more strangely, the light changed colour, and then began to form into a picture. He could see a remarkably convincing image of grass and trees. There was a low stone wall, and in the far corner what seemed very like the altar in Poussin's painting in the Louvre.

'Now,' Rosie said, 'this is not a joke, not a film, not a television. Do you see those people there?'

Lytten looked carefully at a few figures who had appeared at the side.

'Jay, Pamarchon, Henary, Catherine,' Rosie continued. 'All perfectly real and—'

'That other one. She looks like you.'

'Apparently it is me.'

'Very clever. When did you two do this? I must say, it is very like what I had in mind. They all look remarkably as I imagined them. And that arena. Shrine of Esilio?'

'That's right.'

'Wherever did you film it? Or get weather like that?'

'You don't listen, do you? It's real. Angela made it. From your head.'

Lytten shook the very same head, trying to think a way round the joke. It was Rosie's seriousness that unnerved him. He had a great deal of experience of undergraduate pranks and student acting. There was something unusually convincing about her intensity.

'According to Angela,' Rosie went on, 'it's a universe. A different one from ours. I think that's what she said. But time is short. I certainly don't understand enough to explain properly and I can see it's going to be hard to convince you. So you'll just have to go and look for yourself.'

She stopped. 'Oh, heavens! I'm coming over. You stay there. I'd better get out of the way.'

She scuttled off to the side in a hurry, leaving Lytten looking blankly as a differently dressed Rosie appeared in the pergola. Manifestly the same person, but . . .

*

'Professor!' Rosalind through the pergola called. 'I'm so glad to see you!'

'Rosie?' he replied carefully. 'Is that really you?'

'Yes, yes. It's me. The one and only Rosie. You've no idea what's been going on in the last few days. We really need your help here. Who killed Thenald?'

'What are you talking about?'

'Thenald; you must remember. Catherine marries Thenald. Thenald gets murdered, she inherits. You wrote all that.'

'Did I? I remember killing him off, I don't remember spelling out what happened to him.'

'No, he was murdered. So who did it? You must tell me. It's important.'

'Why? It's only a story.'

'That's the point. It's not. It's here and it's real. The whole thing. I'm in it. Listen, I'll come through and explain it all. It's time I was back, anyway. They'll be furious with me at school. Just a minute . . .'

'No!' said Rosie on Henry's side of things. 'She doesn't know about me. She mustn't. Stop her.'

Lytten didn't know what was going on, still assumed it was some elaborate joke of unfathomable purpose, but Rosie's tone held no joke in it. She was panicked.

'How can I stop her?'

'Do as I say. Walk through yourself and have a look. It's not dangerous. I've done it. Well, you can see that. If I'm talking rubbish, then the only danger is that you'll bump into the wall. When you're through there, by the way, there's one really important thing you have to do.'

'What?'

'Pretend it's a play. You're an actor in it. You have to get into your part. Don't look at me like that; I know what I'm talking about. It's the only way of not going a little bit crazy. You'll be fine. You wrote the play, after all. Think of yourself as an actor-manager, or something.'

Lytten noticed she was looking very serious. She, evidently, didn't need to step through a pergola to go a little crazy.

'Ridiculous,' he said again. Then, determined to end this nonsense once and for all, he did as instructed.

587

54

I hadn't been in prison since an unfortunate evening in late 1938 when I got into a brawl in a bar in Marseilles. I badly misinterpreted the friendliness of some strangers, one thing led to another, and I spent the night in jail. We all became good friends eventually.

The police being the British police of course were terribly good at arresting me, but hadn't got a clue about what they should do after that. Questioning, they said. By whom? What about? Three of them stood in the corner, muttering to each other and occasionally glancing in my direction, while I smiled sweetly and fondled the old shopping bag I had brought as a prop. Bolt upright, knees together, I was the embodiment of innocence, which was fair enough; I hadn't a clue why I was there, but I was sure I hadn't done it.

Eventually one of the officers came over. 'I'm afraid, Mrs Meerson . . .'

'Miss, Miss,' I said. 'Once spoken for, never collected, that's me. Just an old spinster, you know.'

'Very far from that, I'm sure, miss. I'm afraid we must ask you to stay here for a few hours, until Mr Wind returns to question you.'

'How exciting. Will you lock me in a cell? It'll give me something to tell the girls at our next luncheon.'

Lovely. A nice quiet cell and a few hours of undisturbed

rest. I persuaded them to bring me some water, popped another half tab and settled down to do a bit of serious work.

*

I should explain how this operates. What you do is unpack all the raw material and turn it over to the stimulated part of the brain. The result is presented a little like the memory of a dream; that is, through symbolism and association. The knack is to unwrap the significance of the images afterwards in order to retrieve the detailed calculations underlying them. In that sense it is a bit like the Tsou script, but vastly more subtle.

I assembled my information, inserted my problems – the arrival of Chang, an entire transcript of his conversation, Rosie, the difficulties of shutting down the machinery, Lucien Grange, Emily – and lay back.

What I had at the end was the most complex piece of work I had ever achieved. A railway line with points, and a train waiting. I, Rosie and Henry were passengers. Henry was shouting something about Shakespeare, but Wind was hitting him, rather like a Punch and Judy show. On the ground, an old man was reading a book given to him by a young girl dressed like a peasant. He pulled a lever and the train began to move. As it went over the points, the girl laughed, ran to the train and jumped on. Rosie tried to get off, but couldn't open the carriage door. The old man was left behind as the train vanished down the tracks.

So what did this mean? Henry shouting about Shakespeare was the easiest. Once, in the South of France, he gave me an impassioned discourse defending Shakespeare's plots, saying that outrageous coincidence was more natural than carefully formed, reasoned action.

Rosie was also simple; she couldn't come back. I had set the machine to prevent anyone from Anterwold wandering into this world. Rosie had come back and the machine would now think the copy was indigenous to Anterwold. Changing that would mean rebuilding the entire machine and there wasn't going to be time. If she stepped through, then she would simply vanish, from this world and from Anterwold.

Next came the image of the train. The old man looked triumphant as he changed the points and the train went forward again, down a different track. The girl jumped onto the train. She looked a bit like Rosie in my mind, but was not.

That took the real work to understand, but the result was devastating. All causes are balanced by consequences, and each is merely a different form of the other. They are interchangeable, like energy and matter. What I had done by creating Anterwold was not just the cause of history changing; it was the consequence of it as well.

There is no difference between cause and effect. That is an illusion created by belief in time. If I drop a cup, the cup breaks. The dropping is the cause, the breaking is the effect, because one happens after the other. Remove the notion of time and that no longer works. Each is the required condition for the other to take place. As the cup breaks, I am required to drop it. It is like the pair of scales again, where conditions in one pan determine the state of the other one.

Ordinarily, it is relatively simple to calculate such things as there is only one line of existence. However, my experiment had created another one and they were interacting. I could not close Anterwold because Rosie was in it. If she had come back then I might have kept control. But she split in two, because she was wearing rings on her toes.

The same applied to the Devil's Handwriting. It existed because of actions taken in my future. But those actions equally depended on its existence.

That was it. In my vision, nothing was done by any of the actors on the train. They just watched out of the window. The central actions came from outside, from the man pulling the lever.

It was obviously Oldmanter; I had never met him nor seen a photograph but my unconscious always had a weakness for poor puns. The girl telling him what to do could only be one person. That's why I was worried. I wasn't battling Hanslip, or even Oldmanter; I could outthink them easily. I wasn't certain I could outthink my daughter. I'd seen her file. She was possibly smarter than I was.

From that point it was fairly simple to sketch out a potential chain of events. Chang told me Hanslip knew of the Devil's Handwriting. Hanslip would assume there was a reason this document was hidden where only a historian would be able to find it. So he sends More to contact Emily. Of course he does.

More goes south. Oldmanter would certainly track that; it was clear from Grange he wanted my project. Emily would be attracted to More – I found him rather handsome and we would have a similar outlook on the subject. Besides, she would be intrigued by the connection to me.

But how does the data get to Oldmanter, and why would he not conduct rigorous checks to ensure it was safe? Here conjecture had to come in, but the only variable I had left was Emily.

I could not see her agreeing to help find the data unless she knew what it was; she would discover it was not only valuable but also dangerous. Of course she would; she would not assist merely so some institute could make money. To get her help, someone like More would have to tell her that finding it was important for the safety of the planet. She would understand immediately that it offered the chance of accomplishing in an instant what she was otherwise prepared to wait for over centuries. As a renegade, she believed the world of science would bring about its own ruin; this would be a spectacular demonstration of that.

Rather than making sure it was never used, she would do her best to ensure it was. But at the cost of her own life, and of those who thought like her? Not if she was like me. How could she possibly accomplish that, though? That I couldn't figure out. I didn't have enough information. What was Oldmanter going to do to change the points on the railway line? What form would his intervention take?

I was getting close now, I could feel it, but I would have to test the conclusions thoroughly. What I had was only marginally more likely than many alternatives; it was not solid enough to rely on.

Then that stupid man Wind arrived and interrupted me yet again. Worse still, I was heavily under the influence, so I didn't make a very good impression.

*

592

'I need some answers,' he said as he came into Angela's cell and sat down. 'Are you all right?'

Angela was sitting on the bench that doubled as a bed. Her eyes were wide and her pupils dilated, and she twitched almost uncontrollably as he spoke to her. She seemed to him as though she was having a panic attack. Guilt? Or just plain fear? he wondered.

'Perfectly,' she replied. 'Fabulous. I am asking myself questions as well, so you can't bother me at the moment.'

'I'm afraid I must insist.'

'On your head be it, then.'

'Are you ill? You look very odd.'

'Oh. No. It's a sort of . . .' She waved vaguely at her head. 'Comes on me, every now and then. Nothing serious. Did you say you wanted something?'

'I need to ask you about the man who vanished.'

Angela wrinkled her nose in disappointment.

'Eh? Oh, him. An extraneous factor, doesn't really affect the outcome. Just a data store, really.'

'Do you know who he was?'

'I have never seen him before.' She giggled. 'That is the truth, because "before" is such a useful word. Germanic roots, I think.'

'What are you talking about?'

'I'm so sorry. Mind all over the place today.'

'I have been going through your files.'

'I didn't know I had any.'

'There is no trace of you whatsoever before 1937. We have been unable to track down your parents, old addresses, anything.'

'Not very good files, then.'

'We have established that information you gave when you became a translator in 1940 was false. Schools, addresses and so on: none checked out.'

'Doesn't say much for your vetting procedure.'

'The form was, in fact, filled in for you by Henry Lytten, who also acted as your referee and sponsor.'

'Because of my languages, you see. There was a war on. All hands to the pump, he said.'

'We also noted that between 1945 and 1952 you came to England for a brief stay, then went on trips – to Vienna, Berlin on one occasion, Stockholm and Geneva. Why?'

'Henry asked me to deliver manuscripts for him. He didn't trust the post and he was keen to rebuild the academic community. I helped out, and always took a little holiday while I was at it.'

'I see. Let me ask about yesterday. This mysterious stranger. Bringing him to the house was your idea, so the policeman says. Did he say why he was watching Henry's house?'

'I didn't ask him. It was none of my business.'

'How did he escape?'

'You were the one guarding the place. Now, are there any more questions? Is that what you came for?'

Angela moved close to him. Her eyes cleared and she held him by the chin as she studied him, then tittered in a high, slightly hysterical laugh. 'Oh, I see what you are getting at.' She let him go, then pushed him away and leaned back against the wall. 'Of course. That's how it might work. You are such a silly man, Sam Wind. Has anyone ever told you that?'

55

'We must go to the circle soon, so that we may welcome the suppliants,' Henary said to Rosalind the following morning.

'You said there must be someone to preside. Who will that be?'

'The spirit of Esilio presides,' he said with a smile, 'but as this procedure has not been employed for a very long time, I really do not know how it will work. I have read as much as possible in the last day, but there is little to discover. For Jay even to think of it was very ingenious and unorthodox. I suspect it will take the form of an ordinary trial, which would mean that the spirit will move through the most qualified. I'm afraid that will probably be Gontal, now that I am bound to Pamarchon.'

'That's no good,' Rosalind said.

'Perhaps it will not be so bad. He has an interest in seeing both of them found guilty. As that is not an option, he will have no choice but to be scrupulously fair. He is not a bad man, really, although he is full of his name and greatly desires power. He is generally saved by his reverence for the Story.'

The pair walked out of a side door, through the courtyards used mainly by stable boys and those who worked in the kitchens; Henary was concerned to ensure that Gontal did not notice them, lest he intercept Pamarchon before he could claim the protection of the Shrine.

'Tell me about this Shrine,' Rosalind said as they walked. 'Why is it so special?'

'It is the grave of Esilio.'

'He's the man I read about. Who was he?'

'There are many opinions. Some hold that he was simply a courageous leader who brought us back from exile to settle the land. Others think that he was – or is – a god. The god, perhaps, who created us then abandoned us. This view holds that he will return and judge whether we have lived well enough to be forgiven the sins of our ancestors.'

'Which sins are those?'

'They are said to be so grave that they were hidden, lest we despair of redeeming ourselves.'

They walked round a curve in the track and there before them was the stone circle – more an oval, really, Rosalind thought – with the monument inside where she had first encountered Pamarchon. Only what? Five days ago? It seemed like an age to her.

As they entered the circle there was a movement in the bushes at the far end, and three figures emerged. They hurriedly crossed over the line into the sanctuary.

'Done it,' said one. 'That's a relief.'

There they all were. Jay, Pamarchon, Kate, and Henary looking at them. The four people, Rosalind realised, she liked most in the world. This world, anyway. They were all safe, for the time being.

She gave every one of them an enormous hug, leaving the last and biggest for Pamarchon, who wrapped his arms around her and nestled his head against hers. 'I'm so happy to see you again.'

'As am I.'

They were interrupted by a discreet cough in the background.

'Oh, yes. Introductions. If you don't mind I will dispense with your formalities. I don't like them, and I'm not in the mood. Pamarchon, son of – someone or other. Henary, scholar of Ossenfud.'

'Welcome back, my Lady,' Henary said. 'You have led us a merry dance for the past few days. I am glad to see you looking so well.'

Catherine acknowledged Henary with a warm smile, then turned to Pamarchon.

'I no longer need your protection, Pamarchon, son of Isenwar,' she said. 'Our truce is at an end. When I came to you first, you thought me a mere servant, yet you treated me with consideration. You not only followed the dictates of kindness but went far beyond them. You have given protection according to your position. I offer you my thanks. What must happen here cannot be changed. But I will not fulfil my part in hatred.'

'It seems that I am not very good at seeing the truth in women's hearts, or am too trusting of their words,' Pamarchon replied. 'I briefly thought the woman I loved most in the world was a mere boy; I thought the woman I hated most in the world was a mere servant. One I love because of who she is, the other I hate only because of what she has done. Separate person and deeds, and my hatred dies like a plant deprived of water.'

Rosalind sighed. They were off again. But the others seemed highly satisfied.

'The deeds and the person will be separated at the end.'

597

'Deeds and those who commit them are not always the same.'

'One can be many and yet—'

'Enough. Enough, you two,' Rosalind interrupted. 'I know you enjoy it, but don't we have more urgent things to do?'

They scowled at her, but Henary came to her support. 'She is right; we must summon the domain. You are aware, Catherine, that time is short. The assembly begins at dusk.'

'I will take care of it,' she said.

'By what right? You are no longer the Lady of this place. You have no more authority than the servant you were not so long ago.'

Catherine gave him what Rosalind thought was a very nasty look.

'Jay! Go as quickly as you can to the Chamberlain. Say he is to ring the bell for a trial. Tell him who and where, and say it must begin within the hour. Then go to Gontal and tell him. You will not get a good reception, but I'm afraid you will have to put up with that.'

'Then should I come back here?'

'As you choose.'

'It's just that I have to prepare.'

'For what?'

'I am to defend Lady Catherine.'

Now it was Henary's turn to be astounded. 'Whose idea was that?'

'We agreed,' Catherine said. 'Who has been chosen for Pamarchon?'

'I have. I could not refuse,' he said.

It was a hastily assembled procession, but a large one. First came the Chamberlain, hurrying through the thickets with only a few followers. Next a gaggle of servants from the house, then ever more people from the nearby fields, abandoning their tools to see what was going on, and villagers from the settlements all around. Finally Gontal arrived, bringing with him his soldiers. Bit by bit, more than a hundred gathered.

No one, though, dared step into the circle except Gontal.

'What exactly does all this mean?' he asked, then stopped as he realised who everyone was. 'Catherine. I am glad to see you restored to us, lesser in rank but whole in person.'

She eyed him coolly but did not reply.

'The choice and acclamation of the new ruler of Willdon must take place at dusk,' Henary said. 'You will present yourself as next in line, I have no doubt. One of these will do so as well. One will take on the guilt that lies between them and so, purified of any taint, the other will offer themselves. Both have claimed the privilege of Esilio, as laid down in the Story, and their wishes cannot be ignored.'

Gontal's eyes flickered between Henary, Pamarchon and Catherine, trying to work out whether there was any way of stopping what he considered to be a devious piece of trickery. He grunted and walked swiftly over to the Chamberlain. They had a hurried, quiet conversation; Gontal's face darkened, and he stamped his foot in frustration. Then he walked back.

'Very well,' he said. 'I imagine I must be the judge of the proceedings.'

'Absolutely not,' said Pamarchon and Catherine to-gether.

'Then who? Who has a better right than I?' He smirked at the crowd gathering around. 'Let any with greater authority than I present themselves to judge this matter.' He called in a loud voice, 'I command them to come forward!'

No one answered, all were looking at him anxiously. Except for Rosalind, who suddenly took a few steps and then started gesturing, speaking to nothing.

*

To say that what happened next caused terror and chaos would be to understate matters considerably. Rosalind ran over to an empty part of the clearing and could be seen speaking fluently and quickly, making gestures of com-mand and respect. She was talking to nothing, but as she spoke she was illuminated by a faint, heavenly light. Only Jay had ever seen anything like it before; only Henary had ever heard of such a thing. He knew enough of the Perplexities to realise his worst nightmare was coming true. What had he done? He had never really believed in it, even after his conversation with Rosalind. His curiosity had set this in motion. Now it could not be stopped. Gontal had spoken in the circle, summoning one greater than him-self, someone with more authority, knowing that no one on earth could have any such authority. His presumption had been answered.

He could not hear what Rosalind was saying; it was too fast and quiet, too far away. But he heard her last words. 'Please come,' she said, then stepped back.

Henary's stomach curdled as a shape appeared and took on a solid form. Cries of lamentation went up; where there had been only a faint light, a figure, a man, was now standing, resplendent in red robes, tall and powerful-looking. He did nothing, said nothing, but smiled at Rosalind. They felt the power of his glance as it swept over them.

All fell onto their knees in reverence; a collective groan went up; some screamed and began sobbing in shock. Many covered their eyes, and those who did not looked in awe at the way that Rosalind, now revealed as a woman of great spiritual power, perhaps even the Herald of Doom itself, approached the spirit without fear. They had all seen it, they had witnessed with their own eyes something they would have dismissed as madness otherwise.

The spirit, meanwhile, appeared sombre, frightening in his authority and wrath. He held up his hands when he saw the crowd that was kneeling in fear of him, and made a gesture that seemed to be an order to step back from his presence. They obeyed without question, scarcely daring to look. Only Rosalind stood her ground, taking her eyes off him briefly as the light behind him flickered and then vanished.

Gontal was trembling, Pamarchon terrified, Catherine stood stock still. Henary looked as though he was about to be violently sick.

'Master,' Jay whispered, for fear that the spirit would hear. 'What is happening?'

'It is the end, Jay. The day spoken of, when the god judges us. He returns, and either sets us free or destroys us utterly.'

'That's a myth, an allegory. You said so yourself.'

'I was wrong. This is my fault. I meddled with things I should have never ever touched. That manuscript foretold it all. You on the hilltop, the coming of the Herald, the return of Esilio. And next, the judgement.'

'Rosalind? She is the Herald?'

'The messenger who prepares the way for the return of the god.'

'You knew this?'

'No. I wanted to prove it was nonsense.'

'It's not possible,' Pamarchon said.

'Why not?'

'Well . . . she agreed to marry me. If all went well.'

'If what went well?'

'The trial.'

'Which trial? Your trial, or the trial of Anterwold? Did she say?'

'This is not in the Story,' Gontal objected. 'These are just superstitions. There is not a single text which states anything like this. You know this, Henary. You have studied them as well as I have.'

'This may be older than the Story,' Henary replied. 'Far, far older.'

56

'Well? What do you think?' Rosalind asked enthusiastically as she examined Lytten's bemused expression.

For a long time, Lytten could think of nothing to say. The smells were real, the warmth was real. The sunlight through the tall trees was real. 'This is . . . very peculiar,' he said lamely.

'You sort of get used to it after a while. Professor, could you do me a favour? I think it's normal to go into the am-I-dreaming routine. I did. But you aren't. So please just concentrate on what is important. You may be here for some time, as the light has gone out, so you might as well make yourself useful.'

Lytten looked. True enough, the light he had just walked through wasn't there any more. 'Angela said something about opening it up at dusk, I think. Where am I?'

'You are in Anterwold. To be precise, at Willdon, in the stone circle of Esilio. Do you remember that?'

'Of course. I thought it up as a sort of sacred spot. I never figured out its precise importance, though. I didn't get round to that bit.'

'It acts as a sanctuary. People are safe from the law here. They throw themselves on the judgement of Esilio, the all-wise. That's you.'

'Me?'

'Who else is going to pop up out of nowhere in the

middle of his own shrine? Apparently your coming has been foretold for generations.'

'But I'm not.'

'Are you sure? As you're here, you might as well play the part. We have two people accused of murder, and they are appealing for judgement on which one is guilty. They will naturally expect you to take charge of things. So, tell me now. Who did kill Thenald?'

'How should I know?' Lytten said, still looking around him at the scene he had somehow entered.

'You must. You wrote it.'

'Well, I'm sorry to disappoint you, but I never wrote that bit. I sketched it out years ago, but I can scarcely remember it.'

'You've got to remember, Professor,' Rosalind said desperately. 'You've got to. If this goes wrong, all sorts of horrible things are going to happen. There may be a war. We have soldiers here, and outlaws around us. It's all your fault.'

'Why is it my fault?'

'It is your fault because you never finished it. You've been writing that book of yours for years, and now it's fed up waiting and is trying to finish itself. You should tidy up loose ends. Agatha Christie does.'

'But I'm not Agatha . . . Listen. I've had enough of this. This is simply absurd. I don't believe any of it.'

'It doesn't matter what you believe. It's what they believe that counts at the moment. You have now appeared out of thin air. You can guess how that seems. Your word is law. As long as you don't make a mess of it. Who is Esilio, anyway?'

'No idea. He's just a sort of foundation figure. Like

Solon the lawgiver for Athens. A mythical character who gets everything going.'

'According to Henary, the Story says he reappears, and when he does all sorts of things start to happen. Like the end of the world. You judge your creation and destroy it if you find it wanting. You can see why you've scared the life out of them.'

Lytten snorted. 'Just because people believe things it doesn't mean they happen. Esilio's not meant to be a god, anyway. I try to avoid gods. Tricky characters.'

'You'd better tell them that. But please will you help now you're here? Listen to what they have to say? It might jog your memory. You can see for yourself they are all real people. Prick them and they bleed, you know.'

For the first time, Lytten smiled. 'Do I have any choice?'

'Yes. You have a choice between seeming like a god and seeming like a right idiot.'

*

His face fixed in an impenetrable mask, Lytten walked around the stone circle, out to the edge where ever greater numbers of people were gathering. They stiffened with fear as he approached. They had seen his appearance with their own eyes. They were terrified that, if they said or did anything wrong, he would raise his arms and bring the vengeance of the heavens down upon them. This was the day of judgement. Everybody now knew it was true.

He studied their faces carefully. Good solid faces, he thought; well fed and healthy. Their clothes were simple but comfortable and practical. They were not so very poor, these people. Anterwold could support itself well; he'd done a decent job there. He caught himself. He was even beginning to believe this nonsense.

'Stand up, man,' he said to one kneeling figure. 'Don't be afraid.'

Slowly, eyes cast still down, the man he had picked out stood.

'Look at me,' Lytten said. 'What is your name?'

'Beltan, Majesty,' he said, choking in fear.

'Are you afraid of me?'

'Of course.'

'Then stop, please. If I remember correctly I made you a tailor. Is that right?'

'Yes, Majesty. A good one, I hope.'

'A rather lovely wife as well. Jolly and kind. Renata, no? I hope you are good to each other.'

'We are very happy, and always have been, Majesty.'

'Excellent. Give her my best wishes. You live well, without cheating anyone?'

'I do.'

'Where do you get your cloth?'

'Mostly from the towns and villages nearby. Sometimes a trader comes through with foreign stuffs.'

'I see. Where do those foreign stuffs come from?'

A puzzled look passed over the rubicund, simple face. 'I don't know.'

'Then I command you to find out.'

Lytten walked on thoughtfully, stopping and questioning the occasional person whose face struck him as interesting.

'Who are you?'

'My name is Aliena, Holiness.'

'Do stop the Holiness. You're the singer, correct?'

'Yes.'

'I think I gave you the most beautiful voice in many generations. Do you use it well?'

'I . . . try to follow the rules.'

'I very much hope you do not. That would be a terrible waste. Sing what is in your heart, not what is in the rule-book.'

After many minutes he turned to Rosalind, who had been tagging along in case he panicked and needed encouragement.

'Extraordinary,' he said. 'Some people here I put in my notes. Others seem to have come from nowhere. And they do all seem to be real.'

'Told you.'

'What do you think of this place?'

'I think it needs a bit of a shake-up. They are a bit stuck in their ways, somehow. We can talk about that later. Are you convinced?'

'For want of a better explanation. Like falling downstairs and getting concussion.'

'Will you help sort out the mess you've caused?'

'I don't see why it's my mess, you know. Angela made it, apparently, not me.'

'Angela? That friend of yours?'

Lytten glanced at her. 'You've not met her, have you? I'd forgotten that. Yes. This seems to be all her doing. Don't ask how or why, because I don't know. She's going to get an earful when I see her again. But I still don't know the answer to your question. It was never in the slightest bit important what happened to Thenald.'

'It is now. If you listened to the arguments, maybe you'd get an idea . . . ?'

'I suppose that's possible. Who are the suspects?' he asked with a tone of irony.

'Catherine and Pamarchon. He's the one I'm going to marry.'

'Oh, good Lord! I certainly didn't put that in. Aren't you a bit young?'

'Not here.'

He groaned. 'Yes. That's true. I'd forgotten. My memory, really. Well, congratulations, then. I think. I'm not too sure your mother . . . What's he like?'

'Oh, he's wonderful, he's everything he should be. Unless it's a trick, and you made him like that so he'd be the last person I would suspect.'

'Not consciously. So, Catherine, then.'

'No! She's really nice too.'

'Which one is she?'

Rosalind pointed her out.

'Good heavens! She looks a little bit like Angela. I suppose that one is Henary.' Lytten examined him dubiously for a moment. 'Does he look like me?'

'Just a little.'

'Dear God!'

'You're much more handsome, though,' Rosalind reassured him.

'I'm glad to hear it. What about the others?'

'Jay and Pamarchon.'

Lytten studied the taller man for a moment.

'Yes, well. All stories must have a love interest, eh? If I remember, that was your idea, so you can't blame me for that. He's a handsome devil, though; I see what the appeal might be. He looks very like a student I taught years ago. Nice young man. I think he went into the army. It's very strange, all this. An awful lot of people resemble people I know, or knew. There's even someone who looks like that odd fellow who was watching my house. See him? Over there, next to the tailor.'

'You may have got that from *The Wizard of Oz*. You steal ideas from everyone.'

'Do I?'

'Yes. There's everything in here. Could you concentrate on the main task?'

'You understand that I'm not at my best? It's not as if this is – you know – normal.'

'You'll stop noticing soon enough. Why are you dressed like that?'

'It's my dressing gown. I've just had a bath.'

'Hence the heavenly odour of sanctity which seems to be so impressing everyone.'

'Old Spice.'

'You look the part, you see,' Rosalind continued. 'As far as they are concerned, you have been summoned to sit in judgement.'

'Why is the result so important?'

'Because if it goes wrong, Willdon is inherited by Gontal, merges with Ossenfud and ...'

'... the combination is overwhelmingly powerful and the whole of Anterwold is unbalanced. Yes, yes. I remember. Hence the need for a figure of Solomonic wisdom.'

'Probably. But all we have is you, who can't even remember his own plot. So will you just listen and look solemn? At least it will gain us some time. Go and sit on that stone thing over there. I will concoct some ceremony, and you act the part of a spirit of awesome power.'

'I still think it is all ridiculous.'

'Can you come up with a better explanation of why you are standing in the middle of a field, surrounded by worshippers while dressed in your bath robe?'

'Very well. I will do my best. But stay close, in case I need your help.'

*

'Do any here deny the evidence of their own eyes? Do any here deny that Esilio has returned as foretold?' Rosalind intoned, once the manifestation had taken his place on his own tomb. 'Do any deny that he has been summoned, to this place and to this moment, for a purpose beyond understanding? Do any think they are greater than he? That they have a greater claim to sit in judgement?'

Not a whisper. She stared pointedly at Gontal for the last one, but he pretended not to notice.

'Do any doubt that if his will is gainsaid in any way, then his wrath will be more terrible than the land of Anterwold has ever witnessed?'

A quiet muttering, which sounded like assent.

'Pamarchon and Catherine, accused. Jay, defender, Henary, defender. Step forward.'

Henary moved first, if anything more nervous than his pupil. He went to the altar and bowed. Jay followed his lead. Both were conscious of the calm, wise gaze examining them with what seemed like curiosity and, in a way, kindness.

Before he could say anything, Gontal also stepped forward and approached the figure on the altar. 'I humbly request the right to speak, lest a great injustice occur,' he said.

'You must be Gontal,' Lytten said. 'Putative heir to this place, known to friends and foes alike as Gontal the Fat. Is that so?'

Gontal shuffled from one foot to the other.

'What is the injustice you are worrying about?'

'Henary cannot speak for Pamarchon,' he said. 'It would compromise the validity of the trial.'

'Your reasons?'

'He is a close friend of Catherine. All would be concerned that he did not argue Pamarchon's case well enough, out of favour for her.'

'What is your recommendation?'

'That this trial be postponed until a more suitable advocate be found.'

'Your point is a good one, Gontal the . . . Yes, a very good one. Do you not think so, Henary?'

'I would speak as my duty compelled,' Henary said.

'And very unpleasant it would be for all concerned, if I understand things properly. Gontal here does not wish you to be put in an unfortunate position, though. Very kind and thoughtful of him. Good for you, sir.'

He nodded approvingly at the now smiling Gontal. 'You are quite right, Gontal. Henary must not speak for Pamarchon. Fortunately, a suitable advocate is to hand, so there is no need to postpone.'

'Who is that?'

'Why, you, man. You. I know full well that for the

past few years you have studied in minute detail every circumstance of this business, hoping to find some way of dislodging Catherine from her place. You have lain awake at nights rehearsing the speech you would give that would cast her out. Now's your chance! How fortunate, eh?'

'I am very much afraid that I must refuse.'

'I am very much afraid you will do no such thing,' came the thunderous reply.

Gontal stared at the figure which seemed to know all about him.

'You will speak for Pamarchon. There is no more to be said.'

Gontal bowed and withdrew.

'How was that?' Lytten whispered to Rosalind.

'Pretty good,' she said. 'You're a natural.'

57

Lytten hoped very much that the participants would talk for as long as possible. Rosie, the one in his house, had told him that Anterwold existed, but he had assumed that she was talking nonsense. Yet here he was, listening to people act out his own book. Except that they weren't. He had jotted down notes on the death of Thenald, but only as a device to explain Catherine. It was not something that he had ever intended to explore in any depth. He had only very vaguely forged a link between Pamarchon and the death, and then once more to explain his existence in the forest, so he could discourse on the young and those outside the law. Not for a single moment had he thought about drawing all the threads together into a murder. He wasn't writing a detective story, dammit.

Yet this – thing – this invention, this whatever it was, had developed some huge crisis out of it all. Taken a few pencilled jottings and extrapolated outwards, adding the details he had never bothered with. This trial, for example. The legal method, the stone circle, the crime, the participants. Idle musings had come together in ways he had never thought possible. And there they were. Gontal talking, laying into Catherine, while Jay stood stony-faced, no doubt wondering how he was going to reply. Catherine and Pamarchon, standing apart on opposite sides. Henary, who currently felt that he had failed everyone. He didn't know how lucky he was.

Had this been Shakespeare or Sidney, it would all have been easy. In *As You Like It* a goddess comes down and sorts it out. In *A Midsummer Night's Dream* the action is controlled and directed by Oberon. Homer also, when he gets stuck, sends a god from Olympus to intervene. Modern novelists of a lesser variety have recourse to a man jumping through a door holding a gun. But, of course, that was exactly what was happening. He was the coincidence, the god descending. He had appeared out of nowhere and was now meant to wave his magic wand and sort everything out. He was Oberon, Athene, even Poirot himself. The trouble was that he had no magic wand, and he hadn't a clue how to sort it out, and his little grey cells were not at their best this morning. He hadn't even had time to finish his coffee.

He listened to Gontal's speech, and it didn't help him in the slightest.

Gontal scarcely touched on the subject of who had actually killed Thenald. Lytten hoped for detail, evidence, background, something to give him a hint. He got none of it. Gontal defended Pamarchon by barely referring to him. The man began with motive, hammering away at the fact that Catherine had gained the most from her husband's death. That this was the best reason to suspect her guilt. That she had no other claim to Willdon, and could not have taken it unless both her husband and Pamarchon were either dead or discredited, preferably both. That she was, therefore, a monster of unparalleled duplicity.

Hardly based on solid evidence, but the trouble was that Gontal didn't even stick to this line of argument. Rather, he picked out minor details, then referred them to some part of the Story and launched into a lengthy piece of literary criticism. The object seemed to be to find which story was the closest parallel. The more the parallels, the greater the proof. Gontal's entire speech, in fact, was a complex exercise designed to persuade the audience that the murder of Thenald most closely resembled a story in which a wicked stepmother steals from her husband and blames his son. 'For what is murder, except the theft of life?' Gontal intoned gravely to make an entirely specious link between the two.

He finished with a positive broadside of quotations, voice rising melodramatically, right arm extended. Lytten knew where that came from. A performance of Racine in France when he was young, the static, ponderous, overwrought declamation, the mannered pose, the over-abundance of language. Yes, that was it, and it was evidently as big a success here as it had been at the Comédie-Française: the audience was cowed. Gontal had a smirk of satisfaction on his face as he turned with a flourish to Lytten, then to Pamarchon, then to the people watching, silent in admiration for the man's skill and learning. Gontal felt sure it was in the bag. How could a seventeen-year-old student stand a chance against such overwhelming erudition?

Lytten looked at the slender figure and crooked his finger to summon him.

'You seem afraid, young man.'

Jay nodded.

'I believe I made you a little ill-disciplined. Would you agree?'

Jay said nothing.

'I made you so for a reason. Use my gifts. Do not try to be a second-rate Gontal, but speak as you feel. Remember, your job is to convince me, not anyone else, and I really don't care for extraneous literary allusion. If I have to sit through another speech as dull as that one, I will conclude that I have created the most boring world that could ever exist, and will erase it and start again. It is your job to redeem this place. Do you understand?'

'No, Majesty.'

'Get to the point. Speak of the world and of people and deeds. Not of books and precedents and quotations. Make your learning serve your heart, not the other way around. Be yourself, dear boy. Use what you know.'

Jay bowed and faced the crowd. He took a deep breath and began.

*

'People of Willdon,' Jay began conventionally enough, 'you have heard Scholar Gontal deliver a fine discourse, as it should be delivered. He is a great scholar, intelligent and learned. I am not. I cannot deliver my discourse with the power that he can summon. I will not pronounce in the correct forms, with the proper weightings and with an impeccable structure. I can only speak the truth, simply and directly. I must confine myself to what happened, and to what I know.

'So let me tell you plainly that he is wrong when he says that Pamarchon is innocent, Catherine guilty. You noted, I am sure, that Scholar Gontal said little to defend Pamarchon. He briefly told you that he was innocent, but

616

his main point was to insist that this was only because Catherine is guilty. That was his entire case. He besmirched the reputation of both.

'I do not accept his conclusion or his method. I will do the opposite, and defend Catherine by defending Pamarchon also. I ask you to decide that both are innocent.'

He turned round briefly to see what the reaction was so far. Rosalind winked at him supportively; the spirit on the tomb nodded, as if in approval, encouraging him to continue. Jay tried to keep them in mind and not Henary, who he was sure would be horrified by his approach.

'Let me start by speaking in favour of the man I am supposed to be accusing. Pamarchon, the outlaw, the bandit, the murderer. I have spent several days with him, and seen him with many people. He rules his band with justice and care; he takes pains not to abuse those he lives near. His followers are with him out of love, not fear. He shows no man violence and no woman indignity. Think back to the days before his fall. Did he not intervene to cool the wrath of his uncle? Is that the behaviour of a violent murderer? Was there anything, any deed or statement, which made you think him capable of such a crime? If there is, then speak.'

No one did, fortunately. It was a risk, asking an audience for a reaction and staking all on getting the right one. If Gontal had had more time to prepare his followers, Jay's entire strategy could have collapsed then and there. Still, his luck held.

'I see that I have had some success in damaging my own case. For I have strengthened the case against Catherine, and it is not a bad case at all. Did she love her husband?

Possibly not, but then nor did anyone else. Did she move quickly to take control of Willdon on his death? Most certainly. Does she have the intelligence to do something like this? Very definitely. She is a woman of great resource, courage and daring. You know this, you who know her better than I do.

'Cruelty cannot be hidden. It does not well up once and then go away for ever, never to be seen again. A woman that cruel, that violent, that cunning would have such traits deep in her soul. They would show themselves again and again, in a word, a deed, a thought. They would have to, for "cruelty owns the soul, and bends men to its will".

'Where is that cruelty? In what way has the Lady of Willdon shown it? In her punishments of transgressors? I think not; she is known for her mercy. In her rapacity over taxes? She is known for her generosity. What about the way she treats those who work for her? She is greatly loved and respected, is she not? So where does this cruel beast linger? Tell me who has ever glimpsed its claws, or been stung by its fangs.

'No. We must search elsewhere to understand the death of Thenald. Listen to me, and I will tell you where to direct your gaze.

'Two days ago, I was summoned to the bedside of Callan, son of Perel, forester of Willdon, familiar to many here. He was on his deathbed, and I was asked to take his story. I am not allowed to tell you what he said, you all know this. However, I intend to do so now, because Callan urged me to use what he had said at the proper time. It is not something I do lightly, but I believe custom should serve the truth, not obscure it. You may judge whether I have acted correctly when I am finished.

'I met Callan when I was eleven; he was a soldier then, and took me to Ossenfud. This was shortly before the death of Thenald. When he delivered me to Ossenfud, he said he was going straight back home to Willdon. Not long after, Thenald died and, curiously, Callan hurried back to his barracks and signed on for another term of service, even though he hated the life of a soldier, even though he missed his forest. He did not return to his home for three years.

'When I took his story, he told me he left Willdon out of fear. He was afraid of being condemned for the murder of the Lord of Willdon.'

A nicely timed pause here. Jay gave the audience a moment to absorb his words. Many knew Callan and were shocked by what he had said.

'It was Callan's knife that had inflicted the wounds, his knife that cut Thenald's throat and stopped his heart. It had happened in a part of the forest where he lived. All knew that Callan had hated Thenald for the reckless way he was chopping down trees without thought or caution, for the cruel way he exploited the laws.

'He had the chance to kill, he had a reason, and the weapon was his. He told me that he pulled the knife from the body, wiped it clean, and returned to the army until he judged it was safe. He never spoke of it to anyone.

'Here it is. This is the knife which killed Thenald.'

Jay took out the knife and held it aloft, then walked round the circle. All gazed transfixed at it, and at him. Many nodded in recognition as Jay then placed it at the base of the altar.

'It would be easy for me to win my case by saying

that Callan had murdered Thenald and confessed on his deathbed. You would take my word for it, as I am bound by the story-taker's oath. There is no one to contradict me. I will not say it; Callan was a good man, and my friend, and I will not tarnish his memory by accusing him of a crime he did not commit. Too many have suffered that already.

'So I say that Callan pulled the knife out of Thenald's heart, but he had not thrust it in. Who did, then? Was it Pamarchon? No, Callan said, may he forgive me. I saw him an hour later, coming back to the house from an entirely different direction. He could not possibly have done it. Was it Catherine? This was no woman's crime, he said. Only a strong man could have driven that into Thenald's chest. Then who? Was it . . . Scholar Gontal, perhaps?'

Jay pointed at Gontal. You see, the gesture suggested, I will be as ruthless as you are, if I must.

'I do not know that name, Callan told me, but he was no scholar. He was a stranger to these parts, asking the way to Willdon. I fed him, let him sleep in my hut. The next morning he had gone, and my knife also. I never saw him again.

'What was his name? I asked. He did not know. The man had said he did not have one. No name, no family.

'So I asked him: if he knew who had done it, why did he run? It was simple, he replied. He was ashamed. He allowed Pamarchon to take the blame, for fear of being blamed himself; he did not think anyone would believe his story of a mysterious stranger stealing his knife. No one else had met or seen this man, after all. He thought people would say he had invented it as a weak excuse to hide his guilt. Can anybody here say they would not have done as Callan did in such a circumstance?

'He kept that knife until he was close to death himself, and gave it to me yesterday, as payment for taking his story and in the hope that I might correct the wrongs he had committed.

'Then my friend, the good forester, lapsed into silence, perhaps his last. I have his story; if I lie now, you may soon enough look for yourselves. But remember: the one person with any real knowledge of this crime was prepared to use his final breath to tell me that both Catherine of Willdon and Pamarchon, son of Isenwar, were wholly, completely and totally innocent of Thenald's death. Think of that as you reach your verdict, I beg you.'

*

Jay had departed so far from orthodoxy that no one had any idea what to do when he fell silent and retired to the side, shaky from his effort. Certainly Jay had no idea. His refusal to make his case in the required way so disrupted proceedings that, in effect, the trial collapsed. Ordinarily, he would have finished his speech; the accused – both of them in this case – would have delivered a shorter discourse disputing the use of quotations by the other; the presiding authority would have made some remarks; and the assembled multitude would have voted.

That, clearly, could not happen now. No one knew what to do, or what they were supposed to vote for or even – now that Esilio had appeared among them – whether they were meant to vote. This gave Gontal his chance to reassert himself.

'A poor speech, excusable in one so young, I suppose. I would have expected better from Henary's star pupil. What? Not a single reference to authority? A case so thin it can claim no parallel to anything in the whole of the Story Hall? Revealing the contents of a story while the teller is still alive? I could depart from custom as well, were I also undisciplined and lazy. I could say that Pamarchon and Catherine were in league together, for example. Certainly a shadow hangs over both. I recommend once more that the question be postponed. Willdon needs a new Lord urgently, but it cannot possibly choose anyone with the faintest hint of crime about them. Either or both of these two may be guilty still; Master Jay's speech has cleared up nothing.

'I am prepared to accept that neither can be convicted, and so will not press for penalties against them. But unless the truth is revealed, will you dare choose one of them as your Lord?'

*

Lytten weighed up his options. How did this work? Did whatever he said instantly become true because he had said it? Did reality conform to his thoughts, or was it now that his thoughts had to conform to reality? A most peculiar question, a dilemma that he imagined no one else had ever had to deal with.

'Rosie? What do I do now?'

'I don't know. But it had better be quick,' she said in an undertone. 'I don't like the look on Gontal's face. He looks like someone who is thinking of testing your spiritual qualities with an arrow.'

'Is he indeed? The cheek of the man.'

Lytten prepared his best lecturing voice, honed over the years so that it was clear and penetrating. He prided himself on being able to wake up a slumbering undergraduate at thirty paces, when in the mood.

'I call before me Antros, friend of Pamarchon,' he said loudly. Antros was shocked and came forward with the greatest reluctance.

'I am under the special protection of Willdon,' he said defiantly as he approached.

Lytten smiled. 'I'm very glad to hear it,' he said. 'I would like to ask you a favour, if I may. I imagine that there are some of your merry band of outlaws carefully scattered around in case something goes wrong here, is that the case?'

Antros didn't reply. 'Please go and get them prepared,' he said quietly. 'Gontal is in a bad mood, and may soon be in a worse one. Can you tell me which of you is the best archer? It would be good to have someone who is calm and self-confident close by.'

'I am easily the best,' Antros said. 'Better by far than even Pamarchon.'

'Then you are my man. Now, I would like you to be ready for all eventualities. Settle yourself down in the bushes there.' Lytten nodded towards his left. 'Out of sight, if you please, but ready with your bow.'

'To do what?'

'You will know if you see it. Just do not be afraid, and trust your instincts. Go now.'

Antros bowed and walked swiftly out of the circle. The encounter had disturbed the crowd, which was now restless in a way which Lytten's experienced ears knew was

623

impatient, annoyed even. Time to take control properly.

'Silence!' he roared suddenly, and the noise shook the clearing like thunder.

Lytten stood up and spread out his arms, the red cloak billowing from the movement.

'People of Anterwold! People of Willdon! Hear my words!'

Silence fell, absolute and total, as he gazed around him.

'That's no good,' he said. 'I do not intend to shout. You,' he gestured to Catherine and Pamarchon, Henary and Jay and Gontal, 'come and stand over there. Everyone else come closer. Yes, yes. Into the circle. Step over those stones. They are just stones, nothing more.'

Even so, they were reluctant. But soon enough one person stepped over and, emboldened, so did everyone else, then rushed forward until they were gathered around the stone tomb, looking up in awe at the figure standing on it.

'Good. I will give you my decisions. They are final, not subject to any query. My words will be obeyed. They are the law, unbreakable and eternal.' He spoke with magnificence and authority, rather like reading the rules of a final exam to a hall of students, but with much greater impact.

'Firstly, stop looking at me like a bunch of sheep. You believe that I called the Story into being. So I did. It was to help you, not hinder you. To open your minds, not close them. I wish you to question, not obey. Doubt, not trust. That is the purpose of the Story, but you have missed the lesson, if Gontal is anything to go by.

'It contains your past, I say. It does not contain your future. I have not written that. No one has, and from now on you will be the only people who can write it. Do not rely on words written by the long dead, as Gontal did in his speech. Erudition is no substitute for wisdom. Take what is good and useful in the Story, but do not treat it as a book of rules. Change it as you wish. You have the Story, but you also have your intelligence and humanity. Use all the gifts you have been given.

'Now, Jay, student of Henary, step forward. Pamarchon, son of Isenwar. Oh – and Aliena, student of Rambert. Let's have you as well.'

That caused another stir; no one could understand why they had been called, but Jay stepped forward and, after a moment, Aliena also emerged from the crowd, looking alarmed, and took her place beside him.

'Might as well take care of the star-crossed lovers first, eh? That's a quotation, by the way. Rosalind will explain it to you. Now, Pamarchon. What can we say of you? Despite Scholar Gontal's efforts in your defence, I do not find you guilty, tempted though I am to punish his tediousness. I consider innocence to be a considerable failing on your part. You witnessed the injustices of your uncle but didn't do nearly enough to stop them. I suspect your rather ridiculous deference to your family name always got in the way. Do stop going on about your lineage. It's tiresome. I do not mean you should have killed Thenald, but I provided everything you needed to challenge him and you didn't use it. Only when you were forced into the forest did you start to consider anew. Better late than never, but unimpressive. I hope you have learned your lesson, because it seems I am giving you Rosalind here, as beautiful and remarkable a woman as has ever lived, with a lineage that goes back through all of time. She bears a name bestowed by the greatest man in history, a giant among giants. She is, in that sense, the daughter of the gods. I am not entirely convinced you deserve her, but she says she loves you, for reasons which rather escape me, so make sure you earn that love every day of your life that remains. Otherwise, you'll be in very big trouble, young man. If you mistreat her in any way you will discover what the wrath of heaven really means.'

Pamarchon bowed.

'Right. That's you sorted. Now, Aliena. I am pleased to see that you are as pretty as I hoped, or would be if you didn't look such a grouch. Stop hitting Rambert, girl. He has been good to you. He is proud of you and loves you. You are his greatest achievement and he knows you will far surpass him. He accepts that, and it is no small thing in a proud man. You owe him gratitude, and the best way to repay him is to sing with a beauty that no one has ever heard before. He will accept it, if you stop using your skill to hurt him. Ask Rosalind about Ella Fitzgerald. You should worship her, not me.

'In your case, Jay, your speech showed your best and worst sides. Lovely delivery, dramatic and theatrical; you spoke with your heart and ignored convention. Well done. But a bit loose on the finishing. You built up the audience beautifully – then left them hanging there. No conclusion; no dramatic unmasking at the end. If you are going to give a speech like that, it must come to a suitable climax. Who did it? Eh? The evidence is there, you know, although now I come to think of it, it is possible you do not know. Still, master the facts in future, please, and only then join them to the rhetoric. You will find the combination serves you well. Details, my boy. Details. The grand themes must always be married to a body of fact.

'On the subject of marriage, I intended you for a terribly pleasant young girl in Hooke; you would have met her on your next visit. But I think, on reflection, that she is not for you. You need someone to keep you on your toes a bit more. It occurs to me that you and Aliena are soul mates. You don't see it, I imagine, and you may not even like each other too much yet. But there we are. My mind is made up. You will each encourage the other, and stop each other getting sloppy. You need each other and will love each other as well. Take your time, though. You are both young. No hurry.'

He beamed at the stunned pair standing in front of him. 'I'm beginning to enjoy this. Gontal! Step forward.'

Gontal, poor man, had already endured a hideous day, seeing all his hopes slowly being prised from his chubby fingers. He had given the speech of his life, and the one person he had hoped to impress had looked as though he was about to fall asleep. He had heard the drivel Jay had delivered, and seen the spirit nodding in approval. Still, the air of command bathing the circle was so strong that he did not even hesitate. He stepped forward and bowed, ignoring the disapproving look of Rosalind, who was standing beside the altar.

'To you, Gontal, I apologise,' Lytten said. 'I should have fleshed you out. Not in body, as you are fat enough for two, but in spirit and character. I made you pompous and self-satisfied, but failed to add much depth to you. That was lazy of me; I'm afraid I just never got around to it. But I put enough in there for you to work on. Henary likes you despite everything, and he is a man to be trusted. I made you funny and cantankerous and intelligent. These are good qualities. Concentrate on them and give up the ambition. It does not suit you, and it has eaten you away a little. You would be a poor ruler of Willdon. Do you understand?'

Gontal stared stonily at the ground.

'Go back to Ossenfud and finish that damned book of yours instead. How long have you been working on it?'

'Twenty years, my Lord, but . . .'

'Believe me, I understand. But you must get it done, man. Oh – and you shouldn't drink so much either. Those bottles in your room when no one else is there?' He wagged a finger. 'Very bad. Very bad.

'Next!' he said cheerfully. 'Catherine of Willdon, come here. Henary as well. Go away, if you please, Gontal.'

There was a silence until Gontal was well out of earshot. 'Coincidence,' he said eventually. 'An entry here, an exit there. Shakespeare knew all about it. So it is the case now. A ring on a doorbell, a chance meeting, and everything would have been different. I am beginning to think that such accidents are significant. I imagine, Scholar Henary, that you do not have the faintest idea what I am talking about.'

'Indeed not, my Lord. Your wisdom surpasses my understanding.'

'I know it does,' he replied. 'It's rather surpassing mine as well, at the moment. So let's have a look at this tale and see if we can pick out some sense from it, shall we? It is a question of the balance of characters, you see. Why, Catherine, do you exist? Why did I create you? Why did I make you such a remarkable person?'

Catherine said nothing, so he continued.

'I didn't,' he said apologetically. 'You were a backdrop only, I'm afraid. A minor figure, there merely to give Henary someone to talk to. That's all. Yet you seem to have turned into a major character. I find that perplexing. You have taken on a life of your own through sheer force of personality. I congratulate you on that, but it means that you are a bit difficult. Such a person could easily harbour dark thoughts and motives without me knowing about it.

'Henary knows all about you, of course, which is why he was so relieved when I removed him as Pamarchon's advocate, no? What were you going to do, Henary? Make out a devastating case against Catherine, as you were obliged to do? Or keep quiet, and betray the honour of your calling, by failing to defend Pamarchon to the best of your ability?'

Henary took a deep breath.

'A problem, eh? Catherine was alone in a rigid, unforgiving world. I know; I made it so, although it was not my intention.' He pointed at Henary. 'You knew that she was nothing. Nothing. No family, no position, not a great lady from a grand family. All she said was one lie after another. She was just herself, a fraud. But what a remarkable self. Clever, spirited, resourceful. Everything you admired. Everything I value. Did you know Thenald was going to put her aside, before he was murdered? In your speech for Pamarchon, you would only have needed to lay out the facts.

'So wasn't it lucky that Gontal tried to take advantage of you? That I sided with him and against you? Your honour was spared. Tell me now. What would you have done? Do you know?'

Henary looked squarely at the apparition. 'No. I don't know.'

'Let me tell you. You would have walked away and incurred disgrace by failing in your duty as advocate. You would have laid down your honour and reputation for your friend. As any good person would, if put into an impossible situation. What does that say about you, Scholar Henary? The two most important people in your life are Catherine, a fraud, and Jay, whose lack of discipline undermines the Story you so reverence. You admire others who do the things you dare not do yourself. Time to change. Etheran showed you how. Do you really think this woman murdered her husband?'

'I will not think it.'

'Just as well. I may have only sketched her out, but I'm sure I didn't give her the soul of a murderer.'

'Then who did kill him?'

'Now, this is the clever bit. This is where you redeem yourself. It is not for me to say. I will cause the truth to be unveiled. That does not mean handing it to you on a platter, my good fellow. You know who killed him. Now that Jay has so usefully provided the missing details you need, and shown you how to make a proper speech.'

'I don't . . .'

'I will give you a hint. Look around you. Who do you see? Cast your eyes over this crowd of people and find someone you know, someone who should not be here, someone who is not part of my story. I will say it once more: what use is Anterwold if intelligent men do not use the gifts they are given?'

He folded his arms and looked down at Henary from

the tomb. 'Bring this to an end, Henary.'

'I need time to prepare, and to think.'

'You can't have it.'

As Henary turned away, Lytten glanced quickly at Rosalind, who was looking puzzled.

'What was all that about?'

'It was all I could think of,' he said. 'Thenald died. I didn't have him murdered. That wasn't in my story at all.'

Henary, meanwhile, had put his hands together as he surveyed the crowd, first this way, then that. Finally he saw the only person who fitted the apparition's words. 'Someone you know, someone who should not be here.' Someone who could have no purpose here. Could that possibly be the answer? He covered his mouth with his hands as he prepared, and closed his eyes. It was a terrible risk, one he would never have dared take, had not the apparition himself all but ordered him to do so. That gave him the confidence to proceed. He stood for many seconds before his body relaxed and he began to speak.

*

'People of Willdon,' Henary said when he finally accepted that he had to obey the apparition's orders, 'I stand before you a man ashamed, unworthy of my name and rank. I have been chastised by the very heavens themselves. Do any now doubt that Catherine and Pamarchon are both innocent of the terrible charges laid against them? The spirit has spoken and delivered its verdict on them both. We have been told that they are innocent, and we are bound by that judgement. Both must go free.

631

'More, I have been told to seek the murderer in my own knowledge and say who killed Thenald and why, for his murder remains to be avenged, a stain on this place which must be removed once and for all.

'So let me state it clearly: I was the cause of Thenald's death. Let me explain.

'For many years now, I have worked quietly in the realm of forbidden knowledge, seeking out hidden truths about the Story, investigating prophecies and the speech of mystics. My master, Etheran, talked to those whose opinions are normally ignored, to itinerant Storytellers, to hermits and to false prophets. He began to see the outline of a story that existed outside the Story, but he died before he could complete his work. I studied his papers when I wrote his own story after his death.

'I found two letters written to Etheran by a man called Jaqui, a hermit. Curiously, I had already met this man once. In the letters there was a prophecy.

'It seems strange to attribute any importance to such things, certainly to introduce them now. We live under the great prophecy that one day we will be judged but we ignore it, not least because no one knows when that moment will come. The Hermit of Hooke thought he did know, and put a time on it. The fifth day of the fifth year. That is what he wrote. The end will come on the fifth day of the fifth year.

'I thought it was meaningless rambling, of course, but here we are; now his words have meaning indeed. Today is the fifth day of the fifth year. The fifth day of the fifth year of Lady Catherine's accession to the lordship of Willdon. This is the day the Hermit of Hooke said the world would end, which meant also the day Esilio would return. Do any doubt now that he prophesied correctly?'

Henary paused to let this sink in.

'When we met, I told Jaqui that Thenald was ruler of Willdon, and had been for seven years already. I even told him that he was in good health. He must have realised that if that was the case, then this fifth day of the fifth year, the end of the world he so desired, would not come for many years. He had to change that; he was so mad that he thought, no doubt, he was divinely appointed to bring this about. This is what I believe took place.

'Jaqui left Hooke and travelled to Willdon, fell in with the forester Callan and waited. A wanderer, a man of no name or place, Callan called him. He stole the knife which was next seen buried in Thenald's chest.

'Then it seems he returned to Hooke and took up his life once more, waiting for the day he believed would prove his own importance. This is the only account which makes sense.

'Certainly Jaqui was at Hooke until a few weeks ago, but as the day he had awaited approached, he left for the last time. I sent my student to find him, but he had gone. He was on his way here, to witness his triumph.

'The rest is clear. He perpetrated the most terrible crime to summon the gods, perhaps in revenge for the way he had been treated in this life. He dared to return to this place, to defile the sanctuary of Esilio. Such evil impiety could not be tolerated. The monstrosity of the deed caused the heavens themselves to protest. The spirit did not respond to Gontal's call for someone with more authority than himself. Rather, he responded to the sacrilege of a murderer daring to set foot in his sanctuary, and claiming the sanction of the gods for evil deeds. Jaqui's foul presence summoned Esilio to this place to right the crimes and false accusations he has brought down on us.

'His presence, I say. For the hermit Jaqui is amongst us now.'

Henary lifted his arm and pointed at the figure the apparition had told him to look for. 'There he is. There is the murderer of Thenald. Bring him forward.'

*

Lytten saw from the corner of his eye that Antros went down swiftly on one knee as Henary finished his dramatic speech and reached for an arrow to slot into place. About thirty feet, Lytten guessed. An easy shot.

It wasn't necessary, though. The man Henary pointed out did not try to run. Nor did he shout or protest. He simply stood there, and when a couple of the soldiers of Willdon approached he allowed them to take him by both arms and lead him forwards. There was an odd smile of satisfaction on his haggard face, half obscured by the tangled mat of hair.

They walked him towards the Shrine, and there he struggled free. 'Get off me,' he said. 'I'm not going anywhere.'

They did, but stayed close as the man walked slowly forwards.

58

'I'm afraid we've never been introduced properly, even though we met briefly in my driveway. My name is Henry Lytten,' Lytten said, once the bedraggled figure stood in front of him and he had waved the crowd away. This was not a conversation either wanted overheard.

'Alexander Chang.'

'And you are?'

'I am – or was – a member of the research institute which employed Angela Meerson. I was sent to find her before she kills us all.'

'You are beginning to have my sympathy there. What is this place, Mr Chang? Do you know? I'm afraid I have only the faintest idea, and that doesn't make much sense.'

Chang laughed harshly. 'Well now,' he said. 'That's a long story.'

'I know. It's my story. But it seems very real at the moment. Is it?'

'As real as you and me. Which is to say, not very, but all we have.'

'You seem to have had a rough time in the last couple of days.'

'I've been here for more than five years.'

'I saw you two days ago.'

'Accidents happen when Angela is involved. Why did she get you to come here?'

'She didn't. She's under arrest at the moment.'

'Good,' Chang said vehemently. 'I hope they use the pliers on her.'

'The what?' Lytten was puzzled, but passed over the remark. 'How did you end up here?'

'She needed to know what this place is, and I needed to hide from you.'

'Did you find out?'

'Oh yes.'

'And?'

'You will forgive me for being blunt, but as you can see my situation is not good here. I'm afraid knowledge has its price.'

'What is yours?'

'I need to stay alive for a few more hours. Angela said she'd open the device for me here at dusk.'

'I see.'

'Dusk on the fifth day of the Festivity of the fifth year. They don't have a universal system for dating, and that was the best direction she could come up with. But Thenald was in his seventh year, and young and healthy, as Henary said. I was afraid I'd be stuck here for ever. I had no choice.'

'So you really did kill Thenald? Henary got it right?'

'I had to. It was the most horrible and revolting thing I've ever done in my entire life. I'm a scientist, for heaven's sake, not a cut-throat. Take it as a measure of how desperate I was. It took me months to recover, and I'm not sure I ever did. I still have nightmares about it.'

'How did you get Catherine on the throne?'

'I didn't. It didn't matter to me who took over. As

636

long as the clock was set to zero, so to speak, it was of no importance who it was.'

'Then tell me—'

'No. I'm not saying any more unless you promise to get me out of here. This place is unstable. Besides, even if they don't kill me, I'll kill myself if I have to stay much longer.'

'I'll see what I can do. Just answer my questions as I pose them.'

*

'The matter is settled,' Lytten said in a booming voice. 'You will all hear the truth from his own mouth. Jaqui, Hermit of Hooke, do you, freely and without force, confess to the murder of Thenald, Lord of Willdon?'

'I do,' the hermit said defiantly, causing a wave of relief to spread through the crowd, followed by a murmur of anger.

'Did you do this on behalf of any other person?'

'I did not.'

'Did any other person know of your intention before you committed this terrible deed?'

'No.'

'Did you ever meet, know or communicate with either Pamarchon, nephew of Thenald, or Catherine, widow of Thenald?'

'I did not.'

'Then I say to the people of Willdon that they should find you guilty of this most terrible crime. Do you so find him guilty?'

There was a roar of assent from the crowd, accompanied by shaking of fists.

'Silence! Do not approach. Punishment is my prerogative.'

There was a long pause until the noise died away.

'The punishment for the crime of murder is death, with the additional penalty of being refused the right to lay down your story. That is inadequate in this case. I say your very body will be expunged from this earth. As dusk falls, I will return whence I came and I will take you into the darkness. You will vanish as if you had never existed and will endure, for all eternity, the punishment due to someone who dares take the life of another. That is my judgement. If the people of this land accept it, then I declare the End of Days will have come and will have passed, never to return.'

He paused, then said in a voice so powerful it brooked no dissent, 'If you do not accept it, I will destroy Anterwold so completely not even a memory of it remains.'

Even the most bloodthirsty and vindictive of people had never heard of any pronouncement so terrible and cruel. A groan of misery, almost of sympathy for the poor man who was to bear such punishment, rose up.

'This man's deeds called me here. Does anyone question my rights?'

No one dared respond.

'Then go now. The matter is decided for ever. Settle the lordship of Willdon and restore harmony to this land.'

As the crowd slowly began to follow his instructions and started drifting away, Lytten turned to Catherine and Pamarchon. 'I see that Gontal is already heading off,' he said. 'I would hurry as well, if I were you.'

'I will leave guards to make sure that this man does not try to escape,' Pamarchon said.

'He will not. Besides, I think your men may have better things to do. I sense that I was not as persuasive with Gontal as I had hoped. He looks unhappy, and I know what that look means. He wants to be ruler of Willdon so very badly, poor fellow, and this is his last chance. And do not suddenly become tempted by power yourself, young man. I do not want you to have Willdon, and you could win it only at the price of losing Rosalind.'

'I am a man of my word.'

'Good. That doesn't mean, by the way, that you should abandon your comrades. Tell Catherine that I say her secret must be paid for.'

'I do not understand what you mean, but I will tell her.'

'Splendid.'

The young man bowed once more and followed the crowd to the place where domain business was conducted. Catherine had already gone.

'May I go with him for a bit?' Rosalind said.

'Of course, my dear. But not for long. We need to talk. You, Jay, should go with Henary. I suspect he needs company. I imagine you have a few things to talk about with Aliena as well.'

Rosalind grinned and skipped after Pamarchon, catching him up and taking hold of his hand. Arm in arm, they walked into the trees and disappeared.

59

The following morning, as day broke over the hills, Jack woke and swiftly got up. He had a long day ahead of him; Emily had offered to drive him to a refuelling station, and there he would try and get a lift north. After that he would make it up as he went along. He didn't dare travel on ordinary transport, as he would be spotted the moment he bought a ticket, so he would take a longer, more complicated route that gave him a reasonable chance of going into hiding. Then he would blend into the background, unnoticed amongst so many millions of people.

'Are you ready?' Emily always seemed to be up before he was, bright and fresh.

'Yes. If I can take some bread with me . . . ?'

'Of course. We can go in an hour. There's not much point leaving before that, as there won't be anything on the road yet.'

'I'd rather go now.'

'I have a few things to do first.'

He supposed that she was worried. If anything went wrong and it became clear that she had been helping him, then the consequences would be bad for her. He was grateful she had offered, and even though it was somewhat selfish, he had accepted without hesitation. It saved him a six-hour walk.

'Very well. I'll go and collect the document. I'll need to wrap it well.'

'I'm not sure Kendred has quite finished.'

She led the way into the next room, which had been set up as Kendred's laboratory. Jack had spent an hour in there with him the previous evening, watching to make sure he did not in any way damage anything. He was impressed by his care; Kendred snipped off only a tiny amount of paper to run his tests and for the rest of the time examined it carefully under an old-fashioned microscope, saying nothing and grunting occasionally. He was still working when Jack had left, and looked now as though he had been up all night.

'Are you nearly finished? Jack wishes to leave.'

Kendred stretched himself. 'Nearly.'

'What are your conclusions?'

'I am absolutely certain that this is a genuinely old document, dating back to the eighteenth century. The paper is certainly that old, the ink is of the same age. I have found nothing in the other papers which refers to it. So how do we explain it? The script cannot have been written then.'

'Luckily, I do not have to worry about explanations,' Jack said. 'I was told to find it and return it. More than that I cannot . . .'

A low throbbing sound in the air had been growing steadily as they spoke. Jack had noticed it in the back of his mind but had paid no attention. He should have been more alert. Even Emily was quicker; she walked outside to look in the direction of the noise.

'Helicopter,' she said.

'Several of them,' Jack said as he joined her. 'Big ones. That's bad.'

There was no point in trying to run or hide, even if they had wanted to. Jack knew full well that advance soldiers would have surrounded the retreat already, taking up position and checking for any threats before the helicopters arrived. This was the end of the operation, the grand finale, not the beginning. There was nothing to do except stand and wait. Somehow or other they had been tracked and followed.

Four huge helicopters flew overhead, making last-minute checks, then pulled back into the middle distance. Jack didn't want to think how many guns were now trained on them, but he warned the others – the Retreat had only a dozen or so inmates and they all came out to look at the noise – to move slowly and deliberately, to keep their hands away from their clothes, to do nothing which might even be thought of as threatening.

They nodded nervously as he told them what to do, and watched as another machine – vast and terrifyingly noisy – loomed overhead, then settled down like a metal insect in the field opposite. Ten soldiers jumped out and spread across the ground, weapons at the ready. Two ran towards Jack and Emily; they did not speak, did not explain themselves, and no one was foolish enough to protest. Jack put his arm round Emily, both to give comfort and to warn her not to move. He knew from experience how nervous the soldiers would be. 'Gently,' he said quietly. 'They're doing their job. Let them get on with it.'

Then came the grand climax of the event, which was, he realised, choreographed to perfection. As the helicopter's

642

engines died and the huge rotors stopped, two more men leapt out and opened the doors; they put a set of steps up to the side of the machine. Then a small figure appeared at the doorway, blinked in the bright morning air and came down the steps, assisted by a guard who, almost touchingly, held his arm to steady him. He walked slowly towards them, then went straight past into the building. From the gestures of the soldiers, Jack gathered they were meant to follow, so he gripped Emily by the arm even more firmly. 'Come with me. Don't be alarmed,' he whispered. 'It's a good show. It's meant to frighten. If he'd wanted anything else we'd all be dead by now.'

*

Oldmanter was sitting in the one chair by the fire, which he briefly gazed at with what seemed almost like appreciation. Jack, Emily and Kendred were lined up in front of him. The bodyguards took up position at the doors and windows.

'You understand my caution?' he asked, gesturing at the guards with a lazy flick of the hand.

'They are not necessary,' Emily replied. 'You know we do not approve of violence in our group.'

Oldmanter ignored the remark and looked around him at the room, which was bare and whitewashed, with wooden floors that had been scrubbed so often they were almost white as well. 'Unusual. Not healthy, but appealing to the eye.'

'Would you care for some refreshment?'

'Would I care to drink some unhygienic muck that is not

scanned in advance, out of a receptacle which has not been properly sterilised?'

Emily flushed.

'No, thank you. I haven't survived as long as I have by taking unnecessary risks. Shall we get down to business, or do you prefer a leisurely period of polite conversation first of all?'

'I would like to know why you have come here. We have done nothing wrong.'

'You think not? I could give you a very long list if I had the time. Unregistered Retreat, harbouring a fugitive. In fact, you know perfectly well why I am here. I want that document. Would you hand it over, please?'

'I'm afraid I cannot,' Jack replied. 'You know that I am duty-bound to Dr Hanslip.'

'He is under arrest and has been stripped of his status.'

'Since when?'

'Since we raided his institute last night. I took the precaution of bringing him here to demonstrate, in case you doubted my word.'

The old man flipped a hand and one of the guards walked out. They stayed there – Oldmanter sitting, the others standing, the guards with their backs to the wall, eyes flitting nervously everywhere – until the door opened once more, and two guards brought a dishevelled and badly beaten Hanslip into the room.

Far from being one of the rulers of the world, if only a minor one, Hanslip now seemed like one of the criminals Jack had arrested in the past. His face was filthy and bruised, and already it was scored with that look of defeat and resignation which he had seen so often.

'Well, Hanslip?' Oldmanter said – not harshly or cruelly, Jack noted. There was no tone of victory or triumph in his voice. 'You see how well your employee serves you. He will not hand over the manuscript until he is certain his contractual obligation to you is at an end. Please confirm it now.'

Hanslip continued to look as though he didn't quite realise where he was or understand what was going on. Eventually he attempted a weak smile, which made him grimace from some hidden pain.

'I'm sorry to see you like this, sir,' Jack said, 'but you must answer the question. Am I now free to hand over the document to Mr Oldmanter?'

'No!' Hanslip croaked. 'No! Never. You must not! It is mine! No one must have it but me . . .'

He got no further. One of the guards clubbed him sharply from the rear with his gun, and Hanslip sank to his knees, his head bowed. Oldmanter regarded Hanslip with what looked surprisingly like sympathy. 'Oh, shut him up!' he said, then turned back to More. 'I am not to be trifled with. This is too important. Mr More, you no longer owe loyalty to that man and all contracts and loyalties have passed to me. You must surrender the document. That is now a direct order.'

'I would do so,' he said, 'but unfortunately I do not have it.'

'Then who does?'

'I do,' said Emily from the corner of the room. 'It is concealed, and if you try to take it by force it will be destroyed. From what I understand of its nature, merely rendering a small section unreadable will make the whole thing useless, is that not the case?'

'Then I ask you to give it to me.'

'Certainly. By all means.'

Kendred instantly rounded on her.

'Are you mad, girl? Don't you know who this is?'

'I do. This is the man who controls the fate of the world, whether we like it or not.'

Oldmanter's eyes showed his amusement. 'Quite right.'

'Unless I destroy that little booklet,' she continued, 'in which case the machine you are all so interested in will be just a useless piece of ironware. Correct? You are not clever enough to reproduce Angela Meerson's work and this is the only copy of it.'

'An interesting opening, young woman. Let us say, for a moment, that your statement is correct. What do you do next?'

'I make modest demands that you will find easy to accept, in exchange for giving you what you want.'

'Oh, dear! You are going to beg me to abandon the campaign against the Retreats and the renegades. How wearisome of you!'

'No. I want you to increase it.'

'I beg your pardon?' Oldmanter visibly perked up at hearing something new for once.

'Shut them down. Gather the inmates together, by force if necessary.'

She got no further, though. Kendred, his face white with fury, spoke once more. 'Stop this now.'

'I know what I'm doing.'

'We must talk. Now.'

He all but dragged her from the room. Oldmanter did not move to stop them, but nodded to one of the guards.

'Watch them. If either makes any dangerous moves, then shoot them both.'

Then he turned to Hanslip, who was still standing in the corner, watching in shock. 'Oh, take him away,' he said. 'I can't stand to look at him.'

*

The room was empty except for Jack and Oldmanter, who sat there and hummed to himself for a while.

Eventually, though, he spoke. 'Are you surprised, Mr More?'

'By you allowing them to leave the room, or by what she just said?'

'The second. It is obviously safer if it is handed over voluntarily. As she said, it is unwise to risk damage to the text. If I have to use force, then I will. But I would prefer not to.'

'I did not expect it.'

'Nor I. She is an interesting young woman. But each must use such advantages as they have, and what loyalty does she owe to any of us? Can anyone offer her a better price than I can, do you think? It is sensible to sell the information to the highest bidder, although I must admit I assumed the stupid principles of these people would get in the way. They always seem to prefer suffering and self-sacrifice to common sense.'

Oldmanter moved slightly in his chair and Jack saw again how very old and frail this man really was. 'I was impressed by your behaviour,' Oldmanter continued. 'You must have known I might have ordered your execution for disobeying me just now.'

'I gave my loyalty to Dr Hanslip,' Jack said. 'I was bound until it was clear the tie was dissolved.'

'And now it is. So what will you do?'

'Look for another job, I suppose. Unless you plan to have me locked up.'

'I do not punish loyalty. Besides, I can think of a better use for you. You will continue in your present employment, but obedient to me directly. Do you accept?'

'Of course.' Jack spoke without hesitation.

'That is settled then.'

'What will you do with Emily?'

'Are you worried for her? Don't be. I will give her everything she wants. I imagine her demands will be limited.'

'Why would she trust you?'

'Because I am a man of my word,' he said in a slightly hurt tone. 'It is my pleasure to be so. I do not win by cheating. Where is the achievement in that?'

'Hanslip said this technology is too dangerous to use.'

Oldmanter laughed. 'A remarkable change of mind, don't you think?'

'You think he was lying?'

'I know he was. There were very advanced plans to use that machine lying in his desk when we took control of his institute, and we have not found a shred of evidence to suggest it is dangerous. Besides, we have analysed the problem ourselves. I put the matter to a committee of the most senior figures in physics. We will not take undue risks, I assure you. It is in good hands; rather better than it was before.'

*

Emily was expressionless as she led Kendred back into the room.

'Have you persuaded your associate?' Oldmanter asked.

'You may have the document.'

'The trouble with that,' Oldmanter said, 'is that once you have done so, you will have no way of ensuring that I keep my side of any bargain. Mr More here pointed that out, which was quite offensive of him, but it has a measure of truth to it.'

'I know. But you will.'

'Why do you think that?'

'Because my price will accomplish your greatest desires, provide you with an interesting experiment and gain you worldwide applause,' she said.

'You are very attentive to my needs. Go ahead.'

'I want a universe.'

Oldmanter paused, genuinely caught on the hop for the first time in decades. 'How splendid!' he said. 'That is what you meant by a modest demand, eh?'

'As fast as is reasonable,' Emily went on, 'you will make your machines operational. You will then transmit those members of Retreats who wish to depart. You will announce the discovery and, as a way of demonstrating its power, announce also that you are financing a programme to rid the world of all subversive, non-productive influences like us. The acclaim will be considerable. Then you can get on with whatever you have in mind.'

Oldmanter was impressed. Jack, standing to one side, could see that he was following her train of thought as fast as she was laying it out; the two of them were in step. It was an extraordinary thing to witness.

'Now that, young lady, is a proposal worth listening to. I am inclined to agree just because of the scale of your nerve.'

'Think of the new data you will gather, the organisational expertise. Think of the gratitude as well. You will recoup the cost in no time, and most will be research expenses you would incur anyway.'

'What a shame,' Oldmanter said appreciatively, 'that you are a renegade. If only my employees had half your imagination. I don't suppose I could tempt you . . .'

'No.'

'Ah well.'

'Ah well, indeed,' Emily said. 'That's the deal. Accept and you can have the data. Refuse and you can't.'

Oldmanter was not a man to hesitate. His success had been built on seeing an opportunity and grabbing it wholeheartedly.

'Obviously I accept. As you say, it is greatly to my advantage.'

'Good.'

He nodded. 'We will go to Mull, set up and calibrate. As long as there has been no substantial damage and my people haven't gone overboard and razed the place, it will take a couple of weeks. Then we will have to test it with a few volunteers to make sure it is functioning properly. We will construct a bigger machine, building in what we have learned. Then perhaps five thousand a day, working up to ten thousand as more machines come on stream. This will continue until all volunteers have gone.'

'Then you will leave us alone.'

'Oh, certainly. We will switch to a different universe for our purposes. You may have a life of rustic bliss festering in primitivism until the day every single one of you dies.'

'One more thing. I would like that poor man to have the chance of coming too. Hanslip.'

'Why?'

'Just a pointless act of kindness.'

'If you want him, you can have him. We can say he died in captivity. Suicide or something. It may be as good as suicide anyway. You know that, don't you?'

'I am quite aware of the risks.'

Emily walked over and gave him the Devil's Handwriting, hesitating for only a fraction of a second before putting it into his hand. 'We have established, by the way, that it is of very recent vintage. It looks old and was evidently meant to convince people it is old. It defeats most tests, but it is quite definitely a fake. Don't believe anyone who tells you differently; we are experts in this field.' She gave Kendred a severe look as she turned away again.

Oldmanter flicked through its pages with deep interest for several minutes, then let out a sigh of satisfaction. 'We will leave for Mull in an hour.'

*

For Oldmanter, having the girl voluntarily give him the manuscript was yet another extraordinary piece of good fortune. A more sentimental man would have wondered if fate wanted him to have this technology.

He could most definitely afford to appear generous, not least because no generosity was involved. He would dispose of the renegades and they would make the task easier by rushing to volunteer. They would herd themselves into the transportation device, beg to be dispatched. If anything demonstrated their unfitness to live, that was it.

Of course, it wasn't that simple. There were the needs of research as well. This was brought up the following day, when he settled down to map out the schedule with his closest advisers.

'Every single one?' they asked. 'There must be millions of them.'

'It will be spread over a period of years. I agreed to send them; I did not agree to a timetable. We get rid of them, at any rate, and subsequent developments can be kept pure of social infections. In due course proper colonists will arrive and they will need labour. Has there been any work on which period is best suited for colonisation?'

'As you know, sir, the greater the distance, the greater the amount of power needed.'

'Meaning?'

'Ideally we would send people to an epoch when there are no human settlements, but that would require huge amounts of power and they would arrive with nothing. If we could commandeer existing infrastructure and send them less far, then we could keep costs down dramatically.'

'I thought that was ruled out because of the difficulties of dealing with the indigenous population. I remember talking to Grange about it.'

'Yes, sir, but that was when the plan was to invade and conquer, then use the indigenous population as slave labour. Hanslip sketched out an alternative which makes this notion more viable. He was toying with the idea that the cheapest approach would be to encourage the native population to kill themselves by exploding a bomb at a period of heightened tension during the nuclear age. Each side would blame the other, and the subsequent war would do most of the work for us; if need be we could unleash biological weapons on any survivors. When the world is clean and empty, we can begin transporting the settlers. It would mean moving people only a couple of hundred years, and despite the damage there would be substantial infrastructure still available. It is a highly imaginative solution, and very cost-effective. The added virtue of the plan is that we could begin almost immediately.'

'What period?'

'The memorandum pinpointed the most vulnerable moments, running from 1962 to 2024. We will use one of them.'

'No moral objections from anyone? I don't want to be hauled in front of some ethics committee.'

'There can be no moral obligation to people who are both long dead and, as far as we are concerned, do not exist. We have tested that hypothesis thoroughly.'

'No safety issues? For us, I mean.'

'No. Again, the panel of physicists has reviewed the matter and finds no problems. They dismissed Angela Meerson's theories as absurd.'

'Then I suggest you start the preparations. The sooner we see if this thing works, the better.'

'There is one other thing. We only got the vote from the physicists by promising one of them that we would conduct experiments into future transportation. He is preparing a paper based on some of the captured material and wants to ensure that we can send people forwards, as well as back. We'll need to do something to keep him happy, and we will have to explore this in due course anyway to maintain proper communication between worlds.'

'I do hate these people,' Oldmanter said. 'Still, give him what he wants. And I think it would be best to terminate Dr Hanslip. It occurs to me that if we send him with the renegades, he may have sufficient knowledge to re-create the machine eventually. If I am going to spend a fortune to get rid of them, I don't want them turning up again in a few generations.'

60

Pamarchon walked hand in hand with Rosalind on his way to the meeting hall, neither saying much for some time, and both merely content that the other was there.

'Better than I could have hoped for,' she said. 'One might even say it is a miracle.'

He took his hand away from hers and looked at her with a worried expression.

'What's the matter?'

'It is a miracle. So how can I ask you to be my wife now?'

'Whatever do you mean?'

'I have seen who you are. How could I presume to ask for your hand now?'

'Oh, stuff and nonsense, Pamarchon, son of whoever. Stuff and nonsense. Don't you dare talk to me like that,' Rosalind replied in alarm. 'Listen, I will tell you once, and once only. There is nothing magical about me. There is nothing even particularly special or beautiful about me either, unless you choose to see me like that.' She paused. 'You can, you know,' she hinted. 'If you want to.'

'But back there . . . ?'

'It's a long story, and a strange one. I know it seems very unlikely and everything. That's just because you don't know the whole story, you see? Everybody only knows a bit of it. So they think there must be something incredibly meaningful about it. Why, Henary thought the world was going to end.'

'Esilio, though . . .'

'Ah, yes. He's a bit difficult to explain. But I'll tell you one thing. He had no more idea of who killed your uncle than anyone else. All he did was sit there and get everyone else to do the work for him. He didn't figure out how or why Jaqui killed your uncle; Henary did. He hadn't the faintest idea what was going on. Not a clue. He was very good at hiding it, but then he is a professor.'

'Everyone saw his apparition.'

'True. He popped up out of nowhere. But then, so did I, and there's nothing strange about me. I've been trying to tell everyone this for ages. If it's any help, I don't understand it either, but there we are. I'm here, I'm real and I have already agreed to marry you, and I expect you to keep your side of the bargain. As you get to know me a little better, you will see how ordinary I really am.'

'You will never be that.'

'That's sweet, but you haven't responded.'

'Were it possible to want you even more than I already did, then I do. Of course I do.'

'A subjunctive! Well done. That's settled then.'

It was a diversion, that last remark, as she didn't want him to see the tears of relief and happiness welling up in her eyes. She disguised her feelings by hurling herself at him and wrapping her arms tightly round his neck. They stood there for some time, until he finally pulled away.

'I have work to do,' he said.

'I'd better get back to the Shrine. I promised.'

'Do you want company?'

'It'll be fine. You go to this assembly thing.'

He watched until she had disappeared down the track to

the Shrine, then continued on his way. He had only taken a few paces before he saw Lady Catherine.

*

'I owe you an apology, it seems,' Pamarchon said as he approached.

'Less than the one I owe you.'

'Then let us both accept the other's regret, and settle this last matter swiftly.'

They walked together for a while before Pamarchon said, 'I was told to say something to you. I do not know what it means.'

'Then speak.'

'He told me to say that your secret must be paid for. What does he mean?'

'He means that I should renounce Willdon and acknowledge you,' Catherine replied quietly.

'Why?'

'Thenald had discovered that I was not a woman of great family. I was, and am, a fraud and he was about to put me aside in disgrace. That is my secret, the one Henary should have revealed in his defence of you. It is why Esilio spared him the task.'

'You are an imposter?'

'Yes. Now you know it, I could not oppose you even if I chose to do so. I will withdraw. I ask only that you preserve my secret as he did, for kindness' sake.'

'I do not think that was the price he had in mind,' Pamarchon said. 'Why, otherwise, did he make Gontal speak? He wasn't protecting Henary alone, but you as well.

657

I believe his meaning is different. He wants you to remain as Lord of Willdon.'

'You can't know that.'

'He knows my heart. He knows I yearn to voyage, see things no man has ever seen before, and I could not do that if I was tied to this place. You must rule Willdon, and in return I ask that you look after my people. They followed me, and I owe them that. That is the price he meant.'

'How many are there?'

'About six hundred, if you count women and children.'

She thought swiftly, the practical woman of business once more. 'I'd have to extend the boundaries of the domain, clear some forest.' She turned to Pamarchon. 'Will they settle? Abandon forest life?'

'Most will. The others you must help as they wish. I will not have them hounded or driven into poverty.'

'You will have to stay for a while. They would not trust me, and I do not know them or understand them. You would have to help.'

'Agreed.'

'Afterwards I will look after them as well as you have, and as well as I do everyone else. Are you sure that is his meaning, and are you certain it is what you want?'

But Pamarchon had come to a halt. He touched Catherine gently on the arm and stopped her as well.

He put his finger to his lips. 'When I speak, do exactly as I say,' he said, so softly she could scarcely hear him. 'Do not doubt me, or hesitate.'

Catherine could hear nothing, but knew someone like Pamarchon could understand noises that meant nothing to her.

'This way,' he whispered. 'Quickly!' Grabbing her firmly by the arm, he led her off the path and into the trees.

Catherine followed him without questioning, keeping as quiet as he evidently wanted her to do. He paused, made her go in front of him, guided her carefully to avoid making too much noise, then pulled her down onto the ground.

'Soldiers,' he said. 'At least a dozen. They are not mine and, I'd guess, not yours either. They're making far too much noise for people used to the woods.'

'Are you sure?'

'Yes. It is the reason I am still alive. I don't make mistakes about things like this. Do not move a muscle.'

'I have to breathe.'

'Must you?' He flashed her a reassuring grin, then vanished.

He disappeared into the undergrowth so carefully that not a branch broke or leaf rustled. Catherine crouched down, listening intently; faintly, in the distance, she heard voices, shouting, the clang of metal. Pamarchon had been right. They could not be her people.

Any further thoughts were interrupted by the elegant, almost dainty way he slid back down beside her. 'Yes,' he said with a certain satisfaction. 'They are Gontal's men. He seems to have decided to take by force what he is unlikely to have by right. Any ideas?'

'You are asking me?'

'I am. I have my men, but they are some way off and I do not want bloodshed. Not least because I do not know what side your own people would join. That would be a disastrous end to this. I assume we need to get you to the assembly square?'

'I imagine people will be gathering there already. They will choose from candidates who present themselves in person.'

'So Gontal's aim will be to stop either of us getting there. The Chamberlain will start the meeting, call for candidates, and only Gontal will be present. We may protest afterwards, but it will be too late. If we try to fight our way through, then Gontal will feign outrage at our unwarranted assault.'

'So,' she said, 'we sit here until it is too late, use your men to unleash a bloodbath we might lose, or risk arrows in our chests by trying to get in unnoticed. Gontal, I fear, has gone too far to be squeamish.'

'Surely Esilio will not allow this to happen?'

'I think he would say this is our business.'

'In that case,' he said, 'we will have to make Gontal see the error of his ways.'

*

Catherine hoped that Pamarchon knew what he was doing. Certainly he seemed very sure of himself when he explained what he intended; for her part she could see no way of avoiding a direct confrontation. They hurried towards the great house, but could only get to within a few hundred yards before the open spaces meant there was no chance of concealment.

'It never occurred to me that these gardens might serve a purpose. They make a curiously useful defence. Ah, well. Do you understand what you must do?'

'Yes, General,' Catherine said. He looked at her. 'A joke,' she said.

660

He grunted as she prepared to stand.

'Catherine,' he said, and held out his hand. She looked a little puzzled, then took it. 'Do be careful. I have just acquired a family member I value. I don't want to lose you so soon. I will cover you from here with my bow, but be prepared to run.'

The rest was simple. She walked boldly towards the house, and within a minute Gontal's soldiers appeared, swords and bows at the ready. This was the dangerous bit; if they had been given orders to kill her on sight, then all the plans would come to nothing. That was why they had had an argument. She had insisted she should go; he had refused. It had become quite childish, for a moment, until she had said:

'Why shouldn't I do it?'

'Because it was my idea. And I'm bigger than you.'

At which she sniffed disapprovingly and he, realising how absurd he was, laughed. 'I can't get at my men and I can't command yours,' she pointed out, 'and we may need them. Besides, I can frighten Gontal better than you. I know him. He will not dare kill me. He wouldn't hesitate to kill you.'

He had agreed very reluctantly indeed, but he knew she was correct.

So she marched up to the men and spoke before they could apprehend her.

'Go and tell your master, Scholar Gontal, that he must come here immediately, or the wrath of Esilio will be let loose on this place and the whole of Anterwold destroyed, in punishment for his disobedience.'

'Have you noticed, Gontal, how the spirit operates?' Catherine said when the fat scholar waddled towards them ten minutes later. They had stood uneasily with Gontal's guards as one of their number ran off to find their master. No one had said a word; Pamarchon had seemed entirely relaxed, which made the soldiers even more nervous.

'Prophecies are fulfilled by men,' Catherine continued. 'Judgements and decisions are carried out by men. There is no magic, no spells, no supernatural interventions. Just the acts of men and women. Esilio proclaimed that Pamarchon and I should present ourselves as candidates to the assembly. That was part of the judgement condemning Jaqui, and if it was broken then Anterwold would be destroyed in its entirety.'

'If they are fulfilled by men then I have nothing to fear,' Gontal replied. 'No man could destroy Anterwold, and if the gods do not intervene, then it will continue.'

'That is not true,' Pamarchon said. 'I can destroy it. I will do so.'

Gontal laughed. 'You? With your little band of outlaws? What are you going to do? Tear up the mountains, stone by stone? Drink the rivers and the seas?'

'Those are just rocks and water. They are not Anterwold. Anterwold is the people and the way they live. The things which bind them together and make them know who they are. Anterwold is the Story. And yes, I will destroy it, with my little band of outlaws.'

Gontal gestured to his men, who drew their swords.

'No, you won't. You will die first, and you will even give me a justification for killing you.'

'Then you will destroy it, and you will be cursed for ever.'

The calm way that Pamarchon spoke made Gontal pause. The young man did not seem afraid, and he did not seem to be threatening. He seemed to be setting out the facts.

'When I thought of retaking Willdon, I knew that it could only be done by force. I had enough men, and perhaps I could have succeeded. But many would have died, and I did not want that. Why should the people of Willdon suffer for what others had done to me? So I thought of a different way. Two days ago I talked to four of my best men, people who owe me everything, people I could trust to do what I asked without question. I sent them to Ossenfud with orders to conceal themselves inside the Story Hall. Catherine would be given the choice: resign her position, or the Story Hall would be burnt.

'If I did not appear within five days they would know that I was dead and our hopes had gone. They would leave, setting it on fire. The entire building. The whole Story, every last roll and document, would burn.

'You cannot possibly find them or intercept them in time. If I am not in Ossenfud within the next three days, they will carry out my orders. Everything Anterwold is, all its memories and knowledge, will be destroyed. So Anterwold will be destroyed, as the spirit promised. If you wish I can summon my closest companion, and he will confirm everything I say.'

Gontal studied Pamarchon as he spoke. Could he be

serious? Was he, was anyone, that ruthless and depraved? He could not read him, could not tell. Catherine, standing slightly apart from them, tried to guess which one would break first. She had nothing to say here; this was not her contest.

'Well, Gontal? I know you are wondering if this is a trick, whether I am lying. But I also know something of you. You are a man of learning. I know that the spirit gave you advice, even though I did not hear it. What did he say? Take Willdon for yourself? Brush aside all opposition whatever the consequences? Is that what he recommended?'

Catherine knew Pamarchon had won, even before Gontal did himself. She saw the hesitation, the way his body softened and folded as he realised that he did not dare take the risk. The Story was everything. He would die for it, if need be.

He nodded to his men. 'Let them go,' he said.

Pamarchon took Catherine by the arm. 'Before he changes his mind . . . ?' he said quietly into her ear.

He led the way past Gontal, past the soldiers and into the assembly, where their entrance was greeted with an enormous cheer that could be heard far away, even by the occupants of the Shrine of Esilio.

61

'Now, Mr Chang. I think we have a little time. The sun is getting lower in the sky, but there is a way to go until we get to dusk. Why don't you explain a bit more? You see I fulfilled my side of the bargain. Perhaps you might start by telling me who Angela is, and how she did all this?'

'She is a mathematician. She comes from what you would term the future. As do I.'

'Oh, of course she is. If you say so.'

'She developed a technology which is supposed to hop from universe to universe. In fact it seems to hop from time to time. There was a dispute over its use, and Angela went into hiding here, taking the data with her. I was sent to find her.'

'Then what is this place?'

'An experiment of hers. Just to see if it could be done, as far as I can tell.'

'What is it? I mean, I know what it is, but . . . what is it?'

'It is a very crude alternative version of the future. It's only a prototype, and it's not working very well. As I say, it is becoming dangerously unstable. It was meant to be isolated in time, simply a snapshot, if you like. Unchanging and fixed.'

'It doesn't seem to be that.'

'No. As long as it was insulated, then the normal conditions of cause and effect were suspended. Nothing

665

could happen, because there was no cause of anything happening. Similarly, without effects, there could be no causes. That was to ensure it could have no past or future.'

'She got it wrong?'

'No. That girl messed it up, and you don't seem to have helped just now either.'

'Rosie? How?'

'She walked into it. You say hello, they say hello back, which they otherwise would not have done. Cause and effect, you see. Anyone who says hello must be real. They must have parents, grandparents, all the way back. That girl started this frozen experiment moving and developing, and that is causing it to join up to the past and future. When I arrived, the effects had already spread back that far. It is now clear the shock waves have spread very much further.

'This Anterwold of yours was built to be an artificial, disconnected creation existing in a bubble, but it might not stay like that for much longer. If it continues to exist, the accumulation of causes will connect it back to the earliest moment in the universe, and the effects will also link it to the last moment of the universe. Then there will be two different futures, and according to Angela there can be only one. Others exist only as potential. So either this world exists, or mine does. If this one exists, ours cannot. It will be the worst catastrophe in the history of humanity.'

'Really?' Lytten said, looking around him. 'Surely not? I designed it to be peaceful and quiet. It's not as if they can do much harm with swords and arrows, you know.'

'Swords and arrows, precisely. My world staggers through, cruel and mean though it is. This Arcadian idyll of yours requires the wholesale destruction of nearly all of humanity and hundreds of years of misery and despair. It is built on corpses.'

'What nonsense! I didn't put in anything like that.'

'You did. When Angela created it as an actual place, it had to bear some relationship to your present. Past or future. You made it the future.'

'How?'

'They eat potatoes and tomatoes, which only came to this island after about 1600. You gave them their mythology of the giants. They know about bacteria, even if they have forgotten the details. Many other things. I mean, look at this place. In comparison to your time it is technologically primitive. It has lost much of the art of engineering, knows little about chemistry. No concrete, no large-scale use of steel. By logical extrapolation, which is how it develops, there is only one way that could happen.'

'Which is?'

'A massive dislocation which pushes technological development into reverse. A war, Professor. A nuclear one. That's the fundamental proof that this is in your future. There are parts of the country still dangerous from radiation. I spent two years travelling the country, and I checked my findings many times over.'

'So when are we now?'

'That's difficult to say. What they call the Exile, when most of the world was dying, seems to have lasted about two hundred years. That was enough for the worst of the radiation to fade, for the plagues to burn out and the forests to regrow. As far as I can tell from examining ruins the Return was a good four centuries back. So at least six hundred years from you, but that's not anything more

667

than a rough guess. I could do better with some proper equipment.'

'When is this war?'

'Also difficult, but after the moment Angela created this place, and before nuclear weapons were brought under unified control. My best guess would be the second half of the twentieth century. All I know is that if Angela is going to stop this, we need to get out of here.'

'What happens then?'

'She pulls the plug. No one here will know. It's not like killing people, you know. Anterwold will not exist, will never have existed, except in your mind. As it should be; then history will have no alternative but to head to my future, which avoids a catastrophe.'

'What about Rosie?'

'She must leave Anterwold. She must. Otherwise Angela won't be able to close it.'

'She may not want to.'

'Then you have to make her.'

Lytten did not like that. If what this man told him was true – and he had heard and seen so many absurdities that he could no longer tell what was reasonable or not – then he might well be correct.

'Here she comes now,' Chang said. 'Please, do as I ask. It is the most important thing you have ever been called on to do.'

*

Rosalind was bounding through the trees, waving cheerfully, a look of deep happiness on her face.

'I left him to it,' she called out. 'It should be settled soon enough.' She ran up and gave Lytten an enormous hug. 'Thank you so much! You were brilliant! I couldn't have done it. You got the hang of it so quickly!'

'Thank you. Not that I had much choice. Believing it all was easier than not, if you see what I mean.'

'I know. You forget about home completely.'

'Ah,' he said. Better get it over with. 'Home. I need to talk to you about that. It seems that the way home will open very soon and probably for the last time. There will not be another chance.'

'Oh, Professor! No! Not yet!'

'I'm sorry. Don't ask me to explain, because you know I can't. Angela's colleague' – here he waved at Chang – 'assures me this is so. This is Mr Alexander Chang, by the way.'

Rosalind look at Chang, who smiled wanly. 'Her colleague?'

'Yes. He says we have to go, urgently, otherwise terrible things will happen. Besides, think of your parents,' he continued. 'Think of your friends, family. Jenkins. Me. We'd all miss you.'

She bit her lip to stop it trembling, then reluctantly nodded, tears beginning to roll down her cheeks.

'I suppose so,' she said, 'but does it really have to be so soon? Now or never?'

'Now or never. I'm sorry.'

*

The timing was perfect; just as the sun dipped below tree level and the light began to fade quickly, Rosalind heard

669

the now almost familiar hum, and there, exactly where it had been before, was the faint blue light, shining out of nothing. This time, though, she did not hurry towards it. But what could she do? Live in a dream world or, whatever their faults and failings, go back to her parents and her real life?

Of course she had to go. There was nothing to be said for it, but how she wished she could stay a little longer! See the world with Pamarchon, travel to all those exotic places, find out things no one else knew or cared about. She wiped away the tears and stood up straight. Don't slouch, Rosie. Ladies don't slouch.

She was glad there was no one else here; if Pamarchon had been with her, they would have had to say goodbye. She knew that one word, one look from him would make her change her mind. So it had to be like this. Chin up, Rosie.

She took a deep breath and stepped forward to peer into the light, her eyes adjusting until she could see through more clearly.

She stopped, her heart suddenly beating far harder even than before. What on earth . . . ?

'Professor!' she called over her shoulder. 'Professor! Come and look!'

Lytten hurried over, worried by the tremor in her voice. 'Look! Is that . . . ?'

Rosie was pointing through the light at herself.

'Yes. That is difficult to explain . . . It's you.'

'What do you mean? How can it be me?'

'How should I know? There's two of you. One went home, the other stayed here. So I'm told.'

'That's impossible.'

'You would think so, but I have talked to both of you. In fact, I am the only one who has. It is a very strange experience.'

Rosalind looked appalled. 'That's horrible.'

'It's not so bad. Both of you are perfectly normal and happy.'

'Do I know about me?'

'Yes. Although you were keen to keep yourself hidden. You didn't want to upset you.'

'What if I go home, though? I mean, who gets my bed? What will my parents say?'

'I know it is hard.'

'Hard? It's a bit more than hard. And what about that nonsense you told me? About my parents and friends. How much they would miss me. They won't miss me. You tried to trick me. You knew all about this. How could you be so deceitful?'

'Well . . .'

'I decided I had to go because of you. But now . . . No. No. You lied to me. I will not go. Nothing you can say will change my mind. I'm not needed there. And what sort of life would it be, sharing everything like that? What am I meant to be? A long-lost twin?'

'It may make it impossible for Angela to shut . . .'

'To shut . . . ? To shut what?'

The question received no answer as a loud cry of protest from Chang interrupted them.

'You can't stand there talking,' he said. 'There is no time to lose. We have to go. It won't stay open for long.'

'We haven't finished,' Rosalind said tartly.

'If we don't go now—'

'It will just have to wait.'

'Mr Lytten, go through, quickly.'

'I don't think . . .'

'Go!' Chang screamed. 'There may only be seconds. Quickly!'

His voice had become so hysterical that Lytten, although he hesitated, began to retreat. 'Rosie?' he called out.

'You can go,' she said. 'Go on. After all, you're not needed here.' It was clear she had not forgiven him.

There was a pause as Lytten cast one last glance at her. Then he stepped forward, and his body fragmented and became translucent. A new, shadowy outline formed on the other side. He had arrived safely.

Chang grabbed Rosalind roughly by the arm. 'Now you. Quickly,' he said. 'We have to shut down this ridiculous place. It's dangerous and unstable. We have to go before it's too late.'

'No,' said Rosalind. 'I'm not going.'

'I have been waiting for nearly six years and I'm not going to risk being blown to pieces so you can stay in your childish playground. Do as you are told. Don't you understand what is at stake here, you stupid girl?'

Rosalind glared at him. 'Right,' she said. 'That does it. I'm not moving.'

62

'Thank heavens I found you! Welcome back, Professor!' Rosie cried as Lytten stumbled through the pergola and shook his head in relief and surprise. 'Now do you believe me?'

Lytten didn't answer, but leaned against the old sink, breathing hard. He seemed suddenly very tired.

Rosie was surprised; she had recovered relatively quickly, she thought. It wasn't her story, though; maybe that made a difference.

'What's been going on? Has something terrible happened?'

Lytten pointed back at the pergola, still glowing faintly in the corner. Rosie turned to see what was so obviously causing him concern. 'Chang,' he said. 'What's he doing?'

'Who?'

He was too appalled and fascinated to reply. Instead he stared at the scene of Chang and Rosalind struggling together in full view of both of them in the cellar.

*

Chang grabbed hold of Rosalind and was gripping her tight. In the half-light metal briefly glimmered, a knife to her throat, the knife Jay had presented as the weapon which had murdered Thenald, and which he had placed as evidence by the altar for all to examine. Rosalind fought back, trying to kick him, stand on his foot and wriggle free, but he paid no attention. Instead he was forcing her ever closer to the light, dragging her backwards, looking over his shoulder. He was much stronger than she was, and there was enough light to see the terror on her face, the tears rolling down her cheeks.

Step by step, ignoring her screams and attempts to bite him, he manoeuvred towards the light, occasionally almost picking her up and swinging her off her feet. There was no one to assist; no one could possibly intervene. The stone circle was deserted.

He stopped, panting with the exertion, but the girl kept struggling. One more heave, though, and it would be done. Already they were close enough for the light to illuminate their bodies, the short girl and the powerful man locked in a bizarre embrace. He bent slightly, summoning all his strength, one arm still tightly around her waist, the other hand holding the knife to her throat. Then he relaxed. She screamed one last time and fell from his grip onto the grass, rolling away from him, scrabbling to get away from the knife.

He shuddered for a moment, then fell sideways as if he had been pushed, blood pouring from a wound in his leg. Rosalind looked back at her attacker as he stood there, pulling at the arrow that was sticking out from him, blood splashing onto the ground. With an agonising look of pain he succeeded, but only at the cost of opening a jagged, bloody wound as the barbed end tore through his flesh. He wavered, now very unsteady on his feet, but focused on Rosalind lying on the ground. He still had the knife in his hand, and with uncertain steps he began to come towards her.

There was a shout in the distance from the bushes. Antros was hurrying towards them, as he was afraid of hitting Rosalind if he fired again, but he was too far away to reach them in time. If Rosalind got up and ran for safety, she would get a knife in her back, without a doubt.

So she did the opposite. With one almighty effort of will she launched herself forward and cannoned into Chang as he advanced towards her.

It was enough, but she paid a price. The weakened Chang toppled backwards into the light, but not before he made a desperate stab with his knife into Rosalind's side. She screamed out in pain as a pair of hands grabbed her from behind and prevented her from following him through.

With one strong movement Antros all but threw her to one side and she fell heavily onto the ground. He stepped back, pulled another arrow from the sheath, metal-tipped like the first, strung it and pulled back. With one smooth movement, he aimed directly at the shadow on the other side and released it.

*

'Look out!' Rosie cried, and pushed Lytten to the left just as he tried to push her to the right. The result was that neither moved. Both crouched down fearfully and glanced towards the pergola. As the arrow entered the light, there was a sharp bang and fizzing, and Lytten's cellar was plunged into total darkness. Not only had the machine evidently closed down, it had also short-circuited the entire house. Chang was screaming in agony in the darkness, which at least gave Lytten something to do. Taking a box of matches out of his pocket, he carefully found his way to the fuse box in the corner by the stairs.

'Come and hold this, will you?' he said. Her hands were trembling. 'Steady,' he said in a surprisingly calm voice. 'Ignore Mr Chang. We can't help him until we can see what we are doing. Concentrate on holding the match still.'

She managed, just, and the match – several of them, one after another – gave enough light for Lytten to extract the fuse, find the wire and repair it. Then he pushed down the main switch and the dim light bulb hanging from the centre of the room came on again.

'Thank heavens for that,' he said. 'Now, go upstairs and phone an ambulance. This poor man needs to get to a hospital. Go on.'

He almost pushed her up the stairs, and then began to deal with Chang. It was a nasty-looking wound, but Lytten – whose eye was more expert than he liked – reckoned that it was not mortal, as long as the bleeding could be staunched. He ran upstairs and got some clean cloth, then knelt by the injured man and pressed hard, reassuring him with touching gentleness as he waited.

Rosie did a good job. The ambulance came swiftly, and Chang was taken off their hands after some emergency first aid as he lay on the dirty cellar floor. He was all but unconscious from the shock and pain, but at least it meant he had fallen silent.

'How the hell did this happen?' the driver asked. 'Why is he in fancy dress?'

Good questions. 'The police will explain,' Lytten said curtly. 'I'm afraid I cannot. Or rather, will not. Just do your job.'

Then he turned to Rosie. 'We have a lot to discuss, but not at the moment. I have something I need to do, and according to Mr Chang it is urgent. You can go home or stay here. Or, if you are up to it, you could accompany Chang and see he is all right. It is entirely your choice.'

Considering that Chang had just tried to stab her, in a manner of speaking, Rosie was understandably reluctant to go anywhere near him. 'I want to come with you,' she said in a frightened voice.

'You can't. What time is it?'

Lunchtime, she told him. He had been gone for a couple of hours. She'd had a bit of difficulty resetting the machine, and it had taken longer than she thought.

'Is that all?'

'How long do you think you were gone?'

'About six hours. Maybe more.'

'What are you going to do now?'

'First of all, I am going to get out of this dressing gown. I look ridiculous. Then I will go to the police station to talk to Detective Sergeant Maltby about Mr Chang. And I need a chat with Angela.'

'What happened in there? In Anterwold?'

'Well,' he said, after a moment to arrange his thoughts into something which passed for coherence, 'I played the role of a returning deity.'

'Goodness.'

'And I had to preside over a trial to decide who killed Thenald.'

'Who did you decide had done it?'

'I didn't. I didn't have the faintest idea. Henary figured it out. It was Chang. He is some sort of associate of Angela's. At least, that's what he says. Oh, and Angela is a time traveller from the future.'

'I know that,' she said, as though it were not so very interesting. 'How am I? The other me, I mean?'

'Until Chang intervened you were blossoming, my dear. Healthy, self-confident and rather forceful. You seem quite decided to marry Pamarchon, and he seems suitably enamoured of you, so I'm sure you'll live happily ever after.'

'Oh. That's nice.'

'Pamarchon is the spitting image of an old student of mine. If he has his character, you will get on very well.'

'So I don't want to come back?'

'No. You and I parted on rather bad terms because of it, I'm afraid. That's what I need to talk to Angela about.'

'Henary looks like you, you know.'

'Yes. I feel a little embarrassed about that. Jay looks remarkably like another student of mine. Gontal is clearly based on an unpleasant chemistry teacher who gave my cat his name. Antros was a corporal in the army during the war. In fact, nearly everybody seems to have been dredged up from my memory. It was very peculiar. Just as well I never met Hitler. I really do think you should go home, by the way.'

'After all this? Not forgetting the spies, the people being arrested, the blood on the cellar floor? You think I can just go home and do my prep?'

She had a point.

'Very well. You can sit over the road from the police station and wait, if you really want to.'

678

*

It wasn't hard for Lytten to see Angela at the police station; after a long conversation with Maltby and a phone call or two to London, all objections were waived. In the end, Lytten promised to write a letter of commendation praising Maltby for his intelligence and diligence, Maltby promised to make sure nobody asked too many questions about Chang, and finally Angela was let out. She looked a little tired.

'Henry! How lovely,' she said distractedly when the cell door opened.

'I'm sure. Can we get straight down to business, please?'

'The Volkov business?'

'No. The cellar business.'

'Ah. That.'

'I've just spent nearly six hours in that invention of yours.'

'Oh, dear. Rosie should not have done that. That was really rash of her. Where is she, by the way?'

'One is over the road, the other is still in Anterwold. I did my best to persuade her, and Chang tried to use more forceful methods. But she stayed. I gather that may cause you problems.'

'Potentially, but it doesn't surprise me. What about Chang?'

'In hospital. One of my more dramatic literary creations shot him with an arrow when he attacked Rosie.'

'That fits as well. He is having a difficult time, poor man. He's not made for an active life.'

'Nor am I any more.'

679

'He was meant to find out where Anterwold came from. Did he manage that?'

'He did,' Henry said. 'He came to the conclusion that Anterwold is our future, or will be once a nuclear war intervenes. Humanity has to be nearly wiped out to prepare the ground for this paradise of mine. A dark age, lasting centuries, with only a few survivors holding on in the furthest reaches, preserving what little knowledge they can by weaving it into stories that are transmitted by word of mouth, then written down as the Story.'

'I see,' she said. 'I was afraid of something like that.' She looked up at him. 'Is it what you had in mind?'

'I didn't have anything in mind. It was just a few jottings in a notebook until you got involved.' They stared at each other for a few seconds. 'Well?' he prompted. 'What are you going to do now? Are you just going to sit there?'

'Of course not,' she said, her face clearing suddenly. 'I am going to try and save the universe, or rather, see if it can be saved. If that sounds a little ambitious, then I am going to visit your aunt. Oh, by the way, Sam Wind was here. He thinks you are a Soviet agent. I hope that's all right.'

*

It took some time to persuade Rosie to stay behind; she was very upset and wanted to be around the only people who understood why. But Angela was adamant. There was nothing she could do. If she wanted to be useful, then she should go back to Lytten's house and stay there. Make sure nobody came in, and allow no one, under any circumstances, to go into the cellar. Shoot them, if necessary. If she wanted to clear up the blood, though, that would be most helpful.

Rosie most certainly did not, but she agreed to the rest and went off, although not very happily. Angela then led Henry to her car and they drove to Tudmore Court, near Devizes, Wiltshire.

'How did you get me out?'

'Surprisingly easy. I can be very persuasive when I have the head of MI6 on the phone to back me up.'

'Isn't that just grand of you.'

They didn't talk much; Angela was working and driving at the same time, while Henry was lost in thought. Only after an hour, her calculations finished, did Angela say:

'What did you think of Anterwold?'

'Oh, it was . . . astonishing. It works quite well. But I don't know how it will behave when its horizons expand. I knew I'd imagined it as a variety of England, but I suppose there are other people scattered over the world. Are they at the same technological level? I didn't bother with any of that. How does that work?'

'Those elements will be produced by logical inference from the basic information in your notebooks. For example, I remember you state that no one has troubled the place greatly for a long time and that the occasional coastal raid is easily dealt with by a militia. That supposes low population and a matching technological level elsewhere. It doesn't sound as though you're suddenly going to get Panzer tanks landing in the south.'

'I wish more things survived. Of us.'

'You'd be surprised what they will find if they look. Think how much survived the dark ages. It's probably there, if they only search in the right places. Lord only knows what they'd find in that Story of yours if they read it properly. And, of course, a Rosie is there to help them. She'll be instructing them in Shakespeare and *Julius Caesar* soon enough.'

'I made Catherine look like you.'

'Really?'

'Yes. She surprised me. I scarcely sketched her at all, but she took on the appearance of a major figure in my real life.'

'I'm flattered. How closely does she resemble me?'

'Not identical; a long way from that, but you can see the relationship. Everything that happened in there was because of her, and I didn't think of any of it. It was odd.'

Angela took a corner at an alarming speed, then said, 'Interesting. I don't think you should go back into Anterwold, you know.'

'I don't want to. Besides, I thought you were going to close it down?'

'I don't know that I can. All I can hope to do is modify conditions to prevent the original machine being used. If I get that right, then preceding events will change. With luck either I will not create Anterwold or Rosie will not go into it. If that happens we will never know about it, of course, because none of this will have happened. This trip is to find out if that is possible.'

'How?'

'I want to see if it is possible to destroy the Devil's Handwriting. If I can't, then I'll have to think again.'

'Do you know what's really strange?' Henry said, once he had decided not to query her on that remark.

'In comparison to . . . ?'

'I've been reading a manuscript by a colleague of mine, Persimmon. He lays out what he thinks is the perfect technocratic society. Hell on earth.'

'So?'

'He is quite stupid, you know, but he has forecast the future remarkably well. The nightmare he conjures up is extraordinarily like the one you and Chang describe.'

Angela fell silent for a long time.

'Now,' she said eventually, 'you're just trying to give me a headache.'

63

It was the pigeons in the great entrance hall which convinced Angela that Henry was telling the truth when he said that his great-aunt's house was semi-derelict. The 'semi' bit was the only part she disputed. His aunt Gertie matched the place perfectly as well, more a character out of a Gothick novel than somebody real. She was dressed in ragged velvet, carried a huge candelabrum about with her and smelled as though she had not had a bath for months. Her hair was thin and unkempt and her conversation bizarre.

Henry, though, was delighted to see her. He gave her a big hug and she examined Angela closely by thrusting the candlesticks into her face and squinting up at her. 'A pretty one, eh?' she cackled. 'That makes a change. Are you here to fix the plumbing?'

'No, Auntie. Just to collect a few papers,' Henry bellowed into her ear.

'They've stopped delivering. Say I don't pay the bills.'

'Manuscripts, darling. Not newspapers.'

'You can read it over breakfast, like your uncle Joseph. Have you seen him?'

'He died in 1928.'

'Really?'

'Yes. He drove his car off a cliff, remember?'

She shook her head. 'Tell him to be more careful when you see him.'

'I will. Now, you go and sit down and pour yourself a nice gin. I just want to go upstairs and collect this thing I'm after. Then, I'm afraid, we'll have to run off. Angela and I are in a bit of a hurry.'

'Angela?'

'This is Angela.'

She peered again. 'A pretty one, eh? That makes a change.'

'Blimey,' Angela said as she followed Henry to the door. 'She's very sweet, and I love her dearly, but my head starts to spin after half an hour with her.'

'She's right about Uncle Joseph, you know.'

'Don't you start.'

*

Henry left me to deal with his aunt and disappeared up the stairs to go to the family archive. It would, he said, only take a few minutes.

Oddly, I have always found the company of the ancient relaxing. What is condemned in this brutal age as dementia, senility and worse is, in fact, a substantial step forward which aligns the mind rather more accurately with reality than our normal state.

Aunt Gertie could not tell the difference between 1928 and now. Uncle Joseph was dead and alive. In other words, she grasped the essential non-existence of time. Generally speaking, our minds impose an entirely artificial order on the world. It is the only way that such an inadequate instrument as our brain can function. It cannot deal with the complexity of reality, so simplifies everything until it

685

can, putting events into an artificial order so they can be dealt with one at a time, rather than all at once as they should be. Such a way of interpreting existence is learned, rather in the way that our brain has to turn the images which hit our retinas upside down in order to make sense of them.

Children have little sense of time; nor do the very old. They live in an ever-present now, which stretches into the past and off into the future. Effect triggers cause, and both happen at the same moment, be that yesterday or tomorrow. Aunt Gertie sensed this because all the acquired mental discipline of the years was falling away from her. Once you realised this, her conversation was perfectly comprehensible, even if it did make me a little dizzy.

Alas, I didn't have long enough for a proper talk; Henry was as good as his word. He returned dusty but triumphant.

'Got it,' he said. 'Just where I thought it would be.'

It was a thin tome, bound in red morocco and calf skin, with no lettering, but I knew the moment I opened it that he had indeed found what I was looking for. Page after page, all in Tsou, meticulously written out by hand. I was astonished at the workmanship. Tsou is a very dense script; the slightest error and it is gibberish. Doing it by hand must have taken years. Despite myself, I felt a little surge of admiration for Lucien Grange, or sympathy for the desperation which pushed him to even contemplate such a task. He must have had a perfect copy in his head even to attempt the job. That answered the question of who had accessed the computer before I left.

I checked through as much as I could to make sure. All was well; it was a fine summary of my work, except for the last symbol, which seemed a little odd. That one I absorbed properly and decoded, and unravelled instructions in plain English. Crop yields and rentals, folios 27–8.

'Henry?' I said. 'What does this mean?'

'What it says, I imagine. In the archives there are shelves of accounts in chronological order according to the estate's different sources of income.'

'Can I look?'

'I'll go for you, if you like.'

'No!' I said. 'You have a good chat with your aunt here.'

'As you please. Second floor, third door on the right. I left it open. If you get to the servants' staircase you've overshot. Do you want me to destroy this, by the way?'

'Not yet. I'd better find out what this reference means first of all. It can wait for a bit.'

So I went, leaving the Devil's Handwriting with Henry, who stowed it carefully in his jacket pocket. Another coincidence, you see. I could easily have taken it with me, or had him set light to it in the fireplace.

*

'To whom it may concern,' began the piece of paper, which I found after only ten minutes of searching. One thing about these aristocrats, they were always very tidy when it came to money.

'I very much hope that one day someone capable of understanding this letter finds and reads it. My name is Charles Lytten, although I took his identity many decades ago when I arrived in this place. Before that I was called Lucien Grange, and I was an administrator, first class, in the research institute of Zoffany Oldmanter. Unless this means something to you, you might as well stop reading now.'

On it went in a somewhat self-pitying fashion. Grange had written down the code in the hope that someone might find it and get him back, although quite how he expected this considering that he clearly believed he was in a parallel universe was unclear. I suppose he was desperate, and willing to clutch at straws. As I read I could understand why. He had made a decent fist of living in the eighteenth century, and had adapted well, but was worried nonetheless.

'My concern is that the colonisation programme will wipe out the indigenous population with me still in place here. I beg anyone who reads and understands this to ensure I am recovered before any such attempt is made.'

That was the last piece I needed. A programme to clear out a world and make it available for colonists from my time. Of course that would appeal to a megalomaniac like Oldmanter. It was obvious how it would be done, as well. Oldmanter liked money; he would choose the quickest and cheapest option, and the further you went, the more power would be required. How to clear a world of its population quickly and efficiently? The evidence of Anterwold gave the answer.

*

This was where the next significant coincidence came in, the final proof, if you like. As I walked to the door I heard a noise through the window which looked out over the main driveway – once a fine avenue of trees, now more like a weed patch. Still, there were remains of old gravel covering

688

it, and it was the crunching of this which made me look to see what was happening. A black car and a plain van were pulling up outside. From the car, I could see the unmistakeable figure of Sam Wind get out.

That was not good. They would knock, Henry would answer, they would find the Devil's Handwriting and think it was some code for communicating with the Soviet Union. Sam Wind always had a limited imagination. I would not be able to destroy it. It was required to survive. Or rather, probability dictated it was more likely to than not.

I could hardly hang around to argue about it; I didn't intend to go back to jail merely for the satisfaction of demonstrating that history cannot be greatly influenced by the actions of a single individual. I still wanted to prove that wrong. There wasn't much I could do for Henry, but at least I might be able to save myself.

I tiptoed down the servants' staircase at the far end of the corridor, down into the bowels of the old kitchens, and, when I was satisfied that Henry had unleashed the full conversational power of Aunt Gertie on them, slipped quietly out of the tradesmen's entrance and across the grass to the nearest trees, then circled round to the road where we had left the car. I drove to Hereford, left it in a side street and took the train back to Oxford.

*

The cars that arrived while Lytten was waiting for Angela to come back down were very quiet, he had to admit. When the doorbell rang he was sitting, unsuspecting, across from his aunt, concentrating hard to make some sense of her

689

increasingly bizarre conversation. Perhaps that was why he had not been as alert as usual. Once upon a time he would never have been caught out so easily.

He looked out of the window. A little posse led by Sam Wind was already at the door, grim and determined. Not much to be done; he was far too old for gymnastics and anyway his mind was on other things. One by one they filed through, but Lytten was already walking silently back to the sitting room.

'Our dinner guests!' screeched Aunt Gertie. 'They're early!'

Sam ignored her. 'I'm afraid it's all over, Henry,' he said.

'It is, I fear. I'm disappointed in you, Sam, coming all this way when you have better things to do.'

'What did you come here for?'

Lytten took the thin volume from his pocket. 'You won't find it very illuminating.'

Sam looked at it. 'What the hell is this?'

'Ah, now. I suppose you will decide it is some abstruse code. It isn't. At least, not the variety you want it to be.'

'When did you become a Soviet agent, Henry? During the war, or was it before that?'

'What a lazy idea,' Lytten said mildly. 'I'm quite offended.'

'Years of leaks and betrayals. You were untouchable, Portmore's golden boy throughout the war. No one ever thought of you, you were so protected by his aura. Age, my friend. You should have given up years ago.'

'You are probably right there,' Lytten said.

'The final proof was that man who showed up, and the attack on Volkov.'

'I see you have been thinking hard. Are you planning to whisk me off somewhere?'

'Yes.'

'Then before we leave, Sam Wind, I would like a word in private, if you don't mind. It won't take long.'

Wind looked suspicious, then nodded.

'I think the study still has some glass in the panes. If your friend would stay here . . .'

Lytten led Wind out of the doors and across the entrance hall. 'Poor fellow. Half an hour of Gertie and he'll be the one who goes over to Moscow.'

*

The room was dark, cold and dusty. It had been his great-uncle's once, and Lytten thought he could just make out the last whiffs of the pipe tobacco the man had smoked, a peculiar concoction, cherry-flavoured Cavendish, that he had blended specially for him in a tobacconist's on Holborn. Lytten stood by the fireplace – why he wasn't certain, as it had not been lit for years. It was where his great-uncle had liked to denounce the iniquities of the unions, or the socialists, or the Germans, or anyone who had recently incurred his wrath.

'Right then. Sit down and listen, if you will. It won't take long, and then you can take such action as you please. You believe I have incriminated myself. You decide to take Volkov away, so I immediately summon aid from the Soviet embassy, which organises a rapid assassination attempt. Or maybe it was Chang. Rather peculiar behaviour, don't you think? I may be getting addled, but I am not so far gone

691

that I could not have killed Volkov myself the moment I saw him in Paris.'

'Volkov is in hospital with a bullet in him.'

'So you tell me. How is the poor fellow?'

'He will survive. He was damned lucky.'

'Good, good.' Lytten paused for a moment to reflect. 'That makes it all much easier. Although it is going to be very difficult to explain to him.'

'I'm sure he understands all too well.'

'I'm sure he doesn't. It's not what he signed up for.'

'What does that mean?'

'His name is David Kupransky. A part-time lecturer in Russian literature. Always a bit short of cash since his wife left him. She had the money, you see. A great pity, but she found his extravagant White Russian ways a little too much after a while . . .'

'Henry!'

'Hmm? Oh. Yes. I offered him a little money to take part in some amateur theatricals. I wrote the note, sent it to myself via Portmore, and packed him off to Paris, just to see what would happen when he said he could identify a traitor in the service. He was very convincing, I must say, although he hammed it up rather. The point is, I would hardly go to such lengths to shoot a colleague. Common-room politics can get nasty on occasion, but rarely that bad.'

'You can prove this?'

'Of course I can. Very easily. Even if he dies, his wife will be able to identify him.'

'So what about Volkov? The real one? Was there a real one?'

Lytten shrugged. 'I knew someone of that name in

Berlin, but I've not heard anything of him since. He might have been shot, for all I know.'

'All of this was a trick? Why?'

'To catch you. Portmore's orders. Or rather, not to catch you.'

Sam Wind tried to take up a pose of knowing lack of concern, and Lytten leaned against the mantelpiece and wished he had a pipe.

'I have gone through everyone over the last two years, Sam. Portmore was convinced there was a traitor and told me to find him before he retired. I didn't want to, but you know how persuasive he is. So I did as he asked, ticking you all off my list, one by one. Slogged through the papers, the old reports. I laid little traps to see who responded. Nothing. Two years of work, and nothing. Not even the suggestion of a bite.

'So I was down to you. Everyone else could be cleared. You were the last. Poor old Portmore was getting very agitated by this stage, or as agitated as he ever gets, and I felt sure I was close to finding out. You were the only person I hadn't checked on.

'Then it occurred to me that I should be thorough. There was a huge gaping hole in my investigation; one other person I'd left out. So I decided to do both at the same time.'

'Who was that?'

'Portmore himself,' Lytten said. 'I could see a trial where some defence counsel tried to get you off by besmirching his reputation, making innuendos and asking why he hadn't been subject to the same investigation as everyone else. So I gave some information about Volkov to you, some to Portmore.

'I told him I was going to Paris, but I didn't tell you, and I was followed. I told you, but not Portmore, when Volkov was coming to Oxford, and that man Chang showed up.

'So it was even. Either of you could be the one. Except that Mr Chang, my watcher, was a nobody. He's reappeared, by the way, and you can talk to him yourself. The point is, he is completely harmless and was only interested in that manuscript you just took off me. I came to fetch it as I felt somewhat guilty about him getting an arrow in his backside.'

'A what?'

'A long story. The point is that I didn't have any proof one way or the other, so I had one last go. When you stuffed Volkov into a van and packed him off to a secure location, I rang Portmore to say where he was going and when he would arrive. Two hours later, he was shot. Couldn't have been you. You were with me all the time, or with that young man from counter-intelligence next door. You didn't make a phone call. You could not possibly have ordered the attack, and only one other person could have done it. As I say, it is going to be hard to apologise enough to Kupransky. Do you think you could get him a proper lectureship in London? Something with a nice pension?'

'Henry, you are being—'

'Portmore isn't afraid of handing the Service over to a Russian spy when he retires, Sam. He is afraid of not handing it over to a Russian spy.'

Lytten now sat down next to Wind, rubbing his hands together to ward off the cold. 'You are – must be – a front runner for Portmore's job. He wanted you out of the way and discredited so his own candidate would succeed. He even told me he thought it necessary to bypass all the senior candidates. If I could somehow nail you that would have been good, but I'm sure his idea was that I should come up with nothing conclusive. He would then argue that a shadow hung over everyone, so you would all have to be passed over just in case. Gontal gave me the idea.'

'Who?'

'Doesn't matter.'

'Who is his candidate?'

'I have no idea. We will just have to wait and see.'

'You mean leave him in his post? That's ridiculous.'

'Think of the entirely false information you can funnel to the Russians. Think of the ways you now have of guarding the few people we have left. Think of the pleasure of waiting until his chosen successor is named, then grabbing both of them.'

'Are you sure of this?'

'I have tried not even to think about it too much. But yes. I am sure.'

Wind sat disconsolately on the settee, looking, for the first time in years, incapable of dealing with the situation.

'I'm sorry, Sam. I have had longer to get used to the idea than you have. I revered Portmore as well. He was – and in his way he still is – courageous and loyal. He was magnificent during the war, but I am certain he is the spy we've all been hunting for so many years. If you set up a proper investigation I'm sure you will find enough to confirm it.'

'It is a thin case.'

'At the moment. It would not stand up in court, and if the Americans ever find out that every secret they shared was as good as posted direct to Moscow, we would never be able to hold our heads up in public again.'

'So?'

'Quiet retirement, a knighthood, maybe the master of a Cambridge college, in exchange for a full accounting and his protégé's head on a platter. Not much choice, really. Besides, he once really was a hero. We owe him that.'

Wind leaned forward, his hands together against his mouth. 'Jesus,' he said softly. 'When did you work this out?'

'I didn't suspect him until I had to. I took him for granted as the best and most doggedly loyal of men. Which he was, of course. Just loyal to something else.'

*

'I wonder where Angela is?' Lytten asked, after a brief search of the house produced no sign of her. 'Sam, could you send some of your minions round the back to see if the car is still there?'

They came back ten minutes later to report that there was no car, just some fresh tyre tracks.

'She must have heard you arrive and feared the worst. Not surprisingly, I suppose; she's already spent much of the day in a cell, and she's a bit busy at the moment. Her opinion of you will probably never recover.'

'I will apologise unreservedly when I get the opportunity.'

'I just hope she doesn't do anything rash, like disappear for good.'

'How could she do that?'

'You'd be surprised. Now I'm stranded. You'll have to drive me home, Sam. I can't stay here.'

'Not immediately. I must see Volkov first, or whatever his name really is. I need a statement from him, and I'll need one from you as well. That can't wait. I can get you to a train in the morning.'

'Very well,' Lytten replied. 'I don't suppose a few hours will make any difference.'

So Sam dispatched his men, while Lytten said goodbye to his aunt and promised that he would come again soon.

'Bring that nice young girl with you. Very charming, she is.'

'I will if I can,' he promised.

Then he and Wind walked out into the evening air.

'At least it's not raining,' Lytten said. 'Quite a pleasant evening, in fact.'

'It won't last,' Wind grumbled. 'You'll see.'

64

As the train lumbered along, I sat in the dimly lit and blessedly empty carriage and reassembled my calculations. The massive run of chance events which both brought the Devil's Handwriting into existence and stopped it being destroyed made me realise that a simple solution was no longer available. It was not that I would be unable to try again, perhaps, but I calculated that random events would again prevent me from being successful. The chances of everything turning out as it had, I reckoned, were tiny, almost as small as the chances the computer simulation had calculated of avoiding nuclear war. In fact, I realised as we passed through Swindon, it was highly likely that they were identical, that the one was an inverse image of the other, on the microscopic scale.

A surge of excitement ran through me. What an idea that was! Now, if I could only pin it down and produce the maths that would firmly link the two, then I would have a really interesting paper to present to . . .

Well, to whom, exactly? No one could understand it where I was, and in the not too distant future everyone who might do so was likely to be wiped out. Was I responsible for that? I had to bear my share of blame. But (I reassured myself) I had not brought the Devil's Handwriting into existence, nor did I ensure its survival, nor did I use it. That strand of things was independent of me. I had established to my satisfaction, after all, that if my creation of Anterwold was generating a nuclear war, the nuclear war was simultaneously generating Anterwold.

I had neither the time nor the energy to do the calculations. Even thinking as much as I did had to be squeezed in between stops at railway halts, where I looked out of the window anxiously to see if any policemen were standing there, waiting for me.

They weren't. Even at Oxford there was no one and I walked out of the station a free woman, then took a taxi up to Henry's house.

I let myself in, drew the curtains, then collapsed in exhaustion on the settee in Henry's study. I was so tired. I should have done something, but all my spirit had left me.

There was nothing I could do. I heard the sound of footsteps. It had to be one of Wind's people. I prepared to meet my fate. Accessory to treason or some such?

The door opened and Rosie put her head through. I could have kissed her, I was so relieved.

*

'So what is going on?' Rosie asked.

'Well, Henry has probably been arrested as a spy and I am a fugitive. I don't have the Devil's Handwriting, I can't destroy it and the world is about to descend into nuclear war. Apart from that . . . How are you?'

'The Professor has been arrested as a spy? Why would anyone think that?'

'Maybe he is. How should I know?'

'Don't you care?'

'Not in the slightest. I am a bit worried about what Wind might do to him. I really don't want him locked up for the next decade. I need his help.'

'What are you going to do?'

For the first time, Angela frightened her. She had always seemed so competent. Now she looked defeated.

'I can't do much about Henry; even looking after myself will be hard. If I stay here then Sam Wind will lock me up as well. I'd be stymied in a prison cell.'

'How much time do you need?'

'A decade at least, but even if I don't spend it in prison, we are likely to have a holocaust before I can figure out a new approach.'

'Why?'

'Probability. The probability that the Devil's Handwriting survives, that it falls into the wrong hands and that it is used to clear the world for colonisation. They think they are going to let off a bomb in an alternative past. In fact it will be this one, and perhaps soon.'

'Surely—'

'It's simple, I think. What will happen if a nuclear bomb goes off in Berlin? The Russians will know they didn't do it, the Americans will know they didn't either. Each will assume the other is starting hostilities and let rip with everything they have. They want an empty world to colonise and this is the easiest way to get one. Cheap, simple and efficient.'

'That's what's going to happen?'

Angela nodded. 'I think so. I've been going about it the wrong way, you see. Anterwold isn't just the cause of a war, it's the consequence of it as well. I can't shut down

Anterwold unless I shut down the ultimate causes of its existence.'

'You created it.'

'We are all creatures of history.'

'How long do we have?'

'I would guess any time in the next seventy-five years. More or less. I can't say more precisely than that.'

'Could you stop it? If you had time?'

'Where there's life, there's hope.'

'Then you must go into Anterwold. You'd have all the time you need.'

'I can't. I can't influence my future from a different one. I have to be on the same line. As this is the last moment which is connected to both, I will have to stay here. I'll go back to France and lie low. I'll have Chang to help, of course, and that will be useful. Assuming he survives, poor fellow.'

'He'll be fine. I rang the hospital. What about me?'

Angela smiled thoughtfully. 'You want to help?'

Rosie hesitated, then nodded.

'For some reason that makes me very happy.' She paused, then became practical once more. 'If I understand your peculiar educational system here, you can leave school next year?'

'Yes.'

'If John Kennedy wins the election next month, we have at least until October 1962, I think. That's the Cuban missile crisis. If we get through that then we might well be safe until 1976. If Nixon wins, then everything becomes unpredictable, but at least I will be sure that history is changing seriously. Assuming all goes well, though, then in nine months' time you can leave school, pack your bags and come and live with me in the South of France. How about that? I've got plenty of money and Chang's perfectly pleasant once you get to know him.'

'That sounds lovely.'

'It will be. Unless we fail, in which case it won't be lovely at all. But then we can gather as many people as possible and head off into Anterwold. I should add that I can't think of any reason why you shouldn't go now, if you really wanted to.'

Rosie shook her head. 'No. I've thought about that. A lot. But as you keep on telling me, I'm there already. One's company.'

'Two's a crowd?'

Rosie smiled. 'A complication. The other me will be happy because I am here with my parents. Someone will have to look after Jenkins if Professor Lytten is in jail. I have a life here. It's not brilliant, I sometimes think, but, you know . . .'

'In that case, we had better succeed,' Angela said. 'Come on. I'll walk you home. There's nothing more to do here tonight, and I must get out of the country as quickly as possible. I need to pack and find my passport.'

A few minutes later the two left the house, and Angela locked the door carefully. 'Quite a day,' she said. 'Let's see how tomorrow entertains us.'

65

Jack was shocked at the state of the island when the helicopters flew over it before settling dustily onto the landing site. Big black holes had been blown into what once had been gleaming white roofs covering the main part of the institute; the wreckage of the defensive outposts still smouldered in the light breeze, on the far side of the island a fire still burned and half a dozen of the small ferries half poked above the water, bombed and sunk as they were, tied up to the quayside. Oldmanter's military had done a thorough, rapid job of it.

Already the repairs were under way. As they landed, he saw other large machines bringing in the equipment needed to patch holes, get power working again. Supplies of all sorts were stacked in neat piles everywhere. His experienced eye scanned the site as they came lower, but he could see no pens for prisoners, no marks of freshly dug graves.

Some had already returned to work under their new master; others had left to fend for themselves as best they could. The place was half empty, quiet, gloomy with lack of purpose. The few dozen people brought up from the Retreats were under guard.

Jack managed to get permission to see Emily, for he was restored to his previous position, awaiting transfer to another part of Oldmanter's vast empire. He had been offered promotion, everything he might need. Oldmanter was a generous man.

'He is going to keep his word,' he said to her. 'The preparations are being made. You still have time to change your mind, though.'

'Why would I want to do that?'

'It's dangerous.'

'It is hardly safe for people like us here, either.'

'How did Oldmanter know where I was? How did he find me so quickly?'

'Simple enough. I told him. It was obvious he was going to win. You would have died, and so would we. This seemed a good way of saving something from the wreckage.'

'You told me the document was old, and told him that it was a fake.'

'That's the sort of imprecision you get from people who do not have a thorough scientific training, I suppose.'

'Hanslip says it is dangerous.'

'But to whom, do you think? What about Hanslip?'

'I have permission to see him tomorrow.'

'I liked him. Tell him I know what I am doing.'

*

'I will try to get your conditions improved before I leave,' Jack began when he came into Hanslip's cell the next day and looked around at the damp walls and filthy floor with distaste. 'There is no reason for you to be treated like this.'

'Have I disappeared?' Hanslip's voice was surprisingly clear and strong for someone who had evidently suffered very bad treatment. Jack looked at the bruises, the black

704

eye, the bandages over his hands. Primitive. He hated that.

'I'm afraid so. The electricity surge has been officially attributed to terrorists and the authorities are responding with mass arrests. The institute never existed, nor did you.'

Hanslip nodded to show he had understood.

'And you?'

'Oldmanter offered me a job. I had little choice, so I accepted it. He has also agreed to send the renegades to their own world in exchange for Emily Strang's cooperation. It will be a reservation, in effect, where they will live undisturbed.'

He considered this. 'I see. Why have you come today?'

'To say goodbye, I'm afraid. You are to be shot. And I wish to apologise to you. One of Emily's conditions was that you should be offered the chance of going with the renegades. Oldmanter agreed, but he has changed his mind. I have been instructed to tell Emily that you refused the offer.'

'Lying for Oldmanter already? Will you do that?'

'Yes. I must.'

'Do you realise how dangerous using that machine could be? Does Oldmanter?'

'I know nothing. You tell me it is dangerous, Oldmanter is sure it is not. As he is the most successful person on the planet, then his opinion is likely to prevail. Emily told me she knows what she's doing.'

'Did she indeed?' Hanslip's eyes narrowed as he thought. Then his face cleared and became almost contented. He nodded to himself and almost smiled. 'Yes. Maybe she does. She's her mother's daughter, after all. I told you that Angela was a ruthless woman. Would you tell Emily that I understand what she is doing, and wish her luck? Also that she can count on me.'

'If you wish.'

'Thank you, Mr More. I appreciate your kindness in coming to visit me. Good luck to you, as well. You will need it more than any of us, I think.'

*

That evening Jack, with three armed soldiers, got Emily from the enclosure once more and walked her along the corridors into the open air. He led her through, then ordered the guards, 'Keep far away. Within eyesight, as I suppose you must, but in the background, please.'

'A man of authority,' she commented as the guards dutifully fell back and allowed them to head down to the shore unaccompanied.

'That's me. They're all right, those three. They don't really care what happens as long as they don't get into trouble.'

'Like most people.'

'I suppose.'

They walked along in silence for a while, Emily absorbing the fresh air. 'It's empty up here. I like it.'

'Good. You will be getting to know it quite well.'

'Why?'

'It's your destination,' he said simply. 'They've decided it is too expensive to move you geographically. So whenever you arrive, it will be exactly at the point where you left. On this island, in fact. You'll have to make your own way after that.'

'How many of us will go?'

'Just you, to start off with. I'm afraid they intend to use you as an experiment, to see if it works. If you think about it, it shows they are taking it seriously. They want to do it properly.'

'That's unfortunate. When will the rest follow?'

'You are asking the wrong person. I am only a security officer, remember.'

'Then I must hope he will keep his word.'

'He will, I think. In his odd way it is important to him. But it's not too late to change your mind if you have any doubts.'

'I might, if I could think of anything better. What date am I going to?'

'I've no idea.'

'Have you seen Hanslip?'

'I have. He does not wish to go. He also said that he understands what you are doing and wishes you luck. And that you can count on him. What does that mean?'

'Are they going to kill him?'

'Yes.'

'Then it means that he has grasped that it doesn't matter if they do or not. He is going to die anyway if he doesn't come with me. Why don't you come instead?'

'You must be joking.'

'I really do know what I'm doing.'

He eyed her curiously, trying to understand what she was saying.

'Won't you trust me?' she added. 'It's important. I cannot tell you why.'

He hesitated, then shook his head. 'No,' he said. 'You're

a renegade. I don't share your opinions or values, even if I do not object to them as much as most people do. Besides, everything I want is here. I am secure, I have proper privileges for the first time in my life. I have a place and a value. I know that doesn't mean much to you, but it is all I want.'

She nodded. 'I suppose. Still, I tried. Let's go back.'

*

Jack had seen it all before, but while the transmission of Alex Chang had been low-key and without ceremony, this time it was done with considerable fanfare. It was recorded, for one thing, so that in due course Oldmanter could present his discovery to an awed world in a suitably spectacular fashion. He even allowed himself to be filmed, for the first time in decades, so important was it to his power and reputation.

They were also using the new machine, unfinished when Angela fled but now completed and equipped with sensors to give a much better idea of where the subjects landed. It was in a large room, dramatically lit and prepared. A suitable hush attended the technicians, hunched over their instruments and concentrating hard, the very picture of technocratic excellence. The volunteer was led in and received a round of applause as she mounted the podium. No one said she was a renegade; rather she had been given the profile of a heroic explorer, a pioneer wishing to better humanity. The child of distinguished scientists ready, yet again, to demonstrate the devotion of her calling to the betterment of mankind. She sat down, nodded to say she was ready, and the magnetic field was raised, trapping her inside.

The cameras focused lovingly on her face until it disappeared into the blue darkness; pretty, fresh and uncomplicated, everything the viewers would like to look at.

Then the room itself darkened until only the blue light could be seen, pulsating rhythmically. Ordinarily the transmission was instantaneous; one moment the subject was there, the next it was gone. This wasn't good enough; the publicity department had insisted on something more visual and dramatic. Can't you keep it going for longer? We need a sense of journey, and what you've got is about as exciting as switching off a light bulb.

It could be done, but only by keeping the volunteer in a state of artificial non-existence for that time. As long as the power was running through the system, she would be kept in limbo; they could add in lighting effects, cut to anxious looks on the faces of technicians, have a commentary building up to the moment when the power shut down and the traveller – presumably – exited at her destination. The lights would come on to reveal the now completely empty podium. It still wouldn't look much, but it was better than nothing. Eventually it had been arranged. The transmission would be dragged out as required. They didn't tell Emily about this, in case she worried. The producers needed her to smile.

Oldmanter watched from the side; he had set it all in motion and was more than happy to leave the technical operation to others. When the theatricals began, he became impatient and walked to the room down the corridor containing the smaller, older machine, the one used in the days of Hanslip. On the transmission pad was nothing but a black metal sphere, about two feet across. Jack went with him; he was instructed to make sure no one else came in.

'I thought you might like to see this,' Oldmanter said as they walked in. 'It is the more serious experiment taking place today.'

'What was that down the corridor?'

'A little publicity. Sending one girl isn't going to accomplish anything. But she looked good and will tug at people's heartstrings.'

'So what's this, then?'

'This, Mr More, is a nuclear bomb. You can have no idea how difficult it was to get hold of it. They are very well guarded, as you can imagine. It's small, but unfortunately that is the maximum density this device can cope with. Sending metal of any sort requires gigantic amounts of energy. The world, I'm afraid, is about to suffer another major power failure.' He turned to Jack with a smile. 'These terrorists, eh? There's no limit to their audacity.'

'What are you going to do with it? What's the point?'

Oldmanter smiled. 'We are going to clear a world for colonisation. Might as well get started to test the practicality.'

'With one bomb?'

'Just one. We can rely on the inhabitants to do the rest for us. It's cheaper, you see. Otherwise we have to go back further and that is more expensive.'

'I hope you're not sending it to the same world as Emily has gone to?'

'Unfortunately we have to,' he said with a slight tone of regret. 'There is a little technical hitch, and we can only access one universe at the moment. No one knows why, but

710

until we sort it out, there is nothing we can do.'

'She'll be killed.'

'No. We decided to send her forwards. No one has ever done that, and one of our consultants is desperate to find out if it is possible. If there is to be communication between the worlds, we need to establish if forward transmission is possible. She will go as far as the power available permits.'

'So you lied to her?'

'I said I would transport the renegades to a different world, and I will do so. I didn't say I'd send them all to the same time zone, nor did I promise not to send a nuclear bomb as well.'

'Where has she gone?'

'Nowhere yet, as far as I understand it. She will arrive when the power to her device cuts off. That will be about ten minutes after this experiment finishes. At the moment she is in a fascinating state of non-existence. Now, if you will excuse me . . .'

A technician had come up to him, bearing a piece of paper.

'The list of options, sir, for your final approval. We will be ready in five minutes.'

Oldmanter took the piece of paper and glanced casually at it. Berlin, October 1962; London, November 1983; Calcutta, May 1990; Beijing, July 2018.

'Which is recommended?'

'Analysis suggests all will work perfectly well. You may choose whichever you prefer.'

Oldmanter ticked a box, initialled the bottom and handed it back.

'Go ahead then,' he said, and walked out of the room

to where Jack was standing in the corridor, looking at the artificial window.

'You find me brutal, Mr More. That, I am afraid, is the nature of discovery. We do not wrest nature's secrets from it by asking nicely. We have to tear them out using whatever ruthlessness is needed. You are worried for that girl, I suppose. But she is just one person amongst many billions who need help and resources. Humanity has a long future ahead of it now. It is worth sacrificing one person for that.'

'She thought that this world would destroy itself through its knowledge,' Jack replied.

'She was wrong.' He glanced at the clock on the wall. 'I will prove it in twenty seconds from now.'

'Are you sure? Would it not be better to wait?'

Oldmanter grunted dismissively, and he and Jack turned to the projection of tranquillity in front of them; another ideal landscape, and still Jack had no idea why anyone bothered to install it. But they both seemed to find it distracting as, behind them, the monotonous tone of a technician called out the last seconds.

'The world is about to change for ever, because of what we are doing here,' Oldmanter said quietly. 'We can make something truly wonderful of it.'

66

'Master Henary!' Jay called, running after the heavy figure walking slowly back towards the great house. 'Wait!'

Henary stopped as the boy – maybe not so much a boy any more, but still distressingly young – caught up with him.

'Master Henary,' Jay repeated, then stopped. 'I don't know what to say.'

'For the first time in my life, Jay, I am disappointed in you,' Henary replied mildly.

'What has happened?'

'I have no idea. Except that you have demonstrated what a magnificent teacher I am. You have kept calm through heaven knows what difficulties, you have made your first speech and defeated one of the finest orators in Anterwold, and you have stared a spirit in the eye without flinching. I claim some credit for your achievement.'

'By all means.'

'Alas, not much. You will far exceed me. I will be known to future ages only as your first teacher.'

'Hardly.'

'You took risks I would never have dared take and triumphed.'

They continued on, heading for the assembly, until Henary spoke once more. 'We have seen marvels today. The fulfilment of a prophecy, the descent of spirits, the end of the world. A great injustice rectified. Extraordinary things. Do you know, a part of me really does feel almost disappointed.'

'Why?'

'Because all I heard was common sense. Esilio descended and all he told us was what we already knew. What we should have known, at least. Strange, don't you think?'

'It was terrifying, though.'

'It was. And the news will spread across Anterwold like a forest fire in summer. It will change everything, and for ever. We may perhaps help it to change in the way the spirit instructed. I would say I needed your help, but let me rather offer you such assistance as I can.'

'I . . . well . . .'

'There is so much to do, Jay. It will be wonderful and frightening for us all. Do not think everyone will agree with us. We will need to argue, persuade and cajole.'

Jay smiled. 'What do you think we should do first?'

'First? Well, first we go and watch this ceremony. Then we go to Ossenfud. Do you know, I think it would be good to get there before Gontal does. After that, well, that's when the fun really begins. Now, what I suggest is . . .'

And the large old man and the thin young boy walked, laughing and talking, into the darkening night, each more excited than ever before in their lives, until they came to the large courtyard where the assembly was being held, in front of all the adults of the domain who had managed to get there in time. The atmosphere was one of high tension and great noise. The Chamberlain was already speaking when they arrived, but was having trouble being heard. Twice he had recited the required words, but had to shout them out for a third time before enough calm descended for the ceremony to continue. Who, he almost shouted, presented themselves first to the assembly?

Catherine walked forward, looking like a lord despite her clothes. Many scarcely recognised her, but when they did a loud murmur of approval ran through the courtyard, and then a stamping began, a few first, then everyone joined in, beating their feet on the ground, shouting and cheering to see her again. For once she broke protocol and, tears streaming down her cheeks, acknowledged their welcome.

'Does anyone claim a better title? Is there any member of the line of Thenald who wishes to present himself?'

All stared at Pamarchon. This was the moment he had dreamed of for years. The moment he had suffered for and plotted to achieve. He stepped forward confidently and in a clear, loud voice exclaimed so all could hear: 'Not I!'

'That is your final word?'

'It is.'

'Then does any other member of the family wish to present themselves?'

It was the measure of Gontal that he had not left already; a lesser man would surely have done so, walked away from the defeat and the humiliation. But Gontal was made of sterner stuff. He was a man of propriety and rules. They had sustained him and guided him all his life, and he felt obliged to honour them even now. That didn't mean, of course, that he had to enjoy it. Still he was there, standing proudly and stiffly as the question was posed. He stood forward also, head upright as he said: 'Not I!' although many noted that his tone was rather less enthusiastic.

There was much more for the Chamberlain to say, but no one heard it. It had been a week without parallel, and only a few hours previously many there had been in terror of their lives. They had seen things that would be talked of for generations. Their Lord had been lost and found again. They had come close to war. The prophecies of old had been fulfilled in ways which had terrified them.

Now all was restored and forgiven. Ossenfud and Willdon had been returned to harmony. The stain on the family of Thenald was wiped clean. The innocent had been forgiven, the guilty punished. The day of judgement had come and gone, and they had been freed from servitude.

No wonder no one heard the Chamberlain pronounce, 'Then I declare the Lord of Willdon is Lord once more, and this election is at an end,' although he tried his best. Everyone was simply too happy, too noisy and too excited to pay a blind bit of attention.

Amid the bedlam, Pamarchon came over to be the first to acknowledge Catherine, ensconced once more on her seat of office.

She smiled. 'You owe me no obedience,' she said as he made to bow to her. 'You know that as well as I do. Go. Find that wife of yours. If you are going to reverence anyone, she deserves it more than I do.'

'Then with your permission . . .'

He scuttled out the door.

And came straight across Antros, bearing Rosalind in his arms, with blood streaming down her dress.

*

With a cry of despair, Pamarchon ran across the lawn to where Antros now stood. 'What happened? What's the matter with her?'

'Jaqui,' Antros said. He was breathing heavily from the effort of carrying Rosalind so far and so quickly, terrified that if he was too slow she might bleed to death and that if he ran he might cause her pain. 'The spirit went back into the light, and Jaqui tried to make Rosalind go as well. He was pulling her into it and I fired. The spirit had told me to, I think. He had that knife, and cut at her before Rosalind pushed him through. He has gone.'

While he was speaking he laid Rosalind on the grass and Pamarchon, who was skilled at such things, looked carefully. A bad cut across the ribs, where Jaqui's knife had caught her as she pushed him through the light. It was bleeding heavily, but looked worse than it was. She opened her eyes at his touch and smiled as she saw his worried face. 'I'm really not that bad,' she said. 'I am quite capable of walking, thank you.'

'Don't you dare.'

Rosie lay still as he examined her and then smiled at Antros. 'That is the second time you have rescued me, Antros the brave,' she said faintly. 'I do hope the Professor hasn't been reading about Launcelot and Guinevere as well.'

Pamarchon picked her up himself and walked towards the house, with Antros running ahead to summon a healer. Catherine came out, and immediately abandoned the ceremony of installation to hurry over as well. Then the healers took over and banished them, laying her on soft sheets and getting clean cloths and astringents to clean the wound before binding it up.

'Stop looking so frightened, young man,' one said to the panicking Pamarchon. 'Anyone would think you had never seen blood before. Now go away. She does not need you, and nor do we. She needs calm and quiet. You may see her when we are done. It is not such a very bad wound, so stop fretting.'

And Pamarchon, in the company of Antros and Catherine, had to wait, pacing up and down, constantly sending in messages to ask how she was.

'Anyone would think he was in love,' Catherine remarked to Antros quietly as they watched him. He laughed softly.

'It seems you did very well back there,' she added.

'I followed instructions.'

'I suspect you were given none.'

'Perhaps.'

Antros, though, had other things on his mind.

'Pamarchon?' he asked. 'What about Ossenfud?'

He nodded. 'After I see Rosalind, I will go. I'll have to hurry; I need to get ahead of Gontal's party. I'm sure he must have dispatched people already but he is still here. Catherine, could you make sure he doesn't leave until tomorrow morning?'

'I will smother him with kindness and hospitality. If that doesn't work, then I'll break open some of Willdon's best barrels of brandy. By the time I'm done he won't even remember what Ossenfud is.'

'Thank you. Antros, you must return to the camp, say what has happened. Keep everyone calm. Tell them I will explain on my return.'

*

Pamarchon returned two days later, exhausted, but satisfied. He had done everything he needed, raced ahead on one of Catherine's finest horses and intercepted his troop of men some fifteen miles outside Ossenfud. The expedition, he said, was no longer needed. Wonderful things had happened in Willdon . . .

They had camped, and he had regaled them with a tale such as no man had ever heard before. He told it well, from their march to the Shrine to the appearance of the spirit, the trial, the unmasking of Jaqui as the murderer.

'The spirit moved Catherine to end this feud. Those who wish can take up their lives, with land and in freedom. Those who do not will be rewarded, pardoned for any crime, and will be free to go as they wish.'

'What about you?' It was Djon who asked.

'Ah, my dear friend! I will marry my fairy and I will help settle my people. Then I will get a ship, the finest ship ever built, and I will set sail.'

He looked at their faces in the flickering flames, saw how he had astonished them with every part of his narrative. 'I will need a crew, of course,' he said. 'A job for the adventurous, the daring, the reckless. Do you by any chance know where I might find such people?'

Aching and tired, dirty, hungry and thirsty, he arrived back at Willdon and slid off the beast which was as exhausted as he was. Was Rosalind recovered? Had they lied to him or made a mistake? What if she was in a coma, infected, even dead?

He hurried across the beautiful gardens as the sun set to the west, and saw a slim, youthful figure running out of the healing rooms, waving at him.

He felt a surge of relief that banished all tiredness and began to run as well.

'You must be very nice to me, Pamarchon son of,' Rosalind said, when each was finally prepared to let the other go. 'For as long as we live. You know that, I hope. I cannot go home now. Not ever. I made my choice and it was you. I hope you haven't changed your mind.' It was three days since the tumultuous events of the Shrine, and already it felt as though it had never happened. Already she could feel a difference in the way that people were opening up, looking about themselves. She had heard people talking differently. 'I will go . . . When I went . . . Next year . . . Many years ago . . .'

'I am more certain than ever.'

'Did you tell me the truth about voyaging? Or do you plan to settle down on a farm with pigs in your yard and chickens in your bed?'

'I will be ready when you are. I would go tomorrow if you would come with me, or stay here for ever if you changed your mind.'

'Silly,' she said. 'I won't change my mind. Seeing the whole world will be easy in comparison to what I have seen already.'

She smiled her sweetest smile at him and he took her in his arms once more.

*

'Lady Rosalind,' Catherine said, when the girl had finally left Pamarchon and gone into the house. 'I am glad to see you rested and recovered. Are you well?'

Rosalind nodded. She had been in bed for three days – two days longer than she thought necessary, in fact; her wound was on the mend and even the fussiest of the nurses had reluctantly conceded that there was no reason she should not be allowed to dress and leave the healing rooms. She had put on fresh clothes brought over from the house, and walked into the gardens just as Pamarchon had arrived. Now she was in the room of records where she had first talked to Catherine after her arrival. She no longer had any idea when that was; sometimes she thought it was only a week, sometimes it seemed like years.

'I am very well. It looked much worse than it was. It was kind of you to come and visit me so often.'

'I had to deploy all my authority to be allowed in. The nurses are tyrants in their domain. We were all very anxious for you.'

'Where is everyone?'

'Henary has gone to Ossenfud; he wants to mend fences with Gontal by proposing they collaborate on the Shelf of Perplexities. He is hoping that you will help him there. Bait, if you see what I mean. Gontal is rather afraid of you. Jay is still here, striking up awkward conversations with Aliena which are a joy to overhear, and that splendid young man Antros has disappeared back into the forest. Pamarchon, as you are well aware, has just returned.'

Rosalind blushed and smiled shyly.

'Do you really plan to voyage?'

'Soon enough, although I can't refuse Henary's request, and one of the nurses pointed out that spring would be a better time to set off. So in about nine months' time we will leave, I hope.'

'And see the world in all its majesty.' She smiled. 'Rain, fog, snow, danger.'

'That's it,' Rosalind agreed happily. 'And beautiful, wonderful things as well.'

'Until then, I hope you will stay here as much as possible. I could use your assistance too.'

'With pleasure, my Lady.' Rosie curtsied, and Catherine laughed.

'Ah, no. You do not call me that. You of all people. In fact, it occurs to me that we have never actually been introduced. Not properly.'

'Then let us do it properly. I present myself to you as Rosalind, betrothed of Pamarchon, son of Isenwar. But I think I know your name already.'

'Do you indeed?'

'I think so. It was what the Professor said, how you became a major character in his story all on your own, a bit like I did. That made me think that perhaps you are not from here either.'

'Go on.'

'I think,' here she paused for a moment, a little uncertainly, 'I think you must be Angela Meerson. It is the only explanation which makes sense to me.'

Catherine smiled. 'Good try. But I am not.'

'Oh, what a pity! I was certain that you had to be.'

'You were very close. My name is Emily Strang. I am Angela's daughter.'

'Now that I did not expect,' Rosalind said with a hint of disappointment in her voice. 'But then I didn't know she even had a daughter. I never met her, you see.'

'Nor I.'

722

'Really? Your own mother? Poor you.'

'She has looked after me in other ways.'

'How on earth did you get here?'

'Now that is a whole story of its own, and a very great one. It will take many hours to tell, but it is worth hearing. I hope you will stay long enough, because I will tell you of my mother and her work, of the Exile and the Return, or at least what I think it must have been. I have seen extraordinary things and would like to tell the one person who will understand, and perhaps help me unravel more of the truth. There is much I do not know.'

'I'd love to.'

'But that is for another day; there is no hurry. Now we must celebrate and be happy.'

She turned to look out of the window, over the broad gardens of Willdon, across to the woods beyond.

'It is beautiful here, you know,' she said quietly. 'We can make something truly wonderful of it, this time.'

Acknowledgements

With thanks for help, support and advice to Ruth Harris, Alex Pears, Michael Pears, David Brown, Felicity Bryan, Catherine Clarke, Bouzha Cookman, Loren Eskenazi, Josie Gardiner, Michael Holyoke, Andrew Katz, Bill Lehr, Lyndal Roper, Mark Rowse, Sarah Savitt, Alex Scott, Nick Stargardt, André Stern, Henry Volans, Simon Whitaker.

A Note from the Author

There are many different ways to tell the story of *Arcadia* and the book you hold in your hands is only one of them.

When I began writing, I also wanted to do something new. I wanted to give you the freedom to put the tale together in your own way.

To take the route through *Arcadia* which most pleases you, download the *Arcadia* app for iPhone and iPad from the App Store.

IAIN PEARS

Find out more at: arcadiatheapp.com/enter

ff

Faber & Faber – a home for writers

Faber & Faber is one of the great independent publishing houses in London. We were established in 1929 by Geoffrey Faber and our first editor was T. S. Eliot. We are proud to publish prize-winning fiction and non-fiction, as well as an unrivalled list of modern poets and playwrights. Among our list of writers we have five Booker Prize winners and eleven Nobel Laureates, and we continue to seek out the most exciting and innovative writers at work today.

www.faber.co.uk – a home for readers

The Faber website is the place where you can find all the latest news on our writers and events, and browse and buy in the Faber shop. You can also join the free Faber Members programme for discounts, exclusive access to events and our range of hand-bound Collectors' Editions.